EYE SPY

Also by Jimmy Sangster

Your Friendly Neighborhood Death Peddler

The Touchfeather Series
Touchfeather
Touchfeather, Too

The John Smith Series

private i (aka The Spy Killer)
Foreign Exchange

The Jimmy Reed Series

Snowball
Blackball
Hardball
Fireball

EYE SPY

Four Full Novels

Touchfeather
Touchfeather, Too
The Spy Killer
Foreign Exchange

JIMMY SANGSTER

The Spy Killer was previously published under the title private I

ISBN-13: 978-1-7358517-0-9

Published by
Brash Books
12120 State Line #253
Leawood, KS 66209
www.brash-books.com

To Sydney

PUBLISHER'S NOTE

This book was originally published in England in the late 1960s and reflects the cultural and sexual attitudes, language, and politics of those turbulent times. This new edition also retains most of the original British spellings, grammar, and punctuation.

AUTHOR'S NOTE

To the best of my knowledge and belief there is not—and never has been—a Katherine Touchfeather on the roster of air hostesses employed by BOAC, TWA, PanAm, Air India or any other member of IATA. Katy, as my story makes clear, is employed by Mr. Blaser. How he contrives to have her appear in the right aeroplane at the right moment, wearing the right uniform and exhibiting the ready smile and warm friendliness of the perfect air hostess, is his secret. I would like to assure SAS, United, Quantas, American, Lufthansa and all other member companies of IATA that I make no suggestion that any of their employees could, or should, do the things Katy does—despite some recent airline advertisements which may have given their readers ideas to the contrary, e.g., 'Save Friday night for Ingeborg Bechtel. She puts the fun in flying'. Or 'Sometimes our hostesses take young men home with them'. Katy Touchfeather is to be regarded entirely as fiction. Whereas my admiration and affection for that unique race of young women, the air hostesses, is demonstrably fact!

J.S.

ONE

Katy Touchfeather. I mean, what sort of a name is that to hand a girl? The Katy is all right, or Katherine as my parents put on my birth certificate. But Touchfeather! It doesn't sound any better in French either, nor for that matter in Spanish, German or Italian. I know, because I speak all of them to some extent. Still, that's just one of the crosses I have to bear. The other is Mr. Blaser. Considering that he is the most important man in my life, it's remarkable how little I know about him. C. W. Blaser, CBE; the C. W. must stand for something, but I haven't the faintest idea what. To me, he's Mr. Blaser or, more usually, 'sir'. Handsome? I suppose so, in an ex-naval, pride-of-the-quarterdeck sort of way. He's about fifty years old, with iron-grey hair, and a face made up of clefts and creases. There are clefts in his forehead, and creases around his eyes; he has two deep clefts angling down either side of a thin, hard mouth, and he has a cleft in his chin which could make him look like Cary Grant, but which doesn't. His eyes survey the world from beneath a formidable pair of eyebrows; they are greyish eyes, not quite blue, and not quite any other colour. There is a basilisk quality in the way he uses them, and over the years I have learned to fix my own gaze on a point just above the bridge of his nose; I find him less intimidating that way.

But the most disconcerting thing about him is that he never looks at me as a woman. Not that it would do him any good, but it's discouraging when every man looks at you in one way, while the one most important in your life looks at you in an entirely different way. Earlier on in our association, I must admit

1

to having tried some of the feminine wiles on him, hoping at least for *some* sort of reaction. I didn't try the low-cut blouse, or the black suspenders under a short skirt—which can be effective, but which I find too personal for mass consumption—but I paid particular attention to my hair, which is reddish, and I fluttered my eyes, which are greenish, and I poked out my chest, which is largish but firmish; and I licked my lips a couple of times, and crossed my legs, and sighed a little. Nothing.

I decided much later that when he thinks of me, which can't be very often, he thinks of me as a Fred. But then I suppose he's on the right track; if he thought of me as a Katy, he'd never ask me to do some of the extraordinary things he does ask me to on occasions. As long as he is the boss and I'm just a simple employee, it's better that our relationship remain on the completely negative level that it has done up to now.

I'd only been in from New York for two hours when his secretary called me.

'Mr. Blaser would like to see you,' she said.

'I'm in the bath.' I was, too—a hot, steaming, overful bath laced with Fenjel and Epsom salts. There's nothing like Epsom salts for easing the aches out of insteps that have practically cracked under the strain of walking across the Atlantic. I'd been up and down the economy class aisle so many times that my arches felt like they had been fractured. It's not so bad on TWA or Pan-American because they provide inflight entertainment in the form of movies. This keeps the passengers quiet for a good ninety minutes, and gives one a breathing space. I don't wish to appear unpatriotic, but BOAC plays hell with its long-distance hostesses; with no movie to pass the time, the passengers get bored, and when they get bored they invariably buzz for the hostess. They're never quite sure why they send for her. Most of the time they don't ask for anything particular; they just talk, and we, the hostesses, just listen and make suitable comments where necessary.

But at least I'm not tied to BOAC like some of the girls. One day I'll be BOAC, all trim and navy blue, but the next I'm as likely to turn up in the pale blue of PanAm or the red of TWA or, my favorite, the sari of Air India or Pakistan. There's something terribly elegant about a sari; it's both sexy and practical, whereas most sexy getups are uncomfortable to wear and, on occasions, downright embarrassing. Not that I'm anti-sex by any means; given a combination of the right time, the right place and the right man, I'm all for it. I take my pills regularly and I can honestly say that, providing the three conditions just mentioned are there, Katy won't be found wanting. But I was a well-brought-up young lady, a credit to my parents and a virgin longer than ninety percent of my friends. Still, there comes a time … There always does. I learned to take my pleasures, kicks, jollies, whatever you like to call them, when they were presented, without too much thought for the morning after. Because in my line of business I can never be sure there's even going to be a morning after. And when I say that, I'm not thinking entirely of air-hostessing.

After Mr. Blaser's secretary had hung up, I hauled myself out of the bath and started to dry off. If Mr. Blaser said 'Jump!' one jumped. He wanted to see me, so that was that as far as I was concerned. BOAC or TWA may have been picking up my tab on the surface, but I worked for Mr. Blaser first, last and in between. I dressed quickly, but carefully; Mr. Blaser liked his people to look right. I'd been in disgrace for a whole week once when I had turned up with a ladder in my stocking.

'We pay you a very generous clothing allowance, Miss Touchfeather. Please see that you use it in the manner for which it is designed.'

There was no point in telling him that the clothing allowance barely covered cosmetics and dry cleaning. He wouldn't have understood; he didn't wear cosmetics and I'm sure that he had a wife hidden away somewhere who sponged and pressed his suits religiously.

I had a reasonably heavy date for later that evening so, as it was already past seven, I settled for my little black number, the dress that nearly makes me look like a lady. That's another thing about Mr. Blaser—he likes his people to look as though they could have been brought up in Cheltenham or Tunbridge Wells. The fact that I was Streatham born and bred he chooses to ignore.

When I was ready, I unwrapped my genuine, natural wild-mink stole from its polythene cocoon and called a mini-cab. The mink most certainly hadn't been bought out of my clothing allowance, but the less said about that the better. Five minutes later the house phone rang.

'Miss Smith?' enquired a voice. I confirmed that I was Miss Smith and that I would be right down. I have found that it saves a great deal of trouble to use the name Smith when it's not important. Imagine what I've had to go through with Touchfeather, especially with some of the more chatty cab drivers and such like. This one wasn't chatty and gave me no trouble at all; he was too busy trying to find the address I had given him.

Thirty-two Pandam Street is an adjunct of the Ministry of Civil Aviation. It's an old building sadly in need of demolition. It houses, among other things, the department whose job it is to investigate air disasters after the investigators have investigated. In other words, when the official boys have finished sifting the wreckage and made their findings, the lads from Pandam Street swipe all the files and try to discover what *really* happened. Not, I hasten to add, that they ever find a discrepancy in 'cause of accident'. They're not interested in that; they're interested in the 'cause of the cause'. A bomb in the luggage compartment has got to have been placed there by someone; a failure of two engines simultaneously or a malfunctioning altimeter may be just that, but there has to be a reason for the failure which sometimes goes beyond the mere collapsing of tried and tested equipment. They usually check the passenger list first, and it's surprising how much information can be gleaned from a list of names, especially when that list can be checked against every other list in existence, whether it belong to MI6, the CIA or, on one momentous occasion, the KGB. But apart from that department, with which I have very little to do, 32 Pandam Street also houses Mr. Blaser.

I paid off my mini-cab and, mounting the four steps to the front door, rang the bell. The door was opened by Bill Banks, who grinned lecherously when he saw me.

'Ah, Miss Tootchfeather,' he said. That was the way he pronounced it. 'Nice to see you, very nice indeed.' I gave him my number-one-type smile, the one reserved for friends, and then slapped his hand as he pinched my bottom in passing.

'Careful, Bill. Someone might see us.'

'There's no one here,' he said, reaching out again. I sidestepped smartly and planted a big wet kiss on his cheek. 'That'll keep you going for a while, you dirty old man!'

He wheezed into laughter, blasting out a smell of camphor and Guinness.

'I'll be all ready for you when you finish with 'im,' he said, nodding towards the stairs.

'I can hardly wait,' I said. Bill Banks was seventy-two, but even though he was one hundred percent talk, I never travelled in the elevator with him; it had broken down between floors on one occasion, and I had been stuck with him for ninety minutes. He hadn't tried to rape me or anything like that, but the smell of camphor and stout in a confined space can be pretty overpowering after the first ten minutes.

I ducked past him to the stairs and walked up the two flights to the door marked records. I knocked and went in. Miss Moody was still at work. I think she must live in Mr. Blaser's pocket, because I've never been in that office when she hasn't been there, and I've visited at some very strange hours. She's a little, grey-haired body of indeterminate age, and she never smiles. This isn't to say that she is unfriendly, but she possesses the most atrocious set of false teeth, which have on occasions been known to drop out onto her lap. So she tries to keep her mouth tightly shut all the time, talking as much as possible through her nose.

'He's waiting for you,' she said as I walked in. 'You look very nice.'

She always gave me a morale booster before I went into Mr. Blaser's office, because she knew I wouldn't get one once I crossed the threshold. That was just one of the things that made me fond of Miss Moody. There were others, like the fact that she was responsible for checking my expenses, and she had been known to pass items that Mr. Blaser didn't even know existed. I tapped politely on the door and waited for the light affixed to the lintel to turn green. Miss Moody gave me a nod of encouragement, and I walked in.

TWO

The first time I met Mr. Blaser I had been an air hostess pure and simple—well, simple anyway. To be an air hostess had been my ambition since I was fourteen years old and, as one of the prime requisites was at least one foreign language, I surprised all my teachers by shining in French, while at all other subjects I was never more than three away from the bottom of the class. And because languages seemed to appeal to me, they took me off domestic science and gave me Spanish, and off biology onto German. Italian I picked up in my spare time. So, by the time I was old enough to apply for the job as air hostess, I was fluent in four languages and could say 'No!' in half a dozen more. I enjoyed the training enormously, not least because of the uniform I was issued on the first day. I have a good figure and, never having had too much money to spend on clothes, the first putting on of my uniform remains one of the red-letter days of my life, like the first time you kissed a boy, or the first time you... only I hadn't at the time. I romped through the training, passing out with the highest marks anyone could remember.

My first flight was also memorable in that I fell in love with the Captain. He was tall, handsome, amusing and very, very gentle. He could ease a 707 onto the ground as softly as a falling leaf, his large hands coaxing maximum reaction from his plane with minimum fuss. We stopped over in Beirut for two days, during which time I learned what his plane felt like. I wasn't very 'with it' in those days. To me, the verb 'to seduce' was something the male practised on the female. Apart from fluttering my eyelashes, I had no idea how to go about getting the man I wanted, but I wanted to go to bed and apparently I put the message across, because that's where we ended up. It was the first time for me and I was desperately frightened that I would be a disappointment to him. I started out nervously, trying to remember all the things I'd read and heard about that were supposed to please a man. But it is something you just can't learn from books. After five minutes with those gentle hands, I mislaid my mental manual and the whole operation was taken over by an automatic pilot I wasn't even aware I possessed. Two weeks later we were married in Mexico City, and three months after that I was a widow.

I try not to be maudlin about this. It happened three years ago. I tell myself that had he lived our marriage would automatically have descended from its elevated plane to the more mundane world of diapers, hot stoves and the seven-year itch. But it never had a chance to come down from the metaphorical honeymoon we were still having. After Tom died, I mooned about for a couple of weeks, completely lost and loathing myself because I wasn't pregnant.

Then the airline called me and asked me to go back to work. I refused at first. Then I began to wonder what I was going to do for the rest of my life on my widow's pension. That did it—the words 'widow's pension'. They had a connotation of middle-aged, deprived women drying up until they blew away. So I went back to work. It was all very depressing at first; I'd be meeting people we had known together and going places we had both been. The first time I returned to Beirut I cried like a baby all night. But everything passes except memory. In a couple of months I had pulled myself together sufficiently not to feel sick every time I saw a man with four gold rings on his sleeve.

And it was about then that Mr. Blaser entered my life. Considering the subsequent impact he was to have on it, it was surprising that he entered with so little fuss. I was ten minutes from boarding a flight to Nassau when the Duty Officer told me that I was wanted in Flight Control. I'd never been in Flight Control before. Our job is to keep the passengers happy and healthy; the men up front look after everything else. With no idea what it was about, I checked that my seams were straight and reported to the office.

Mr. Blaser got to his feet as I came in. It was the first and last time he ever did so and he shook my hand dryly when I introduced myself. He indicated for me to sit down and then he slid back into the chair from which he had uncoiled.

'Very sorry to hear about your husband, Miss Touchfeather,' he said. I had reverted to my maiden name when I returned to work. It had been ten weeks by then, and I was able to accept condolences without bursting into tears. So I sat there, making the appropriate inane remarks one does in such situations, and wondering why this strange man should be sorry. To the best of my knowledge he hadn't even known Tom. Which shows how wrong you can be.

'I knew your husband very well,' he said. 'He worked for me on and off.'

I nodded, feeling that nothing was required of me at this stage. I was wrong again.

'Aren't you interested in what he did?'

'He was a Captain,' I said.

'Among other things,' said Mr. Blaser. 'Among other things.'

'What sort of things?' I asked, not too keen to know. My memory parcel was all neatly tied and labelled and I didn't want anyone messing about with the knots. But, before enlightening me, he shot off on a tangent which I had some difficulty in following.

'I've examined your personal file very thoroughly,' he said. 'When you were seventeen you visited West Berlin. What was the purpose of this visit?'

That was something I knew wasn't in my personal file, and I said so.

'Not your employer's file, Miss Touchfeather. Mine.'

'Why have you got a file on me?' I said, feeling a little shirty. 'I don't even know you.'

'I hope to rectify that,' he said smoothly.

'I've got to go,' I said, getting to my feet. 'My flight is due to be called.'

'I've had you taken off the flight,' he said.

I sat down again. I didn't know who he was, but he just had to be someone; normally you had to lose a leg to be taken off a flight at such short notice.

'West Berlin?' he said.

'I went with a school party. There were six of us taking "A" level German.'

'Yes?' he prompted.

'We stayed for five days in a crummy little hotel, speaking nothing but German and visiting the museums.'

'That's all?'

'What else?' I said, still a little miffed.

'You didn't visit the Eastern sector, did you?'

'Good heavens, no!' I said. 'What on earth for?'

He looked at me steadily for a long moment. 'Good,' he said. 'I thought it must have been something like that, but we like to be sure.'

'Sure of what?' I asked, genuinely mystified.

But he'd finished on his tangent. He ignored my question and went straight on. 'Your late husband was one of my couriers,' he said.

I stared at him, blank faced. There didn't seem to be anything to say. So Tom had been a courier; lots of Captains run errands on the side, strictly legal and aboveboard. Some deliver diplomatic pouches; others carry personal mail for overseas employees; it happens all the time.

'It was in the course of his work for me that he was murdered,' Mr. Blaser went on.

I remained blank faced, but only because everything had gone numb suddenly. He gave me thirty seconds to deanaesthetise before continuing. 'I, that is my department, thought you might want to assist in the apprehension of those responsible.' He talked like that occasionally, using long words where short ones would have been more effective. I clenched my teeth once to make sure everything was working. When I spoke, even I was surprised at how normal my voice sounded.

'My husband died in an automobile accident,' I said.

'Quite,' said Mr. Blaser. 'But did you never wonder what caused the accident?'

Actually, I had wondered. It had been reported that he had driven into a brick wall at seventy miles an hour, just outside Rome. At the inquest a number of theories had been advanced, from the condition of the road, which was bad, through the fact that it was an unmarked dangerous bend, down to mechanical failure somewhere in the car. Accidental death had, of course, been the verdict, but the positive cause of the accident had never been clearly established. I had wondered at the time, because Tom drove a car with the same gentle care that he flew an aeroplane, or made love to a woman. Crashing into a brick wall at seventy miles an hour just didn't fit the image. But I had been wallowing too deep in misery and self-pity to pay much attention to the coroner's findings, and anyway I had been fifteen hundred miles away from the proceedings.

'What caused the accident?' I asked, not really sure that I wanted to know.

'This,' he said. He pulled something from his pocket and dropped it into the metal ashtray on the desk in front of him. It hit the ashtray with a solid clunk that stiffened my spine and froze me to my chair. Even from where I was sitting I could see what it was, and I just didn't want to know. I wanted to get out of the office; I wanted to scream out loud; and I wanted to cut Mr. Blaser's throat. But I did none of these things. With an admirable sense of the dramatic, Mr. Blaser waited for my reaction, knowing what it would be before I did myself. Hypnotised by what was in the ashtray, dreading what I was doing, but unable to help myself, I stood up, took a step towards the desk, reached down and picked up the small piece of flattened lead, feeling its rough contours between my fingers, unable to put it down, my hand shaking.

'It's a three-oh-three rifle bullet,' said Mr. Blaser. 'It was removed from your husband's head during the postmortem.' The little lead slug weighed a ton, but still I couldn't put it down. Mr. Blaser continued. 'For reasons I won't go into at the moment, it was expedient not to bring this out at the inquest.'

Suddenly the full impact hit me; this insignificant piece of distorted metal had crashed into Tom's skull, splattering blood and bone, extinguishing in a blinding flash everything I loved and lived for. It seemed to grow red hot suddenly and I dropped it back onto the desktop. It rolled off, onto the floor and under Mr. Blaser's chair. He made no attempt to retrieve it.

'Sit down, Miss Touchfeather,' he said. I sat. 'I'd like you to answer my question,' he continued flatly.

'What question?' My mind seemed to have blanked out completely.

'Would you be interested in helping us apprehend the man who murdered your husband?' I still didn't grasp what he was saying, but I must have nodded, because he suddenly got to his feet.

'Good,' he said. 'Let's go back to town.' I got up and followed him like a trained seal.

It seemed pretty cruel at the time, but looking back on the whole thing I believe that the dramatics with the bullet were necessary. After all, I was only an ordinary sort of a girl, and it needed something pretty drastic to shake me out of the lethargy I'd dropped into. Knowing Mr. Blaser as I do now, I doubt that the bullet was, in fact, the one that killed Tom, but it served its purpose admirably. We drove to Pandam Street in absolute silence, during which time I started to boil. Slowly at first, but by the time we arrived I was willing to take on any and everything required to avenge Tom's death.

What was required of me turned out to be considerably less than I was prepared to give. I made a contact in Rome; I identified a man I had met on one occasion with Tom; and then I enticed the man into a place and situation from which, I strongly suspect, he never emerged alive. But I didn't know that at the time. The knowledge of what I was doing and whom I was working for came slowly, piece by piece.

Mr. Blaser never spoke to me about the first job after it was over, but he must have been satisfied because two weeks later he contacted me again, and suddenly I found myself flying with PanAm and keeping a rendezvous in Washington DC, where a dishy man, who said he was with the CIA, flew with me as a passenger on to Honolulu, handed me a small sealed package and told me to deliver it to a Japanese Colonel in Tokyo. This time, when I reported back to London, I found that I had been taken off the airline availability list and reassign. Nobody ever told me to whom I was reassign, and I don't know to this day. That is, I know I work for Mr. Blaser, and he keeps referring to his department, but to the best of my knowledge, it has no official name, and very little official recognition. He's got a 'hot line' on his desk, painted bright blue, but it is connected to I know not where. I don't ask—and if I did, he wouldn't tell me.

After my second job, and my transference to Mr. Blaser's department, I was taken off flying duties for a short time and sent back to school. The school was a dignified country house, high on the South Downs, a sort of lightweight Roedean from the outside. But there the similarity ended. The curriculum was strictly St. Trinian's for adults. I was shown how to use a gun, how to kill a man and how not to kill him, how to mix a mickey finn from the ingredients normally found in any women's handbag and how to hide things like microfilms in the most extraordinary places.

All this knowledge and a great deal more was imparted to me by a WRAC Sergeant of terrifying proportions and strong lesbian inclinations. She was rather a dear actually, and once I'd got the message across that I wasn't interested, she didn't bother me. She had a hatred of men that was almost pathological, and when describing the six most efficient ways to disable a member of the opposite sex, she would grow almost lyrical in her prose. Bessie was her name, and I have had cause to thank her many times for what she taught me. Her lessons have got me out of serious trouble on a number of occasions and I hope for her sake that some of the knowledge of what I have done has leaked back to her. I can imagine her beady little eyes sparkling as she reflects on the men I have left strewn in my wake. Her greatest disappointment was that I didn't share her butch tendencies, not because she fancied me herself, but because she considered that what I possessed was far too good to throw away on any man's altar.

I don't agree about that, of course. To me, sex is fun—and I don't go along with the theory about men needing it more than women either. Most women need it just as much, but they're more capable of controlling themselves if they're not getting it. Being a freelance air hostess has its advantages; one gets to meet a vast number of good-looking, eligible men, with the added bonus that there's very little chance of them tripping over each other. Not being a greedy girl, I make do with three on a semi-permanent basis. One of them is the airport manager in one of the South American countries; another is a Flight Captain on the New York–Los Angeles run; and my home number is just a nice guy who sells motor cars and considers a trip to the Isle of Wight as foreign travel. They're all nice men, and I suppose I'm a little in love with all three of them. They all want to marry me to a greater or lesser degree, but I've had my fill of marriage for the moment and I've no wish to settle down yet awhile. Besides, masochistic as it may seem, I actually enjoy working for Mr. Blaser.

There are occasional drawbacks, of course, like the time I was locked in a cellar for three days with two Sicilian founder members of the Mafia, but I have learned to relegate such incidents to the realm of occupational hazards, and the drawbacks are amply compensated for by the enormous satisfaction I get occasionally over a job well done. I'm good at my job. Fortunately I don't need Mr. Blaser to tell me this, because he never says a word. But the fact that I never seem to stop working, combined with the knowledge that I usually accomplish exactly what I've been asked to do, makes me secure in my self-confidence.

To put it a different way, I flatter myself I'd have made a hell of a James Bond, if it wasn't for the fact that I'm not a fellow. As you'll gather, I'm not modest either!

As I came into the office, Mr. Blaser was rummaging in the centre drawer of his desk. He told me to sit down without even looking up. I pulled up a chair, sat down and crossed my legs. With skirts the way they are these days, there's not much one can do about decorum. Not that I cared much. I may be a Fred to Mr. Blaser, but a girl can't help but keep trying. Finally he produced what he was looking for, a pipe scraper. With it he proceeded to gouge out the interior of his evil smelling pipe, sucking at the stem occasionally, making a noise like the bath water running out.

'You're due a few days off, Miss Touchfeather,' he said.

'Yes, sir.' I was due about six weeks off as a matter of fact, but there was no point in mentioning it.

'I'm afraid I must ask you to postpone it for a few days,' he said, blowing down the pipe stem and sending up a cloud of ash from the bowl.

'Yes, sir,' I said. There was no point in pressing him; he wouldn't get to the crunch until he was good and ready.

'Filthy weather we're having,' he said. I agreed we were having filthy weather, but as I had just spent two weeks in Nassau, perhaps I wasn't as sympathetic as I might have been.

'What do you know about Gerastan Industries?' he shot at me suddenly.

'Absolutely nothing,' I said.

'You should,' he said, sourly. 'They make half the instruments that keep you up in the air.' And then I recalled vaguely having seen the name Gerastan printed on some of the dials that festooned the flight decks. 'But no matter,' he continued, deciding to ignore my ignorance. 'Gerastan Industries, apart from making aircraft instruments, are leaders in the field of electronic research and development.' I tried to look interested, no easy feat in the circumstances. 'They are basically an American corporation with a large United Kingdom offshoot. The parent company holds United States Government contracts worth billions of dollars, mostly connected with missile development. The United Kingdom offshoot concerns itself mainly with computer development and aircraft instrumentation.

'However ...' he said more loudly, and I jerked myself awake. 'However, there is a small research unit in this country which has been doing some very important work. It is with this unit that we are concerned.' He tipped himself back in his chair to an alarming angle before continuing.

'Such is the value of the work done by this unit, that the parent company have repeatedly tried to get them to move to the United States. But the head of the unit, a Professor Partman, flatly refuses to go. He is too valuable to lose, so Gerastan have been forced to allow him to work on here in England. Two weeks ago, in Bombay, a man was fished out of the sea. He had been dead about two days. He was unidentifiable, but on him was found a microfilmed report on the work that Professor Partman's boys are working on. There's no need for you to know what that work is; you probably wouldn't understand it anyway.' Thank you very much, I thought. 'Sufficient that the work is classified up to Maximum Red.'

Now I was impressed. Maximum Red is as maximum as you can go without climbing off the top of the scale.

'It has been impossible to trace back the leakage, and we still have no idea as to the identity of the dead man. It is unlikely that we shall ever know. But we are reasonably sure that, since he still had the film on his person, he had not passed on any information. We think he was merely a courier, a contact man, and he died, or was killed, before he could complete his assignment.'

I thought that hereabouts I had better start contributing something. 'If he didn't manage to pass on his information I don't see that there's much to worry about. Surely it shouldn't be too difficult to find out where the leak is at this end, and then block it.'

'We've found out,' he said.

I felt like saying that he didn't have any problems, then. But if that was so, what was I doing there? I soon found out.

'Professor Partman has booked a first-class reservation on Air India 102 to Bombay tomorrow,' he said.

THREE

They call it the Maharajah Service. It's only another aeroplane trip, but they dress it up a little. We hostesses wear saris, and we put our palms together and bow our heads instead of saying good morning. All I needed as a supplement to my permanent tan was a dark wig and a caste mark on my forehead, and I looked Indian enough to fool anyone but another Indian. My instructions were pretty flexible: I was to keep my eye on Professor Partman during the trip, and later, too, if I could work it. The fact that he was unmarried and forty-two years old made me think that there was every chance that I *could* work it. The trip took fourteen hours, and if I couldn't charm him in that amount of time, then I was in the wrong job. However, if he turned out to be a misogynist or a fairy, and I was unable to keep contact after we landed, I was to report to someone in Bombay, and that would be an end of it as far as I was concerned.

Of course, my first question had been why were they letting Partman fly halfway round the world if they didn't trust him? According to Mr. Blaser, there was no way they could stop him. It seems that Professor Partman was one of that vanishing breed, an individualist. He had even refused to sign the Official Secrets Act. If he felt like going to Bombay or Timbuctoo, there was no way of stopping him, bar breaking both his legs. I must say, I built up a pretty wild picture of him from the background file that Mr. Blaser made me read. I constructed an image of a wild-eyed, shaggy-haired, scruffy extrovert, a cross between Albert Einstein and Rasputin. Nobody had seen fit to provide me with a photograph, so when a man who looked like a cross between Gregory Peck and Prince Philip took the seat allocated to Partman, I tried to turf him out. He flashed a blinding smile at me and explained in a soft, slightly burred voice that he was Professor Partman. Then he added something in what I could only assume was Hindustani. I bowed my apologies, explaining that I didn't speak my native tongue because I was only half Indian, my father having been one of the last survivors of the British Raj, and I had been educated at Roedean. He seemed to accept this and, girding my sari, I set out to make his trip as memorable as possible. This was no hardship, because I fancied him from the moment of that first smile.

We were by no means full, so I had plenty of time to spare, and after lunch had been cleared away, I broke the rules and accepted his invitation to sit with him for a while. The Chief Steward glared at me, but he'd obviously had some sort of instruction from higher up, because it went no further than that. By the time we reached Khartoum, we were old friends and, what was more important, we had a date for dinner that evening. He told me he was staying at the Taj Hotel, which automatically became the hotel I was staying at. An hour later we had arranged to drive in from the airport together and I was beginning to think that the person who had been detailed to take over surveillance was going to earn his money the easy way.

Bill, because that's what I was calling him now, explained that he was visiting Bombay partly for pleasure and partly because he had promised to read a couple of papers at Bombay University. He had been in India during the war, and had always promised himself he would one day return to the country that had so fascinated him.

The trouble was that about here I began to think that Mr. Blaser was barking up the wrong tree; this dishy man couldn't possibly be what he was suspected of being. And this is where a serious flaw in my training started to show up. If I was a man, they'd say I was a sucker for a pretty face. In my case, it means that at a certain stage my emotions take over, and where I should be judging a man from the documented facts, I start judging him by my pulse rate. A quick count showed that Bill Partman was having more effect on me than I had any right to let him, and I was positively drooling at the thought of having dinner with him. I said he was a dish. Well, it went deeper than that. It was painfully obvious after the first hour that he reminded me too much of my husband to be healthy. I've met all sorts of men in all sorts of situations, but the deadly ones, as far as I am concerned, are the big, gentle-eyed, soft-spoken men with large capable hands, and a way of looking at you as though you are the only other person who exists. They have other characteristics, these men, but they are too subtle and too personal to put into words. I've only met three of them. I married the first; I made a complete idiot of myself over the second, who was already married; and Bill Partman was the third. I hoped that Mr. Blaser and his informants were hopelessly wrong and, if they weren't, wondered whether or not there was anything I could do to lessen the ultimate fate that would befall Bill Partman. Of course, there wasn't, so I clung desperately to my first hope, that the whole thing was a ghastly mistake.

We met headwinds on the last leg of our journey across the Indian Ocean and put down at Bombay Airport, Santa Cruz, ninety minutes late. Bill promised to meet me outside customs and I practically ran off the plane, clearing my own baggage in nothing flat. I made my contact and told him that I would continue to handle the situation, and would he please pass the word back to Mr. Blaser. He agreed to stay on the job anyway—he was drawing expenses and didn't particularly want to go back to the office.

Then, like a schoolgirl on her first date, I went to meet Bill. As we drove in from the airport he wanted to know what some of the new buildings were, and why had they pulled down so and so. Fortunately I had been in Bombay earlier in the year and I knew most of the answers. Those I didn't know, I made up. And by this time I flattered myself that he felt pretty much the same way as I did.

Within two minutes of checking into the hotel I was moved out of my original room and into one next door to Bill's. This had been arranged on the phone by the contact I had met at the airport. Then I had to act all surprised and bashful as I pulled open the connecting door and discovered Bill in the middle of his unpacking. We went down to dinner together and spent an indecent time lingering over the coffee. Bill had thoughtfully brought a flask of brandy down with him, and by the time we started back upstairs I was three parts tiddly. Outside my room I allowed myself to be kissed chastely, and then I let myself in and started to get ready for bed, waiting for the inevitable.

It came ten minutes later, a discreet tap on the communicating door. I wrestled with my conscience. I really did. Here was a man I hadn't known existed twenty-four hours ago, a man who could possibly be a traitor, and who I would have to turn in if he was. I was responsible for keeping a watch on him and reporting the least sign of anything suspicious. Added to that, he believed I was an Anglo-Indian with hair as dark as night and a body to match. It was feasible that I could keep my wig on through anything that might have followed, but how was I going to explain away those white slashes of flesh across my breasts and hips, standing out against my tan like a transparent bikini? The scales were weighted too heavily against me, I decided, and I took the only way out. I ignored the tapping on the door and, after a few minutes, when he gave up, I quietly cried myself to sleep.

When one considers some of the situations I have been in since working for Mr. Blaser, it's strange that I am still capable of behaviour like falling for a man and wanting him with all the intensity of a twenty-year-old. But the fact remains that somewhere not too deep inside me is a core of solid marshmallow that thrives on kind looks and gentleness and warmth. I've managed to construct a pretty hard shell around this softness, but it's still there, and has the habit of leaking out through the shell at the damnedest times. Fortunately the men I generally come across in my professional capacity arouse in me nothing but distaste and I can perform my duties in a detached and, I hope, efficient manner. Then, just as one is feeling safe and secure, along comes a Bill Partman, and my insulation is cracked to hell and gone.

We had breakfast together the following morning and he made no reference to his unsuccessful bid to storm my ramparts. For my part, I was too embarrassed to look up from my orange juice and coffee. He was to be met that morning by a man from the University and taken on a tour, ending with lunch with the faculty. The first of his papers he was to read that afternoon. Knowing my contact would pick him up as soon as he left the hotel, I saw him off after breakfast, standing outside the hotel until his car was out of sight. Then feeling like an absolute bitch, I let myself into his room and proceeded to dissect his luggage. After two hours I felt better; if he was carrying anything that he shouldn't be, it certainly wasn't in his room. And if it was as valuable as Mr. Blaser made out, he'd hardly be likely to cart it around with him. So, from my biased viewpoint, I surmised that the whole thing was a mistake and that Mr. Blaser had got his wires crossed somewhere.

I had lunch alone in the huge dining room of the hotel, surrounded by a dozen waiters, all regretting the passing of the Raj. Then I went back to my room. I stripped off completely and climbed under my mosquito net where I drifted off to a never-never land, where all the men looked like Bill and I was the only woman left alive.

The phone jerked me back to reality at five-thirty. It was my contact. Bill Partman was on his way upstairs. He had read his paper and been dropped back at the hotel. He had been in contact with no one other than the people at the University. I passed along my bit of news about having found nothing in his room. Then I got out of bed and started to make ready for another frustrating evening. We went for a *ghari* ride after dinner. Bombay is pretty depressing in the daytime, but at night its ugliness fades into the shadows and only beauty remains. This is especially so when you are sitting in a horse-drawn carriage, clip-clopping along, holding hands with a very attractive man. Mellowed old buildings, bathed in moonlight; giant moths fluttering kaleidoscopically in the lamplight; the smell of the sea, and the warmth of the night air; the sound of a street vendor's call, high and plaintive; and the distant hoot of a departing liner. By the time we arrived back at the hotel, I was a gone gal.

I allowed Bill to lead me by the hand up the huge curved staircase, not wanting to share our intimacy even with the elevator boy. He took my key from my nerveless fingers, opened my door and pushed me in gently. I didn't move a muscle as he kissed me, and once again my conscience and I joined battle. This time, my conscience lost. I stood still while he unwound my sari and allowed it to slip to the floor. He hadn't turned on the light, so the room was in semi-darkness, and if he noticed anything, he didn't say. Not that I would have cared much anyway. He unclipped my bra with such gentleness that I was hardly aware of it until I felt his hand curl round my breast. My nipples hardened under his touch and I shivered although the night was very warm. Then he pulled me towards him and we were kissing again. Our tongues met briefly and then more urgently. 'You can have my resignation, Mr. Blaser, as of now,' I said to myself as he led me towards the bed.

He was gentle, as I had known he would be, but he was firm and positive as well. His hands were insistent, caressing my

breasts, my stomach and my thighs, opening me up as though
I were a ripe fruit. It's madness, I thought, complete and utter
lunacy; what happens tomorrow if I have to … But tomorrow
was impossibly far away. Any latent reluctance buried in my
subconscious slowly seeped away under the persuasion of his
hands and mouth. Finally it was pure instinct that led me on,
all reason having long deserted me. And still he continued to
stroke reactions from my body until I begged him to make real
love to me.

'Now, Bill. Please. Now!'

He rolled over and I was conscious of his weight for a brief
second. Then all feeling other than the concentrated focal point
left me. Movement became urgent and autonomic, building up
towards that impossible climax which it should, and so often
doesn't, reach. I wanted it to last and last, and yet I chased it to
its end, searching and finally achieving what I was at the same
time trying to delay. And we matched each other perfectly. It was
as though we had been making love to each other all our lives. I
lay still for a long time afterwards, holding him close almost as
though I were frightened to let him go. He was the one to eventually break the spell. He lit two cigarettes and passed one to me. I
rested in his arms, pulling myself together slowly, piece by piece.
Finally I judged I was sufficiently in control to say something
reasonably lucid.

'I wondered why they called you Professor,' I said. 'Now I
know what you're a Professor of.'

'You weren't too bad yourself,' he said generously. 'Even if
you are not what you would have us all believe.'

I went cold suddenly and tried to keep myself from stiffening
in his arms. 'How's that?' I said innocently.

'You're no more an Indian than I am,' he said. 'And I come
from Bognor Regis.' Obviously the darkness hadn't been as complete as I thought. 'Your tan is an outside-in one, rather than the
other way round.'

'You won't tell anyone, will you?' I said.

'Tell them what? That my brown love wears a white bikini made of skin?' His brown love; I liked that. One more lie, I thought; then we'll forget the whole thing.

'Air India like their girls to be Indian,' I said. 'And I like working for Air India. As long as none of the paying customers finds out, they're happy, and so am I.'

'This paying customer is happy,' he said, reaching his hand for me again. But I beat him to it; after all, he had found out all about me, so it was about time I started to find out some things about him....

Later, as we lay there, warm and peaceful, he told me about himself. William Partman, age forty-two, unmarried, parents killed in an automobile accident when he was seven years old. There had been no brothers or sisters and he had been brought up by an aunt. He had won a scholarship to a redbrick university which had been delayed for a couple of years by his National Service at the tail end of the war. Then came four years of concentrated study, after which he passed out with more honours than any one man has a right to receive. He had declined the offer to stay on at the University in a teaching post, and moved out into industry to make his fortune. He hadn't made a fortune for himself, but he had for his employers, who marketed one of his computer developments and made ten million dollars in the process. When his contract had expired he had told them politely to get stuffed, and even the offer of a five-pound-a-week rise in salary didn't get him to change his mind.

Then, all on his own, he invented a small gizmo which meant absolutely nothing to me but obviously did to someone. He patented it and then leased the patents to the Gerastan Corporation on a royalty basis, thereby securing himself a yearly sum of money which would continue to the day he died and beyond. He refused to tell me how much at first, but as I was already entertaining serious designs on this man, I tickled him into eventual submission, and he told me.

'My God,' I said. 'I'm in bed with a millionaire!'

'Only if I live to be a hundred and sixty-two,' he said.

It seemed that Gerastan Industries were so happy with the situation that they allocated him unlimited funds to work on anything he chose, providing they had first option on anything he came up with. This happy state of affairs had existed for the last eight years, during which Bill had grown even richer. Then they had the only disagreement of their association.

'They wanted me to go to America,' he said.

'What's so bad about America?' I asked.

'Nothing, if you're an American. Personally, I can't stand the place. It's all neon and freeways.'

'I rather like it.'

'People can change their minds,' he said.

'Yours or mine?'

'I don't know yet. We'll work on it.'

Anyway, he had flatly refused to go when they asked him, and there was nothing the Corporation could do about it as long as they wanted to hang on to his services. Apparently he had even been interviewed by the almost mythical Roger Gerastan himself, a man who hadn't been seen in public now for as long as anyone could remember.

'Sent his own aeroplane to London for me,' said Bill. 'A bloody great DC-8 with a crew of six. Flew me all the way to California to his own private airfield. He lives in this extraordinary rambling sort of place, full of armed guards and man-eating Alsatians.'

But even the power of Roger Gerastan had failed to work with Bill, and the following day he had been flown back to London. All that had been a year ago, and since then he had continued to work on happily somewhere down on the South Downs, while the security forces of the West chewed their fingernails impotently. And that seemed to bring us back to square one and, before he got too tired from talking, I dragged him back into physical involvement.

Bill was scheduled to read his second paper at nine o'clock the following morning. I don't know how he made it, because we didn't get to sleep until five a.m. When I woke up it was eleven and he had left me a note on the pillow. 'Stay in bed. I'll be back for lunch.' I felt so marvellous that I had forgotten for a moment the reason I was here. Then I remembered—and at the same time I remembered that, while he was at the University, someone else was watching him. Not that there was any further need; of that I was convinced. But until I reported in, no one else was.

I debated for a time whether or not to call Mr. Blaser; then I decided against it. If he agreed with me that he had been wrong about Bill, then he would very likely order me home on the first available plane, whereas if I kept quiet I could stay with Bill under the guise of doing the job I was sent out to do. And anyway, Mr. Blaser was going to require more proof than the fact that one of his people found the subject under surveillance a marvellous lover. He just isn't the type to be swayed by such considerations, and it's no good waving things like woman's intuition at him. As far as he is concerned, if such a thing exists, it's to be viewed with considerable scepticism.

So I made no phone call. I turned on the bath and rang for the room to be done while I was in the tub. Then I ordered lunch for two to be sent up to the room, including a contraband bottle of champagne, which in Bombay is like ordering the crown jewels. By the time Bill arrived I was ready for him, having even discarded my wig, which had somehow remained in place during the previous night's exercise.

'My God,' he said when we had kissed, holding me at arm's length. 'My brown love is copper-topped with it.'

'Genuine, too,' I said.

'I don't believe it. That colour just can't be natural. It goes against nature.'

'I can prove it.'

'So prove it.' While the champagne cooled in the ice bucket, I proved it.

We spent a childish afternoon playing silly games which I hope my children, should I have any, don't play until they're over twenty-one. Then we dressed reluctantly and meandered down to dinner. Over dinner he told me that he had received a call, via the University, that he must return to London as soon as possible. It was rotten news because he had hoped to spend at least a couple of weeks in India, revisiting some of the places he remembered. But his employers, it seemed, thought otherwise, and could I use my influence to get him on the next flight to London? Nobody had reported to me about any long-distance telephone calls, but my sphere of influence didn't extend to the University switch-board. So, feeling completely happy, I went to the lobby to make my own phone call.

My intuition had been right. He had delivered his lectures and now he was going home. No secret meetings in back alleys. No suspicious rendezvous. Everything exactly as it appeared to be. I phoned my contact and made the necessary arrangements and reported them back to Bill. I was due out on the London flight tomorrow morning, and I had reserved a seat for him.

'You will personally be looked after by the best-looking, sexi-est hostess on the route,' I told him.

'I thought you were coming along,' he said. And the whole evening went like that, silly jokes that kept us both in stitches, while we both wondered how early we could decently escape back upstairs. Eventually we did, and that night was even bet-ter than the previous one. Now we were armed with an intimate knowledge of each other's bodies which made lovemaking less of an adventure, but more of an experience. As I drifted off to sleep, I was composing in my mind the letter of resignation I would hand to Mr. Blaser as soon as Bill asked me to marry him.

FOUR

To cope with the business of organising the flight, Bill and I parted company for a couple of hours the following morning. I noticed that he was still being watched by my contact. If it made the department happy, good luck to them. They certainly weren't going to find anything on my boy. As he came aboard with the other passengers, I pressed my palms together and bowed low. He didn't bat an eyelid as I showed him to his seat. I promised to come and sit with him as soon as the takeoff paraphernalia was completed; then I moved off to settle the other first-class passengers. There were only four of them, two Indians, one Asiatic and a European. One of the girls from the economy section remarked that she only had twenty people aboard and the airline wasn't going to get very rich on this trip.

I paid my respects to Captain Singh immediately after takeoff. I had flown with him before, and if he wondered why I was a red-haired English girl one day, and a raven-haired Indian the next, he didn't say so. I collected his and the rest of the flight crew's order for lunch and passed it to the Chief Steward. And that seemed to be that as far as I was concerned.

There were two other girls working the cabin and, with only five passengers including Bill, they weren't going to be rushed off their feet. So I went to sit with Bill. We held hands surreptitiously, twining fingers while we gazed into each other's eyes and spoke volumes without saying a word. I left him for half an hour while lunch was being served, and each time I passed his seat, I stopped for a moment and he stroked my leg. It was all very childish and extremely bad behaviour for an air hostess, but I couldn't have cared less. Later we sat and talked the afternoon away. I told him about Tom and he squeezed my hand sympathetically, and he told me about the girl he had been going to marry who had died of leukemia and I squeezed *his* hand.

But whatever my training had lacked in the emotional area, it had still been thorough enough to prevent me from telling Bill what I really did for a living. Of course, it may have been a sneaky feeling of shame on my part that made me keep my mouth shut; he might have confused my motives for being with him, and I didn't want any of that at this stage. Later I would tell him everything, but at the moment it was sufficient that I was an air hostess and I spent most of my time living in London where I had a cosy little flat which could possibly be rearranged to accommodate two.

The headwinds we had met going out were now helping us, and we put down in Khartoum thirty-five minutes ahead of schedule. The passengers who were travelling on remained in the designated airport area, while the half a dozen who were leaving us disappeared through customs and immigration. And here we in first class picked up two more passengers. They were Americans by the look and sound of them. They were deeply engrossed with each other, no doubt talking about the oil refinery they had just sold, or the diamond mine they had just bought. Immediately after takeoff I offered them a drink, which they refused a little impolitely, and then I rejoined Bill. With nothing much to worry about any longer, and with the comfort of Bill sitting next to me, I dozed off. I'd had very little sleep the past two nights, and there was a lot of catching up to do.

When I opened my eyes I had no idea how long I had been asleep, or what had awakened me. I wasn't sure, but there seemed to have been a slight change in the pitch of the engines. If one flies a great deal, one becomes very conscious of the slightest variation in the established flight pattern. I was facing Bill as I opened my eyes. He was sitting on the inside seat, and I started to smile, until I noticed that he was staring past me into the aisle. I turned to see what he was looking at so intently and found myself peering down the barrel of a gun, held inches away from my face. It was being held by one of the Americans who had boarded at Khartoum.

Even as I saw the gun, it swung away from me to embrace the other passengers. All of them, that is, except the Asiatic gentleman who had been with us since Bombay. He was standing in the centre aisle facing the economy section. I couldn't see his hands because his back was towards me, but from the faces of the economy passengers, he was obviously holding a gun, too. I looked round for the other American. The door to the flight deck was open and I could see him leaning over the co-pilot, talking to him. I could also see Captain Singh's arm hanging limply over the side of his seat. Groping my way up out of sleep as I was, it took a full three seconds for all this to sink in. We were being hijacked. It was almost too ludicrous to be true, but the whole thing was confirmed as I made to shift my position. The gun held by the American swung back lazily, until I was looking down the snout once more.

'Stay where you are, darling,' said the American. 'No fuss, no trouble.'

I reached out blindly for Bill's hand and clutched at it. It should have been a comfort, but it wasn't; all I could see was the gun. With it went the knowledge that we were flying at twenty-nine thousand feet and, should the American be misguided enough to fire it, he'd puncture the pressurised cabin and we'd all be dead. I wondered whether he was aware of this fact. Better mention it, I thought.

'You're not going to fire that gun, I hope,' I said tentatively.

'Not if I can help it, darling,' he said.

'You'll puncture the cabin if you do.'

He grinned at me equably. 'I know it, darling,' he said. 'But don't worry your pretty little head about it. We won't be up here for long.'

I noticed then that our flight path was a descending one. I glanced past Bill out of the window. We were flying over desert and were already far lower than I had thought. I shifted my glance to Bill, who squeezed my hand.

'How long was I asleep?' I asked.

'Thirty-five minutes.'

I tried to work out quickly where we were. Assuming we had kept roughly to our original course. Cairo couldn't be far off. This was small comfort considering the relationship that Nasser had with most of the world. What on earth were we carrying that could interest these modern-day pirates? I had no idea what was on the cargo manifest but, whatever it was, it must have been a pretty big prize. I mean, people just don't go around hijacking two-million-pound VC10s unless they've got pretty strong reasons.

I looked out of the window again. Cairo it was. I could see the Nile, and to the East the high cliffs of the Mokattam Hills. I'd only put down there a couple of times, but there was no mistaking it. I looked back towards the flight deck. The second American had stepped back from the co-pilot and was letting him fly the aircraft. It was just as well, because a VC10 is a lot of aeroplane and needs a great deal of care and attention, especially when you're only a copilot and not supposed to have to handle it by yourself.

I slipped on my seat belt and told Bill to do the same, wishing that the American had had the sense to disable the co-pilot and not Captain Singh. The other American, the one standing close to me, made no effort to sit down. Neither did the Asiatic who was watching the economy section. Perhaps if the aircraft was put down heavily enough they'd be knocked every which way and we'd have a chance. But I realised almost immediately that it was a stupid hope, because even if they were all knocked out, the aircraft would be on the ground and too far along the runway to take off again without taxiing back. And if we were expected, as we obviously were, whoever was waiting for us wasn't going to allow us to taxi anywhere, except where he wanted.

There was a baby crying in the economy section and, for a moment, I thought of asking whether I could move back there. Then I realised that I couldn't see any of the other girls; they must have all been back with the other passengers. So I gritted my teeth and mentally joined the co-pilot to help him land the air-craft. It was a creditable effort considering all that he had against him but, as the reverse thrust of the engines roared out halfway along the runway, I felt Bill gently disengage his hand from mine. Glancing down I could see the deep indentations made in his palm by my fingernails. I looked at him, wanting to apologise, but he wasn't really with me. I'm sure that if I hadn't been sitting between him and the American, he would have made a grab for the gun. But Bill was a professor, a man of books, a gentle man. I, on the other hand, had seen what a bullet can do to a human being, and I didn't want to see it happen to Bill. I took his hand again quickly, trying to distract him. For one moment I thought I hadn't succeeded; I could feel the muscles in his hand and arm standing out stiffly.

'No, Bill,' I whispered.

He glanced at me as though he didn't recognise me; then the staring look in his eyes faded and I felt the muscles relax. I breathed again as we turned off the runway onto a taxiing apron.

From the window I could see that we weren't heading for the main airport buildings; they were way over to our left. We were making for a group of maintenance hangars on the edge of the airfield. The American on the flight deck stayed where he was until the engines were switched off. In the silence that fol-lowed, the child crying in the economy section sounded almost deafening.

Then there was a clattering against the outside of the aircraft and one of the Americans moved to open the main passenger hatch. A moment later the aircraft seemed full of small brown men in ill-fitting dark suits. One of them spoke rapidly to the American in a language I didn't understand and gestured angrily towards the passenger cabins. The American replied then turned to his companion, who nodded.

'Everybody out!' he barked.

The second American repeated the order to the Asiatic then moved to the front of the cabin as we unbuckled our seat belts and stood up.

We were led out of the aircraft into the baking heat outside and quickly ushered across the few yards that separated us from one of the hangars. Inside, it was even hotter, the sun's rays magnified by the high metal roof of the hangar. The child started to cry again. I wished I had been a few years younger, then I could have joined her.

We were herded into a group, thirty bewildered souls, while our American cousins and a couple of the Egyptians kept a steady eye on us. One thing I was glad to see was that Captain Singh had recovered sufficiently to make his own way from the aircraft. There was a thin streak of dried blood coming from beneath his turban, but all he looked was livid. He started by shouting at one of the Egyptians, but when that had no effect, he switched to one of the Americans.

I picked out phrases like 'international incident', 'freedom of the airways', 'piracy' and the like. But one of the Americans shut him up with a jab from his gun and, looking like a man whose whole world had suddenly disappeared in a puff of smoke, Captain Singh moved over to join us.

I was still standing hand in hand with Bill, so I was in a good place to hear and see everything that followed. A man appeared suddenly, outlined by the glare of the sunlight in the hangar door. At this distance, dwarfed by the dimensions of the hangar, he looked small, but as he walked towards us I could see that he was in fact enormous. Not only was he well over six feet six inches tall, but he was built with mountainous proportions, barely concealed by a sweat-soaked suit.

One of the little brown men fell into step beside him, taking three strides to his one. One of the Americans moved to meet him. Then the three of them came towards us. As he drew nearer I realised that it wasn't just the size of the newcomer that impressed. He was completely hairless, without even eyelashes, and his skin was almost dead white, as though it had been bleached. His features were generally Mongolian and his eyes were two small black buttons, dull and opaque. I've met some pretty frightening customers in my time, but this one was the daddy of them all. The child behind me started to scream now, and I didn't blame it one little bit. But worse was to come. He stopped three paces away from Bill and me, and the smell of his huge body was almost overpowering, a sickly sweet smell of sweat and cheap toilet water. He glanced at me briefly and then his eyes switched to Bill.

'Professor Partman?' His voice was high-pitched and sibilant, incongruous with a man of his size. I felt Bill stiffen beside me, but his voice was level and controlled as he answered.

'Yes, I'm Professor Partman.'

'You will come with us, please.' The man turned on his heels, about to move off, when Bill spoke again.

'I'll do nothing of the sort,' he said.

The big man turned back, a glimmer of surprise on his face; obviously he was accustomed to having his orders obeyed without question. Bill continued levelly.

'You have committed piracy, kidnapping, assault, theft, diplomatic mayhem and God knows what else. Why should I do anything you say?'

'Because there will be serious trouble if you do not,' came the sibilant hiss.

'You don't even know the meaning of the word,' said Bill. 'But, by Christ, you will when this lot gets out. There'll be an international clang all the way up to the United Nations.'

'You are one of thirty people, Professor Partman. The fate of the other twenty-nine rests entirely in your hands. You come with us and the others will be able to continue their journey immediately. You give me any trouble and I'll kill everyone, starting with her.'

He pointed a stubby finger at me like the barrel of a gun, and I felt my knees go weak. I knew the difference between threats that were idle and those that were genuine. This one was as genuine as I had ever heard—and Bill knew it, too. There was a moment's pause and then I felt him gently disengage his hand from mine. I tried to keep the contact, scrabbling for his fingers, but he moved away from me, and when I tried to move after him one of the Americans blocked my path.

'You stay right here, darling,' he said.

'Bill!' I said. He turned. I felt the tears well up in my eyes and I couldn't say another word. He smiled at me then, that gentle smile that had come to mean everything to me during the past couple of days. Then he turned and moved off after the big man. As he moved away to an office at the side of the hangar, the little brown men among us started to urge us back towards the main doors.

I walked with the others, but my eyes were fixed on Bill. I saw the group enter the office and, through the glass in the wall, I saw the big man turn and say something to Bill, who shook his head. I paused for a moment at the hangar door, still looking back, and I wished from the bottom of my heart that I hadn't. I saw the big man reach into his pocket. There was a metallic flash as he moved quickly, his arm crossing in front of Bill's face. Bill dropped back out of sight. A second later he was dragged back into view by the two Americans who were standing one on either side of him. Even from this distance, I could see that his face was covered with blood.

FIVE

I was barely conscious of getting back on board. By the time I had pulled myself together, we were airborne with a course set for Rome. Captain Singh was on the radio almost before we got off the ground, speaking ahead to Rome and setting in motion the wheels necessary to blow the whole thing into the international scandal it undoubtedly was.

For me, though, it was just a personal tragedy. The broader implications meant nothing as far as I was concerned. Realising that there had been something between Bill and myself, the other girls left me alone on this stage of the journey, doing my work for me. The passengers were excited now that everything was over. They had been part of something they would be able to talk about for the rest of their lives. Fear was replaced by ebullience and they chattered among themselves like a flock of starlings. The economy section had been opened up into the first class and drinks were being served free. Amid all this I remained a small oasis of misery, staring unseeing out of the window.

I had been right about Bill; that much was plain. And I consigned to the bottomless pit those faceless individuals who had allowed him to travel. It was painfully clear that whoever had failed to pick up the original microfilm had done the next best thing and gone straight to the source. There could have been nothing on that film that wasn't locked in Bill's head, and now they were in the process of unlocking it. I prayed hard and long that Bill wouldn't be stupid enough to try to hold out on them. I had learned since working for Mr. Blaser that there is no man living who can hold out against a determined and knowledgeable adversary who holds all the cards. There are ways of making a man talk that defy description; even hearing about them during my training had been sufficient to make me feel physically sick. And from what I had seen of the big man, he probably knew things that I hadn't even heard of.

Dear Bill! Darling Bill! My Bill, who had called me his brown love. I couldn't help it. The tears just wouldn't stop. They poured silently down my face. I tasted their salt and I died a little during that flight.

Our arrival at Rome had to be seen to be believed. There were a dozen cars and two dozen motorcycle police waiting for us on the arrival apron. All the passengers and crew were whisked into the cars and driven past mobs of screaming reporters to some airport offices set aside for the purpose. There we were received by officials from the Indian, British, American and Swiss Embassies, together with half a dozen members of the Italian Government and one extremely embarrassed gentleman from the Egyptian Consulate. But every time he opened his mouth everyone shouted at him, so he didn't make much of an impression.

We were questioned together and individually as the officials tried to build up a picture of what had occurred. It was plain that we were already an international incident and the world press were howling like a pack of wolves outside the door. I answered the questions as best I could, which wasn't easy, as each time I thought of Bill and his blood-covered face, I started to cry again. None of the officials interviewing us was cleared as far as I was concerned, so I couldn't beg off. To them I was just another hostess, with no deeper involvement than that which appeared on the surface. If Mr. Blaser had wanted me to make my true position known, he would have got word to me somehow. He hadn't, so I played it straight.

After a couple of hours the passengers were all loaded into another aircraft to continue their journey to London. The crew were to rest overnight and then fly back to Bombay the following day. Deprived of the passengers, the press seemed to grow tired of the whole thing, and we were loaded into a minibus without too much trouble. The drive into the city was conducted in absolute silence, except for Captain Singh, who every now and then uttered one short, sharp expletive that did nothing to relieve the tension we were still under. The tears had dried up by now; there just weren't any more to shed and I had practically succeeded in anaesthetising myself by the time we reached the hotel. We checked in and departed to our various rooms without a word to each other. Everything that could be had already been said.

As soon as I reached my room, I phoned Mr. Blaser. I was tired and I felt sick. I didn't want to go to Bombay the next day; I wanted to go home, and I told him so.

'Why?' he asked.

'Because I'm tired and miserable and sick to the teeth of you and your whole bloody department,' I said. Then my training got the better of me. 'Sir,' I added.

There was a long pause before he spoke again.

'The fact that you failed on an assignment isn't sufficient excuse for rudeness, Miss Touchfeather.' He continued before I could explode. 'And please remember this is an open line.'

I told him what he could do with his open line and something of my misery must have communicated itself to him, because when I ran out of anything more insulting to say, he still hadn't hung up.

'You're obviously upset about something,' he said, with sparkling insight. 'You will be contacted before midday tomorrow. Until then, stay in your hotel room, and talk to no one.'

I said a rude word to him, but he had already hung up. There had been no point in asking him if he knew what had happened to Bill. If there was any way of knowing, then he already knew it, and if he didn't want to volunteer the information, there was no way on earth that I could get it out of him. Apart from that, I knew enough about the ways of the world he and I moved in to want to remain ignorant; it could only have been something terrible, and my heart was bleeding sufficiently already without twisting the knife in the wound. I took three sleeping pills, which knocked me out as efficiently as a pole axe, and it was ten in the morning before I emerged from a completely dreamless sleep.

As I swam to the surface, the whole thing came back to me with the force of a steam hammer. But while I had been sleeping, my body mechanism had been working hard. The agony I had been through had been gathered together and locked away in a small compartment reserved for such material. There was still pain, but it no longer washed over the whole spectrum of my mind; it was confined to one small area where it could be controlled. This is a facility which is a direct result of my work and my training. Pain, both physical and mental, cannot be allowed to clutter up the smooth working of the machine which I am supposed to be; it must be quickly classified and then stored away in the memory banks where it can be referred to occasionally, but only when the machine considers it necessary.

So, dry-eyed now, I climbed out of bed and started to get ready for the day ahead. I sent a chambermaid out to buy me some new clothes, and then I gave her the sari because she looked as though she wanted it. The loss of it would appear on my records the next time I was required to fly Air India, but I couldn't have cared less at the moment. And, as I lay in the tub, I realised that I was already thinking in the terms of 'the next time I fly Air India'. More basically, this meant that I had no intention of giving up my job in spite of what I had said over the phone to Mr. Blaser. There is a certain comfort in continuity, and the best way to stop myself from re-ascending the heights of misery was to continue doing what I had done in the past. I was even rational enough to hope suddenly that I hadn't burned my bridges with

Mr. Blaser. I'd said some pretty strong things to him last night, and he didn't like his people to get emotional; it clouded their judgment, he said. Still, there was no point in worrying about it at the moment. I'd know soon enough. I climbed out of the bath and dressed in the new clothes I'd ordered. Then I sat down to wait.

At eleven forty-five the phone rang. Would I be kind enough to come to the offices of the Ariadne Import and Export Company on the Via Veneto. I confirmed that I would be there in twenty minutes and hung up. I stuffed my passport and papers into my new handbag and went to keep my appointment.

Ariadne Imp. and Ex. was housed in two small offices above one of the better known cafes on the Via Veneto. It took me twenty minutes to walk there through the midday Rome traffic. Arriving, I reported to Signor Bertelli, whom I had met before and who never failed to make a pass at me. I think he only did so because he felt that, as an Italian, it was expected of him. But obviously Mr. Blaser must have had words with him, because he leapt to his feet as soon as I was shown into the office, and proceeded to treat me with a charming old-world courtesy I didn't think he knew existed. The hands I had learned to dodge relieved me politely of my handbag and then pushed a chair under me. He moved back to his desk and, sitting down, placed his fingertips together, elbows on the desk, and regarded me solemnly from sad, brown eyes. He sighed deeply a couple of times before speaking to me in Italian.

'Poor Miss Touchfeather. Mr. Blaser is an admirable man, extremely knowledgeable and efficient. But he is an Englishman. What can he know of affairs of the heart?'

Someone had been talking, I decided. Then I realised that I had done nothing to conceal my feelings for Bill and it could have been any one of half a dozen people who had reported back to Mr. Blaser. Apart from the contact in Bombay, it could have been someone else whose identity I didn't even know. We worked in very tight, self-contained cells. Mr. Blaser liked it that way. It had been known for three people to be on the same job at the same time, each one believing he or she to be the only one. He acted on the assumption that the less we knew about each other the less chance there was of giving away a colleague. Basically this was a good premise, but it had been known to backfire. On one occasion I had been hit over the head, tied up and incarcerated in a dirty cellar for twenty-four hours by a fellow operative, who had thought I was a member of the opposition.

But Bertelli was still talking. 'It's only someone like myself who can appreciate the suffering you must be enduring right now. Mr. Blaser sees people as cyphers, not as warm, passionate, hot-blooded creatures who love and who are loved back.' He sighed again. 'Poor Miss Touchfeather. Poor, poor Miss Touchfeather.'

I thought I had better put a stop to this before he got me going again. 'You're very kind and understanding, Signor Bertelli. But I'd rather not talk about it.'

He looked uncomfortable suddenly and his hands started to move involuntarily, as though they didn't know where to go. Finally he used his left hand to pin the right one down on the desktop. 'I am terribly afraid that we *must* talk about it,' he said. 'It embarrasses me, but ...' His right hand tried to escape, but he recaptured it quickly. 'You understand, I have no choice in the matter.'

I nodded. 'I understand, Signor Bertelli. You're extremely thoughtful, and I am grateful.'

He smiled sadly and, having received my absolution, he got right down to business. 'Mr. Blaser would like a full report. You will fly to London this afternoon, as a passenger.' He pushed a ticket across the desk towards me. 'In the meantime I am to speak to him on the telephone and tell him anything that you feel he should know.'

'Like what?' I asked.

Bertelli cleared his throat before continuing. 'He wishes to know as soon as possible ... He wishes to know whether ... He would like to know ...' He stopped and started all over again. 'Considering the nature of your relationship with Professor Partman, is there nothing you can tell us that we do not already know?'

'Tell me what you already know, and I'll see.'

'We know that Professor Partman made no contact in Bombay and that he was taken off the aircraft at Cairo. Nothing more.'

'There isn't any more.'

'But did he not tell you anything while you were ... Did he not tell you anything?'

All I could remember was that he had told me that he loved me, but that belonged to me alone and I wasn't going to share it with Bertelli, or Mr. Blaser.

'Nothing,' I said flatly.

'He gave you no clues as to the reason he was in Bombay?'

'Of course he did,' I said. 'He was reading two of his scientific papers at the University.'

Bertelli dismissed this with a wave of his right hand, which had somehow escaped. 'That is what we have all been told,' he said. 'But it does not necessarily make it so.'

'What other reason could there be?' I asked, genuinely surprised.

'Mr. Blaser had hoped that you would be able to tell us.'

'Tell Mr. Blaser ... No, I'll tell him,' I said, getting to my feet.

'Tell him what, Miss Touchfeather?' Bertelli's eyes had gone cold suddenly, and he didn't even look like an Italian any longer. I remembered a story I had heard about him, how during the war he had worked for the Italian Resistance and had personally done to death one of the Gestapo chiefs, along with the German's wife and five children.

'Tell him that whatever it was that Bill Partman's unit were working on is probably known to the other side by now. Tell him that the people who decided that a man with his knowledge should be allowed to travel to a place they were already suspicious of should have their heads examined. And tell him...'

'Wait, Miss Touchfeather. Why are you so sure that Professor Partman will have given away the nature of his work?'

'You didn't see the bald man. I did. He looked efficient enough to...'

'Bald man? What bald man?'

'The one who was waiting for us at Cairo.'

'Describe him to me, please.'

I realised then that I hadn't actually described him to anyone. In my earlier reports, made at the airport, I had just referred to the men who had hijacked us, not identifying any of them as individuals. I described him to Bertelli, not a very difficult task. Halfway through my description, he was reaching for his keys. By the time I had finished he had produced a file from his safe and, rather like a magician producing a rabbit from a hat, he reached into the file and flipped a photograph across the desk towards me. It didn't take two looks to recognise the man from the Cairo airport.

'Who is he?' I asked.

Bertelli shook his head and made clucking sounds. 'He is a very dangerous man, very dangerous indeed.'

'That much I know,' I said. 'But who is he?'

'We don't know his real name. We call him the Eunuch.' That figured, I thought, remembering the size of the man and the timbre of his voice. 'If the Eunuch was at Cairo, then you are probably right. Professor Partman would not have been able to resist him for long.'

I was starting to feel a little sick; the office was far too hot and there was an overpowering smell of garbage leaking up through the rear window. 'If there's nothing more, Signor Bertelli, I'd like to go now.'

He became all Italian again, leaping to his feet and rushing around to usher me out of the office, to the accompaniment of small bows, and with eyes that were sad once more. He kissed my hand courteously and even came downstairs to find me a taxi. It was lunchtime, and the city had curled up inside itself, leaving its carcass to be picked over by the tourists. Bertelli scuttled across the pavement to the head of the taxi rank and opened the door for me. He kissed my hand again as he passed me into the taxi. Then he leaned in the window.

'Arrivederci, dear Miss Touchfeather. Please come to see me the next time you are in Rome. I will try to dispel some of your sadness.'

He was beginning to revert to form, so I wound up the window and told the taxi driver to take me back to the hotel before Bertelli forgot himself sufficiently to climb in with me. It was only a five-minute drive back to the hotel, so after seven minutes I started to worry. I hadn't paid any attention to our route and, looking out of the window, I realised I had no idea where we were. I leaned forward and tapped on the partition separating me from the driver. The stolid-looking head in the front remained facing forwards and I knew I was in trouble. There wasn't much point in trying the door or window handles, but I tried them anyway. They were mechanically locked. So was the partition.

I examined the contents of my handbag to see whether I had anything that could conceivably be of any use. But, unlike some of the glamorous agents of fiction, my lipstick wasn't a small-calibre pistol and my compact wasn't a two-way radio; both were useful if I wanted to look my best, but they weren't going to be any use at this moment. My nail file was made out of thin wood and was just the thing for filing nails. My cigarette lighter was out of fuel. That exhausted my handbag. I felt down the sides of the seat and came up with a handful of dust. I groped around on the floor and got my hands dirty. There was nothing else for it. I settled back in my seat and just hoped that whoever was kidnapping me was going to be civilised enough not to want anything from me that I wasn't going to be able to let him have.

SIX

We changed cars somewhere out on the Appian Way, about twenty minutes from the city. The taxi pulled off the main road and bumped along a rutted track for a few hundred yards. Then it stopped and, a moment later, the door was opened from the outside.

'Hello, darling,' said the American from the aeroplane.

He looked different now. The first time I had seen him he had been just another passenger, an unidentifiable face among twenty-five others. Later, when he had pulled a gun and assumed an individual identity, I had been far too concerned with what was going on to really look at him in any detail. He was of medium height and build, about thirty-five years old. He sported a crew cut and beneath it his face was lean and hard, his eyes cold and blue. He looked like a high-powered executive in a large efficient organisation. Considering the manner in which the VC10 had been handled, his organisation was certainly efficient, but who they were or what they did, when they weren't kidnapping scientists, I had no idea.

He wasn't carrying a gun, probably considering that with just little old me to look after he didn't need to. Here I showed him how wrong he could be. I stepped out of the taxi when he told me to and kicked him very hard where it would do the most good. Bessie, my old WRAC instructor, would have been proud of me. He doubled over and collapsed to the ground while I started to run. The taxi driver, who was half out of the taxi, started after me, but he needn't have bothered. Out of all the directions I could have taken, I chose the wrong one. I was ten feet away from the trees that surrounded the clearing when the other American materialised in front of me. Unlike his companion, or probably because of him, he was taking no chances. He held a gun pointing at me and it stopped me dead in my tracks.

'Naughty girl,' he said. 'Jack isn't going to like what you just did to him one little bit.' He spoke with the accent of the New York waterfront, and while Jack looked like a hardcase business man, this one looked exactly what he was, a hood, pure and simple.

We went back to pick up Jack, who had staggered to his feet and was behind the taxi being sick. He emerged looking like the wrath of God. To show how much he appreciated what I had done to him, he hauled back and slapped my face with his open hand, so hard that I would have been knocked fifteen feet if his colleague hadn't been standing behind to catch me. He was about to follow up with a second blow when Hank, which I learned later was his name, called a temporary halt.

'Not out here, Jack. Wait till we get her home.'

I thought for a moment that he hadn't got through to Jack, but then the fire went out of his eyes, and he pulled himself together. He even managed a smile, which carried about as much humour in it as a starving leper.

'Didn't mean to lose my temper, darling,' he said. 'Shall we go?'

The taxi driver had already returned to his vehicle and, as we moved away from the clearing, he started the engine and turned the cab back towards the main road. I memorised the number in case I was ever in a position to do anything about it, but it was probably false anyway.

Fifty yards through the trees there was another small road and parked there was a small black saloon. Hank climbed into the driver's seat and Jack pushed me into the back and got in after me. He shoved me, facedown, on the floor, not being particular where he put his hands. Then he placed both his feet in the small of my back and kept them there. Forewarned is forearmed and, to be sure, he now had a gun in his hand which he held inches away from my face, which was pressed into the dusty carpet.

After we had been driving for a few minutes, he removed one of his feet from the small of my back and used it to kick back the skirt of my new dress so that it settled round my waist. I waited a tense moment for what was to follow, but all he did was to replace his foot on my back. He was content just to look, it seemed. And if looking at my legs as far up as my waist would keep him from doing anything else, he was welcome. I had once been modest, but that was a long time ago; modesty, like innocence, can only be sustained during one's tender years. My tender years had ceased abruptly the day I had met Mr. Blaser.

We drove for twenty-five minutes, and by the time we stopped we could have been anywhere. All I saw, as I was hustled from the car and into a building, was a narrow street lined with houses whose front doors opened directly onto the road. It looked like the street of a small village, but could equally well have been a backstreet in Rome itself. Hank stayed behind the wheel of the car and, as we got out, he drove away. Jack ushered me through the front door into the only ground-floor room the house contained. There were a couple of dirty-looking beds, a table, some straight-backed chairs and very little else. Some stairs led upwards and some more led downwards. Jack pushed me towards the latter. I must have hesitated for he smiled again, the same humourless smile.

'Go on, darling,' he said. 'Give me trouble.'

If trouble was what he wanted, he wasn't going to get any from me, and I did as he asked and headed down the stairs. He followed me, still holding his gun. The stairs were cut out of stone, chipped and ancient. They curved downwards to a door at the bottom.

'Open it, darling,' he said.

I pushed it open and descended two more steps to the floor level. There was sufficient leak light from upstairs for me to look around while Jack lit an oil lamp that was hanging on a nail beside the door. The room was bare except for a large chair against one wall. It was an elegant chair, high backed, and with intricately carved arms and legs. There was a coat of arms embossed into the wood of the back and the whole thing looked completely incongruous in this ramshackle house, as though it had been recently looted from some palazzo.

'Sit down, darling,' said Jack, who had got the light burning. 'Make yourself comfortable.'

I sat, and tried to look as though I wasn't terrified out of my life, which I was. I was so bloody *alone*; Bertelli had seen me off in what appeared to be a normal taxi and, until I didn't get off the aeroplane in London, not a soul would know I was even missing. Jack sat on the bottom stair, nursing the gun on his knees, and waiting for the fun to start. Five minutes later there was a noise upstairs and Hank appeared.

'Where did you put the car?' asked Jack.

'Usual place,' said Hank. Then he looked across at me. I had already got Jack tagged as a looker, but Hank didn't seem that way at all. There was an animal quality about him that made me think he was going to need a lot more than a look to satisfy him. He turned back to Jack and I noticed that he was carrying a coil of thin rope.

'Shall we start?' he said.

'Might as well,' said Jack.

He got to his feet and both men came across towards me.

'On your feet, darling,' said Jack. I stood up.

'Take off your dress.' I hesitated a moment and Jack hit me again. The next time he asked me, I did as I was told. I stepped out of my dress and stood holding it, wondering what I could do with it. Hank took it from me and threw it across the room casually.

'Sit down, darling.' I sat down again and, as ordered, placed my arms along the arms of the chair. In forty-five seconds Hank had me tied securely, my arms to the chair arms, and my legs to the legs of the chair. For good measure, he passed a couple of loops round my waist and finally secured the rope at the back of the chair, which they had dragged away from the wall. Jack was reasonably happy; he could look to his heart's content. My legs were spread to each chair leg, and my bra and pants were chic, but hardly conducive to concealment. Hank had started to colour up a bit and breathe harder than normal.

'Take her brassière off,' he said.

Jack moved round to the back of the chair and started to grope for the hooks. I pressed my back against the chair, making it as difficult as possible for him without trying to look too unco-operative. And then Hank started talking obscenities, spewing them forth in an endless stream that made me feel cold and sick. He paused only long enough for Jack to explain what it was all about.

'It's like this, darling,' he said from behind me. 'You spent a couple of days with your boyfriend before we got hold of him. We want to know what went on between you.'

'Bill?' I'd almost forgotten Bill temporarily.

'That's right,' said Jack. 'Bill. Now he must have given you something apart from a good time. Or told you something?'

I hadn't the faintest idea what they were talking about, and I told them so.

'He must have talked about his work. He must have given you something to look after for him. A little package perhaps?'

'Nothing,' I said.

'Come on, darling, don't be difficult. We've got all the time in the world.'

'I told you it was a waste of time,' said Hank suddenly. 'All he gave her was a roll in the hay. Pretty good roll, too, I'd reckon.' He was looking at me like someone looks at a piece of meat on a slab.

'Did he tell you he gave me anything?' I asked, trying to get Hank's mind off what it was dwelling on.

'He didn't tell us anything,' said Jack. 'Someone got clumsy.'

I jerked my head round, trying to see him behind me. 'What do you mean?'

'The big fellow—you remember the big fellow. He lets his enthusiasm run away with him at times. He starts to enjoy himself too much, and before you can stop him he's gone too far.'

'Bill's dead,' I said. It was a statement, not a question. I think I'd known it all along.

'He's as dead as anyone I've ever seen,' said Jack. 'Ain't that so, Hank?'

Hank nodded and grinned. 'Never seen anything like it before,' he said. 'And I've seen it all.'

'So be a good darling,' said Jack. 'Tell us all about your boyfriend. What he told you, what he gave you, and who he told you to deliver it to.'

I explained again that Bill had told me or given me nothing that could be of the slightest interest to either them or anyone else. Hank was inclined to believe me, but not Jack. But all Hank really wanted was his kicks, and he started on again about what he was going to do with me. Jack gave up trying to undo my bra from the back and, moving round to the front, he stuck his hand between the cups and jerked hard. It was a good bra, but it wasn't designed to stand up to that sort of treatment.

Jack sucked in his breath suddenly and even Hank shut up for a second. Then he got busy with his hands and I started to feel sick. I tried to separate the conscious from the subconscious and retreat into the latter. I tried to think about nice things, normal things like Hyde Park and the Albert Hall. I almost succeeded, too. Then Hank stopped using his hands and Jack lit a thin brown cigarette. He puffed at it a couple of times so that I would get the full message. What he did next sent me skidding off to hell and gone.

When I came round I was alone. A squint down at my chest showed me that I had grown another nipple, an angry red mark an inch away from its more conventional partner.

I tried not to, I really did, but when someone has hurt you and there is no one around to see your shame, you can't help crying. At least, I can't. The tears welled up and spilled over. But they were tears of anger as much as anything else, anger at myself for doing something that could go so far wrong as to put me where I was now. If it had been my own fault I wouldn't have felt so bad, but it wasn't, and the absolute bloody injustice of it all brought on a fresh onslaught of tears. But I'm a practical sort of girl, and while shedding tears can be a comfort at times, they don't really serve any useful purpose. If I didn't want a fourth nipple I was going to have to get out of there before my two chums returned.

The rope was pretty well tied, but not so well that there wasn't sufficient slack to allow me a fractional movement of my right arm. If I sucked in my tummy I loosened the turn that Hank had made round my middle, giving me enough extra slack that I was able to work along to the arm. Never tie anyone with one coil of rope, Bessie had always said. Divide the rope and use a separate piece for each limb. She was right, because after three minutes I had wriggled the looseness in the rope sufficiently far along the arm of the chair to try and slip my right arm out from under. It didn't work for a couple more minutes as the rope kept snagging on the more intricate carvings in the wood. But finally I managed to pull a badly grazed arm from beneath the rope and, sixty seconds later, I was on my feet, climbing into my dress.

My bra was useless, but I don't think I could have managed to wear it with that burn. Anyway, this was Italy and, according to Sophia Loren movies, no one in Italy wears bras.

There wasn't a sound from upstairs, but that meant nothing. I looked around for some sort of weapon, but the best I could come up with was one of the chair arms, which I managed to detach with a couple of judicious kicks. I now had to make the decision whether to wait for them to come downstairs again or go up and find them. I chose the latter.

The door at the bottom was open and I prided myself that a mouse couldn't have moved up those stairs quieter than I did. As my head came level with the ground floor, I risked a peep over the top. The place seemed empty and it was dark outside. I came up the remainder of the stairs and moved quickly over to the window that looked out onto the street. I ducked back immediately as a swathe of light suddenly bathed the window and I heard the engine of a car. They'd come back for me.

I moved behind the door and waited, praying that one of them would stay with the car. One of them did. The door opened, with me behind it. As it started to close again, I saw Hank at the same time that he saw me. I would have preferred Jack, because my breast still hurt like hell, but he would come later. To give him credit, Hank didn't bat an eyelid when he saw me. The only part of him that moved was his right hand, streaking under his jacket. But he really didn't stand a chance. Kicking the door completely shut, I hit him with the arm of the chair across the side of the head. I hit him so hard that the chair arm broke. His feet left the ground completely and he landed on his face six feet away.

Without looking at the mess I had made of him, I fished out the gun from the waistband of his trousers and checked it over. It was a forty-five automatic, as large as a tank and about as powerful. I moved over to the window and peered out towards the car. Jack was behind the wheel, waiting. There was a sudden flare of light as he lit a cigarette, so there was no indication that he knew anything had gone wrong. I waited to allow the time that Hank would have needed to go downstairs and fetch me. Then, holding the gun in both hands behind my back, I moved over to the door and kicked it open. As I stepped out into the street I turned back towards the doorway.

'All right,' I said. 'You don't have to shove.'

Apparently satisfied, Jack leaned across the back and opened the nearside rear door.

'Come on, darling,' he said.

I put one foot inside the car and then showed him the gun, practically shoving it up his nose. I suppose he thought that, because I was a girl, I wouldn't use it. That's happened to me before. He took one second to make up his mind. Then he went for his own gun. There really was no alternative; there wasn't sufficient room to swing back and hit him, and I could hardly have turned tail and run. So I shot him.

SEVEN

'You realise, Miss Touchfeather, that it was an extremely unwise thing to have done?' said Mr. Blaser.

'I'm sorry, sir. I didn't have time to weigh the pros and cons.'

He looked at me steadily for a moment. He was absolutely livid. That much I had learned from Miss Moody before coming into the office. And, when he was angry, Mr. Blaser could be a very unpleasant man indeed. He didn't shout, or even raise his voice, but he could send you out on an assignment that could have easily been done by a disinterested girl guide and then proceed to forget you until he felt you had done sufficient penance.

On one occasion, when I had displeased him, he assigned me to keep an eye on a pilot who flew for some outlandish airline, possessing two Dakotas and a war surplus Avro Anson. We flew between what used to be called the Gold Coast and one of the offshore islands. The temperature never dropped below 96 degrees and the passengers always brought their goats along with them. He kept me on that little job for eight straight weeks, during which time the man I was supposed to be watching chased me from dusk to dawn. Fortunately they'd never heard of an automatic pilot, or I'd have been running all day as well. But before Mr. Blaser consigned you to hell and beyond, he invariably dissected the operation that had displeased him, holding up for examination what he considered your errors, so that you could identify them and not make the same mistake next time.

We had covered the whole thing once and we were halfway through the second time around. I had tipped the unfortunate

Jack out of the car and driven back to Rome where I had contacted Signor Bertelli. I told him that he had better get busy
disposing of one dead and one near-dead foreigner, whom I had
left in some village I didn't even know the name of. By the time
he had finished his work, I was halfway back to London, and it
wasn't until I saw Mr. Blaser that I learned that Jack had been
found per schedule, but that Hank had disappeared, leaving
nothing behind him other than a couple of pints of blood. In
spite of Bertelli's connections, which were considerable, Jack was
proving quite a problem to bury discreetly, and this was just one
of the things that Mr. Blaser was miffed about. There were a lot
more.

'Am I actually to understand, Miss Touchfeather, that you
became on intimate terms with Professor Partman?'

'You are, sir,' I said.

'Completely intimate?'

'As complete as possible.'

'And am I to understand that this intimacy was not confined
to the merely physical?'

'If you mean did I fall in love with Professor Partman, yes,
I did.'

He shook his head. 'I really don't know what to make of you,
Miss Touchfeather.'

He was a loathesome old hypocrite. If I had gone to bed with
Bill purely in the line of duty, he would have been happy. That
was one of the reasons he employed good-looking birds. But
because I'd committed the unpardonable sin of enjoying it, he
was all set to roast me over a slow fire.

'We will go into the deeper implications, insofar as they
affect your status here, later,' he went on pompously. 'But more
important at the moment is to try to judge how much they may
have learned from Professor Partman.'

'Nothing,' I said flatly.

'You sound very sure.'

'If Bill...if Professor Partman had told them what they wanted, there would have been no need for them to pick me up in Rome. My abduction was a last-ditch attempt to rectify an error.'

'How so?' asked Mr. Blaser.

'Having killed Professor Partman through...' I recalled Jack's words. '...through over-enthusiasm, they staked everything on the fact that he might have talked to me about his work or, better still, given me something to look after for him.'

'And had he?'

'No, sir, because there was nothing to give. I've said it before and I'll say it again. Professor Partman went to Bombay solely to read his papers at the University. The fact a man was fished out of the sea there a couple of weeks ago is a complete coincidence. Fortunately for all concerned, Bill Partman died before they extracted from him the information they were after.' I became a little wet eyed stating it so baldly, but it was something I was going to have to learn to live with.

Mr. Blaser still wasn't happy. 'You didn't actually see Professor Partman die, did you?'

'No, sir. But I saw the Eunuch do something to him and I saw him covered in blood. Fortunately I had to get on the aircraft immediately after that, so I was spared the rest.'

He looked at me as though he didn't consider it fortunate at all. 'This American you were misguided enough to shoot. Have you been able to pick him out of the files?'

'No, sir.'

'So the only identifiable person in the whole mess is the...er...Eunuch.'

'Yes, sir, and it was Signor Bertelli who picked him out. I still don't know who he is.'

'You haven't been doing your homework, Miss Touchfeather,' he said nastily. By homework, he was referring to the loads of bumph we were supposed to wade through in our spare time. It included, among other things, items from various intelligence units spread throughout the world and a rogues' gallery of photographs of the most wanted and dangerous individuals. But spare time was something he hadn't allowed me much of in the past few months and I'd let my reading slip behind.

'I'll rectify it, sir,' I said.

'Do, Miss Touchfeather. If you had known his identity from the outset we might have been saved considerable trouble.'

I failed to see how. Even if I had known who the bald man was, I had hardly been in a position to do anything about it. But there didn't seem to be any point in mentioning it, so I kept quiet.

'You feel, then, that in the circumstances, we can mark the Partman file as closed?' he asked. That was all it meant to him, a file to be marked closed and shoved away in a dusty cabinet.

'Yes, sir, I do.'

'Are you sure there is nothing you have forgotten?' I shook my head. 'You disappoint me, Miss Touchfeather.'

'I'm sorry about that, sir. May I ask why?'

'Think back, Miss Touchfeather. Think back.' I thought back and could only see Bill, not as I had last seen him, but as I had first seen him, getting on the aircraft, when I had tried to turn him out of his seat.

'No, sir, there's nothing … Wait a minute! Yes, there is.'

'Ah!' said Mr. Blaser, as though I had just discovered the Holy Grail.

'I'm sorry,' I said. 'You can't mark the file closed.'

'Why not?' he prompted.

'Because of the man you fished out of the sea. If Professor Partman wasn't the leak from his unit, then the leak still exists.'

'Bravo, Miss Touchfeather. Bravo. And …?'

'They've tried twice. It's reasonable to assume that they will try a third time.'

'Exactly,' said Mr. Blaser. He nearly smiled, but only nearly. Still, it was his problem, and I didn't volunteer anything further. 'Fortunately that problem now shifts out of our hands,' he said. 'I told you before that the Gerastan Corporation wanted Professor Partman's unit to work in the United States. With Professor Partman no longer alive, there doesn't seem to be any obstacle in the way of that any longer. I imagine the entire unit will be leaving the country within the next six or seven days.'

'Is there any point? Professor Partman is dead.'

He smiled nastily. 'I'm aware that you are biased, Miss Touchfeather. But Professor Partman was not the be-all and end-all of the unit. Research is a joint effort and, while he may have been the guiding light, I imagine that his work will continue very well without him.'

If someone had handed me a knife and told me I could stick it in either Mr. Blaser or the Eunuch, I think at that moment I'd have chosen Mr. Blaser. Then he shifted to the area I was dreading. It was no good my telling him that I wouldn't have behaved the way I did if Bill had been guilty as suspected; he would never give me credit for being a sufficiently good judge of character. All he could see was that I had become emotionally involved with a man who could have turned out to be a traitor and worse.

'What would you have done, Miss Touchfeather, had you subsequently discovered that what we believed of Professor Partman was true? For instance, what if I had asked you to kill him?'

'I would have killed him,' I said. 'As long as I was sure that he was guilty.'

'As long as *you* were sure?' I nodded my head reluctantly. 'Regardless of what I told you?' Right again. 'Well, at least you're honest,' he said, as though it were a dirty word. 'I think it's about time you took some leave.'

'Yes, sir,' I said. The thought of having to take leave right then made me go quite cold, but if that was what Mr. Blaser had in mind, there was nothing I could do about it. Then he pitched me a lifeline.

'I can take you off all duties, or you can keep flying. Whichever you prefer.'

I grabbed the line he was offering me. 'I'll keep flying,' I said quickly.

'Very well, Miss Touchfeather. Tell Miss Moody the route you would like to fly. She'll arrange it.'

'Thank you, sir,' I said, getting to my feet. I went to the door; then I turned back. After all, he was three parts right, and it wouldn't choke me. 'I'm very sorry, Mr. Blaser. It won't happen again.'

He looked at me almost like a human being for a moment. 'Perhaps the third time will be lucky for you, Miss Touchfeather,' he said. 'But do try and do it in your own time.' I must have looked bewildered.

'Do what?' I said.

'Fall in love,' he said. And, although the light was bad, I could have sworn that he blushed.

EIGHT

The phone was ringing when I let myself into the flat. It was my car salesman, wanting to know whether dinner was on the cards. I told him that it wasn't and that I would call him. The department doctor, a dour, uncommunicative Scot, had dressed my burn, but it still hurt, and that, combined with the inside hurt that still nagged away, made me feel anything but sociable.

I had arranged with Miss Moody that I would be ready for work in three days. I had opted for the New York–Los Angeles run, on United Airlines. They're a large, well-run airline and, apart from that, my American Flight Captain flew for one of the opposition and, if I played my cards right, I didn't have to bump into him unless I wanted to. I chose the New York–Los Angeles run because, in spite of what Bill had said, I enjoyed America. I liked the contrast between East and West Coast: New York, brusque, brash and efficient, and Los Angeles, sprawling, warm and more leisurely. Flying from coast to coast seemed as good a way as any of nursing myself back to a normal state of mind. It was a busy route and I wouldn't have much time to get too sorry for myself.

The three days' notice I had given Miss Moody I intended to spend by myself, fortifying and crystallising my memories of Bill. I wanted to establish him more securely in my memory, giving him a permanent niche that wouldn't suffer from the ravages of time. There was nothing morbid in this; it was merely that I wanted to remember him, and I had so little to hang on to. We had known each other for three days and, apart from the potted autobiography he had given me, I knew nothing about him. Just once I wanted to see the place where he lived and worked, and perhaps meet some of the people who had known him.

Cumming-on-Hardy was as difficult to get to as it sounded, but I finally made it by four-thirty the following day. There was one pub in the village and, although they didn't normally let rooms, the landlord and his wife were pleased to see a new face and, while I protested feebly, arranged for their son to move in with his baby sister while I took over the boy's room.

Unpacking my small bag, I began to feel like a human being again. The room was small, but reassuring in its normality. There were pictures of the Beatles and Sandie Shaw stuck on one of the walls, and three badly made model aeroplanes suspended from the ceiling; one of these I knocked down within two minutes of coming into the room and I made a note to buy a replacement later. Doris Grierson, the lady of the house, had cleared out one of the drawers, into which I put the contents of my overnight bag. She had also cleared a small space in the wardrobe and lent me a couple of hangers.

After tidying myself up a little, I went downstairs to accept the Griersons' invitation to have tea with them. They were a youngish couple, fresh back from Aden, where they had run a small import-export business. Not visualising much future once the Union Jack had been lowered, they had packed up and come home and used their savings to buy the only pub in Cumming-on-Hardy. They weren't going to make a fortune out of it, but all they wanted was a living and this seemed as pleasant a way as any to go about earning it. Jim Grierson was a little too 'hail, fellow, well met' for my taste, but Doris was a sweety. Within half an hour I had offered her the loan of my flat any time she wanted to come to London for shopping or the theatre.

The bar opened at five-thirty, but no one arrived until half past six, when suddenly the place seemed to be full of large men in tweeds and Wellington boots. Every girl likes to be the centre of attraction at times; it's good for the morale. That evening my morale received a five hundred percent shot in the arm. The men were all pleasant, and rather like excited schoolboys at having a stranger in their midst, especially since she was female and came from London and wore a moderately short skirt and didn't mind a not-too-dirty story. It was about half past eight and the bar was packed, when Doris leaned over the bar and pointed towards the door.

'Here come a couple of Professor Partman's people now,' she said.

Through the press of bodies I could just see two men who were removing their topcoats. One was middle-aged, a donnish-looking man, dressed in a neat dark-grey suit. The other was younger, dressed in a scruffy sports jacket and untidy slacks. He was about thirty years old and looked more like a rugger player than a scientist. His nose had been broken somewhere along the fine and it gave his face an attractive, beat-up appearance. Doris called out to them and they forced their way through the press of bodies until they were standing next to me.

'Don Scamper, Mr. Carter, this is Katy Touchfeather. She's a friend of Bill Partman's.'

Immediately both men became a little confused. On the one hand, they wanted to show distress over what had happened and, on the other, they wanted to show pleasure at meeting a friend of Bill's. Added to this, the younger one, Don Scamper, could hardly contain his exuberance at having struck so lucky as to meet what he obviously thought was a swinging-type bird in a place like Cumming-on-Hardy.

'How well do you know Bill?' asked Carter, after glasses had been refilled.

'Very well,' I said. 'But not for all that long a time.' There was no point in telling them that I had been on the plane; they'd only have wanted to know all the details and I didn't feel up to going through the whole thing again.

'Funny he never mentioned you,' said Carter.

'It would have been funnier if he had,' said Don. 'Very sensitive about his personal life is our leader.'

There was a faint edge of sarcasm in his voice, which grated suddenly. Carter looked sideways at him, and he had the good manners to realise that he had dropped a brick; he coloured slightly and buried his nose in his tankard.

'We all miss Bill very much,' said Carter. 'But not as much as you, I imagine?' It was a direct question, and I realised that he was fishing.

'Yes, I miss him,' I said. 'Even though it's only a short time.' He was dying to ask me how long, but he didn't.

'Terrible business,' he said. I agreed that it was a terrible business. 'Of course, we don't actually *know* what has happened to him. There may be a perfectly reasonable explanation and he'll explain it to us all when we see him.'

Then I realised what had been troubling me since they arrived; they were all speaking about Bill in the present tense. They didn't know he was dead. All they knew was that he had been taken from an aircraft and then disappeared. I'd dropped a clanger there, I thought. Watch it, Katy. But nobody seemed to have noticed, and Carter continued to probe delicately.

'I'm surprised you bothered to come down here, knowing that Bill was missing.'

Don Scamper removed his nose from his tankard. 'Don't knock it, Harvey,' he said.

Carter smiled. 'I'm not knocking it. I'm truly delighted to be in such charming company. I just said that I was a little surprised.'

'I was in Brighton on personal business,' I said. 'I thought I'd drop in here on my way back. Bill's told me so much about the place.' Don Scamper accepted this at face value, but Harvey Carter still wasn't convinced. He was going to give me trouble, and I was already beginning to regret the impulse that had brought me down here. I was saved further discomfort though as Don spotted an empty dartboard.

'Do you play darts, Katy? May I call you Katy?' he asked.

I agreed that I played darts and that he could call me Katy.

'Next up!' bellowed Don, as he pushed his way through towards the dartboard, gaining possession a second before a couple of the locals.

'May I join you?' enquired Harvey Carter as I climbed down from my stool.

'Please do,' I said. 'You can give me moral backing. I'm a terrible darts player.'

'So is Don,' he said. 'But he won't admit it. I'll fetch you another drink.'

By the time he joined us at the dartboard, I was already trying to throw my darts everywhere except at the target; I was so far ahead of Don Scamper, who hadn't yet managed to get his opening double, that it was embarrassing. Not that he seemed to mind. Full of boyish exuberance he continued to hurl his darts so that they stuck a good inch into the board and required considerable effort to get them out.

'She's more than just a pretty face, this one,' he said, as he took the drink Carter handed him.

'I'm sure she is,' said Carter, making the remark for me alone.

The next time I threw the darts, I didn't have to aim badly for them to go off target; Carter was making me nervous.

At half past ten, Jim Grierson started to bellow 'Time!' and by ten to eleven the place was empty, apart from the Griersons and myself. I'd sidestepped an invitation for lunch and dinner with Don the following day, but I had as good as promised he would find me propping up the same corner of the bar the following evening. I helped the Griersons gather up the empties and dried while Doris washed.

'Nice men,' she said, meaning Carter and Don.

'Very,' I agreed.

'Harvey Carter's a bit of a stodge at times, but he's very charming when he relaxes.'

'What does he do exactly?' I asked.

'Who knows what any of them do up there? All I know is that it's a bit hush-hush and no one's allowed past the front gate, not even the tradesmen.'

We finished tidying the bar and retired to the kitchen for a cup of chocolate. By midnight I was tucked in to my junior-sized bed trying to count the number of John Lennons on the opposite wall by the light that came in from the street outside. I'd got to about eighteen before I drifted off.

I was still sound asleep at nine-thirty when Doris woke me with a cup of tea.

'There's someone downstairs to see you,' she said.

'Who?' Apart from the two men I had met last night, I didn't know a soul for fifty miles in all directions.

'His name is Beamish. He works up at... you know, Bill Partman's place.'

'What does he want?'

'I want to see you, young lady.' We both looked towards the door. There was a man standing there. I hastily tried to gather my modesty around me, being addicted to sleeping in the nude, while Doris performed the indignant bit on my behalf.

'Really-Mr. Beamish, this is a bit much,' she said, angrily. 'I told you I'd give Miss Touchfeather your message.'

'Didn't want her hopping out of any windows. Eh? What?' He actually said 'Eh? What?' I'd thought up to then that Englishmen only said those words in American movies. He was a small, wiry-looking man with a bright-red face and slicked-back, sandy-coloured hair. He wore the conventional tweeds and Wellington boots with a checked shirt and a lemon-coloured tie which did absolutely nothing for his complexion. The whole thing was topped by a duffle coat two sizes too big for him. He looked like someone attending a bloodstock sale until one saw his eyes, which were pale and rimmed with pink. They looked like pig's eyes, and I didn't like him one little bit.

'Hopping out of windows?' said Doris. 'What on earth are you talking about?'

'Ask the lady, Mrs. Grierson,' he said, nodding towards me.

Poor Doris was completely bewildered, and she took the only course left open to her. 'I'm going to fetch my husband,' she said.

'Don't bother, Doris,' I said. 'If Mr. Beamish wants to see me this badly, he must have good reasons.'

'Sensible girl,' said Beamish. 'Toddle along, Mrs. Grierson.'

'You toddle along, too, Mr. Beamish,' I said. 'I'm going to get dressed. I'll see you downstairs in fifteen minutes.'

He glanced towards the window, and decided that it was too small for me to abscond through. 'Rightyho,' he said. 'Fifteen minutes.' He turned and walked from the room, leaving Doris looking at me with an expression compounded of equal parts confusion and curiosity.

'Who is he, Doris?' I asked, getting out of bed.

'Something to do with security,' she said. 'He doesn't use the pub much. Don't *you* know him?' I admitted I didn't. 'And what did he mean about hopping out of windows? Really, it's a bit much. You expect this sort of thing in Aden, but not in Cumming-on-Hardy.'

'Don't worry about it,' I said. 'I'll see what he wants and then send him packing.' She nodded, reluctantly, and left me to get dressed.

Beamish was waiting for me in the empty bar. I could hear Jim Grierson pottering around in the cellar, and Doris had decided to leave us strictly alone, disappearing into the kitchen as soon as

I came downstairs. He got to his feet as I came into the room, but I don't think it was out of politeness. If he considered me capable of jumping out of first-floor windows, he probably thought I wasn't to be trusted.

'You're a friend of Professor Partman?' he asked, without preamble.

'I may be,' I said, and had the satisfaction of seeing him look a little confused.

'You told Harvey Carter that you—'

I cut in on him, wanting to set the record straight as soon as possible. 'What I told Harvey Carter is none of your business,' I said. 'And, while we're on the subject, I don't like you, or the way you burst into bedrooms making stupid remarks, embarrassing me and my hostess. And I don't think I'm going to tell you one little thing that you're obviously dying to know.' So put that up your nose and sniff it, I thought.

His red face went even redder, except for two white spots that appeared high on his cheekbones. He wasn't used to being talked to in this way, especially by a chit of a girl.

'Now just you listen here, Miss Touchfeather—if that is your real name.'

'You don't think I'd make it up, do you?'

'It is my duty to investigate any person who behaves suspiciously in this area. And from what I heard of last night, you fall into that category.'

'I beat Don Scamper three times at darts and I bought him and Harvey Carter a pint of bitter each,' I said. 'If you call that behaving suspiciously.' But I was playing for time now.

'Do you deny that you are a friend of Professor Partman?'

'I don't deny it at all.'

'That's more like it,' he said, feeling himself on firmer ground. 'What is the nature of your business in Cumming-on-Hardy?'

'Didn't Harvey Carter tell you that as well?'

'I want to hear it from you.'

'I had personal business in Brighton and I thought I'd call in here on the way back.' It didn't sound as convincing as it had last night.

'Knowing that Professor Partman wasn't here?' I nodded, wondering what had possessed me to come on this bloody trip at all. 'I'm not entirely satisfied, Miss Touchfeather,' he said pompously.

'I don't really care whether you are or not, Mr. Beamish,' I said.

He ignored this. 'I would like you to come along with me to answer a few questions,' he said.

'I'm sorry,' I said.

'What do you mean, sorry?'

'I mean I'm not going anywhere, except back to London by the first available transport.'

The white spots appeared on his face again. 'Now see here, young lady—' he started.

But I decided I had better try to finish the whole thing here and now. 'No,' I said. '*You* see here. You may be all sorts of a big wheel where you work, but you don't work here. I assume your job is looking after security at Professor Partman's establishment. I suggest that you attend to it, and stop bothering me, before I call the police and have you charged with breaking into a woman's bedroom.' I turned and started out of the bar.

Then, like an idiot, I fired a parting shot. 'Perhaps if you'd been doing your job better, you'd have talked Bill into not taking that trip. Then none of this would have happened.'

That did it. I think I realised it before he did, but even so, he was quick. He shot across the room and grabbed my arm in a tight hold.

'Why should Professor Partman not have taken the trip?' he asked, his pig eyes positively glowing.

I tried a bluff which I didn't think would come off. 'He'd be here now if he'd stayed in England.'

It didn't come off. His grip tightened; he was surprisingly strong for so little a man. 'But why should I, as a security officer, have cause to warn him off?'

'Take your hands off me, Mr. Beamish,' I said.

'You haven't answered my question.'

I gave him one more chance. 'If you don't let me go, I shall break your arm,' I said. He tightened his grip, beginning to enjoy his work now.

While I didn't actually break his arm, I made a considerable dent in his dignity. He picked himself up from the floor, looking hate at me and at the same time wondering how such a thing could have possibly happened. Then he turned and opened the door and called outside.

'You two! In here!'

A moment later the bar seemed crowded as two men came in. Both were dressed in a security police style of uniform, not unlike blackshirts, with breeches and leather boots. If this was the type of private police force Gerastan Industries ran, it wasn't surprising that Bill had been impressed when he visited California. Both the men were young and very large. I think I could have taken them both had surprise been on my side, but I had made enough scenes for one day, and I went like a lamb.

We drove out of the village for three miles and then turned into the gates of what had been a large country estate. There was barbed wire on top of the original brick wall, and another line of wire ten feet inside it. There was an impressive-looking guardhouse, with two checkpoints separated by a kind of no man's land. Then we were bowling up the drive towards the main buildings. The original house was still there, but it had spawned a group of newer buildings which grew out from it in all directions. We turned off the main drive fifty yards before we reached the house and drove between some low, squat buildings, pulling up eventually outside the last in the line. Beamish, who hadn't spoken a word during the journey, now told me to get out of the car. This I did, following him into the building, with the two large young men on either side of me. We marched down a corridor and into an office where I was told to sit and wait.

Beamish left me with the two young men and, while they couldn't see how someone my size, shape and sex could be any problem at all, they didn't take their eyes off me for a second. For my part, I was worried stiff. I had made a monumental error of judgment, and I didn't see how I was going to get out of it. Beamish had probably been through a lot over the past couple of weeks, ever since it had been discovered that there was a security leak, and now he was presented with a stranger who knew more than anyone had a right to. He was obviously burning up the telephone wires to London at this moment. Of course, there was one very simple way I could clear myself. A phone call to Mr. Blaser and I would be on my way, but I'd also be out of work. I was going to have to get out of this one all on my own, and I didn't have the faintest idea how I was going to go about it.

Beamish came back in five minutes. He hesitated at the door for a moment, wondering whether it was safe to dismiss his heavies. Then he decided that I would hardly get tough on his home ground and told them to leave us alone. But he also told them to wait outside the door, so he couldn't have been all that sure of himself. Then he peeled off his duffle coat, hung it behind the door and sat down behind his desk.

'Let's start at the beginning, Miss Touchfeather. Item one, who are you?'

'Katherine Touchfeather,' I said, and gave him my address for good measure.

'Item two, *what* are you?'

'I'm an air hostess.'

'For which airline?'

'Air India.' If he knew that Air India only employed Indian girls, he didn't show it.

'Item three, what are you doing in Cumming-on-Hardy?'

'I was in love with Bill Partman. I wanted to see where he worked.'

His piggy eyes grew as wide as they physically could.

'"Was", Miss Touchfeather?'

'I beg your pardon?' I said.

'You used the past tense referring to your feelings. Do you mean you are no longer in love with him?'

'I was referring to Professor Partman,' I said.

'In the past tense?'

'He's dead, isn't he?'

Now he'd really got me, he thought. 'How do you know he's dead?' he asked, using the question like a club.

I've found on occasions the best way to lie your way out of a situation is to tell the truth, or at least enough of it to provide the other side with something they can check up on. So I told Beamish how, as a hostess for Air India, I had met Bill. I told him about our three days together. I told him about Cairo and what I had seen; and, for good measure, I told him about Rome.

'You mean to sit there and tell me that these men actually tortured you?' he said. It was no time for modesty. I undid my dress, pulled back my bra and showed him. I think that was what did the trick. The scar was ugly and was going to need a skin graft at some later date. In spite of what I had done to him he started to get all masculine and sympathetic.

'Please excuse me, Miss Touchfeather,' he said and left the office. He could do any one of half a dozen things now, depending on how suspicious he still was, and how efficiently he ran his organisation. He could phone Air India. He could phone the Taj Hotel in Bombay. He could phone the police in Rome, who would switch him straight through to Bertelli, and not mention it. He could phone Captain Singh, if he could find him. And he could run a quick check on my identity at Somerset House, at the passport office, or with my landlord, bank manager, hall porter and, if he was so inclined, my window cleaner. Anything, just so long as he didn't call Mr. Blaser. But that wasn't likely since he probably didn't know Mr. Blaser existed. Very few people did. Who he eventually did contact I never found out. He returned to the office half an hour later and told me I could go. He walked back to the car with me.

'Tell me one thing, Miss Touchfeather,' he said before we said goodbye. 'Where did you learn to throw a man like that?'

'It's part of the regular training for air hostesses,' I told him.

'Really!' he said. 'I never realised.'

Back at the pub I packed my bag and made my apologies to the Griersons. Suddenly I didn't want to stay in Cumming-on-Hardy any longer. The idea had been a bad one to begin with and it had run rapidly downhill. I had a local taxi take me to the nearest main line station. Two hours later I was in London and three hours after that I was on my way to New York.

NINE

Like I said, I find New York invigorating. The people I know there are mostly fun people, and normally I manage to swing there harder and more often than I do anywhere else. But while I was glad to be back, I wasn't in a swinging mood. As soon as I got off the aircraft I took a cab straight to the downtown office of Walter Martin. He is Mr. Blaser's American opposite number—an ex-CIA man who had come in from the cold when someone had broken both his legs by driving a twenty-hundredweight truck over them, after letting all the air out of the tyres first.

He is about forty-two years old, but looks like an overgrown college boy. It's the freckles that do it, that and the fact that he's so exuberant it's exhausting. If he could have done, he would have jumped to his feet when I was shown into his office. As it was, he paddled his wheelchair from around behind his desk and drove it straight at me, knocking me off my feet so that I landed in his lap. There he pinned my arms to my sides and kissed me enthusiastically.

'Katy, me darlin',' he said, in an atrocious takeoff of an Irish accent. 'How are you after keeping your beautiful, sexy colleen of a self?'

I had tried to explain that just because I was called Katy and had once flown Aer Lingus, it didn't make me Irish. But he wouldn't have it. He released me suddenly and propelled himself over to his desk again. He picked up a slip of paper and waved it at me. 'London told me you were coming over. I've been holding my breath ever since.'

'That's because you're a sex maniac and can't wait to have your wicked way with me.' He'd never made so much as half a pass at me during the two years I had known him, and I'm sure that if he had I would have succumbed, wheelchair notwithstanding. He was such a *nice* man, one couldn't help wanting to do things for him.

'Ah, Katy, migirl. You've brought the sun out in this raddled old metropolis. Come and give us another kiss.' I gave him another kiss, and then sat down on one of his low office armchairs. 'I hope you're not intending to venture forth during the daylight hours in that skirt,' he said. 'You'll be locked up.'

'I wore it especially for you,' I said. 'All the best swingers in London are wearing it this length.'

'Ah, London,' he said. 'Would that I could gaze on her dreaming spires once more.'

'That's Oxford,' I said. 'You gaze on the Hilton, the Playboy Club and the American Express in London these days.'

'There's progress for you!' he said. 'You're two days early.'

'You're complaining?'

'Perish the very idea. No, just curious. And it says here that you are on plain flying duties. That makes me curious, too.'

'There aren't any snags, are there?'

'No. I've fixed it up with United. But tell your uncle Walter what's really going on.'

'Nothing,' I said.

'Come on, Katy. Admit it. Old Blaser is onto something he doesn't want to spread around. What is it?'

'Honestly, Walter, there's nothing. I'm a little tired and I asked for a normal flying job without the side issues. That's all there is to it.'

'But why us?' he said. 'Has England run out of airlines along with everything else?'

'I wanted to come to America,' I said. 'It's as simple as that.'

'You mean you couldn't go on any longer without seeing me—that's it, isn't it?'

'That's it exactly.'

He looked at me for a moment, his face suddenly serious. 'You look a little bruised around the edges, Katy. It doesn't suit you.'

'It's not just the edges,' I said. 'It goes clear through.'

'*Affaire d'amour?*' he said, evenly.

I nodded. 'That and the fact that Mr. Blaser thinks I made a botch of a job.'

'Did you?'

I nodded again. 'I suppose I did in a manner of speaking.'

'Wanna tell me about it?'

'What, the job or the other?'

'Either, or both. I've got the broadest, most comfortable crying-on-type shoulders this side of the Atlantic.'

I settled for telling him about Bill. He knew the basic background from the intelligence reports, but he didn't know about Bill and me. And that is what I talked about. He was a good listener and he let me talk myself into the ground before he interrupted me, pointing out that it was dark outside and asking how would I like some dinner. Taking into account the five-hour time differential, it was way past midnight by my clock, but I wasn't tired and I didn't want to spend my first few hours in New York on my own.

'I haven't found anywhere to stay yet,' I said.

'*Voila!*' he said, pressing the buzzer on his desk. A moment later the door opened and Robbie Brightwell came in. She's Walter's secretary, a startlingly beautiful girl of twenty-seven extremely kind years.

'Who's using the apartment?' he asked.

'Nobody,' said Robbie.

'Wrong,' he said. 'Irish is using it.'

She smiled at me. 'I'll let you have the keys on the way out, Katy,' she said, and left the office.

'Why don't you marry her?' I said as she closed the door behind her.

'She hasn't asked me yet.'

'She's besotted with you—and you know it.' He looked sad suddenly, glancing down at his legs. Then, in case I'd noticed it, he smiled at me broadly.

'Where shall we eat?' he asked.

'You choose,' I said. 'I'm off to make myself beautiful. Pick me up in an hour and a half.'

'Wear that skirt,' he shouted after me as I left the office. Robbie handed me the keys of the apartment and on impulse I asked her what she was doing for dinner.

'Nothing,' she said.

'Then join Walter and me.' Before she could think of an excuse, I told her to be at the apartment in an hour and walked out. Going down in the elevator, I felt like a meddling busybody, but although I always seem to fall on my backside in the hearts and flowers department, I'm still an incorrigible matchmaker when I like people as much as I do Walter and Robbie.

Walter had laid on the full important-client service. There was a uniformed chauffeur to meet me in the main lobby and he escorted me to the company car, parked just outside the main entrance. Walter, like Bertelli in Rome, used a cover. Mr. Blaser is the only one who doesn't hide behind some other occupation. I'd like to believe it's because he's incapable of doing anything other than what he does and that, if he had a cover, he'd make such a botch of it he'd be spotted a mile away. But the actual reason is because, as the operational head of the organisation, he's far too busy to be bothered with even the smallest outside encumbrance.

The area controllers, however, aren't so busy, and just as Bertelli's Ariadne Export and Import Company do in fact export and import things, Walter's public-relations outfit really do public relate. And I believe he's very good at it. Like all successful public-relations outfits he keeps a company car and a town apartment for the use of visiting firemen or, in my case, fire-women. It's a comfortable apartment in the upper Seventies, and I like using it. The chauffeur dropped my bag in for me and, after I'd wandered round and turned down all the central heating, I poured myself a drink and took it to my bath.

It would have been nice to say that the evening was an unquali-fied success, but it wasn't. Once Walter had got over the initial surprise at finding Robbie was to dine with us, he behaved like the perfect host.

'The two best looking girls in New York, and I've got them both,' he said. But his heart wasn't really in it. Or rather it was too far in it for him to be his normal exuberant self. It was pain-fully clear, and had been for a long time, that he adored Robbie Brightwell, who was one of those rare creatures who managed to combine the glacial beauty of a *Vogue* model with a homemak-ing heart as big as a house. It was a crying shame. They couldn't have been more right for each other. But because of his legs he wasn't going to make the first move—and she was too unsure of his reactions to make it herself. I did the best I could, glad to have someone else to worry about apart from myself. But the evening finally ground to a halt shortly after a man whom Robbie knew vaguely came over to the table and asked her to dance. She was all set to refuse when Walter opened his big mouth and practi-cally forced her onto the floor.

'You're a stupid bastard,' I said.

'I know it, Katy,' he said. 'And I'll thank you to mind your own bloody business.'

And that was that. The party broke up ten minutes after Robbie returned to the table. Walter dropped Robbie off first, and then me. I asked him in for a drink, but he declined.

'See you tomorrow,' he said. 'Come round for some lunch.'

It was late, but I still wasn't tired. You can't walk the New York streets alone at night and for a moment I debated whether to call my American Flight Captain. But I decided against it. What he would want I didn't feel in the mood for. So I settled for *The Late Late Show* and fell asleep in front of the television half an hour after it started. I woke up two hours later, staggered to bed, where I slept until eleven a.m., which was when Robbie Brightwell phoned me.

'A photograph has come through on the wire. You're to come down to the office and look at it.'

'Who says?'

'Your Mr. Blaser,' said Robbie.

'I'll be there in an hour,' I said. I made some coffee while I was getting up. The fridge was stocked with everything, but I'm a no-breakfast girl, so I didn't bother with anything else. One thing I found encouraging, Mr. Blaser still acknowledged my existence.

Robbie made no reference to the previous evening as she showed me into Walter's office.

'Top of the mornin', Irish!' said Walter. 'Come and look at this.'

The 'this' he referred to was a wire photograph, not a very good one originally, and the transmission hadn't been up to much either, but clearly recognisable nevertheless. It was of Hank, Hank of the dirty hands and the foul mouth and the Roman cellar. Just looking at the photograph made my breast start to smart again.

'Do you know him?' asked Walter.

'I know him,' I said.

'Rotten company you keep,' he said, putting the photograph away.

'Why? Do you know him?' I asked.

'Hank Almedo, long time bad guy, not big, but bad just the same. Sells his muscle to the highest bidder and doesn't care how he's asked to use it.'

'I know it,' I said. 'I've scars to prove it.'

'He usually travels around with another hood, name of Jack Kelly,' said Walter.

'I know him too.'

'You've been getting around.'

'I always got around,' I said. 'But these men sound like home-ground operators.'

'They are. Alcatraz Island is about the furthest they've been from the States.'

'They're broadening their horizons,' I said. 'I met them in Khartoum, Cairo and Rome.'

'What the hell were they doing there?'

'One of them was dying,' I said.

'Which one?'

'Jack Kelly.'

'It couldn't have occurred to a better person. What happened to him?'

'I did,' I said modestly.

'What did you do? No, don't tell me; it may spoil some of the illusions I have of you.' Then, when I said nothing, he asked again impatiently, 'Well? What did you do?'

'I shot him,' I said.

'Me darlin' Katy. No wonder Ireland is such a marvellous country, with the likes of you populating her shores. Why didn't you shoot Hank too?'

'Sorry,' I said. 'No could do. But I did hit him ever so hard with a piece of four-by-two.'

'Not hard enough, it seems.' He pressed the buzzer on his desk and Robbie came in. 'Message to Mr. Blaser. Miss T. identifies Hank Almedo. Record following. Get onto the FBI and ask them to courier all they have on Almedo to London.'

'May I add a PS?' I asked.

'If you make it short. Cables cost money.'

'Tell him I've also identified the one I ... the one who stayed in Rome.' I didn't know how sanguine Robbie was; perhaps she wouldn't want me as a friend if she knew I went around shooting people.

'Rephrase that, Robbie,' said Walter. 'Miss T. identifies Hank Almedo and the late Jack Kelly. Records on both following.' Robbie nodded and went out.

'I suppose this means you won't be staying with us,' said Walter.

'Nothing's changed,' I said. 'Mr. Blaser is just tying up his loose ends.'

He took the photograph of Hank from his drawer and looked at it again. 'Funny,' he said. 'Hank's a muscle man. He's got about as much intelligence as a four-year-old village idiot. What the hell were he and Jack doing on the wide screen? They're strictly nickelodeon boys.'

'They were doing what they were told.'

'I know that. But by whom?'

'The Eunuch?' I ventured.

'No. He's big-time intrigue stuff. State secrets and anyone want to buy an atom bomb? He'd never use a couple of hoods. Not American hoods anyway.'

'Well someone was using them. They knew what they were after.'

'Did they hurt you, Katy?' he said softly.

'Not much,' I lied.

'Poor Katy. Why aren't you married to a broth of a boy, living in an Irish bog, digging peat and raising a pack of redheaded IRA recruits?'

'For two very good reasons. I only like the Irish when they're drunk. And I like my work.'

'You're a masochist,' he said. 'Let's go and have some lunch.'

I didn't make the mistake of asking Robbie to come with us again, and we lunched at the back of a small French restaurant where they knew Walter and even had boards ready to put down so that he could wheel himself down the two steps to the rear. We were onto our coffee before he remembered something he had to tell me.

'Your assignment from United has come through,' he said. 'You fly the lunchtime flight to LA tomorrow.'

'I haven't got a uniform yet.'

'Robbie's having it picked up this afternoon. They know your size. When will you be back?'

'When United tell me,' I said. 'I'm strictly a working girl for the next few weeks.'

'And then?'

I shrugged. 'If Mr. Blaser forgives and forgets, it'll be back to the old grindstone.'

'I saw Mike Fellows last week,' said Walter, from left field. Mike was my American boyfriend, the one I hadn't called last night.

'How is he?'

'Fine,' said Walter. 'Are you seeing him?'

'I shall play it by ear,' I said. 'Why, are you jealous?'

'Terribly,' he said. And the sad thing was he almost meant it.

I picked up my uniform from Robbie, did some window-shopping on Fifth Avenue, then took myself to a movie. Dinner I cooked for myself in the apartment. Then I packed my flight bag and stowed the rest of my luggage in one of the closets in the spare room of the apartment. Then I went to bed. I phoned Robbie from Kennedy Airport the following morning and told her to collect my stuff if Walter wanted to use the apartment. Then I said goodbye and joined the ranks of the working girls.

TEN

There are basically two types of people who travel on aeroplanes: those who travel for business and those who travel for pleasure. The business ones enjoy themselves; the ones travelling for pleasure have a terrible time. The business man opens his briefcase as soon as he embarks, and only looks up from his work long enough to shovel food into his mouth, or pour down the booze. But the others don't want to miss a thing. If they're sitting on the right of the aircraft, everything they want to see is out of windows on the left. If the movie doesn't come on in time, they complain, and when it is on, they're forever letting up the window blinds to make sure they're not missing anything thirty thousand feet below them. They complain if we're late and they complain if we're early. They complain if the weather is rough, and if it's smooth, they complain that there's no excitement. They snigger at the hostess as she goes through the oxygen-mask and life-belt drill. Then they complain because they haven't understood it. Some of them leave their arms dangling in the aisle so that they can give you a surreptitious feel every time you pass by, and nearly all of them proposition you at least once on the trip—and this isn't only confined to the men. Through all this you're supposed to move serenely, always smiling, always cheerful, always reassuring, a cross between Florence Nightingale, a wet nurse and a backstairs skivvy.

'Miss, there's a bolt missing from the wing.'

'Miss, what was that bump I felt?'

'Miss, isn't that Cincinnati down there?'

'Miss, the coffee is cold.'

'Miss, will you go to bed with me tonight?'

So, with all this going on, why does anyone want to be an air hostess? I don't know. You tell me.

We had our usual crop of difficult customers on the Los Angeles flight, but I wasn't really bothered. I did my job, walked a blister onto my heel and, six hours later, as we fastened our belts for landing, I was tired and reasonably content. It was dark and Los Angeles was spread out like a magic neon carpet below the aircraft as we put down. I stood at the hatch and smiled my goodbyes at the faceless people I had been cooped up with; then I joined the crew in the staff commissariat for a cup of coffee before we all dispersed to our respective hidey-holes. Being an out-of-town girl, I was given an expense chit entitling me to bed and meals for as long as I stayed in LA. The hotel wasn't what I would have chosen myself, but like most American hotels it was clean, efficient and impersonal, which suited my mood completely. I ate in the nearly empty restaurant, then went to my room with every intention of having an early night. The phone was ringing as I let myself in.

'Katy?'

'Who's that?'

'Mary Youngman.' Mary was the English girl who had achieved what every hostess dreamed of. She'd married a millionaire she had met while she was working.

'How did you know I was here?' I asked.

'Robbie Brightwell called me from New York and told me you might be lonely.'

She knew Robbie purely as a friend of mine; Mary had been just a normal hostess before she struck lucky, and while she obviously wondered how I could turn up in half a dozen different uniforms in as many weeks, she never embarrassed me by asking. I was fond of Mary for a number of reasons, not least of them being the fact that she had introduced me to my husband. She had been the senior hostess on my first flight and, while the Captain was generally considered a perk for the senior hostess, she was already involved with her millionaire. She had been matron of honour at our wedding, and on hand three months later when I was widowed. Six weeks after that she had been married and disappeared to America, where I managed to see her whenever I was in town at the same time as she. It wasn't as often as either of us would have liked, because she and her husband owned six different places in America alone, and God knows how many others scattered throughout the globe.

'You really are an old bag,' she said. 'Why didn't you call me?'

'I only just got in,' I said. 'I'm going to bed.'

'You're not,' she said. 'The car will be out front of the hotel in thirty minutes.' Then she hung up on me, giving me no time for argument.

Why not? I thought. It was off-day tomorrow as far as I knew, so I didn't have to get up early. I put on a fresh face and then wondered what the hell to wear. One never knew with Mary Youngman whether one was going to a white-tie-and-tails affair or a swimming-pool party. I settled for a blouse and skirt; if I was wrong, Mary would lend me something. We were near enough the same size to make no difference.

Thirty-five minutes later I was sitting in the back of a Rolls Royce, driven by a coloured chauffeur who had problems. He kept the partition down so that he could tell me all about himself and his wife, who had the shingles; and his son, who had just been expelled from UCLA for smoking pot; and his daughter, who showed every sign of becoming a whore if her mother didn't take a club to her pretty soon.

I said just now that Mary's husband, Skip, was a millionaire. Actually he was a millionaire thirty-two times over, and he lived as though he couldn't wait to get rid of all thirty-two of them. The house in Beverly Hills had eighteen bathrooms. It had other rooms as well, but I had always been so impressed with the first statistic that I had never bothered to enquire how many. There was also a swimming pool, whose mosaic-tiled bottom could be raised to make a dance floor; two tennis courts, one grass and one hard; a squash court; an eight-hole golf course; and a garage to hold eight cars. There was a living-in staff of five and an army of little Japanese gentlemen who swarmed all over the gardens during the daylight hours.

Mary was waiting for me at the front door and we fell into each other's arms while the butler and the chauffeur looked on impassively. Then I was dragged indoors to say hello to Skip. Millionaire he might have been, but he couldn't really help that, and he was a charming little man who had never quite got over the surprise that somebody as lovely and as elegant as Mary could have fallen in love with him. He pecked me on the cheek and told me how glad he was to see me. The nice thing about it was that I knew he meant it. He worried sometimes about the fact that he had plucked Mary from the bosom of friends and family, so when any of those friends turned up in Beverly Hills, or any place else for that matter, he bent over backwards to please them, knowing it was what Mary wanted. The silly thing was that he didn't have to worry one little bit about Mary. She adored him and would have married him even if his father hadn't left him thirty-two million dollars. He's a little man, as I said, not yet forty, with bright-blue eyes in a tanned, well-ordered face. He doesn't drink to excess and he doesn't chase girls. His whole life revolves round Mary, and hers around him. They're an attractive couple and I'm very fond of both of them.

After the initial greetings, Mary dragged me upstairs while she changed out of the jeans and shirt she had welcomed me in.

'We're going to The Factory,' she said. 'OK?'

'Anything you say,' I said.

'I've got a fellow for you. He's meeting us there.' I must have pulled some sort of a face, because she immediately backtracked. 'I can always cancel him if you'd rather not.'

'Not at all,' I said. 'Who is he?'

'Friend of Skip's. He's got some oil wells some place. He's a nice man. You'll like him. And he's single.'

She threw the last remark in, hoping I'd take it as an afterthought of no consequence. Mary had never really got over her good luck, and she was always trying to find spare millionaires for her unmarried friends. In the past she had paired me off with a Greek shipping tycoon in Monte Carlo, and a Venezuelan oil millionaire, who had all sorts of things on his mind, marriage not being one of them. But she pressed on regardless.

We piled into the Rolls and the chauffeur drove us to The Factory. The usual group of young actors and actresses were playing pool, and everyone looked towards us as we came in. Then, realising that we were nobodies, they continued where they had left off.

My millionaire date turned out to be six feet tall and one of the most beautiful men I had ever seen. His name was Marvin Torbay and it took me all of five minutes to work out that he was as queer as a two-pound note. He was only twenty-six years old, and some of the big husky men around the room looked daggers at me when they realised that I was his date. His manners were impeccable, and he spoke with a soft Southern accent which could have been sexy, but which wasn't because of certain inflections in his voice which left no doubt in which direction his urges took him. But he was off duty this evening and he made a charming companion. I don't know what Mary had told him, but he treated me like a cross between a maiden aunt and a sixteen-year-old girl on her first date. Mary trapped me in the toilet the first chance she got.

'I'm terribly sorry, darling. Honestly, he seemed so butch the last time I met him.'

'You were drunk,' I said.

She admitted that she might have been, and only cheered up when I was able to convince her that I didn't mind his being queer at all. And I didn't. I was enjoying myself and I was going to be spared the inevitable end-of-evening complications. After we had returned to the table Marvin asked me if I would like to Frug.

We were busy shaking it all over the place when I caught sight of someone across the room who looked like Mike Fellows, my American boyfriend. I didn't want to see him that night, so I asked Marvin to take me back to my table where I could see without being seen. Mary and Skip had moved to another table and were talking to someone they knew, and Marvin started telling me some of the more unimportant things about himself and his friends. I was still keeping an eye open for Mike Fellows, and I suppose I'd half switched off to Marvin's conversation. Suddenly I switched on again quickly.

'Who did you say?'

'Gerastan. Roger Gerastan.'

'What about him?'

'I just said that the newspapers and the magazines print a lot of rubbish about him. They don't know anything about him so they make it up.'

'You know him?'

'You haven't been listening to me, Katy darling.'

'I'm sorry,' I said. 'But do you?'

'I told you. I was up seeing him this afternoon in that great mausoleum he lives in.'

'Tell me about him?' I asked.

'What's to tell? He's one of the three richest men in the country and he likes his privacy.'

'I know that,' I said. 'But what's he *like*?' After all, this was the man who had employed my Bill for five years, the man who had flown him seven thousand miles for a chat, and had grown even richer than he already was from the fruits of Bill's inventiveness and brilliance. But before Marvin could go on, Mary and Skip came back to the table.

'Tell you what,' said Marvin. 'Next time you're in town, I'll take you up there. It's only a couple of hundred miles. He'll adore you.'

'Who will?' said Mary, ever attentive.

'Roger Gerastan.'

I'm sure nobody noticed it except me, but I happened to be reaching for my drink at that moment, and I was looking straight at her. It was only momentary, but it was there nevertheless: at the name Roger Gerastan, Mary suddenly looked very, very frightened.

As though to confirm what I had noticed, Mary announced five minutes later that she had a splitting headache and please would Skip take her home. Skip offered to send the car back for me, but Marvin said that he would drive me back to my hotel. For the first time since I had known her, Mary didn't suggest that I stay with her and Skip. I think Skip noticed it, too, because he started saying something to her as they walked away, glancing back at me. She said something back to him and a moment later they were gone. I played around with the conversation for a few more minutes before steering it back to where I wanted it.

'Do Skip and Mary know Gerastan?' I asked.

'Good heavens, no!' said Marvin. 'At least, I think Skip knows him, but he can't stand the man, positively loathes him.' Skip is a bit of an idealist. To him, no one is wholly bad, just ignorant. Roger Gerastan, on the other hand, is so far to the right as to be practically out of sight. If you're not white, Protestant American, you don't rate.'

'Mary doesn't know him though?'

'No fear! Skip wouldn't allow it. He's got open house, has Skip, but let Roger Gerastan set foot over the threshold and he'd set the Dobermans onto him.'

'It still doesn't sound like Skip,' I said.

'You're forgetting one thing,' said Marvin. 'Mary's Jewish.'

I *had* forgotten. But that couldn't have been why she was frightened. What had made her react the way she did at the sound of Gerastan's name?

'Did you mean it about introducing me to Gerastan?' I asked.

'Next time you're in town,' he said. 'Providing he approves.'

'Why shouldn't he?'

Marvin looked at me critically. 'You're not Negro. And you're not a communist, are you?'

I shook my head. 'I'm not American either.'

'He doesn't mind the English,' said Marvin. 'In fact he's quite fond of them. He reckons that you're idiots to have given away your empire, especially as you gave most of it to the blacks, but he still has a bit of a soft spot for the English. Apart from that, he's a dirty old man. He'll approve, I think.'

'Thank you very much,' I said. 'Now, as long as you keep your hands to yourself, you can drive me back to my hotel.'

He grinned at me; he really was one of the most beautiful men I had ever seen. 'Half the men in the room would just love to be in my place right now,' he said.

'That makes us quits,' I said. 'The other half would love to be in mine.'

He grinned again to show there was no offence taken. That was another thing I liked about him. He was as camp as a row of tents, but he didn't give a twopenny damn. It was a criminal waste; that's what it was, and I told him so. 'I've got a good mind to take you back to my place and seduce you,' I said.

'That would take more than a good mind,' he said cheerfully. 'Life's too short. Let's go to a place I know and tie one on.'

I agreed, and an hour later found us driving along the coast searching for a turnoff that Marvin was convinced we'd missed half a mile back. There was a heavy sea mist rolling up across the beach and spilling onto the road, which had become wet and slick. No cars were foolish enough to try to overtake us in the mist, but those going in the opposite direction glided past us silently, the lights from their headlamps feeling the way for them like a blind man's cane.

'There it is,' said Marvin suddenly.

He swung off the main road so quickly that, to the man driving behind us, it must have looked as though the ground had opened up and devoured us. We started to climb up out of the mist on a long road that kept doubling back on itself in a series of hairpins that would have been unnegotiable in a larger car. But Marvin was driving a neat little Mercedes, and he threw it round the hairpins like a man who had decided that life held nothing more for him. Fortunately, I had drunk sufficient to keep me from worrying too much.

I wanted to ask him more about the Skip-Mary-Gerastan situation, but when I started to frame a question, he took his eyes off the road. So I dried up quickly and let him get on with his driving. After twenty minutes of climbing, we levelled out, and two minutes later he turned into a drive framed with two large concrete pillars. Fifty yards further on we pulled up behind half a dozen other cars. The house was a single-storey affair, meandering over the uneven ground as though it couldn't make up its mind where to settle down. In spite of the cars in the drive, there was no light showing in any of the windows, but I could just hear the sound of oriental-flavoured music from inside. We crunched across the gravel towards the front door.

'I'm not going to wake up in Buenos Aires, I hope,' I said.

Marvin was holding my hand, and he gave it a squeeze. 'Nice people,' he said. 'You'll like them.'

I doubted it, but I let it go. The front door was off the latch and we walked straight into the main room, which stretched to the rear of the house and beyond that to a terrace with the inevitable pool. There were about fifteen people in the room, but I only made it out to be this many after the third count. The room and the terrace were in almost total darkness, relieved only by small pools of light from concealed sources. Three couples were moving around the centre of the room, more or less in time to the music, while the others were sitting, standing or laying wherever the fancy took them, and I do mean laying.

Orgies I can take or leave, but given the choice, I prefer to leave them. To my way of thinking they fail to live up to any of the promises they're supposed to provide; they're a dead loss as far as sexual satisfaction is concerned, and as an exercise in community sociability, they fall flat on their multitudinous backsides. The few I have attended have started off full of embarrassment and deteriorated into near anarchy. So and so, who is terribly broad-minded, suddenly realises that he doesn't appreciate the things being done to his equally broad-minded wife by the boyfriend or husband of such and such, and Mrs. So-and-so starts to worry that her old man might be enjoying himself too much with the eighteen-year-old nymphomaniac who arrived with the dyke who has already started to upset the hostess. Call me square if you like, but that's the way I am. In my book, sex is something personal, to be enjoyed by two people alone with each other, without the benefit of audience or extra participants.

Marvin introduced me to our hostess, a strikingly beautiful Negress wearing a caftan which effectively masked the body beneath it, but not enough to hide the fact that it must have been magnificent, if the way she moved and carried herself was any indication. I was offered a cigarette which turned out to be very good quality pot, so after a couple of drags, I stubbed it out surreptitiously and substituted one that might give me lung cancer, but at least allowed me to keep my feet on the ground while I was getting it. Not Marvin, though. He had come for a static trip, and he took off ten minutes after we arrived. I wandered around for half an hour, becoming more bored and disinterested by the minute. There didn't seem any point in waiting for Marvin to drive me home; he'd gone so far out he'd not be back for twenty-four hours. So I located him on the terrace and asked him for his car keys. He didn't even know who I was, but he handed them over regardless. I scribbled a note for him, letting him know where he could pick up the car and, tucking the note in his jacket pocket, I kissed him on the forehead. He beamed at me from twelve miles away as I slipped off towards the front door.

'You leaving us, honey?' It was my hostess.

''Fraid so,' I said. 'I'm a working girl.'

'Aren't we all?' she said, flashing her magnificent teeth. 'Mind how you go!'

I pointed the car downhill and twenty-five minutes later I hit the coast road. An hour later I was tucked up snugly in my lonely, virginal bed—and delighted to be so.

Mary called me the following morning.

'Are you working today?'

'No,' I said.

'I'll pick you up for lunch at eleven-thirty.'

I looked at my bedside clock, which showed ten-thirty. Something had to be wrong with Mary. She never got up before eleven and didn't consider that the day started until teatime. She met me outside, driving herself in a Triumph sports car that she could have lost in the trunk of any of her other automobiles. I'd only managed about four hours' sleep, but next to her I looked like a baby. There were lines of worry and concern around her eyes that I could have sworn weren't there last night, and she drove the car as though it were going to blow up at any moment.

We drove out to the beach, where she pulled in at a small fish restaurant which looked as though it were going into immediate bankruptcy. It was empty when we arrived and, by the expression of the faces of the two queers who ran it, it looked as though it was going to be the same way when we left. The food explained it all, but neither Mary nor I was interested in what we were eating.

She managed to hold off until she had downed two drinks while I was still blowing the froth off the first.

'Don't go and see Gerastan!' she said suddenly. I'd been expecting something like this, but it still managed to surprise me.

'Why not?'

She didn't want to tell me, but she realised that she was too far in to change direction. So she took a deep breath and told me.

It was all very ordinary, really, but quite nasty nevertheless. She had met Gerastan before she married Skip. She had been going three parts steady with a Flight Captain named George Random, who had applied for a flying job with the Gerastan Corporation. He had subsequently been screened through half a dozen personnel executives and private secretaries, until it only required the stamp of approval from the great man himself. The job was that of chief pilot for Gerastan's own personal fleet of aircraft, so the old man wanted to make the final decision himself. At the same time, he asked George to suggest a couple more people who might like to change their jobs—a first officer and a hostess. Naturally enough, George asked Mary if she was interested. She was, and it was arranged that she, George and the prospective first officer would be flown out to meet Gerastan.

The interviews had gone well, it seemed, and the three of them were asked to stay overnight at the Gerastan place. Roger Gerastan had walked unannounced into Mary's bedroom in the middle of the night and, when she showed unwilling, he had raped her with the assistance of two of his henchmen, who hadn't batted an eyelid throughout the entire operation.

The following day, the three of them had been informed politely by a secretary that they weren't suitable, and they had been flown back to where they had come from. But Mary, not unreasonably, decided that she would make a fuss. Unfortunately she made the mistake of announcing her intentions before she pitched in. Next day, she was visited by one of Gerastan's lawyers, who showed her his latest set of photographs. Now, even if a girl is being raped, there are odd moments when it *can* look as though she is a willing partner; a camera shutter clicks very fast, and an expression of pain, if caught at one-five-hundredth of a second, could feasibly be one of pleasure. Out of the three hundred odd photographs taken from a concealed camera let into the ceiling, a dozen had been selected. According to Mary this dozen had been beautifully doctored, and not only did it look as though she were having a ball, but somehow Gerastan had disappeared completely from the scene, leaving just herself and the two henchmen. The lawyer went to great pains to point out that everyone would be a lot happier if Mary forgot the whole unfortunate episode. So forget it she did, and a year later she was married to Skip.

Six months after that, Skip's business advisers had come to Skip and told him that the Gerastan Corporation were trying to buy a tract of land that Skip owned in Arizona. They wanted to build a missile factory or some such. The price offered was fair and the advisers suggested that Skip accept. But Skip didn't rate Gerastan at all. He despised the man's politics and had said so on a number of occasions. Added to this there was a background of double-dealing and high-powered chicanery which had taken place sometime in the past over a business deal, when Skip's father was still alive and Skip had just started working for the company. So Skip told his advisers that he wouldn't sell a glass of water to Roger Gerastan if the man was stranded in the middle of Death Valley.

Skip's advisers duly reported this to Gerastan's advisers, and two weeks later Mary received one of the photographs in the mail, with a little note signed by Gerastan. How she managed to talk Skip into selling, I don't know, but she did. She had to. And that, more or less, was it. Gerastan still had the photographs, and she could never be quite sure that one wasn't going to land on her breakfast table one morning, should Gerastan ever feel disposed to want something from her or Skip.

'Why didn't you tell Skip the truth?' I asked. 'He'd have understood.'

'Perhaps he would,' she said. 'But it's too late now. I can't take the chance. He's very narrow-minded, in his own way. Perhaps if it had been anyone else but Gerastan, but ...' She reached across and pressed my hand. 'Don't go up and see him, Katy. Don't go near him. Whatever Marvin says about him, he's an evil man. You could get into trouble, serious trouble.'

It wasn't quite right somehow. I knew that Mary was very fond of me, but that hardly seemed sufficient reason for her telling me what I'm sure she had never told anyone else. She knew I was a big girl now and could look after myself in the clinches. All in all it didn't gel, but there was no point in pursuing the matter. I agreed that I wouldn't go and see Gerastan, even if I was invited, and she seemed vastly relieved. We finished our lunch and paid a bill large enough to stave off bankruptcy for the next three months.

Mary drove me back to my hotel. 'I'd like to ask you round tonight,' she said. 'But Skip has to go out of town and I'm going with him.'

I told her I was working the following day and needed an early night anyway. As I watched her drive away, I thought I saw a car drive past that I had noticed earlier, parked across from the restaurant while we were lunching. But most American cars look the same to me, and I could have been wrong.

ELEVEN

I spent a wallflower-type evening. Even Marvin didn't call, but he probably hadn't yet got back from his trip. I was flying to New York the following morning, so I had an early night, trying to catch up on some of the sleep I hadn't had the night before. Bright and early I greeted my sixty-two charges and held their joint hand as we crossed the continent from West to East.

Walter was out of town, so I had dinner with Robbie in the apartment. I tried to steer the conversation around to her and Walter, but like he did, she politely told me to mind my own business. I decided that matchmaking was for the birds, and we spent a pleasant evening talking about absolutely nothing.

The following morning I welcomed aboard seventy-eight people who could have been the same ones as yesterday, so anonymous do passengers become when one is flying regularly.

With the time differential on my side, I was back in Los Angeles by three-thirty p.m. local time. Same hotel, different room. I called Mary's number in case she had changed her mind and not gone away, but was informed by the butler that Mrs. and Mr. Youngman had departed yesterday for parts unknown and he didn't know when they would be back. I would have called Marvin, but I didn't know his number, so I called American Airlines and asked if Captain Fellows was in town. He wasn't, and that seemed to cover the whole spectrum of my social life.

I spent a couple of hours by the hotel pool and then I had my hair done. About seven, I hired a self-drive car and drove around town trying to pick out a suitable-type restaurant for lonely spinsters, one where their loneliness would be respected, and where they wouldn't be required to fight off equally lonely bachelors. I didn't find one, so I drove back to the hotel where I phoned United and practically begged to be given a flight the following day. The supervisor called me back an hour later and told me that a girl had gone sick, and I could take her place on the afternoon flight the next day. Then I went to bed.

Ten minutes later the phone rang. It was Mike Fellows. He had just got in and they had told him that I had called earlier.

'Can I come round?' he asked.

'It's late,' I said, knowing that he would give me an argument. He gave me one, and twenty minutes later I answered his gentle tap on the door and let him in.

'What did you do? Bribe the house detective?' I asked after the welcomes were over.

'It cost me ten dollars,' he said, starting to undress.

Like I said, I'm a bit in love with Mike Fellows, or rather I used to be up to a week ago. He's a neat, compact man, with a tidy, well-put-together face and the bluest eyes I've ever seen. He has a gentle, humorous mouth and he's a marvellous lover. We'd had some pretty wild times in the past, but something had gone wrong tonight and it could only have been my fault. He was the same as always, but he felt like a stranger to me. I tried very hard, but it was because of this that I gave myself away. After ten minutes he rolled away from me, his blue eyes regarding me steadily.

'What's the matter, Katy?'

'Nothing.'

'Yes there is. You've met someone.'

There didn't seem any point in lying to him. 'He's dead,' I said.

'Poor Katy!' He took me in his arms again, but it was no different this time. After a few minutes he drew back again. 'I'm sorry,' he said. 'But you shouldn't have let me come round.'

'I phoned you, remember?'

'Because you were lonely?'

'Perhaps.'

He kissed me again, gently, without passion. It was nice, lying there in his arms, comfortable, and I didn't want him to leave me. And after a few silent minutes I realised that perhaps I did want a little more from him. I'm a normal, healthy girl and these things happen, however screwed up one may be inside. And he really was very sweet, and I was terribly fond of him, and he smelled nice, and he was cuddly. It turned out to be almost like old times. I woke up once in the night, coming up from a dream of Bill, which left me shaking and covered with perspiration. But Mike wrapped his arms around me again, and after a while I drifted back to sleep.

We had late breakfast sent up to the room. Then he watched me while I got dressed and we made vague plans for the following day, should I get back to Los Angeles. I kissed him goodbye and went downstairs to check out. Five minutes later I caught the crew bus to the airport. Fortunately, I was early. My flight wasn't due to be called for an hour yet, and that's how I saw Hank Almedo.

He was getting out of a taxi outside the American Airlines terminal. I didn't recognise him until he turned back to pay off the cab, and by then we had already driven past. But it was him right enough, with one side of his face looking like a Turner sunset. I yelled for the bus to stop and I had jumped out before the driver really knew what had happened. I ran back to where I had seen Hank, but he had already disappeared into the terminal building. This suited me fine. I went in through the end door and looked along the two hundred feet of lobby. He was checking in at the fourth booth and, even as I saw him, he turned away and headed towards the bar. The sign above the check-in counter showed that he was going to Chicago, departing in thirty-five minutes. I ran across to a line of phone booths and then realised that I had left my handbag in the bus. I dialled the operator and asked for a reverse-charge call to Walter in New York.

'There's a twenty-minute delay to New York,' reported the operator happily, so I asked for the supervisor, and when she came on the line I gave her the code number Walter had told me to use any time that it was urgent.

Two minutes later Robbie put me through to Walter. 'I've just seen Hank Almedo,' I said.

'Where?'

'He's flying to Chicago in thirty-five minutes.'

There was a moment's pause, the long-distance wire humming gently; then Walter made up his mind. 'Go with him. I'll contact Blaser and have instructions waiting for you when you arrive.'

'I don't know, Walter,' I said. 'I'm supposed to be nonoperational at the moment. Mr. Blaser might not like it.'

'I'll take care of Mr. Blaser. You do as I say. What's the flight number?' I gave him the Chicago flight number and heard him call it out to Robbie; then he was back on the line with me. 'What are you supposed to be doing?' I told him I was due out for New York in an hour and gave him the details. 'Check in for the Chicago flight in ten minutes. There'll be a ticket waiting for you. Fly as a passenger in whichever class Almedo isn't. Clear, Irish?'

'Clear,' I said, and hung up.

I ran all the way to the United terminal, where I collected my handbag. Some enterprising person had already put my suitcase aboard the flight to New York, so I borrowed a topcoat from one of the girls and slipped it on over my uniform. Walter had worked fast; I'd already been taken off the New York flight and the supervisor was livid because it meant that they were going to have to fly one girl short. There didn't seem much point in offering my apologies, but I did anyway. I needn't have bothered, because they weren't accepted.

Then I ran back to the American building and checked in at the same desk Hank Almedo had used. My ticket was made out for economy class, which meant that Hank was travelling first. Walter had arranged that I board the aircraft with the cabin crew and, as the flight hadn't yet been called, I got aboard without even seeing Hank. I saw him board with the other passengers and take a seat halfway along the cabin. It was a window seat, so he wasn't going to be able to make any rapid getaways when we reached Chicago, which was a relief, because until we landed there and I picked up my instructions, I didn't know what I was going to have to do.

The flight was uneventful and it was quite a change to be sitting down in an aircraft while the other girls fetched and carried. Five and a half hours later I was first off the plane, running down the covered gangway hoping that whoever was supposed to meet me would see me before Hank Almedo did. There was an airline man waiting at the end of the gangway.

'Miss Touchfeather?'

When I agreed that I was, he handed me an envelope. I tore it open quickly. There still wasn't another passenger in sight.

Stay with him. Report whenever possible. B.

And that was it. No matter that I didn't know Chicago, nor that I was still wearing a uniform covered only by someone else's topcoat, nor that I had only about six dollars in my handbag, nor that if Hank recognised me he would no doubt get very ugly. Mr. Blaser, three thousand miles away on Pandam Street, had made his decision and it was not my place to reason why. I cursed the fact that I had decided to report for work early. If I hadn't I would probably have missed Hank altogether. A pox on everyone, I thought. Then my breast started to itch where it was healing up, and I thought about that cellar again, and I thought of Bill and how Hank had been partially responsible for what had happened to him. That made me feel better about the whole thing, and by the time Hank Almedo came out through the first-class exit, I was already across at the other side of the lobby, waiting for him. I had decided what I was going to do. I would follow him to his hotel, and after he had checked in, I would check into the same place and then phone Walter to wire me some money. I had sufficient in my bag to cover my cab trip to town, and that was about all. I still think it was a good plan, and it wasn't my fault that when Hank reached town he checked in at the YMCA.

'Where are you?' asked Walter.

'I'm in the bar across the road,' I said. 'And they're already starting to gang up on me.' I was referring to the half a dozen predatory-looking men who had sparkled into life as soon as I had walked into the bar; none of them could wait for me to finish in the phone booth.

'Oh, Katy, Katy!' said Walter, uselessly. 'What price that Irish bog now?'

'It would be a help if you'd stop being facetious and get someone over here double quick,' I said icily.

'I thought you enjoyed your work.'

'What work?' I asked. 'I can't check into the YMCA, and I can't stay here, and I've got no money, and I've got no clothes, and there are some men outside who look intent on rape, and I'm miserable because I'm cold and I don't like Chicago, and I think you're an absolute pig.' I'd practically talked myself into tears by then, and at that moment Hank Almedo came out of his hotel across the road.

'Christ, he's just come out! Bye!' I hung up before he could say a word. I ran out into the street and hailed a cab going in the opposite direction to the one Hank was climbing into.

'Follow that cab,' I said, trying not to sound like something from a B movie.

'What cab, lady?' said the driver reasonably.

'That one over there. Oh, he's getting away.' But I'd obviously touched some sympathetic chord in my cab driver.

'Oh no, he ain't,' he said, and swung his cab into a U-turn that nearly finished everything there and then. There was a squeal of brakes and a screech of rubber as the drivers behind us, barely avoided collisions and a moment later we were tucked in behind Almedo's cab.

'What's the creep done to you, lady?' my cab driver said, companionably. 'Given you the bum's rush?'

I admitted that he was my husband and had just run out on me and the kids. The cabby glanced at me in the driving mirror.

'He wants his marbles counted,' he said. 'You sure you want after him? A good-looking broad like you is probably better off without the creep.'

'You're probably right,' I said. 'But I want to know where he's going.'

'Want to get the dirt on him, eh? What are you, anyway—a GI bride?'

'Why?'

'You're English, aren't you? I'd know that accent anywhere. I saw *Blow Up* four times. Dirty picture.'

'I haven't got any money,' I said, deciding that I'd better throw myself on his mercy.

'That figures,' he said equably. 'None of the English have. But don't worry about it. You can send it to me when you start getting your alimony.' All this time he had been driving practically in the trunk of Almedo's cab, and I started to worry a little.

'Wouldn't it be a good idea to drop back a little?' I said. 'He might see us.'

'Whatever you say, lady,' said my cabby, and promptly allowed four cars to get between us and Hank Almedo. And we lost him, of course; we were bound to. My cabby just wasn't cut out for the cloak-and-dagger bit. We cruised around for half an hour trying to find him again, until I told the cabby to drive me to the best hotel in town. There, I took him into the lobby with me and told him to wait. I phoned Walter and told him what had happened.

'Not to worry too much, Katy,' he said. 'We'll pick him up again when he returns to his hotel.'

'You pick him up,' I said. 'I quit.'

He chuckled and asked me where I was phoning from. I told him and he asked me to wait in the main lobby for twenty minutes. I rejoined my cab-driver friend, who wasn't at all abashed at the tuxedos and tiaras. We talked of this and that for twenty minutes until an elegant young man in a Brooks Brothers suit came into the lobby and headed towards us.

'Miss Touchfeather?' When I had established this to his satisfaction, he handed me an envelope, tipped his narrow brimmed hat and walked out. I opened the envelope and extracted ten fifty-dollar bills and a typewritten note. One of the bills I gave to my cab driver, who told me that I was a doll, even if I was English. Then I read the note.

Return New York first available transport. Report for further instructions.

The note wasn't signed. I tore it into tiny pieces and dropped them in one of the large ashtrays that dotted the lobby. I said goodbye and thank you to the cab driver. Then I went to the reception desk and asked for the best room in the place. They looked at me a bit askance when they realised that I had no luggage, but I flashed around my newfound wealth, ordering toothbrushes and six-course dinners and the like, and they finally gave me a room. 'First available transport' indeed. I'd get to New York when I was good and ready, and it certainly wasn't going to be tonight. I sent my uniform to be pressed and I washed out my smalls. Then, wrapped in the huge towelling robe provided by the hotel, I sat down and ate the meal I had ordered. I ate the lot, starting with the caviare, and moving right through to the

Souffle Grand Marnier to finish up with. Then, feeling a little sick, but quite content, I went to bed.

Walter was quite excited when I saw him the following afternoon. But he wasn't the only one; Robbie looked as close to tears as I had ever seen her. A lovers' tiff, I decided, and asked her about it. But she wasn't telling, and she ushered me in to see Walter before I could ask too many questions.

'What's the matter with Robbie?' I asked as soon as she left us alone. 'Have you been a bastard to her?'

He started to say something, then changed his mind and became all official. 'You're to report back to London right away.'

I said a rude word and for once he didn't come back with a smart remark. There was something wrong in this office, and I didn't think any longer that it was as simple as a lovers' quarrel. Anyway, I was too choked with Mr. Blaser's peremptory instructions to dig into the matter.

'I'm supposed to be non-operational. What does the silly old fart want?'

'You'd better go and find out,' said Walter flatly.

And that was all that I could get out of him or Robbie.

TWELVE

My apartment smelled like a disused tomb. I had forgotten to leave a window open and the central heating seems to gang up on me when I'm away, turning rotten any food I leave lying around. My instructions from Walter had been explicit. I was to report to Mr. Blaser the moment I set foot in London. But it was I who had taken the night flight; hadn't slept; and was feeling tired, dirty and irritable, and I wasn't reporting to anyone until I had a chance to repair some of the damage. I took a hot bath, soaking for an hour; then I made myself up leisurely, dressed in something suitable for the occasion and drifted around to Pandam Street at eleven o'clock.

'Where have you been, Miss Touchfeather?'

'In America, sir.'

'I'm referring to the fact that you arrived at London Airport at eight a.m. It is now eleven.'

'I didn't realise there was any urgency,' I said.

'Mm!' he grunted, ominously. 'I've heard you had quite a time of it, including stranding yourself in Chicago without any money.' Wait until he saw the expense sheet that would eventually be passed through from Walter. Let's see him argue *that* through Exchange Control.

'I managed, sir,' I said.

'From what I hear, all you managed to do was to lose the man you were supposed to be following.' There didn't seem to be much of an answer to this, so I didn't bother trying to invent one.

'Still,' he said, after a moment. 'One good thing has come out of it. Your seeing the Almedo man may go a long way towards re-establishing a lead.'

'A lead to what, sir?' I asked politely.

'The Partman affair, of course,' he snapped.

'I'm sorry, sir; I thought that was no longer any concern of ours.'

'Who said so?' He was quite irate.

'You did. You said that once Professor Partman's unit went to America, they would cease to be in our province.'

'That's right,' he said. 'I did say that, didn't I? Well, something has cropped up since then, and I have revised my thinking.' He would tell me if he wanted to, so I didn't press it. He continued after a moment. 'It has been established that detailed plans of Professor Partman's latest project are already in the hands of . . . of a foreign power.'

'You knew there was a leakage of information from Cumming-on-Hardy,' I said.

'True. But we are sure that security has been one hundred percent effective since the death of Professor Partman.'

'What you're saying is that the information was known to the other side before Bill . . . Professor Partman was killed.' He nodded.

'That's stupid,' I said, forgetting myself for a moment. 'In that case, there would have been no need to kill him.'

'I didn't say how long before, Miss Touchfeather. We think it was in the course of giving this information that Professor Partman was killed, either by accident, or because they had no further reason for wanting him alive.'

'So you're now saying he *did* talk under torture,' I said, feeling a little sick.

'That is exactly what I am saying.'

'Then why did they bother with me in Rome, if they already had what they wanted?'

'I don't know,' he said, evenly. 'That is what we have got to find out.'

It seems that Mr. Blaser's theory was all based on the timing of events. An agent who had proved thoroughly trustworthy in the past had contacted Mr. Blaser and informed him that the Russians had already started work on a missile-control unit that would obviate the efficacity of the anti-missile device that Bill had come up with. Suddenly the Americans weren't two years ahead of the Russians; they were running neck and neck, and the President of the United States was about to ask for an appropriation of another umpteen million dollars to develop an anti-anti-Russian-anti-USA-anti-missile device to ... and about here I got lost. The point was, though, that the Russians had started work at such a time as to put it after the man had been fished out of the sea near Bombay, and before the time that I reported back to London, badly singed, from Rome. The only possible supposition was that Bill had given way under pressure. But if this was the case, why had Hank and Jack bothered about me in Rome?

'How are we going to find out?' I asked. After all, I was more than just casually involved, and I firmly believed that I had a right to know.

'If Mr. Almedo fails to give us a lead on his own, then we shall have to have him picked up and ask him to point the way.'

'He struck me as being a man who would need quite a little persuasion.'

'We shall do our best to accommodate him,' said Mr. Blaser. He really had a very nasty streak in his makeup, and the only strange thing was that I was still capable of mild surprise when he exhibited it.

'What has he been doing?' I asked.

'Since you lost him?'

'Since I lost him.'

'Apparently he disappeared for three hours, and then returned to his hotel. About the time you must have been flying to New York, he was on his way back to Los Angeles. He is at present staying in a motel just outside Los Angeles and, from all accounts, he shows no signs of going anywhere in the immediate future.'

'Did anyone meet with a sudden fatal accident while Almedo was on his own in Chicago?' I asked.

'As a matter of fact, yes,' he said, as though he were reluctant to give anything away.

'Anyone I know?'

He looked a little embarrassed suddenly. I'm not going to like this, I thought. I repeated the question to show him that I wasn't just making small talk.

'Anyone I know, Mr. Blaser?'

He cleared his throat. 'I'm afraid so, Miss Touchfeather. I understand that the deceased was a good friend of yours. That is one of the reasons why I had you called back to London. I thought it better to give you the news myself. Walter Martin offered to be the one to tell you, but I wanted to have you where I could keep an eye on you, in case you took it into your head to do anything foolish. Apart from that I—'

I interrupted him, probably the only time I ever had. 'If you don't tell me, Mr. Blaser, I shall scream out loud.'

'Yes,' he said. 'Well, we don't want that, do we? I'm sorry to have to tell you that Mrs. Mary Youngman was shot to death outside her Chicago home, the night before last.'

Perhaps I should have told Mr. Blaser about the conversation I had had with Mary right away, but at first I could see no possible connection between what she had told me and what had eventually happened. The actual shooting had been classic prohibition period. Mary and Skip had come out of their house, heading for the car. They were dining out and both were in evening dress. The chauffeur was holding open the rear door of the car and, as Skip stepped aside to allow Mary to get in, there had been three shots, without even the suggestion of an interval between them. Mary had been wearing an off-the-shoulder gown and she must have presented a beautiful target, the whiteness of her flesh framed against the dark material of her dress. The shots had landed within three inches of one another, just below her left breast.

It was shooting of the highest order, and nobody had the faintest idea from which direction they came. The chauffeur had called the police on the car telephone while Mary bled her life away in Skip's arms. Whether or not she said anything to him during those last few seconds, nobody knew; neither did they know whether there had in fact been any last few seconds, or whether Mary had been killed instantaneously. Skip, it seemed, wasn't talking. The police had moved quickly, but not as quickly as the men Walter had alerted. What should have been a front-page story in two-inch type was squashed quickly and effectively. And while the Chicago police turned over the underworld, looking for the killer, Walter's men kept their mouths shut about Almedo and allowed him to leave for Los Angeles the following morning. In flight transit, Walter had had Almedo's bags searched and the murder weapon was found, clipped to a false bottom in his suitcase. The gun was left where it was, and as far as Almedo was concerned, he had performed a very efficient job, with no comebacks or repercussions.

'You saw something of Mrs. Youngman while you were in Los Angeles?' asked Mr. Blaser. It was the following day. He had allowed me to go home after breaking the news to me. Next morning, having decided that I had mourned long enough, he'd had Miss Moody summon me back.

'We went out one evening and we had lunch together the following day. The day she left for Chicago.'

Mr. Blaser cleared his throat, a sure sign that he was going to say something unpleasant.

'I think it is stretching coincidence a little too far,' he said.

'What is?'

'You have a connection with this Almedo man. You also have a connection with Mrs. Youngman. The two things must be related somewhere.'

'No, sir,' I said emphatically. He was as good as suggesting that it was because of me that Mary had been killed.

'Put your personal feelings aside for a moment, Miss Touchfeather. Consider the facts.' I considered them and was forced to admit that the old bastard was right.

'Let us examine what we have,' he said, 'and see where it takes us. The Almedo man was working for someone when he was involved in the Professor Partman affair; he was working for the same party when he abducted you in Rome. It is reasonable to assume he was still working for the same party when he shot to death Mrs. Youngman.'

'Yes, sir,' I said.

'So we must ascertain the identity of his employer.'

'Roger Gerastan,' I said, not knowing why I said it. Mr. Blaser didn't know why either, but to give him credit, he didn't throw up his hands in horror, or even look surprised.

'Why do you say that, Miss Touchfeather?'

'I haven't the faintest idea, sir. But he's the only person I can think of who was even remotely connected with Professor Partman and Mary Youngman.'

'How connected?'

'He was Professor Partman's employer, and he also held blackmailing information on Mary Youngman.'

'What information?' I told him and he clicked his tongue a couple of times. 'Very nasty,' he said. I agreed that it was. 'Why didn't you mention it before?'

'Nobody asked me. And anyway, it was a personal confidence between Mrs. Youngman and me.'

Mr. Blaser strongly disapproved of his people sharing confidences with anyone except himself, but he allowed it to pass.

'I still fail to see where the tie-up lies,' he said.

'So do I,' I replied. 'But I'll find out.'

He mounted his high horse quickly. 'You'll do exactly as I tell you, Miss Touchfeather. Nothing more, nothing less.'

'Yes, sir,' I said.

There was a pause after that, and I started to fidget. When Mr. Blaser wandered off into the realms of speculation, there was no telling how long he would leave you alone. He returned about three minutes later.

'Let us assume for one moment that you are right, Miss Touchfeather, and that Roger Gerastan is somehow linked with the whole business. How would you go about proving it?'

'Since when have we had to prove anything, sir?' It was a reasonable question. Proof was for the law courts, and the law courts very rarely saw any of the people we came up against. Mr. Blaser comprised his own judge, counsel and jury. Once he was satisfied as to a person's guilt, he called in his own hatchet men, faceless individuals I'd been fortunate enough never to have met, and they did the rest.

'We are dealing with an extremely important national of a friendly nation, residing in that country. If he is in fact guilty of any of the things you seem to think he is, it's the Americans who will have to take action. And they will not act without proof.'

'They're not fools.'

'No, they're not. But they're politically hag-ridden. Their civil service is tied to the current administration to a large degree. There is very little of the autonomy we enjoy over here. In a matter such as this, everything would have to be explained in detail and justified with documented proof. Only then would they act.'

'I suppose there's no chance that you could send one of your own people over there. Make it look like an accident?'

He looked horrified. 'Absolutely not, Miss Touchfeather. The repercussions could be astronomical. Anyway,' he added, getting closer to the core of his reasoning, 'from what I have heard of the man, Gerastan would be a very difficult man to, er … eradicate. No, proof of complicity is what is required.'

'I'll get it, sir,' I said. And, come hell or high water, I would, too. First Bill and then Mary. I could hardly wait. But Mr. Blaser is a bright man when it suits him.

'You're not letting emotion get the better of your judgment again, are you, Miss Touchfeather?'

'Perhaps I am, sir, but don't worry. It won't affect my work.'

'Don't prejudge things, Miss Touchfeather. Approach every-thing with a completely open mind. Make your decisions on the facts as they are presented to you. Don't try to bend them to fit your preconceived ideas.' That was page-one stuff from the train-ing manual, but he was justified in mentioning it. I'd already got Roger Gerastan hung, drawn and quartered.

'Have you any idea how you would start work on this—just assuming I assigned you to it?'

'I have an invitation to visit Mr. Gerastan at his home,' I said a little smugly.

'You have!' He was genuinely surprised. 'How did you man-age to arrange that?'

'I didn't. It just came to me out of the blue.'

'If your suspicions are correct, you'll be entering the lion's den as it were.'

'Daniel did it,' I said, getting bold now. But he slapped me down coldly.

'I'll think about it, Miss Touchfeather. Wait at home until I call you.'

Outside his office I handed Miss Moody my current expense sheet.

'You're non-operational,' she said.

'I know.'

'I'm sorry, dear. You're not entitled to expenses when you're non-operational.'

Mr. Blaser kept me waiting for two days. During this time I stayed in my apartment, only going out when it was absolutely necessary. Each time I returned after one of these sorties I phoned in, just in case I'd missed his call. Each time Miss Moody told me politely that no, Mr. Blaser hadn't called me. But it was only a matter of time, and on the third morning I answered the phone at nine a.m.

'Mr. Blaser would like to see you,' said Miss Moody.

'Thank you,' I said. 'I'll be there in half an hour.'

I was there in twenty-five minutes, and Miss Moody wouldn't let me go in.

'He's busy right now,' she said. 'And as long as you're here, I've had an extraordinary note from Mr. Martin in New York. He says he gave you five hundred dollars in expenses last week.'

'That's right,' I said. She looked at me wide-eyed.

'That's over two hundred pounds.'

'Yes.'

'What did you *do* with it?'

'I spent it.'

'Mr. Blaser will have to pass it, I'm afraid,' she said. 'Exchange Control regulations, you understand.'

'Perfectly,' I said. 'The green light's gone on. May I go in, please?' She nodded and I went in. Mr. Blaser was disembowelling his pipe once more. He didn't look up.

'Sit down, Miss Touchfeather.' I sat. 'I have considered carefully what we talked about the other day and I have come to a decision.' What he meant was that he had called around and realised that he was up against a brick wall.

'Yes, sir,' I said politely.

'If, as you say, you have an entrée to Mr. Roger Gerastan, I suggest that you use it.'

'Yes, sir,' I said, and got to my feet.

'I haven't finished,' he said. I sat down again. 'I would like you to know, Miss Touchfeather, that I ... this department ... consider this as a last resort. In the normal course of events I would never countenance an action of this sort. It's speculative and based purely on intuition and inconclusive information. Unfortunately we have no alternative.'

'You mean he wouldn't talk, sir?'

'Who?'

'Hank Almedo.'

At least he was man enough to admit it. 'There was a slipup. Typical American, I might add. The men sent to apprehend Mr. Almedo were overzealous. Mr. Almedo attempted to avoid capture and ...' He shrugged.

'Dead, I take it?'

'That is the case, I believe.' He gave an extra savage dig at his pipe and I heard the bowl crack clear across the room. His anger abated somewhat, turning to dismay as the pipe bowl came apart in his hands. Then anger returned.

'Really, it's too much. Everybody in America seems to be either a cowboy or a gangster. You give them a gun and they shoot at anything that moves. Didn't they realise how important this man was to us?'

'Knowing Almedo, they probably had to shoot to avoid being shot,' I said.

'That's hardly the point, Miss Touchfeather.' What he meant was that he would have expected one of his people to have been shot to hell and gone before damaging the merchandise. He laid the broken body of his pipe reverently on his blotter, gazed at it sadly for a moment, then looked up at me.

'Well, what are you waiting for? Miss Moody will give you your ticket. You leave this afternoon.' I headed for the door.

'One thing more, Miss Touchfeather.' I turned back. 'Due to the precarious position of the pound sterling, I would consider it a personal favour if you took extra care over your expenses while in the dollar area.' I didn't reply. The day I considered doing a personal favour for Mr. Blaser would be the day they lowered me six feet under.

THIRTEEN

It was necessary for me to re-enter Marvin's life in the same guise as I had left it. So I checked in with Walter in New York and he fixed me a United flight to Los Angeles. He also told me what he knew of the Hank Almedo affair. When Hank had shown no sign of moving from his motel, Walter had, on instructions from Mr. Blaser, arranged to have him picked up. Questioning was to follow, and I'm not sure that Hank wasn't better off where he was. But anyway, three very discreet men Walter had borrowed from the CIA moved into the motel where Hank was staying. They watched him closely for twenty-four hours to establish a behaviour pattern; then they moved in professionally. But Hank was of the old school. Nobody was supposed to know he was staying at the motel, so a knock on the door could only mean trouble. Apparently he had pulled his gun and gone out through the window, just as the second CIA man was coming in the same way. Hank had shot him, not fatally as it turned out, and as the third CIA man, who was stationed twenty-five feet away in the next bungalow, yelled for Hank to drop his gun, Hank had loosed off a shot at him as well. By this time number one had come in through the door and had drawn a bead on Hank through the window. Again Hank decided not to heed any warnings and the first CIA man, standing at the window, had to make up his mind very quickly whether to shoot or be shot. He chose the former, and shot Hank in the knee, just as the third man, the one in the bungalow across the road, decided to do the same thing. Unfortunately, by the time he had loosed off his shot, Hank was scrabbling at his shattered leg, and his head was where his knee had been a moment before. Exit Hank Almedo. The hatchet men were sent home, the questionnaire torn up, and re-enter Katy, stage left.

I landed in Los Angeles at four p.m. local time, checked in at the same hotel and called the number that Walter had told me was Marvin's.

'Hello, doll,' he said, when he knew who it was. 'Where you been?'

'New York,' I said.

'What did you do with my car?'

'I left you a note.'

'No note.'

'I put it in your jacket pocket.'

'No jacket.'

'It must have been some trip.'

'It was. When I landed, I was in San Francisco. I think I walked all the way, by sea. What are you doing?'

'Waiting for you to ask me out.'

'I've got a little party going up at my place. Come along,' he said.

'I left my orgy kit at home.'

He chuckled. 'Not tonight,' he said. 'Strictly hetero and Lucky Strike.'

I took down his address and told him that I would be along. Almost as an afterthought he asked me if I had heard anything from Skip and Mary.

'No,' I said, 'I don't even know where they've gone.'

'Me neither,' he said. 'See you, doll.' And he hung up.

I was better equipped in the luggage department this trip and I chose something simple but sexy. I might have been working, but while it would have no effect on Marvin, it was a party after all, and a girl never knew when she might strike lucky. Poor Mary had had the right idea and Beverly Hills was supposed to be swarming with millionaires.

Marvin's pad was smaller than Skip's, but not much, and the joint was really jumping by the time my cab dropped me off. One of the servants pointed me in the direction of my host and then left me to push my way through three hundred assorted movie and oil people until I managed to reach Marvin. He greeted me like a long-lost relative and proceeded to introduce me around as Lady Katherine Touchfeather from England. I must say this went down well with the Americans, but I looked a bit stupid when I found myself shaking hands with Don Scamper, late of Cumming-on-Hardy and a disastrous game of darts.

'Charmed, Your Ladyship,' he said, bowing over my hand.

'Countryman of yours,' said Marvin. 'Mr....'

'Scamper,' said Don. 'But Katy knows that already.'

'That right?' said Marvin. 'Then I'll leave you both to talk about whatever it is old friends talk about.' He smiled at us and moved off to mingle with his other guests.

'Surprise, surprise!' said Don.

'Isn't it just,' I said. 'What on earth are you doing here?'

'I work here, remember? I told you we were coming over to the States.'

'I remember,' I said. 'When did you get here? How are you enjoying it?'

'Whoa back there, Katy! One question deserves another.'

'Yes?' I said, knowing full well what was coming.

'What the hell are *you* doing here?' Somehow he looked shrewder than he had over a pint of bitter and a dartboard.

'I'm an air hostess,' I said.

'That's what we heard. Air India, isn't it?'

'It was. I work for an American company now.'

'That's chopping and changing a bit, isn't it?' There's no point in being an attractive female if you don't use it sometimes. I touched his arm and gave him one of my fourteen-carat smiles.

'You sound like your Mr. Beamish,' I said.

He looked a trifle embarrassed suddenly. 'That was none of my doing, Katy. It was Harvey Carter. He said—'

'I don't want to know what Harvey Carter said. I want you to fetch me a drink.'

'Yes, of course.' He headed towards one of the bars like he was trying to make a touchdown, and I took a quick look around to see if I could locate Harvey. I didn't think I would need too much wool to pull down over Don's eyes, but I would need a polo-neck sweater to fool Harvey. I hadn't spotted him by the time Don returned, flushed and triumphant.

'Is Harvey here?' I asked, when I had thanked him and fluttered the eyelashes a bit.

'Nope,' he said. 'He's working.'

'Why aren't you?'

'Because until he finishes what he's—' He stopped, realising that perhaps he was being a little indiscreet. Still, I had the whole evening in front of me and, when he suggested a walk on the terrace, I tucked my hand under his arm and trotted along obediently.

'Bit of luck finding you here, Katy,' he said. 'Like a drowning man spotting an oasis.'

'You're mixing your metaphors, Don,' I said.

'Am I? It's the booze they serve here. You ask for a whisky and they give you some stuff that's fit to gag a buzzard.'

'You must ask for Scotch,' I said, aware that he was drunker than I had at first thought. It was going to be a walkover. The fresh air didn't help him either and, after two more drinks, during which time I managed to keep him away from the food, I gauged that the wheels were oiled sufficiently to start the motor.

'I think it's rotten that Harvey can't be here,' I said. 'What could be so important that he couldn't get away for a party like this?'

'He's head man since poor old Bill disappeared. Not that Harvey's as good as Bill, but he's bright. Bill was a bloody genius—blinding revelations and all that sort of thing. Harvey's a slogger. It takes him a year to arrive where Bill could in twenty-four hours. But he gets there eventually. This new thing we're working on—Bill would have had it by now. Harvey takes his time.'

'What new thing?'

Drunk he might have been, but not that drunk.

'This and that, Katy, this and that. What about this place, then? Bloody extraordinary, isn't it?' He was referring among other things to the fact that there was a portable bar in the pool and four of the guests, swimsuited, were helping themselves to drinks from it.

'Are you going to like it, Don?' I asked.

'What? America? Certainly I'm going to like it. I was just talking to an actor fellow. He says they've got a cricket team right here in Hollywood. If they're bright enough to play cricket, I might be able to get a game of rugger.'

'You're living here in Hollywood, then?'

'No. Actually it's about three hundred miles from here. That's another thing. People over here think nothing of travelling three hundred miles for a party. Back home it was a drama travelling three hundred yards. I came down tonight in an aeroplane, a company plane all to myself.'

'He obviously looks after his employees,' I said.

'Who does?'

'Roger Gerastan, of course.'

'I suppose he does. I hadn't thought of him being responsible. It's just the Corporation as far as I'm concerned.'

'He *is* the Corporation, isn't he?'

'Not as far as I'm concerned. Never seen the fellow. He's a bit like that other chap, the one who makes aeroplanes and movie stars and has just bought Las Vegas. I'll tell you something though, Katy, the setup here makes old Beamish's lot look a bit sick. There's a bloody great private army out where we work. Getting in and out of the place is a full-time operation.'

'They're very security conscious over here,' I said.

'I think they overdo it a bit. Come on, I'll get you another drink.'

'How about taking me up for the weekend?' I said, before he could drag me back into the party.

'Up where?'

'Where you work.'

'Couldn't do that,' he said. 'They'd cut my balls off. Sorry! Didn't mean to be crude. Must have had one too many.' He took my arm firmly and started to lead me back into the house.

'How come you're at Marvin Torbay's party?' I asked him. 'Do you know him?'

'Met him up at the plant last week. He said if I was ever in Los Angeles to look him up. Glad I did. Talk about how the other half lives!'

'What on earth was he doing up at the plant?'

'I don't know. Wandering around.'

'With such tight security?'

'Didn't seem to bother him. When you've got his sort of loot I don't suppose it matters.'

This was interesting. It pointed to the fact that Marvin was connected with Gerastan on more than just a social level. I decided that about here I'd better start working on Marvin; after all, that was the reason I was here. I let Don wander off to get me a drink and then I started to search for my host. He was surrounded by half a dozen people, holding forth in a gentle denigrating way on how it felt to have been left twelve million dollars and a thousand acres of oil by a fond father, thus obviating having to work for a living.

'As long as that stuff keeps slurping up out of the ground, I guess I'm never going to know the joys of an honest day's toil.'

There was a fluffy little blonde thing hanging on to his every word. She clearly hadn't got the message as far as he was concerned, because she looked daggers at me as I moved up to the group and latched on to Marvin.

'Where have you been, Katy?' he said, dragging me into the circle. 'I've missed you.'

'Don Scamper and I have been waving our Union Jacks and saying what a good job it was we gave you your independence.' One of the men in the group snorted and would have said something rude if Marvin had let him. But he overrode him neatly and politely.

'Katy is one of my favourite people,' he said. 'Even if she does go around stealing automobiles.'

'You don't!' said the blonde girl. 'Really?'

'Only when I'm hard up,' I said.

'You're joking,' she said. I admitted I was joking. 'Why do you steal them, then? For kicks?'

'She's a kleptomaniac,' said Marvin. 'She'd steal anything.'

A cold glint came into the blonde's baby-blue eyes, flashing at me from beneath her contact lenses.

'Yes,' she said. Then she took the arm of the man who had been about to insult the Union Jack. 'Let's go get a drink, honey,' she said, and they moved off.

Marvin took my arm and steered me across the room towards another group of people. I could see Don out on the terrace, glass in each hand, moving around like a retriever who had lost the kill.

'I wish you'd stop introducing me around like a prize heifer,' I said to Marvin before we reached the new group. 'Like water, I can find my own level.'

'I'm sorry, Katy,' he said. 'I thought it was what you wanted.'

'No,' I said.

'Then what?'

'I thought you were going to introduce me to Roger Gerastan,' I said.

'I was?'

'That's what you said.'

'But he's not here. He never goes to parties.'

'I didn't think he was. But you said you were going to take me up to that place where he lives. Or was it the booze talking?'

'Of course it wasn't. Do you really want to meet him?'

I nodded emphatically.

'Why?'

'He's a legend. I always like to meet legends. It'll give me something to tell my grandchildren.' He looked doubtful for a moment; then he smiled his beautiful smile.

'How long are you in town?'

'Three or four days.' It could have been three or four weeks if necessary.

'I'll call you tomorrow,' he said. 'Now do you want to find your own level, or do you want to meet some fascinating bores.'

I reached up and gave him a little kiss on the cheek. 'You're a darling. I'll find my own level.'

He touched his cheek where I had kissed him. 'Mind how you go, Katy. People might start to get the wrong idea about me.'

'Like blondie?'

'Oh, she knows. She just isn't letting on. Twelve million dollars can keep an awful lot of urges under control. If I gave her the nod, she'd sew herself up.'

'It would take more than twelve million dollars to keep that one out of circulation,' I said, in true Hollywood fashion.

He smiled at me again. 'Don't try to be bitchy, Katy. You wouldn't even be a starter in this town.'

I looked at him speculatively. 'You could be quite a challenge for a girl,' I said.

'If anyone could do it, you probably could,' he said. 'Even if you don't look much like a fella.'

I left Marvin and went to relocate Don. He'd drunk my drink as well as his own, and was now well under the weather.

'Want me to drive you home, Don?' I asked him.

'No need, Katy. Staying here. Houseguest.'

'Marvin's idea or yours?'

'Marvin's. Nice fellow.'

I hoped that they would be very happy together and I left the party without a ripple to disturb the surface. The butler called a cab for me, and half an hour later I was back in what I was rapidly coming to think of as home.

I thought long and hard that evening, trying to marshal some sort of order out of the chaos of what had occurred over the past couple of weeks. Mr. Blaser had unbent sufficiently before I left to allow me to look at some of the files, and I had spent a boring hour in an outer office while a security man disguised as a canteen worker had peered at me through the glass partition in the door to make sure I didn't make off with anything I wasn't supposed to. There was a great wodge of material covering the work that Bill had been doing, and I spent most of my time trying to reduce the semi-technical data to a state where my extremely lay mind could understand it. It wasn't easy.

Missiles come in all shapes and sizes. There are air-to-ground and vice versa, ground-to-ground and air-to-air; there are missiles that home on heat, noise, vibration; and there are missiles that can be guided visually onto targets no larger than a hole in a man's head. There are anti-tank, anti-aircraft, anti-warship, antipersonnel and anti-missile missiles; there are attack missiles and defence missiles. But the granddaddy of them all, the number-one, top-grade, copper-bottomed, highest-rated, most closely guarded missile of all is the ICBM; the intercontinental ballistic horror designed solely to lift a hydrogen bomb around the globe from East to West, or vice versa, and drop it neatly on New York, Moscow, Pittsburgh or Leningrad. They are very sophisticated items of technology indeed, and the amount of machinery they carry, apart from the nuclear device, is staggering. But nobody is going to sit still and just let one of these things land on them. They're going to try to intercept it and get rid of it while it is still up in the stratosphere; there it will harm no one except the few millions who will be poisoned by radiation in the next couple of generations, when the fallout has leaked back into the atmosphere.

So, built into the ICBM are all sorts of devices to counteract the machinery which might be hurled up against it. There are anti-heat-seeking devices, anti-vibration seekers, radar scramblers and infrared baffles. And as fast as one side comes up with something new, then the other side goes to work on something newer. And so the race goes on, each side leapfrogging over the other with the development of something that nullifies what has just gone before. And billions of dollars and roubles are poured into this fantastic race. The only time there is any relaxation is when one power gets far enough ahead of the other to sit back and say, 'There you are. What are you going to do about *that*?'

But this doesn't happen very often, and when it does, it is purely temporary. As witness the case in hand. America had been two years ahead of Russia up to a few weeks ago, but before they could even stick their two fingers up in the air, the Russians chopped them off. Bill had developed a small electronic gizmo which, when fitted to an anti-ICBM missile, effectively scrambled every known device the ICBM carried. Fitted with Bill's invention, America could effectively seek out and destroy everything that the Russians could send up against them. So up yours, Tovarich! One week with the details of Bill's device and the Russians were able to tighten a nut here, change a washer there, and the device became nothing more than excess baggage. Now it seemed that America was falling over herself to find a new piece of machinery that would do what Bill's had, before the Russians learned its secret. And that was all it boiled down to.

America *had* been ahead, and now Russia had leapfrogged over her. It was now up to America to regain the lead. And until she did the Comrades in the UN were throwing their weight about trying to rush all sorts of things through before the status quo was reversed. As the Gerastan Corporation were the leaders in this particular field, thanks largely to Bill, the US Government had opened up the purse strings. They only scribbled one qualification across their carte blanche—money no object, but get a bloody move on.

These, then, were the broader issues, all very straightforward. It was only when one came down to personalities that the whole affair started to cloud into confusion. Bill, the Eunuch, Jack Kelly and Hank Almedo, Mary Youngman, Marvin Torbay, Beamish, Scamper, Carter. Some of them fitted into the pattern quite neatly, but most of them didn't.

And the biggest question mark of all, the person who could hold the key to the whole mess, or could equally not have a clue, was the man I hadn't even met yet. Roger Gerastan.

FOURTEEN

'The man's a nut,' I said to Marvin. We were in Marvin's small private plane flying over the most inhospitable bit of country I'd ever seen. I'd probably flown over it many times before, but at thirty thousand feet, who the hell knows what is below? At three thousand feet one is still basically earthbound, and what I could see from the window just wasn't worth looking at. Marvin was flying the plane one-handed. The other one he was using to do a crossword puzzle in the *Los Angeles Times* which he had folded open on his knee.

'Who's a nut?' he asked, without looking up. 'Six letters—a songbird?'

'Bobolink... Roger Gerastan.'

'That's not six letters... Why?'

'Nobody could *like* living out here.'

He glanced out of the window. ''Tis a bit bleak, isn't it?' he agreed. 'Still, he doesn't live in a tent.'

The radio suddenly crackled into life. 'Aircraft approaching Santhoma, identify yourself please.'

Marvin flipped the transmit switch. 'Santhoma. This is Marvin Torbay and guest. Over.'

'Hiyuh, Mr. Torbay. You're clear to come straight in. Watch out for a couple of tractors at the east end of the runway.'

'Roger, Santhoma. Out.'

I looked at Marvin. 'Santhoma? That's Saint Thomas isn't it?'

He grinned. 'He could hardly have called it Sanroger, could he?' he said. 'Kneads into lump—five letters?'

'Balls,' I said.

The first thing I saw was the airfield. I had thought that the land below us was flat, but as we started to descend, I realised that it was a series of lowish hills running parallel to each other like rippling water. Then there was a cut through one of the hills and the runway stretched out beyond it. Just before we put down, I thought I caught a glimpse of gleaming white rooftops away over to the left, but then they were masked by the hills on either side of the runway. It was a single runway, long enough to take a Concorde—and, if all I had heard about Gerastan was true, he'd probably be first in line for one when they started to come off the production line, ahead of BOAC and Air France.

There was a DC-8 standing to one side of the runway, with a couple of smaller aircraft sheltering beneath her wings. There was a maintenance hangar, surrounded on three sides by some small huts, and it was towards this that Marvin taxied. Before we had stopped, a car had appeared along the only road that led from the airfield. It pulled up, waiting for us. A couple of mechanics, beefy-looking men, chocked our wheels, while a third moved round to help me down from the plane. I was wearing a shortish skirt, and as he lifted me down he pulled me close, making it appear even shorter. But one never knows when one is going to need a friend, so instead of breaking his arm, I gave him a smile.

'Thank you,' I said.

'Thank *you*, lady,' he replied. I may not have made a friend of him, but he was going to think twice before deciding I was an enemy. He glanced across me towards Marvin, who was just climbing down.

'Nice to see you, Mr. Torbay. How are you making out?'

'Not as well as you, Bud,' said Marvin, seeing the way I was being held. But Bud obviously knew which side Marvin's bread was buttered and he only grinned.

'This is Miss Touchfeather. Katy, this is Bud. He knows more of what goes on inside an aero engine than the Wright brothers.'

'How fascinating,' I said, wishing he'd get his dirty mechanic's hands off my backside. Then he stepped smartly away from me as the driver got out of the car and came towards us. I hadn't seen him before, but I might just as well have. He was of the same mould as Jack Kelly and Hank Almedo, pure hood. He was dressed in semi-Western gear which was part Roy Rogers and part Al Capone. His hair was jet-black and lacquered solid. He wore a six-gun at his hip like a stage cowboy; only this gun was for real. He flashed his sparkling teeth at us.

'Hi, Marvin! How's it been?'

'Hello, Angel. Katy, meet Angel. Angel, Miss Touchfeather.'

'Miss *who*?'

'Touchfeather,' I said. I was used to it.

'I'll call you Miss T. if I may, Misty.' He held out his hand and I shook it. It was dry, yet giving the impression it was clammy. It was an extraordinary sensation, like shaking hands with a snake.

'Mr. Gerastan sent me down to pick you both up, personally,' he said, leading the way to the car. 'Hop in!'

The three of us got into the car, and as Angel swung it round, heading back towards the road, Bud called after us.

'When d'you want the plane again, Mr. Torbay?'

'About five,' shouted Marvin.

'You're staying over,' said Angel. 'Mr. Gerastan arranged it.'

I glanced sideways at Marvin, who shrugged. 'But I haven't brought any clothes,' I hissed.

Angel answered for him. 'Not to worry, Misty. You'll find everything you need up at the house.'

He called it a house, but I suppose it was just familiarity breeding contempt. Although it was all under the same extended roof, it was more of a village than a house. The road curved away from the airfield through a cut in the hills and, half a mile away, headed through a pair of gates, which opened automatically as we approached them. A fifteen-foot wall extended from either side of the gates in an unbroken line. I couldn't see any barbed wire along the top, but that was probably because they found electrification of the top three feet of wall more effective. Just inside the gates, two men dressed the same way as Angel were lounging against the wall. As soon as we were inside the gates it was like being in another world. Outside it was barren scrubland; in here it was like Kew Gardens: great sweeps of lawn, high magnificent trees and shrubs blazing with colour.

'I thought water was supposed to be scarce out here,' I said to no one in particular, noticing that the whole place was a forest of sprinklers.

'It is,' said Marvin. 'Roger sunk a well.'

'He sunk six wells,' said Angel. 'And the way he throws the stuff around he'll have to sink another six before long.'

'When they dry up he'll pack his bag and leave this place to the natives,' said Marvin.

Angel laughed shortly. 'You may just be right there, Marvin.'

We turned a bend in the drive, and the house was in front of us. Like I said, it was all under the same roof, but it spread over about two acres, a series of long, single-storey buildings, linked by covered passages. The basic style, if it could be said to have one, was *House & Garden* hacienda. The whole place was painted a glaring white, which was blinding in the sunlight.

The car headed straight through an archway and stopped in a courtyard framed by half a dozen of the sections, all facing inwards. Three more make-believe cowboys were lounging around, apparently minding nobody's business but their own. One of them was throwing chunks of raw meat to a couple of dogs, half Alsatian, half Doberman and all mean. The dogs looked up at us incuriously as we drove in; the men didn't even bother to do that.

Two Mexican house servants ran down from the front door and opened the car doors for us as we stopped. We all three got out and Angel ushered us through the main entrance into what I assumed must have been one of the main rooms in the house. It was about sixty feet long, pine panelled and cool. Comfortable armchairs and settees were scattered about as though the owner had no further use for them. Passages led off from each end of the room and we headed down the one to the right. The walls here were hung with early Americana, bows and arrows, tomahawks, buffalo-hide shields and a few untidy scraps that looked uncommonly like scalps.

At the end of this passage we emerged into another room, and I revised my opinion about the first being one of the main ones; it was just a lobby compared to this. Eighty feet long, thirty-five feet wide, with one wall all glass, it opened up onto a terrace and a gentle slope of lawn running down to the pool. At the far side of the pool there was another slope of lawn leading up to another section of the house. The pool area was enclosed on all four sides by the house, and in each direction I looked I seemed to see another room similar to the one we were standing in. At first glance it seemed there wasn't a room in the place too small to hold a hunt ball.

'Misty's in the blue room, Marvin,' said Angel. 'Show her where, while I tell Mr. Gerastan you're here.'

He headed off towards the terrace, leaving me with Marvin.

'Cosy,' I said, trying not to be awed.

'Come on, Katy; I'll show you to your room,' said Marvin. He looked a little subdued, not at all the Marvin I knew. We headed down another passage, hung with Navaho rugs and other relics of the first Americans. Then, turning right, Marvin opened a door and stood aside for me to go in.

'Jesus!' I said, irreverently, as I crossed the threshold. The blue room was just that. Every damn thing in it was blue, from the carpet to the bed linen, from the wallpaper and the drapes; even the mirrors along one wall were tinted blue, as was the glass in the windows looking out across the formal gardens.

'I'll go blind,' I said as Marvin followed me in.

'Bathroom's over there,' he said. 'Dressing room there. There's a small sitting room just beyond the dressing room.'

'Where's the poolroom?' I said. Marvin sat down on the bed, a huge monstrosity that looked large enough for a family of twelve, while I opened a few doors and peered into a couple of drawers.

'Sorry about this, Katy,' he said.

'It's just a little blue.'

But he was serious. 'This staying-over bit. I didn't know.'

'We don't have to, if you don't want to,' I said, hoping that he did. But I needn't have worried.

'If Roger says stay, we stay.'

'Even if you don't want to?'

He got to his feet and shrugged. 'That's the way it is, doll. You'll find clothes in the dressing room. Put some pool gear on. I'll meet you there in twenty minutes.' He went out looking miserable.

I peered into the bathroom. That was blue, too, with a sunken bath like something out of a Cecil B. DeMille movie. I wondered which of the gold-plated taps one turned on for asses' milk. The dressing room was lined with closets, and it took me five minutes to work out how to open the damn things. Then I found a small switch and the doors slid silently open, revealing enough clothes to restock Bergdorf Goodman. I have an inbuilt reluctance to wearing secondhand clothes, but I needn't have worried; everything was brand-new. There were drawers full of undies, still in their original wrappings, ranging from the practical to the wildly exotic. The dresses, slacks, shirts, blouses and every other damn thing came in three of each of eight different sizes. The sizes were fine for any young girl of reasonable proportions; obviously Mr. Gerastan didn't entertain any middle-aged or fat women. Not in the blue room at any rate—unless they brought their own luggage. The swimsuits were in the far cupboard.

I chose a one-piece because a bikini allowed my Rome scar to show. Wondering which of the mirrors was a two-way job and who was watching, I stripped off and put on the swimsuit. I took a towelling robe and then set out to find my way back to the pool. It was no trouble, because Angel was waiting for me outside my bedroom door.

'All set, Misty? Mr. Gerastan and Marvin are down by the pool.'

He led me back the way I had come, and on the terrace he left me, disappearing back into the house. As I walked down towards the pool, two men who were standing on the far side turned towards me. One was Marvin, who looked even more beautiful undressed, and the other was Roger Gerastan.

I must confess to disappointment when I first saw him. The man with Marvin was short, barely five feet eight inches, with snow-white hair. His body was well kept and very brown, and he moved easily like a man who knew how to take care of himself. It wasn't until he reached me that I realised one didn't even notice his height anymore. He had the lightest blue eyes I had ever seen, like pieces of chipped ice. He had a long, straight nose and a mouth that looked as though it had been chopped into his face with a clean blow from a sharp machete. His eyebrows were white, as was the hair on his body; his hands were small and beautifully kept. But it was the eyes that both fascinated and repelled at the same time; they had a near-hypnotic quality which made one forget that the man behind them was only five feet eight inches tall, and not at all attractive.

Marvin introduced us and I had to strain to hear what Gerastan said. He spoke very softly and slowly, as though he were examining each word carefully before putting it into circulation.

'It's very nice of you to come all this way just to see an old recluse like me,' he said. 'You should have told me she was beautiful, Marvin.'

'I did.'

'You didn't do her justice,' he said. 'I hope your room is comfortable.'

'I love blue,' I said, wishing that he would stop looking at me with those chips of ice. He hadn't even stopped when he was talking to Marvin, continuing to regard me with a steady gaze which gave me absolutely no clue to what he was thinking.

'We were just going to have a drink,' he said. 'Come.' He took my elbow and led me towards a small bar set up at the edge of the pool. 'Champagne, of course,' he said.

'Of course,' I agreed. He opened a bottle deftly and poured three glasses. He handed me one and allowed Marvin to get his own. Then he raised his glass.

'Welcome to Santhoma, Katherine,' he said. 'I don't like abbreviated names. You don't mind?'

'I like it very much.'

'Good. Come and sit with me.' He led the way towards a couple of lounging chairs, ignoring Marvin, who stayed at the bar. 'I've heard a lot about you, Katherine,' he said.

'From whom?'

'From Marvin, of course.'

'I've only met him a couple of times,' I said. 'And one of those he was away on a trip.'

'Marvin's like that,' he said. 'But he doesn't do anyone any harm.'

'Except himself, perhaps.'

'Perhaps,' said Gerastan. 'But that's his problem.'

There was silence for a moment, during which he continued to regard me steadily. I tried to fill it in.

'This is a beautiful place, Mr. Gerastan.'

'Roger, please.'

I smiled gratefully, with just sufficient demureness to fit the occasion.

'Why did you want to meet me, Katherine?' I should have had notice of this question, and I tried to make the answer sound as convincing as possible without going over the top.

'What girl wouldn't want to meet the mysterious Roger Gerastan,' I said. 'You're quite a celebrity.' If he thought I was flattering him, he didn't acknowledge it.

'Any other girl, perhaps. But not you, Katherine.'

'What's so different about me?'

'Come, my dear. You're too intelligent to ask me a question like that.'

'I am?'

He didn't bother to answer. 'It may interest you to know that if you hadn't asked Marvin to bring you out to see me, then I would have asked him.'

'You would? Whatever for?'

'I was interested. Very interested.'

'In little old me?'

'Stop that nonsense, Katherine. It doesn't suit you and you're not very good at it.'

'At what?'

'The "little old me" type of line belittles you.'

'You seem to have a very clear idea of the sort of girl I am, Mr. Gerastan.' If he noticed that I had used his surname, he didn't say so.

'Bring us some more champagne, Marvin,' he called. Marvin fetched the bottle and refilled our glasses. He was looking more like a house servant every moment, and I didn't like to see it.

'Why don't you join us, Marvin?' I said. I saw him flash a look at Gerastan, and although I'd swear Gerastan didn't move a muscle, Marvin obviously saw some sort of message, because he smiled apologetically at me.

'Not just now, Katy,' he said. 'I'm dying for a swim.'

He turned and dived into the pool and started to swim up and down vigorously, making plenty of noise to let us know where he was.

'The picture I have of you is not as complete as I would like,' said Gerastan, continuing the conversation as though we had not been interrupted. 'You are something of an enigma.'

I started to say 'little old me' again, but thought better of it. 'You flatter me,' I said instead. 'I'm just a working girl, plain and simple.'

'You're certainly not plain, and I doubt very much that you are simple. As to being a working girl, you may be telling the truth there, but working at what?'

I told him, although I was pretty sure by now that he wasn't going to believe me. 'I'm an air hostess.'

'So you would have us all believe.'

'It's true,' I said. 'Whether you believe it or not.'

'I'm sure it is,' he said. 'But is it the whole story?'

'You mean, do I have a job on the side?'

'Do you?'

'I wish I had,' I said. 'We're not paid all that much. It's not the glamorous career that it's painted.'

'Why do you do it, then?'

'It's a living. Better than being a secretary or a shop assistant.'

'Or a policewoman.'

'Or a policewoman,' I said.

He looked as though he were going to say something else; then he glanced towards the terrace. Angel was standing there and, as Gerastan looked at him, he made some well-concealed signal. Gerastan turned back to me.

'Enjoy yourself, Katherine,' he said. 'I'm afraid I must leave you for a while. I shall see you at dinner.' He got to his feet and headed towards Angel.

How much did he know about me? That 'policewoman' remark hit below the belt and it hurt. And, just as important as how much he knew was from whom he had learned it. I was still trying to sort this lot out when a dripping Marvin joined me, flopping down on the chair vacated by Gerastan.

'What do you think of our man of mystery?' he said. He seemed more at ease now that Gerastan was no longer with us.

'Like you said, a man of mystery.'

'What were you talking about?'

'He seemed to doubt that I was an air hostess. He thinks I've got other interests. What did you tell him about me, Marvin?'

'Nothing much. I said there was an attractive girlfriend of mine who was dying to meet him.'

'Did you mention my name?'

'Certainly.'

'And that's when he agreed to have you bring me up here?'

Marvin suddenly looked thoughtful. 'That's funny,' he said.

'What is?'

'What you just said. It was exactly like that. He started to give me an argument and I said Katy would be disappointed. He asked me, "Katy who?" and I told him. Then he agreed that I could bring you over.'

'Which presupposes he knew my name,' I said.

'I don't see how.'

'Nor do I at the moment,' I said. 'Perhaps you could find out?'

'Not if he doesn't want to tell me.'

'What's with you and him, Marvin?' I asked. 'You're a different person when he's around.' He looked away from me nervously. But I pressed on. 'Are you frightened of him or something?'

He smiled ruefully. 'It shows, does it? If you must know, my inquisitive little Katy, I'm mad about him—and he scares the living daylights out of me.'

'What do you mean "mad about him"?' I asked, a little naïvely.

'Just exactly that,' he said. I stared at him long and hard, and at least he had the grace to blush.

'Does he know?' I asked, finally.

'Of course he knows. He gets a minor kick out of having me hang around like I do.'

'So why do it?'

'He throws me a crumb occasionally.'

'You mean he's bent?' I was astonished.

'Like a hickory stick,' said Marvin.

'You told me he was a dirty old man.'

'So he is, but heterosexuals don't have a monopoly of that condition.'

'You said he liked pretty girls.'

'Most of us do, darling.' He had never looked so queer as he did at that moment. But this wasn't what concerned me. If what he was saying was true, and there didn't seem any reason to doubt him, then Mary had been feeding me a lot of rubbish. Queers just don't go around raping their female houseguests.

We were asked whether we wanted lunch indoors or outdoors, and we opted to eat by the pool. The lunch was a cold buffet, but it was magnificent, served by two more Mexican house servants who might have learned their business at the Tour d'Argent. After lunch Marvin asked me if I would like to see around the grounds. What I really wanted was to be on my own, where I could indulge in a little top-level thinking. But a conducted tour of the place couldn't do any harm; one never knew when this sort of knowledge would turn out to be very useful indeed. So I returned to my room and changed into slacks, a shirt and a magnificent pair of Western boots that could have been made for me they were so comfortable. I topped this sartorial binge with a wide-brimmed Stetson and, feeling like Calamity Jane, I went to join Marvin.

Nobody looked at us as we walked out of the courtyard, but later I noticed that the two men who had been lounging against

the front door when we came out seemed to be lounging whichever way we turned: against the tree over there, behind those
shrubs. I mentioned this to Marvin after twenty minutes.

'Doesn't he trust us?' I asked.

'Who?'

'Gerastan. We're being followed by Wild Bill Hickok and
Wyatt Earp over there.'

'It's their job,' said Marvin.

'I don't like being followed.'

'It happens all the time at Santhoma.'

'Not to me. I'm going to do something about it.'

He tried to dissuade me, and when he couldn't he opted out
altogether and headed back towards the house. Wild Bill started
to follow him but, when he realised where he was going, changed
his mind and came back to join Wyatt, the two of them meaning
to keep an eye on the wandering stranger. I realise now it was
a stupid idea, but I was bored and a little annoyed, and more
important, I thought it would serve as a dummy run and give me
a good idea of the efficiency of their security precautions. I played
it very cool, lulling Wild Bill and Wyatt into a sense of false security. I sniffed some flowers, admired the lake and picked a couple
of rhododendron-like shrubs. Then, about ten minutes later, I
disappeared.

It was very simple, actually. I shinned up a tree and waited
in a lower branch. Wild Bill and Wyatt wandered into view, saw
that I had gone missing and, still not over-concerned, split up
and circled around the area where I might have gone. Five minutes later they realised that they were in trouble, but by then they
were out of my sight.

From my position in the tree I was able to see a good portion
of the grounds and of the house, enough to notice that the wall
circled the entire property without a break except for the gate we
had come through on our way from the airfield. All this was very
interesting, and I was about to climb higher when all hell broke

loose. A siren started up from the house, and a moment later the grounds seemed full of cowboys and bloody great dogs. Two helicopters appeared overhead and I could see men with binoculars leaning out, searching the ground beneath them.

Fortunately, I played it the correct way. I stayed up in the tree and whistled a couple of the dogs over. Then, when they were leaping and slavering around the base of the tree, I started to scream for help. Two minutes later the dogs had been leashed and Angel was helping me down from the tree.

'What were you doing up there, Misty?' he asked.

'Getting away from those bloody great hounds,' I answered. 'And don't try to tell me their bark is worse than their bite.'

He grinned. 'No, it's not,' he said.

'If I hadn't been near that tree I'd be dogs' meat by now,' I said.

'How come the fellows lost you?' he asked.

'You'd better ask the fellows,' I said, full of righteous indignation. 'All I know is that I was minding my own business, and the next thing the hounds of the Baskervilles were baying at my heels.'

I don't know whether he believed me or not, but he wasn't about to call one of the houseguests a liar.

'Don't wander around alone, Misty. It could be dangerous,' he said, walking me back towards the house.

'Could be! It bloody well is! What's the point? What's it all about?'

'Mr. Gerastan is a very big man,' said Angel. 'Lots of people would like to do him harm. We're here to see that they don't.'

'You do it very well,' I said.

I left him at the front door and went back to my room. There I stripped off for siesta. But sleep wasn't part of the plan. It was thinking time again.

From whom had Roger Gerastan learned so much about me? It couldn't have been Marvin, because he didn't know anything.

Don Scamper? But he's never met Gerastan. Then, of course, it came to me, and once again I started to curse the sentimental impulse that had taken me on my pilgrimage to Cumming-on-Hardy. It had to have been Mr. Beamish of the sandy hair and nasty disposition. As security officer, he had no doubt put the details of my visit on the teletype to all branches of the Gerastan Corporation. My name and description would have been checked against files just to make sure I hadn't turned up anywhere else with a different cover story. And from somewhere along the line an order must have come back to him to release me. But by that time I would have been labelled and docketed in every Gerastan security file throughout the world.

Obviously Roger Gerastan had come across my name, or perhaps he had been informed that the Katherine Touchfeather, who wanted to meet him via Marvin Torbay, was already on the security files. Whichever it was, he would know I wasn't just a fan blinded by the glory of his name. This led me to my second problem. If he knew I wasn't what I purported to be, why had he agreed to receive me at Santhoma? And what were his intentions? I was in the eye of the hurricane, and if I couldn't find out, then I was in the wrong job.

In spite of my good intentions, I dozed off, waking up about five o'clock, a little hungover from the champagne and the wine we had drunk with lunch. I climbed off the bed and started to run myself a bath. Then, still naked, I padded into the dressing room to pick out what I was going to wear for dinner. I wanted something elegant, but very feminine; if there was going to be any rough stuff for dessert, I didn't want anyone forgetting I was just a girl. I was poking through the wardrobe when suddenly I remembered that when Marvin had shown me to my room, he had said something about a small sitting room leading off from the dressing room. I'm not even sure why I was interested; I suppose it was just curiosity, or maybe I wanted to see how many more shades of blue had been dreamed up by the designer of the place.

Still naked, I opened the door and stepped through. The blue was all there, like the bedroom and the bathroom, a small, comfortable-looking room with a bar against one wall. I was delighted to see the bar, because suddenly I needed a drink very badly. Because blue decor and bar notwithstanding, the first thing I saw when I opened the door from the dressing room was a man sitting in an armchair, obviously waiting for something. I shouldn't have been surprised, I suppose. But I was, and I was delirious, too, and ecstatic and terrified and horrified and just plain dumbfounded. It was Bill.

FIFTEEN

'Hello, Katy,' he said.

Now, Katy girl, I thought, training to the fore, self-control; play it cool. No panic and no hysteria.

'Excuse me,' I said. I turned back into the dressing room, selected a robe and I pulled it on over my nakedness. Then I took a deep breath to stop myself from passing clear out, and walked back into the sitting room. He smiled at me as I came back in, that gentle, slightly crooked smile that I loved... Steady on, Katy! Forget the love bit for the moment. There's sorting out to do first.

'Modest, Katy?' he said as I came back in. 'That's new.'

I sat down on a chair facing him, gently as though my backside were made of eggshells.

'Well, well,' I said. I couldn't think of anything else.

'How are you, Katy?'

'I'm fine, thank you. How are you?'

'Fine. You look well.'

'So do you.' And that seemed to exhaust the platitudes.

'Don't you want to know what I've been doing?' he said.

'Only if you want to tell me,' I lied.

'I thought you would have been a little more enthusiastic,' he said.

'I'm sorry, Bill.' There, I'd said his name. 'But no doubt when the numbness wears off, I'll behave more to pattern.'

'That's more like the Katy I know,' he said. He got to his feet and for one awful moment I thought he was going to cross the room and touch me. But then he turned and moved over to the bar.

'Drink?' I nodded and watched him while he mixed it. There was no need for him to ask how I liked it. He knew already. He carried my drink over to me and returned to his chair. Then he raised his glass towards me.

'To what might have been,' he said. I raised mine.

'To what nearly was,' I said. We both took a drink and I waited for him to start talking. I would have started myself, but there was nothing to say.

'Shall we start with apologies?' he said.

'For what?'

'For disappearing. For making you think I was dead. For Rome.' He knew about Rome, then. My hand went to my breast involuntarily.

'I didn't know about that until afterwards,' he said. 'They promised they wouldn't hurt you. Does it still hurt?' I shook my head. 'The scar will go?' he asked. I nodded. 'Good,' he said, for all the world like a family doctor pronouncing on a case of chicken pox. 'You had your revenge though. That should be some comfort.'

'It's a great comfort,' I said.

His eyes crinkled at the corners as he grinned at me again. 'Dear Katy, trying to play it cool as a cucumber. I'll bet you're like jelly inside.'

'No, Bill,' I said. 'Not jelly. A little ice perhaps.'

He shook his head admiringly. 'You're quite a girl, Katy. Quite a girl.'

'So you said once before.'

'I meant it then and I mean it now. Well, I've apologised. How about you?'

'What have I got to apologise for?'

'For deception, Katy. For deception.'

'You knew I wasn't what I appeared to be. You saw my tan.'

'I'm not referring to the fact that my brown love turned out to be not so brown. I'm talking about the deeper deception.'

'I don't understand you,' I said, trying forlornly to buy a little time in which to sort out some of the new material I had just been handed.

'I know that you're a good air hostess,' he said. 'But not so good that you can work for Air India one day, BOAC the next and United any time you feel like it.'

I didn't reply to this. He was prepared to go on talking and, since I had nothing to say, I let him.

'That's the deception I'm talking about, Katy, that and the fact that a lovely girl can mew like a kitten in my arms at one moment and shoot a man's head off the next. Which one is the true Katy? The kitten or the tigress?'

'You tell me,' I said. 'You obviously know the answer.'

'I honestly don't. I thought the kitten was genuine—and I'm sure the tigress was.'

'A kitten can turn into a tigress when something she loves is taken away from her.' There, I'd said it.

'Loved, Katy? Really loved?'

'Really loved,' I said. 'And you knew it.'

He gave a small sigh. 'I think I did,' he said. 'And, believe me, it didn't make things any easier.'

'If it's any consolation, it wasn't planned.'

'I'm sure it wasn't. These things can't be legislated for. But what *was* planned, Katy? Why were you told to follow me to Bombay?'

There didn't seem much point in trying to deny the fact. 'I was sent along to make sure you came to no harm.'

He smiled. 'Very delicately put,' he said. 'You were there to see that I didn't pass any information, weren't you?'

'That, too,' I admitted. 'They didn't know about you.'

'Were you surprised when I didn't?'

'No. Others may have been, but I knew you by then.'

He stopped smiling, his face relaxing into what could have been sadness. 'You were wrong, Katy. They were right. I *was* going to pass information.' I started to say something, but he stopped me. 'We'll go into cause later,' he said. 'Let's get rid of effect first. I *was* going to pass information, but due to your efficiency and that of your compatriots, I was unable to. You see, there was nothing written down, nothing photographed. It was all up here.' He tapped his forehead. 'It required a couple of hours at least to get across what I had to. And your people didn't give me a couple of minutes. So the hijacking of the aircraft was arranged. The reasons were twofold. One was the actual passing of the information. But more important was the consideration that whoever you work for would know I was responsible, so it was necessary at the same time that I should bow out of the current scene.' He stopped there, watching me closely for any reaction. I was still a little too numb to come up with anything bright; I could still remember his face covered with blood, and the way the sight of it had made me feel.

He continued after a moment. 'So we played our little pantomime in Cairo. Designed so that, when it was eventually discovered the information had gone and me with it, it would be assumed that it had been tortured out of me and that I had been killed. Another drink?'

I shook my head; I'd hardly touched the first one. He stood up and moved over to the bar again. 'You're going to ask me the necessity for Rome now, aren't you?' he said from the bar. I hadn't been going to, but I nodded nevertheless. 'It was designed purely as a means of letting the world at large know that I was dead. As a bonus it also meant that for a few days at least, no one would know that the information had already been passed. It gave us time to clear it before the real panic started.'

He walked back from the bar, carrying his drink. 'You were meant to escape and report what you had been told. The boys were going to drive you back towards Rome and then rig an accident and allow you to slip away. But you rather took things into your own hands there. Nevertheless—I've said it before and I'll say it again—at no time were you meant to be more than just frightened; anything that happened on top of that was none of my doing. And that was to be an end of the whole affair. Bill Partman is dead; rest in peace.'

I seemed to have thawed out a little by now, enough to start asking some questions anyway.

'Why, Bill?' It wasn't much as questions go, but it was the best I could do for the moment.

'Why what, Katy? Why did I want to betray my own secrets?'

'That'll do for a start,' I said.

'I'll let someone else explain all that to you. He does it better than I do.'

'Gerastan?'

'A brilliant man, Katy. Intellect like a razor. One of the most intelligent, farsighted individuals I've ever had the fortune to meet.'

'Queer, too,' I said, unable to resist it.

He laughed. 'I believe he is,' he said. 'But what has that got to do with anything?'

'I don't know. Ask Mary Youngman.'

He stopped laughing suddenly. 'She was a friend of yours, wasn't she?'

'You know she was. Otherwise she'd be alive today.'

'Roger knew that you had seen her. He didn't know how much she had said, or would say in the future. It was the only way.'

'If he convinced you of that, he *must* be bright,' I said. 'What was her part in all this?'

'In this, nothing,' he said. 'But she knew Roger before.'

'That's what she told me,' I said.

'Not the truth though.'

I had to admit that from what I had learned about Gerastan, he was probably right.

'She worked for him before she married, when she was still an air hostess.'

'Worked at what?' I asked.

'Fetching and carrying mostly. Nothing very dramatic, but sufficient to prove an embarrassment should it have come out.'

'And?'

'Roger had been prepared to leave her alone after she got married. After all, she couldn't hurt him without hurting herself. And everything was all right until she started getting chatty with you. Then I'm afraid things became a little too dangerous.'

'I've known Mary for years. Why *then* all of a sudden?'

'Because we haven't known *you* for years, Katy.' Poor Mary, I thought, all that time with something like that hanging over her head. And she had tried to warn me in her own way. 'Don't go to see Roger Gerastan; it could mean big trouble.' Well, she'd been right there.

'What happens now?' I asked.

'Now we change for dinner,' he said. 'Unless you want to come dressed like that.' He stood up and walked over to me. He put out his hand and touched my cheek, and I am delighted to say I didn't feel a thing, no electric shocks, no weak feeling behind the knees; apparently I'd just become immunised.

'What's going to happen to us, Katy?'

'That's rather up to you, isn't it?'

'No, my dear,' he said. 'It's going to be entirely up to you.'

I decided that femininity wasn't going to be too important to establish at dinner; they already had me established as a girl of considerable resourcefulness, and a frilly dress and a glimpse of lace wasn't going to impress anyone. So I grabbed the first dress in my size and went into the bathroom to find that I had left the taps running, and the place was knee-deep in water. I thought about ringing for someone to come and clean up the mess; then I didn't bother. Fat lot I cared if the carpet went mouldy. So I sloshed my way over to the bath, had a quick rinse, then went back into the bedroom to review strategy. But I was rather in the position of a tennis player who couldn't make any plans until his opponent sent the ball over to him. It was in their court and I was going to have to wait until they served it before I could work out how I was going to play it. One thing was clear: I didn't have an ally in the whole bloody place. Apart from the fact that Marvin was besotted with Gerastan, it was a pretty fair chance that Gerastan also had something on him, so he was out. Perhaps I could pitch a few of my curves at Bill, relying on memory of things past to do the rest. But we would have to wait and see about that later.

At six-thirty there was a tap on my door and Angel stuck his head round before I could tell him to come in. He looked a little disappointed to find me fully dressed, but then he announced that the other guests were gathered for cocktails and would I like to come along.

I followed him into a section of the house I hadn't been in before, along half a dozen passages and through two more vast rooms. Then he tapped on a door and pushed it open. The room was smaller than the others and distinguished by the fact that there was a huge log fire blazing away in an open fireplace. To compensate for this, the air-conditioning was turned up full blast. It wasn't as disastrous as it sounded; the temperature was comfortable and one had the visual benefit of the open fire. Not that I looked at it for long; as soon as I came into the room with Angel, Roger Gerastan, dressed in a dinner jacket, came over and took my arm.

'You look enchanting, Katherine,' he said, in his soft voice. 'I think you know everyone.'

He turned with me into the room. I knew two of the other guests, Bill and Marvin. The third I knew only by sight. But he had been a part of my bad dreams for so long now that I felt we must have been better acquainted than we were. It was the

Eunuch, the firelight sparkling off his shiny baldness, his huge bulk encased in a badly fitting dinner jacket.

'I don't know him,' I said, nodding towards the Eunuch, who was regarding me flatly across the room.

'No, of course not,' said Gerastan. 'I'm sorry.' He guided me across towards the Eunuch, who continued to watch me expressionlessly as I approached.

'Hamid, this is Miss Touchfeather. Katherine, Hamid El Mullah.'

The Eunuch inclined his head a fraction of an inch, making no other acknowledgement of the introduction.

Then Gerastan steered me past him over towards the bar. 'Martini?'

'I'd prefer it with vodka,' I said.

'Of course.'

I watched him while he mixed my drink expertly. Everything he did he seemed to do with a minimum of fuss or wasted effort; he was neat, compact and efficient, and I think I disliked him even more than I disliked the Eunuch. There was enough tension in the room to suffocate a person sensitive to atmosphere. I had noticed it as soon as I had come in. Most of it was coming from Bill and, to a lesser extent, Marvin. Gerastan didn't seem to know the meaning of the word, any more than the Eunuch did. I wondered whether I could funnel any of this atmosphere to my own benefit, but until I knew the cause I'd have to wait to see. Gerastan handed me my drink. Naturally it was completely perfect.

'I hope William didn't give you too much of a shock,' he said, after allowing me to take a swallow.

'Who?'

Then I remembered that Gerastan didn't like shortened names. I glanced across at Bill. Funny, I'd never thought of him as a William before. I decided to try to do so from now on; it might help me to detach the past more effectively. He looked as miserable as hell. So did Marvin, and I wondered what they had been talking about before I came in. Gerastan answered my unspoken question.

'We were just talking about you, Katherine,' he said.

I could only play it by ear until I knew more of what was going on. 'That's nice,' I said.

Gerastan grinned. 'What a very normal female reaction,' he said. 'When a woman hears she is being talked about, she automatically assumes that it is something pleasant.'

'It's a defence mechanism,' I said. 'We can't afford to analyse the situation too clearly in case we find out we're wrong. If we were, then we'd rather not know about it.'

'It's gratifying to discover that a girl in your line of work is still capable of ordinary female self-deception,' he said.

'I'm not sure what you mean by "my line of work", but surely self-deception isn't the prerogative of the female. Don't you all indulge in it?'

'Do we?' said Gerastan. 'Tell us. Tell us about our self-deception.'

Here goes, I thought. Bull by the horns and all that jazz.

'Let's take Marvin first,' I said. Poor Marvin, I was about to cut his throat, but he probably deserved it, if the facts were known. 'Marvin feels that he is the queen of the fairies around town. The big swinger, carousing with the kinkies, flying with the junkies, every pansy's dream of home.'

'Whereas?' said Gerastan, enjoying himself.

'Whereas he's just a sick little man involved in an unrequited love affair with another man who would as soon step on him as look at him.' Gerastan chuckled. Marvin didn't say a word, but I'd hit him hard enough to make him bleed.

'And Hamid?' said Gerastan.

'I don't know Mr. Mullah,' I said. 'But anyone who looks like he does must indulge in self-deception. If he didn't he'd cut his own throat.' The Eunuch didn't move a muscle, nor did his expression change. It would obviously take a larger knock than that to make a dent in his monolithic hide.

'And William?' asked Gerastan. 'What about William?'

I looked across at Bill. 'On William I am an expert,' I said. 'The urbane, sophisticated, brilliant Professor Partman—'

'Stop it, Katy,' said Bill.

'Go on, Katherine,' said Gerastan.

'A wow with a transistor and a devil with the ladies is William. But what is he really? He's a man with an obvious talent for getting mixed up with things and people so far out of his league as to be laughable. He's a man who'd sell out what he creates because another man tells him it's the thing to do. He's worse than Marvin in his dependence on this other man; at least Marvin's hormones are bent and he's got the excuse that his dependence is physical. Whereas William is allowing himself to be seduced mentally.' Bill had turned away from me, ostensibly to sit down, but he had sat with his back towards me so that I couldn't see his face.

'And what about me, Katherine?' said Gerastan, still enjoying himself. 'Where's my self-deception?'

'It's all around you,' I said. 'It's in those guards, with their dogs, and the helicopters and this ridiculous place built in the middle of nowhere. You are deceiving yourself into believing you are valuable and important enough to need all this protection. Nobody is that important. I think you indulge in this pantomime to feed your own ego. Nobody is that bothered about you, Mr. Gerastan. If they were, they'd do something about it regardless of where you are, or how well you're guarded.'

'Is that all?'

'No. Whatever it is that you are doing, it is for your own self-gratification. You've constructed a legend around yourself and your whole life is devoted to feeding that legend and keeping it alive. I'm not quite sure what it is you're up, to but whatever it is, I'll bet your motives aren't what Bill and Marvin think they are. You use them all for your own self-aggrandisement, sniggering up the sleeve of your five-hundred-dollar suit because they allow themselves to be used.' Even Bill had turned round now and was looking towards us. But Gerastan refused to be put out. He allowed himself a smile before taking me apart.

'What about you, Katherine?'

'What about me?'

'Shall we examine the circumstances that brought you here?'

'Do,' I said. 'If it will please you.'

'You no doubt consider yourself an able person, one who does her job efficiently. But let us look at the facts. One, you were recognised for what you were the moment you boarded the flight to Bombay. In actual fact I knew about you before you boarded. Your employers aren't the only people who have an entrée to airline personnel. Two, you allowed yourself to be seduced by the man you were supposed to be watching, and don't try to excuse it by saying it was all in the line of duty. We know better. Three, you made it ridiculously easy for my men to abduct you in Rome. Four, having escaped from the lion's den once, you were stupid enough, not only to reenter it, but to place your head in the lion's mouth. Five, you will no doubt consider it unjust when the lion closes his mouth with your head still inside.'

Every shot a bull's-eye, I thought. Thank God Mr. Blaser wasn't there to hear my deficiencies laid out on the line like that; he'd have sent me back to school at best, or pensioned me off at the other end of the scale.

'And now I think we'll go into dinner,' said Gerastan, while I was still reeling from his justifiable denigration of my capabilities.

The first part of dinner was taken up with the business of eating. I'm sure that the food was magnificent, but to me everything tasted like sawdust. Touchfeather, I thought, you're in very deep water, and there just ain't anyone who is going to throw you a life jacket. I looked around the table. Bill and Marvin were just plain miserable. The Eunuch was shovelling the food into his mouth, obviously tasting nothing and just performing a biological necessity. Only Gerastan seemed to be enjoying himself. It may have been an act, but I doubted it. He commented on the wine. He complained mildly that the entrée could have done with another forty-five seconds in the oven; and he sent the coffee back because he said it had been standing too long before we reached it. Apart from that he managed a line of small talk which was endless, but which didn't say a thing. He waited until he had sampled the brandy before he got down to business.

'Tell us about yourself, Katherine, and the people you work for.'

'United?'

'No, my dear. Nor Air India, or BOAC, or any other airline. The people you *really* work for, the people who employ Signor Bertelli in Rome and Walter Martin in New York.'

'I don't know what you're talking about,' I said with remarkable lack of invention.

'I didn't suppose you would straightaway,' said Gerastan. 'Still, we have plenty of time.' I saw Bill and Marvin both glance at him quickly, but he didn't even acknowledge their looks of enquiry. Instead he addressed himself to the Eunuch.

'Hamid, we must talk,' he said. Then he turned to Bill. 'William, take Katherine back to her room. Don't bother retiring, Katherine. The night has only just started.' Then almost as an afterthought he turned to Marvin. 'Is your plane ready?'

'I think so.'

'I shall want you to return to Los Angeles later.' He stood up and turned to me. 'I have some business to attend to. It will take me exactly one hour. Please use that time to consider your position here. Afterwards I shall ask you the same question again, along with many others.' He bowed slightly, and he and the Eunuch walked out, leaving me with Bill and Marvin. There was a long moment of silence broken by Bill, who turned to Marvin suddenly.

'You bloody fool,' he said savagely. 'Why did you bring her here?'

I answered for him. 'I asked him to,' I said. 'Not that it would have made any difference, eh, Marvin?'

Marvin shook his head. 'If she hadn't asked, I was to bring her here anyway,' he said. 'Those were Roger's orders.'

Bill looked at him for a further moment, then got to his feet. 'Come on, Katy,' he said. Marvin started to say something else; then he changed his mind. I stood up.

'You're a bright pair, aren't you?' I said. 'The master says jump and you both react as though he had put a rocket up your backsides. Marvin I can understand, even if I can't condone. But you, Bill, what's the matter with you?' He glanced towards Marvin as though for help, but he was going to get no assistance from that one. Then he turned back to me.

'Come on, Katy,' he said.

He tried to take my arm, but I shrugged his hand away and walked ahead of him. My grand exit was a little spoiled outside the door due to the fact that I didn't know whether to turn left or right. Bill steered me correctly without attempting to take my arm again, and three minutes later we were back in the blue sitting room.

During that three minutes I had done some fast thinking. He headed for the bar as soon as we entered the room, while I sat down and wondered how I could make my move without appearing too obvious. But I only had an hour, so I couldn't afford to hang about too long.

'Bring me a drink, please, Bill,' I said. He poured me one and fetched it over.

'You don't understand Roger Gerastan,' he said, still looking for his own justification.

'Explain him to me,' I said, deciding to sacrifice five minutes if it would help me understand things better.

'You think he's some sort of a traitor, a man who sells stuff to the other side. Well, he doesn't. He gives it to them.' The idea was so ludicrous that I nearly burst out laughing. But I didn't.

'Roger maintains, and I agree with him, that the only way to prevent the world from destroying itself is to keep an even balance of power. If one side gets too far ahead, they have no need to fear the other any longer; they can do what they like. This can only lead to the Holocaust.'

'And Gerastan gives away his country's secrets to keep this balance. Is that what you're saying?'

'It works both ways. Hamid feels the same. If either East or West gets too far ahead, then these two men try to even it out. As long as one nation is as powerful as the other, there can be no war. It's as simple as that.'

Nothing could be that simple—except perhaps Bill for believing it. But believe it he obviously did; it was too daft for him to have made it up. Obviously the academic life had addled his brain.

'So you should be grateful to men like Roger Gerastan. He risks his name, his reputation, even his life to maintain a spot of sanity amid the insanity that threatens to explode all around us.'

'Yes, Bill,' I said, and emptied my drink over my lap. I jumped to my feet and he started to make clumsy efforts to mop me down.

'Just a minute,' I said. 'I'll change.' I went into the dressing room and stripped down quickly. Then I started to rummage in the closets. I had no scruples about what I was going to do; neither did I have any false hopes as to its efficacy. But I couldn't think of anything else. I had to get Bill into bed and there point out the folly of his ways; there's not much point in carrying the equipment I do if I'm not prepared to use it when the time is ripe, and I couldn't remember one riper. Bra, I thought, in case the sight of my scar turned him off before he started, but flimsy bra so that he could see the treasures that lay buried beneath. Is he a black-stocking-and-suspender man? I wondered, then quickly decided that they all were. So on they went—and a pair of pants on top, in case he thought I was throwing it all at him too hard. There was a flimsy negligée which allowed everything to show through and, thus armed to the teeth, I galloped back into the fray.

I started by appealing to his better nature, which got him across the room and onto the settee beside me. Then, involuntarily, I placed my hand over his, emphasising a point I was trying to make, and two minutes later he covered my hand with his other. Eyes widening a bit, I reminded him of what we had meant to each other and how I had felt when he disappeared from my life. I even managed to squeeze out a tear, and that provided the catalyst. In a moment I was sobbing my heart out on his chest and he was 'there there-ing' me all over the place. One thing led to another, and five minutes later one of my breasts had found its way into his hand, and a moment later into his mouth. Then, with thirty-five minutes still left of my hour, he was carrying me into the bedroom. I discovered there that he wasn't all that much of a stockings-and-suspenders man after all. He had them off me in thirty seconds flat.

I've always maintained that one should grab one's pleasures when and where you can and, having satisfied my conscience in the matter, I went on to enjoy myself. I mean, there was no telling; it might be the last time, and it would have been hypocritical of me to fight against the physical enjoyment. Apart from that, no girl can fake an orgasm like the real thing, and Bill knew from experience the way I reached my climax. So I let nature take its course, and, five minutes later, I was gasping his name and chewing my lower lip to a frazzle. It was a repetition of that first time in Bombay. The only concession I made to the occasion was that I pulled myself together a lot quicker than I would have done normally. I'm a girl who likes to unwind slowly. There aren't all that many men who can give you a decent, first-class, deluxe trip, and when I've got one, I try to make up for all the wasted times, when I've started out and never quite made it. But this time I sorted myself out almost as soon as it was over, leaving him hanging way behind.

'Oh, Bill, that was wonderful. God, you're marvellous!' And having given his vanity a boost, I started down to serious work. 'What are we going to do, darling?'

'I don't know, Katy. I really don't know.'

'You'll think of something,' I said, doubting it. He chewed on this for a few moments.

'If only you could see how right Roger is,' he said finally. 'What he's doing, he's doing for all of us.'

'Even if I did, would he accept it?' I said. 'He thinks I'm all sorts of a Mata Hari.'

'Not without cause,' he said gently.

'People can change their ideas as well as their allegiances,' I said.

'You really mean it, don't you, Katy?' I assured him that I meant it, but would Gerastan believe me?

'You could be an enormous help to our cause,' he said.

My God! It was a 'cause' now, with Roger Gerastan mounted on a snow-white charger and bearing a strange device, the keeper of the world's peace while he got fat in the process. And it was only at that moment that I suddenly realised what his motives were. What had Mr. Blaser said? America had cut back her missile-development programme because she was so far ahead of the Russians; then, because the sides had drawn level again, Uncle Sam had opened up his bottomless purse, shovelling money at the Gerastan Corporation like there was no tomorrow. Fifty, a hundred, a thousand million—you name it, Mr. Gerastan, sir; we'll just sign the cheques. Just so long as we can draw ahead again. But not too far ahead, says Mr. Gerastan, or the purse strings will be pulled shut again. And if a man like Bill comes up with something to upset the balance, then for God's sake let the other side get it as well and, what is more important, be seen to get it. As for friend Eunuch, he was no more an agent working in Russia than Mr. Blaser. Because this trade was strictly one way, from West to East. If Russia managed to draw ahead by her own effort, then the effect for Gerastan would be the same, the bottomless purse again. It was just that the Comrades couldn't always be relied upon to do it on their own, so Gerastan gave them a boost every now and then. The Eunuch was just a high-powered, international hatchet man, nothing more. And Roger Gerastan was a money-grubbing maniac who didn't mind using treason as a means of getting fat.

It must have been a pretty sweet setup: a couple of Government auditors on the payroll and he could milk as much as forty percent out of what the Government was paying him. Research and development is a notoriously difficult thing to budget for and, added to this, there were the fifteen-odd factories around the country turning out machinery that was designed to be obsolete before it ever got off the production line. And forty percent of figures with eight noughts at the end added up to a great deal of loot in anyone's language. As long as he had people like Bill to come up with fresh gizmos every now and then, and Uncle Sam didn't run out of money, it could go on forever.

But there would be no point in trying to explain my new-found theory to Bill. If he hadn't caught on by now, he wasn't going to. He was blinded by the reflected glory of Gerastan's great peace motives. It was going to take more than a quick fuck to get him to change his ideas.

'I don't think Mr. Gerastan will trust me, whatever you tell him,' I said, cuddling close. He was obviously thinking the same thing, because he didn't answer right away, and when he did, it wasn't to give me an argument.

'If there was some way for you to prove to him that you're on his side,' he said finally.

'Like what?' I asked.

'I don't know. Tell him what he wants to know about the people you work for. That would help.' It would help me get hung, drawn and quartered if ever I got out of this, but I doubted that Roger Gerastan would be very impressed, whatever I told him. If I could have cut Mr. Blaser's throat in the middle of Oxford Street at high noon, I think I could have won Gerastan over, but I didn't see doing it with much less. But now I had to convince Bill of this, at the same time keeping him sufficiently hung on me to go along with my next suggestion. To state it baldly, this was to get me the hell out of there before Gerastan set the Eunuch onto me. I rated my chances at double zero with the hairless horror. Just looking at him was the equivalent of someone else using thumbscrews.

'I've got to get away from here,' I said. 'It's the only way.' Bill had his face tucked into the angle made by my shoulder and neck. He removed it to grunt something unintelligible and then he went back to his nuzzling. 'Then when I don't do anything, he'll know that I go along with his ideas.' It sounded pretty lame, and simple as Bill might be, he wasn't *that* simple. He removed his face once more.

'He'd send someone after you,' he said. 'He'd have you killed.'

'I think he might do that anyway,' I said, trying to get his two feet on the ground.

'Not while I'm around,' he said. 'He wouldn't dare.' Dear, brave Bill. He didn't realise it, but he'd probably cut my throat himself if Gerastan ordered it.

'So what is he going to do with me?'

'Nothing, so long as you tell him what he wants to know. And don't try to lie to him, Katy. He's too bright.'

'Even if I tell him what he wants to know, he can't very well let me go afterwards if he doesn't trust me.'

'You'll come with me,' said Bill.

'Where? You're supposed to be dead.'

'A place he's got in the Eastern Mediterranean. We'll stay there until this whole insanity has sorted itself out and Roger can come out into the open.'

That'll be the day, I thought. Bill didn't realise it, but he was as dead now as he would be when they lowered him six feet under.

'All right, Bill,' I said. 'I place myself in your hands entirely.'

It was what he wanted to hear, probably what he had been sent to my room for, and I heard him breathe a sigh of relief. Then, to seal our pact as it were, he started to make love to me again. I went along with it for a few minutes. I was just beginning to enjoy it again when he rolled over on top of me. It was now or never. I wrapped my legs around his neck, and before he realised that I wasn't motivated by passion, I'd nearly throttled him. I rolled out from under and in two minutes I'd tied him with half a dozen elegant-looking belts I found in the dressing room. I stuffed a silk scarf into his mouth and tied it with a sexy little suspender belt. I made sure he could breathe and, although he hadn't yet regained consciousness, I planted a kiss on his forehead for old time's sake. Then I scrambled myself into a pair of slacks and a shirt and pulled on my boots.

SIXTEEN

The tinted glass of the bedroom windows gave a beautiful blue sheen to the moonlit grounds, but that was all it gave. The glass was an inch thick and unbreakable. And it was set into metal frames. Air-conditioning gave all the fresh air that the blue-room guests could require and, unless one happened to have a stick of dynamite handy, these windows just weren't for opening. So it had to be another way.

They must have assumed that I would be safe in Bill's care because there was no one outside my bedroom door. Turn right along the passage, through one of the large rooms, another passage, into the room I had seen on first entering the house, and there was the front door. If memory served, there would be two cowboys propping up the pillars just outside, so I gave the door a miss, crossed the room and ran down another passage, trying to keep an outside wall with me all the time. A right angle in the passage and another window letting onto the gardens. But it was the same sort of window as the one in my bedroom and I still had no dynamite with me. I tried to remember the house as it had looked from outside and whether there were any other doors. But to the best of my recollection everything was built facing inwards and, apart from these stupid immovable windows, nothing faced out onto the grounds. So, cowboys or no cowboys, I was going to have to use the front door.

I backtracked along the passage, gathering an Indian memento in the form of a club en route. Then, feeling like Geronimo about to make his last stand, I opened the front door and stepped outside. I was only half right: there was one cowboy propping up the house, not two. It was Wild Bill from that afternoon. He'd obviously been chewed off a strip for allowing me to make an idiot of him, and he wasn't at all pleased to see me.

'Good evening,' I said, both hands behind my back.

'Where are you going?' he asked.

'For a walk.'

'Nobody told me nothing about that,' he said. He turned and reached into a recess for the house phone. I hit him hard enough to lay him out, but not hard enough to kill him. At least, I didn't think so, but they were pretty crafty those Indians, and perhaps the club was better balanced and more deadly than it seemed. Anyway, I wasn't going to wait around to find out and, as he slid quietly to the ground, I relieved him of his gun. Five seconds later I was out through the archway and into the grounds. The two dogs chained in the courtyard hadn't even given me a second look; apparently they only chomped and slavered when they were off their leashes. So there I was, trotting down the drive, keeping to the cover of the bushes and shrubs that bordered it, and I still had five minutes before my hour was up.

The garden smelled enchanting and the thin moon gave me just sufficient light so that I didn't trip over anything and fall flat on my face. But what had seemed a short distance in the car that morning was a hell of a lot further on foot, so I had plenty of time to plan the strategy I was going to employ when I reached the gates. Unfortunately time was all I did have, because as I stopped behind a tree and looked at the gates twenty-five feet in front of me, I still had no idea how I was going to get through. There was a small lodge just inside the gates; the door was open and there were two men half in and half out of the place. They were talking quietly and one of them had his left boot off and was sitting on the ground, massaging his foot. I could see a small table inside the lodge and, on the table, the house phone. Two men weren't going to be as easy as one, even taking into account the fact that I now carried an equaliser. I could hardly go banging it off all over the place. I still had a fair way to go, and I didn't want to travel it in front of a pack of bloodthirsty hounds.

So Katy played it cool. I left the gun behind the tree and sauntered out into the light from the lodge. The first cowboy jumped to his feet while the second started to struggle back into his boot.

'Good evening,' I said.

'Evening, miss,' said number one, doubtfully. 'Anyone know you're out on your own?'

'I'm not on my own,' I said. 'Mr. Gerastan's back there chatting to a couple of your campadres.' They started to pull up trousers and tuck in shirttails. By then I had reached them, just as number two got his boot back on and stood up, preparing for the CO's inspection. I turned and called back into the comparative darkness of the grounds, 'Come on, Roger dear.'

They both looked past me as I stepped between them and relieved number one of his gun. A quick-draw holster is a very picturesque piece of dressing, but it's a hell of a thing to be carrying a gun in if someone wants to take it off you. The heavy gun slid out of the holster as though it were greased, and I had it jammed into number one's back before he was even aware that it was missing. He wasn't very bright because he still wasn't sure.

'Careful, miss,' he said. 'It's loaded.'

'You're kidding,' I said—and he still wasn't sure.

'Honest, miss,' he said. 'And there ain't no safety.'

Then, to cap it all, they both looked out into the darkness, hoping the Boss would appear and take this kinky houseguest off their hands. As number two still had his gun in its holster, it was him I hit, using the barrel of the six-shooter I was holding. And before number one could gulp twice I had it jammed into his back once more. The expression on his face, as he watched his companion fold up, was comical. Then he realised that he was in trouble and he started to do something stupid. There was a rifle propped up against the wall of the lodge and he made a grab for it. Using both thumbs I clicked back the hammer of the gun, hoping he wasn't deaf. It sounded like the crack of doom and froze him rigid. There was a moment's pause as he started to sweat.

'Christ, lady, watch it!' he said finally. 'That thing's got a hair trigger when it's cocked.'

'I don't believe you.'

'So help me, it'll go off if you look at it cockeyed.'

'Prove it to me,' I said.

He finally got the message, strength five. 'What you want?'

'I want to go down to the airfield nice and quietly, with absolutely no fuss at all.'

'Mr. Gerastan will skin me alive.'

'He won't get the chance if I don't get to the airfield,' I said. There was a moment's pause, and I could feel through the gun between us some of the tension leave him. He'd obviously come to grips with the situation and decided to play it the only way he could.

'You wanna drive or walk?' he asked.

'We'll drive if you've got the transport.'

'There's a patrol jeep outside the gate.'

'Fine, let's go ... What's your name?'

'Harold.'

'You drive, Harry. I'll sit behind you.'

'Take the gun off cock first,' he said. 'If we hit a bump I'll lose my head.'

'I'll do that when we're on our way,' I said. He'd grown the faintest bit too amenable for my taste. 'Now come on; I'm in a hurry.'

'I'll have to phone in and tell them I'm opening the gates,' he said.

'Why?'

'Because if I don't an alarm will go off as soon as I open them. And you don't want that, do you, lady?'

I agreed that I didn't want that at all, and I allowed him to make his call.

'Harry here. I'm going outside for half an hour. Yea, Lee's staying here at the lodge.' Lee was the man on the floor, bleeding quietly from the head. Harry hung up the phone and would have turned on me if I had given him a chance, but I reminded him of the edge I was holding over him and he changed his mind and headed for the gates instead. He opened them, then closed them behind us.

The jeep was parked against the wall, just off the road. He climbed into the driver's seat and I clambered over the side so that I was sitting behind him. Then I pressed the gun up against the base of his skull and delicately removed it off cock. It was as though I'd lifted a ten-ton weight off his back; he relaxed so much I thought he was going to fall out of the jeep.

'What d'ya wanna do, lady? Drive right onto the airfield or creep around a bit?'

'We'll creep,' I said. 'Cut your lights before they can see them; coast in as far as it's safe. I'll take it from there.'

'You're quite a gal,' he said companionably, as he started the engine. 'How you get out of the house?'

'I managed,' I said. He started to shake his head admiringly until I stopped it with the barrel of the gun. 'Just drive, Harry. You can hand around the bouquets later.'

'I hate to say it, lady, but it'll likely be at your funeral.'

'We'll share them, then,' I said.

The jeep jerked into motion, nearly throwing me off the back seat.

'I told you to take the gun off cock,' shouted Harry above the engine noise. 'I'd be without my head by now.'

'There's still time,' I said, rearranging myself. 'What happens down at the airfield?'

'What d'ya mean, what happens?'

'How many men down there?'

'There's Bud and a couple of mechanics. Then there's the crew for the DC-8, when the Boss needs them.'

'Are they there now?'

'Don't think so. He hasn't used the big one for a coupla weeks. He flies the crew in from LA when he needs 'em.'

'So it's just Bud and the two mechanics, then?'

'That's about it, unless the chopper crews are down there, too.'

'Are they usually?'

'No, the choppers park up back of the house. The boys live up there most of the time.'

'But they *might* be there?'

'Lady, anybody and his mother might be there. I'm just giving you the facts as I know 'em. How you handle them is your concern. But I can tell you right now, you're wasting your time. The Boss'll send some of the fellows after you. You ain't got a chance.'

'I got this far.'

'That ain't nothing,' he said. 'Once he sets someone like Jack Kelly on your tail you may as well curl up and die.'

'Jack Kelly's dead.'

'No kidding? What happened to him?'

'I killed him,' I said dramatically.

'You're having me on. No, maybe you ain't,' he said, changing his mind.

'That's right. I ain't,' I said. 'Now is there anything you haven't told me that you feel I should know?'

'Bud carries a heater; the mechs don't. And he's fast with his hands.' You're telling me, I thought.

Suddenly he cut the lights and the engine at the same time and we coasted to a silent stop.

'What's wrong?' I asked, reminding him that I still carried the gun.

'Nothing wrong, lady,' he said. 'We've arrived.'

There was a low hill, around which the road curved out of sight. The airfield buildings must lie just around the bend, I thought. I climbed out of the jeep, still keeping the gun on Harry.

'What you going to do with me, lady?' he asked equably.

'Is there any rope in the jeep?'

'There is, but I'd prefer it if you'd belt me. It'll look better when I explain things. The Boss don't like slipups.' So I belted him, just above the ear. If he'd had time, I'm sure he would have thanked me. As it was, he curled up quietly in the front of the jeep.

Three men in the past ten minutes—you're quite a girl, Katy Touchfeather. Bessie would be glowing with pride if she knew. I could have done with her company right then. If there had been anyone who could have subdued quick-handed Bud, it would have been Bessie. But Katy was on her own and Katy was going to have to do it herself. It wasn't as difficult as it could have been, and I think it was about here that the little man in my head started to wave his warning flags. But he wasn't waving hard enough yet for me to pay him much attention and, tightening a metaphorical notch in my belt, I started to creep up towards the only one of the airfield huts that showed a light. There was jazz music playing inside which effectively masked any noise I might have made, and a quick glance in the window showed me all the opposition in one place. Bud and the two mechanics were seated around a table playing poker. By the amount of money lying around, they must have been grossly overpaid. Moving back from the window, I looked out across the airfield. The DC-8 was parked where I had last seen it, with its two chicks still nestling beneath her wings. Marvin's Piper was a hundred and fifty yards away, facing towards the runway. 'Is your plane ready?' Gerastan had said to him. 'You're to return to Los Angeles later.'

So there she was, all fuelled up and waiting to fly me out of here, just as soon as I could think of a way of getting aboard. I tried to remember what I knew about a Piper, but it had been a long time since I'd done any of my own flying and I never was much good at it. The ex-RAF instructor who had steered me through the course had been stuck on me, and he would have passed me out even if I'd never taken my feet off the ground. To him 'solo' meant that he wasn't allowed to come up with me, so my whole course had been a dual effort with me paying more attention to seeing that his seat belt stayed fastened than to actually doing any flying. However, I *had* flown and, what is more important, I had flown a Piper.

I visualised the cockpit, wishing I'd paid more attention to Marvin that morning. Self-starter for both engines, warm-up time about three minutes, longer if possible. I weighed this against the three men inside the hut and decided that I'd chance the plane. If I cut the warm-up time, I should be able to start taxiing as soon as the engines fired. The plane was a hundred and fifty yards from the hut and it would take Bud and the others about twenty seconds to reach it from the moment they heard the first cough of the engines. Assuming the engines started the first time, I'd probably make it. If they didn't, I was going to have to leave off long enough to shoot three men on the hoof, very likely while I was being shot at at the same time. Still, life's a gamble at the best of times—and this wasn't one of those.

So I left Bud and his companions to their poker and walked out to Marvin's plane. The wheels were chocked and I removed these quietly. I checked that the wings weren't tied down; I didn't want to take off dragging two lumps of concrete with me. Then I climbed onto the wing, opened the hatch and slipped down into the driver's seat. I closed the hatch and laid my gun down on the seat beside me. The array of needles, dials and levers in front of me was a little intimidating, but not as much as what I had left behind me. I counted to three; then I turned the key in the ignition and watched the needles jump. The little man in my head was waving his flags madly, and still I didn't take any notice of him. I checked the fuel tanks: full. Fingers crossed, hand on throttle levers and eyes down for a full house. I threw the starter and both engines caught immediately without the faintest trace of a cough. Without even bothering to glance back, I fed them as much juice as I could without choking them to death and started to taxi out towards the runway. I remembered that the apron met the runway about halfway along its length; since it was long enough to take a DC-8, there should have been enough room in front of me to take off twice.

As I gathered speed into the darkness, I glanced back towards the huts. I could see three figures running towards me, but they didn't stand a chance. I checked the speed, then pulled the wheel back into my stomach. I bounced once, and then I was clear.

I couldn't remember how high the hills were at the end of the runway, so I aimed for as much height as possible. At one thousand feet I levelled off and took the first breath I could remember all evening. I looked down at the instruments: oil pressure OK, fuel gauges OK, engine temperature OK. And finally my little man with the flags got through to me. The engine temperature was normal for running, but I'd only started the bloody things two minutes ago. They couldn't have warmed up that quickly, not unless they had already been run up. Oh sister, I thought, you're up here in this aeroplane because that's just where you're supposed to be. The adrenalin had been pumping so hard for the past half an hour that I hadn't bothered to think how ridiculously easy the whole thing had been. I'd been so proud of myself for getting out of the lion's den that I hadn't been able to see that it was only because the key had been left in the door. And, if someone back there wanted Katy up in this aeroplane, then Katy wanted to be somewhere else, anywhere else.

A nice little accident halfway back to Los Angeles. Poor Katy Touchfeather. She wanted to fly back on her own. We tried to get her to wait, but she was a bit tight, and you know how things are...

Halfway back to Los Angeles was about an hour's flying time, but I didn't stay off the ground for more than ten minutes. As soon as the lights of the house and the airfield had faded, I switched on the spotlight below the fuselage and started to lose some height. At two hundred feet by the altimeter I eased back a little, my hands starting to sweat. Outside, the ground hurtled by beneath me at a ridiculous speed, and the spotlight seemed to find an uncommon amount of boulders and stunted trees. Still, I wasn't about to fly around looking for a bowling green to put down on. It was going to have to be one of those sink-or-swim affairs. And I came very near to sinking. I went lower and started to cut the speed, looking for a stall, but not before I was near enough to the ground to cope with it. Stall I eventually did while I was still fifteen feet up. I had a moment of warning during which I balled myself up as tight as I could with my head tucked well under my arms. I just had the presence of mind to switch off the ignition before all hell broke loose. Twenty minutes later I came round and started to unwrap myself from the wreckage.

SEVENTEEN

The dawn comes up early in those parts, but it comes up cold as well. The blazing Piper had kept me warm for an hour, but that was long gone; it had even stopped smouldering as the desert dew, rising from God knows where, effectively dampened the whole thing down. I was sitting on a small rock fifty yards away from the burned-out wreckage, practically freezing to death.

Once I had detached myself from the crash-landed plane, which had ended up on its nose, I had counted my arms and legs. Then I had groped around until I found the gun I had left on the seat beside me. After that, I had opened up the fuel cocks and thrown a match into a pool of gasoline. It went up like a bomb and I nearly got killed all over again. The light from this fire would be visible for miles in the desert, and if anyone was watching from Santhoma, I wanted to let them know that everything was proceeding according to plan. I had a long way to go and I didn't want anyone to come looking for me too quickly.

Ten minutes later, when the main part of the fire had died down, I had started walking. And fifteen minutes after that I had realised that walking in the middle of the desert at night, with nothing to guide you, was strictly for the birds and, unless I wanted to get lost ten times over, I was going to have to wait until daylight. So I had crept back to the wreckage, which was still smouldering, and sat down to wait for sunup. I was banking on someone from Santhoma coming along before the general 'aircraft missing' call went out. They would want to make sure everything was kosher before they made their calls to the state officials. The actual discovery would be made by someone else, someone official and aboveboard.

I'd had plenty of time for thinking during the night. It hadn't kept me warm, but it had served a purpose of sorts. Why should Gerastan want to know about the people I worked for? He knew enough about them already. He knew of Bertelli and Walter, and he knew about me. I suppose I could have told him a few things about Mr. Blaser, but I don't think he would even have been interested. What he wanted was to get me out of the way without upsetting Bill more than necessary. He needed Bill too much. And I had given him exactly what he wanted. Well, not quite exactly because I wasn't dead. But he didn't know that.

I'd begun to see what Bill had meant when he said he was a very bright man. He had plotted my every move for me, even to dropping the hint at dinner that Marvin's plane would be fuelled up for takeoff. Fuelled up, yes, but warmed up, no. If it hadn't been warmed up, it might not have started the first time. Bud would have had to come running, and I might not have got away. Probably Bud was the only person on the Santhoma staff who knew what the plan was. I doubt that Gerastan would have told the guards. He couldn't have relied on their acting capabilities to make it look real. Instead, he had relied on my inventiveness to find my own way out, and if I killed a couple of the guards on the way out, instead of hitting them on the head, then so what. And Bill, of course, would be convinced, especially after the way I had left him.

'I'm sorry about Katherine,' Gerastan would say. 'But she brought it upon herself. I had nothing to do with it. If she couldn't fly, she shouldn't have stolen an aeroplane.'

But Mr. Roger bloody Gerastan was going to be in for some nasty shocks. I was angry now, and we Touchfeathers get awfully mean when we're angry. I was also desperately cold and hungry, and if I hadn't been so furious, I would have been frightened, too. My watch had broken in the crash, so I had no idea of the time except a vague notion that the sun came up in these parts about five a.m. That made it about five-fifteen when I started back towards Santhoma for the second time. Twenty minutes later I bit the dust as a helicopter flew low overhead, searching for the wreckage. They would find it and, after sifting through the ashes, would report back that Katy had gone missing. All hell would then break loose and Gerastan would call out full-scale search parties. But they would expect me to be heading for the nearest point of civilisation, anywhere, in fact, other than back to the lion's den. And the reason I was going in that direction was not from any sense of bravado, but purely because I felt that it held the best chance of my staying alive.

I was damn sure Mr. Blaser wouldn't approve, but Mr. Blaser was seven thousand miles away and I could hardly check with him. Anyway, he usually wrapped up a case by judging ends, not means, and without the means I hoped to use, there just wasn't going to be any end for him to judge. Because, whichever way you sliced it, I had absolutely nothing on Roger Gerastan except what I had guessed. Proof was what Mr. Blaser had asked for, and proof I just didn't have. I suppose Bill was something of a find, but he was about to disappear to the Eastern Mediterranean, there to lie low and continue the good work.

If I had been able to report my theories to Mr. Blaser right now and assuming he went along, he would have had only one course open to him; he'd have had to summon his hatchet men and have them arrange an accident for Mr. Gerastan. Apart from the fact that this would be very difficult to do, considering how well he guarded himself, there would be a fuss kicked up that would make the Bay of Pigs look like a PTA meeting. No, Katy was in the best position to carry things through to their conclusion—the only position in fact.

It was a long, hot morning. By eight-thirty I was praying for a return of the damp and cold of the night. In these parts, once the sun eases up over the horizon, it doesn't hang about; it climbs fast and hot, until fifteen minutes after it first appears it seems to be hanging dead overhead. I'd had nothing to drink since God knows when, and walking showed me that my high-style Western boots weren't as tailor-made for me as I had thought. I also began to appreciate the full benefits of air travel; I'd been in the air for about ten minutes last night, and I suppose I'd covered just about twenty miles. It hadn't seemed very far then, but the thought of walking it now would have made me go cold if I hadn't been so hot.

Added to the vagaries of climate and feet, I had to make sure I wasn't spotted by anyone from Santhoma. The helicopter knew exactly where I had crashed, so the search parties used that as their starting point. They headed straight there from Santhoma in their jeeps, and then they fanned out and started to scour every inch of desert between the wreck and Los Angeles. But Katy was travelling the opposite way, so apart from making sure they didn't spot me on the way to their rendezvous, it wasn't too much of a problem. Two choppers had arrived back on the scene twenty minutes after the first one had located the wreckage. By then I was three-quarters of a mile away, and only had the barest glimpse of this operation as I crested a small rise. Not long afterwards I saw the two choppers suddenly rise from behind the low hills and start to fan out on a search pattern moving in the opposite direction to the one I was travelling.

I travelled a path about a mile East of the trail between the wreckage and Santhoma and, aside from the inconvenience of having to hit the dirt each time I saw an approaching cloud of dust, it served as a useful guideline for me to follow. I am notoriously lacking in sense of direction, and without this aid, it is quite possible I would have walked in a complete circle. Fortunately, dressing hoods up as cowboys doesn't make them anything more than hoods dressed up as cowboys; a real cowboy would have been able to follow my trail blindfolded, even though the desert ground was nearly rock-hard. But there was nobody on Santhoma who had been born further West than Chicago, except the Mexicans, and they were merely house servants and had nothing to do with the serious business of manhunts.

Like I said, it was a long, hot day, the longest and hottest and dryest and hungriest twelve hours that I have ever experienced. I took a one-hour rest about halfway through the day and very nearly didn't start out again. I made the mistake of taking my boots off and, when the time came for putting them on again, I thought for a couple of minutes I wasn't going to make it. Fortunately I had a hanky to stick on top of my head, but the sun played merry hell with any part of me it could find, which included my face. And, of course, I thought of water: running water, static water, tap water, spring water and rainwater; I thought about swimming pools and lakes, of streams and rivers; I thought about the six wells at Santhoma, and the way hundreds of sprinklers threw the precious stuff around, drawing it out of the earth simply to put it back again so that Roger Gerastan could have a green lawn and a couple of trees. I didn't know that there were so many combinations and permutations all to do with water, and a couple of hours after my rest I became a little light-headed, beginning to think I was paddling in water, then wading and finally even swimming a couple of strokes. Then I imagined that there was a cloudburst and stood like an idiot, with my mouth open, looking up at the sun, trying to catch the drops as they fell.

I'd probably still be standing there now if the sound of an aircraft hadn't pulled me round. I flopped to the ground and lay there, twisted round so that I could see the source of the sound. I spotted it about a thousand feet up, still making height. This put the airfield closer than I had imagined, which was encouraging. It was climbing too fast and too high to be a search plane, but I recognised it nevertheless as one of the aircraft that had been parked beneath the wings of the DC-8. I wondered briefly who was flying out, and hoped that it wasn't Gerastan. The only occupant of Santhoma I would have liked to have seen on the plane was Marvin. He was a poor, weak-minded fairy, but it wasn't really his fault and I didn't suppose he had much of an inkling as to what his lover boy was up to. If he wasn't in that plane, then he would be mixed up with the nastiness that was going to follow, and while I didn't want that to happen, it certainly wasn't going to make any difference to the way I played it. I watched the plane almost out of sight, glad of an extra excuse to take a rest; then I pulled myself together, hauled myself to my aching feet once more and plodded on.

A couple of hours later the sun seemed to get bored with the whole bit and decided to turn it in. It had raced to its zenith almost as soon as it had peered over the low hills at dawn; now it started to dive for the opposite horizon as though it were fed up with trying to fry Touchfeather and couldn't wait to get to bed. It was standing balanced on top of a distant hill, taking one last look round, when I realised that I had arrived. I had crested a small rise, and three low hills beyond where I was standing I caught a brief glimpse of the main house, surrounded by its wall and greenery. The walls were bathed in red for a moment from the reflected sun, and then the whole thing disappeared like a mirage as I moved down the opposite side of the rise. At the same time the sun packed up, and within fifteen minutes it was totally dark.

I wasn't keen on the house. What I intended had to be done at the airfield. So, having fixed my bearings during that momentary glimpse of Santhoma, I changed direction. Now that the sun had gone down, the aches and pains of the day became less of a problem. I was still desperately thirsty, but it wasn't torture any longer, and even my feet didn't hurt as much. I located the road between house and airfield and, keeping to the edge so that I could duck if there were any vehicles about, I reached the point where Harry had dropped me off the night before.

I moved round the edge of the hill and started to survey the general situation. There was no sign of Bud, nor was the small aircraft back yet. But the DC-8 was receiving attention. It had been towed across the apron to a refuelling point, and I could see one of the mechanics scrambling about on the starboard wing, dragging a thick fuel line which led back into an underground tank. I also noticed for the first time that the aircraft carried long-range fuel tanks, which was unusual on an aircraft the size of a DC-8. The mechanic was smoking, another sure sign that Bud wasn't around.

If they were making ready the big one, it supposed that Gerastan hadn't yet left, but he sure as hell was going to have to pretty soon. When the search parties returned without Touchfeather, he was going to be a worried man. He wasn't going to be able to appear anywhere until he was sure I was out of the way. I wished I had been around to see his face when the chopper pilot reported me missing. He would picture me at the nearest telephone, calling New York and London, and while he didn't know I had guessed what he was up to, he did know that I could tie him in with Bill and the Eunuch. Explaining that away could keep him busy for a long time. The only thing he could do was to disappear for a time and hope that his organisation could find Touchfeather before Touchfeather found a telephone. And once he was safely away someplace with Bill and the Eunuch he could only play it one way. He would have to pitch Bill and the Eunuch to the wolves: have them killed and then turn up and say that he had just discovered their duplicity. He would apologise all round and, after a suitable lapse of time, he'd find someone else to do his dirty work. So whichever way it came out, find Touchfeather or don't, he would be all right in the long run. The second alternative would just prove a little more inconvenient.

I was still sitting there working out the finer points of how I was going to handle it when the landing lights suddenly went on, cutting a great swathe across the desert air strip. A moment later I heard the sound of the approaching aircraft and, sixty seconds later, the small plane I had seen earlier was taxiing onto the apron. It stopped and Bud got out. He was followed by two men I hadn't seen before and who I could only assume were the crew for the DC-8. Two men *can* fly a DC-8, especially if they are not governed by the rules of IATA which stipulate a minimum crew for airline purposes. It's better with four, of course, but, if the Boss is in a hurry, no one is going to hang around waiting to pick up extra personnel. Still, two suited my plans about twice as well as four would have done, and I was eminently satisfied.

As they climbed down from the small plane, they said something to Bud and then both of them headed towards the DC-8, while the mechanic on the wing doused his cigarette quickly. Bud moved over to the airport office, probably to call up to the house. If Gerastan was going off somewhere quiet, it was a fair bet that he would be making for his place in the Eastern Mediterranean— the one Bill had mentioned. If it was quiet and discreet enough to keep Bill hidden from the eyes of the world, it was going to be ideal for Gerastan as well. There weren't all that many places in the Eastern Med where one could land a DC-8, but Gerastan had already shown how good his relations with Cairo were, and you can't get much further East than that. If he managed to get there, he'd be as safe as if he'd gone to the moon.

I didn't know how many people he expected to take aboard his DC-8; it's a big aeroplane and there's room aplenty. But however many passengers Gerastan reckoned on, he was going to be carrying one extra—to wit, Katy.

EIGHTEEN

What I had been through before was child's play compared to what was to come next. Somehow I had got to get aboard the DC-8. I could hardly go up to Bud and ask for a boarding card, and there was only one gangway in position, at the entrance that is normally used by the first-class passengers, the one up front. One of the crewmen had used it and I could just see his head at the flight-deck window as he made some of his pre-flight checks. The other crewman was standing with the refuelling mechanic, and at that moment the second mechanic came down the gangway and moved towards the hut where Bud had gone. Five men in all, and more to come at any moment. Whatever I was going to do had to be now, before the passengers came down from the big house. A diversion was needed, but a natural diversion, not one that could only be created by a body bent on mischief.

I skirted round the back of the hangar, looking for a service door. I found one and let myself in. It was large and empty. The two big operational doors at the front were open and I could see the DC-8 on the apron beyond. Along the left wall was a workbench, loaded with enough paraphernalia to keep BOAC in the air; there was also an overhead chain tackle for lifting out engines, a couple of forklift trucks parked against the far wall and a few packing cases distributed indiscriminately around the place. But all this was lost to me at first because just inside the door, fixed to the wall, was a handbasin and, glory be, a tap. So as not to make any noise, I contorted myself and managed to twist my head around so that I could clamp my mouth completely over the end of the tap before turning it on ever so gently. The water was ice-cold and tasted to me like a particularly good year's Dom Perignon. I wanted to bathe my sunburned face, but I was too frightened of making a splash, so I contented myself by allowing just a little water to trickle down my chin; it felt like cold velvet. Then I turned off the tap, and not until I was sure there were no drips hanging around did I remove my mouth. I straightened up, breathed very deeply for a couple of moments to try to slow down my pulse rate, belched once and then moved round to see what was happening outside.

I could still see out to the apron, secure in the darkness of the back of the hangar. The crewman now said something to the refuelling mechanic and then headed back towards the gangway. Still five men: two in the aircraft, two in the office and one on the apron. Perhaps the crewmen hadn't been told anything about me, but I couldn't chance it; even if they hadn't, they weren't going to assume that I was a houseguest looking the way that I did. I couldn't see my face, but I could feel that it was a bright, peeling red and my lips were cracked; my clothes were scuffed to hell and gone. I'd been in a couple of fights, an air crash and a twenty-mile trek. And my hair was a mess. So I was going to have to get everyone in one place, concentrating on one thing, all at the same time. There didn't seem to be anything else for it. I set fire to the hangar.

A small tin of turpentine, a small pile of rags, and all I needed was a match. Fortunately, America is a country that abounds in matches. Everyone has personalised books of matches and restaurants can't give them away fast enough. There were a dozen half used books of matches strewn along the workbench, from the Whisky a Go Go and Pink Pussycat in Los Angeles to 'Hank loves Dolly'. I struck one, threw it into my pile of turpentine-soaked rags beneath the bench and ran. I made for the side of the main doors where I crouched behind two disembowelled packing cases. I could just see through a crack in the wood out onto the apron. Everyone must have been awfully busy out there because the hangar wall was blazing merrily before anyone noticed it.

The mechanic on the apron was the first. He yelled at the top of his voice and headed into the hangar at a gallop. He was the one with the careless cigarette and he probably thought the whole thing was his fault. The two crewmen were next, hurrying down the gangway. By the time they reached the fire the mechanic was already busy with an extinguisher. I prayed that he wouldn't get it out before Bud and the other mechanic arrived. He didn't, and a few seconds later Bud and companion, each carrying an extinguisher, dashed past my hiding place. There they were, five men, all in the same place at the same time, and all busy. Now or never, Katy. Ten seconds later I was on board the DC-8.

I'd flown DC-8s for three different airlines and, apart from the décor, they're all built the same way. As you come in through the front hatch, the door to the flight deck is on the left, and on the right is a small bar-lounge area, with a circular seat around a low table. Opposite this is the first-class galley and two toilets; beyond lies the passenger compartment. I'd already decided that I was going to hide in one of the toilets, so I felt like a right twit when I stepped on board and found there weren't any. Neither was there a galley, nor a bar area. I had stepped straight into a living room right out of *House & Garden*. Not content with spending a million odd pounds on the aircraft, Gerastan had had the interior torn out and redesigned. What can be cramped for one hundred and forty people leaves an awful lot of room for one. The place I found myself in was forty feet long and as wide as the aircraft. It was furnished expensively, but with a casual, informal touch so that I wouldn't have been surprised to have seen an open fire burning. But I wasn't here to admire the furnishings. I was here to hide.

I couldn't see anywhere in this section, and I didn't want to risk examining the rear. If I went through there and couldn't find a handy place, I might not have time to get back. So I turned the only way I could, sharp left onto the flight deck. And I struck lucky. There was a toilet just inside the door. I suppose Gerastan didn't approve of the hired help using the same toilet as he and his guests, so he gave them one of their own. Hoping the crew were efficient enough to know about the 'not while standing at the station' bit, I went in and sat down. I couldn't lock the door in case they noticed the 'engaged' notice on the other side of the door, so I crossed my fingers, checked the gun which I had hung on to during all my trials and tribulations and, feeling unduly vulnerable, I prepared to wait it out.

It was half an hour before the engines were started. During that time I sweated a great deal at what was taking place outside the door. Immediately after I had settled down, all I could hear was the crackle of the fire from outside and the shouts of the men who were fighting it. Ten minutes later there was no more crackling, and five minutes after that the two crewmen came back on board. Separated from them only by a thin partition, I didn't even have to strain my ears to hear what was going on. The Captain was doing most of the talking; the other one was just replying in monosyllabic grunts. And the Captain was in a foul mood. One, he hadn't filed a flight plan, and didn't the old man know it was illegal to take off without filing a flight plan? Two, he couldn't have filed a flight plan anyway, because nobody had had the courtesy to let him know where he was supposed to be going. Once he got off the ground he didn't know whether he was supposed to turn left or right. Three, he didn't approve of complicated pieces of aeroplane like DC-8s being kept on private airfields with a small staff, especially if he was going to fly them. Four, he was a pilot, not a bloody fireman. And five, he'd been given twenty minutes' notice for this flight and couldn't even tell his girlfriend when he'd be back, let alone his wife.

Having got all that off his chest, he started his pre-flight check. Five minutes after that the other crewmen pointed out that there were headlights on the roadway from the house, and the Captain, still grumbling, went to meet the man who paid his wages. A few minutes later I heard everybody come aboard. Gerastan had told the Captain where they were going, and now he was even more bad-tempered.

'It's about fourteen bloody flying hours,' he said. 'Especially going the way he wants us to. And knowing him he's just as likely to want to come back half an hour after we arrive.'

But I had stopped listening to him and was trying to hear what was going on in the passenger lounge. I recognised Gerastan's voice, and Bill's, too. The Eunuch might have been there, but he never had much to say, and I didn't hear him speak. Just before the Captain started the engines Gerastan came onto the flight deck.

'How long after takeoff will we be in radio range?' he asked.

'You keep a very tight beam here, sir. Not more than thirty minutes.'

'Tell them to keep in touch,' said Gerastan. 'If they have any news, any news at all, they should call us and we'll come back.'

'Yes, sir,' said the Captain.

'After we're out of range get them to phone any news through to the Gerastan Corporation in Tampico. We'll pick up a signal from them.'

'Yes, sir,' said the Captain, and I heard Gerastan move back to join the others. I had been right, then. He was still hoping for news of me that would obviate the necessity for his having to take this trip.

'Where we going, then?' asked the co-pilot.

'Cairo,' said the Captain. Right again, Katy.

'So what are we doing over Tampico?'

I would have asked the same question if I had been in a position to do so.

'Don't ask me,' said the Captain. 'We fly Southeast down to Mexico and turn due East over Tampico. We overfly Cuba, the Sargasso Sea, pass to the North of Cape Verde, change course East-Northeast, overfly the Sahara, Southern Libya and into Egypt.'

'It's a hell of a way to get to Cairo,' said the co-pilot.

'Stop griping,' said the Captain, who had been doing nothing else all evening, 'and go plot me a course. We're to make no land calls except Tampico until we're over Africa, so make it a good one.'

'You're kidding! We'll be lost seventeen times over,' said the co-pilot.

'That's what the man wants,' said the Captain. 'Now unless you want to go back there and tell him, you do as you're told.'

A moment later I heard the Captain speak over the landline to the mechanic who was waiting to start the engines.

During the business of takeoff I tried to calculate how long it would take us to get over the sea and whether either of the crew was likely to want to use the toilet before that time. It was about twelve hundred miles to Tampico. Then we were due to turn due East and we'd have another nine hundred miles to go before overflying Cuba. There wasn't much traffic in the Gulf of Mexico, and what there was was unreliable, so what I wanted to do would have to wait until we were past Cuba and overflying the Southern Bahama Islands, say one hour's flying time after Havana. Altogether about six hours—and if someone didn't want to use the toilet in that time, he had something seriously wrong with him. So I was going to have to play it by ear and hope their bladders would stand the strain as long as possible. Because once I was discovered I was going to have to work very hard, and it was much too comfortable sitting there, lulled by the engine noise, and with no passengers to fetch and carry for. But play it by ear as I might, my ultimate objective was crystal clear, and during the long time following takeoff, during which I heard the Captain make his last call to Santhoma, I had plenty of time to reflect on what I had to do.

Both pilots were kept pretty busy. Although they were unable to transmit, they could receive beacon signals, and they used these to keep a check on their course. A couple of times we were called to identify ourselves, having been picked up by ground radar. But we were heading out of the United States at seven hundred miles an hour and nobody on the ground bothered to send anyone up to press the issue. We picked up the beacon at Tucson, and fifteen minutes later we were out of America and over Mexico. There was another beacon over Saltillo and then the Captain told the co-pilot to switch to the Gerastan Corporation's Tampico frequency and ask if there were any messages for Mr. Gerastan. I knew what the answer would be. As the Captain signed off he spoke to the co-pilot again. 'I'll break the news to the old man,' he said. 'We've got a long night ahead of us.'

I couldn't hear what was said in the passenger compartment, but whatever it was, it didn't take long. I heard him come back onto the flight deck, mumbling to himself, and at that moment he decided he would take a pee. When he saw me sitting on the toilet with the gun pointing at his navel, he very nearly did.

I stood up slowly, so's not to frighten him into stupidity, then I nodded to indicate that he should get out of the way and let me out onto the flight deck. He backed away like a lamb, his eyes rivetted on the gun, only flicking occasionally to my face to see if I really meant it. I moved out onto the flight deck as he continued to back up until he bumped into the rear of his seat. The co-pilot sensed he was there and spoke without turning.

'We should be fixing to change course in a couple of minutes,' he said.

I indicated with the gun for the Captain to take his seat. It was the first time I had seen him up close. He was getting on, pushing fifty-five by the look of him, a retired airline Captain drawing his pension and twice as much again from Gerastan. He looked very tired, as though he could suddenly see his entire life flying out of the window. He had a wife and a girlfriend, probably a couple of kids at college and a hefty mortgage. Apart from all that he didn't like his employer. He was going to be no trouble at all.

I wasn't so sure about the co-pilot. I saw his face for the first time as he looked sideways at the Captain, and then followed the Captain's stare, homing onto me. He was much younger, about thirty, and if he had ever worked for an airline, he hadn't retired; he'd been kicked out. He had a hard, truculent mouth and cold eyes. He didn't bat an eyelid when he saw me and my gun.

'Lady, we only work for him,' he said. 'If you've got any bones to pick, go do it in there.' He nodded towards the door leading to the passenger section. It was a good job, he reminded me. Keeping my eye on them both, I backed to the door, fiddled around behind me and clicked the lock. Then I moved up forward again. I saw the co-pilot glance at the Captain and, realising he was going to get no help there, he decided he would be a hero all by himself. Perhaps he thought Gerastan would give him the Captain's job. He started to get to his feet and I stuck the barrel of the gun into his ear. He sat down again, a little subdued, but not enough.

'You shoot that off in here, lady, and we'll all be dead,' he said. I knew the line. I'd used it myself. I angled the gun so that it was still stuck in his ear but pointing downwards.

'It's got your breastbone, your stomach, your backside, the seat, the cross bulkhead and whatever you've got stored below,' I said. 'If it's got any power left in it after passing through that lot, it may fracture the pressure hull, but I doubt it.' He doubted it, too, because he stayed where he was.

'So what happens now?' he asked. He may have been doing the talking, but the Captain was flying the plane, so I spoke to him.

'Isn't it about time you changed course?' I said. He pulled himself together like a man coming out of deep shock.

'Where do you want to go?' he asked.

'You've got your instructions,' I said. 'Turn East over Tampico, wasn't it?' He nodded mutely and read off the new course to the co-pilot. There was no immediate reaction, so I waggled the gun about in his ear until he responded. I felt the great plane bank gently beneath my feet, and waited until the artificial horizon settled down again before continuing.

'How long to Havana?' I asked. The Captain looked more frightened than before. I even got a reaction out of the co-pilot. 'Don't worry,' I said. 'I'm not going to turn you over to Fidel. We're going further on.'

'There isn't anything further on,' said the co-pilot. 'Not till we get to Africa.'

'We'll talk about that later,' I said. 'How long?'

The Captain checked his course and speed quickly. 'Ninety minutes,' he said.

'Less,' said the co-pilot. 'We're beginning to pick up a tailwind.'

'That's fine,' I said. 'Now do I keep this gun in your ear, or do I take it out?'

'Take it out, lady. It makes me nervous.'

'I'll take it out, but I won't put it away,' I said.

'Suit yourself, lady,' he said. 'But for forty thousand dollars a year I'm not about to get shot.'

'Just remember that,' I said, backing away to the seat normally occupied by the Flight Engineer. 'And remember one other thing. I've been around aeroplanes for a long time. I know what keeps them up in the air, and I know how they should be treated. So fly this one as you've been taught to. I'll know if you don't.'

That seemed to cover everything, and we spent the next twenty minutes in a companionable silence, with only the noise of the engines between us. Then the co-pilot tried to get chatty.

'What's he to you, doll?' he asked.

'Nothing,' I said.

'You're taking an awful lot of trouble over nothing.'

'It's in my nature,' I said. 'Now please shut up.'

'Just as you say, lady.' He was getting cocky, too. Another twenty minutes and the only conversation was an interchange between the two of them, talking about altering course two degrees to allow for drift. The co-pilot started to explain to me all about drift and I told him to shut up again.

'How about a cup of coffee?' he said twenty minutes later. I was dying for a cup of coffee, for anything in fact, but I didn't trust that one moving about.

'No coffee,' I said.

'Suit yourself, lady,' he said. 'But do you mind telling us what you intend doing?'

'Later,' I said.

'I love a chatty dame,' he said, and that finished that particular round.

Fifteen minutes later we picked up a beacon from Havana. You can't trust anyone in Cuba these days, so we swung North and passed Havana a hundred miles to seaward. We were flying along the Tropic of Cancer and twenty minutes later we picked up the beacon from Nassau, a couple of hundred miles to our North. All right, Katy, enough sitting around. Time to get to work. I stood up and moved forward again.

'Put her down,' I said. They looked at one another, then back at me. The co-pilot even grinned.

'Sorry, lady,' he said. 'There's nowhere down there.'

'He's right, miss,' said the Captain. 'There's only a couple of small islands. Nothing that will take a DC-8.'

'I know what's down there,' I said. 'And that's where we're going.'

'Into the sea?' said the Captain.

'Into the sea.'

Then the co-pilot really started to give me trouble. So much so that I had to hit him over the head to stop him getting to his feet and strangling me. He subsided gently and the Captain nearly passed out cold in sympathy. But it served a dual purpose because the Captain decided that he was more frightened of me than he was of putting the aeroplane down in the sea. The aircraft at his fingertips was reasonably predictable in its behaviour and would do what he told it to, but as for this kookie, red-faced madwoman, who the hell knew *what* she would do next? If an aircraft is under full control, a water landing is no more difficult than a belly landing on dry land, which is another way of saying that it is very difficult indeed. But my frightened Captain had learned his business in the thirty-odd years he had been flying.

'I'll have to warn the passengers,' he said.

'Do,' I said.

He switched on the intercom. 'This is the Captain speaking, Mr. Gerastan,' he said. 'Due to circumstances beyond my control I am forced to make a landing in the sea. We will be down in about five minutes. I will give you another warning about thirty seconds before we hit. At that time brace yourselves as best you can. Do not inflate your life jackets until you are clear of the aircraft.'

He clicked off the intercom and I gave him a pat on the shoulder by way of encouragement. A moment later I heard the handle of the door being rattled. Nobody could put Roger Gerastan down into the sea unless Mr. Gerastan knew the reason why. When the door didn't open, I heard Gerastan start to thump it.

'Tell them we're going in now,' I said to the Captain.

He clicked on the intercom again. 'We are going to hit in forty-five seconds,' he said.

The hammering stopped immediately, and I gave the Captain another pat. We were descending quite fast now, but were still a few thousand feet up. I found three life jackets and slipped one on myself. I managed to wriggle the unconscious co-pilot into another and I helped the Captain into the third. Then I strapped the co-pilot securely into his seat and gave the Captain his final instructions. He nodded that he had understood them and, now that he had accepted the inevitable, he was all concentration, flying the aircraft as though he were part of it. I moved back and strapped myself to the Flight Engineer's seat, put a pillow on my lap and, ten seconds before contact, buried my face in it.

Twenty minutes later I was swimming away from the DC-8 making for the life raft that held the Captain and the barely conscious co-pilot.

NINETEEN

'The whole operation sounds ill-conceived, badly planned and abominably executed, Miss Touchfeather,' said Mr. Blaser. 'I would be extremely gratified if you would tell me the whole thing again, during which time I shall do my best to follow you.'

I took a deep breath and explained it to him again. As soon as we had ditched—a remarkably good ditching it had been, too—I lifted my face out of the pillow, unstrapped myself, and opened the door to the passenger section. The three passengers were still picking glass and furniture out of their hair. Gerastan was seated, well strapped in and, as expected, looked the least troubled of the three of them. The Eunuch's vast bulk had ripped his seat belt from its fastenings and he was flat on his face against the bar, just beginning to stir. Bill's chair had broken away from its moorings and slid across the room against the far bulkhead.

There were only three of them. Apparently Marvin had got out while the going was good. Everything that hadn't been double-fastened down had broken adrift and the place looked a shambles.

Gerastan saw me first. I would like to be able to say that he looked shocked or terrified, but he didn't even register surprise. He reached down to unfasten his seat belt.

'Leave it, Mr. Gerastan,' I said. The sound of my voice pulled Bill's head round towards me.

'Katy!'

'Stay there, please, Bill,' I said.

He had bumped his head and there was a cut just below his hairline. I felt one brief moment of weakness, but I stifled it quickly. Now the Eunuch rolled over to a sitting position, his back against the bar, staring flatly at me. He'd give me no trouble. If he moved, it would be to break my neck, and he wouldn't stir a muscle until he was sure that he would succeed. For a long moment we all looked at one another, the only sound the sea lapping against the side of the plane. We were still dead level, well afloat, and the rocking motion of the floor was a little nauseating. Gerastan spoke first.

'I assume that you, Katherine, are the "circumstances beyond his control" that the Captain referred to?' I nodded.

'Are you all right, Katy?' This from Bill.

'I'm not dead, Bill, if that's what you mean.'

'Thank God,' he said. And he meant it, too, which didn't make things any easier.

'What happens now, Katherine? A Nassau-based British gunboat?'

'No, Mr. Gerastan, that would be too complicated.'

He raised his eyebrows. 'Complicated how?'

'International complications,' I said. 'CIA and the State Department knocking on the door. "Please can we have our United States citizen back?" Questions in Parliament. Questions in the Senate. Too much trouble all round.' I think he started to get an inkling of the idea about then, but he didn't show it.

'What, then?'

'Wait and see,' I told him. The floor below me gave a sudden lurch and we developed a definite forward angle. Although we could still hear only the gentle, deceptive sound of the calm water outside, I knew that we must be shipping the stuff very fast from below. The rocking motion of the floor had grown sluggish. I risked a quick glance over my shoulder onto the flight deck. The crew escape hatch was open and, as I looked back, I could see the legs of the co-pilot disappear through it as he was dragged from outside. At least the Captain was doing what I had told him.

'Katherine!' I looked back at Gerastan. 'You realise, of course, that this aircraft will only stay afloat for fifteen minutes?'

'Twelve,' I said.

He inclined his head slightly. 'I bow to your superior knowledge.'

'I thought you were dead, Katy,' said Bill. 'You told me she was, Roger.'

'Wishful thinking, William,' said Gerastan. Bill looked from him to me, then back to him again. Then he decided that they had better move. He bent over to unfasten his seat belt.

'No, Bill,' I said.

He looked up at me. 'We've got to get out, Katy. We'll be going down soon.'

'Stay where you are.'

'Now come on, Katy. We haven't got much time.'

'I know,' I said evenly. He still didn't understand; he had no idea what I was getting at.

'Katy, we're sinking. We've got to get out,' he said, as though he were speaking to a child. Gerastan explained things for me.

'She knows that, William. Unless I'm seriously mistaken, that is the object of the exercise. Right, Katherine?'

'Right, Mr. Gerastan.' I started to explain to Bill, attempting to justify my actions to myself at the same time.

'You're a fool, Bill,' I said. I went on to tell him all about Gerastan, his motives and his plans. I even told him how Gerastan had tried to have me killed in the aircraft crash, purely to keep him happy. Still he didn't believe me.

But by then we were beginning to run out of time. The forward tilt of the aircraft was much more pronounced now, and I could hear the water slopping onto the flight deck from the open escape hatch used by the Captain.

'You realise, Katherine, that if the three of us rush you, you'll never be able to kill us all? One of us is bound to get to you.'

'You, Mr. Gerastan, I'll shoot the moment you try to undo your safety belt,' I said.

'What about me, Katy?' asked Bill, beginning to understand at last.

'I'm sorry, you, too, Bill.'

But the Eunuch didn't have a safety belt and he decided that he wasn't going to wait around just to drown. He started to get to his feet slowly. I swung the barrel of the gun towards him, but his mind was made up. Both Gerastan and Bill watched him in hypnotised fascination as he started towards me. He didn't rush, but came at me with a slow, measured tread. He looked like a tank bearing down on me and, for one brief moment, sheer terror paralysed me. Surely there wasn't a bullet made that could stop this advancing monolith. In fact, one bullet didn't. It took three, each one thudding into his great body with frightening impact. The first rocked him back on his heels; the second brought him to his knees. And still he continued towards me, crawling on all fours, his eyes black with hate; his lips drawn back over his teeth in an expression compounded of pain and superhuman effort. The third bullet killed him. It also killed Gerastan and Bill, too, in that they made no attempt to move after that. Gerastan offered me a million pounds, and Bill said he loved me. By now the water was around my knees and rising rapidly as the nose of the aircraft dipped lower. I stood watching the two men and they sat staring back at me. Time ceased to exist; every second took an hour; every minute took a day.

'You know the rest,' I told Mr. Blaser. 'We were picked up from the raft four hours later, in response to the Captain's Mayday signal. The DC-8 was long gone by then.'

'I suppose you know that the Captain and the co-pilot wanted to bring charges of piracy and murder against you,' said Mr. Blaser.

'Yes, sir. I thought they might.'

'It took a great deal of persuasion to get them to change their ideas.' I thought about the truculent, cocky co-pilot with a sore head.

'It must have done,' I said.

'There is considerable tension between us and the Americans because of this whole disgraceful affair,' said Mr. Blaser. That was his problem; at least he'd been saved the embarrassment of sending hatchet men onto foreign soil.

'There will be a very full enquiry into the whole matter,' he went on. He was being sour about the whole thing because that was his job, but I knew him well enough to know he was delighted at the way things had turned out. There had been no proof of Gerastan's guilt and he had been spared the problem of manufacturing any. The world press had announced the unfortunate demise of that great industrial empire builder, Roger Gerastan, in an aeroplane crash, and the CIA would make sure the air crew kept their mouths shut until the crack of doom. It wouldn't do their image any good to have it known that a foreign agent, or whatever, had taken the law into her own hands on their home ground. They weren't even convinced of Gerastan's complicity in the matter of information leakage, but there was absolutely nothing they could do about it.

'Is that all, sir?' I asked.

'You tell me,' said Mr. Blaser.

'That's all, sir,' I said. He looked at me for a beat; then he nodded. Crafty old devil, he knew there was something I hadn't told him. But it wasn't going to alter things and he knew that, too. So he let it go.

'Very well,' he said. 'See Miss Moody on your way out. She's worried about something to do with an extraordinary indent for five hundred dollars from your Chicago jaunt.'

I called my motor salesman that evening. It had been so long that he told me he thought I'd died or got married. We had a nice quiet evening together in a restaurant just off the King's Road, and then we went back to his place.

I awoke in the middle of the night, struggling up from a dream of Bill. I knew then that if I ever thought about him in the future, it would have to be as I had first seen him, not as I had left him. Because no man is going to sit still and allow himself to be drowned, even if he is threatened with a gun. It becomes a case of six of one or half a dozen of the other. And I had miscalculated, as is sometimes my wont. When I had judged that the time was exactly right, and that he and Gerastan wouldn't be able to reach their emergency exits, I had waded back onto the flight deck. It had been my intention to close and lock the flight deck door behind me. But, due to the water being chest high with the slope of the floor, I couldn't budge the door, and Bill and Gerastan had come wading out behind me.

There had been no alternative, I'm afraid, and it is something I shall regret to the day I die. The only spark of hope in the whole thing is that Bill truly didn't believe that I would do it, until it was too late. I had to shoot them both. My motor salesman calmed me down from my bad dream, and five minutes later I drifted off to sleep again.

TOUCHFEATHER, TOO

To Julie

PUBLISHER'S NOTE

This book was originally published in England in 1970 and reflects the cultural and sexual attitudes, language, and politics of the time. This new edition also retains most of the original British spellings, grammar, and punctuation.

AUTHOR'S NOTE

To the best of my knowledge and belief there is not—and never has been—a Katherine Touchfeather on the roster of air stewardesses employed by BOAC, TWA, Pan Am, Air India, or any other member of IATA. Katy, as my story makes clear, is employed by Mr. Blaser. How he contrives to have her appear in the right aeroplane at the right moment, wearing the right uniform and exhibiting the ready smile and warm friendliness of the perfect air stewardess, is his secret. I would like to assure SAS, United, Quantas, American, Lufthansa and all other member companies of IATA that I make no suggestion that any of their employees could, or should, do the things Katy does—despite some recent airline advertisements which may have given their readers ideas to the contrary, e.g. 'save Friday night for Ingeborg Bechtel. She puts the fun in flying". Or 'sometimes our stewardesses take young men home with them". Katy Touchfeather is to be regarded entirely as fiction. Whereas my admiration and affection for that unique race of young women, the air stewardesses, is demonstrably fact!

ONE

"Gold, Miss Touchfeather," Mr. Blaser had said. "Gold. That's what we are looking for." I refrained from commenting "Aren't we all?" and he continued in that self-righteous, pompous way that I used to find quite impressive, but which now annoys me intensely. I even made up my mind to tell him about it once, but he frightens me too much.

"This gold," he said, "is being smuggled into South America, and the man you are being sent to follow is the one who will be carrying it."

"Follow" had been Mr. Blaser's word for what I was doing, although it hardly seemed to fit the situation I was currently involved in. Here I was, wrapped in a large bath towel, in a luxurious suite on board one of the most glamorous yachts in the world, busily going through the luggage of one of Spain's great heroes of the bullring, while said hero snored lustily in the background, dreaming no doubt about the Great Bull that all matadors are supposed to dream about; or perhaps just dreaming about me and the rather energetic couple of hours we had just spent together.

I'm a pretty dab hand when it comes to searching someone's personal effects, but I was handicapped slightly in this case in that I didn't know what I was looking for. I knew what it was, but not what it would look like.

Mr. Blaser had been his usual enigmatic, pompous self when he briefed me: "If we knew what it looked like, Miss Touchfeather, we would simply bribe a member of the crew or a harbour official to take it from his cabin. But that is not the object of the exercise. If it was, we would not be spending good money to send you on this high-life jaunt where no doubt you will have a most enjoyable time at Her Majesty's expense."

He was right there. I'd had a ball. I've always had a soft spot for Spaniards, and when that Spaniard turns out to be a bullfighter to boot... Well, all I can say is "Ole!"

"We know this bullfighter has an invitation to join one of Galipolodopolo's yachting orgies in Cannes. You will endeavour to effect an introduction before that time and use your... ingenuity to be invited on the same trip. Do I make myself clear?"

"Perfectly," I said.

"I have arranged for you to fly on his flight from Mexico City to Madrid. It is a ten hour journey. You shouldn't have any problems."

I pulled my skirt a little lower down my thighs and tried to look prim but when you're built like I am and have been dragged from a swinging party somewhere off the Kings Road at quarter past midnight on a Saturday evening, neither one's state of mind nor one's wardrobe is conducive to primness. It had been a friendly party too, and I'd had a couple too many to drink; while not actually falling all over the place, I was nevertheless reasonably high. I hadn't mentioned this to Mr. Blaser, of course. It's doubtful that he would have appreciated or made allowances for such a lapse on the part of one of his people; we weren't supposed to have any spare time in which to indulge ourselves. If he had had his way we would all have been locked up in a sterile padded cell each time we finished a task, there to languish until he decided he needed us for a fresh piece of nastiness. And there's no point in asking me what Mr. Blaser himself was doing in his office at 0015 hours on a Sunday morning. Even if I'd asked him, which I wasn't about to, he wouldn't have told me.

"You will fly to New York tomorrow," he had said. "And from there, straight to Mexico City. Your man is booked out on the midday flight on Thursday. The three days beforehand you will spend in Mexico City brushing up on your Spanish. To that effect I have arranged that you will fly a local airline between Mexico City and Tampico."

I knew those local flights. The passengers all had ten pairs of hands and brought their goats along with them. I could as well have brushed up on my Spanish lying by a pool in Acapulco; but there didn't seem to be any point in mentioning it. Then Mr. Blaser removed his pipe from his mouth and proceeded to gouge out the bowl, spilling ash all over his blotter. Here comes the crunch, I thought. He always started to disembowel his pipe when he had something unpleasant to say.

"Should you meet with any unforeseen complications when dealing with this man, you will do everything you consider necessary to cover up your tracks. The man himself is of no importance, but it is essential that his companions do not learn they are under any sort of suspicion from any source. Understood?"

Here he raised his eyes from the business of the pipe and fixed them on me. They are greyish eyes, perhaps more blue than grey, but grey nevertheless. Buried beneath a pair of formidable eyebrows, they peer out at you like a predator watching from beneath a shaggy bush.

"Yes sir," I said.

Virtually he was telling me that if anything went wrong, I was expected to push my man overboard or poison his aperitif or fuck him to death; in any event, to call an abrupt halt to his short, happy life.

Fortunately, up to now, nothing had gone wrong. Antonio, who was rather a sweety, was snoring away contentedly whilst I was busy disemboweling his personal effects. It had all been ridiculously simple and remarkably enjoyable. Two hours after taking off from Mexico City wearing the neat uniform of an Iberian Airlines stewardess, I had emptied a tray of dry martinis into his lap. By the time I had sponged him dry and dried him out he had plotted my seduction to the last gasp. So as not to appear obvious, once we got to Madrid, I had made him lay siege for a few days. Finally after a particularly good afternoon in the Plaza de Toros, where the President of the *corrida* had awarded him two ears, I awarded him the tail ... mine. Two days after that we had flown to Nice, driven from there to Cannes and boarded the *Maria*, the Galipolodopolo yacht.

If Mum could only see her Katy now, I had thought as soon as I had discovered who our fellow guests were. Apart from Galipolodopolo himself, reputed to be among the five richest men in the world, if one excluded the Arabs, there was his current (number three) wife who was conveniently named Maria. This stroke of fortune had saved Galipolodopolo from changing the name of the yacht when he married her; it had been named after his second wife who was also called Maria. She was a quiet little Greek girl, twenty-five years his junior, and quite plainly terrified of her husband, his friends, the crew, the sea and everything else. Her one comfort and joy was a nasty little Pekinese which followed her everywhere and bit the crew constantly. I gave the dog three days before it disappeared mysteriously overboard. Then there was Gary Brian, forty years old, American, top box-office draw in the cinemas of the world for the past five years, and as camp as a row of tents. The only problem I had with this one was keeping him away from Antonio. There was Sir Roger Bleak, thirty or thereabouts, accompanied by a predatory little dolly bird whose name I never did get, but who obviously proposed to change it to Lady Bleak or die in the attempt. There was an Italian Count with a roving eye and hands to match and his lesbian wife, and there was a French textile magnate who distinguished himself by bringing three girls along and insisting that all four of them share the same stateroom. The girls were lean, cool, brown, and as near as made no difference, identical. Then there was Antonio, number one Matador de Toros, and of course there was Katy; in with the jet set at last and at this moment rifling the personal belongings of her lover.

I glanced at him as I finished the top drawer and started on the next. Apart from being a sweety, he was also a dish. Twenty-six or thereabouts, and unlike most of his contemporaries in the bullring, from a very good Spanish family. He hadn't started to fight bulls from hunger, but because he wanted to. The critics had started by saying he would never make a truly good matador because he had never starved. And it was probably true he would never be a Manolete or a Belmonte, but he was bloody good from where I was sitting. I'm neither pro nor anti bullfighting, and I suppose if I were asked to analyse it I would have to admit that it is basically cruel; but then so are *paté de foie gras* and battery chickens. Having convinced myself of that, I become an *afficionado*. With someone like Antonio, it had been easy. There's something about sleeping with a bullfighter that's like nothing else. I suppose a racing driver might be similar, but not to such a large extent. It's the proximity to death that does it. It heightens sexual awareness; each time you get into bed may be the last, so everything becomes that much more important.

There was nothing in the first two drawers and I started on the third.

"Why not have the customs go through his bags and take it off him?" I had asked Mr. Blaser, not unreasonably I thought.

"We are not interested in the gold, that's why," he said.

"Oh." I said, not sure where on earth we were going.

"Allow me to enlarge on that," he continued. Thank you very much, I thought. "We are not interested in preventing the smuggling of the gold, only in ascertaining what kind of gold it is." To me, gold was gold; obviously I'd been wrong all my life. "What do you know about the refining of gold, Miss Touchfeather?"

"Absolutely nothing, sir,"

"I thought as much." He tossed a folder across his desk towards me. "I suggest you read this as soon as possible."

"What is it?"

"It is a short report on the methods and processes involved in the refining of gold."

It was about an inch thick and looked as short as a telephone directory. I pulled it towards me and flipped back the cover; single space typing on foolscap sheets; it would take me a week to wade through. But I started anyway.

"Later, Miss Touchfeather," snapped Mr. Blaser.

I sat back quickly. "Yes, sir."

"When you locate what we are looking for you will take a sample and then replace the gold so that no one will know it has been disturbed. Clear?"

"Not very, sir."

"When you have read that, it will be," he said.

I doubted it, but the after effects of my party were beginning to creep up on me, and I wanted to go home. I got to my feet and headed for the door.

"Miss Touchfeather," he said just before I went out. I turned back to him. "The next time you come into this office, try to do so sober."

Which only goes to show that he is not as dim as I would sometimes like to believe.

❧ ❧ ❧

The third drawer yielded nothing either, and I was beginning to get heartily sick of the whole affair. Antonio was still rumbling away in the background and I dearly wanted to join him. But duty called, and I started on the built-in wardrobes. Gold can be disguised into practically any shape, but even I know that it ends up still being metal; it may be sprayed silver, bronze or grey but, however ingenious the smuggler is, he can't make it look like a Christian Dior necktie or a pair of silk Y fronts. And all this speculation seemed pretty stupid when I reached the second wardrobe, because that's where I found it. It wasn't disguised as a model of the Eiffel Tower or a "present from the Cote d'Azur"; it wasn't disguised at all. In the bottom of one of Antonio's small hand cases, the sort that one usually carries onto the aeroplane, were three gold bars. And that's exactly what they were, bars of gold, ingots, or whatever they're called. I lifted one gingerly from the bottom of the bag. God, it was heavy! Multiply it be three and one had to admire Antonio; I knew he was pretty strong in more ways than one, but to heft that bag around making it look as though it carried nothing more than a toothbrush and a pair of pajamas was going to take some doing. He would have to carry it as hand luggage, that way he could avoid having it weighed at the airport. And for Antonio, the celebrated Matador de Toros, Customs would prove no problem either out of Spain or into South America.

I replaced the ingot next to its companions and scampered back to bed. Shaving samples off gold bars wasn't something that one could do at dead of night with someone sleeping not ten feet away. But at least I had located the stuff, and tomorrow or the next day I would find time to do the necessary. Antonio grunted something as I grabbed my share of the sheet, but he didn't even wake up. Normally, after making love long and well, all I want to do is sleep, but this time I was so wide awake I doubted I would ever sleep again. I lay on my back for a while, contemplating the ceiling and wondering how much trouble Antonio was going to get into as a result of all this. And wondering why. Because he didn't need money. Apart from the fact that his family seemed to own two-thirds of Spain, he earned enough each Sunday afternoon to keep an average family in luxury for a year. But then, everyone aboard the *Maria* was filthy stinking rich; one of them must have passed the stuff to Antonio, because he certainly didn't have it before we came aboard. I suppose it was just a case of the more you've got, the more you want.

Mr. Blaser had been tight as a clam; just get the samples and turn them over to the first contact I could make. Then I was to extricate myself from the high-life and return to London. Whys and wherefores weren't my concern, apparently.

I tucked myself into the crook of Antonio's body and tried to persuade myself into sleep. But it still wouldn't come and after ten minutes the sweat created where our bodies touched became uncomfortable. I rolled clear again and continued my earlier contemplation of the ceiling. And, as is my wont on occasions like this, my reflective turn of mind carried me back beyond the present assignment, beyond even the previous ones; right back, in fact, to the time when Mr. Blaser entered my life.

Six months before meeting Mr. Blaser, my existence had been neat and well ordered. I was an air stewardess. We used to call ourselves hostesses, but the connotation smacked of night clubs and call girls; and while most of us enjoy night clubs, and some of us even moonlight in the latter profession, it wasn't the image we wished to put over to the travelling public. So there I was, free, white and twenty-one, a fully fledged, paid up, member-in-good-standing, air stewardess. Then I met this sweet, lovely man. He was captain on one of my early flights to Beirut. I fell like a ton of bricks, and our two day stopover in Beirut turned into a sort of pre-nuptial honeymoon. We were married very soon after, and three months later I was a widow. An accident, they had said; and I had believed them because I was like that in those days.

Then Mr. Blaser crept into my life. He convinced me that it had been no accident, and he presented me with a formidable pile of evidence to back up his claim. My husband had been murdered. The Touchfeather blood started to boil and I greedily accepted Mr. Blaser's offer to square the books. One thing led to another and, before I fully realised it, I was no longer a common or garden air stewardess, but a cross between a female James Bond and Mata Hari.

I still flew, but one day it would be for BOAC, the next Air India and the third Pan Am. This was what they call in the trade my "cover". Mind you, I'm a good air stewardess, too. I'm built right, everything evenly distributed; my bust is a little prominent perhaps, but I've never found that a particular disadvantage. My reddish hair and greenish eyes seem to go well with most of the airline uniforms I'm required to wear, and I can pour a martini, serve a meal, empty a sick bag, calm a frightened passenger and fend off a wandering hand, all at the same time if necessary.

Mr. Blaser started me off on nice simple jobs when I first entered his department; I suppose he hadn't wanted to scare me off before I found my sea legs. There were a couple of simple tailing jobs from London to Tokyo and back, via Sydney and Calcutta. I delivered some mysterious packages to equally mysterious individuals in Tangier, Beirut, Bombay and Rangoon.

Then, apparently satisfied, he sent me back to school where I was handed over to the care of a WRAC sergeant of vast proportions and strong lesbian inclinations. Bessie was her name and she was rather a sweety, actually. She taught me the six most horrendous things a girl can do to a man. I've only used two of them since and I still go quite cold when I recall the effect they had. She also taught me a great many other things which have got me out of trouble on more occasions than I can even remember. I've cause to be grateful to Bessie, wherever she is. She did try to teach me the joys of lesbianism as well but, while I have dabbled – I'll try anything once – it isn't really my speed at all.

What I really mean is that I like a man involved somewhere and, provided I am equally involved, as frequently as possible. I don't go along with that theory about men needing it more than women. Most women need it just as much, but they're better equipped mentally to control themselves if they're not getting it. Being a freelance air stewardess has its advantages: one gets to meet a vast number of attractive men, with the added bonus that, if one is careful geographically, there's very little chance that they'll trip over each other.

Not being a greedy girl, I make do with three on a semipermanent basis. One of them is the airport manager in one of the South American countries; another is a flight captain on the New York-Los Angeles run; and my home number is just a nice man who sells motor cars and considers a trip to the Isle of Wight as foreign travel. They're all nice men, and I suppose I'm a little in love with all three of them. No doubt all three would marry me if I gave them the faintest encouragement, but marriage I can do without at the moment. Besides, working for Mr. Blaser, I'd have made a helluva fine wife. And, strange as it may sound, I actually enjoy working for him. It has its drawbacks of course; like the time I was locked in an Italian cellar with two crazy American hoods who were making patterns all over me with lighted cigarettes, but they're both dead now and there's not much point in bearing grudges.

In any event, such situations I have learned to relegate to the area of occupational hazards, and the drawbacks are amply compensated for by the enormous satisfaction I get from a job well done. And I am good at my job. Fortunately I don't need Mr. Blaser to tell me so, because he never says a word except to criticize. But I usually accomplish what I set out to do, and up to now I've managed to stay in one piece. I have scars, of course, but you can get scarred from knocking over a frying pan, or banging your foot on the vacuum cleaner. All in all, I am a pretty well adjusted girl who enjoys her work and does it well. I'm not overly modest either, but you will have probably gathered that.

I drifted off to sleep about four a.m. so I was a bit miffed when Antonio woke me up at ten-thirty. Then I realised why he had awakened me, and it was alright again. We made soft, gentle love most of the morning and probably would have gone through the best part of the afternoon as well, except that the engines stopped suddenly. Antonio tottered over to the window and looked out.

"Where are we?" I asked from the bed.

He came back towards me shrugging. "Everywhere looks the same at sea." he said. He climbed back into bed.

"Let's go ashore for lunch," I said.

"You're all I want to eat right now," he said, reaching for me again. He really was the most marvelous lover. His body was hard and lean and, if one discounted the scars of his profession, each one looking dramatic enough to have killed six ordinary men, he was also very beautiful. I felt a rush of tenderness towards him and he started nuzzling me gently, driving me right up the wall. If that was how he wanted to take his lunch, who was I to argue? I rolled myself around and joined the feast.

Afterwards we dozed off again, and I woke up half an hour later still in his arms. He smelled warm and very sexy. I'm a great one for smells as long as they're clean and, lying there with him sleeping all over me, I'm damned if I didn't start to turn on again. Enough Katy, I thought, this is ridiculous. I slid away from him gently and padded over to the bathroom where I had a quick shower and slipped into a bikini. Then I tip-toed back into the stateroom. He was still asleep. I planted a little kiss on his bare backside and went up on deck, feeling as warm towards him as I had towards anyone for a long, long time. This, of course, exposes an essential flaw in my makeup; one that I have tried to suppress, but which every now and then rears its ugly head inconveniently. The flaw is simply that I am still able to become personally involved with people I have no business to. Mr. Blaser had made it very clear that, should things go wrong on this job, I was expected to do something about removing Antonio from the scene permanently. I suppose, if it came to the crunch, I *could* do it, but it would keep me awake nights for at least a week.

The deck was as hot underfoot as the sun was overhead, the dry, flat heat of the Mediterranean. I love the South of France; I suppose you could call me a France-ophile (as opposed to a Francophile). Gary Brian was the only one of my fellow guests present. He had a large drink in his hand and a jaundiced look in his eyes. I sat in the chair next to him and ordered a champagne orange from the steward who had appeared beside me instantly.

"Godawful trip, darling," Gary said for openers.

"I'm having a ball."

"I'm not surprised," he said. Then he leaned forward. "I suppose there's no chance you might get tired of your beautiful bullfighter?"

"By him, not of him," I said, a little smugly.

He relaxed in his chair. "It figured that way," he said without rancour. "Godawful trip."

"Why don't you go ashore?" As soon as I had come up on deck, I had recognised that we were lying off La Siesta at Antibes. I knew the place well. "You're bound to get lucky there."

"Too risky, sweety. Before I get involved I've got to inspect the pedigree. Vulnerable, that's my problem."

"Once bitten?" I asked, rather liking him.

He gave me a wicked grin, the one that had formed queues outside more cinemas than I have had hot dinners. "More than once sweety. Delicious."

"Antonio's not right for you, anyway," I said.

"I can see that by the bags under your eyes. I'll be alright once we get to St. Tropez. I have my contacts there. But that's a couple of days away."

"Why don't you go ashore and drive there? It only takes an hour. You can pick up the boat again when we arrive."

He gave the suggestion a moment of quiet thought, then got to his feet abruptly. "Brilliant, darling. I'll see you on Thursday. Make my apologies." He loped off to find a boat to take him ashore. I felt I'd done him a big favour he looked so happy.

The steward brought me my drink a moment later. Not just a glass, of course, but a bottle of Dom Perignon in a silver ice bucket, and a beautiful cut glass jug of fresh orange juice. He opened the champagne immaculately, tipped ice out of the glass, and poured my breakfast, half champagne, half orange juice. Then he stood respectfully while I tasted it.

"*Formidable,*" I said. He bowed and disappeared as quietly and as efficiently as everything else on this floating palace. A word about the *Maria:* everyone has heard of the *Christina;* well add an extra quarter of a million pounds and you've got the *Maria.* It is impossible to describe the indescribable, so there is no point in wasting my time trying. I took another sip of my drink. My God, Katy, this is the life, I thought. I'd had my share of luxury since working for Mr. Blaser, but there was usually something pretty nasty lurking in the vicinity; something I had just done, or was about to do. But in this case I was required to harm no-one; a simple two minutes alone in our stateroom; a contact in St. Tropez two days from now, and that was that. In the meantime, eat, drink and make love. Life was very good and I raised my glass in a silent toast to Mr. Blaser. Perhaps it was that which did it; one shouldn't provoke the deities and Mr. Blaser is the only deity I know personally. If I'd kept my mouth shut and just drunk my champagne, perhaps things wouldn't have gone as wrong as they sure in hell did.

The other guests drifted back to the boat about five-thirty. They'd had too much food, sun and booze and looked a pretty bedraggled lot; all except the textile man's three companions who looked as cool as three glasses of iced lager, complete to the frosting on the outside. And Galipolodopolo looked as smooth as he ever did. He must have been at least sixty years old, but he looked a well preserved fifty, and very dishy if one liked one's men short, dark and Greek. Personally I don't, but if the world's press were even half way accurate, there were plenty who did. His name had been linked with every international beauty on the scene for the past fifteen years, and this notwithstanding the fact that he had been married all that time. Much to my surprise he came over and sat down next to me while everyone else staggered below to sleep off the day.

"I'm sorry you weren't able to join us for lunch," he said.

I pointed to the remains of the caviar the steward had brought me. "I was well taken care of."

He smiled showing his immaculate teeth. "I'm glad. And Antonio?"

"Still sleeping."

"I envy the ability of the young to sleep," he said. "If I manage more than four hours out of each twenty-four, I consider myself lucky. You are a very beautiful girl, Katherine."

This caught me way off guard on two counts; first he tucked the phrase onto the end of his sentence without pause or change of tone; and second, I wasn't even aware that he knew my name. We had been introduced, of course, when we first came aboard, but that had been the sum total of our acquaintance to date.

"Thank you," I said and, believe it or not, I started to blush. I mean, I know I'm quite attractive and all that, but when one of the richest men in the world tells you you're beautiful...well, it just gets to a girl where it matters.

"I would like to make love to you," he said, still without changing his tone. The blush, which had started to recede, now reblossomed like the rising sun, and for a moment I really couldn't think of anything to say. Then I did the unpardonable: I giggled; not chuckled or laughed, but giggled like an embarrassed schoolgirl. His eyes didn't go cold because they were always that way; in fact, his expression didn't change one iota. He looked at me steadily for a few seconds, then he got to his feet. "Let me know when, Katherine," he said, and walked away without a backward glance.

Not let me know "if", but let me know "when". Antonio would probably run him through with his *espada* if I told him. But then again, he probably wouldn't. The group of people I was now moving with passed their girlfriends round like cigarettes, and all of a sudden I decided I didn't care as much for the highlife as I had at first thought. Galipolodopolo's remark had even cast a shadow over my relationship with Antonio. But it was just as well I suppose; I had started to forget my position in the whole affair. I was here to work, so the best thing I could do would be to get the work done and get out of here while my sense of values was still intact. And, as though to help me on may way, Antonio came on deck at that moment, looking quite beautiful in his swimming trunks and with a towel slung over his shoulders. He came over to join me.

"I woke up and you weren't there," he said.

"I'm resting up."

He reached out and gently squeezed one of my nipples through my bikini bra. I felt it creep to attention. "I'll have a swim and then we'll find out how much good your rest has done you. Alright?"

I nodded. "I'll go down and make myself sexy."

"Twenty minutes," he said. "Then I'll make you sexy."

"You already have," I said, removing his hand gently.

I watched him move over to the deck rail. He threw his towel onto the deck, jumped lightly onto the rail, posed for a brief moment, and then dived overboard into the incredible blue of the sea. There was a pool on board, of course, but Antonio was a long distance swimmer; he didn't believe in paddling about splashing water on each other. He liked plenty of space and I knew he would swim at least half a mile from the boat before turning back. That gave me the twenty minutes he had promised with a probable fifteen more on top. I got to my feet and went below.

Gold: a dense, bright yellow metal; symbol Au; atomic number 79; atomic weight 197.2. The dossier handed to me by Mr. Blaser had started out like that. Then it had gone on for sixty-two closely typed pages which, if I had read and understood them, would probably have told me more about the stuff than anyone needs to know. As it was, I had skimmed through it, missing out the parts that seemed too complicated, comprising about two thirds of the report, but at the end I still knew more about gold than anyone not intimately connected with the stuff. And I think it was just bloody mindedness on Mr. Blaser's part making me read it anyway, because all I had to do was to take the samples. I wasn't going to be the one who had to analyse them.

The stateroom struck very cold as I came down from the deck. I turned down the air conditioner and wrapped myself in a towelling robe. From my manicure case I produced a small, scalpel type knife which had been provided by the department. Had anyone been interested in my manicure case, the knife *could* have been something to do with nail paring or cuticle cutting; but in fact it was as sharp as a razor and God knows how many times tougher. It would cut gold like an ordinary knife cuts butter, I had been told. I hadn't believed it particularly, but now was the time to find out.

I removed one of the gold bars from Antonio's case and carried it over to the light. I examined it carefully for any markings, but it was as clean as a whistle. I had been told to expect none but to make sure just in case. Then I took the knife and placing the blade flat along the base of the gold bar, I drew it towards me. Whoever had designed the knife, knew his job. There was a fractional curve along the flatness of the blade, invisible to the naked eye. But this curve sliced a sliver of gold from the base of the bar thinner than a cigarette paper. I drew the knife towards me half an inch, then relaxed the pressure slightly. As I did this, the wafer of gold was detached. Holding my breath in case I blew it away, I picked it up with a pair of eyebrow tweezers and slipped it into a small plastic envelope. It was so thin that when I held it up to the light I could see through the gold as well. I examined the gold bar minutely before I replaced it. A microscope might have shown where I had removed my sample, but you certainly couldn't see anything with the naked eye; at least, I couldn't.

I repeated the whole business with the other two bars, replacing each one exactly where I had found it. The knife and the plastic envelope I replaced in my manicure set, the envelope slipping neatly between the lining and the case. And that was it. That was what I had travelled half way round the world for. All that remained was to pass it to a contact in St. Tropez. If for any reason we didn't go to St. Tropez, then the contact would be made at the first port of call we *did* make. And then Katy could go home. But that was two days away which meant that I had forty-eight more hours of the high-life, if I could stand the pace.

I went to the bathroom, stripped off and showered. Then I settled back on the bed to wait for Antonio to finish his swim and get down to work again. I must have dozed off, because when I next became aware of the time, more than an hour had passed, and I was very cold. I got up, turned the air conditioner off altogether and, pulling on a pair of slacks and a sweater, I went up on deck to find out what had happened to my bullfighter.

There was no-one around, which wasn't surprising when one remembered the condition they had all been in when they returned from lunch. I didn't expect any of that lot to put in an appearance before nine p.m. at the earliest, if then. The sun was going down in a molten sky behind the old fort and the sea was as calm and flat as a sheet of polished glass. Two miles away a speedboat swept out from behind the Cap, heading across towards Nice, but apart from that nothing moved except for the cars just visible on the road backing the long stretch of stony beach. Antonio's towel was still where he had dropped it before going in for his swim. Quite suddenly, cold as I had been, I became even colder. I rang the bell for the steward who appeared as though he had been waiting on tenterhooks all day for this summons.

"Have you seen Senor Fuentes?"

He shook his head. "No Madame."

I thought about it for a moment. "Would you tell the Captain I'd like to see him," I said.

He bowed and disappeared, leaving me looking out to sea, searching for I know not what. The Captain, a Greek of indeterminate age and antecedents, joined me in less than a minute.

"I know this may sound silly." I said. "But I think we"ve lost Senor Fuentes."

"Lost?"

"He went for a swim. He doesn't seen to have returned."

"How long ago?" Not much concern yet.

"Over an hour." A little concern now.

"What makes you think he hasn't come back on board?"

I pointed to Antonio's towel. "It's exactly where he left it when he dived in."

The Captain digested this for a moment, then he saluted politely and walked quietly away.

I remained where I was while the boat was searched, and I remained there when the others came up on deck to watch the crew launch the two speedboats. I was still there two hours later when Antonio's lifeless body was carried back on board.

TWO

"You seem to have mismanaged the whole affair abominably, Miss Touchfeather," said Mr. Blaser.

"Yes, sir."

"A perfectly simple task which could have been carried out by a disinterested girl guide. And what do you do?"

"I ball it up, sir."

He frowned, the lines in his already weather-beaten face becoming positively canyon like. "If I thought for one moment that you were treating this affair with anything but deadly seriousness, I would take you off duties and bury you so deep you'd never emerge again." He wasn't given to idle threats; but then neither was I trying to be facetious.

I *had* balled it up, and that's all there was to it. He settled back in his chair. "Perhaps I have missed something, Miss Touchfeather," he said. "Shall we go over the whole thing once more?"

He had missed nothing, but we went over it again anyway.

Antonio had been fetched aboard and laid out on the deck. Resuscitation had been attempted in the speedboat as soon as he had been dragged from the water. But he was long dead and, once he was lifted aboard the *Maria,* all they did was to spread a blanket over him and wait for the arrival of the police who had been summoned by ship to shore telephone. My fellow passengers grew very bored very quickly, and after a short time I was the only one of us who remained with Antonio. Galipolodopolo had tried to talk me into going below, but I had shaken my head through a mist of tears and he had diplomatically left me to wallow in my misery.

The police arrived half an hour later. They asked me some preliminary questions and we were about to get down to serious business when the very junior man in charge took a look at the passenger list. He wilted visibly and disappeared into the radio shack for a few minutes. When he re-emerged he walked as though on broken glass, taking care not to step on any of the very influential toes the *Maria* abounded with. Very politely he asked the Captain if he would ask Mr. Galipolodopolo if he would mind terribly putting into Nice for a short time. He didn't mind, and that's where we went.

Someone on board had got a big mouth for, when we arrived an hour later, there were enough people on the quay to seriously disrupt the traffic. We were all requested to remain aboard, and Antonio's body was carried ashore and driven off in an ambulance. A strong police guard was put on the gangway to stop unwelcome visitors from overrunning us and, a few minutes after we docked, a full blown Chief Inspector lumbered aboard, looking like a cross between Maigret and Robespierre. We were all questioned as the Inspector endeavoured to put together the facts. Not that there was much problem. Antonio had gone for a swim, something had happened, and he had drowned; all very unfortunate, but straightforward.

Half an hour after the Inspector came aboard, the Captain informed him that Mr. Galipolodopolo wished to take the *Maria* out of Nice as soon as possible and would the Inspector kindly remove his finger, as Mr. Galipolodopolo didn't like to be kept waiting. The Inspector didn't like to be talked to in this fashion and, naturally enough, he became a little stroppy. But the poor dear man didn't stand a chance; within fifteen minutes there arrived on board a Frenchman with diplomatic corps written all over him. He was accompanied by a Superintendent of police and a man from the Mayor's office. There was a fourth man, too, who claimed to be a junior police officer, but who I knew was no such thing. I'd met him before a couple of times and, while he may have appeared to work for the Nice police department, he also worked for the Deuxième Bureau, the CIA, MI5, 6 and 7 and, for all I knew, the NKVD and KGB as well. He also worked on and off for Mr. Blaser, which is why I recognised him.

While the heavy guns were attacking the Chief Inspector, beating him over the head with his pension, my man managed to get it across to me that I was expected to leave the boat there and then. And that's exactly what I did do. I started to cry all over again. The first time had been when Antonio had been lifted aboard, and that had been for real. This time I squeezed a few tears and managed a minor attack of hysterics. Shouting that I couldn't bear to remain aboard for another second, I staggered ashore. Unfortunately, I forgot to take my luggage with me. And in my luggage, of course, reposed the object of the whole exercise, my gold samples.

"Perhaps you had too much sun," said Mr. Blaser.

"Yes, sir." I felt the less said the better at this stage.

"Have you *no* excuses?"

I did have a slender one and I thought that here was as good a time as any to try it out. "It would have been alright if you hadn't recalled me."

"I recalled you for the simple reason I assumed the whole venture had aborted."

"Why?"

"Your instructions were that if you got into trouble you were to … dispose of the man. I assumed that was what you had done. I merely wanted to get you out of the predicament I thought you had got yourself into."

That was nice of him, I thought.

"With you dead or incapacitated," he continued, "I would have to have assigned someone else to the affair, and at this moment there is no-one else available."

So up you too, I thought. But I threw him a crumb. "Well I didn't kill Antonio," I said. "Someone else did."

He didn't bat an eyelid.

"The Coroner in Nice describes it as death by drowning."

"And no doubt that's what it was," I said. "But there is more than one way to skin a cat."

"Stop being obtuse, Miss Touchfeather."

"Sorry, sir. There was a frogman lurking around."

I had been on deck when the speedboats had left to search for Antonio and, because I'm trained for such trivialities, I had noticed something that none of my fellow passengers had. The boats had left with four crew members apiece; one of them had returned with five. Later, on our way to Nice, I had taken a quick look into this boat, which had been hoisted back on deck. Under the rear seat squab had been a frogman's suit, and it was still wet.

"You are suggesting that someone from the *Maria* swam out after this man and deliberately drowned him?"

"I'm not suggesting anything, sir. I'm just telling you want I saw."

"Assumptions?"

"As long as you're asking, sir, yes, I do think someone from the *Maria* drowned Antonio. He was a magnificent swimmer and in perfect physical health. There can be no other explanation."

"Reason?"

"You've never told me what this is about, so how can I be expected to come up with a reason?" This was a little bold of me but, after all, he had asked. He digested this for a moment, making up his mind whether to tell me anything or not.

"Mmm," he said, after a few seconds. I waited, and after another lengthy pause, he said "Mmm" again. Finally he dragged himself back to awareness of me.

"Could you get back on board?"

"The *Maria?*"

He nodded.

"If it's the gold samples you're worried about, surely the easy thing to do would be to have my luggage picked up at their next port of call?"

"Answer my question, please, Miss Touchfeather."

I thought about Galipolodopolo. "Tell me when Katherine" he had said. He wasn't bad looking; and he *was* one of the richest men in the world; and I badly wanted to have a go at someone for Antonio; and Mr. Blaser was the boss.

"Yes, sir," I said.

"When?"

"I'll have to send a cable."

"Send it."

"From Nice. That's where I'm supposed to be."

"Miss Moody will take care of it."

"Then I've got to be invited. " I added.

"See that you are," said Mr. Blaser, and that seemed to be that.

Miss Moody took down my cable for me. She is Mr. Blaser's secretary-cum-right hand; a little grey haired body of indeterminate age who never smiles. This isn't because she is unfriendly, but she possesses a very badly fitting set of false teeth which on occasions have been known to drop out in her lap. So she tries to keep her mouth shut at all times, talking as much as possible through her nose.

"You look lovely and brown," she said, after dispatching my cable through the Nice office. I liked Miss Moody. Apart from the fact that she usually says something nice to me, she is the person responsible for checking my expenses and she has been known to pass items that Mr. Blaser didn't even know existed.

She had looked a little puzzled when I dictated the cable, but she hadn't said a word as she took it down. I asked her to take a copy in to Mr. Blaser. Let him work that one out, I thought.

GALIPOLODOPOLO SS MARIA C/O GALIPOLODOPOLO ATHENS WHEN STOP WHERE QUERY KATHERINE

Galipolodopolo would get it even if Mr. Blaser didn't. And I hied me to the South of France once more.

The Hotel Byblos at St. Tropez is truly a wondrous place. It's about the best hotel for a hundred miles in any direction but, even if it wasn't, it would still be my idea of heaven. It is a low, rambling place, cool and faintly Eastern in design, with all the luxuries of the West thrown in. There are beautifully tiled courtyards, small arches leading to enchanting little hideaways, and a split level bar that perches out over the swimming pool. The service is impeccable, with just the right mixture of the personal and impersonal. Film stars stay there, so do film producers; millionaires stay there either *en famille* or most definitely *sans famille;* the only qualification the Byblos makes of its guests is that they be rich; it provides the best that money can buy and you need plenty of money to buy it. But I was a guest of Galipolodopolo, and I received the bridal suite and the royal treatment. A reply to my telegram had been phoned through from Nice within two hours of sending mine.

TOUCHFEATHER NEGRESCO NICE.
SAINT TROPEZ THURSDAY WAIT AT BYBLOS CON-
STANTIN

As I wasn't supposed to have any luggage, I caught the first plane back to Nice. There I checked into the Negresco, arranged to have a bill falsified and back dated two days, and promptly checked out again. I hired a car and drove to St. Tropez. At the Byblos I was greeted like the Queen of Sheba. I was informed deferentially that instructions had been given that I was to buy anything I wanted in the town and charge it to my hotel bill. Never having been one to miss an opportunity, and mindful of my role as that of a jet set courtesan who would have no scruples in that direction, I trotted down to the town and spent a fortune on clothes I would probably never wear, but which were fun to have lying around. This was Wednesday and the *Maria* wasn't expected until the next day. I wasn't supposed to know anyone in St. Tropez, so I was agreeably surprised when my phone rang at six o'clock, just about cocktail time. It was Gary Brian.

"Katy, darling. I heard you were in town. Are you in mourning?"

"Not particularly."

"Oh, the fickleness of youth. Meet you in the bar in ten minutes. I've something to show you."

The something turned out to be the most beautiful boy I have ever seen. His name was Gaston and he was tall, willowy, with coal black hair and light blue eyes and a mouth to send anyone wild. He smiled gently at me as Gary introduced us and took my hand in his. He had a grip like a steel trap and then, as he bent low over my hand, he tickled my palm with the tip of his forefinger. Poor Gary, I thought; here was one pedigree he hadn't checked too carefully. But it turned out that Gaston did what he did for a living and, be it with male or female, he believed in giving value for money. Gary was ecstatic.

"It's all your doing, beloved," he told me. "It was your idea that I came here in the first place." Then he remembered suddenly that I'd had a personal tragedy, and he went all Hollywood on me. "What can I say, Katy? You poor, poor child! What you must be going through." and all that jazz. I stood it for a couple of minutes then I drew the line.

"I'm rejoining the *Maria* tomorrow," I said.

"Oh! Under whose auspices?"

"Constantin Galipolodopolo's."

He patted me on the head. "There's a brave girl," he said. "Clever, too."

And in truth I wasn't mourning any longer. Anger, yes; misery, no. Because, in my line of business, reflecting on the past is strictly for the birds. I had been fond of Antonio, yes; but I hadn't been in love with him. We had swung together and it had been simply marvelous. But now he was dead, and tomorrow was another day. We Touchfeathers are realists, if nothing else.

I had dinner with Gary and Gaston on the poolside patio of the hotel, where it seemed half St. Tropez had come to dine. All the women fancied Gary, all the men fancied me, and all the in-betweens fancied Gaston. We were the centre of attraction as everyone tried to work out what sort of arrangement we had going between the three of us – who had who while who did what. We were the best looking *ménage a trois* you ever did see, and I felt like the belle of fifteen different balls all at the same time.

Afterwards we went to *Les Caves du Roy,* the club built beneath the hotel where the noise was stupendous and the atmosphere stifling. Then we moved on to the *Voom Voom* and, later, the *Papagayo,* our party growing larger by the minute. It was half past five when we started back to the hotel. We were tottering along the quay playing hopscotch over the mooring ropes of the floating gin palaces that seem to spend their entire sea-going lives tied up in exotic ports, when Gary suddenly hove to.

"Ship ahoy!" he said.

I looked out to where he was pointing. Just outside the harbour bar, riding gently in a lazy swell, lay the *Maria.* Fun over, Katy, I thought. Back to business.

Gary opted out of rejoining the boat. Gaston couldn't or wouldn't get away and Gary decided that where Gaston stayed, he would stay, too. He sent a message out to the *Maria* and had his luggage brought ashore.

I travelled out to the Maria on the same speedboat that had carried Antonio's body and was delighted to find I didn't feel a thing.

Constantin Galipolodopolo was waiting for me at the top of the gangway. He kissed my hand elegantly and said how delighted he was to see me again, then turned me over to a steward who escorted me down to a stateroom. Not the same one used by Antonio and me, but one which had a connecting door to another stateroom; and it didn't take much working out to know where the owner's cabin was located. My luggage from the previous voyage had been transferred and I watched while the steward hung up and put away all the new stuff I had picked up yesterday. Then, as soon as he left, I made a beeline for my manicure case. My samples were still there.

"We still need those samples Miss Touchfeather," Mr. Blaser had said. "And the same arrangements will apply. There will be a contact waiting for you in each port you call at. As for this new business, if you have any information to pass, you will do so at the same time that you pass the samples,"

This new business was simply for me to find out as much as I could about Antonio's death. Not who killed him, because apparently that wasn't important; all that mattered were the reasons for his being murdered. And finally Mr. Blaser just had to tell me the details of the whole affair. He explained it to me once and, in case I hadn't got it, he explained it a second time.

He told me Galipolodopolo was engaged in smuggling gold. "So what?" I had replied. "Everybody smuggles gold these days." But it seemed that the gold that Constantin was shifting all round the globe had no business being in existence in the first place. The world supply of gold is kept under pretty tight control; the people whose job it is to know about such things keep accurate reports on how much gold is dug out of the ground; how and where it is refined; and what happens to it later. So much is used for jewelry, *objets d"art* and other trivialities; so much is returned to the ground from whence it came in innumerable vaults, banks, safe deposits, tin trunks and old boxes; so much is shipped back and forth between Governments trying to balance their budgets; and so much just disappears, God knows where. But, at all times, a check is kept on it to the nearest five or six million dollars' worth. In other words, it is known at any one time that there is umpty-four million dollars worth of gold floating around somewhere, and everyone is reasonably happy knowing more or less where it is.

But during the past couple of years the boys with their adding machines had started to get worried. It seemed there was no longer umpty-four million dollars' worth, but umpty-five or even six. And no-one knew where it was coming from. The Russians, notoriously tight-lipped normally, had been approached through tortuous channels to find out whether they were digging out more than usual, but it turned out that they were just as concerned as were our lot. They'd noticed it, too, and had wondered themselves. They were asked if they could make discreet enquiries from the Red Chinese, but Russia and Red China weren't talking any more and they had declined.

About here I had made one of my stupid remarks which I occasionally do, and which never fails to get up Mr. Blaser's nose.

"Surely," I had said. "The more gold there is, the better?"

He doesn't often actually snarl at me, but he did this time. He must have been getting it pretty strong from up top, I decided.

"Controls, Miss Touchfeather! We must have controls. Think for one moment what would happen if there was a sudden glut of gold."

I thought, and I must admit the idea sounded attractive.

"Chaos," said Mr. Blaser. "Absolute chaos. The monetary systems of the world would collapse." I hung my head, not quite knowing why. "International finance is a delicately balanced operation," he went on. "Our entire economy is built on gold. Flood the market with gold and gold becomes worthless. Now do you understand?" I didn't, but I let him go on. "Gold is appearing all over the world," he continued. "Gold which, to the best of our knowledge, doesn't exist. It has been mined and refined by people we know nothing about in a place we can't identify. It may be Red China, it may be one of the emergent African nations, it may be South American in origin, we just don't know. But we must find out. Right?"

"Yes, sir."

"That is why we want the samples that you idiotically forgot about. It may be that the analysts will be able to ascertain point of origin from the chemical properties. Gold dug up in Africa differs from gold dug up in Alaska. Most of the differences are refined out of the finished product, but we may be lucky." He offered me one of his wintry smiles which, if anything, are worse than his snarls. "If you'd had even half your wits about you, we would already have completed that phase of the operation, Miss Touchfeather."

"Yes, sir," I said.

There had been a little more. It seemed that Constantin Galipolodopolo had been tied into the whole thing somewhere along the line. On three occasions the pirate gold had been traced back as far as him. A distributor he most certainly was; my job was to try to find out if he was anything more and, if he wasn't, to find out who the hell was. Antonio must have been some sort of courier, carrying gold into South America or Mexico or Spain. Being no end of a celebrity in bullfighting countries, he was never likely to have trouble with customs, so he was ideal for the job. The only point that still puzzled me as far as Antonio was concerned, was why someone as rich and successful as he would even have bothered. I mentioned this to Mr. Blaser.

"Mr. Galipolodopolo is also rich and successful, Miss Touchfeather. Much more so than your late friend who fought cows for a living." And that had been that.

Now here I was, a member of the jet set once more, and about to be seduced by one of the richest men in the world. My seduction was obviously going to take place on the high seas because, before I had been in my stateroom for ten minutes, I felt the engines start up and we were under way again. I mooned around the stateroom for another half hour, then I decided that I had better put in some sort of appearance for the benefit of my fellow passengers. It would be as well to set the record straight as far as they were concerned as soon as possible. I climbed into a bikini and, wearing one of the toweling robes supplied by the *Maria,* I wandered up on deck. With the rather obvious exception of Mrs. Galipolodopolo, they were all there, all except Constantin. Sir Roger, the Count, the Countess and the textile magnate were playing bridge on the aft deck; the other ladies were engaged in oiling themselves, swimming in the pool and generally doing what everyone does on a million pound yacht in the middle of the Mediterranean. Sir Roger's little bird flashed me a glacial smile; the three companions of the Frenchman didn't even bother to do that. They formed a complete entity in themselves; their lack of communication with the rest of us was complete. They would murmur quietly among themselves and only address an outsider with a request to pass the salt or pepper. Trying to work out what went on between the three of them and their lord and master once they were all tucked away in their communal stateroom, was something that had occupied everyone else on board at one time or another.

I borrowed some sunoil from Sir Roger's lady friend, desperately trying to remember her name. She was exceedingly frosty at first, until I casually mentioned that I had rejoined the party at the request of our host. After that she started to blossom. Poor dear, she had been worried that I might be after the title that she was angling for. Looking across at Sir Roger, it could only have been the title. He was rich, admittedly, but it all ended there. He was a shade under six foot tall, with sandy coloured hair, a minimal chin and red-rimmed pale grey eyes; he possessed very prominent teeth which weren't particularly clean, and when he talked he managed to drench you before he had squeezed out two sentences. He was perhaps the only man on board who didn't fit the pattern. The French textile man was a hard, cruel, barrel-shaped man who had hacked his own way to the top; the Count was smooth and bland and as tough as granite; Constantin, we all knew about. But Sir Roger ... I just couldn't see it at all. I decided that he was along for window dressing, like Gary Brian had been.

We lolled away the afternoon, becoming stupefied by the sun. About four p.m. I thought I heard a speedboat starting up somewhere nearby, but I wasn't paying much attention and nobody else seemed to bother, so it made no real impression. Then at five o"clock I decided that I'd had enough sun for one day and staggered down to my stateroom for a bath and a nap before the evening's festivities. As I opened the door, the first thing I saw was an envelope lying on my bed, propped up against the pillow. It was addressed simply to Katherine. I opened and read it.

Katherine my dear,

A thousand apologies, but business has dragged me away. I will be returning to the *Maria* at Capri in two days time. Until then, anything you want, just ask.

Constantin.

So my honour was to remain intact for at least another forty-eight hours. I have to admit, I wasn't sorry. I hadn't been looking forward to going to bed with Constantin Galipolodopolo; not that I doubted for a moment he was very adept in that area, but I really do prefer to choose my own lovers rather than have Mr. Blaser do it for me.

So Capri was going to be our next port of call. No doubt Mr. Blaser already knew about it and was arranging my contact there.

I spent half a day poking around and asking questions of any member of the crew who would stand still long enough to talk to me. One never knew, perhaps I would turn up new information on the death of Antonio. But they were either very well trained or extremely stupid, because nobody knew anything. So now I had nothing to do except enjoy myself. But somehow without Antonio, the gilt seemed to have worn off the jet set bit and, as I bathed and tried to decide what I was going to wear for dinner, all I could see before me was two days of stupefying boredom.

And that's how it turned out. In fact I spent most of the time in my stateroom, sleeping. I had my meals sent in, dispatching apologies to my fellow guests. They probably imagined that I was heartbroken that Constantin had deserted me as soon as I came back on board and, apart from fighting off the Count once, when he took it upon himself to come into the stateroom to enquire about my health, nothing else happened to break the monotony until we reached Capri.

We dropped anchor at six o"clock on the evening of the second day and everyone immediately piled shore. I accompanied them, and we climbed up to the main square where two tables had been commandeered for us, to take care of the cocktail hour. As always, the arrangements had been impeccable, our arrival having been announced and prepared for. Within seconds of sitting down the booze was flowing like water and nothing to pay, of course.

The evening promenade in Capri is a sight to behold. It seems that the entire island moves into the main square, there to see and be seen. There are the boys and girls, the boys and boys and the girls and girls. There are the middle-aged, trying to recapture something; and the downright old who gave up trying to recapture it years ago and now while away their lives in sorrowful reminiscing. There are the starlets and the film men, the has-beens and the never-weres; there are the Italians and the Germans and Scandinavians, a few French and practically no English. And there are the Americans, the individual tourists and their package counterparts, the women with blue hair and the men in Bermuda shorts, festooned with Japanese cameras. And, of course, there is my contact whoever and wherever he is.

But it turned out that I didn't have to worry. I spotted him almost at the same time as he spotted me. It was an old friend, Signor Bertelli, who ran Mr. Blaser's Rome operation. He was sitting at a table a few yards from ours, sharing it with a group of young people who were chattering among themselves in Swedish. Here then was my contact. It would be interesting to see how he would go about it. Perhaps he would signal for me to go to the ladies, or some-such; perhaps he would follow us later and try to waylay me in a dark alley. But whatever he decided to do, I knew it would be efficient. Because beneath the appearance of a lightweight de Sica, Bertelli was solid steel. He had been a founder member of the Italian Resistance during the war and, if the records were accurate, he had done some things to make even my hair curl. So I sat back and waited for him to make his play.

I didn't have to wait long. He finished his drink, left some money and, getting to his feet, he started to thread his way through the tables, no easy feat considering how closely packed they were. Then came the acting bit. He pretended to see me for the first time, then he did a double take as he looked again. A smile came over his face and he changed direction and started to plough his way towards our table. He started speaking while he was still a good ten feet away, oozing Italian over everyone.

"Miss Touchfeather! Dear, dear Katherine! Is it really you? Can it be you? Dear, dear Katherine…"

Everyone was looking at him by now, and by everyone I don't just mean my party, but practically the entire square.

"Dear sweet Miss Touchfeather… Katherine! After all this time. Say it's you… Say you remember me…"

Tripping over a pair of legs he finished up practically in my lap, grabbing my hand and then kissing it as though his very life depended on it.

"Signor Bertelli!" I said, trying to appear surprised, which wasn't all that difficult after watching his performance. "How nice to see you again."

He looked crestfallen. "Umberto, please! Not Signor Bertelli! After all we have been to each other, it must be Umberto."

The others were agog, and even I was beginning to think he was piling it on a bit thick.

"It's been a long time, Umberto," I said, trying to drag his feet back onto the ground.

"Too long, dear Katherine… Katy… Dear, dear Katy!"

"I'd like you to meet my friends," I said, wanting to step out of the blinding limelight that his entrance had switched on. Immediately he released my hand and stood to attention.

"Signor Umberto Bertelli," he said, damn near clicking his heels. I floated through the names I could remember, stumbling a little over the textile man's three companions. But no-one seemed to notice unduly. Then Bertelli took over once more, which was just as well, because I hadn't the faintest idea how to play it.

His face crumpled suddenly. "You deserted me, Katherine. You left me without a word." He looked at the others. "She left me without a word… at dead of night. I wake up one morning and she is gone… all her luggage is gone… I am devastated."

He looked back at me. "Why Katherine? Why did you do it?" I thought about here that I had better take a hand.

"Please, Umberto!" I said. "Not here."

"Not here? Why not here? Are you ashamed? Tell me truly, are you ashamed?"

"Please, Umberto, that's enough."

"You are ashamed! I know it! You are ashamed of what you did to Umberto Bertelli."

I got to my feet and turned to the others. "Please excuse us," I said. "I'll see you back on board." I took Bertelli's arm but he was enjoying himself far too much to leave without a final flourish.

"On board? On board what? What are you on board?"

"Please, Umberto..." I pleaded, practically dragging him away. And finally he decided that he'd had his fun.

"We will talk Katherine, you and I." He turned to the others. "You will excuse us, please." He bowed once more; then allowed me to drag him away.

We found a quiet little cafe away from the square where we chose a table at the back, away from any chance of being overheard.

"What the bloody hell was all that about?" I said.

He smiled. "Good?"

"It'll take me a week to explain it all," I said. "Especially as I've got to make everything up."

"But it could have been, Miss Touchfeather. It could have been," he said, reaching for my hand again. He never failed to make a pass at me. I think he did so because he felt that as an Italian it was expected of him, a matter of national honour. I retrieved my hand quickly.

"We're alone Signor Bertelli There's no more need for acting."

"I am not acting," he said, breathing heavily.

"Yes, you are," I said. "And if you don't stop, I shall tell Mr. Blaser." This didn't seem to deter him unduly, so I added my topper. "And Signora Bertelli as well." That stopped him dead as it always did, and he immediately became very businesslike.

"You have the samples?" I took them from my purse and passed them to him beneath the table. He slipped them into his pocket without even looking. "And information?" he asked.

"No information."

"Mr. Blaser will not be pleased."

"Tell Mr. Blaser that Galipolodopolo hasn't been around since we left St. Tropez. He's supposed to be rejoining us here."

"Then you will go to bed with him."

I put on my icy expression. "That's none of your business, Signor Bertelli," I said.

He looked at me steadily for a brief moment, his eyes calculating and shrewd. Then he nodded.

"You are right, Katherine. It is none of my business. But one day, one fine day..."

"Don't hold your breath," I said.

He smiled at me. "Have fun, Miss Touchfeather," he said, and a moment later he was gone.

We all had dinner ashore that evening. Constantin still hadn't turned up when we went back to the boat to change, but dinner had been arranged at one of the best restaurants and we were all ferried there in taxis. Nobody mentioned the encounter in the square, which was just as well because I hadn't quite got my story worked out. Sir Roger's bird looked at me a little slant-eyed a couple of times during the evening, wondering I suppose whether there would be any profit in mentioning it to Constantin, but that was all. I'd found out her name by now, it was Deirdre as if it could have been anything else. I decided that I hoped Sir Roger would pop the question soon; they deserved each other.

After dinner the others decided to go dancing. I begged off and walked back to the boat alone, hoping that Constantin still hadn't put in an appearance. He hadn't, and by midnight I was tucked up safe, sound and alone. Mr. Blaser had told me to hang around a bit after passing the samples, so nobody would get suspicious by my taking off in a hurry. I was still wondering just how long I was going to have to hang around when I drifted off to sleep.

The steward brought me my breakfast the following morning at nine o"clock, which was a bit inconsiderate of him, because I hadn't ordered any breakfast. There was a small note on the tray saying would I please see the Captain at my earliest convenience, and in any event before ten o'clock.

The Captain was in his cabin when I went to see him. He was very polite and most apologetic. Mr. Galipolodopolo had telephoned the previous night; unfortunately he was unable to rejoin the *Maria* at this time and, that being the case, was sure that Miss Touchfeather would understand that there was little point in her remaining on board. The steward was already packing my things, a speedboat was waiting to take me across the bay to Naples, and here was a first class one-way ticket from Naples to London. It's been very pleasant, see you again sometime.

Two hours later I was at Naples airport. I managed to bung off a cable to Mr. Blaser telling him I was homeward bound, and two hours after that I was in London.

When I fly into London Airport I usually check at the office Mr. Blaser keeps there to see if there are any messages or instructions; also to bum a lift into town. That was my intention this time. I came through immigration and out into the customs hall. I was waiting for my bags to come up when a porter sidled up to me.

"Porter, Miss?"

I agreed that I needed a porter and I identified my bags for him as the conveyor regurgitated them onto the turntable. He collected them all and I headed over towards the green customs exit.

"This way, Miss," said my porter, heading towards one of the red exits. "It'll be quicker."

It wouldn't be quicker, but I knew he must have his reasons, so I followed him to the end bench. There I waited behind a young couple who were frantically declaring all their cigarettes and duty-free liquor in the vain hope that the inspector would overlook the camera they had bought as well. He didn't, and I waited patiently while the invoice was made out and the duty paid. Then it was my turn.

"Have you read this?" said the Inspector, shoving the board at me. I said I had read it.

"Have you anything to declare?"

"No," I said, looking him straight in the eye.

"Would you open that one," he said, pointing to the case holding all the gear I had bought in St. Tropez. I opened it and waited while he rummaged through it, carefully checking all the St. Tropez labels in the dresses. Then he closed the case, snapping it shut.

"Thank you," he said. He looked past me at the porter who was still hovering. "You may take the lady's cases to the bus."

The porter nodded, gathered up the cases, and I followed him out. A nod is as good as a wink they say and, if someone wanted me to take the bus, that was it. I climbed aboard, paid my seven shillings, and forty minutes later I was deposited at the West London Air Terminal. There I hailed a taxi and twenty minutes after that I was home in my own little pad.

The place smelt musty with disuse and the first thing I did was to go round and open all the windows in the sitting-room. Then I moved through into the bedroom and noticed imme-diately that the cleaners had delivered back to me my Iberian uniform. This was a little odd because, apart from the one trip I had made with Antonio, I hadn't flown that airline for months and the uniform I'd been wearing on that particular occasion I'd mislaid somewhere in Madrid.

I opened the suitcase that had interested the Customs Inspector, and the note was just under the top dress. "You're being followed," it said, and that was all.

I burned the note and set about opening a few tins for my dinner. It wasn't much after the gastronomic high-life I had been living over the past few days, but even baked beans can taste good after all that caviar, pheasant and stuff. So I had a fry up, just like my Mum used to do, and washed it down with Brooke Bond "69.

So I was being followed; that meant I would have to play the game according to the pattern I had set myself. I had met Antonio as an Iberian stewardess, and that was supposed to be what I returned to now that my jaunt into the high-life was over. I called in to the airline office and reported myself for duty. They were expecting my call. A flight to Mexico City tomorrow, departure from London, ten-thirty a.m. "Thank you very much," I said, and that was that. I brushed my teeth, switched on the television and settled down for a domestic evening. But the television wasn't particularly absorbing and I found myself wondering.

If I was being followed, it had to be from the *Maria,* to see where I went and with whom I made contact. And if I was being followed today, it was a pretty fair bet that I was being followed yesterday. And if I had been followed yesterday, then they, who-ever they were, would also have followed Signor Bertelli after his diabolical acting bit in the main square. I hoped he was alright, because in spite of the occasional disagreements we have, I quite like him, and he really is very good at his job. But I was good at my job, too, so why was I being followed? Where had I slipped up?

But I didn't spend too much time wondering about this, because I knew that if I had made a mistake, Mr. Blaser would tell me in his own good time, hammering it home with consider-able relish. About half-past nine, I debated whether to call my

motor car salesman, but decided not to; I had to get up reasonably early next morning and fly the Atlantic. So instead I took a
sleeping pill and went to bed.

In fact I flew the Atlantic three times the following week. I was
on the regular duty roster and I worked just like all the other
girls. There wasn't a word from Mr. Blaser, so I assumed that I
was still being followed. Whoever was responsible for watching
me was doing a very good job and must have been using a dozen
different people, because never once did I get the slightest clue
that I was being tailed; and never once did I spot anyone I even
vaguely recognised. They must have been spending a fortune
on aeroplane tickets alone. I think Mr. Blaser assumed that if I
continued to play the part I had been cast in, they would eventually give up. But he was wrong there. They were prepared to
play a waiting game, but they weren't going to wait forever. They
allowed me eight days to make my move and when I didn't they
moved themselves.

I was picked up in London. I was tired and a little grotty after
a particularly nasty flight and I accepted a lift into town with a
captain I knew rather than take the crew bus. He tried to talk me
into coming out to dinner with him, but I begged off. Sulking, he
dropped me off outside my apartment and drove off, no doubt
going home to his wife. I picked up my suitcase and headed
towards the front door, feeling pretty bloody about everything.

The man was waiting just inside the front door of the building. The landlord didn't consider it necessary to light the hall
and passages and a small army could have lurked in our building
unseen.

"Miss Touchfeather?" enquired the man politely. He was
short. That much I could tell from the level that his voice was
coming from, but that was all.

"Yes" I said, too tired to even suspect anything.

"I wonder if you'd mind coming with me?" he said. And still I didn't get it.

"Where?" I asked, wondering what the hell he was talking about.

"We'll talk about it in the car," he said. He got through to me then alright. Play it cool, Katy, I thought. I didn't doubt that I could take care of the man in front of me. After all, that's what I'm trained for, but I didn't know how many there were behind me and, even more important, I had been playing the role of an air stewardess all week, and air stewardesses just don't go around breaking men's arms and suchlike. So I did my indignant bit.

"I don't know who you are," I said. "And I'll thank you to get out of my way."

"Don't give us any trouble, Miss Touchfeather." He was still being polite.

"Look here," I said in my best Roedean accent. "If you don't leave me alone, I shall call the police." My eyes had become used to the darkness now and I could see him better. He was smiling, actually enjoying himself.

"I shouldn't do that," he said. I was inclined to agree with him, but I was still acting a part, so I had to follow it through.

"I'll scream," I said.

"No you won't," he said equably.

Let's see who's right, I thought, knowing full well that he was. I opened my mouth to yell, and that was that. He poked four stiff fingers into my midriff, just below and between my breasts; then he caught me as I fell. I was still tying to get a breath of air into my tortured lungs when he swung me up into his arms. Then he carried me out of the door, across the pavement and deposited me in the back of a waiting car. It had all been so simple and straightforward. There were even people walking about in the street, but no-one took a blind bit of notice. This goes towards proving a theory of mine; you can commit a major crime in full view of umpteen people and, providing you don't make too much noise about it. the chances are that no-one will notice and, if they do notice, they won't do anything about it in case they make fools of themselves.

My abductor got into the back of the car with me and I saw that there was a driver sitting in the front. Without a word, the driver started the engine and the car pulled away. I lay where I was for a good ten minutes trying to get my breath back, while the cause of my trouble just ignored me. I took a closer look at him, seeing him clearly for the first time. I was right; he was short, but barrel shaped and obviously very strong. He had fair hair and a nothing sort of face, except for the mouth which was thin and hard. You wait, my lad, I thought. One day I'll get you when I'm not pretending to be someone else, and that will be a day you'll remember for a very long time. We can be very vindictive, we Touchfeathers.

By the time I pulled myself together, we were out of London on the Western Avenue and, as I noticed this, I started to worry about something else. If my captors weren't concerned that I knew where they were taking me, then it was a pretty fair assumption that they didn't think I was going to be in any position to do anything about it at a later date. Very ominous, I thought. I gave the indignant bit one more try.

"I have never ..."

"Shut up," said my companion. Soft soap then, I thought.

"Please, won't you ..."

He told me to shut up again, and this time there was a look in his eyes which warned me to take notice. I didn't think there would be much point in chatting up the driver: apart from leaning over to open the door when I'd been shoved into the car, he had done nothing but drive, and hadn't said a word. I tried to see what he looked like through the driving mirror, but it was angled wrongly. So I gave it up, sat back, and tried to prepare myself for what was bound to follow.

I may be all sorts of a tough chick when it comes to handling myself; turn me loose with most people and providing the odds aren't too heavily stacked against me, I can generally make out. But this doesn't mean that I enjoy violence and particularly not when it's directed at me. After all, I *am* a girl, a member of the weaker sex and, like ninety-nine per cent of my sex, my basic desire is to be cossetted and nurtured, looked after and loved. I don't like hurting people and, even more, I don't like being hurt. If I read the signs correctly, I was due to be hurt extensively when we arrived at wherever it was we were heading for. These people had been following me for a week, hoping that I would give something away. I hadn't, and now they were tired of waiting; they wanted me to start talking and I had no illusions about how they would go about it. I felt very vulnerable all of a sudden, wishing I had taken up cooking or drama instead of my chosen profession.

We drove for two hours, turning off the main Oxford road on the other side of High Wycombe, there losing ourselves in the maze of small country roads that interlace the Chilterns. Although I didn't reckon it would do anyone any good, I kept a check on where we were going. In the unlikely event that I would be given a chance in the future, at least I'd be able to find my way back. Then abruptly we turned off the road through a pair of high, ornate wrought-iron gates, and headed up a long drive flanked by parkland. It was very dark and all I could see was the area picked out by the headlamps, which wasn't much.

The house lay at the end of the drive; a vast, hideous Victorian folly that looked as though demolition would be doing it a kindness. The car stopped and the driver got out. He was almost as indistinguishable as his companion, an anonymous sort of man whose face looked as though it had been put together by an Identikit. I was urged out of the car and across the ten feet of drive to the front door. One of my escorts opened the front door, not even having to use a key, and we went through into the hall. Somewhere somebody clicked the lights on.

The house was as ugly inside as it was out. Perhaps some of the furniture may have been good, but it was all covered with dust-sheets so I couldn't see. And it was very cold, the dank cold of disuse. I almost expected to see water running down the flock wallpaper. I was nudged across the hall and through a pair of doors into what I assumed was the sitting-room. Sixty feet long and as inhospitable as the rest of the place.

"Sit," said one of my companions. I sat in the high back wing chair he indicated and a small cloud of dust blew up from the sheet that covered the chair. The two men didn't even bother to sit; they took up station, one leaning against the fireplace, the other with his arms resting along the back of what I took to be a settee. And they just looked at me, neither of them making any sort of move at all. So it seemed that if nastiness were to follow, they weren't going to be the ones to inflict it. The house had had the emptiness of a tomb about it when we arrived, so I assumed that the principal in this little drama wasn't even here yet.

This was confirmed twenty minutes later when we all heard a car crunch across the gravel outside. One of my escorts detached himself from the fireplace and walked out into the hall. I heard the low murmur of voices and a moment later he came back, followed by the new arrival.

It was a woman. She was about thirty years old, very dark, and with a strong Eurasian look about her. I'm not particularly charitable when it comes to describing members of my own sex, but even I had to admit that this one was very beautiful indeed. Her skin was a pale creamy colour, her eyes black and enormous; she had a classic line to her cheekbones, and her mouth was very full, the sort of mouth to drive men crazy. She was wearing a full length sable coat over a white evening gown.

She hardly glanced at the man who had been standing watching me. She came straight over to my chair and stopped about three feet away. A swift kick with my sensible stewardess type shoes and I could have crippled her for life. But there didn't seem much point unless I could incapacitate her two heavies with the same kick. Instead I thought once more that I had better try to recapture my supposed identity.

"I don't know who you are," I said in my best outraged manner. "But I demand to be released."

"My name is Lucia," she said. She pronounced it Luchia. "And yours is Katherine." She spoke quite softly, even gently, her accent carrying strong French overtones.

"Alright, Lucia," I said, continuing to flog a dead horse. "What is the meaning of this outrage?"

"Please, Katherine, don't waste our time or yours by continuing this act. Just answer my questions and we can have an end to the affair."

I knew what the end would be, too, as far as Katy was concerned.

"What questions?"

"Very simply, who do you work for?"

"Iberian Airlines."

"We know that, dear. Who else?"

"No-one else," I said.

She looked at me for a beat then she opened her handbag. From it she took a small, leather case. She opened it and drew out a hypodermic syringe and a small phial containing a colourless fluid. Whoops, I thought, here we go with the truth drug. But I must admit I felt a slight feeling of relief. At least they were going about this in a civilised way, thumb screws obviously weren't their speed at all.

"Do you know what this is, Katherine?" she asked, as she expertly charged the hypodermic, drawing into the shaft what looked like a half pint of drug.

"No," I said.

"It's a truth drug," she said. "With this in your veins you will be incapable of lying to me. Incidentally, it will also kill you fifteen minutes after administration."

That didn't sound like any truth drug that I had ever heard of, but I believed her implicitly. And if I was going to die in fifteen minutes, I thought that about here I had better do something about it. After all, it wasn't as though I had anything to lose. And anyway I *hate* injections. The one leaning against the fireplace looked the most dangerous, if you discounted Lucia who was more dangerous than the two of them lumped together and multiplied by four. But he was ten feet away from me, and that was an awful lot of ground to cover. God only knew what weapons he was carrying on him, but at least they didn't want me dead before I had talked so he probably wouldn't do anything too drastic. I glanced quickly at the other one. He was still leaning up against the settee watching the whole business with a casual disinterest as though he had no part in it. Then Lucia did me a big favour.

"Come and hold her," she said.

Both men approached my chair as Lucia held the needle up and squirted out the air. The men took up station either side of me.

"Roll up her sleeve," said Lucia. One of them started to do just that, and Katy did what she had to do. I broke his arm quickly and painfully. The crack of breaking bone sounded like a pistol shot, riveting everyone in the room for the brief moment I needed to deal with the other one. To him, I did Bessie's number three trick for disabling a man. It worked like a charm. Unfortunately I had underestimated the calibre of the first man. Broken arm he might have had, but he still had one good arm left and a job to do. As I turned back to him he had just finished pulling a wicked looking cosh from his pocket. I tried to grab his wrist, but I was off balance. The first blow caught me on the shoulder, knocking me to my knees. I heard Lucia scream something at the man

before he hit me again. Then came a roar like thunder, and I slid
off to hell and gone.

"Fortunately we arrived on the scene at that precise moment,"
said Mr. Blaser. By "we" he didn't mean himself personally, but
the two men who had been following me to find out who was
following me, if you get my point. They had seen my abduction
from outside my apartment and had tailed the car, only breaking
into the house just before Katy was beaten to death by an irate
man with a broken arm.

"What happened to them?"

"Your two kidnappers are under lock and key," said
Mr. Blaser. "Both in hospital I might add."

"What about Lucia?"

"I assume by Lucia you mean the woman?" I agreed that I
meant the woman. Mr. Blaser cleared his throat. "Unfortunately
she escaped. Those responsible have been severely reprimanded."
I started to say something, but he continued, "In any event, it is
doubtful that she would have led us anywhere, so there is no real
harm done."

"She was going to kill me," I said.

"I know," said Mr. Blaser. "We analysed the chemical she was
going to inject you with. Most interesting."

"Can the men tell you anything?"

"They're just a couple of small time criminals engaged for
one job only."

"Engaged by whom?"

"By the woman, Lucia."

"Cosy," I said. Then I had an idea. "What about the house? Is
there a lead there?"

"That at least proved interesting," said Mr. Blaser as though
everything else was a crashing bore. "It belongs to Sir Roger Bleak."

"The plot thickens," I said.

"Not for you it doesn't, Miss Touchfeather. You are no longer of any use to me on this venture. You have been identified."

"But I didn't say anything," I said. "They could still think I'm what I claimed to be."

"Airline stewardesses don't have special agents coming to their rescue when they get into trouble." He said it as though he regretted having rescued me in the first place. But he was right. My cover was blown, as they say in the trade.

"What about Galipolodopolo?"

"What about him?"

"Aren't you going to do anything about him? I mean, he was responsible for all this."

"Come, Miss Touchfeather. That blow must have affected your thought processes." Again he was right. Nobody could tie Galipolodopolo in with my abduction, except perhaps Lucia, and she was long since gone. All that we had left were two unfortunate heavies who had been paid for a job that had gone sour, and who knew nothing about their employer except that she was female.

"So what happens next, sir?"

"As far as you are concerned, nothing," said Mr. Blaser. "You will be re-assigned as soon as I have something else for you to do."

I grew bold here; after all, I was interested and I knew the people involved. "No, sir. I mean, what happens about the whole gold business?"

Mr. Blaser looked at me as though I had just committed sacrilege. "You know better than to ask a question like that, Miss Touchfeather."

"Yes, sir."

And the miserable old idiot was right again. It was bad organisation to allow too many people to know what was going on; the less anyone knew, the more secure the whole operation. Just before I left the office, I asked him something I had been wanting to for quite a long time, and hadn't up to now in case the answer upset me.

"What happened to Signor Bertelli?"

"Nothing," said Mr. Blaser. "Why?"

"As they were on to me I assumed they would be on to him as well."

He smiled at me thinly. "Fortunately all my people are not as inept as you, Miss Touchfeather," he said. "Good day."

The next three days I spent on the London-New York run, behaving like any normal air stewardess, which of course I am when I'm not doing things for Mr. Blaser. It makes quite a pleasant change knowing that the passengers are just passengers and not assorted villains liable to beat you over the head, shoot you, or stick needles into you. Not that the normal passenger can't be a menace: some are positively diabolical in their cunning. They devise elaborate schemes to harass the stewardess, and one such individual can make a girl's life a living hell for the six or seven hours it takes to cross the Atlantic. I had one on my second trip, a sandy haired lecher of twenty-two, who behaved like every dirty old man who had ever existed. He pestered me rotten, and every time I came anywhere near him, he tried to look down my blouse or up my skirt. Two hours out of New York, he nearly succeeded in trapping me in the toilet and it was only the timely arrival of the Captain, doing his rounds, that saved me from a fate worse than death. What some people expect for the price of an aeroplane ticket is quite extraordinary. The other trips were uneventful and, whereas normal scheduled flying can make a pleasant change, it can also turn out to be a drag if it goes on too long.

I was soaking in a hot bath after my fourth round trip, wondering how many more times I was going to have to walk across the Atlantic, when the phone rang. It was Miss Moody.

"Mr. Blaser would like to see you," she said.

"Tomorrow?"

"Tonight."

"It's ten-thirty already."

"Is it as late as that?" she said. "I hadn't noticed. How long will you be?"

"I'm in the bath."

"Shall we say an hour then?" And she hung up before I could think of an excuse. A pox on the both of them, I thought, as I clambered out of the bath. Then the thought of not having to fly the Atlantic again tomorrow cheered me up a little. I dressed, put on my war-paint, called a minicab, and went to see what little goodies Mr. Blaser had in store for me next.

THREE

Borami is a country, believe it or not. It has its own President and elected representatives; the only trouble is that it is the President who elects them. It also has a huge hydro-electric project in the pipeline, and the Russians and Chinese fighting with each other over who is going to pay for it. Once it is completed it will provide electricity for the whole of Borami; and it is a matter of record that only two per cent of the population of the entire country are equipped technically or psychologically to handle electricity. Borami also has its own bank, a seat on the United Nations, its own import and export councils and, of course, like all emergent African nations, it has its own airline.

I looked up the airline in the trade books; two 707's and three Dakotas. One of the 707's was reserved exclusively for the President himself and, as the Borami people were notoriously frightened of flying, the other was used almost entirely by foreigners who flocked to the country, vying with each other to see who could offer the largest bribes thereby landing some of the huge contracts which were being financed by rubles or yen or dollars. Borami was like a very small boy with three frantically rich uncles each of whom, for reasons best known to himself, wanted to become the only uncle, and was willing to empty his pockets for the privilege.

Miss Moody gave me her customary nod of encouragement as I waited for the light on Mr. Blaser's door lintel to change to green.

"You look very nice dear," she said.

Before I could reply, the light went to green and I tapped on the door and went in. Mr. Blaser unbent sufficiently to ask how I was, but he didn't wait for me to tell him before ploughing straight on.

"Borami, Miss Touchfeather. You're due there the day after tomorrow."

"Yes, sir."

"You fly BOAC to Nairobi and check in with Borami National Airlines there."

"Yes, sir."

"You will report direct to Captain Chalmers and no one else. He knows about you."

"What does he know?"

"He knows that you are going to report to him," said Mr. Blaser crossly. "Naturally he doesn't know what your assignment is."

That makes two of us, I thought.

Then Mr. Blaser went on to explain what it was all about.

And that's why I was standing in the Main terminal building at Nairobi Airport, while the public address system searched for Captain Chalmers on my behalf. The air conditioning had broken down about ten minutes after I arrived, and the temperature had rapidly climbed up into mid-nineties. The journey from London had been grotty in the extreme; the job I was supposed to be doing was pretty foul viewed by any standards; I hadn't slept a wink in nineteen straight hours; I hadn't even bathed for seventeen. All in all I felt like half a dozen different versions of hell rolled into one.

I had reported to the Borami Airlines desk as soon as I arrived, asking for Captain Chalmers. The desk was manned by a snotty-nosed adolescent with pimples, who told me to wait. I waited for half an hour while he did absolutely nothing, so I asked him again. He exposed some very grubby teeth at me and told me to wait some more. I told him to go and take a jump at himself and asked the main information desk if they could assist me in locating my Captain Chalmers. They started by telling me to check with the Borami Airlines desk. I told them I had already done that and if I had to go back there I would probably commit homicide. They must have had dealings with my pimply adolescent, because I detected a note of sympathy as they promised to try to locate Captain Chalmers for me. And locate him they did.

As he introduced himself I thought that here was the only good thing to happen to me for over a week. He was a large, slow-moving man, fair, with blue eyes and little wrinkles in the corners that came from long hours spent staring out of flight deck windows. He was just like a commercial for an airline captain and he was exactly my type. Because, although I might swing with the Antonios of this world, it is usually in the line of duty and, if the truth be known, I have a very soft spot for these large capable men with gentle voices and even gentler touch. I cursed the fact that I looked such a mess, but he didn't seem to notice; or, if he did, he didn't show it. In fact he looked as agreeably surprised when he saw me as I felt on seeing him.

"Miss Touchfeather?"

"Captain Chalmers."

We shook hands, In spite of the heat his hand was cool and dry and I wished I'd wiped my palm before offering it.

"Sorry you've been kept waiting."

"Snot nose at your counter was no help at all," I said.

"He never is. Let's get out of here."

We went to the crew room, where miraculously the air conditioning was still working. Fortunately the place was empty so we were able to talk.

"I know almost nothing of why you are here, Miss Touchfeather," he said, when he had assured himself that I was comfortable and wanting for nothing. "I was asked by certain parties in London to get you the job of junior stewardess on the presidential 707."

"How did you manage?" I asked.

"When the junior stewardess went sick I put your name forward. I'm in charge of recruiting personnel for our illustrious airline."

"She went sick very conveniently, didn't she?" I asked.

He looked puzzled for a moment. "Funny about that," he said. "The doctors say it was food poisoning, but as far as I know I'd eaten the same food as she had for the previous twenty-four hours." I detected the long arm of Mr. Blaser here, but I certainly wasn't going to say anything.

"Well," I said. "All's well that ends well."

He looked at me steadily for a moment. "I'm sure it will end very well indeed," he said.

Why not, Katy? I thought. After all, I didn't have a regular boyfriend in Africa. If I was going to be in Borami for any length of time, I was going to be seeing a great deal of Captain Chalmers and, from where I was sitting at this moment, I had to admit to liking the idea.

"I suppose you can't tell me what it's all about?" he asked.

"What?" I asked innocently.

"The reason you're here."

"You needed a stewardess. You've got one."

"I could have picked up a stewardess here in Nairobi," he said. "Not that I'm complaining," he added quickly.

"Then how did you manage to get me engaged all the way from London?" And here he actually started to blush under his warm brown tan. "I had to tell a couple of lies."

"Affecting me?"

"Actually yes," he said. "I'm in the President's good books at the moment. He likes the way I fly." That'll make two of us, I thought. "Anyway, I told him I had a girlfriend ... a sort of fiancée ... in London, and please could I give her the job?" Better and better I thought, all the ground work had already been done for me. Then he returned to his original question about what I was doing here.

"I don't think the certain parties in London would be too keen on my telling you," I said, trying to make it sound as pleasant as possible. "In fact I would get into terrible trouble if they thought..."

He leaped in like the gentleman I knew he was. "Enough said. Not one more word. And now I'll take you to your hotel."

⚜ ⚜ ⚜

He picked up my bags from where I had left them and ten minutes later we were in a car heading into town.

"What's our flying programme?" I asked. Then I remembered that I was junior stewardess and he was Captain. "Sir," I added.

"That's alright for the flight deck," he said. "Otherwise it's Peter."

"And I'm Katy," I said coyly.

"As to our flight programme, we act on the whim of the President. He's in Nairobi conferring with other despots at the moment. When the fancy takes him, he'll expect to be whipped out of here at one hour's notice."

"Back to Borami?"

"I think Borami's the only other country that'll put up with him."

"What's wrong with him then?"

"Delusions of grandeur. A third rate, coffee-coloured Caligula. I don't know why old man Kenyatta even allows him into Kenya."

"Politics," I said, as though it covered the entire spectrum of human behaviour.

Peter nodded his big, beautiful head. "You're right, Katy. It's a great comfort to have an honest trade at one's fingertips."

I didn't want to disillusion him too soon in our relationship, so I kept my mouth shut on that one. Five minutes later he handed me the key to my hotel room and told me he would expect me downstairs for dinner at seven p.m.

The room was airy and cool. I stripped off everything and threw it in the dirty linen basket. Then I took a long cool bath. While I was soaking I went over my last conversation with Mr. Blaser.

"Politically Borami is a powder keg, Miss Touchfeather. The President is playing all ends against the middle. America, China and Russia are all pouring money into the place in an attempt to buy the old pirate's allegiance. But as long as the money continues to arrive, he's going to remain firmly on the fence. Her Majesty's Government, needless to say, are extremely interested in the outcome of this sordid affair. After all, we ruled in Borami for over a hundred years, and we *know* President Calmooni. Despot and tyrant he may be, but he still has a hearty respect for the British. It is not beyond the bounds of possibility that he will take all the money that is handed out, and eventually throw out the Americans, the Russians and the Chinese, and return to the fold. After all, Borami *is* a member of the Commonwealth. Should any of the three Big Powers get wind of this, it is quite likely that they will work towards having the President removed permanently and replaced by a man who is more sympathetic to their own particular cause. Chaos would of course result, forcing Her Majesty's Government to send troops to restore order. Needless to say, we have neither the desire nor the facilities to mount an operation of this sort. Apart from that the publicity would be extremely bad. 'Colonialist' has become a dirty word, Miss Touchfeather." He paused.

"Now, as to your specific instructions, they are simply keep your eyes and ears open. You will be working aboard the President's own aircraft. When he is not using it, it is employed extensively to fly foreign diplomats in and out of Borami. You will merely listen, take everything in, and send your reports back to me from time to time. You will make no attempt to evaluate what you hear. You're not equipped for that kind of work. In the event, however, that you hear something that you feel requires immediate action, you will be given a contact you can approach in Borami. That's all, Miss Touchfeather."

"How long will I be there, sir?" I had ventured to ask.

"As long as I choose to keep you there," he said.

I should have known better than to ask.

✤ ✤ ✤

Bath over, I managed to get a couple of hours' sleep before going down to meet Peter. We had a slow, leisurely dinner and he behaved like the perfect gentleman afterwards, leaving me outside my room with just a brotherly peck on the cheek by way of good night. But the chemistry between us was right; we both knew it and we both knew that it was only a matter of time. A couple of days lolling around the pool, I thought; perhaps a drive up country to the National Parks; a few more cosy meals *a deux* and we'dbe away. With this pleasant thought at the back of my mind, I drifted off into the best nights sleep I'd had for a long time. I awoke about eight o'clock and wondered why I was feeling so good; then I remembered and started to plan the day. Peter had promised to call for me at about ten o'clock, so there was no hurry. I phoned down for my breakfast and prepared to spend a quiet couple of hours getting ready for the day. At eight-fifteen the phone rang. It was Peter.

"We take off at ten-fifteen," he said.

"Take off what?" I wasn't quite awake.

"The President, God damn his soul, has decided he wants to go home. I've got to go straight out to the airport to file a flight plan. Be there no later than nine-thirty."

"It's a quarter past eight already," I wailed.

"Be there, Katy." Then, in case he had sounded too authoritative and grotty, he added, "Please..."

"Yes, sir," I said and, for the same reason, I blew him a kiss over the phone. I heard him chuckle just before he hung up.

I leaped out of bed and into the bathroom. My breakfast arrived and I ate it while I was getting ready. It was only when I went to the wardrobe that I realised that I had no uniform. There was no point in calling Peter because he would have already left for the airport, and I certainly wasn't going to call the airport office in case snot nose answered the phone. Finally I decided that the President would have to take me as he found me. I chose my most conservative suit in pale blue linen and, with a white blouse underneath, I had to admit I looked pretty svelte.

Then came the problem of my luggage. Were we coming back here or weren't we? I decided better to be safe than sorry and repacked everything, bidding a fond farewell to the stuff that I had sent to the cleaners the night before. I would put in an expense chit when I returned to London. Miss Moody would see me alright. I rang for a porter to carry my bags down, and when he arrived travelled down in the elevator with him. My bill had already been taken care of by the airline, and I asked for a taxi. But the porter who had brought my bags down indicated that he had put them in a waiting car. I walked over to the car, climbed into the back, and met Gloria.

Gloria Glover was the senior stewardess, and my superior. A startlingly beautiful girl of twenty-seven or thereabouts, with the blondest hair I had seen for a long time. She smiled a big smile as I parked myself next to her and the driver started the car.

"You're Katy. I'm Gloria. Call me Glo," she said.

"Hello, Glo."

"Peter asked me to pick you up." I felt my hackles rise slightly. This was competition with a capital C.

"That was nice of him."

"He's like that," said Glo. "He's going to be our best man."
I warmed towards her immediately. Lovely girl, I thought. She
chattered on as we drove to the airport. It seemed she was about
to marry a Great White Hunter she had met in Nairobi. The only
trouble was he kept running off on safari and she couldn't pin him
down long enough to name the day. Glo was an American; a former TWA stewardess, who had met her GWH on an African trip,
fallen like a ton of bricks, and taken a job which at least allowed
her to see him occasionally. He hadn't wanted her to work but she
had tried the idle life for a few weeks and then given it up.

"He was always dashing off into the bush to kill something,"
she said. "I never knew whether he'd be home to dinner this side
of Christmas."

She was a nice girl, I decided; a little scatterbrained for
twenty-seven, but looking like she did I couldn't see it worrying anyone. Just before we reached the airport, I asked what my
inflight duties would be.

"Keep the booze flowing and your back to the bulkheads at
all times," she said.

"It's like that is it?"

"It's worse than that," she said. "But there's plenty of room
for maneuvering."

I saw what she meant about there being plenty of room, the
moment we went aboard. The original interior of the aircraft had
been stripped out and re-designed as a rather plush, overblown
boardroom-cum-living room, with decoration strongly reminis-
cent of a Victorian bordello. There were numerous large over-
stuffed armchairs bolted to the floor around the outside edge of
the cabin, and a large oval dining table complete with ten chairs
in the centre. This occupied forty-five feet of the aircraft. The rear
end, sheltered behind a bulkhead, was reserved as a private suite
for the President himself. It consisted of sitting room, bedroom,
dresssing room and bathroom. All very luxurious and vastly
extravagant.

The President came aboard about twenty minutes after we did. Peter came through from the flight deck and told Glo and me that the tower had just called to say he was on his way. The two of us lined up inside the open hatch while Peter went down the gangway to meet him. Three Mercedes 600's drew up and out piled about a dozen coloured men and, by coloured, I don't mean their skin. They were black certainly, but it was the clothes they were wearing that blinded. Bright red robes, blue head-dresses, yellow sashes, orange pantaloons sticking out beneath green three-quarter length jackets; feathers dipped in all colours and shades; and the whole group flocking around the President himself, who was dressed in a blue kaftan shot with gold thread. He was a mountain of a man, over six feet tall and weighing somewhere in the region of twenty stone. He had a great moon-shaped face and moved slowly, rather like a hippopotamus, while his minions fluttered around him like a flock of exotic tropical birds. He grinned widely at Peter and shook his hand. Then he allowed Peter to precede him up the gangway into the aircraft. As he stepped aboard I could have sworn I felt the springs sag. He smiled at Glo, then looked at me. Before Peter could present me, he grinned hugely, exposing what looked like enough teeth for three ordinary people.

"You must be Peter's young lady," he said in impeccable English. He held out a huge hand and engulfed mine.

"Miss Katherine Touchfeather," said Peter from behind him.

"Welcome, Katherine," he said. Then he turned to Peter. "Now you are happy, Peter?"

"Very happy, sir. Thank you."

Then he turned further, addressing the entourage who were queueing up behind him, waiting to get into the aircraft.

"This is the fiancée of Captain Chalmers," he said very loudly. "If anyone dares to lay a finger on her, I will have his hand cut off at the wrist." He meant it, too; I could see that by the expression on everyone's face. It was only later that I discovered he was addressing his Prime Minister, Foreign Secretary, Minister of Finance, two Generals and countless Under Secretaries. He certainly had *his* government where he wanted them.

Glo and I settled everyone in their seats, and checked that they were strapped in. President Calmooni patted my bottom as I adjusted his outsized seat belt, but it was avuncular rather than anticipatory, and I didn't mind a bit. Glo and I strapped down on a couple of spare seats, and five minutes after everyone coming aboard, we were up, up and away.

The President's warning seemed to have had its effect and I had no trouble whatsoever with the passengers. I served their booze and, when the time came, their lunch. Glo and I were the only cabin staff. On the flight deck, apart from Peter, there was a co-pilot, a middle-aged Sikh, and the third crewman was an African, a young, gentle-faced lad who never failed to smile politely at me and who called me "ma'am" at all times.

The flight itself was completely uneventful and, once lunch had been cleared away, the President retired to his own quarters and everyone else got their heads down where they were sitting. I had just finished clearing up when the co-pilot came back to ask if I would like to sit up front with Peter for a while. Peter flashed me a smile as I slid into the co-pilot's seat. He was on automatic pilot, with his feet resting on the instrument panel in front of him. I like it on the flight deck, all around is blue nothing; there may be clouds, but they're fifteen thousand feet straight down, and the main impression one gets is of enormous, clear, fresh, space; you feel you can breath better up here.

"I hate to appear ignorant," I said after a couple of minutes' companionable silence. "But how far is Borami from Nairobi?"

"Four and a half hours," said Peter. "We'll be there just before fifteen hundred." As though to confirm this, the polite African handed him a slip of paper at which he glanced. "Fourteen fifty-five."

I looked at my watch. There's a clock somewhere on the flight deck, but who could ever find it with all the other junk that festoons the place? It was already a quarter past two.

"What's Borami like?" I asked.

"Borami is the country. We're going to Calmooniville, the capital."

"So what's Calmooniville like?"

"Hot."

"And?"

"Hot," he said.

"Where will I be staying?"

"The hotel. There's only one."

"Do you live there?"

"I have a house," he said, giving me a sideways glance. "It's a large house."

I'm not usually so forward, but what with the height and the ratified atmosphere, I made my pitch. "Wouldn't it be better if ..." I paused. Perhaps I *was* coming on a bit strong. He helped me off my own hook.

"I was thinking, Katy," he said. "I mean, after all, you're supposed to be my fiancée. It's a big house, four bedrooms actually. Wouldn't it be better if you moved in with me? Strictly kosher, of course." That's what you think, I thought.

"It sounds like a very good idea," I said, as though I hadn't thought about it.

He beamed broadly at nothing in particular. "I've got a couple of house servants, use of the presidential swimming pool, and a cook I can borrow from the French Embassy from time to time. How does it sound?"

It sounded marvelous, and I said so.

Ten minutes later I went back to the cabin to wake everyone up for the landing. Glo did the necessary with the President, and five minutes before touchdown he lumbered out from his own quarters and subsided into one of the armchairs. I decided that he was a bad daytime sleeper, because he was foul tempered. The Prime Minister said something to him in language I didn't understand, and promptly got his head bitten off at the neck. After that it was dead silence until we had landed and taxied to our dispersal point.

The original designer of Calmooniville airport had visualised nothing larger than an occasional Dakota, and when in a fit lunacy the airline bought two 707's an extra mile of runway was slapped onto the end of the one already in existence. The wind was always blowing in the same direction in Calmooniville, so there was only need for the one. Then, in another fit of national pride, work had commenced on the airport buildings. Something like a cross between Kennedy and Heathrow had been proposed; foundations had been dug; and work had started. Six months later everyone seemed to get fed up with the idea, and it had just stopped. There remained a couple of acres of half-built terminal buildings, and a small corrugated iron hut which had originally been the site foreman's office. This hut now housed customs, immigration, passenger waiting area, the lot. There was a maintenance hanger on the far side of the main runway, and at least this was run efficiently. Peter saw to that. Major maintenance had to be done elsewhere, but at least he could replace a gasket or mend a puncture on his home field.

Two Rolls Royces and a Cadillac followed the aircraft for the last half mile of taxiing and, by the time we had stopped and opened the hatch, the gangway was in place and the cars waiting at the bottom. The President and his party piled off the aircraft and into their respective cars which drove off to God knows where. I waited for Peter while he turned the aircraft over to the co-pilot with his instructions as to its disposition. Then he joined me and I set foot on Borami soil for the first time.

Peter had been right about the heat. As I stepped onto the gangway and allowed the sun to give me its first belt, I damn near passed out straight away. It must have been well over a hundred degrees and in two seconds I was soaking wet and feeling like hell. Peter took my arm as we walked down the gangway.

"Good job we didn't arrive at noon," he said. "It's as hot as hell then."

He must have been here longer than I thought. He had a small saloon car parked at the back of the unfinished terminal building. It was standing out in the sun and I drew back as we approached it.

"I'm not getting into that," I said. "I'll cook."

"No, you won't," he said.

Two Africans were already stowing our luggage in the boot and I noticed the engine was running. When Peter opened the front door and pushed me in, it was like getting into an ice box.

"It's refrigerated," said Peter, climbing in beside me. "They come across from the control tower and switch it on when I make my last approach call." My God, was he organised!

The drive from the airport to his house was unrelieved in its depression. Calmooniville had started off as a few mud huts a hundred and fifty years ago. The British had done their bit and put up a few hideous Victorian style buildings, which since Independence seemed to have been left strictly alone, apart from the groups of squatters that had taken up residence. So there were still mud huts, and shanty-like buildings, and a couple of grubby houses, and more shanties, another relic of the Raj, and a few more mud huts. And suddenly there was the Palace. Originally Government House, it had been extensively enlarged and renovated; what had been good enough for a succession of Governor Generals and High Commissioners certainly wasn't good enough for a home-grown President.

I saw it all later, and from that time on I never wondered where all those millions of dollars of aid had gone. But that was later; right now, Peter drove round the perimeter of the palace walls to an area which had been neatly laid out like a very upper class American suburb. There were cool, elegant houses, with well-kept lawns and gardens, and a proper road meandering through the whole area. I could see gardeners working industriously and, in a lot of cases, built-in lawn sprinklers were throwing water around every whichway. It looked like any normal Sunday in Beverly Hills.

Peter's house wasn't quite as grand as some of the others, but it was pretty nice from where I was sitting. It was on the far side of the development, a couple of miles from the Palace. A lawn sloped up from the road to the house itself which was surrounded by a screened verandah. It was a one storey building and it looked cool and inviting. As we drew up two jolly looking Africans came bowling out of the place and running down to meet us. They greeted Peter in atrocious English, exposing masses of teeth and rolling their eyes.

"Diogenes and Archimedes," said Peter.

"You've got to be kidding,"

"So help me God."

"Which is which?"

Peter shrugged. "I don't know."

He managed to get it across to them that I was to be a house guest and their delight knew no bounds. They fought over my luggage fiercely, and then compromised by dividing it between them; Peter's they left by the side of the road. They preceded us up to the house, looking back over their shoulders to make sure I didn't disappear in a cloud of smoke. One couldn't really blame them I suppose, but they dumped all my luggage in Peter's bedroom. When Peter made them take it out they looked almost as disappointed as I did. Still, if he wanted to play it all proper and above board, I wasn't about to give him any arguments. I allowed myself to be led to the room he had chosen for me and was considerably encouraged to find there was a connecting door to his. I had a spot of trouble stopping Diogenes and Archimedes from doing my unpacking. I finally got them out of my room, but they continued to stick their heads round the door every two minutes giggling something or other to me which I didn't understand. Finally I heard Peter bellow something at them and they didn't appear again until dinner time.

Obviously this was one of the nights when Peter hadn't been able to borrow the Embassy chef, because the food was pretty grotty. But I didn't mind, because everything else was pure romance; the soft night outside, the candlelight, good wine, and dinner *a deux*.

And after dinner? Well, it was inevitable. We had both made up our minds on that ten minutes after we met. He allowed me thirty minutes before he had tapped on the connecting door. I had made the best of that time, too. I looked smashing and I smelled divine. He was very gentle as I had known he would be. I've had my share of kinks and the caveman bit, and they're all very nice if the company and the situation is slanted that way; but basically I'm an old fashioned girl and I like it warm and tender the first time round. He kissed my breasts; he nuzzled around my navel with his tongue, and he put his finger where he had no business to, but which I approved of most highly. I tried to get him inside me after five minutes, but he was having none of that for some time yet. He had the willpower of a superman and he did everything to me that I had ever heard of and a few things that I hadn't before he finally came to the crunch. He woke me up twice during the night for repeats. I don't know what the staple diet is in Borami, but it certainly worked wonders for Peter. I mean, it wasn't as though he were twenty any longer. But he managed to have me begging for mercy before the dawn sun edged through the Venetian blinds. He left me at seven a.m. and I zonked out until after mid-day.

Archimedes woke me up, or was it Diogenes? I managed to make enough of his garbled English to learn that I had a visitor. I must have nodded my head or something because he suddenly disappeared and a moment later Glo was pushed into the room. She slapped his hand away vigorously, and after getting him out of the room she slammed the door in his face.

"My God, you look terrible," she said.

"So would you," I replied smugly.

"Funny really," she said. "I never fancied Peter."

"Start now and I'll cut your heart out," I said. I meant it, too. She smiled. "Don't worry I've got all I can handle."

"That's in Nairobi."

"I didn't say that," she said, and we left it at that. "Peter asked me to look after you today. He had to go to the airport," she went on.

"I'm a big girl now."

"You are indeed," said Glo, eyeing my breasts which were sticking out over the sheet. Hello, I thought, had I missed something in the beautiful Gloria's hormone make-up? I stored the idea at the back of my mind where I kept other such trivia.

"He told me to show you the sights," she said.

"Are there any?"

"You'll be surprised. Don't wear slacks or a mini," she added, and left me to get dressed. That rather put the knockers on my entire wardrobe, and I was wondering what the hell I was going to do, when I made a discovery. Diogenes and Archimedes had been very eager to unpack for me yesterday and I had assumed it was because they wanted to fondle my undies or somesuch. When they had reluctantly surrendered the privilege at my insistence, they had nevertheless shown me the closet I was to use. Now, in my sleep dazed way, I climbed out of bed and opened the wrong closet. It was crammed with clothes, women's clothes. Some were new, some were used. My opinion of how well organised Peter was shot up fifty per cent. Also I felt a little disappointed. Unreasonable of me I know, but show me the girl who wouldn't be. I rifled the closet and came up with a sari that looked as though it could have been made for the Begum.

Hoping that wherever Glo was going to take me, I wouldn't bump into the owner of the sari, I bathed quickly and wrapped myself in its soft coolness. It's a delicious thing to wear is a sari;

sexy, subtle, comfortable and elegant. On the odd occasions I had flown Air India I had worn one and, once I had got into the habit, I'd gone out and bought myself a couple for my personal wardrobe.

Half an hour after waking up, I was ready and I went to see what little treats Glo had in mind. She made an "Oooh" of approval as I swept in, and Diogenes and Archimedes went into paroxysms of ecstasy when they saw me. So we set forth.

Peter had left his car and, with the refrigeration turned well up, we took the full tour of Calmooniville. My first impression hadn't been all that wrong, but what I hadn't seen was the new town that was going up. It was a sort of poor man's Brasilia, being constructed ten miles from the main town. A huge area had been chopped out of the jungle, and here were the high buildings, the massive sculptures, the landscaped architecture and the immaculate planning of a bankrupt nation. Mind-boggling schemes had been started, but over all hung the hideous certainty that none of it would ever be finished. Like the grand new airport, interest had seemed to fade about halfway through the operation. There were odd groups of dispirited looking Africans moving around wheeling barrows and mixing cement, but they looked as though they would still be at it a hundred years from now. And as though to confirm everything I was thinking, the jungle was starting to creep back in to reclaim its territory.

"The money is running out," said Glo. "Everyone leaped in with open purse strings at first; then when the Russians found they were working next to the Americans with the Chinese in between they all decided they were being taken for a ride. Which they were, of course. So the bottomless purse was snapped shut. It only opens nowadays for things like power stations, dams, irrigation projects and factories; something that the financier can point to proudly at the end and say "Look! We built that. Aren't we kind, generous and far sighted?"

It was all very depressing, and I said so.

"You'll get used to it," said Glo.

We spent a couple of hours viewing the remains; then we headed back towards town.

"Where now?" I asked.

"The Club," said Glo. It seemed that the entire social life of Borami revolved around the Club. Everyone who was anyone, and a good few people who were nobody at all, used the Club as their meeting place, and as the clearing house for information and gossip. Nothing happened in Borami without news of it going the rounds at the Club almost simultaneously. Glo told me all this on the way back into town, so I was half expecting everyone to know who I was and with whom I was staying; I also had a sneaky feeling that everyone would recognise the sari I was wearing; which turned out to be exactly right.

The Club was housed in a new building on the outer perimeter of the palace grounds. The President was fully aware of its value in keeping him informed on who was doing what to whom in his little domain, so he had presented the land and donated a considerable sum towards its construction. Then he made sure that at least seventy per cent of the staff were on his own payroll. He never used the place himself, but he knew more about what went on under its roof than the resident manager. The place was crowded when we arrived, the car park full of opulent looking automobiles of British, Russian and American origin.

"It's always crowded," said Glo, as we headed across the cool green lawn to the clubhouse. On the left I could see the swimming pool, and beyond that half a dozen hard tennis courts, none of them being used. "Eighty per cent of government and ninety per cent of commerce is done from here," she added. It sounded the right sort of place for me, bearing in mind my current assignment.

I was introduced to the manager as soon as we set foot on the terrace that surrounded the whole building. He was a sandy coloured Englishman with piggy eyes and a mean looking mouth. His name was Beamish and he had once served a two year stint in the Navy.

"Welcome aboard, Miss Touchfeather," he said, stripping my sari from me with his first glance. "We're delighted to welcome any friend of Captain Chalmers."

He made "friend" sound like a dirty word and I decided that I didn't like Mr. Beamish one little bit. I found out later that very few people did, but that he was good at his job. He ran the place well without putting his hand too deep into the till, so he stayed where he was. He escorted us straight through to the bar, which covered one entire half of the building, opening on all sides to the terrace. The place was crowded and until the moment I arrived, it was noisy too. Then, as I appeared, there was an abrupt and absolute silence for one brief moment. Every eye in the place swiveled towards me; everything was noted, clear down to my false eyelashes. Then, as though by command, all eyes swung away and the noise was resumed at exactly the same level. Welcome to Borami, I thought. But one pair of eyes had not swung away and now their owner bore down on us like an eager little retriever fumbling his way towards the kill.

"God," said Glo. "Here comes the Henry Henry."

That's not a misprint, his family name was Henry and his parents in a fit of lunacy had christened him with the same given name. He was a little, roundish man about thirty-five years old. He babbled effusively, but always with a faint underlying impression of panic. It was as though one only had to say "Boo!" to him and he would collapse into floods of tears. Glo introduced us.

"Katy Touchfeather. Henry Henry." I must have looked a little surprised, but obviously he was used to it. He smiled rather sweetly.

"Terrible, isn't it? I thought about changing it, but I never quite got round to it." He seemed the sort of man who would never quite get around to anything in this life.

"I'll call you Hank," I said.

The poor darling nearly kissed my hand. "Would you?" he said. "Would you really?"

"Hank it is," I said, feeling impossibly noble.

"Please come and have a drink with me to celebrate my new name."

I glanced at Glo, who shrugged, "Love to," I said.

I started towards a corner of the room, but imperceptibly Hank touched my elbow, steering me in the opposite direction, It was only much later that I learned he had spotted the owner of my sari sitting with a party at the far side of the room, and wanted to keep me as far away from her as possible. I was rather sorry when I found out because I would have liked to have taken a look at her. But when I did find out, it only confirmed the nice feelings I already held about Hank. I don't know what it is, but queers like me. I mean it's not as though I'm butch or anything like that, but for some reason they take to me on sight and remain dear and devoted friends; at least until such time as I have my eye on a fellow they also have designs on. Then they can be bitchier than any woman born. But in general, they like me, and I like them. They're invariably good company, polite, amusing, and there's never any complications at the end of the evening.

We spread ourselves around a spare table and Hank ordered the drinks. Then he beamed at us both.

"The two most beautiful girls in the room, and I've got them both." he said.

"No, you haven't," said Glo.

Hank was about to say something; then he shut up. Glo got to her feet, excused herself and headed across the bar towards a group of people who were standing on the far side. Hank smiled at me, apologising for her.

"Gloria has so many friends," he said. I could see one of them from where I was sitting: six feet two, fair haired, brown as a berry, and looking as though he had just stepped off a movie set.

"She'd only need one like that," I said.

"Karl Brenner," said Hank. "He fools around with a small import export business."

"That's not all he fools around with," I said. He was leaning over Glo and whispering something to her, his arm wrapped around her in a proprietary fashion.

"They're very discreet," said Hank. It didn't look that way to me, but I let it go. "How do you like Borami?" he went on.

"Not much," I said. "Although it does have its compensations."

"Everyone loves Peter," he said.

I fluffed the edge of my sari at him. "I'm beginning to find that out," I said.

He smiled apologetically. "It can get very lonely out here. After all, it's not as though he really means anything to you."

"He's my fiancée," I said. "Where I come from, that means something."

"Ah, yes," said Hank. "Your fiancée. And who's going to give you away at the wedding? Mr. Blaser?" Big deal, I thought. So now I know who my contact is.

We talked inconsequentials for the next half an hour. A couple of people drifted over, were introduced, and left again. Hank gave me a brief rundown on the social and sexual lives of most of the people in the room and it all sounded highly entertaining, rather like *Peyton Place* in a hot climate. Then Peter joined us, thanked Hank for looking after me and dragged me off.

"We're going to a palace reception" he said.

"Who's being received?"

"The usual. Diplomats, business men, promoters and gangsters. You name it and it'll be represented there this evening."

"Do we have to go?"

"I do," said Peter. "I suppose I could make excuses for you."

"I was just wondering if one of your ex-girlfriends has as good a taste in reception type gowns as she has in saris?"

He didn't bat an eyelid, for which I was grateful. "You'll find something," he said.

"Just so long as no one is going to come up to me in the palace and rip it off my back."

"The only ripping will be done by me, and it won't be at the palace," said Peter. And with that thought to warm me for the evening, I went to get ready for my first palace reception.

President Calmooni headed the receiving line, which was composed of the Prime Minister, the Minister of Finance, and assorted males and females whose names and functions I never quite did get hold of. But it wasn't really my fault, because the moment I walked into the reception room, before I had even started along the line, I recognised someone across the room. He saw and recognised me at the same moment. I would like to have said he blanched or rocked back on his heels or somesuch. But he didn't. But then men like Constantin Galipolodopolo very rarely do.

FOUR

I managed to locate Hank without too much trouble. He, too, was at the reception. It was only later that I learned he was at all the Palace binges; he was a sort of unofficial master of protocol. President Calmooni relied on him to make sure that the functions he gave were reasonably well run and the social gaffes not too monumental. Peter had me chatting with a party of Americans when I caught Hank's eye across the room. I made some vague sort of signal in his direction which he must have understood because a moment later he moved over to our group. He stood chatting for a few minutes, then asked Peter if he could borrow me for a short time. Peter agreed, and Hank led me back across the reception room towards what he hoped would be a quiet corner. At one moment I saw the cold eyes of Constantin resting on me from across the room, but he made no attempt to make any sort of contact. Finally Hank thought we had sufficient privacy for whatever it was that I wanted. But he thought he would do me a favour before we got down to the nitty gritty.

"Do you want to meet one of the richest men in the world?" he asked.

"I most certainly do not," I said. "I already know him. And I want you to let Mr. Blaser know he's here and what am I supposed to do about it?"

"Like for instance?"

"Like run like bloody hell before Galipolodopolo sets his dogs on me again."

"Oh dear!" said Hank. "Oh dear me." Which didn't strike me as being any help at all.

"How long before you can get word back?" I asked.

He glanced at his watch. "A couple of hours," he said.

"Then be a love and get moving. In the meantime I'll plead sick and go home." He offered to escort me back to Peter, but I didn't want to risk that walk across the room again. The longer I remained here, the more chance there would be that I would be confronted with Galipolodopolo; and I had absolutely no idea how I would handle the situation. Added to all this, there was a fair old chance that Constantin would tell everyone that I was not all that I was supposed to be. Altogether it seemed that I was batting on an extremely sticky wicket and the quicker I extricated myself, the better.

Hank left to do the necessary with his radio, and I sent a message to Peter saying I'd come over queer and had to go home. I located the car in the forecourt, maneuvered it out, and drove back to the house. Archimedes and Diogenes fussed around me like two mother hens when they heard I wasn't well. I managed to prevent them calling a doctor and, after considerable effort, I also managed to dissuade them from undressing me and putting me to bed. I allowed them to bring me a medicinal brandy, then sent them both to bed. After that, I just waited. It was an even money bet as to who would get to me first: Hank, with some sort of instructions; Peter with tender solicitude; or Galipolodopolo with a meat axe.

Fortunately Hank arrived first. I heard him arguing in the hall with Archimedes-or-was-it-Diogenes and, after making out phrases such as "Missy sleeping" and "Missy not well" and "No disturb Captain's lady," I pulled on a dressing gown, courtesy of another Captain's lady, and went to learn my fate.

"Did you speak to him?" I asked. Hank looked horrified, as though I'd asked if he'd spoken to God.

"Of course not. Not personally anyway."

"But you found out what I'm supposed to do?"

"Well yes, in a way."

"In what way?" I asked, not liking the sound of it at all.

"Your instructions are to play it by ear."

More specifically, the report had come through that Miss Touchfeather was to use her discretion in the matter. I thought of the hundred times that Mr. Blaser had told me that I was totally lacking in discretion.

"Are you sure you contacted the right Mr. Blaser?" I asked. Hank looked horrified again.

But those were the instructions and Katy prepared to play it by ear. And the first thing my ear told me to do was to get the hell out of there; to put as much distance between myself and Galipolodopolo as I could. Because it was a pretty fair bet that where Galipolodopolo lurked, then not far behind lurked Lucia of the happy hypodermic. Truth drugs are all very fine in their place, but truth drugs that kill you stone dead I can do without.

Then reason prevailed. If Galipolodopolo was going to go after me, it was a pretty safe bet that somewhere, sometime he would eventually get me. And apart from all that, I couldn't see myself sitting across from Mr. Blaser and telling him that I had run because I was scared. His people weren't supposed to get scared about silly little things like their own skins. So I decided to stay where I was. Perhaps if Galipolodopolo was handed enough rope he'd hang himself; my main concern was that he would do it before he hanged me.

I thanked Hank and asked him to keep an avuncular eye on me for the next couple of days in case I suddenly dropped from view.

"I could get you a gun," he said doubtfully.

But guns are for shooting people and there didn't seem to be anyone around I could shoot, except myself, so I declined the offer. Apart from that, a girl like me, with a trim little formfitting uniform to wear, has absolutely no place where she can conceal a gun, except in her handbag; and my bag is always so full of junk, I'm hard pressed to find room for a spare lipstick. So I patted Hank's cheek, thanked him very much, and sent him on his way. Then I went to bed.

Peter crept home an hour or so later. I heard him open the connecting door between our rooms and stand there looking towards my bed. But I just wasn't in the mood, so I breathed steadily and pretended to be asleep. He tiptoed out a moment later and two minutes after that I really was asleep. It's a funny thing with me; when all around is grotty in the extreme and disaster lurks around every bend, all I want to do is sleep. I know I shall miss the Day of Judgment because I'll be asleep at the time; and this night I died for ten straight hours.

When I emerged it was after ten and the day's heat had started to build up alarmingly. I rang for Archimedes-or-was-it-Diogenes and asked him what had happened to the air conditioning which, along with every other electrical appliance, wasn't working because the electricity supply had packed up again. Apparently it did this with monotonous regularity. Archimedes-or-was-it-Diogenes explained that the power station usually remained out of action for five or six hours so there was nothing to worry about. I disagreed with him; it meant a day without air conditioning in a temperature that reached 110° in the shade at noon. I thought for a moment about going to sit in the car all day, but that didn't seem very practical. Nor did it seem practical to go swimming, either at the Club or at the Palace pool which Peter had use of; either of these places could be swarming with Galipolodopolo.

So I took a cold shower, wrapped myself in a damp sheet and prepared to sulk the day away. Peter had gone out to the airport at nine o'clock and wasn't expected back until the evening. He had left a note for me in which he hoped I was feeling better and would look after myself and have a nice day. I wandered round the house for a couple of hours being nosy and pretending I was looking for something to do. Peter's library was woefully inadequate, all James Bond and technical journals. I found a couple of minor pornographic works on one of the top shelves, but I don't go much for solitary reading of pornography and, anyway, I'd read them both before.

I was still sulking around the house two hours later when Peter called from the airport.

"How are you feeling?" he asked. I told him I was feeling fine. "Good. There'll be a car there in fifteen minutes. We're flying upcountry."

"Where's upcountry?"

"Manboola," said Peter, leaving me none the wiser. "There's a uniform in the closet that should fit you. It may be a little tight around the bust though," he said, no doubt recalling the chest measurements of its former owner.

"They don't build them like me these days."

"They certainly don't," he agreed, and hung up.

Delighted to have something to do, I showered again, made up, and climbed into the uniform of Borami Airlines. It wasn't bad as uniforms go, lightweight and not as tight around the bust as Peter had supposed. Obviously his memory of things past was going. Then I made the mistake of telling Archimedes-or-was-it-Diogenes that I was going to Manboola. I only told him because he asked me if I would be back for dinner and I said I didn't know because I didn't know how far away Manboola was. His eyes opened wide, as did his mouth, and he yelled excitedly for Diogenes-or-was-it-Archimedes. He gabbled something to him and there was the same reaction. Immediately they started running round in circles, and ten minutes later, just as I was about to leave, they handed me an old carrier bag, containing God knows what. It seemed they had three or four aunts and untold cousins in Manboola, and would Missy be so kind as to locate one of the clan and hand over the carrier bag. It contained, they assured me, scraps from Peter's table, food that would otherwise be thrown out, but which would be very gratefully received by the poor, half starved upcountry cousins.

On the way to the airport I peered into the carrier bag; among other things were two jars of caviar, a bottle of scotch, one of gin, and three tins of turtle soup; hardly perishable foodstuffs, but then obviously Peter could afford it, and it wasn't really any of my business anyway.

Peter met my car at the airfield. "We've got a very very V.I.P. today," he said, when he had given me a kiss.

"Don't tell me," I said. "Let me guess."

And of course, I was right.

It seemed we weren't taking the 707 because the airfield at Manboola wasn't big enough to accommodate it. Today it was to be one of the renovated Dakotas. As we walked across the baking apron towards the aircraft, I started to plot and scheme. Perhaps I should just throw a faint here and now; perhaps I should tell Peter I couldn't fly when I had the curse, which I didn't have; perhaps I should say Dakotas made me air sick; or perhaps I should just cut my throat and call it a day.

Then Peter handed me the topper. "I was going to use Gloria on this trip," he said. "But our V.I.P. asked for you especially."

With the scales weighed that heavily against me, there didn't seem much point in fighting it any more. I grinned weakly and allowed Peter to take my hand and lead me up the short gangway into the aircraft.

"Incidentally, you must have made quite an impression on him," said Peter, just before he went forward. "I didn't know you were at the reception long enough to meet anyone."

This meant that up to now, my antecedents weren't being shouted around. I didn't know whether to be relieved or otherwise; and on reflection it didn't seem to make much difference either way. I moved around the aircraft numbly, getting things ready for the flight. It was only two hours, so no food was to be served, but we had enough ice and booze on board to stupefy a regiment.

"How long are we going to be gone?" I asked Peter, just before the passengers came aboard.

"We'll be back this evening," he said. "Galipolodopolo just wants to visit the mines at Manboola."

"What does he want to do that for?" I asked, thinking that I might as well continue on the job up to the bitter end.

"Who knows why a man like him does anything?" replied Peter, and with that I had to be contented.

The two engines were run up and we taxied as close to the airport entrance as we reasonably could. The passengers arrived in two of the palace cars. The group consisted of three Borami representatives and three Europeans whom I took to be Galipolodopolo's men. And, of course, Constantin himself. He came up the gangway first while I buried my head in the galley and hoped he would forget I existed. Then, as Peter moved back onto the flight deck, I was simply forced to put in an appearance. I moved down the aisle checking the seat-belts, and eventually I came face to face with Constantin.

"Is your seatbelt fastened correctly, sir?" I asked feeling like a complete twit.

He looked at me steadily with those cold brown eyes of his and, if you think it's difficult for brown eyes to be cold, you should take a look at Constantin's.

"I would still like to make love to you, Katherine," he said. And that was all. Not "Sorry I had you kidnapped and tried to have you killed at the same time"; not "Now you're in for it, Katy Touchfeather"; not even "You're looking well," or "Longtime no see." Just "I would still like to make love to you." Sex mad, that was his problem.

He gave me absolutely no trouble on the trip. When I asked him if he would like a drink, he thanked me very much and said he'd have a vodka on the rocks. When I asked him if he would like another, he said, "No, thank you." And that was the extent of our inflight communication.

Two hours later on the dot Peter announced that we were about to land. Seat belts were fastened and I sneaked a look out of the window. For a moment I thought Peter had suffered heat stroke or something, because it seemed we were going to put down slap in the middle of the jungle. And it was real jungle. Even from up here one could tell that. This wasn't a Hollywood jungle with Tarzan swinging through the trees; absolutely nobody or nothing could swing through that tangled mass of vegetation that stretched as far as the eye could see. It looked like a very shaggy green carpet that went on forever. Then, as we dropped lower and lower and I could still see no break in the surface, I thought that perhaps we were going to land on top of the trees, they certainly looked solid enough. We seemed about to do just that when a gash opened up in front of us, cement stretched out ahead, the wheels banged down onto something solid, the brakes screamed, held, and we had arrived. We turned at the end of the runway and taxied back along half its length. Then we turned off onto a tiny apron, and a moment after that the engines started to wind down. Peter appeared up front.

"I don't know how much business you have to conduct here, gentlemen," he said to no one in particular. "But I would be grateful if you would allow me to take off before dark. There are no runway lights here and things get a bit tricky come nightfall."

It was Constantin who answered him. "We will be exactly two hours, Captain. Will that be alright?"

Peter glanced at his watch. "That will be fine, sir. Thank you."

The gangway was trundled up outside and the passengers disembarked to get on with their undoubtedly nefarious business.

This left Peter and Katy alone together.

"Drink?" suggested Peter.

"Drink," concurred Katy.

We walked over to the corrugated iron hut that was the only building in sight, and while Katy belted a large scotch on the rocks, Peter had a coke. Being a well brought up flight captain he never touched a drop of booze when he was working. And I needed that scotch. Apart from the flight which had been nerve racking in the extreme, Manboola was enough to drive anyone to drink on its own account. It had been chopped out of the jungle and consisted of a collection of huts crouched among the trees which loomed over the settlement as though they were about to devour it. Three Land Rovers had met the aircraft and the passengers, Constantin included, had driven off into the jungle. Peter explained that the mine was about two miles from the airstrip and he had never seen it, because he had never been asked. Indeed, on one occasion when he had expressed an interest in visiting the place, he had been convincingly dissuaded. He hadn't actually been ordered not to visit the place, but it had been made clear to him that a lot of people in high places would have disapproved strongly. So he hadn't bothered.

"What do they mine up there?" I asked.

"Manganese," he said. "Or is it nickel? Anyway, there's a railway line that goes through to Calmooniville. They ship the ore there, then it's switched to the main line and goes on to the coast."

"What's so secret about a nickel mine?" I asked.

He shrugged. "Perhaps they're digging up uranium at the same time." He didn't really care, and there was no reason why he should.

"May I have another scotch?" I asked. He looked at his watch. There was still an hour and a half before the passengers could reasonably expect to be back, so he agreed.

"A small one this time," he said. Then he trotted out to supervise the refueling and check on the weather for the return flight. The waiter serving us spoke English so I asked him if he knew any of the cousins of Archimedes/Diogenes. He did better than that, he *was* one of the cousins. So I gave him the carrier bag I had toted from Calmooniville, and won a friend for life in the process. No, he had never been up the mine, but three of his cousins worked there, and would I like to meet them? I said I would like to very much, but there wasn't much chance as we were due out in the next ninety minutes. Never mind, he said, next time. I agreed that next time would be fine and I ordered another scotch. Landing here had been pretty traumatic and I wanted to be well insulated by the time we came to take off again. He brought me my scotch and, because we were now bosom buddies, it was a big one. I'd like to think it was this that set my head reeling five minutes later; after all I had started with a double, then a single, now another double; five scotches may not sound too much, but in that stupifying heat, and with my nerves being as uptight as they were, it seemed a reasonable enough explanation. I stood it as long as I could, then I told my newfound friend to tell Captain Chalmers that when he needed me I'd be in the ladies loo, throwing up. I never even made the ladies; I hit the sun outside, the sun belted me back, and I keeled over. I was vaguely aware of catching my elbow an awful bang as I tried to break my fall, and that was all I remembered.

When I emerged, it was to see a rather pleasant face bending over me, the face of a blond young man with blue eyes and a nice smile.

"Hi!" he said.

I tried to reciprocate, but nothing came out. I tried again.

"Hi yourself," I managed.

"Feeling OK?" he asked. I shook my head, then grabbed it before it fell off and rolled under the bed.

"Take it easy," he said. "Drink this." He held me partially upright while I swallowed some vile tasting concoction which surprised me by muffling the bells that were ringing in my head.

"What happened?" I asked, when he had lowered me back onto the pillow.

"You passed out and you were brought here."

"Where's here?"

"The hospital."

"What hospital?"

"Manboola Mining."

"Oh," I said. "Where's Captain Chalmers?"

"He and his party left hours ago. You've been out for quite a time."

"Galipolodopolo, too?"

"I believe so." At least that was relief. "I'm Doctor Petrie," he went on. "You're Katy Touchfeather."

"I wouldn't bet on it," I said, still feeling like absolute death.

He grinned pleasantly. "You're a real treat for me," he said. "All I usually get here are VD cases and broken arms."

"Shouldn't there be a nurse in the room or something," I said, recognising a far off gleam in his blue eyes.

"Don't worry," he said. "You're far too sick for me to take advantage of you. Not that I wouldn't like to."

"What's wrong with me?" I asked, trying to change the line of the conversation.

He shrugged. "I don't know," he said. "I thought you might be pregnant, but you're not."

"I know it," I said. "How do you?"

"I looked." Fair enough, I thought. After all, he was a doctor. "Food poisoning probably," he went on. But he didn't sound to happy about that either.

"So what happens now?" I asked.

"As soon as you're well enough, I call Captain Chalmers and he'll come and fetch you."

"How about calling him now?" I didn't fancy staying in Manboola any longer than was absolutely necessary.

"Let's leave it until tomorrow," he said. "Is there anything you want?" I shook my head again, and this time it stayed in place. "I'll send a nurse in to give you something to help you sleep. See you in the morning."

"Are we actually at the mine?" I asked, game to the end.

"We're in the compound," he said. "There's no hospital at Manboola proper."

"I thought this place was off limits to outsiders."

He looked puzzled. "Who told you that?"

"Well, isn't it?"

He shrugged, "We don't get many outsiders here I admit, but that doesn't mean they're not welcome. You're very welcome."

"I must have misunderstood," I said.

He smiled, rather sweetly. "If I played my cards right I could keep you here for a couple of weeks," he said. "Doctor's orders."

I managed a smile in return. "I'm a pretty generous type girl," I said. "But never when pushed."

He looked at me from the door for a moment, a speculative gleam in his eye. Then he smiled again.

"See you tomorrow," he said, and left.

I looked around my room. It was sterile, functional and completely without any warmth or charm whatsoever. There was a small wardrobe in one corner, one chair, a wash basin and a bedside table. That was it; exactly the sort of hospital room one would expect to find anywhere in the world. But I wasn't anywhere in the world. I was in Manboola, in the middle of the jungle and a thousand miles away from absolutely everything. I didn't like it and I started to feel miserable; really miserable. At times like this Mr. Blaser invariably comes to mind, because he is the one who is responsible for me being where I am. "Play it by ear," indeed.

Had he any idea at all what he was talking about, the silly old fool. I'd like to play it by his ear, all around Calmooniville, Manboola and points between. Still, Constantin Galipolodopolo was gone, so I didn't have to worry about him any longer, which was a consolation. And having indulged myself in a small ration of self pity, I started to cheer up again.

The nurse arrived ten minutes later, a cheerful coloured girl. I thought I was going to get a sleeping pill, but she had other ideas. She prepared an injection, swabbed down my arm, and shot me full of something that perched me for a moment on the edge of a delightful cottonwool abyss, and then slid me gently over the edge, way over my head.

This was some drug I had been given. It was better than an LSD trip. There were hallucinations, colour, movement, noise, people, more movement and more noise. All this was interspersed with periods of nothing. It was exactly as though I were lightly sleeping and occasionally surfacing to wakeful-ness when I would grasp an impression of something, and slip back to sleep once more. All very cosy, I thought, in one of my semi-lucid moments. I must remember to get the name of the stuff. Whoops, now I was flying. Not by myself as in a proper LSD trip, but in an aeroplane, a warm comfortable aeroplane. I've always said that the best way to fly is by aeroplane. Then off to sleep again. Perhaps the next time I surfaced I'd be floating. But I wasn't, I was still flying. Cheap old drug I thought. It doesn't even vary the pattern. I dozed off once more and, damn me, if I wasn't still flying the next time I emerged. Ridiculous, I thought. This needs investigation.

So I fought against drifting back to sleep this time and managed to stay awake initially for thirty straight seconds. After that, it was no problem because my fright pumped enough adrenalin into my system to keep me awake for the next ten years. Because Goddamn it, I *was* flying.

Without advertising the fact, I took a peek around. I was in a small cabin holding six very luxurious seats with plenty of leg and elbow room. I was at the back, and there may have been someone else in the cabin with me, but they would be obscured by the rear of their seats. The engine noise was that of a jet, and glancing out of the window I could see by the vague light of the night sky that there were no wing engines. That meant aft engines. So what did we have? One; a small aircraft. Two; rear mounted jet engines. It had to be the sort of aircraft owned by film stars and captains of industry – the executive jet, they call it. And it didn't need three guesses to work out which executive *this* aircraft belonged to.

After five minutes I managed to convince myself that I wouldn't drop off to sleep again. I thought about now would be a good time to try to garner some information. I unfastened my seatbelt and lurched to my feet. I wasn't as well as I had supposed, because if I hadn't been able to grasp the backs of the two seats in front of me, I would have fallen flat on my face. But, standing up, I was able to see across the backs of the other seats. I was alone in the cabin. This was a certain comfort, but not much, because I obviously wasn't going anywhere except where the aircraft took me. I tottered towards the front of the cabin where the door led through to the flight deck. Should I try it or not? It would probably be locked, and in trying it I would only advertise the fact that I was up and about. The best thing I could do would be to make what preparations I could for the nastiness that was to follow.

By now I had worked out exactly what had happened; a mickey finn in one of my scotches, sufficient to make me pass out and be taken to hospital; something heftier and more subtle in my late night injection. While all this was going on,

Galipolodopolo would have arranged for one of his private air-craft to slip into Manboola and have me lifted out of there at dead of night. Altogether a very smooth operation especially if one bore in mind Peter's earlier statement that there were no runway lights at Manboola. Whoever was up front driving this thing was a hell of a pilot.

I spent a few minutes working out the permutations that would follow my disappearance. No doubt Peter would call to see how I was. If Doctor Petrie was in on the deal, then I would be reported as OK but not yet well enough to travel. If Petrie wasn't in on it, then he would tell Peter that I had disappeared in the middle of the night. And what would Peter do then? And would Hank hear about it? And if he did, what the hell would Mr. Blaser be able to do about it? Because one thing was for sure, wherever we were heading, it was a pretty fair bet that very few people would get to hear about it and Mr. Blaser was way at the bottom of the list. No, Katy was strictly on her ownsome, and pretty sick about it to boot.

A look out of the window told me absolutely nothing, except that dawn wasn't far away. Below there was just cloud. The first light of the day did tell me we were travelling roughly north west, but that was all. If there had been a parachute available I would probably have used it, preferring the unknown to what I reck-oned was waiting for me. But there wasn't a parachute so I was saved from making the choice. But while there wasn't a para-chute there was something else. In the rear bulkhead there was a hatch marked "Emergency Equipment".

This seemed as dire as an emergency as would come my way for quite a time, so I opened the hatch. Behind it was a deep locker holding a couple of inflatable rubber dinghies, half a dozen inflatable life jackets, and a small box marked 'survival kit.' I opened the box and sorted through the glucose tablets, seasick pills, water purifiers, chocolate bars and first aid gear until I found what I was looking for. It was a roll of fine nylon thread on a spool, half a dozen extremely large fish hooks and a knife. Every survival kit worth its salt carries the equipment necessary for fishing, and for gutting the fish if you're fortunate enough to catch anything. The knife was very sharp, with one plain and one saw edge. This I tucked down the back of my blouse, flat under the back strap of my bra, giving silent thanks to whoever it was had dressed me at the hospital. God knows where I would have hidden the knife if I hadn't been wearing a bra. I wasn't quite sure what use the fish hooks would be, but they were very large and looked exceedingly vicious; these I hooked into the underside hem of my skirt. The nylon cord I started to wrap around my waist under my blouse and skirt. When I had wound what seemed like ten miles of the stuff around my middle, I pulled the knife out again and cut the cord; then I tied the end so that it wouldn't unravel and fall around my ankles. I put everything else back in the emergency locker, closed it, and resumed my seat at the rear. When we landed it would be advisable to look as though I had just regained consciousness. That way they wouldn't bother to poke around my person wondering if I had been up to anything.

It was almost daylight now, but there was still one hundred per cent cloud cover below, so it was no help. What I did manage to see was the aircraft registration letters. They showed that the aircraft was registered in Greece. Surprise, surprise! And then, just as I was about to drift off to sleep again, having nothing better to do, the door to the flight deck started to open. I closed my eyes quickly and tried to look unconscious. I sensed someone come into the cabin and then there was silence. I stood it for as long as I could and then I risked a peek. A rather dishy face was a foot away from mine, brown eyes regarding me steadily. I squeezed out a little groan, closed my eyes again, opened them once more and rolled them about a bit. All told, not a bad performance; at least it managed to convince him.

"How do you feel?" he asked.

I focused once more. He really was dishy; dark, with soft brown eyes like Omar Sharif. He wore a plain blue uniform with no sleeve rings, and he smelled faintly of an expensive after shave lotion.

"Oh dear," I groaned. "Oh dear."

There was a flash of concern in his eyes; a hell of a kidnapper this one.

"What is it? Can I get you anything?"

"I'm going to be sick," I said.

He moved quickly and returned a moment later with a sick bag. He handed it to me, and then, because he was obviously a gentleman, he turned his back to me so I wouldn't be embarrassed at throwing up in front of a complete stranger. He was the one to be embarrassed. I made convincing throwing up noises just for the time necessary to unstrap my seat belt and reach into the back of my blouse for the knife. The first intimation he had that all was not as it should be was when I struck the point of the knife up under his ear. He wasn't used to this sort of caper because he made the mistake of trying to turn round to see what was going on, and I had to jab the knife in a little way.

"Perfectly still," I said. "Or it goes all the way in."

He looked so shocked I almost felt sorry for him, especially as there was a trickle of blood running down his neck into his clean white shirt collar.

"Madre mia!" he exclaimed. "Be careful with that knife."

"Sit down!" I said. He sat, while I kept the knife stuck where it was. "Anyone else up front?"

He was about to nod, then, working out he would probably impale himself, he settled for saying, "Yes."

"Just one?"

"Yes."

"Where are we going?"

I think about here he decided to see if I was bluffing, because he shut his mouth firmly and a small jab with the knife, while making him wince, didn't open it again.

"Is the money Galipolodopolo pays you worth getting your throat cut for?" I enquired politely. Still he didn't answer.

This would be quite a problem I thought. I could hardly stand there digging him with the knife if he was determined not to say anything. And at any moment his companion might come trotting through the door. I didn't want to cut his throat because, believe you me, the mess is indescribable. I hardly had time to tie and gag him, and I hadn't got a club to beat him over the head with. So, hoping I remembered the anatomy that Bessie had taught me, I reached for the vital pressure point that could cut off the flow of blood to the brain. I gave it a good whack with the edge of my free hand and he keeled over as though he had been poleaxed. For a moment I wondered whether I had killed him. But I wasn't about to waste time finding out. Leaving him where he was, I moved up to the front part of the cabin. He had left the door half open, and peering through it I could see his companion flying the aircraft like he didn't have a care in the world. Maybe at that moment he didn't, but he sure as hell did ten seconds later when I came up behind him and clouted him with the fire extinguisher I took from the wall just inside the flight deck. He keeled over and the aircraft immediately put its nose down in sympathy, starting earthwards at a vast rate of knots. I dragged him clear, slipped into the seat, and leveled off five thousand feet lower down. I located the automatic pilot, switched it on and checked for a moment to see that it was operational. Then I slipped out of the seat again and went to tidy up. Ten minutes later I was back, looking at the controls and trying to work out how to fly the bloody thing.

By now, my two companions were back in the cabin, wrapped up in fishing cord. Even when they regained consciousness, they weren't going to be able to do anything except strangle themselves if they struggled too hard. Katy was on her own with five hundred and fifty miles per hour of aeroplane at her fingertips, and without the faintest idea what to do with it. I'd flown aeroplanes, of course – all part of the training – but there is a vast difference between a conventional prop aircraft and a jet. Books have been written about this difference, but unfortunately I'd never read any of them.

I looked at the dials and levers and gadgets for a full five minutes before I said the hell with it. But one thing I could do was to go down and take a look at what was below. The fuel gauges read half full, so there was no screaming rush to land, or anything like that, but it would be comforting to know roughly where we were. Then perhaps if things worked out I could take a chance on the radio; one never knew who might be listening in.

I dipped the stick forward and started a long, gentle downward track. The clouds came up three minutes later and, gritting my teeth, I continued to head downwards. There may have been a mountain lurking someplace but I had to take a chance. The altimeter was reading six thousand feet when we went into the cloud and two thousand when we came out. As soon as I saw the ground, I eased back on the stick and leveled off. I wish I hadn't bothered. I should have left the flying to the two boys back in the cabin. At least they knew where we were going, and how to get there. We were flying over desert; not your Californian type desert, or even your Arizona type desert. This was full blown, king-sized number one, top grade, umpty thousand mile type desert. Seeing as we were still travelling roughly north west, and bearing in mind where we started from, it had to be the Sahara; the daddy of all deserts. Sand went on forever, without any sort of a break, not even a camel to relieve the monotony. Alright Katy, I thought, what are you going to do now? Either you can fly this thing until you see something below you, or until you run out of fuel; or you can go back into the cabin, untie the pilot, apologise, and let them get on with what they are equipped for, namely to take this flying coffin to someplace where they can put it down on the ground. Because even if I found a place I considered good for landing, I didn't think I would be able to do it. It was all to do with stalling speeds, flap angles, drag and inertia, and a few things I'd never even heard of, let alone understood. Perhaps I could force one of the pilots into flying me to where I wanted to go. Let's give it a try I thought.

I reset the automatic pilot and went into the cabin. Both men had regained consciousness and both started talking as I came in.

"Please, lady, you'll get us all killed."

"Let me fly the aeroplane."

"Do you know what you are doing?" And similar remarks in that vein.

I chose the pretty one, the one I had stuck the knife into. At least he hadn't received a bang on the head to upset his judgment.

"I'm going to cut you loose," I said. He didn't say anything, but his eyes spoke volumes. "But please don't get any ideas. I may be sugar on the outside, but I'm just plain mean underneath it all. And if I have to stick this knife into you, I'll do it, even if it's only to convince your friend that I'm that type of person. Now, are you going to behave yourself?"

"Yes ma'am."

He sounded reasonably impressed with what I had told him, so I cut him loose. Which only goes to show how you can't trust a soul these days. Because as I cut the last strand of nylon he proved just how untrustworthy he was by grabbing for my wrist where I held the knife. I stepped back quickly but the gangway wasn't all that wide and I didn't have as much room to manoeuvre as I would have liked.

"Get her, Andrei," shouted the one who was still tied. And Andrei did his best. In fact he did so well, I had to do something I'd hoped to avoid; namely stick the knife into him.

The mess was unbelievable, and by the fuss he made you would have thought I'd castrated him. He rolled around the cabin, shedding blood copiously and swearing that he was as good as dead. All I had done was to slash his wrist; painful, yes; bloody, certainly; but fatal, no; not so long as a tourniquet was applied. I told him this and let him get on with it while I untied the second man, who was as quiet as a two day old kitten by now. As I urged him towards the flight deck, Andrei appealed to me.

"Please help me," he said. "I can't put a tourniquet on by myself."

"Use your other hand," I suggested. "Just clamp it above your wrist. Don't forget to ease the pressure every few minutes or your arm will drop off."

With that I escorted the other man through to the flight deck, where I closed and locked the door. He knew more or less what was wanted of him, because he sat straight down, switched off the automatic pilot, and quickly checked all the instruments to make sure I hadn't fouled up anything. Then, satisfied, he turned to me.

"Alright lady," he said. "What happens now?"

Where the other man was Greek, this one was English, obviously ex RAF. He was about thirty years old with a rather tired face as though he had seen it all and didn't much like any of it.

"First things first," I said. "Where are we going?"

"Babout."

"Where's Babout?"

He pulled a flight chart towards him, turned a couple of sheets, and pointed to Babout.

It was, as near as made no difference, slap in the middle off the Sahara.

"What's at Babout?"

He shrugged. "It's an oasis."

"With a private airfield of course," I prompted. He nodded. "Whose?"

There was a moment of silence so I encouraged him with the knife under his ear.

"Constantin Galipolodopolo," he said reluctantly, no doubt seeing his pension going out of the window. I looked at the map again.

"We'll go on to Casablanca," I said.

He shook his head. "Not enough fuel."

"Where have we got enough fuel for?"

"Babout," he said. And so help me if he didn't grin.

"What's your name?" I asked.

"Thomas Wise," he said, not catching the drift.

"Alright, Tom," I said. "Let's see how funny You'll find it with your ear in your lap."

He stopped grinning and went quite white.

"And having exhausted our comical repertoire, perhaps You'll tell me where else we can put down."

"Lady, there isn't anywhere," he said, with shades of panic beginning to edge his voice. "There's nothing this side of Babout and nothing for six hundred miles the other."

"We haven't got six hundred miles?"

"We haven't got sixty if you make me keep to this altitude. We're burning fuel down here like there's no tomorrow."

"Take her back up where you want her," I said.

He breathed a silent sigh of relief, eased back on the stick and we started to climb back into the clouds. I let him fly the aeroplane for the next five minutes, until he had levelled off at his former altitude.

"So tell me all about Babout," I said finally.

It seemed there were a few oil wells, owned by Galipolodopolo, and the great man also kept an establishment there which, while not exactly being a palace, came pretty close. All the world knew of his houses in London, New York, Paris, Athens and Rio, but I was willing to bet that very few people also knew he had a pad in Babout.

"What's going to happen when we land?" I asked.

Tom didn't look pale any more as he realised I wasn't going to try to put us down in the middle of the Sahara.

He shrugged. "I suppose a car will call for you to take you up to the house."

"And then?"

"That's your problem, lady. We were just told to pick you up at Manboola. We've done it before."

"Done what before?"

"Picked up birds ... ladies, and flown them in."

"Unconscious ladies?"

"We thought you'd had too much to drink," he said. "That's what we were told anyway."

It sounded reasonable. They must have had quite a shock when I turned as grotty as I did. Ladies visiting *chez* Galipolodopolo weren't supposed to play around with knives.

"How far is the airfield from the house?" I asked.

"A couple of miles."

"What else is at Babout?"

"A small Arab village, the water hole, the airstrip, the oil encampment, and that's it."

"How does the oil go out?"

"Pipe line."

"Where to?"

"Bir el Mers." That was in Spanish Morocco, on the coast.

"And there's nothing else?"

"Like what lady?"

I didn't know, but somewhere there had to be something I could use. I'd done pretty well up to now; it would be a crying shame if it all went to waste.

"How long before we arrive?" I asked.

"I don't know till I get a fix."

"So get it," I said.

He switched on the radio and I prodded him gently with the knife just to remind him that he still had company. He called Babout and received a strength two reply. He received his fix and, after doing a couple of calculations, informed me that we would be in Babout in a shade under ninety minutes.

Having extracted a promise from him that he would behave himself, I went back into the cabin to see whether Andrei had bled to death yet. I was grasping at straws by now, and there was only one way out that I could see. It wasn't a good one, and I didn't honestly expect it to work, but beggars can't be choosers.

Andrei hadn't bled to death, but he looked pretty sick nevertheless. He was sitting on the edge of a seat, clutching his wrist like it would drop off if he let it go for a second. I fixed a tourniquet for him, and he seemed pathetically grateful.

"Thank you, Miss," he said.

"A couple of dozen stitches and You'll be as right as rain," I said. He looked at me doubtfully and I tried to give him a smile of encouragement. A silence followed which grew positively companiable.

"You'll be judged as accessories," I said finally.

He looked at me blankly. "To what?"

"Murder."

"Who's been murdered?"

"Me, shortly,"

"I don't know what you're talking about," he said, meaning it.

"That won't help you in court," I said. "And rest assured there will be a trial. A lot of people will be looking for me. They're very efficient, and eventually they'll find me. What's left of me," I added.

He shook his head slowly from side to side. "You really are a case. I've flown all sorts of girls all over the world for Mr. Galipolodopolo, but there's never been one like you."

"That's because all the others wanted to go."

"Don't you?"

"Does it look like it?"

He had to admit that it didn't. "So why are you going?"

"Because I was drugged and then handed over to you and your friend Tom."

"They said you were drunk."

"Well I wasn't. And in about five hours from now I'm going to die."

About here he started to take me seriously. He still wasn't convinced by a long chalk, but at least he was listening and taking things in. He asked me a couple of questions and I gave him a couple of answers. They weren't strictly true, but by the time I'd mentioned white slavery a couple of times and repeated the fact that I was going to wind up dead, he had started to look worried.

"Does Tom know all this?" he asked.

"Why not tell him."

He decided to do just that and asked my permission to go forward, which I graciously granted. After all, at this stage there wasn't much that the two of them could get up to and at least I'd got one of them thinking. Perhaps if he could convince the other that they were batting on a sticky wicket, something could be salvaged yet. Andrei was up front about ten minutes; then they both came back looking very worried.

"Is all this true?" Tom asked me.

"I have certain information Galipolodopolo wants from me. After he has got it, he will have me killed," I said, laying it as flat on the line as I could.

"Can you prove it?" asked Tom. Obviously he was to be spokesmen.

"If I was a normal type dolly bird off for a dirty weekend with one of the richest men in the world, is it likely I would have acted the way I did?"

He agreed that it wasn't likely. "Anything else?" he asked.

"How great a radio range have you got up front?"

"On the aircraft radio about five hundred miles. But we've got the guvnor's radio on board as well."

"What's the range?"

"Unlimited, more or less. He uses it to call all over the bloody world when he's flying." That was a bit of luck.

"London?" I asked.

"On the key," he said. "Not on R/ T."

"Good enough," I said. I gave him a call sign, and told him to make the call and verify my identity. I also gave him my code name, always a source of embarrassment to me.

"I beg your pardon," said Tom.

"Virgin," I said. "You heard right the first time."

He would like to have smiled, but the circumstances didn't seem to call for it and, anyway, he already knew the call sign, very hush hush, top secret and all that jazz. Like all pilots he was aware of its existence, but he had never used it. It clears the airways quicker than a Mayday signal. He and Andrei had a couple of quiet words, then he disappeared up front to do the necessary. He came back five minutes later and almost bowed to me, he was so impressed. Then he turned to Andrei.

"She's a big wheel," he said.

They both looked at me as though it was quite beyond all belief, and I only just refrained from gloating as I asked them what they intended to do in the light of their newfound information. And whereas thirty minutes ago, it was me who had no idea, now it was them. They still had to land at Babout, it was the only place, and once they landed things were out of their hands. But then Katy came up with an idea she should have had hours ago.

"Send out a Mayday call," I said. They looked at me blankly for a moment. "Say you *hope* to land at Babout, but you don't know if You'll make it." They thought about it for a couple of minutes.

"It's a good idea," said Tom finally.

And that's what we did. The Mayday call went out on the wavelength reserved for such emergencies, and within five minutes we were being tracked and reported on by a dozen different radio beacons. Fast aircraft took off from Casablanca and Spanish Morocco, converging on Babout. We may have been in the middle of the Sahara, but everyone jumps at a Mayday call because they never knew when they were going to have to make one themselves. We now had so much publicity that Mike Todd would have envied us.

I suggested to Tom that he drop our altitude a little to burn up fuel; it was important to both he and Andrei that they arrive at Babout with empty tanks, hence the reason for the distress call. Also they would be able to tell Galipolodopolo that the wild woman they had picked up had created havoc in the aircraft, slashing wrists and beating people about the head. After all, they weren't supposed to know that I was anything other than just another girl for their master, and they couldn't be blamed when I turned grotty and forced them to fly low and burn up fuel; neither could they be blamed for sending out a Mayday call. Galipolodopolo would be livid, of course, but he wouldn't be able to touch them without giving away the plot.

Then, to make sure we had a good sized reception committee, we continued to call on the radio that we had an injured man on board in urgent need of medical attention.

"Loosen your tourniquet just after we land," I told Andrei. "Spread a bit more blood about the place."

"I don't think I have any more to spare," he said, almost enjoying himself by now.

Ten minutes out of Babout, Tom seriously started to wonder whether we would in fact make it after all. He and Andrei did a quick re-calculation of the remaining fuel and arrived at different conclusions. So we all crossed our fingers and sweated it out together. We did make it, just. We ran out of fuel as we were taxiing back to the dispersal point. Then, before everyone piled into the aircraft, I gave them both a big kiss, apologised for treating them badly, and said I hoped we never met again. They both wished me luck and prepared for their acting bits.

It didn't really need much acting on their parts. All they had to do was to tell the truth. A nutty female had run berserk with a knife, tried to take over the aircraft and forced them to fly low so they burned up too much fuel. Finally they managed to overpower her and here she is. For God's sake take her off our hands. All this to a perfectly charming young Arab police officer stationed at Babout. He met us as we landed, actually driving along the runway beside us as we began to taxi in. Big noises were made over the telephone and, while Galipolodopolo's people stood by impotently, I was locked in a tiny cell to await my fate. The cell was a little larger than an oven, and twice as hot. But I didn't have to put up with it for long. The Arab lieutenant brought me a Coke and told me I was in serious trouble, so serious that one of the aircraft alerted by the Mayday call had been instructed to put down at Babout and transport me direct to Casablanca.

"Why Casablanca?" I asked, not caring.

"The offence you committed was done over Moroccan airspace," said the Arab in impeccable French. "Therefore you will come under the jurisdiction of the Moroccan courts."

"Courts? What courts? What have I done?" I too, could act when necessary.

"You are going to Casablanca to stand charges of piracy," he said. Strong stuff, and music to my tired old ears. "The penalty for piracy in Morocco is death," he added as an afterthought.

All I had to worry about now was whether Mr. Blaser's contacts in Casablanca carried sufficient weight to do the necessary once I got there. It would be an interesting problem for him to work out. Running a worldwide department as he did, he was forever moving on tiptoe along international boundaries taking enormous care not to overstep the laws of any particular country. In a case like this, it would never have surprised me if he were to wash his hands of me entirely and let me take the consequences. However, he was probably thinking that I had suddenly become a mine of information on the Galipolodopolo case, so he would move hell and high water to get me out. Or so I hoped.

My air taxi arrived half an hour later. Papers were signed and exchanged, and Katy, escorted by a young Arab constable who was ecstatic about a free trip to Casablanca, was driven out to the boarding point. As we took off, I could see Tom talking heatedly to the men who had been sent to meet me. A moment before we turned away, heading north, I saw Andrei, his arm in a neat sling, move over to join the group. A lot of people were going to get fleas in their ears over this, and I didn't care one little bit.

FIVE

asablanca; a sea port on the coast of Morocco at 33 degrees 27 north. 7 degrees 46 west. The capital city of Morocco and one of the largest on the African continent. So say the gazetteers. They're undoubtedly right, but all that had nothing to do with the Casablanca that I know. I know the beaches just outside the city, the incredibly white villas along the coast, the languor and indolence of weeks spent there before or after assignments. There are a number of places scattered around the globe that I keep a soft spot for, and Casablanca is quite high on the list. A place is attractive solely through the memories of times spent there, and I had spent some incredible times in Casablanca.

All this was resting comfortably at the back of my mind on our flight from Babout. I knew there would be inconveniences; after all, I was under arrest charged with a major crime. But the Touchfeather optimism is renowned and I was warmed by the thought that as soon as the legalities were disposed of, I would probably be able to con Mr. Blaser into allowing me to spend a week or two recuperating. Which only goes to show how time and distance can dull even the most perceptive of minds. Because in the cold light of day I have long been aware that Mr. Blaser wouldn't offer a dying man a glass of water if he were sitting with his feet dangling in a swimming pool.

The flight wasn't too uncomfortable if one discounted the fact that I was handcuffed to my Arab policeman. I had tried to get him to unlock them after we took off. After all, I told him, I could hardly run away. But he was having none of it. He had been lurking in the background when they searched me at Babout, and had seen them extract the fish hooks one by one from my skirt. As far as he was concerned, any girl who would hide that sort of thing away couldn't be trusted to blow her own nose. Added to that, he made an interesting discovery once we were airborne. Being handcuffed to someone brings you in very close physical touch. He was only a lad, but an Arab lad, and they mature early I've been told. I worked it out that, if my escort was anything to go by, they must mature in the womb. He became hornier than a pond full of toads, pressing up to me, rearranging his legs in seventeen different positions, all of them embarrassing. I may be fluent in half a dozen languages, but Arabic doesn't happen to be one of them. I tried glowering at him, snarling, frowning, scowling; and still he came on strong. I could hardly break his arm or otherwise maim him. I was in enough trouble with the law already. So I put up with it, struggling as far away from him as our united wrists would allow.

We landed at a military airport at Casablanca, the authorities obviously convinced I was far too dangerous to be allowed anywhere near the general public. From there we transferred into a police car and, escorted by three motor cycle outriders, we drove into town to police headquarters. There I was finally cut asunder from my Arab admirer, who disappeared to enjoy the fleshpots of the city before he returned to Babout. I was turned over to an Akim Tamiroff type character, who introduced himself as Inspector Ahmed Ben Mullah.

"Miss Toochfeather," he said, pronouncing it exactly like that. "You will explain your actions, please."

Without guidance from Mr. Blaser, I had no idea how far I was supposed to go in my explanations, so I compromised by asking to see the British Consul. It appeared he was playing golf, so the Embassy sent me a minor Under-Secretary instead. His name was Bernard Philpot and he was remarkable only to the extent of his B.O. He must have been to police headquarters before, because the Arabs, who aren't usually too particular in that area, recoiled visibly the moment he walked into the room. I got the message two seconds later as he came close to me to shake my hand. It had to be glandular I decided, because he looked perfectly clean, in fact well scrubbed. It was a crime sending a man like him to a hot country; in a place like Iceland he could probably have carved quite a career for himself. Here, he didn't stand a chance. Inspector Ahmed Ben Mullah was delighted to leave us alone, rushing out of the room at the first available opportunity.

"Sorry about this," said Philpot, as soon as we were alone.

"About what?"

"The pong," said Philpot. "It's glandular. Can't do a thing about it."

I warmed to him immediately. "It doesn't bother me a bit," I said, lying like a cheap carpet.

"Stay upwind of me and, believe it or not, You'll get used to it. And now down to business. What have you been up to?"

"Haven't you heard anything from London?" I asked.

"Not about you. Should I have done?" I'd obviously drawn the wrong Under-Secretary.

"Would you be an angel and call them for me?" I asked.

I gave him the diplomatic callsign and he turned me back to Ahmed Ben Mullah and toddled back to the Embassy to alert the radio room.

Ben Mullah opened all the windows in his office before coming over to sit down opposite me.

"Filthy pig," he said.

"It's glandular," I offered. Either he didn't know the meaning of the word or he was just plain stubborn.

"Filthy pig," he said, and left it at that.

However, the "filthy pig" had spoken up on my behalf, waving his Union Jack all over the place, and nothing was to be done with me until he contacted the police again. I was shown to a cosy little cell deep in the bowels of the building, which smelled even worse than poor Philpot. When I asked for some nourishment, not having eaten for more than twenty-four hours, I was reluctantly handed a bowl of inedible slop, which I ate anyway.

Two hours after leaving me Philpot was back. I was escorted back to the Inspector's office to enjoy another blast of *eau de Philpot*.

"Would you believe that I've taken two showers since I last saw you?" he said companionably as I came in. At least he had learned to live with his affliction.

"Did you make the call?" I asked.

"The call was made. Strings are now in the process of being pulled."

"When do I get out?"

He shrugged. "It's out of my hands. Whatever happens now is up to the big wheels. I'm only a little one."

"Can you use your influence to get me some decent food sent in?"

He nodded. "If anyone will let me get close enough to talk to them, I'll organise it," he said. He bowed to me, and saying that it was unlikely we would meet again, he wafted out, clearing a wide path in front of him. Ahmed Ben Mullah returned and we went through the window opening bit once more, and then I was escorted back to my cell. An hour later a reasonable meal was brought to me, along with a bottle of dubious wine. I ate the meal, drank the whole bottle and, feeling like I hadn't slept for ninety-six hours straight, I hit the sack.

They had to choose that particular night to raid one of the brothels. I was rudely awakened at three a.m. by my cell door being slammed open. Suddenly I seemed to be fighting for my life. In fact, nobody was attacking me; it was just that six people were now occupying a cell designed to hold one. They were all highly painted, three-quarters nude, very loud and, as it turned out, a load of laughs. After we had introduced ourselves and they had ascertained that I wasn't one of them, they insisted that I retain the bunk, while they all squatted around the floor, cursing the police in general and Ahmed in in particular. It seemed that he was a man of vast and extraordinary sexual appetites; he had slept with all of them at one time or another and not necessarily one at a time. Needless to say, they had let him have it on the house, charging him nothing, him being a police inspector and all, and now he had the barefaced effrontery to throw them all in the pokey. The conversation drifted from there to tales of an autobiographical nature, all wildly erotic, and most of them highly entertaining. Nobody asked me who I was, or what I was in for, and altogether it was quite a pleasant hen party.

At seven a.m. the door crashed open once more and standing there, in a brightly shining newly pressed uniform, was Inspector Ahmed Ben Mullah. He scowled at the whores who all scowled back at him. Then he located me. He beamed and bowed low.

"Miss Toochfeather, can you ever forgive me?"

Obviously the strings had been well and truly pulled, and now Ahmed was dancing at the end of them. He escorted me out of the cell, bowing and scraping and apologising, surreptitiously trying to kick some of my new found companions en route.

"Bye girls," I called out just before the cell door was closed, and they chorused their reply.

"Trash!" said Ahmed. "Gutter scrapings."

"I thought they were rather pleasant," I said. "And they're very cross with you, Inspector."

"Cross with me? Why should they be cross with me? I only do my duty. And who cares if they are cross with me anyway. They are trash."

"The one named Maris said the next time you ask her to ..." I went on to describe one of the wild things I had heard in the cell. It is difficult for an Arab to blush, but Ahmed Ben Mullah managed it admirably. I've never seen anyone so delighted to get rid of me. He turned me over to my new escort and practically bolted. My new companion was a young Frenchman, very handsome and very sure of himself. He greeted me as though we had been on intimate terms for years. This wasn't particularly remarkable because we had, on and off. Pierre Boulard was Mr. Blaser's man in Casablanca, and he was one of the reasons why Casablanca held fond memories for me.

"Katy my darling," he said as soon as he saw me. "You look ..." He groped for the right word and finished up by shaking his head. *"Merde"* he said.

I must admit that up to that moment I hadn't given much thought to my appearance. Now I did, recalling that I hadn't washed for as long as I could remember and hadn't been out of the clothes I stood in since I had been bundled into them at the hospital at Manboola two, or was it three, days ago. And I had complained about Philpot. Bless him, he probably smelled like a rose garden up against me. Doing his best to conceal his obvious distaste, Pierre, who had always been a shade too fastidious for my liking, escorted me from my police headquarters into a waiting car.

"I'll be alright as soon as I've had a bath," I said, settling back.

"There's no time, *chérie*. The aircraft is waiting."

"What aircraft? Where am I going?"

He gave a Gallic shrug. "My instructions were to get you out of jail and take you to the aircraft. I don't know any more than that."

"Was it difficult getting me out?"

He shook his head. "The difficult thing was getting you in. It was the only way we could guarantee your safety at Babout.

Under official arrest even Galipolodopolo wouldn't try to spirit you away."

I thought for a moment about my arrest, my amorously inclined police escort and my night in a dirty cell with half a dozen whores. I opened my mouth to complain, and then I recalled what the alternative could have been and shut it again. Just before we reached the airfield, Pierre overcame his distaste sufficiently to take my hand and turn on the soulful Frenchman bit.

"Dear Katy, is it possible that you will be returning soon to Casablanca? The city is a desert without you." Considering I hadn't been here for close on eight months, he must have been going through a pretty dry time. I tried to get close to him metaphorically; I didn't want to get too close physically in case he recoiled in horror.

"I'll be back as soon as I can, Pierre. I promise you that." After all, a girl never knows when she'll be in need of a friend; and he was a sensational lay.

At the military airfield I had landed at the previous day, I was delivered into the care of an RAF Squadron Leader who looked seventeen years old and behaved like a courteous old man of seventy. I don't know what he had been told about me, but he treated me like he would have the Queen Mother. He actually bowed slightly as Pierre introduced us.

"Have I got time for a bath?" I asked as soon as Pierre left us.

He was desolate. "My orders ma'am. They are specific. We are to leave the moment that you arrive at the airfield." He nearly burst into tears he was so upset at not being able to grant such a simple little request. I didn't want to upset him more than necessary.

"OK." I said. "Lead on."

We drove out to where an RAF Transport Command Comet was waiting, A whole Comet, just for Mrs. Touchfeather's little girl. At least there would be wash and brush up facilities aboard, I thought. Wrong again. The aircraft had been stripped out as a troop carrier, and troops weren't supposed to wash it seemed. So I sat in lonely, dirty, isolation for the hour that it took us to fly to Gibraltar. I had nursed a secret hope that London was to be our destination. Visions of my cosy little pad were floating before my eyes. About the last place I would have chosen to go to right then was Gibraltar. Aldershot by the sea, I called it. However, that's where we were.

My Squadron Leader bowed me off the aeroplane and into an official car driven by a Corporal in the WRACS, who took one look at my condition and came over all smug and superior.

"I suppose I couldn't stop off somewhere for a bath?" I asked, as we swept out of the airfield gates. She looked even more smug in her trim little uniform and deodorised underwear.

"Orders are to drive you straight to headquarters," she said. Then, in case she had misjudged my rank or importance, she took out a little insurance. "I'm sorry Miss," she added reluctantly, not sorry at all.

Headquarters was a nondescript looking building flying the Union Jack. In these troubled times with all the Spanish arguments going on, everybody flew the Union Jack in Gibraltar; it was as though they were beating everyone over the head with how British they really were. Why anyone could actually *want* to be ruled by the current British Government is beyond me entirely, but then I don't live in Gibraltar, so it's none of my business. My WRAC Corporal handed me over to a sergeant in the Royal Marines who escorted me down miles of grey corridor, finally stopping outside an unmarked door. Just before he knocked I tried it for the last time.

"Is there anywhere I can get a wash and brush up?" I asked, almost desperate now. His stubby little moustache bristled as he looked down at me.

"Orders Miss," he said. "You are to ..."

I didn't even let him finish; the whole thing was obviously a conspiracy to keep me dirty. "Never mind," I said.

He knocked on the door and was bidden enter. He opened the door and stood back for me to go in. I went in.

"How dare you come into my office looking like that! For heaven's sake go away and get yourself cleaned up," said Mr. Blaser.

I'd never before seen Mr. Blaser outside his office in Pandam Street, London W.C.2. At one time I had even worked out a theory that he never left the place, living out his entire existence in a small bedroom in the back somewhere. I suppose he must have had a smart little two up and two down somewhere in the suburbs, but I could never picture it; he was part of the furniture and fittings of Pandam Street as far as I was concerned. I couldn't have been more surprised at seeing him here in Gibraltar. It would have been easier for me to accept the presence of the Archangel Gabriel or, to be more precise in my similes, Mephistopheles. But there he was, as large as life and as objectionable as ever.

After being thrown out of his office, I looked around for someone who could tell me where I could clean up and get a change of clothes. The only person I could find was the Marine Sergeant. And I was in luck. It seemed that he had a daughter of my age and build, and he took pity on me. He phoned his wife and five minutes later she arrived at headquarters in a beat up old car. She collected me and drove me to their home in the Naval married quarters. Grace was her name, a homely body of fifty-five or thereabouts, worn down by the uncertainty of being a service wife all her married life.

"Look after her, Grace," her husband told her. "And get her back here as soon as possible."

The bath was heaven and I lay soaking in it until Grace banged on the door for the third time. Then I hauled myself out reluctantly and Grace showed me to her daughter's room. The girl's make-up wasn't exactly what I would have chosen for myself, but it was adequate; about as adequate as the slacks and sweater I chose from the wardrobe. Mr. Blaser hated women in slacks; so up yours, Mr. Blaser, I thought. And an hour later I was shown back into the office that he had requisitioned.

Apart from being his normal grotty self, he was livid at having to come to Gibraltar. This was the week of the Royal Regatta at Henley, a positive must for Mr. Blaser, and he had issued instructions that I was to be flown through to London. But the RAF had dug their heels in, and said they would only transport Katy as far as Gib. Added to that, Mr. Blaser had needed to get into heavy discussions with the Moroccan authorities to arrange my entry and exit. Reasonably enough, they hadn't even heard of Henley and they weren't prepared to travel all the way to London to do Mr. Blaser a favour.

"Sit down, Miss Touchfeather," he said.

I sat, trying to look respectful and mutinous at the same time; I felt in my water that he was about to come up with something pretty drastic for Katy, and Katy was rapidly getting tired of the whole bit. Whatever he was going to ask me to do, I was going to go down fighting.

"You made a bit of a mess of your assignment, didn't you," he said.

"Which one, sir?"

"Both of them. Or, if we go back to the beginning, all three. First you let Galipolodopolo get on to you on his yacht. Second, you blow your cover in Borami..." I started to say something, but he lifted his hand imperiously. "I haven't finished. Then when I send through instructions that you are to play the new situation with the utmost discretion, you get yourself kidnapped ... for the second time. You alert half of North Africa with a Mayday signal;

you force me to go cap in hand to the Moroccan authorities to arrange for your arrest in Babout and your release in Casablanca; you tie up a Comet that I had to borrow from the Royal Air Force; and, to cap it all, Miss Touchfeather, you come into my office looking as if you had slept in your clothes for two nights running."

"I had, sir."

"That's beside the point," he snapped. "I'm seriously displeased with you, Miss Touchfeather. Seriously displeased."

So do me a favour and sack me you silly old twit, I thought.

"I'm sorry, sir," I said.

"Still," he went on. "Perhaps all is not lost." He took his unlit pipe from his mouth and started to gouge away at the bowl with a letter opener. Here we go, I thought, he's about to tell me to go and cut someone's throat or, worse still, my own. I braced myself in the chair waiting for the bomb to drop. When he finally spoke it was without looking up at me.

"As from this moment you can consider that you are off the Borami assignment," he said. I tried to remember what the hell it had been, it seemed so long ago. "I am re-assigning you to the Galipolodopolo case."

It seemed to me that if anyone had done the re-assigning, it had been Constantin himself, but I didn't say so.

"Only we will now approach it from an entirely different angle." He paused a moment, giving his pipe an extra savage stab and breaking the letter opener in the process. He looked at the ruined letter opener and then at his pipe. Satisfied that the latter was undamaged, he stuck it back in his mouth and sucked it experimentally a couple of times; revolting in the extreme, I found it.

"Let us examine your involvement from the point of view of Galipolodopolo's side. They know you are on to them; they know you are working for someone. It is imperative for them to find out who it is and how much we know. To that end, you have been abducted twice. Given the opportunity, they will try it a third time." Fat chance I thought; from here on you wouldn't even find me entering a Greek restaurant. "On our side, it is necessary for us to put a stop to Galipolodopolo's activities as soon as possible."

"What are they?" I blurted out before I could stop myself.

He looked at me a little strangely for a moment, as though he believed I must have suffered a severe blow on the head. Then he decided to pretend that he hadn't heard me.

"To this end I have decided on a course of action which could loosely be described as a last resort."

I decided that I just couldn't let it go. "Please sir, what exactly are Mr. Galipolodopolo's activities that you are going to put a stop to?"

"I thought you knew, Miss Touchfeather. I certainly told you at considerable length, if memory serves me."

"No sir, you didn't. You told me he was digging up gold and not telling anyone about it."

"That's part of it, certainly. But only the visible portion of the iceberg." When Mr. Blaser became metaphorical he sometimes became difficult to follow, so I started to concentrate.

"It is what he is doing with the gold that we wish to put a stop to. As you know, in the vast majority of countries, the barter of gold is illegal. In fact, it is forbidden for any of the citizens to own gold. There are exceptions, of course, but we are not concerned with those. Are you following me so far Miss Touchfeather?" Now he was getting sarcastic as well as metaphorical. It wasn't going to be easy, so I concentrated even harder.

"This state of affairs is designed to maintain an evenly balanced economy. It prevents the outflow of money from the country in question. Let us take a hypothetical case." Let's do that, I silently agreed.

"A Mr. X in India is very wealthy, but he is unable to take his rupees out of India. And he wants very much to take them out because there isn't all that much he can spend them on in his home country. He wants to travel; he wants a house in the South of France and a castle in Spain; he has the money to buy these things ten times over, but he is prevented by law from doing so. Even if he can smuggle his rupees out of India, he can't sell them, because nobody wants rupees. So he buys gold, paying in rupees four times what the gold is worth on the official market. Now he owns gold, which is freely saleable in most countries of the world."

I put in my two cents' worth. "But if Galipolodopolo sells the gold, it means that he now owns a lot of Indian rupees. What does he do with them?"

"He uses the rupees to buy things in India. Things like ships, guns, aeroplanes. He buys them in India and he uses Indian money to pay for them."

"It all sounds very reasonable to me."

"That's because you haven't even begun to grasp what I am getting at, Miss Touchfeather," he said testily. "Let us assume he buys a ship for fifty million rupees. After six months he transfers the registration of the ship to one of his merchant navy flags, and that's the last the Indians ever see of it."

"But he's paid fifty million rupees to the shipbuilder; the money has stayed in India."

"No. The shipbuilder is Mr. X., and the money has left India in illegally purchased gold. Added to that, of course, Galipolodopolo has paid for the ship with money that he purchased at twenty-five per cent of its face value."

It all sounded like admirable business to me. No wonder Constantin was so bloody rich. I ventured to say so.

"Pressure is being brought to bear, Miss Touchfeather. If we continue to use our hypothetical case, the Indian Government become very annoyed indeed and questions heavily loaded with political overtones start to be asked. We need all the friends we can get these days, and we are losing them rapidly because of the activities of Mr. Galipolodopolo."

"Why us? He's not English."

"He operates through two main companies. One English, the other American. Unlike some of his fellow ship owners, he does not operate under a flag of convenience. His fleet, some one hundred and fifty vessels, is divided equally; half of them fly the Red Ensign, the other half the Stars and Stripes. He pays all his taxes, he's on very good terms with the merchant seamen's unions in both countries and, all in all, he provides both the United States and our own Treasury with considerable amounts of foreign currency."

It sounded to me as though we should be giving him a medal or the Queen's Award for Industry. But I didn't bring it up, and Mr. Blaser continued.

"The Americans, too, are feeling the pressure from affected countries, notably those on the South American continent. But while they are embarrassed and even annoyed, they are not prepared to do anything about it at the moment."

"There's not much they can do," I said boldly. "Any more than we can. I can see that what Galipolodopolo is doing is illegal, but it's hardly earth shattering enough to have him locked up."

"Well put, Miss Touchfeather," said Mr. Blaser, leaving me wondering what the hell I had said. "You're quite right of course; our case is hardly one we can bring into International Court. Even if we did have all the evidence, it would still be too tenuous to hold up. Therefore he must be stopped in a different way.

"What way?"

"One, we must find his gold mines."

"I've found one of them, I think."

"Manboola?" He asked. I nodded. "I assumed as much. Then, having found them, we must close them down."

"How do we do that?"

"We simply get the countries where they are located to nationalise them." That seemed straightforward enough. "Two, we must prove to him that he is going to lose considerable amounts of money on the operation. To do that, we must make sure that the gold he is already holding is confiscated."

"Confiscated?"

"Alright," he said testily. "Stolen. And if all else fails, three, we must remove Mr. Galipolodopolo himself."

That was like saying we must remove Mount Everest, but there didn't seem much point in my mentioning it, as Mr. Blaser knew as well as anyone what he was talking about. I thought about here that it was time for me to get down to the crunch.

"How am I to figure in all this, sir?" I asked. "I have no cover as far as Galipolodopolo is concerned."

"Exactly," said Mr. Blaser, sitting back as though he had produced a rabbit out of a hat. I waited for an explanation, not at all sure that I was going to get one. But he gave me one, and listening to it curled my hair.

From Gibraltar to Tangier is a couple of hours by boat. One leaves Gibraltar, which is painfully English, and two hours later one lands in Tangier, which is overwhelmingly Arab. Following orders to the letter, I caught the eight a.m. boat and landed in Tangier at ten a.m.

All this was two days after my meeting with Mr. Blaser, who had climbed on an aeroplane the moment he had briefed me and returned post haste to the wet warm comfort of his Whitehall office and the last two days at Henley.

I disembarked from the ferry-boat and fought my way to a taxi waiting at the dockside. I gave the driver the address of the hotel that had been booked for me. It wasn't one I would have chosen for myself, but I wasn't in any condition to worry about it, To say that I was numb would have been an understatement; I was a walking paralysis case. And having checked in, still following instructions, I prepared to wait. Not that I would have to wait long; that much I was sure of. Because, although Tangier is quite a large harbour, there's not much room to hide a boat like the *Maria*; and it was the *Maria* that had hypnotised me for the last twenty minutes of our trip across the Straits of Gibraltar. There she lay, unbelievably elegant and outrageously opulent. But to me she no longer resembled a rich man's play thing; to me she looked like a stinking prison hulk.

Assisted no doubt by the connivance of Mr. Blaser, the Galipolodopolo organisation knew of my arrival in Tangier before I had even landed. I suppose long distance telephone calls resulted and instructions were issued. The two hours they gave me after checking into my hotel was longer than I could have reasonably expected, and by the time they arrived I was nearly ready for them.

Behaving as I had been instructed, I had unpacked my newly purchased wardrobe as soon as I checked in and spread myself around the suite as though I had every expectation of remaining there for a couple of weeks at least. And, like I said, they gave me two hours. I had just got out of the bath when there was a polite tap on the sitting room door. I wrapped myself in a large bath towel, and went to answer it.

"Who is it?" I called.

"Room service," came the reply. I hadn't asked for any room service. But I opened the door nevertheless and then indulged in the full, indignant, angry, frightened bit, as two men sidled into the room behind two large guns. They were gentlemen of few words and all of these to the point.

"Get dressed," said one; and while I got dressed and he watched me like a hawk, the other one threw all my stuff back into the suitcase. The one who was watching me didn't bat an eyelid while I was getting dressed, having already declined my request that I be allowed to do so in privacy. He just stood there while I fumbled with my pants and bra beneath the bath towel, making like Grandma trying to dress on the beach at Blackpool. In the end I said to hell with it and I dropped the bath towel and got dressed the normal way. After all, my modesty was the least of my worries from this point on. And he still didn't bat an eyelid; although his companion looked up from his packing long enough to go slightly glassy-eyed. They were a couple of real heavies these two; dark skinned, immaculately dressed, cold blue eyes and as alike as two maggots in an apple. They were tidy and professional in their operation. They knew exactly what they were doing and the most efficient way to go about it. They wasted no time or effort, and five minutes after they came into the suite we were all ready to leave.

One of them carried my suitcase, the other held my arm just above the elbow in a grip that looked like cotton wool but felt like a steel trap. We travelled down in the elevator and stepped out into the lobby. While I was escorted straight out to a waiting car, the one carrying my suitcase went over to the reception desk and checked me out. Ten minutes later we were pulling up at the dockside where the *Maria* was berthed. They may have been kidnapping me, but they weren't about to be sneaky about it. I was escorted up the gangway like a very important guest and they even had the Captain waiting at the top for me. He saluted me gravely.

"Welcome aboard, Miss Touchfeather," he said. "It's nice to see you again."

Before I could reply he was already shouting out orders like "single up aft" and "belay the mainbrace" or somesuch. In fact we put to sea so quickly that my two man escort barely had time to scamper ashore before the gangplank was hauled up from under them.

A steward had taken my bag and now he escorted me below. I had given up the protesting bit by now, there didn't really seem much point any longer. After all, not a soul believed me, so I decided not to waste my time or my breath. Believe it or not, they put me in the same stateroom that I had occupied before, the one with the connecting door to the owner's suite. Perhaps I'd got the whole thing wrong; perhaps Constantin was only after my lily-white body. Then I remembered Lucia and her happy hypodermic and I decided that Katy was just pipe dreaming. And as though to confirm this, I tried the stateroom doors only to find they were both locked on the outside. So here we were, Katy. Everything going according to Mr. Blaser's plan.

"You will allow yourself to be abducted by Galipolodopolo," he had said. "Then when he or his employees demand information from you, you will give it to them."

"You bet your life I will," I said. Then I added "sir" in case I sounded too flippant. I mean, honestly, I had escaped the clutches of the arch villain twice, at considerable peril to life and limb, and now I was being told to forget it and start again at page one. It was too much, and I felt like bursting into tears.

"We will of course tell you exactly what you can and cannot say," Mr. Blaser had said.

"That won't be much good if they give me a truth drug."

"It is unlikely," said Mr. Blaser. "The last time they were acting in haste. This time they will have all the time in the world. Added to that there is the fact that information divulged under the influence of a drug is not as succinct and accurate as that given under threat or torture. The subject is not in control of his or her faculties and the information is liable to be bogged down among the rubbish that lies around in the subconscious. It takes someone used to such things to sift out the accurate from the supposed. No, I think they will threaten you with something painful and unpleasant." He was a great comfort was Mr. Blaser. "However," he said. "If they do threaten to use a drug on you, you must feign terror, fear, revulsion, call it what you will, and then divulge your information before they can administer the drug. On no account are you to allow them to weaken your mental defences by allowing them to inject you with any drugs. Understood?"

I was too flabbergasted to do anything but nod my head.

"Good," he said. "Now the *Maria* is due in Tangier tomorrow evening, so we have all night and all day tomorrow to go over what you are to tell them. You will leave for Tangier yourself by the first boat on Thursday morning.

The briefing session had been long and involved. I was tired when it started. I was practically unconscious by the time Mr. Blaser was satisfied that I was reliable enough to be turned loose. And all this accounted for the fact that now, with the engines of the *Maria* throbbing gently under my feet, I decided that the best thing I could do would be to catch up on some sleep. I had no idea when the fun was due to start, but I wanted to be in full possession of my faculties while I still had faculties to be in possession of. We Touchfeathers have always had the ability of being able to drop off to sleep at the damndest of times; one Jeremiah Touchfeather was reported to have snatched forty winks on the tumbril taking him from Newgate jail to the gallows at Tyburn. And feeling that my situation was not unlike that of Jeremiah, I took off my shoes, lay down on the bed and zonked out.

I must have slept for a couple of hours at least. When I awoke the first thing I did was to look out of the window. There was no sign of land and the sea had changed colour from Mediterranean blue to Atlantic green. That meant we had turned left after leaving the harbour, heading out to God knows where. I unpacked my suitcase, hanging up the stuff I had bought in Gibraltar, the inevitable loss of which wasn't going to bother me one little bit. I intended putting in an expense chit for twice what they had cost me as soon as I got back to London; *if* I got back to London. After that, I took a bath. By the time I emerged I was feeling hungry. I was still debating whether or not to ring for the steward when he arrived, bringing me one of the finest meals I have had for a long time. Hoping that it wasn't the traditional "condemned man's breakfast," I tucked in vigorously. Another Touchfeather family accomplishment is that when all around is doom and despair, we can still eat like there was no tomorrow; and, in this case, there quite possibly wouldn't be.

After my meal there was nothing left to do but wait. I assumed that Constantin wasn't aboard, or surely he would have been to see me before now. But on the other hand, perhaps he wished to remain aloof from personal involvement. He had all sorts of minions drifting about, and it was unlikely that he would actually tighten the thumbscrews himself. He wasn't built that way. He was the sort of man who could give the orders quite cold bloodedly as long as there was no chance that any of the blood would splash over his five hundred dollar suit. For carrying out the orders, he had people like Lucia, and it was she who turned up in my cabin twenty minutes later. She wasn't dressed as an inquisitor at all; she was wearing a Pucci style number and looked gorgeous. She had obviously worked out that there was very little I could get up to on the high seas, because she arrived alone and unarmed. She let herself in quietly and stood looking at me for a long moment.

"Hello, Katherine," she said finally.

"Hello, Lucia." There didn't seem much point in doing the ignorant bit with these people any longer; they had me well documented and it wasn't going to fool anyone.

"May I sit down?" she asked politely.

It was interesting to speculate what she would have done if I had said "No," but, like the perfect hostess, I nodded towards a chair and she sat, arranging herself immaculately before she got down to business.

"You are a girl of infinite resource," she said.

"Thank you." There was no point in being ungracious.

"And, knowing this, we wonder why you have allowed yourself to fall into our hands for the third time."

"I didn't arrange anything," I said. "Your thugs picked me up in Tangier."

"But what were you doing in Tangier?"

"Working. At least I was going to."

"Which brings us back to the original question. For whom do you work?"

It would have been so easy right there to trot out my carefully rehearsed story. That way, all the subsequent unpleasantness would be avoided; but, equally, they wouldn't have believed a word of it. Girls of infinite resource only open their mouths under duress.

I smiled sweetly at her. "I can't tell you that."

"What were you doing in Borami?"

"I can't tell you that either."

"Why were you in Gibraltar?" I shook my head, still smiling. She looked at me speculatively for a moment. "This wouldn't be a suicide mission would it, Katherine?" she asked, getting far too close for comfort. "You haven't got a neatly prepared story to tell us?"

"I haven't got anything to tell you," I said. "Except that I shall be missed and people will start looking for me. In fact, they're probably already doing so."

She dismissed this as of no importance whatsoever. "Rest assured they won't find you unless we want them to. Now, you have one more chance. The next time I ask you, you will be made to answer. Who do you work for?"

I just shook my head, wishing like hell I could tell her; because I don't like pain. Especially don't I like it when it is inflicted on me. And Lucia had developed a glint in her eyes which rather pointed to the fact that I was about to suffer considerable unpleasantness in the very near future. She stood up and left the stateroom without a word. More from habit than anything else, I tried the door after she had closed it behind her; it was locked, of course. So I took a couple of deep breaths in an effort to slow the beating of my heart, and then I finished the bottle of very good wine that they had sent me with my meal. Then I lay myself on the bed and prepared myself. One problem that had reared its ugly little head was just how much I should put up with before I trotted out my story. If I threw a fit of hysterics too soon after they started on me and babbled all, there was a chance they wouldn't believe me. In this case it wasn't beyond the bounds of credibility that they would keep on trying, to see whether I came up with anything else. And if they tried hard enough, I sure as hell would. I would tell them the lot, even the colour of Mr. Blaser's waistcoat. On the other hand, I didn't want to last out too long because, as I have mentioned before, I don't like being hurt. So the whole thing evolved into a matter of rather fine judgment—not too soon, not too late; rather like working out how many fingernails one was prepared to let them extract before one called a halt. Two would be insufficient; four would be insupportable.

But, as it turned out, my fingernails were to remain inviolate. It seemed that whatever was to happen, they didn't want to leave any external marks. No doubt the plan was to deposit my remains somewhere, so that death could reasonably be attributed to natural causes. I worked all this out as Lucia got to work on me. And, as it turned out, I didn't have to worry about how much pain I could stand, because I didn't stand any at all; discomfort, yes; pain, no.

She returned twenty minutes after she had left me with three crew members. They must have been lately recruited, because I didn't recall any of them from my previous trips on board the *Maria*. Obviously Constantin kept one crew for pleasure, another for business; and this was definitely the business crew. They were all three vaguely Middle Eastern, large, silent and very capable.

Two minutes after coming into the cabin, they had me as helpless as a babe and stark naked to boot. I was spread eagled on the bed, face down, my wrists and ankles secured with leather belts to the four corners of the bed. I must have looked like a stranded starfish. I twisted my head to try to see what Lucia was doing. I couldn't see her at first, but then she walked into my line of vision. She was still wearing her Pucci number, but she had pulled on a white laboratory overall over the top and she was carrying an enamel tray; the sort that one finds in hospitals, complete to the white towel draped over what it was holding, lest the contents disturb the patient. She put this down on the bedside table and then pulled a chair up so that she was sitting close to me.

"I don't want to do this to you, Katherine," she said. "But you leave me no alternative." I tried to see what was in the tray but the towel covered everything completely.

"Do what?" I asked, not keen to know.

"You'll see," she said. "But first, one more chance."

She ran the flat of her hand down across my back and over my backside. It was gentle, almost a caress. Hello, I thought, perhaps I've read her hormones wrong; but that was the least of my problems at the moment. She allowed her hand to linger where it had no business to for a moment, and then, almost as though she had read my mind, she withdrew it abruptly.

"Just one more chance, Katherine," she said, as though she were reluctant to do what came next.

Enough of this procrastination Katy, I thought. If it's got to happen, let's get it over with.

"Go fuck yourself," I said.

She looked at me steadily for a moment, then she sighed. "Very well," she said. Then she stood up. "I'm going to give you an enema," she said.

I nearly burst out laughing, it was so preposterous. "You're going to do what?"

"You heard me."

She pulled the towel off the tray and, by God, there it was, an ordinary common or garden enema, something I hadn't even seen since I was fourteen years old and had my appendix out. Beside it was an enamel bowl, and beside that a small medical bottle unlabeled.

"This is water," she said, pointing to the bowl.

But I wasn't interested in the water, I wanted to know what was in the bottle.

"This is sulphuric acid," she said.

And naturally, as soon as she told me that, I started singing like the proverbial canary. While I could possibly have withstood the bamboo splinters or hot pliers for a short time, what Lucia was proposing was quite out of the question. In spite of the fact that she intended to use a diluted solution to start off with, I didn't want to know.

She had been very specific, "I will dilute the sulphuric acid in the ratio of ten to one to start with, she said, impassively. "Subsequently, if you survive and don't go out of your mind, I shall decrease the dilution. But I don't think that will be necessary."

I maintained my cool long enough to watch her mix the potion, and even long enough for her to charge the enema. But once she started to reach for the Vaseline, I turned the whole thing in. Visions of that stuff sloshing around inside me, burning holes through the walls of my intestines, swam before me. Enough is enough, and sod Mr. Blaser and everyone connected with him.

"World Bank," I said.

She paused in the business of charging the enema. "What did you say?"

"I work for the World Bank."

Almost reluctantly she put down her equipment of persuasion. She went to the door of the stateroom and opened it. There must have been someone waiting outside because she returned to my line of vision almost immediately carrying a small portable tape recorder. We both waited while she set it down and switched it on. Then she turned to me once more.

"Alright, Katherine, start at the beginning. Who do you work for?"

"Can't you untie me?"

She shook her head. "Not yet. First you talk. Who do you work for?"

"The World Bank."

"Doing what specifically?"

"Investigation."

"What have you discovered about Constantin Galipolodopolo, and why is the World Bank interested?"

"He's mining gold unofficially. He's selling gold illegally."

"How did the World Bank find out?"

"I haven't the faintest idea," I said.

She paused for a moment wondering whether it was worth the effort to get me to try to enlarge on this statement. She decided that it wasn't.

"And what is the intention of your employers now that they have this information?"

"I just investigate," I said. "Then I turn in a report. What happens after that is none of my business."

"You must have some ideas."

"Some," I said. "But they're only ideas."

"Let me hear them."

"They'll close down the mines. Or at least wrest them from Galipolodopolo's control."

"They don't know where they are."

"Yes, they do. At least that's what they told me."

"Is that why you were sent to Borami?" I nodded, no easy feat if you're strapped down face first.

"And is that all they intend to do? Close down the mines?"

"No," I said. "They also intend to confiscate all the gold that Galipolodopolo holds at present."

There was a long pause as she digested all of this. Then she started again.

"That deals with the generalities," she said. "Now let's get down to specifics."

This is where the hard work started; now I had to start remembering details of the briefing I had been given; names, places, more names, dates, memos, code words, and all the paraphernalia that had been so carefully prepared for me under the auspices of Mr. Blaser. Everything would check out, Mr. Blaser had assured me. He knew that nothing I said would be taken on trust and he had prepared everything accordingly. There wasn't one word that I delivered to Lucia that couldn't be proved as fact once Constantin's organisation swung into operation. She untied me after the first half hour and from then on I was allowed to sit in a chair, wrapped in a dressing-gown, while a large seaman with a gun watched me like a hawk and the tape recorder continued to record.

About nine o'clock, Lucia seemed satisfied with all she had learned and decided to call it a day. Before she left me she had one final word.

"I hope that all you have told me so far is accurate," she said. I assured her that it was.

"We will continue at a later date." And with that she left me to my own devices. The seaman cum guard also left and Katy was alone once more. Dinner was brought down half an hour later, but with visions of a burned out digestive system, my appetite seemed to have evaporated, and I was only able to do justice to the wine that accompanied the meal. An hour later I was tucked up in bed and asleep.

The following day I was left strictly alone. I was allowed on deck for a couple of hours, but it was cold and there was a heavy swell running, so it wasn't much fun. It was amazing the difference between the *Maria* I had known before, and this particular vessel. Apart from the fact that the deck furniture and the sun awnings had been stowed away, it was exactly the same ship, but now, instead of indolence she carried an air of efficient menace; efficient because here in the Atlantic she was able to show herself off as a proper ship and not just a floating gin palace; and, as for the menace, well you know all about that. Nobody spoke to me all day, and I didn't see Lucia. While I was on deck, the same large seaman remained within grabbing distance at all times. It was difficult to imagine what they thought I would be capable of, a couple of hundred miles out in mid Atlantic, but obviously they thought that a girl of infinite resource needed close watching.

While trotting around the deck, I relearned the geography of the ship as best I could; quickest way up to the bridge; quickest way down to the engine room; quickest way over the side; stuff like that. I tried pumping the steward who brought me my food, just to find out where we were heading, but if he knew, which was doubtful, he certainly wasn't going to talk about it.

Around nine p.m., just as I was about to go to bed, the engines stopped suddenly. I wandered over to the window and peered out. Three hundred yards away was an oil tanker, her bridge and deck lights blazing. She, too, had stopped engines, and was wallowing gently in the swell. There was some clattering on the deck above me, and a couple of minutes later I heard a speedboat start up. A moment later it emerged into my line of vision, heading towards the tanker. It remained there just long enough for someone to climb down the side of the tanker, then headed back towards the *Maria* carrying one passenger. It passed out of my line of vision beneath the deck rail of the *Maria,* as the Captain appeared from somewhere above me to welcome aboard the owner.

The engines started up soon after, and at the same time the tanker swung away to continue her normal business. I debated for a time whether I should continue what I had been doing, namely going to bed; then decided that it probably wasn't a very good idea. The chances were that Constantin would want to talk to me, and one is at a disadvantage when woken out of a deep sleep. So I got dressed again and, when Constantin arrived twenty minutes later, I was sitting in an armchair reading a particularly dull book. He entered without knocking and, not being a lady, I just glanced up from my book, looked him straight in the eye for a second, and then continued reading. He closed the door quietly behind him and, after a couple of minutes of total silence, I just had to look up at him again. He had remained standing just inside the door, staring at me. He had changed since coming aboard, and was now wearing the standard seduction gear of a smoking jacket.

"I hope you are comfortable, Katherine," he said, when I looked up.

"Not particularly."

"That's a pity, because you will be staying with us for some little time." At least that was a relief; it meant that they had decided not to kill me right away. Now he moved across the stateroom and sat himself down opposite me. "I am still in the process of having your credentials checked," he went on.

"And?"

"So far they seem genuine enough," he said. "Are you sure you left nothing out?"

"Nothing."

He smiled a thin smile. "Lucia is very efficient in affairs of this kind."

"Lucia is going to get her neck broken if she's not very careful."

"Possibly," he agreed. "But not by you."

"Don't take any money on it," I said. "And now, unless you've got anything to talk about, I'd like to go to bed." Then, in case he got the wrong idea, I added a rider. "Alone."

"Aren't you interested in what we are going to do as a result of the information you have given us?"

"Not very," I lied. "But tell me anyway."

"The people you work for are going to close down my mines. This is inconvenient, but not disastrous. Let them go ahead, if they can find them. But, thanks to your timely warning, I am having all the gold already in existence shipped to one place. It's worth a great deal of money, Katherine. Some three hundred million pounds on the black market. So you can see, it's enough to last me through my old age."

"They're also planning to confiscate the gold you already have," I reminded him. "Or didn't Lucia tell you that?"

"She told me," he replied. "But before they can confiscate it, they've got to find it. And they won't."

"Where can you hide that much gold?" I asked. "Fort Knox?"

He smiled again. "That I shan't tell you. But rest assured, no one will get their hands on it. Now, is there anything you need?"

I shook my head. "Just peace and quiet."

He looked at me speculatively for a moment. "I would still like to make love to you, Katherine."

I smiled sweetly. "I'll tell you what you do then. Get half a dozen of your crew in here to hold me down, and then you go ahead. But make sure they're holding me securely, or I shall very likely break your back."

He got to his feet. "You are an extremely exciting woman, Katherine, because I am sure you could do just that if you put your mind to it. And you would do it without second thoughts, without any qualms whatsoever."

"You'd better believe it," I said, and returned to my book.

He left a moment later and I was alone once more. Alright, Katy, I thought, mission accomplished. Mr. Blaser had grudgingly admitted that once I had given them my story, and they had checked it out, then I was on my own with full permission to extricate myself in any way that I could. Meanwhile his people would start to close in on the Galipolodopolo enterprises. Vast amounts of gold need vast amounts of transport and organisation to shift it around. If enough people kept their eyes open in enough places, then somewhere along the line there would be a slip up, and Mr. Blaser's men could swoop. My only other brief had been to try and learn the whereabouts of the gold that Mr. Galipolodopolo already had in stock, and even Mr. Blaser had admitted that this would be difficult; so he had generously left it to me whether or not I should fulfill this last instruction. Also in the back of his mind he obviously thought that I would have very little chance of passing on anything I learned, so there hadn't been much point in his getting grotty and laying down the law about it.

So now all that was left was for Katy to disable a crew of twenty-five, take over the ship, and sail her to a friendly port. So come on, Katy. It shouldn't be too difficult for a girl of your infinite resource. I thought about it for a minute or two. A plan here, a scheme there. I made a couple of mental calculations, permuting a sequence of events. I tore them up and made a few more. And then I decided upon the one thing I was fit and capable of doing at that precise moment. I went to bed.

SIX

The Bahama Islands stretch as a loose group for about a thousand miles. Starting with Grand Bahama, less than a hundred miles from the coast of Florida, they finally trail out into the Turks and Caicos Islands about one hundred miles north of the Dominican Republic. There are big islands and little islands, well populated islands and deserted islands; some are well charted and some aren't charted at all because the last time the charts were revised, either someone forgot to put them in because they were so small, or because at that time they didn't even exist, some undersea upheaval having thrust them up into view without anyone being aware of the fact.

I don't really know for sure how I was aware that we had reached West Indian waters; the weather was better certainly, and the sea was bluer; but that only meant that we had reached a more temperate climate. No, there's something about the West Indies, something in the air that you can't put your finger on, but which, if you've been there, you never forget. Even so, I had no idea what part of the West Indies we had reached, because any land that was visible was never nearer than five miles away.

It had taken us two more days to reach here, and during those two days I had kept myself to myself. Constantin had asked me whether I would like to take my meals with Lucia and himself, but I had told him that it would give me flatulence and heartburn, so he had not asked me again. Apart from that, by taking my meals alone in my stateroom, I had been able to start putting together a small armoury. A steak knife and a lobster pick may not sound like much in the way of aggressive or defensive weapons, but they did wonders for my morale. Also I had rigged up an interesting little electric gizmo, using the stateroom's domestic appliances, whereby I could electrocute anybody who tried to switch on the bathroom light; all I needed was ten seconds notice to join up a couple of wires and *pow*!

It was during these experiments that I made an interesting discovery. Tucked away in the paneling in the far corner of the room, well obscured with carved curlycues and cupids, was the lens of a television camera. It wasn't much of a problem to keep out of its way once I had located it, but it did provide the answer to a question I had almost forgotten existed. Assuming every stateroom was similarly equipped, it would explain away the death of Antonio, my bullfighting lover of what seemed like another age. Having viewed our amatory gymnastics over the course of the few days we were aboard, whoever was watching would have seen me going through Antonio's luggage and, later, slice off my gold samples. They must have assumed that Antonio was in cahoots with me outside the sack as well as in. So exit Antonio. One thing was for sure. If the TV camera was connected to any sort of videotape or film recorder, somebody had some extremely blue movies lying around that would be worth a fortune.

Anyway, here we were, two days after Constantin's arrival aboard, cruising the waters of the West Indies. I was still allowed up on deck for a few hours each day, guarded by one of the crewmen, and I spent a considerable time leaning on the deck rail trying to identify some of the humps and bumps of the distant land line. But it was hopeless; the only way I would find out what island lay off our port bow would be to swim ashore and ask someone. And, bearing in mind it could turn out to be Cuba or Haiti, I didn't give the idea too much consideration. Anyway, most of the time we never came any nearer to land than five or six miles, and I'm strictly a feet on the ground type of swimmer. By that, I mean that I can swim very well, as long as I know the water isn't too deep, but tell me that it goes on down forever beneath me and I start to panic. Silly, I know, and I believe they've even got a medical term for it but, whatever it's called, that's what I've got. So I just continued to lean up against the rail and watch the long line of land drift by in the distance.

My dinner was later than usual. The steward, obviously not real-ising my true status aboard, had the good grace to apologise.

"I am sorry about this, Miss," he said. "But the Captain has had all hands working below."

"What on earth for?"

"Clearing some forward cargo space."

"Cargo? On this boat?"

"Oh, we carry it from time to time. Leastways we've got room for it. There's a big hold up front where we keep junk most of the time. But every now and then the guvnor wants something moved in a hurry, and he uses the *Maria*."

Interesting, I thought. Cargo to be taken on. It didn't take much working out what that cargo would be. Also it didn't take much working out that Katy's days were definitely numbered. If Constantin was going to take on gold, it could only be because he intended to deliver it someplace – the ultimate hiding place. And he wasn't going to do that with me lurking around. The fact that I was still around at all was only due to the consideration that I might be able to answer questions as they came up regarding my fictitious employers. Indeed, Lucia had come to see me on the third day, seeking clarification on a point I had made during our long chat in the shadow of the hot enema. But now had come the crunch, and Katy was going to have to pull her finger out while she still had some fingers left.

After the steward left, I checked over my armoury. Like I said, a steak knife and a lobster pick – hardly the equipment of which revolutions are made. What I really needed was a gun, and as long as I was dreaming there was no point in not throwing in a bazooka and an armoured car as well.

We hove to three hours after I had eaten my dinner. For the benefit of anyone who was looking in on me, I had climbed into bed, but had stayed wide awake. As soon as the engines stopped, I was out of bed and over to the window like a shot. There was a land mass looming up a couple of miles away, only just distinguishable in the clear moonless night. On land there was no sign of any lights at all; either it was a deserted island or everyone had gone to bed early. We lay at rest for half an hour before anything happened, the engines restarting occasionally as we drifted off our point a couple of times. I assumed the Captain didn't want to drop anchor in case a quick getaway was called for. From my window I could see a dozen crewmen and one of the officers gathered at the rail a little forward of midships – it's amazing what three or four days on board a boat can do for your vocabulary. Before I had come aboard I would have said they were hanging around halfway up towards the sharp end. They didn't seem impatient, as though whatever it was they were waiting for would get here in its own good time. And get here it did. There was the sound of engines first, drifting across the water, growing closer and closer; a few minutes later the vague outline of a small coastal cutter could be picked out. The men at the rail doused their fags and prepared to start work. Katy did likewise.

The lock on the cabin door was absolutely no problem; I could have opened it at any time since coming aboard, but there hadn't seemed much point in doing so before now. But now there was and I went into my little pantomime for the benefit of anyone who may have been watching telly. I went back to bed as though I had grown bored with what was going on outside. I turned off the lights and settled down. I lay where I was for five minutes, then got up again and padded across to the bathroom, like any girl who needs to take a pee in the middle of the night. I closed

the bathroom door behind me and dressed in no time flat, using
the clothes I had left hanging behind the door. Then I wired up
my electrical booby trap and, one minute after entering the bathroom, I was out again.

Only this time I didn't cross the room into the range of the
TV camera. I hugged the wall of the stateroom making my way
round to the door. Like I said, it proved no problem at all; a couple
of judicious jabs with my lobster pick and I heard the tumblers
click back. The trouble was that if there was anyone outside, he
would have heard them, too. But I had to take a chance on that.

There was no one. I closed the door quietly behind me and
started up the corridor which led eventually up onto the main
deck. It was as though this section of the *Maria* had been abandoned; there wasn't a soul around. A great deal of noise was
coming from the deck part and obviously everyone was up there,
either helping or just watching. Remembering my geography, I
turned left when I reached the open air and made my way aft to
where we had all sipped our cocktails in happier times. But now
the deck furniture had gone and so had the sun awning.

But one thing had stayed the same, and that was the loca-
tion of the Captain's cabin. If everything I knew about ships and
suchlike were correct, this was where they kept the guns. I'd seen
dozens of movies where the Captain breaks open the armoury
and hands out weapons to his loyal officers with which to defend
themselves against the mutinous dogs clamouring outside.

I was taking a hell of a lot for granted, because apart from
the fact that I may have been seeing the wrong movies, and there
wouldn't be any guns, I was also assuming that the the Captain
himself wouldn't be in his cabin. And that turned out to be mistake number one. I opened the cabin door and there he was. He
was sitting at his desk working on some papers. Why he wasn't
going about his rightful business conning the ship or somesuch,
I don't know. But he wasn't and ten seconds later he was heartily wishing that he had been. He looked up at me as I came in,

and for a moment he didn't get it. He had become used to seeing me walk around the deck during my exercise periods, and he assumed no doubt that I had taken to exercising at night. He even started to smile.

"Good evening, Miss Touchfeather," he said.

"Good evening, Captain," I replied, sticking the point of my steak knife up under his chin. Hardened old sea dog he may have been, but twenty years before the mast hadn't equipped him for this sort of situation. He started to get to his feet until I pricked him with the knife.

"I'll cut your throat, Captain," I said, trying not to sound like Long John Silver. It was very important that he believe me because, if he didn't, I was going to be in trouble; not as much trouble as he would be in, but trouble enough. Fortunately he decided that he did believe me, and he subsided into the chair again, his weathered old hands gripping the arms as though they were my neck.

"I need a gun, Captain," I said. "Two if you can manage."

"There are no guns here," he said, lying vigorously.

"Either you tell me where they are or I'll have to look myself, and I can't do that with you hanging around," I said, and gave him another jab, sending his head snapping back, just so he would understand what I was getting at. Then came the soul searching bit as he weighed up the pros and cons of doing what I asked. On the one hand he would get into terrible trouble with Galipolodopolo, probably lose his job, his pension, and find himself scrubbing decks again; on the other hand he would get his throat cut. It was an unfair contest. The breath went out of his body like a deflating tyre, and suddenly he wasn't the salty old skipper any longer, but a rather tired little man. He nodded down towards the desk.

"Top right hand drawer," he said.

I leaned across him, careful to keep the knife in place and tried to open the drawer. It was locked. I glanced round at him and he almost burst into tears he was so apologetic.

"I'm sorry," he said. "I forgot."

He fumbled in his pocket for a bunch of keys, selected one and unlocked the drawer. He was about to assist me further by pulling it open for me when I stopped him.

"I'll do it, Captain."

I pulled open the drawer and there was the gun lying there in isolated splendour. It was a Colt .45 automatic, a veritable cannon. Anybody firing that who didn't know about guns was liable to get their arm broken. Fortunately I knew about guns. Together with the gun was a spare clip which looked full. Assuming the gun was also full, that gave me sixteen shots – hardly enough to mount a full scale battle, but a hell of a sight better than a steak knife and a lobster pick. I reached across him again and took the gun out. It weighed a ton, but to me it felt as light as a feather.

I think the Captain had worked out what I was going to do next a second before I did it. Now that I had got what I had come for, he reasoned, I was going to have to do something about him. I could hardly thank him for the gun and just walk out. No, he decided, I was going to have to incapacitate him. He started to say something, but we"ll never know what it was because, before he could get a word out, I clouted him gently with the barrel of the gun just behind his ear. All his doubts and uncertainties vanished at once; he slid from his chair as though I had suddenly extracted every bone from his body. And there I was, on my own, with a lovely, lovely gun and sixteen beautiful bullets.

Go down I might but I was going to take a hell of a lot of people with me. Why, if I could line them up in groups of two, I could probably shoot thirty-two of them. I pulled back the breach and fed a cartridge into the barrel. The gun was well oiled and moved like a dream, and suddenly I felt ten feet tall. I hate guns in the normal course of events; they're nasty, vicious, danger-ous things; and, apart from anything else, they can give a person delusions of grandeur. But I had been sat upon, pushed around and threatened with all kinds of nastiness for long enough, and delusions of grandeur was exactly what I wanted right now.

I glanced down at the Captain who was sprawled untidily at my feet. He'd give no trouble for an hour at least. I don't think I had fractured his skull, but he was going to feel like hell when he came round. I turned out the light and closed the door when I left. I didn't know how long I was going to remain undiscovered, but the longer the better.

The deck area outside the captain's cabin was deserted when I came out, which was fortunate for any person who might have been there, because I would have shot them without batting an eyelid.

I suppose I could have swiped a boat about here and just escaped, but I was feeling grotty in the extreme, and I wanted to spread a bit of my grottiness around where it would cause the most trouble.

So now I put phase two of my plan into operation. I called it a plan, but the loose conglomeration of my intentions couldn't really be distinguished with such a high sounding word. A plan is something that has been worked out in detail; all that I had was an intense desire to stay alive and to do as much peripheral damage as possible in the process. As far as the former was concerned, optimist I might have been, but I didn't rate my chances very high; but, as for the damage I could cause, there I was convinced I could pick up top marks.

All the kerfuffle of the loading was still going on on the port side, so I kept to the starboard, making my way forward to midships. I reached the corner of the main deck superstructure and risked a peak round the edge. A portable winch had been rigged and this was being used to transfer stuff from the smaller coastal vessel on board the *Maria*. The deck area in use was floodlit and I could see Constantin and Lucia standing arm in arm watching the proceedings. Whatever it was being loaded – and it just had to be gold – was coming aboard in small wooden crates about two feet by one foot by one foot. They were winched aboard two at a time and lowered onto the deck. Then two men would take one of the crates at either end. And they were heavy. You could see that by the effort the men put into carrying them. Using rope handles fixed to the crates, the men lugged them across the foredeck and down an open companionway halfway up towards the bow. It was a scene of efficient industry, fascinating when one knew what the crates contained. A ship's officer was checking the loading against a manifest, and Constantin was checking the officer. Two shots, I thought, and I would dispose of both Constantin and Lucia. It was a pleasant thought, but hardly practical in the circumstances. Alright Katy, just what in hell are you going to do? I was saved further speculation, however, when there came a sudden scream from somewhere in the ship and simultaneously all the lights went out.

Clever Katy, I thought, someone has tried to switch on your bathroom light. In fact, as I learned later, it was the steward who had been passing my cabin and had decided to collect my dinner dishes. He had put his key in the door, found it already open, and gone in. No Katy, and no light on in the bathroom; better just take a look before reporting to the Old Man. Into the bathroom, switch on the light and, bingo, instant shock. And instant darkness too, by way of a bonus. As the lights went out, the group around the winch froze into temporary immobility. They were still lit by the lights from the other boat behind them, but that was below the *Maria's* deck level, and it was pretty dark by most standards. Added to that, up until a moment before they had all been standing in the bright glare of two powerful floodlights; the sudden contrast must have left them in what seemed like total darkness, while their eyes slowly adjusted.

Constantin pulled himself together first. He ordered the officer to go and check the electrics, then detailed two men to accompany Lucia and himself aft to investigate the scream. As soon as the owner was out of sight, the others all sat down and lit their fags. Now or never Katy, I thought. I slipped around the corner and padded across the deck to the open companion way. Just before I climbed in, I heard a couple of voices cursing from below at having been left halfway down the stairs in the pitch dark. I slipped round to the back of the hatch and waited until the owners of the voices reached the deck once more. Then, as they crossed towards their companions, I ducked round the edge and promptly fell down a flight of metal stairs.

I picked myself up painfully. There didn't seem to be anything broken, but I wasn't prepared to take any money on it. And, having got here, I started to wonder what I was going to do next. Because, apart from the glimmer of light from the open hatchway above me, I couldn't see a bloody thing. The darkness was like black velvet, complete and unrelieved; there was absolutely no point in my trying to move around, because I could break both legs three times over before taking more than half a dozen steps. I was still pondering my predicament and ready to shoot anyone who poked their head over the hatchway, when someone did me a big favour. All the lights went on again. Two seconds to orientate myself, and I was off once more.

I was in a narrow passage, with closed doors either side and one at the end, which was open; it was obviously there that the crates had been carried. Acting on the premise that a place safe enough for all that loot must be safe enough for Katy, I made straight for the open door. I stepped over a rising bulkhead and found myself in what could only be the forward hold. It was as wide as the ship herself, but narrowing rapidly at the bow. The ceiling was low and the whole place was strictly functional in that this was the inside of the hull, and looked exactly that. Elsewhere in the *Maria* the walls may have been decorated with oak paneling or flock paper, but here we were down to basics, and nothing separated the hold from the sea outside other than half an inch of steel plate. I started to look around, and then I decided first things first, and closed the door behind me. It was a heavy door and it fitted in a watertight fashion into the bulkhead. There were four levers for securing it, one at the top, one at the bottom, and two down the edge. They were one sided levers only; and could only be operated from my side. The outside had its own set. I slammed all the levers home, leaning on them to make sure they were secure; and that seemed to be that for the time being. Now I took a closer look around me. The crates had been stacked down either side of the hull and, at first, it looked as though there were hundreds of them. In fact there were two hundred, because I counted them later. Also later, I prised one of them open. It contained twenty gold bars and, remembering some of my homework, I was able to estimate each bar as being worth approximately five thousand pounds. That made it one hundred thousand pounds per crate; and two hundred crates made it twenty million pounds actual value, and probably two or three times that much on Constantin's black market. I'd certainly chosen the right place to make my last stand; around that sort of money everyone would have to tread very carefully. I say "my last stand" because that was what I knew it was going to have to be. I never really expected to hide aboard the *Maria*. By a simple process of searching the ship from stem to stern, they were bound to find me. All I could hope for was to make things as uncomfortable as possible for everyone on board.

It took them half an hour to work out where I was. During that half an hour they had obviously found the electrocuted steward, the unconscious Captain and checked that there wasn't a missing lifeboat. There wasn't and, like I said, after thirty minutes there was a great clang on the door outside. Just to be sociable I pulled out a bar of gold and clanged back at them. That little exchange was followed by two minutes silence, which in turn was followed by another clang, this time more positive. I clanged back a couple of times until between clangs I heard someone shouting from the other side of the door. I pressed my ear up against the cold metal and listened. It was Constantin, obviously yelling at the top of his voice to make himself heard through half an inch of steel watertight door.

"Katherine! Can you hear me?"

"I hear you," I yelled back.

"I will give you two minutes to come out."

"What are you going to do if I don't?" I yelled back at him.

There was a long silence while everyone outside realised that there was absolutely nothing they could do.

After a couple of minutes I grew bored with the silence. "Constantin," I shouted.

"Yes, Katherine?"

"I have a proposition for you."

"What is it?"

"Are you listening carefully?"

"I'm listening." I judged his height roughly, visualising more or less where his ear would be, seeing it pressed up hard against the metal of the door. "Are you sure you're listening?" I screamed at him, just to be doubly sure.

His voice came back to me faintly as he yelled at me. "I'm listening, Katherine."

I drew back the gold bar I was holding and clouted the door so hard I nearly broke my arm. The reverberations were still going through my body ten minutes later when the engine started.

A tomb is still a tomb; even a twenty million pound coffin, despite the elbow room. And taking a good look around me, it seemed that was what I was confined in. Having got myself into it, safely sealed off from the vicissitudes of the outside world, there didn't seem to be a thing I could do except wait for their next move. It was noisy down here with the engines running, a little bit murky, and the place smelled of oil and bilge water. Apart from the gold, there was very little else. There were some links of anchor chain coiled up at the far end, a few miles of rope, some tools, some oxy-acetylene equipment and, rather incongruously, a pair of oars. There were some drums of what I assumed to be oil, but which could equally well have been petrol and, wrapped in protective polythene, neatly stowed away, there was the summertime deck awning. And, of course, there was Katy, all alone and now that the euphoria was evaporating, very miserable. One small consolation was that Constantin couldn't be all that happy either. Bar cutting his way through the bulkhead, there was no possible way that he could get to me or his loot. And that gave me an idea. But before I could investigate its possibilities, a noise from outside the door attracted my attention. I moved back to the door and stuck my ear up against it, then jerked my head back quickly, clapping a hand to my ear. The door was hot and I immediately identified the noise I had heard. It was the roar of an oxy-acetylene torch.

Great minds must think alike. No sooner had I promulgated the theory that cutting his way in was all that Constantin had left, than here he was, doing just that. Well, someone was in for a nasty shock in the very near future. I moved away and sat patiently on a million pounds worth of gold and watched the door turn a dull red on my side. A few minutes later the metal fractured and a lance of flame came through the half inch gap it had cut in the steel. I remained watching the flame as it started to move sideways and ten minutes later there was a four inch slash in the door, half an inch deep. Now is the time, Katy, I thought. I moved over to the door and, keeping to the opposite side to which they were cutting, I risked a quick peek through the slit. I received a vague impression of a man's head masked with heavy goggles and, past him, further down the narrow passage, a couple more men sitting on the steps that led up to the deck; the relief crew, obviously.

Satisfied that my efforts would not be in vain, I pulled out my gun. I lined up the barrel up with the half inch slit in the door and, without bothering to aim at anything, I pulled the trigger. The noise was catastrophic, nearly blowing my head off and setting all the bells in the world clanging in my ears. But that was nothing compared to what happened out in the passage. The bullet nearly clipped the ear of the man doing the cutting, and then went off on a merry little jaunt of its own, ricocheting off the steel walls and taking one of the men on the stairs with it en route. It was bloody marvelous. A bullet fired at an angle into that passageway could do the work of a machine gun.

Feeling safe, I took a good look through the slit this time. The man on the stairs was bleeding profusely. His companion had disappeared entirely. The one whose ear I had shot off was busy crawling on all fours towards the end of the passage, presenting me with the almost irresistible target of his backside scurrying away from me. If it had been Constantin or Lucia, I would certainly have used another bullet, but on some poor fellow I didn't even know, the operation would have been spiteful. So I let him scuttle to safety up the steps dragging his more seriously shot companion with him. Constantin may have been all sorts of an international big wheel, but it wasn't going to count for much in getting any more of his crew down into the passageway, now that Katy had shown her hand.

In fact, they did try it once more, using a large piece of sheet steel carried in front of them. I had been peering through the slit on and off while I was making my own plans, and the first thing I saw was this two feet by three feet piece of flat steel moving towards me. I could see a pair of legs sticking out from beneath it, and had a vague glimpse of a shock of red hair over the top. I let him get halfway down the passage and then, judging the angle of deflection carefully, I fired at the wall halfway between him and me. The bullet screamed off the wall like a banshee. A fraction of a second later the steel shield was dropped and the man was beating it back up stairs dragging a badly bleeding leg. What about that? I thought. I've got a gun that shoots around corners.

And that was the extent of outside interference for the next few hours. I think Constantin must have decided that he would starve me to death because, although I took frequent looks through the slit, nobody appeared again. Between looks I went about my business.

Briefly this was that if they could cut their way in, I could cut my way out. The oxy-acetylene equipment was to hand, and I'd once done a short course on its use when Mr. Blaser had wanted me to take the back off a safe in Rio during carnival week. (Remind me to tell you about that sometime.) I paced around the hold for a few minutes weighing the pros and cons of exactly where I was going to cut a hole in the *Maria*. Eventually I settled for a point about ten feet back from the prow on the port side. The only reason I selected this particular place was because that was where the oxy-acetylene equipment happened to be. The cylinders are very heavy and I didn't fancy having to drag them around the confined space in which I was trapped. I checked the cylinder gauges and the hose connections. Everything looked fine. I calculated the mixture I would need for the most effective cutting flame. I even found a pair of goggles and gloves where they had been left by the last person to use the equipment. I took one more peek down the corridor to make sure I was still on my own, and I was ready for work. But I didn't have a bloody match.

I found one eventually in a box of lifeboat supplies stacked away at the back. Also among the supplies were three bottles of brandy; obviously there for medical purposes, I decided that if anyone needed medicine right now, it was Katy. I broke open one of the bottles and took a couple of healthy slugs. Then, feeling primed like a well tuned pump, I went to work. The first, and most important, calculation I had to make was the height of the waterline outside. I could hear the stuff slopping away against the hull, but it was difficult to judge exactly how high the true level was. We were moving and, by the vibration, we were making good speed. That would mean a bow wave was being sent up, and the true water line would become lower for the first few feet of hull. On the other hand, if I took this level as accurate, when we slowed down or stopped I could find myself trying to cut a hole into the sea. I took another slug of brandy and gave the matter considerable thought; I took one more slug, and nearly decided to forget the whole thing. Then I started cutting. The height I cut at was finally resolved by my taking up the most comfortable position I could find, crossing my fingers, taking another swig from the bottle and praying.

It's a very simple piece of equipment is an oxy-acetylene cutter. It's the same as they use for welding, but it carries an extra jet which blows pure oxygen on to the oxidised metal, shoving it out of the way, thus forming the cut. All things being equal, it can be operated by anyone with a strong wrist and an ounce of common sense. But here, all things were most definitely not equal. The boat was rolling and I was three parts pissed. And that was just for openers. The actual burning flame reaches a temperature of 6000 degrees Fahrenheit and, although that is only a minute portion of the flame, the result can still be a great deal of spread around heat.

After ten minutes I was sweating like a pig and, worse, I wasn't making much of an impression on the hull. What with the heat, the rolling of the boat and the rolling of Katy, I seemed completely incapable of holding the flame still for long enough for it to bite into the metal. All I was getting was a large area of scorched hull and a terrible headache. I decided to start all over again. I switched off the flame, then stripped off to bra and pants. Resisting another pull at the brandy bottle, I took one more peep through into the still empty corridor; then gritted my teeth and really concentrated. Using one of the crates of gold as a support I managed to hold the flame reasonably still, and was rewarded a few minutes later by seeing the metal start to give way under the onslaught. A moment later the sea came in and my torch went out.

It was only a small hole, but it must have been well below the waterline because a sudden jet of water doused the torch and hit me straight on the goggles. Feeling heartily fed up with the whole thing, I tore myself off a strip of polythene from the deck awning wrapping and plugged the hole. It wasn't difficult, but the event did act as a pointer as to what could happen if I cut in the wrong place again. I dried off the torch, relit it, and started cutting two feet higher. This time everything went swimmingly and I even started to hum a little tune while I worked. It must have been the effect of that bloody brandy again because, all things considered, I was in a hell of a mess whichever way you sliced it. Still there's not much point in dwelling on your problems; they don't get any smaller that way. If anything, they seem to get larger. Neither is there much point in projecting your plans too far ahead because as sure as hell something will crop up which you haven't foreseen and which will trip you up leaving you flat on your arse with egg all over your face.

Half an hour later I had a neat cut, eighteen inches long. I paused for a while for a short bout of stock taking. Outside, the sea seemed very close. When the metal had cooled sufficiently, I took my goggles off and had a proper look. My God, it *was* close. I was eighteen inches above the operative waterline, Outside the water seemed to be flowing by at approximately seventy-five miles an hour, and it whispered and gurgled at me in a terrifying manner. I had intended to make the next cut vertically downwards from the first one. To hell with that, I thought, and started the next cut at an angle of forty-five degrees from the original, cutting upwards. I reckoned that if I could remove a triangle eighteen inches by eighteen by eighteen, I would be able to wriggle through; my 36, 24, 36 notwithstanding. It would be a tight squeeze and I would probably scrape myself raw, but that was my plan, And that's what I did.

With periodic checks to make sure I was still being left alone, I managed to cut through the hull within the hour. The last couple of minutes were a bit traumatic as I didn't know whether the section I had cut away was going to fall inwards or outwards. If it fell inwards, it could do Katy a nasty injury. But nothing ventured nothing gained, and I continued to cut away. Fortunately it fell outwards and there I was staring out at sea eighteen inches away from my nose. From this low eyeline it seemed to stretch away forever.

While I was still staring at it, a hundred odd gallons suddenly sloshed through the opening, drenching me and frightening me out of my life to boot. I was still spluttering and coughing when another hundred gallons spilled through. The engine noise was still the same so obviously we hadn't decreased our speed. This could only mean that the weather was getting worse. Just what I needed – with sea water coming in by the ton, and an overloaded forehull, the boat would soon become unmanageable. She'd start to carry so much weight forward that she'd lose steerage-way. At least, that's what I thought. With any luck she might sink too, which raised the rather interesting theory as to what the hell I was going to do if she did. It was alright for that lot up there – they'd got life jackets, boats, rafts, rubber rings and all sorts of stuff for keeping afloat. Me, I had my bra and pants, and twenty million pounds worth of gold; a nice nest egg, but pretty useless when it comes to keeping your head above real wet-type water.

Another couple of hundred gallons of sea sloshed into the hold and the water line outside seemed a fraction closer. The more water that came in, the lower the *Maria* would settle forward, which in turn would let in more water. A vicious little circle, with Katy at the dead centre. More water spilled in, and suddenly the engine noise changed and I heard the far off clang of the engine telegraph. They had obviously noticed the change in the *Maria's* trim and were about to investigate its cause.

So it was now or never. I waded across to the door that led to the passageway and looked through the slit. Two heads were peering down from the top of the stairs, one of them belonging to an officer. I banged a couple of shots and the heads disappeared miraculously as the bullets sang and whistled their way from bulkhead to bulkhead and back again. Then I tore off another piece of polythene from the deck awning cover and used it to wrap the gun in what I hoped was a watertight fashion. I tied this little package around my neck with a short piece of nylon rope, because where I was going I would need both hands free. Then, hoping that I had discouraged outside interference for the next few minutes, I opened the watertight door as quietly as possible. The oxy-acetylene equipment used in the attempt to winkle Katy out was still where it had been abandoned in such a hurry when I had started to make like Annie Oakley. I lit the flame, adjusted it quickly, and in two minutes I had wrecked the hinges of the door, melting them into blodges of shapeless metal. The devil himself wouldn't be able to close that door now.

Fortunately nobody felt inclined to see what I was up to, because in spite of frequent looks over my shoulder, nothing happened at the top of the stairs – which was just as well, because my gun was now nicely wrapped in a waterproof parcel around my neck and it would have taken me five minutes to get it into action once more.

Having sealed open the door, I went back into the hold. The water was knee deep now and instead of sloshing in through the hole I had cut, it had started to flow in steadily. The *Maria* had definitely settled a fraction and, if I knew anything about marine architecture, which I didn't, she was very likely for the knackers yard if someone didn't do something soon. I waded across to my do-it-yourself exit and, gritting my teeth and sucking in my chest, I started to squeeze through. It was no easy feat because, apart from anything else, the water was really coining in now at a steady rate of knots. It had already spilled over into the passageway outside and, in a couple of minutes those on deck looking down into the passageway would be able to see it. When they did, it was doubtful that even the threat of Katy's gun was going to keep them from coming down to investigate.

I managed to get my upper half through the hole and, in imminent danger of drowning, I tried to get the rest of me through. Obviously however, I wasn't the 36-24-36 that I had thought I was. If I was still 36 up top then I must have suddenly developed a frightening 38 down below–the outcome no doubt of too much luxury cruising because I wedged solid. Now I was in real trouble. If anyone decided to risk coming down to investigate, they were going to be presented with Katy's nether regions, apparently growing out of the hull like so many barnacles. Apart from the indignity of the situation, I would be completely helpless. Added to that, I was proving to be an effective cork, because no more water was spilling into the hold, which wasn't the object of the exercise at all. I pulled and I heaved; I wriggled and I squirmed; I braced my arms against the outside of the hull and pushed hard. Nothing! I took a deep breath and tried again; still nothing. One last try, Katy, I thought, then you'd better turn the whole thing in. I sucked in my breath, then I blew it all out; I braced my arms against the hull, counted to five, and then shoved hard. I shot out of that hole like a cork from a well shaken bottle of champagne, and in seconds I was coughing and spluttering with a mouth and nose full of sea water. I righted myself after a moment and took stock. The hull of the now stationary *Maria* rose in front of me as high and as solid looking as the United Nations building. And the water was really making it into the hold now; in fact I had to pull myself along the hull a little way to avoid being dragged back in by the suction. Bullets or no bullets, somebody was just going to have to come down and have a look. Then the fun would start. And by that time I wanted to be somewhere else.

I felt my way along the hull, trying not to think of the mile or so of water beneath me. Fortunately being nose heavy the *Maria* wasn't drifting as much as she might have been and by half swimming and half pushing myself along I made my way aft. The foredeck was going to be as busy as Piccadilly Circus on Cup Final Night, and I couldn't see myself climbing over the deckrail into all that excitement. If anyone managed to lay hands on me, they would probably be so livid with what I had done that they would use me to plug the hole. The further back I moved, the higher the stern seemed to rise. There was a line on the hull down by the water line which had been a foot beneath the sea up front but here, more or less midships, it was a foot out of the water.

I could hear a lot of noise from the deck above me. There was shouting and yelling and running feet and more shouting. Obviously they knew something was seriously wrong up front and now it only remained for someone to pluck up enough courage to go down and have a look. What they would do when they discovered there was a bloody great hole in the ship was anybody's guess. If they got to it very soon they might be able to weld a patch over it, but even that was doubtful because by now the sea must be gurgling in good and fast and, with the watertight door sealed open, it wasn't going to be just the forehold that was flooded. A boat like the *Maria* could cope with that and still stay afloat. But what I had done was to lay open the means for the sea to flood back into the passageway, into the cabins either side, on under the staircase, back God only knew how far; probably between a third and a half of the length of the entire boat. Smashing ship she may have been, but she wasn't smashing enough to hold that much water and still stay on the top of the sea where she belonged.

I was thinking so hard on all this as I worked my way back along the hull that I nearly missed my chance. I had reached about three quarters of the way towards the stern when from a point just above my head and slightly to one side, I heard a thump of sound and something banged gently against the hull. I looked up, and in the vague light that leaked down from the deck above I could just make out the shape of a bucket tied to a length of rope which disappeared up on to the deck. Somebody had been pulling in sea water to scrub the decks or some such and had left his bucket dangling when he had been called away to more important things. The only question now was how tightly he had secured the rope up on the deck. Hoping he had paid attention to his knot-tying instructions when he was in sailors' school, I reached up and grabbed the rim of the bucket with both hands. I gave it an experimental tug and it remained secure. Still, it didn't really tell me much. The only way I was going to find out if it would take my weight was to start climbing the bloody thing. Metaphorically crossing my fingers, I braced my feet against the hull and, shifting my grip from the rim of the bucket to the rope, I started upwards.

Two minutes later my head was just below deck level, and offering up a silent blessing to the sailor who had tied the knot. I shifted my grip to the lower rail. There was a hell of a racket going on above me, but most of it seemed to be coming from the forward area and, apart from a scurrying pair of feet inches from my head just before I reached the top, my part of the boat seemed deserted. I held my breath for a moment, plucking up some heretofore undiscovered courage or fool-hardiness, and then hauled myself upwards.

Two seconds later I was crouched in the shelter of one of the lifeboats unwrapping my gun. I was shivering like a maniac. It was cold, certainly, and I was soaking wet in just a bra and pants.

But it wasn't that cold and I realised that the brandy-induced euphoria of the last couple of hours had been washed away by all that salt water, leaving just a very frightened little girl.

Praying that the gun was in working order, and praying too that I wouldn't have to use it, I poked my head out from my place of concealment. Looking forward I could see what looked like a veritable army of men gathered on the foredeck around the hatch that led down to my passageway and hold. From where they were standing they must have been able to see the water pouring into the passageway and points beyond, but it looked as though, as yet, nobody had decided to risk his neck and go down to take a closer look. As far as they were concerned, down there lurked Katy and her itchy trigger finger. Soon they would work out that it would be six of one against half a dozen of the other; drown or get shot. Then someone would go down. But by then I hoped to be well on my way. Because I had finished playing this affair by ear. Now I *did* have a plan. When we Touchfeather's are frightened, we really come to the fore. I suppose it's all that adrenalin shooting around inside that does it but, the more frightened we become, the more cold bloodedly efficient we seem to act. And I was just about as frightened as any girl has any business to be.

SEVEN

"Alright, Miss Touchfeather. You have described the build up with your customary flair for rhetoric," said Mr. Blaser. "Shall we now get down to what actually happened?"

He's a bastard that Mr. Blaser. He won't give me the satisfaction of basking in my own reflected glory for longer than it takes him to fix me with that basilisk stare of his, bringing me down to earth with a dirty great thump.

It was three days later and I considered that I had dried out sufficiently to make a full report. Had Mr. Blaser had his way, I would have been back two days earlier, but I was in Jamaica and as long as I didn't answer the phone, he couldn't get to me. Of course, he had done so in the end. He always does, practically dragging me back to London by the scruff of my neck. Now, with his tape recorder devouring everything that I said, and without even so much as a "Good to see you're still alive, Miss Touchfeather," he was getting at me again.

"You had regained the deck of the *Maria*," he prompted. "And you had formulated a plan. What went wrong?"

"Nothing went wrong, sir," I said, trying to keep righteous indignation out of my voice.

His eyebrows went up a millimetre. "Do you mean to sit there and tell me that everything that happened subsequently was by deliberate action on your part?"

"Yes, sir," I said proudly.

He still didn't get it. "This fiasco was intended?"

The Touchfeather blood started to simmer gently; it wasn't boiling yet, but it would do so very shortly. "Yes, sir," I said. "This fiasco was intended."

He regarded me steadily for a moment, then something that could have been a sigh vaguely disturbed his frame.

"Very well, Miss Touchfeather. Explain it to me."

The explanation wasn't nearly as difficult as the actual operation. There I was, cold, wet and frightened, standing on the deck of the *Maria,* which had put her nose down so alarmingly that I could almost hear the lutine bell ringing at Lloyds. I had three objectives; the bridge, Constantin and a boat – in that order. Assuming, with all the excitement up front, that the bridge would be sparsely occupied, I made for it straight away. I had been on the *Maria* enough times by now to know the geography accurately, and I went to the bridge by the back way, circling the main deck aft, and keeping as much boat as possible between myself and the foredeck at all times. I was right about the occupants of the bridge; there were only two men, both officers. One was looking down towards the foredeck; the other was in the radio room, just aft of the bridge proper, sending out subtle, ambiguous signals, trying to ascertain whether there were any rescue boats in the area, without actually committing himself until everyone knew what was what. He had earphones clamped to his head, so I ignored him for the moment, concentrating on the other one. So fascinated was he with what was going on below that he allowed me to get right up to him without his being aware that I was there. I peered past him down onto the foredeck where the entire ship's company were standing around the open hatchway.

"What's happening?" I asked.

"Christ knows," he said without turning. "But someone had better go down there pretty bloody soon before…"

Then he twigged. He turned to me and his mouth fell so far open that I could see his back teeth. I had to admit that he had good cause. There was Katy, dripping wet, as naked as made no difference, and with a cannon in her hand. I now stuck the cannon hard into his stomach. That had the effect of snapping his mouth shut again, bringing him back to earth with a nasty jolt. His eyes remained blank for one second, then I read a change of expression in them, It was an expression I had seen many times before. It meant that he was about to do something foolish and, if I didn't nip it in the bud, I was going to have to shoot him. So I nipped. I stepped back a couple of paces to give myself swinging room and, without reversing the gun, I hit him across the side of the head. His mouth fell open once more and this time it stayed that way. He toppled backwards losing all further interest in me, the *Maria* and everything else.

So now all I had to cope with was the Sparks, who was still sitting in the radio room with his back towards the bridge. He was still fiddling with his morse key, wondering whether he dare send out an SOS. Constantin wouldn't want anyone creeping around the *Maria,* with the cargo she was carrying, and he had probably given strict instructions about it. But the radio officer was no fool; he had a slip of paper in front of him giving the exact position of the *Maria* and, orders or no orders, he was going to bang that message out as soon as he felt the need to. But I relieved him of having to make the decision. I crept up behind him and pushed the cold barrel of the gun up against the back of his neck. This one was no hero and, like I said before, he was no fool either. He froze immobile, his hands flat on the table in front of him. In fact he remained like that for so long I wondered whether I had killed him from shock and instant rigor mortis had set in. But he wasn't going to move a muscle until he received permission, so I had to use my other hand to pull his earphones down from around his ears.

"You can turn round," I said.

He did so very carefully, using the revolving seat of his chair. He was sweating profusely and his eyes were glazed with panic.

"Up!" I said.

He stood up. I indicated with the gun that he should move out onto the bridge. After one brief moment, I followed him. He went three shades whiter when he saw his companion stretched out and I thought that any moment now he was going to faint dead away. But he managed to keep his feet by supporting himself on the compass housing.

"Get on the public address and ask for Galipolodopolo to come to the radio room," I said.

He looked at me blankly so I repeated the message, punctuating the words with periodic jabs of the gun into his stomach. At last I managed to get through to him. He switched on the public address and a moment later I saw all heads on the foredeck turn towards the speaker as it crackled into life.

"Mr. Galipolodopolo to the radio room please," the voice boomed out.

I jabbed him with the gun again. "Urgent," I hissed.

"Urgent," he said, with remarkable lack of invention.

I saw Constantin detach himself from the group on the foredeck and head towards the bridge and, joy of joys, Lucia decided to come with him.

"Sorry about this," I said to the radio officer, and dispatched him to join his companion. Then I threw a couple of charts onto the floor, put a match to them, and went out to greet Constantin and Lucia.

"You deliberately destroyed the charts?" said an incredulous Mr. Blaser.

"Yes, sir. I used them to start the fire."

"Why did you need a fire?"

"It seemed like a good idea at the time."

"Couldn't you have used something else? *Anything* else."

"There wasn't anything handy," I said.

He sighed again. "Why did you want Galipolodopolo and the woman?"

"I wanted them with me."

"I realise that," he said tetchily. "But why?"

"After what they'd done to me, I didn't feel inclined to leave them to disappear to some South American haven to live happily ever after."

"Personal revenge?" said Mr. Blaser ominously.

I backtracked quickly before I re-blotted my copy-book. "I needed them to insure my getaway," I said.

There was a moments pause. "Carry on, Miss Touchfeather," he said finally.

I met Constantin and Lucia halfway up to the bridge. I would like to say he looked surprised or shocked when he saw me, but he didn't. Obeying the obvious threat he saw in my hand, he just stopped and waited for me to handle the ball which was so well and truly in my court. Lucia went a couple of shades paler beneath her immaculate make-up, but she too behaved impeccably.

"We're going aft," I said.

He gave me no argument; just turned and started aft, Lucia by his side. He did, however, express a certain amount of interest. "What's aft, Katherine?" He asked without turning.

"The number two speedboat," I said, seeing no reason why I should keep it secret.

"Where are we going then?"

"Anywhere, so long as it's off this ship," I said. "She's about to sink." I detected a slight stiffening of his neck muscles as the impact of this hit him fully.

"The *Maria* is a very seaworthy vessel," he said, fishing.

There didn't seem any reason now why I shouldn't tell him. "Not with a bloody great hole in the hull and a fire on the bridge," I said. And of course they just had to do something. You can push people just so far, then they reach a point where there ain't nothing going to move them any further. Funny, but it was Lucia who reached this point first. She stopped suddenly, turning so that I nearly bumped into her.

"We seriously underestimated you, Katherine," she said coolly.

"Yes, you did, didn't you?" I said with equal aplomb. Constantin had stopped, too, and was watching both of us. "But I haven't got time to stand around and talk about it," I said, waving the gun at her.

But she didn't move. "You're going to have to shoot me, Katherine," she said.

"Don't continue to underestimate me," I said, but she didn't move a muscle. And gradually into her eyes came a gleam of satisfaction like a poker player gets when he calls a bluff and comes out on top. It was that expression that did it, that and the mental images I conjured up quickly of poisonous truth drugs and sulphuric acid enemas. I had to conjure up these to help me do what I did, because I'm not a vindictive girl by nature. It's just that I can get a bit stroppy when self preservation is in the balance.

"You're going to have to shoot me, Katherine," she had said.

"Very well," I said. And I shot her.

The rest was easy. Using the automatic winch, Constantin lowered the speedboat over the side and we both climbed in. As we drew away from the *Maria* we could see just how dire were the straits she was in. She was really settling forward now, her bows six feet deeper in the water than they had any right to be.

That meant that the hole I had cut was way, way below the water line and the sea would be coming in under pressure now. There was absolutely nothing that could keep her afloat much longer. Added, to that, the fire on the bridge was now going great guns and from five hundred yards away, Constantin and I watched the tiny figures of the crew running this way and that, like so many disorganised lemmings. Finally someone must have given the order to abandon ship, because boats started to come down the side. And once the *Maria* decided to go, she didn't hang around. There was a huge, metallic crash that carried clearly across the water, as her machinery gave up the effort of trying to withstand the steep angle of incline, and broke loose. The whole lot must have slid forward, increasing the weight at the bows to an impossible degree. Fine ship that she undoubtedly was, she gave a desperate clang of despair, stuck her nose down, and two minutes later there was nothing left but some isolated pieces of debris and a couple of life rafts which were gradually filling with crew.

"That's all?" said Mr. Blaser.

"You know the rest, sir," I said. "I made land three hours later, reported the wreck and caught the first plane to Jamaica."

"And Galipolodopolo?"

Here was my big disappointment. I had cosseted and nurtured him across three hours of water, beached the boat single-handed because I didn't trust him to do it, and then proudly marched him off at gunpoint to the nearest authorities I could find. I had left him there while I had toddled off to make a couple of calls. An hour later, when I returned, he had gone.

"Did you know that he had a charter plane fly in within the hour to pick him up and take him out?" asked Mr. Blaser.

"No, sir," I said. "But I guessed as much."

"Don't you care?"

I *did* care and, if I had known it was going to happen, I would probably have pushed him over the side before we landed. But there was no point in crying over spilt milk.

"Not much," I said.

He looked at me shrewdly for a moment before continuing. "There's nothing we can do with him, of course. We've clipped his wings considerably. His mines have gone, and from here on he'll have to make his living honestly."

"Not too much of a hardship with a hundred and fifty ships of his own," I said.

"One hundred and forty-nine," said Mr. Blaser. "Which brings me to another point." I knew he would get to it in the end, but it had been interesting seeing just how long he had been able to hang out. "We are very interested in pinpointing the exact position where the *Maria* went down."

"Yes, sir," I said. He waited, and then when nothing was forthcoming, he grew tired of waiting.

"Well?" he said.

I looked at him innocently. "Sir?"

"Come, Miss Touchfeather. You can read charts. Before you burned them didn't it occur to you to check the exact position of the *Maria*?"

"No, sir," I said.

He looked at me steadily for a long time, then growled a dismissal. Before I walked out of the door to present Miss Moody with an expense chit that was going to curl her hair, Mr. Blaser acknowledged in his own way that I had been through a great deal and was entitled to something.

"You can have two days off, Miss Touchfeather," he said.

"Thank you, sir," I replied sweetly, and I left.

⚜ ⚜ ⚜

It's a great comfort to a girl to know that she's got a twenty million pound nest egg. It's a thought that will keep her warm on those long winter nights when, because of the passing years, the phone has stopped ringing. Because naturally I know where that gold is. The position was written on that slip of paper in the radio room and I memorised it very carefully before I threw it on the fire that I had started.

Of course, all this is pipe dreaming. Eventually I shall have to tell Mr. Blaser. It's absolute hell being a basically honest person – it causes one to do the most stupid things. But if I can't keep the money for myself, at least I can use it as a lever. Even Mr. Blaser will budge under the pressure of a twenty million pound solid gold lever. I think I shall ask him for three months leave on full pay and a round trip ticket to Calmooniville. On the other hand, he pulls a lot of weight; perhaps I shall get him to exert some of it to have Peter Chalmers transferred to London for a couple of months. I'd like to see Peter again; we never really got much of a scene going together, what with Archimedes and Diogenes lurking about all over the place and my early abduction. Yes, that sounds like fun. The only trouble comes in knowing just how much pressure to exert on Mr. Blaser. Not enough, and the result is a big fat zero; too much, and the lever is liable to spring back and inflict serious injury on Katy. Push that man too far and he'll have me flying some grubby milk run in the Outer Hebrides for the rest of my working days – probably without the aid of an aeroplane.

THE SPY KILLER

PUBLISHER'S NOTE

This book was originally published in the United Kingdom in 1967 under the title *private I* and reflects the cultural and sexual attitudes, language, and politics of the period. ... as well as the punctuation and spelling.

To John Paddy Carstairs

PROLOGUE

T HE slamming of the door sounded like the last crack of doom. It had an utter finality about it. If I ever heard another voice or saw another person, it would be a surprise. I might as well have been embalmed, placed in a coffin, and buried a hundred miles deep.

For one moment a disembodied eye peered through a hole in the door. Then that was withdrawn and a metal slide replaced it. And there I was, *finis, kaput, terminado*, the absolute and ultimate end.

The straitjacket I was wearing was not looped too tightly, and there's a trick for getting out of them. Unfortunately, nobody has ever taught me the trick, so I lay there with my arms wrapped round myself and tied at the back, like a dressed fowl ready for the oven. The only thing needed to complete the synonym was stuffing, and that had long since gone. It had been beaten, medicated, thumped, interrogated and brainwashed out of me.

I was now classified as an A-1, first class, top grade, number one type lunatic.

My medical dossier, two inches thick, had been stamped INCURABLE and was safely filed away.

The real crunch was that it was all so legal. The certifying doctors, three of them, were pillars of respectability, doyens of their profession. They had examined me minutely over a period of a month. Finally, jointly and severally, as the legal termination has it, they had reached their findings. The three of them had put their names to the certificate of insanity. The poor deluded

buggers couldn't have done otherwise. As far as they were concerned, my symptoms were classic and genuine. There was no
way they could know about the needles I'd had jabbed into my
backside in the middle of the night, needles that ossified my
brain, paralysed my nervous system, and turned me into a gib-
bering idiot for days at a stretch.

As far as they were concerned, Bruno was just another male
nurse. Big Bruno, with a face that looked like a badly packed suitcase, and whose gentle brown eyes stayed gentle while he was
pumping a patient full of Pheno this, Para that, and God knows
what else. Or while he was using those great lumps he called
hands, carefully feeling for the nerve centres where an ounce of
pressure could deliver a ton of pain. I couldn't help but admire
Bruno though, and the day I cut his throat with a blunt penknife,
as I have privately sworn to do, I'm sure that I shall regret the
passing of a true professional. Max should be proud of Bruno,
the last of the Great Inquisitors, the pain maker, the creator of
insanity. But then Max has always chosen his people carefully. I
think the only mistake he ever made was me.

Of course, it would have been far simpler for him to have
disposed of me in the time honoured manner. To give him credit,
he'd tried. But fortunately for us both, he hadn't succeeded.
Because stupid as I sometimes am, I'm not so stupid that I don't
take certain precautions along the line. Now, my life insurance
policies rest secure in two safety deposit boxes, while as an added
precaution my bank manager holds certain documents, about the
contents of which he knows nothing. All that he does know is that
I'm now locked up in a lunatic asylum, and somehow or other he's
going to have to explain away my overdraft to head office.

Had Max disposed of me in the normal way, the documents
would have been forwarded circuitously to the faceless gentlemen who spend their lives in anonymity and wield their power
with awesome indifference. Max, Bruno, Danielle, all of them
would have disappeared quietly, without a ripple to mark their

passing. At least that way I would have had the satisfaction of not going down alone.

It's getting late now. I wonder if Bruno will keep on with the injections now that their purpose has been accomplished. The doctors have all returned to their staid and lucrative practices, there's no longer anyone to whom it is necessary for me to exhibit my lunatic tendencies.

That in itself is a relief. The slipping away of sanity which followed the injection was something to be experienced. One tiny corner of the mind would stand back objectively and watch the remainder dissolve into chaos. And soon even that small core would give way before the onslaught. What followed I never knew. I only know that hours later, when sanity began to return, the same way as it departed, that tiny eye in the mind opened on to things that both horrified and revolted.

Fingernails torn from scratching at the walls, a bleeding scar on the wrist where I had bitten myself; blood, vomit, excrement, and a thin wailing, blubbering gibberish, issuing from a mouth over which at first the mind had no control. This was the evidence of what had gone before. What that was, I have no desire to know. I have never been proud of my body. Unlike some people, it has always been to me a machine that functions well or indifferently, depending on how much work you ask it to do, and how much care and time you are willing to spend on maintenance. I know that I am nearly two stone overweight, that my digestive system plays up constantly, that my teeth aren't particularly good, and that I have suffered periodically from halitosis, B.O., prickly heat and dandruff. But then I have never been particularly ashamed of my body either, not until those moments when I groped my way out of God knows what, and looked upon this battered, stinking, filthy carcass, and shuddered at what I must have turned into under the aegis of Bruno's needle.

There's no doubt that Max could have put me into a permanent state of insanity. A few extra c.c.s of whatever it was that

Bruno used, and I would have slipped far enough over the edge, never to return.

But Max wouldn't do that. If I were truly insane, then I would no longer be aware of my predicament. And awareness was part of the scheme of things. This was Max's way of saying "You've been a bad boy and now you must suffer the consequences." He's a vindictive bastard, and must derive great satisfaction from the knowledge that I could be suffering my punishment for the rest of my life. A bullet or a knife would have been quicker, but the true essence would have been missing. And anyway, there were the insurance policies.

So Max had given me four, blank anonymous walls to live with, and perhaps if I'm a good boy, in a couple of years they'll let me spend an hour a day with the real lunatics who are now my compatriots.

I've seen some of them during my periodic trips along the corridors. They have the vacant stare, the slack mouth, the crafty crazed expression of true madness. They cringe, they whimper, they strut and they shout. There are schizophrenics, paranoiacs, psychopaths; there's every damn shade of lunacy with one common denominator, they're all highly dangerous. They're dangerous both to themselves and to anyone misguided enough to turn their backs for half a second. This isn't one of those "open wall" institutions where the inmates are allowed into the town, there to embarrass the populace. Here, the walls are twelve feet high, the doors are steel, and the beds bolted to the floor. Here, if a man isn't in a straitjacket at least once a week, he's a cissy. This is the place where the male nurses are six feet tall and carry leather covered coshes in their hip pockets.

They strap you to the table to shave you; all food is liquid so there can be no need for cutlery (even a spoon can be broken and used as a gouge). There's no glass, no wire, no fitments, no belts, suspenders or neckties. We wear long cotton shifts, reinforced in the weaving so that they cannot be torn into strips. That is when we wear anything at all; most of the time we're kept stark naked. Our fingernails are kept trimmed very low. Our hair is cut very short. I've a strong suspicion that after a couple of weeks, they pull all your teeth as well, just to be one hundred per cent sure.

Now it seems I have nothing to do for the next thirty-odd years except to think about Max, and about the stupid, idiotic, bloody fool way I managed to get myself into this.

CHAPTER ONE

I T was a Monday, a wet, miserable Monday. I'd spent the weekend following the over-sexed wife of a client and making copious notes. She had fallen in and out of so many beds in the course of forty-eight hours, that I had begun to doubt even my own count. My client had asked for evidence, what I'd got for him was a revelation. The only surprising thing was his wanting a divorce at all. It was a wonder she hadn't killed him from exhaustion years ago.

The weekend, too, had been wet. My shoes had started to leak and I had been unable to find time to get home and change them. I had managed about six hours' sleep, all in the car. I had eaten stale sandwiches and doubtful meat pies, and those only when I could escape long enough from my subject's amatory gymnastics to find a cafe.

I had finally reached home at four o'clock that morning, and now, tired and extremely irritable, I was on the way to the office to type up the notes. They had to be made to sound lurid in the legal sense rather than the erotic.

I was rolling a phrase around my tongue, something like "the subject was observed momentarily at a first-floor window in a state of undress," when I emerged from the Piccadilly Underground to find that it was still raining.

I debated for a moment whether I'd stop at the Corner House for some breakfast. Then I decided that I would treat myself to lunch instead. In my constant battle with overweight, it was always breakfast *or* lunch. I crossed Shaftesbury Avenue and was walking past Cecil Gee's before I was aware of it. The overcoat was still in the window. One hundred per cent cashmere, sixty-five guineas. I tortured myself daily by looking at it.

"One day," I said to myself. "One day."

As usual, the dustbin on the stairs hadn't been emptied, and as usual on a Monday morning, somebody had used the letter box facing into Old Compton Street as a toilet some time during the weekend. So, the passage stank, and the stairs stank and, when I reached the outer office, that stank too. When it rained Miss Roberts' cheap fur coat smelled like a stable that needs mucking out. She smiled at me as I came in.

"Good morning, Mr. Smith," she said brightly. My name really is Smith, and to make it doubly distinguished my parents christened me John. "We are early this morning."

Miss Roberts was about thirty-five and looked fifty. She was a kindly, inefficient body, who seemed to have come with the lease. I shared the premises with a man named Stubbs. We each had our own room leading from the outer office, and Miss Roberts provided the only link between us. She answered the phone, took messages and made the tea. She would tell me everything about Stubbs, and no doubt told him everything about me. Stubbs ran an abortive theatrical agency, and I ran an abortive enquiry agency. Between us, we aborted together, always behind in the rent, the rates, the telephone, and Miss Roberts' salary.

She continued to smile as I crossed towards my own office. I was about to go in when she delivered her news.

"*You* have an appointment," she said.

"I have?" I said.

"Eleven o'clock, a Mrs. Dunning. She phoned."

I thanked her and walked through into my office, leaving her rattling the tea cups. The mail was on my desk, two bills, a circular, and a message in Miss Roberts' spidery hand. Mrs. Dunning. Eleven p.m. I had once spent an hour trying to explain to Miss Roberts the difference between a.m. and p.m.

I hung up my raincoat and took my weekend notes from the pocket. I spread them on the desk and spent the next five minutes sorting them out. During this time Miss Roberts arrived with the first of an endless supply of cups of weak tea. She would keep the tea coming just as long as there was anyone in the office. The fact that one could only swallow so much tea in the course of a day didn't bother her. She would remove the untouched cup, which was now cold, shake her head, and place a fresh cup of the same brew in its place.

However, this was the first of the morning, and I drank it while I reread the notes. Then I pulled the typewriter towards me and started work.

At ten forty-five I had finished. I sorted them, stapled them together, and put them in a neat pile at the side of the desk. My client would be calling for them that afternoon, and was he in for a shock. Then, with nothing to do for the next fifteen minutes, I took stock. This is something I do periodically, an exercise that never fails to depress me. It involves thumbing back through my cheque book, wondering where the hell all the money has gone to. The fact that there is very little money to go *anywhere* makes the task easier. Then come some rapid calculations on the back of an envelope which confirm what I already know, namely that I am spending money at roughly twice the rate I am earning it. As always, this masochistic exercise in personal finance ended by my tearing up the envelope and slamming my cheque book into the drawer. And at this point Miss Roberts announced Mrs. Dunning.

I suppose I should have remembered. Somewhere, somehow, I had heard that Danielle had married a man named Dunning. But that was three years ago, and unimportant information doesn't stick. She looked marvelous, of course. She was one of those flowers that bloom in the warm glow of money, and obviously Mr. Dunning supplied plenty of that. She was wearing a soft suede coat with mink collar and lapels. Her handbag and shoes alone must have cost as much as I earned in three months.

Her face was carefully made up so that it looked as though she wasn't wearing any make-up at all, and as always, her hair was impeccable, red now where it had been blonde.

She smiled as she came in.

"Darling!" she said.

I saw Miss Roberts' expression as she closed the door behind Danielle. What a tidbit for Stubbs *that* would make.

Danielle held out her cheek for me to peck at, and her involuntary withdrawal as I did so was almost well enough concealed for me not to notice it.

Then she sat down, arranging herself tidily on my only visitor's chair, and crossing her legs demurely.

"You've put on weight," she said.

"So have you." She had, too, only on her it looked good.

'We're older, John,' she said.

"A hundred years older," I said, sitting down at my desk.

"You haven't had your teeth fixed yet." She still had the faculty for bringing out into the open the thing which you most wanted ignored.

"I can't afford it," I said.

"Poor John. Business not too good?" She allowed her eyes to flick briefly round the room. "What a very brown room."

It was. It's the *brownest* room I've ever seen. The walls are brown, the floor and ceiling are brown. Not a rich, warm brown, but a dirty beige-type brown that overwhelms with depression so that even the green filing cabinet seems brown.

She looked back at me.

"You're losing your hair, too," she said. The whole conversation needed re-routing before she started to ask whether my sexual prowess had continued to deteriorate along with the rest of me. I knew that she would, too, if I didn't force her to change direction. I should have asked her how she was, or commented on how well she looked, or enquired whether she had been happy since she divorced me. But I didn't.

"What do you want, Danielle?" I asked.

Her eyebrows lifted a fraction.

"To see you," she said finally. I shook my head. She looked at me for a moment, then she lowered her eyes.

"No," she agreed. "I need your help."

Before I could say anything, she continued.

"Professionally, of course," she said. "I want to engage your services."

"What as?" I asked.

She waved her hand.

"This," she said, embracing the office. "John Smith, enquiry agent."

"*Mr.* Dunning?" I said.

She pouted. It was a "little girl" expression which had never suited her.

"I'm afraid so," she said.

I felt easier. Now I was on familiar ground. I dragged a pad towards me and took out a pen.

"Name, address and details of what you want me to do," I said a little pompously.

"Nathaniel Dunning, fourteen A, Eggerton Crescent, South West One."

I wrote it down and waited. When nothing else was said, I looked up.

"Well?" I asked.

"I thought *you* would tell me," she said. "That's why I came."

"Do you want him followed?" I asked.

"That's it," she said. "I want him followed."

"You have reason to believe he is conducting an extramarital relationship," I prompted.

She looked at me for a moment, then she burst out laughing. She threw her head back, exposing her long, fine neck. It was one of her better features, and she had learned to use it. I waited until she had finished laughing. I didn't even smile.

"I'm sorry, John," she said eventually. She stopped laughing with an effort. "Yes, I have reason to believe he is conducting an extramarital relationship." Her eyes still laughed.

"And you wish me to obtain evidence to this fact that will be of use in a court of law?" I said.

"Yes, I wish you to obtain evidence to ..."

"Tell me about it," I cut in, realising I was losing the initiative.

Quite suddenly her eyes and mouth went hard.

"The bastard's having it off somewhere, and I want to know all about it," she said.

This took me by surprise. She had only used vulgar speech, as she called it, when we were in bed together. Outside those unguarded moments she had spared no effort to let me know that she disapproved of it strongly. Some of my surprise must have showed.

"I've shocked you," she said.

"Not shocked," I said. "Surprised."

"I'm different, John. That bastard has changed me. Boy, how he's changed me."

I refrained from saying he deserved congratulations. Any man who had managed to change Danielle for better or for worse must have had something going for him. During the five years we had spent together, she had been as unchangeable as time itself.

"Have you any suspicions?" I asked, dragging it back to the professional once more.

"I *know*," she said. "Suspicions don't come into it."

"Then why do you need me?" I asked.

"I want it all legal, proved and notarised or whatever. I want it so that it will stand up in court."

"All right," I said. "Name of co-respondent?"

"Peter Alworthy."

I looked up.

"That's right," she said. "My husband's a queer. And if you laugh, I'll hit you over the head with that ashtray."

I had no intention of laughing. The whole thing had a poetic justice that was almost sublime. She saw it too, although she would never admit that her relationship with Marianne Pleshet had ever been more than that of a very good friend. The night I accused her of being a lesbian, she had hit me with a flower vase, packed a bag, and moved in— with Marianne. The subsequent divorce was provided by me. When I heard of her six months later, I realised that her lapse into lesbianism had been experimental and only temporary. But the affair with Marianne had not been the sole cause of my divorce, rather had it been the straw that broke this particular camel's back. And now, here she was, attempting to gather evidence for another divorce because her husband was a queer. It wasn't a laughing matter, but it was bloody amusing nevertheless.

"Well," she said, "don't you want to hear more?" I dragged myself back and tried to look professional again.

"Go on," I said.

"Peter Alworthy is a little fag who pretends to be a fashion photographer," she said.

"Pretends?"

"He takes dirty pictures as a side line. Nat sees him three times a week. He may see him more, I don't know."

"Perhaps your husband just likes dirty pictures," I said.

"*Queer* dirty pictures?"

"It's been known."

"He hasn't slept with me for over six months. If I touch him, he jumps a mile, and he insists on having his own bedroom."

"Have you tried to..." For some reason I felt embarrassed. Confessions are never easy, and for Danielle they had used to be downright impossible. But I wasn't her husband any more, I was a disinterested third party.

"I've tried everything," she said. "Barring rape. I'd try that if it wasn't a physical impossibility."

She *had* changed, and suddenly I wanted to get her off the hook.

I took down the name and address of Peter Alworthy and a couple more notes. Then we came to the crunch.

"This may take some time," I said.

"I don't care," she said.

"I *am* rather busy at the moment," I said. She saw what I was getting at.

"Dear John," she said. "You don't think I'd ask you to do this for nothing."

I had thought so, but I wasn't going to let her know.

"What is your normal fee?" she asked.

I added up quickly the amount of money I immediately owed and then added twenty-five per cent. I divided this by the number of days I thought I could stretch the affair.

"Fifteen pounds a day and expenses," I said, trying not to sound too hopeful.

"Do you mind cash?" she said, already delving into her handbag.

"Make it a hundred and fifty," I said. "If I can wrap it up in less than ten days, I'll refund the balance."

She pulled a roll of tenners from her handbag and started to count them off. The sight of all that money was so upsetting that I wanted to look away. I glanced at my notes.

"Where does your husband work?" I said.

She pushed fifteen ten pound notes towards me.

"He's something to do with the Foreign Office," she said.

If I hadn't been watching the money like a hypnotised rabbit, alarm bells might have started to sound there and then. As it was, I was too bloody greedy to see further than the sudden ability to pay the rent and eat well for the next three or four weeks.

I scooped the money towards me and casually slipped it into the desk drawer as though it was something I did every day.

"Have you got a photograph?" I asked, not very hopefully.

"No," she said. "Does it matter?"

I said that it didn't and took down the address of her husband's place of work. Then, because I could think of nothing else to say or do, I got to my feet to signify the end of the interview.

"Will you have dinner with me one night?" she said as I walked her to the door.

"Why?" I asked.

She shrugged.

"Talk about old times," she said.

The 'old times' she referred to seemed, in retrospect, to have been one continuous battle. There didn't seem much point in raking it over.

"Perhaps we should leave it until I've finished this job for you."

She looked at me as I opened the door to the outer office. Then she smiled and nodded.

"If you say so, dear," she said.

She reached up and kissed me on the mouth. Before I could react, she had gone, leaving me standing.

Miss Roberts closed the outer door behind her and looked at me with a new respect in her eyes.

"Ooh, Mr. Smith," she said.

Before she could enlarge on it, I reached for my raincoat, took the money from the drawer, and went to lunch.

With one hundred and fifty pounds in my pocket, it had to be Wheeler's in Old Compton Street. There was a bit of bother getting a table, but finally one was found for me on the third floor. It was practically in the kitchen, but who cared.

I ordered two dozen oysters, a sole *meunière*, and a bottle of Chablis. Then as I pigged it, surrounded by the noisy lunchtime crowd of film and near-film people, I took stock again.

Not financial stock this time. That had been temporarily taken care of. I took stock of Danielle and me, and the five years that had passed since I had left Danielle and the Service.

I always linked the two, because I quit them both at the same time, although in fact they had little to do with one another. Perhaps when I decided to break with the Service, I had sub-consciously wanted to make the break absolute, turning my back not only on my old professional life, but on my old social life as well. Both had been equally unrewarding, if not down-right impossible. The marriage had been conceived in deceit and born into distrust. It had taken approximately two months for us both to realise that we had made a horrendous mistake. We were unsuited physically and psychologically. But having recognised this fact, we allowed the whole thing to drag on for three years before either of us could stir up enough enthusiasm to do anything about it. In actual fact it was on the night I quit the Service that I had accused Danielle of being a lesbian. So I suppose the incidents *were* connected, even if it was only by a disgruntled state of mind.

She was as relieved as I was to have found the catalyst which allowed us to go our own ways. As for my break with the Service, the less said about that the better.

By the time I had finished lunch, it was two forty-five and I was pleasantly drunk. I paid the bill, overtipped, and walked round to the bank two minutes before it closed. I paid in one hundred pounds of Danielle's money, keeping the balance for running expenses. Then I went back to the office.

At half past three, my client called for the weekend report on his wife. I watched his face while he read it through. There were tears in his eyes when he finished reading. He managed to blink them back like the man that he wasn't.

"Will this be sufficient for me to get a divorce?" he asked.

I felt like saying that it was sufficient to get his wife deported if he wanted, but I didn't. He thanked me as though I had done him a big favour, and settled his account. He obtained a promise from me that I would appear in court if necessary, for a fee of course, and he left.

Two pay days in six hours! Business was looking up. If things carried on like this for much longer, I'd be able to buy that cashmere coat *and* keep that long-standing appointment with my dentist to have my teeth capped. Miss Roberts then fed me endless cups of tea until I left at five o'clock.

A hundred yards from my office in Old Compton Street is a shop that sells overalls, jackets for waiters and other such gear. A beige dust coat set me back forty shillings. In a smelly passage nearby I unwrapped the parcel. Using my pen-knife I drilled three small holes into the lapels. Left and right. Where official messengers should wear their Crown-badges. Often they don't because they can't be bothered to change over when they send one coat to the laundry and put on a different one.

It had stopped raining and I walked down through Leicester Square and Trafalgar Square, and into Whitehall.

I called in at a stationer's on the way and bought a blue cardboard file, and half a ream of copy paper. I told the assistant not to wrap either. I put the paper into the file, giving it a nice bulky look. Before I left the shop, I wrote across the top of the file CODE E.2.

The address Danielle had given me fitted her description of her husband being "something to do with the Foreign Office," the building itself being exactly that.

In the street outside the main doors, I took off my raincoat and hung it carefully over the railings. I put on the dust-coat. With the file clutched under my arm, I pushed the door open and walked in. I hurried across to the sergeant's desk.

"Has the Principal Under-Secretary gone yet?" I said urgently.

The sergeant didn't even blink.

"He's still upstairs."

Without thanking him, because my business was far too urgent, I ran up the main stairs two at a time and turned left at the top. Once out of sight of the sergeant, I slowed down and tried to stop puffing and blowing. Any staircase taken two at a time leaves me like that these days.

I chose the third door on the right, Room 43. I knocked and went in.

A tall, dried-up looking man was just putting on his over-coat. He looked at me as I came in.

"Here's the file, sir," I said.

"What file?"

"Mr. Dunning, Room forty-three," I said.

"No Dunning here," he said, reaching for his umbrella.

"This *is* room forty-three," I said.

"That may be," he said. "But no Dunning. This is my office and my name's Ryman. Now if you'll excuse me ..." he started towards the door.

"I'll leave it here anyway," I said, moving over to put it on the corner of his desk.

I saw him looking at it, its size and the cryptic classification on the cover. Whatever it was, he didn't want to be landed with it. Files meant work, and misdirected files meant even more work.

"Hang on," he said. He picked up a phone.

"Dunning, what's his room number?" he said. Then he nodded.

"Thank you." He hung up and turned to me.

"Dunning's in room one-two-seven, second floor. Take it up to him, there's a good chap."

I hesitated a moment, just long enough, then I nodded disagreeably.

"They said room forty-three," I grumbled, heading for the door.

"They also said Dunning. He's in room one-two-seven," he said.

He came out of the office behind me, smiled bleakly, and moved off towards the stairs.

I found room 127 at the end of the corridor on the second floor. I tapped on the door and walked in. Dunning was sitting at his desk working on some papers. He looked up as I came in.

He had a certain flashy dignity about him, and I could see what might have originally impressed Danielle. Thin, well-drawn face, small military type moustache, and very pale blue eyes which could have been intimidating but weren't because of a nervous tick which caused him to blink his eyelids about five times more than normal. He *could* have been a queer, I suppose, but these days who the hell could ever tell. He looked at me enquiringly, his eyelids batting up and down like a semaphore.

"Mr. Ryman, sir?" I said.

"No," he said.

"This is room one-two-seven, isn't it?"

"Yes, it is. I'm Dunning."

I looked disappointed.

"Sorry, sir," I said. "Someone's given me the wrong room number."

He reached for the phone.

"I'll find out for you. Ryman, you said?"

"It doesn't matter," I said quickly. But he had already picked up the phone. I stood there looking humbly grateful while he ascertained that Ryman was in room forty-three. Then I thanked him and left.

I dropped the file in a wastebasket on my way down. The sergeant didn't even look up as I crossed the main hall, and walked out into Whitehall.

My raincoat was still on the railings where I had left it, which didn't say much for my raincoat. I put it on and crossed the road to a line of telephone booths. One was empty. I stepped in and closed the door behind me. Then I dialed the speaking clock.

"At the third stroke it will be five fifty-seven and forty seconds."

"Oh really," I said for the benefit of a man who was glaring into the phone booth, waiting to make a call. Then a booth was vacated somewhere along the line, and he disappeared.

It was quite easy to see the main entrance from where I was, and for the first ten minutes I watched a procession of men and women pour out, with no sign of Dunning. Periodically I disconnected the phone and dialed something else. I allowed my own home number to ring for five minutes; I dialed 999 and reported a multiple rape in Eaton Square; and I dialed TIME again and had spirited conversation with the recorded voice at the other end; and still no Dunning.

The flood of people leaving the building had now dwindled to a trickle, and something else had started to worry me. The combination of a bottle of Chablis and nine cups of tea was putting a serious strain on my bladder, and I knew that inside five minutes I would have to do something about it.

The five minutes passed. I said good-bye to the voice at the other end of the phone, and came out of the booth. There was a public toilet in Trafalgar Square, but that was four minutes' walk. Even if I could make it, I stood a very good chance of losing Dunning. So I lose him, I thought, I'll pick him up tomorrow. I started to hobble off in the direction of Trafalgar Square, and at that moment the inconsiderate bastard appeared.

He stood for a moment at the top of the steps, pulling on his gloves. Then he came down to street level and started to walk in the opposite direction to the one I had been going to take.

So I followed him, staying on the opposite side of the road, and moving like a man of a hundred and four.

He came into Parliament Square, and turned across it towards Broad Sanctuary. I could wait no longer. I raced down the steps of the Underground, spent an excruciatingly pleasant minute in the toilet, and raced up the steps again. I crossed the square at a run and headed down Broad Sanctuary. He hadn't let me down, he was there, five hundred yards in front of me. I walked fast until the gap had been narrowed to a hundred yards, where I stuck.

He turned into a pub in Petty France. He went to the saloon bar, so I went into the public. I ordered a large vodka, and before

I could drink it, I saw him served with a bottle of wine and walk out again. Having paid for the vodka, I swallowed it much too quickly, and reached the street choking. He was fifty yards away. I staggered after him, and when he turned into the house, I was twenty-five yards behind him. He let himself in with his own key, and by the time I was level with the door, he had gone in and closed it behind him.

I walked on past the house to the end of the short street, and after a respectable pause, I walked back again.

The address was the one that Danielle had given me for Peter Alworthy, and I began to think that perhaps Danielle was on the right track.

Dunning had his own key for a start, and secondly the house *looked* as though it belonged to a queer. It was similar to its companions in the street, but it had been fussed over. Pink front door, twee coaching lamps and pretty little window boxes fully of pretty little flowers. The house itself looked like an ageing queen.

I reached the end of the street once again and planned strategy. The bottle of wine pointed to the fact that they were going to dine. I could visualise the whole scene, candles stuck in old chianti bottles, Alworthy making like the little woman in the kitchen and serving *ratatouille*. There would be Ella Fitzgerald on the record player and pictures of guardsmen around the walls. I decided to allow them two hours to eat. Then I would try to get a closer look. Perhaps if things worked out, I'd come back tomorrow with a camera. One photograph was worth a dozen pages of typescript.

I walked back to the pub and this time went into the saloon bar. I ordered a plate of cold meat and potato salad, and a large vodka. I bummed an evening paper from the bartender and tucked myself in a corner to wait it out in comfort.

The bar was pleasantly busy, and after the third vodka I began to feel positively benevolent. A pretty girl in a short skirt was sitting up at the bar, and she occupied my attention for half an hour. I looked at her legs and indulged in lewd flights of fancy. When she eventually left, I felt like I had been jilted. I considered whether or not to call Mary to fix up something for later that evening. I had been having an affair on and off with Mary for three years now, and bloody lucky I was too. She was a slim, sexy blonde of twenty-seven or thereabouts who modelled in a whole-sale dress house. She was not married, but had an understanding with her boss, who was. Saddled with a wife and four children he was forced to play it very cool indeed, and this allowed Mary plenty of free evenings. She was a good-hearted girl who also played it cool for the benefit of her boss who was besotted with her. So on the evenings she didn't see him, she usually stayed home. He had a sneaky habit of phoning her late at night when he was walking the dog, and if she wasn't in, there'd be hell to pay the following day. I'd suggested once to her that it wasn't a very ideal arrangement, and she should consider turning the whole thing in. But she liked her job, she was well paid, and she felt sorry for the poor bastard with his four kids, his dog and his wife who understood him only too well. I had nothing to offer her in exchange, so while not exactly telling me to mind my own business, that's what she implied.

Once or twice a week, whenever the fancy took me, I would call her and we would go out to dinner, or she would cook some-thing in her flat. Bed didn't always follow, but it followed often enough. I'm not very good in bed, but Mary never complained. Unlike Danielle, who had on occasions been known to complain loud and long. This is an area where even if a man knows he's no Casanova, he doesn't like to be reminded of it all the time. In fact, part of the trouble with Danielle had been due to her snide attacks on my virility, which decreased, as far as she was concerned, in a direct ratio to the amount of scorn she poured on it. It had become a descending spiral where the outcome had been that not only did I not want to sleep with her, but on the odd occasions that I tried, I only managed to confirm what she was saying.

Mary, however, never mentioned it, and I was, after three years, beginning to think that perhaps I wasn't such a limp handshake in bed as Danielle had led me to believe.

I looked at the clock on the wall of the bar. If I stayed there another half an hour, and then allowed an hour to prowl around the outside of Alworthy's house, I could be free by half past ten. I used the pub phone to call Mary. She answered a little breathlessly.

"Alone?" I asked. This was the standard opening gambit. My relationship with her was far too tenuous for me to want to queer anything good she might have had going. She always knew who it was.

"Hello, darling," she said. "What are you doing?"

"After half past ten, nothing," I said.

"Will you have eaten?" she asked.

I told her that I would have eaten and she said that she'd see me later. I returned to my drink feeling at peace with the world. I had a ten-day job that I'd probably wrap up in two, a medium-sized alcoholic glow, and a warm bed waiting for me.

During the last half an hour, I managed to find room for three more large vodkas. Then, bidding the barman good night as effusively as if I'd known him all my life, I went out to earn my pay. The fresh air made me suddenly realise that I wasn't as sober as I might have been. I wasn't drunk, but I was more than halfway there.

I wandered up the street past the house once more. The coach lamps were lit, and there was a light showing through the curtains of the downstairs room. There were a few neat plastic dustbins in the road which was a pretty good indication that there was no back entrance to any of the houses. This would have upset me normally as it was far too early to be sure that people

wouldn't still be out and about. But in my present state of alcoholic euphoria, I could see no problems.

Then I had the best idea of the day. Why pussyfoot around
outside? Why not bang on the front door and confront Dunning
with whatever I found inside? Then I could use my natural talent for such things to provide him with enough rope to hang
himself. I realise now that it was the booze doing the thinking,
and even if things *hadn't* turned out the way they did, it was still
a bloody fool thing to do. But it was ten o'clock, and in half an
hour Mary would be expecting me. I had a momentary picture of
her which somehow became mixed up with a picture of the girl
at the bar. The aphrodisiacal effect of this double vision was all I
needed to push me over the edge.

Although normally I'm not a bad enquiry agent, everyone is
entitled to drop a brick occasionally. Hindsight has since shown
me that I had already dropped it, at about five past eleven that
morning. Whatever I had decided to do while I was making up
my mind whether to ring the doorbell or not, it would have made
no difference to what was to follow.

There was a small gate, and six feet of paved garden in front
of the house. I stepped over the gate, straddling it, which showed
how near drunk I was, and walked up to the front door.

I rang the bell, prepared for all eventualities. If Alworthy
answered I would ask for Dunning, and if Dunning answered I
would ask for Alworthy. One way or another I would get into the
house, then, with one or two devastating observations I would
reduce them both to the condition where they would agree to
anything. If no one answered, I was prepared to lean on the
doorbell all night. Or at least until half past ten.

As it turned out, things didn't go that way at all. I'd hardly
touched the bell before the door was flung open by a person I
assumed was Alworthy. He was about twenty-four years old,
dark and willowy. He was wearing a tan coloured silk shirt with

pale olive slacks. I could tell he was wearing make-up because he had been crying and his mascara had run.

"Thank God you've come," he said, and disappeared through a door that led off from the tiny hall. I stepped through the front door. I had been right about the guardsmen, there were pictures of them all over the hall. I followed him through the door into the main room. It seemed expected of me. It was a pretty room, in keeping with its owner. There were chintzy things scattered here and there, lots of low chairs and gaily coloured cushions, and a long settee at right angles to the fireplace.

In a small alcove, there was the dining table and the remains of dinner. Right again—two candles stuck in chianti bottles.

I stood in the door and looked at Alworthy, who was looking at me. The silence between us grew until I felt I had better say something.

"Mr. Alworthy..." I started.

"Well *do* something," he said petulantly.

I must have looked as vague as I felt.

"It's too bad," he said when he realised I wasn't going to be any help. "I call for the police, and they send me... oh really, it's *too* bad."

He had called the police. For what? I looked around. There was no sign of Dunning. Then I realised what it was that had been worrying me since I had first come into the room. It was the decorations; they weren't right somehow. There was too much red splashed about without regard to form or design.

The alcohol I had drunk evaporated suddenly, leaving me stone-cold sober.

I rubbed a finger along a particularly vivid splash of red which crawled down the wall just inside the door.

"It's blood," I said, sounding like an idiot.

Alworthy nearly burst into tears again.

"Of course it's blood," he wailed.

Then I realised that he had moved to the corner of the settee in order to show me something behind it. I had no desire to know what it was, but I looked nevertheless.

Dunning was crouched on his side, his knees drawn up to his chest, his hands cupping his chin. He looked as though he were trying to hide. I touched him tentatively with the toe of my shoe and regretted it immediately. He rolled from his crouched position on to his back, his hands slipping away from his chin.

I realised then that he hadn't been cupping his chin at all. The poor sod had been trying to hold his head on. There was a gash in his throat as wide as an open grave, and damn near as deep.

I was perched on the edge of an armchair when Inspector Diaman arrived, trying to look as though I had every right in the world to be there. The place was already swarming with forensics, fingerprinters, photographers and uniformed men. Two of the latter were keeping a sharp eye on me, but I was far too worried to be any trouble. I was in it up to my armpits and it was getting worse every minute.

My main cause of concern was Peter Alworthy, or to be more precise, the lack of Peter Alworthy. A moment after I had turned Dunning over and he had grinned at us with his throat, Alworthy had excused himself hurriedly for the purpose of throwing up. He had disappeared in the direction of the kitchen and that had been the last I, or anyone else, had seen of him. My observation about there being no back way out of the house had been detection of a similar order to the rest of my performance that day. There *was* a back way out and Alworthy had used it with alacrity. Two minutes after he had left me, and before I had even begun to get suspicious, the police had gonged up to the front door. They had found me poking around the living-room looking for God knows what. I had started to explain about Alworthy but they had told me to save it until Inspector Diaman arrived. They said it with such relish that I expected Torquemada to walk in the door. Perhaps I would have been better off if he had.

His arrival was announced by everyone in the room falling silent. I looked towards the door, and there he was. One of the uniformed men moved over to speak to him, and while he was doing that, I saw Diaman's eyes lift towards me. They were flat, slate grey, with no expression whatsoever. I'd never come across him before, but I had heard plenty. He was one of those policemen who subscribed to the theory that to do his job properly it was necessary to put the fear of God into the criminal classes. If he thumped a man occasionally, it was only so that man would spread the word that Diaman was a very hard case indeed. Law breakers of the lower orders had been known to give themselves up *en masse* when they heard that Diaman had been assigned to their case.

Now the uniformed man stepped back and Diaman came into the room. He ignored me completely. He had a word with the doctor, he looked at the body, he gave permission for it to be removed, he spoke to one of the fingerprint men, he instructed the photographers to pay particular attention to the disposition of the bloodstains, he had another word with the doctor, and then he disappeared for a few minutes to look over the rest of the house. Apart from that first flat stare from the door, he hadn't looked at me once. It was twenty minutes before he condescended to acknowledge my presence.

He sat down opposite me, pulling a chair forward. He looked at me sadly for a moment, then he sighed gently and started.

"Tell me all about it, son," he said. I could probably have given him a year or two, but if he wanted to call me "son", that was his affair.

"Where shall I start?" I said like an idiot.

"Start where you like, son," he said. "One way or another, we'll get it all."

And get it all he did. My training and background has given me pretty methodical thought processes, and I presented him with all the facts, starting with Danielle's visit that morning. It's all very well to be ethical and respect the anonymity of your client, but when it comes to my own hide, I can pitch to the wolves with the best of them.

I was brief, lucid and to the point. He didn't take his eyes off me for a second. He didn't nod, he didn't grunt. He just sat there like a monolithic sponge, soaking it all up. I finished and sat back, waiting for a pat on the head. He continued to stare at me, and I could almost hear the gears clicking in that steel trap he used as a mind. Then he grunted something unintelligible and heaved himself to his feet.

He walked to the door and said something to the uniformed man. Then without a backward glance, he walked out of the front door. I judged that now was the time for me to do the same. I got to my feet and headed for the door. The uniformed man grinned at me, hoping I'd cause trouble.

"Going somewhere, sir?" he said pleasantly.

"Home?" I said.

"Not just yet," he said.

Ten minutes later, I was in the interview room at the police station. Someone took my coat, someone else brought me a cup of tea, and someone else gave me a cigarette. Everyone was so damned pleasant that I began to realise just how much trouble I was in.

I waited for half an hour under the bored scrutiny of a young copper who did me the favour of not trying to start a conversation.

"May I use the telephone?" I said finally.

"I'll ask," he said and disappeared. He came back with the station sergeant.

"Who do you want to phone?" said the sergeant.

"A friend," I said, thinking of Mary.

"I'll ask the inspector," he said.

Two minutes later, he returned with a phone which he plugged in.

"Give me the number and I'll get it for you," he said.

"I've changed my mind," I said. I didn't want Mary dragged into this mess, and having met Diaman, I knew that she would be if I'd given them the slightest lead.

"The Inspector won't like that," said the sergeant. I felt like telling him what the inspector could do with himself, but I wasn't angry enough yet. But I was beginning to get that way, not with the police, but with myself. I had behaved like a first-class nut, first in ringing the doorbell, second in going into the house, and third in allowing Alworthy to get away. I should have stuck with him even if he *had* been going to throw up.

Half an hour later, Diaman sent for me. I was taken upstairs to his office. The first thing I noticed was the presence of a stenographer. Diaman saw me looking at him nervously.

"Just to make a few notes, son," he said.

"I know what he's for," I said.

"Makes it easier it all round," he said. "Sit you down."

I sat me down and waited for him to start talking.

"What sort of business do you do, son?" he asked.

"I told you, I'm a private investigator," I said.

"I know," he said. "But what do you do mostly?"

"Divorces," I said.

"Like tonight?"

"Like tonight."

"Suppose you start at the beginning again. Tell me the story like you did earlier."

If he was expecting me to make a mistake, he was going to be disappointed. I had been telling the truth before, all I had to do was tell it again. I did so, step by step, exactly as I had done before.

"You've got a good memory," he said when I finished.

"It's part of my job," I said.

"It's an interesting story," he said. "Now let's go into it in a little more detail."

I noticed that he had stopped calling me "son".

"I accept the fact that you're a private investigator," he said. "And I accept the fact that your wife…"

"My ex-wife," I interrupted.

"…your ex-wife visited you this morning. Do you know why I accept this?"

"You asked her," I said brightly.

"No, I didn't. I can't get in touch with her. But I asked your receptionist Miss Roberts. She confirms that you had an appointment with Mrs. Dunning this morning."

So Miss Roberts had been contacted. What a marvelous time she would have with Stubbs tomorrow.

"Next you went to the address she gave you and there you identify Dunning so that you would recognise him later."

"Right," I said.

"Next you follow Dunning to Alworthy's house," he said.

"Right," I said.

"Wrong," he said. I waited for him to enlarge on it.

"The house you followed him to belongs to Dunning himself, not Alworthy."

It was a surprise, but not catastrophic. It just meant that Dunning paid the rent for his boyfriend.

"I didn't check the lease," I said.

"I did," said Diaman.

"Is it important?" I said, not seeing how it could be.

"We'll see," said Diaman. "Next, you kill a couple of hours in the pub up the road. Why?"

"I was hungry and thirsty, and it was too soon for anything to happen at the house."

"Anything like what?"

"I was there to collect evidence for a divorce. The best sort of evidence would have been to find them in bed together."

"Dunning and Alworthy?" he said.

"Exactly," I said, wondering where this was leading to.

"So after two hours you leave the pub, walk up to the front door and ring the bell."

I nodded unhappily.

"So if they *had* been in bed together, one of them would have had to get up to answer the door."

"I didn't say I would find them in bed, I just said that would have been the best sort of evidence."

"But by ringing the doorbell you would automatically destroy such evidence," he said. To this observation I, of course, had no answer.

He allowed the silence to grow to embarrassing proportions before he continued. I could see the stenographer chewing the side of a fingernail while he waited for his lord and master to start again.

"The door was opened by Alworthy," he said finally.

I nodded.

"He told you to come in. It is your idea that he mistook you for the police whom he had recently telephoned, and he left you alone with the body while he went out to the kitchen to vomit."

"That's what he said," I said.

Diaman now put his hand flat on the desk and cleared his throat. Something about the way that he did it made me worried about what was coming next.

"There are certain factors about your story about which I am not happy," he said. It was the understatement of the year.

"First, Alworthy and Dunning couldn't have dined together. There was only the remains of one meal at the dining table."

"Perhaps one of them wasn't hungry," I said helpfully.

"Secondly, the call to the police did not come from the house but from a telephone booth some way down the road. A passer-by reported seeing a man trying to force an entry. So we can assume that Alworthy didn't make the call himself. Thirdly, there is no evidence that anyone apart from Dunning, was ever in the house this evening. Fourthly, what happened to Alworthy? Now you're a reasonably intelligent man. What sort of conclusion should I draw from all that?"

I knew, but he could have broken my arm before I'd have said it. So I said nothing, and he provided his own answer.

"There is not and there never has been, any such person as Alworthy," he said. And as far as he was concerned, that just about wrapped it up.

Police station cells are pretty fair as cells go. Mine had a bed, a table and a chair. For washing or going to the toilet, I had to bang on the door and a middle-aged policeman would let me out and accompany me to where I wanted to go. He would stand with me while I did it, then he would take me back and lock me up again.

I had some cigarettes and coffee sent down from the canteen and I reviewed the general situation. From whichever direction I looked at it, it was murky. I tried ticking off the essential points as I came to them.

One: I hadn't been charged with anything. Not a particularly good sign in itself, but at least better than if I *had* been. Two: the problem of the non-existent Alworthy. Non-existent as far as the police were concerned. All the facts pointed to his having done the killing and my interrupting him before he could get away. This being the case he wasn't likely to turn up out of the blue to confirm my story. Three: where was Danielle? Diaman had told me he had tried to contact her, but didn't really know where to start because the only address he had for her was the house where the killing took place. It seemed that the address she had given me for Alworthy was her own, hers and Dunning's. This didn't help my story any, because if it was her own house, why had she given the address to me as the one to follow Dunning to? Four: as long as I was locked up here, I wasn't going to be able to sort out items two and three. And until I could sort them out, I wasn't going to be able to get out of here. Five: I'd had a hell of a day, it was now two o'clock in the morning and I was tired.

So I finished my coffee and went to bed.

Diaman came down to see me at seven thirty in the morning. He too had been on the premises all night, but unlike me, he hadn't slept. He looked like hell.

He stood aside as the door was unlocked.

"Out," he said.

I picked up my jacket and tie and followed him. We went to the interview room. While I was tying my tie in front of the wall mirror, he sat and scowled at me.

"You're a lucky bastard," he said finally.

"You've found Alworthy," I said.

"Don't come that balls with me," he said. He was very angry.

"You fellows think you can get up to whatever you bloody well like. But I'm telling you, Smith, if our paths cross again, look out, because I'm going to jump on you, and jump so hard I'll break your bloody back."

I believed him too, even if I didn't understand him. What I did understand was that I was getting out. Something had come up in the night, something that Diaman didn't like. He wasn't the sort of copper who would get angry just because a prime suspect is found to be clean.

That took a vindictive copper, and he wasn't that. Therefore, he must still believe I'm as guilty as hell. So why was he releasing me?

But I wasn't going to look a gift horse in the mouth. I kept quiet while he continued to snarl at me inwardly. Then I slipped on my jacket, opened the door of the interview room and walked out. The desk sergeant looked up politely when I spoke to him.

"May I have my raincoat please," I said.

"No, you bloody can't," said Diaman from the door of the interview room. "It's got bloodstains all over it. Someone might think you've committed a crime."

This was the first I had heard of the bloodstains. But on considering the amount of blood splattered all over the murder room, it wasn't surprising. No wonder he was so needled at having me walk out of the place.

I turned right outside the station meaning to pick up a taxi to get me home. There was a black Humber parked at the kerb, and as I approached it, the door opened and a man stepped out.

The whole bloody thing fell into place there and then. I damn near turned back to take my chances with Diaman. But the man was leaning against the car smiling at me, and I knew he wouldn't let me.

"Hello, Johnny," he said affably.

"Hello, Max," I said.

CHAPTER TWO

HADN'T seen Max for five years. That wasn't strange because unless you were in the Service you didn't see Max. The last time I had seen him, I had been facing him across his desk. I had stated my case very simply, I wanted out. And he, just as simply, said I couldn't go.

I told him I was sick of the Service, sick of him, and most of all sick of myself.

"We all get low at times, John," he said. "You'll get over it."

"I know I will," I said. "That's why I want out."

"Sit down and tell me about it," he said, adopting his confessor role. I didn't have to tell him, he already knew. But he thought the effect of laying it out on the line might act as a catharsis. I knew the only effective catharsis for me was a lobotomy, but I told him all about it anyway.

I had been back from Algeria for a week, and still I couldn't sleep for more than an hour at a stretch. The whole job had been such a monumental cock up from start to finish, that it was a wonder there was anyone left alive to talk about it. Privately, I knew, Max regretted this fact. He would have preferred a nice clean end to the affair with no loose ends. I was a loose end.

Some anonymous clerk had given the operation the code name Redskin. And that just about covered it. Skin red with blood, floors and ceilings swimming in it, heels skidding in pools of it. Blood over everything, blood on my hands that even after a week's scouring I couldn't seem to scrub off.

MAKE CONTACT WITH ALI BEN AHMED, ASSIST
IN ELIMINATING THE LAGRAVE FACTOR.

That's how the order filtered down to me, and that's what I set out to do. The Lagrave factor was the name given to a group of misguided Frenchmen who, under the mask of the Algerie Francaise movement, were laying the foundations for a Red intervention in Algeria. At least, that's what we had been told.

The Arab Bureau in Algeria couldn't go to the French Bureau, because they were virtually at war with each other, so the whole operation landed on our plate. As long as France and Algeria were fighting each other with no third-party interference, it was no concern of ours. But as soon as information came to hand that there *was* third-party interest, and who that third party was, then something had to be done.

So I packed my little bag and left with George Barnes, another Service man with whom I'd worked before. The operation had been simple, Ali ben Ahmed took time off from slaughtering Frenchmen to show us where and how the renegades were operating. In a week we had the whole thing sewn up. It was too easy, a factor that worried me until I found out the reason, and then it worried me even more. They were amateurs, little more than kids. Embroiled in a war they didn't really understand, they had been a soft touch for the third party. Pictures had been painted of a new, free Algeria owing allegiance neither to Mother France nor the corrupt Arab government who would take over when the French left. And these poor, deluded infants lapped it up.

The normal procedure for eliminating a subversive cell is to first search out the tendrils that radiate from the core. Then when the core is eliminated, the tendrils can be wrapped up quietly, without any fuss. It took George and me four days to discover that there were no tendrils. There was nothing more than a group of kids printing and distributing communist propaganda, which nobody bothered to read anyway.

I sent a cable to London stressing that somewhere along the line we'd been fooled. The Service had been dragged into something for some other purpose than the one stated. It took Max two days to run the whole dirty business to earth. The third party had leaked the information to Ali ben Ahmed, knowing he would get on to London. Then the presence of Service personnel on French territory would be leaked to the French Bureau and a fine old *schemozzle* would result, considerably straining the *entente cordiale* and the Franco-British Nato relations.

But thanks to my cable, Max managed to jump on the scheme before it bore fruit. Two third-party agents in Paris disappeared, and the leak to the French didn't take place. But by now there were a lot of worried men in London, and somewhere along the line, someone panicked. Max was ordered to remove all evidence and get us out of Algeria fast. As far as Max was concerned, people were evidence, and in reply to my cable that the third-party cell should be let off with smacked bottoms, I received a cryptic message from London.

ELIMINATE. MAX.

And we eliminated. Armed with sawn-off shotguns, George, myself and two of Ahmed's men forced an entry into the old house they used as their headquarters. There were twelve of them, not one over twenty years old, and four of them girls.

One girl particularly I noticed, probably because she was the youngest and prettiest. She had long, straight blonde hair, and she was wearing blue slacks and a blue silk shirt. She was making coffee when we arrived, while her companions were moving around sorting out pamphlets, and manning an old printing press in the corner.

Like all the others, she turned towards us as we suddenly appeared among them. Her blue eyes which matched her silk shirt, were wide with enquiry. I wanted to tell her not to worry, that everything would be all right. Then a boy standing close to her, realised what we were going to do, and grabbed at a gun in his belt. I shot him. A sawn-off shotgun isn't the most selective of weapons, that's why we were using them. I killed the boy all right, and I also blew the pretty girl's face off.

In thirty seconds, it was all over. George had a bullet in his chest which was scheduled to kill him half an hour later, and one of our Arabs was nursing a shattered elbow. The other Arab was moving about the room finishing with a knife what the guns had started.

The pretty girl wasn't dead and I wanted to do something for her. Give her a new face perhaps to replace the one I had removed. She lay in a pool of blood making a small whimpering sound and moving her hands spasmodically. Then the Arab leaned over her and deftly slit her throat. He looked up at me and grinned. Another second and I would have shot him, too, but fortunately I chose that moment to be sick. The trouble was that we were unable to get out of that place until the truck we had arranged for arrived to clear out the bodies. And the truck was late, half an hour late. So for half an hour I sat with George while he died, and all around me the young people lay in their own blood, looking like pale orchids on a field of scarlet.

Five hours later, I was back in London. By then I had developed a Lady Macbeth complex. I couldn't stop washing my hands. The psychiatrist told me that it would go away after a few months and I should ask Max for a transfer in the meantime, to some desk job out of the field. I didn't ask him for a bloody thing. I told him I was getting out altogether. When he told me he couldn't allow that, I told him to go and stuff himself. We argued back and forth for a couple of days, but he couldn't shift me. He had to let me go if I insisted, and I insisted. I commuted my pension rights into a lump sum, collected a couple of months' back pay and went on a bender which culminated in kicking my wife out of the house. I never saw Max again. Not until now.

He's a small man physically, with thinning hair and a sharply defined face, all planes and angles. He has a thin, humourless mouth and very good teeth. His eyes are prominent and he's a permanent martyr to conjunctivitis. He uses eye drops as frequently as another man uses a pocket handkerchief, pulling out a small bottle and squeezing the drops into the corners of his eyes.

He did this as I sat across from him in the office I had hoped never to see again. Then he sniffed hard, put the bottle away and looked at me, his eyes swimming.

"Sorry about that," he said. "Same old trouble."

I said nothing.

"You're in a spot of bother," he said.

"You should know," I said. "You got me out of it."

"I did, didn't I? He's quite a bulldog that Diaman. Once he gets his teeth in, he hates to let go. I had to pull some very well-connected strings."

"Why?" I said.

He continued as though he hadn't heard me.

"For a couple of hours last night I didn't think I'd be able to pull it off. But now, here you are."

"Why?" I persisted.

He looked at me levelly. His eyes had stopped watering.

"You know why, John," he said. "I want the notebook."

"What notebook?" I said.

He sighed and scratched the corner of his chin. He needed a shave, I noticed, but then so did I.

"We're professionals," he said finally. "You can fool some of the people all the time, but you can fool the professionals hardly any of the time."

"I'm not trying to fool anyone," I said.

"Then turn over the notebook like a good fellow, and we'll forget all about it."

"What will you do if I don't?" I said.

He looked genuinely concerned.

"Don't say that, John," he said. "I told you I had to pull some important strings on your behalf. I'd hate to see all that effort go to waste."

I was way ahead of him.

"If I let you have the notebook, I'm clean. If I don't, I go back to Diaman," I said.

"That's about it," he said.

"Just say I *do* let you have the notebook," I said. "Who gets the chop for Dunning?"

"The file is marked 'unsolved'." he said.

"Then I'd better let you have it," I said.

He smiled.

"There's a good chap. Just tell me where it is and I'll have it picked up."

"Can't do that," I said. "Must pick it up myself."

He thought about this for a moment, then he shrugged.

"So be it," he said. "When can I expect you?"

"When you see me," I said. I got to my feet. He let me get as far as the door before he spoke again.

"Not like you, John," he said. "A messy job, not like you at all."

"I like to cut throats," I said, and left.

I called in at home where I showered, shaved and changed my clothes. Then I took a taxi to Marylebone Station. I caught an Amersham train, and at the first stop I pretended to be asleep until the train started to move out of the station. Then I made a good show of waking up suddenly like a man who realises he's nearly overslept his destination. The train was doing ten miles an hour and gaining speed fast as I opened the carriage door and jumped out. I just made the end of the platform where it started to slope down to track level. Needless to say, no one got out after me. I thought I had seen a man someway down the carriage look startled when I suddenly erupted, but he could hardly pull the communication cord, and I may have been wrong anyway.

I left the station and walked out into the small town. There I caught a bus to Uxbridge, where I took the Underground back into London. I changed trains and got out at Victoria main line station. There I bought a ticket to Box Hill.

At Box Hill station there were no taxis, so I walked the two miles to Gunther's house. His daughter let me in and said the old man would be glad to see me. She wasn't so glad; she disapproved of me strongly.

Gunther was sitting up in bed wearing flannel pyjamas and an embroidered shawl over his massive shoulders. Even now, after six years in bed, he still emanated strength and vitality. His blue eyes twinkled from either side of his great beaked nose, and his hand, when he gripped mine, did so gently so as not to crack any bones. There was a wooden bar rigged up over the bed, and he used to exercise on this daily, pulling himself up and lowering himself for hours on end. He had no further use for his giant strength, but he kept at it just the same. Below the waist of course there was nothing. A bullet had shattered the base of his spine and paralysed everything below. His legs were like matchsticks, and even if he had been able to stand, they would no longer have been able to bear the weight of his hugely over-developed torso.

As always, he was genuinely glad to see me. For ten minutes, he complained bitterly that it had been more than three months since my last visit. Even after twenty years in England, he hadn't lost the heavy accent of his own country. I sat listening to his complaints like a penitent schoolboy. He grew bored with it after a while.

"So how is the peeping tom business?" he asked finally.

"It's a living," I said.

"What sort of living," he said, his voice full of scorn. "A living by looking in bedroom windows."

"I saw Max this morning," I said.

"Ah," he said slowly. "So now we get down to it."

"I think I'm in trouble," I said.

"I think so too," he said. "Or you wouldn't be here. Tell me."

I told him, exactly as I had told Diaman, but continuing the story so that it included my interview with Max.

He was silent when I finished, and I sat there waiting patiently.

"The notebook," he said. "You know nothing of it?"

"Nothing," I said.

"This man Dunning worked in the Foreign Office. Max is interested. Therefore, the contents of the notebook must be classified."

I nodded. Gunther sorted out the facts in his mind, his eyes going blank with concentration. Then he relaxed.

"So we have a situation," he said. "The situation is this. There is a notebook which Dunning owned and in which he had written certain information. Dunning is killed for possession of the notebook, and you have done the killing, therefore you now have the notebook. Why do you want the notebook? You want to sell it for a big price. The price must be big because the book is valuable enough for very important strings to be pulled to release you, when you should be charged with murder."

"Right," I said. "Except that I didn't do the killing and I haven't got the notebook."

"But you didn't tell this to Max," he said.

"No."

"Why not?"

"The notebook got me out of serious trouble. If Max thought I didn't have it, he'd throw me back in."

"Whereas now he thinks you are going to get it for him and everything will be O.K."

I nodded.

"Then you must get it," he said. "Without it you will be hanged."

"They don't hang people anymore," I said.

"You'd rather go to prison for twenty-five years?" said Gunther.

"I'd rather neither," I said.

"So now we come to Mr. Alworthy," said Gunther. "We assume that he too knew of the notebook and he killed Dunning to get it. Question: has he got it yet? Answer: no."

"Why?" I asked.

"You interrupted him," he said. "If he had already found the notebook, he would not have been there when you arrived."

"Reasonable," I said.

"So you must find it before Alworthy does," said Gunther.

"And give it to Max," I said.

"Maybe, maybe not. Read it first, find out what all the fuss is about. A man dead with his throat cut, a man released from jail when he should be charged with murder. We all know Max. Perhaps the notebook will provide you with a little insurance for your old age, because once you give it back to him, then it is unlikely that you will have an old age."

He nodded his head slowly, liking the idea.

"Find out what is in the book," he said. "*Then* decide what you are going to do."

I thought about this for a moment, then Gunther brought up a factor I had been trying to ignore.

"Danielle," he said. "You've thought about her?"

"She may have been genuine," I said.

"I think it is stretching coincidence further than I like to. Go and see her."

"I don't know where she is," I said.

"Find out. Talk to her. Don't tell her anything, but listen to what she has to say. Make up your mind afterwards."

After that, we talked of other things for an hour. His daughter brought us some lunch on trays, and later she chased me out of the place. As I shook his hand before leaving, he pulled me forward and planted a great wet kiss on the side of my face. He always did it, and it always embarrassed me momentarily. That's why he did it.

"You English," he said. "You are ashamed of emotion between men. You think it is pansy to kiss another man. You are my son, I am your father, so I kiss you."

He wasn't my father, but he was all the father I had, and since his own boy had been killed just before the end of the war, I had taken his place in the old man's affections. I didn't mind, in fact I was bloody glad of it. He'd saved my life once on a job in Finland, and I'd done the same for him a couple of years later. At least our affection for each other was by choice and not forced on us by accident of birth.

On my way back to London, I considered his advice. It was good, as always. That's why I discussed things with him. I would probably have done what he suggested anyway, but I felt better knowing it was what *he* would have done in my place.

He had been the best operative the Service ever had. After the bullet had killed his usefulness, Max had wanted him deported under the Aliens Order. Gunther was Finnish and in Helsinki he would have gone to jail at worst or become a starving cripple at best. Fortunately, I had got wind of Max's plan, and I had threatened to scream so loud, that Max had been forced to back down. Then, in case he should change his mind, I had spirited Gunther away to the place in Box Hill. I'd done it so damn well, it had taken Max eight months to locate him. By that time, Max had cooled down sufficiently that I knew I wouldn't have to worry any more. Added to that, I had started keeping my "Dossier on Max," a fact which I managed to leak to him, and which put the fear of Christ into him.

Gunther still drew his government pension and it was sufficient for him and his daughter to live on. And although his body was now useless, his mind was as sharp as ever. He pretended he had never forgiven me for quitting the Service, but secretly he was glad. He had seen the mess I was in after the Algerian incident.

It was raining when I reached Victoria, and now possessing no raincoat, I treated myself to a taxi home. I'd hardly opened the door when the phone started to ring. I decided not to answer it, then I changed my mind. It was Mary, who only rang me when there was an earthquake or the sun exploded.

"Can I see you?" she said.

"Is it important?" I asked. It was a stupid question.

"Come round at seven," she said.

It must have been important. There was a standing order that I never tried to contact her before eight in case her boss, who always drove her home from work, hadn't left the flat.

I promised to be there. It wasn't too much of an inconvenience. What I had to do that evening couldn't be done until much later.

When she hung up, I rang the office.

"No," said Miss Roberts. "No messages. Mr. Stubbs has signed up a new singer. He discovered him in a coffee bar, just like Tommy Steele."

I hoped he would be as successful, then Stubbs could start coughing up his half of the rent. But I didn't say this to Miss Roberts; she would have thought it disloyal.

I made a quick call on my way to Mary's place to pick up a few things I hadn't thought I'd ever need again. I left them in the car, and went in to see Mary. She lived in one of those genteel, faded houses in Belgravia. Like its neighbours, it had been turned into apartments, some with their own bathrooms and kitchenettes, some without. Mary's was with, a large high room, warm and comfortable.

The street door was open and I walked up the wide curved staircase, a relic of a bygone elegance, to the first floor where Mary had her apartment. I tapped on the door and heard her call for me to come in. The door was on the latch and I slipped the latch back into place before closing it behind me.

"I'm in the bath," she called.

I picked up the evening paper and was about to sit down and wait, when she called me again.

"Come in," she said.

I went into the bathroom and sat on the lavatory. She looked and smelled very sexy in the bath, and I started to think about things I had no business thinking about considering the trouble I was in.

"How's the water?" I said brightly, hoping she'd invite me in to try. But she didn't. She looked at me steadily for a moment, her eyes wide and clear.

"What are you up to?" she said.

"You, if you'll give me half a chance," I said.

She grinned, but only with her mouth.

"I had visitors last night," she said.

"Oh," I said. There didn't seem much else I could say.

"They wanted to know if you'd left anything here," she said.

"Like what?"

"Like an overnight bag," she said.

"You're my overnight bag," I said, trying to make light of something which was plucking at the hairs at the back of my neck. "Who were they?"

"They said they were from the police," she said.

"But you didn't believe them," I said.

"No. Yes, I did. No, I didn't ... I don't know," she said.

That meant that they probably weren't policemen. Real policemen wouldn't have left that much area for doubt.

"What did you tell them?" I said.

"I told them you haven't got an overnight bag, and even if you had, you wouldn't leave it here."

"And ...?"

"They were very polite. Please could they have a look. They were neat and tidy, they put everything back in its place. They scared the shit out of me."

Mary rarely used bad language, an indication of just how much shit they'd scared out of her.

"What were they like?" I said.

"I told you, they were very polite. They went all through my underwear cupboard and didn't bat an eyelid. They even looked under the mattress. Then they made the bed again for me afterwards."

"Why did they frighten you?"

"They were so impersonal. They behaved as if I wasn't even here. One of them had a harelip."

"Can I have a drink?" I said.

"Get me one," she said.

I poured the drinks. The whole thing smelled like a cheap embalming. If they were police, how had they got on to Mary, and what were they looking for? If they weren't police, then I knew what they were looking for, but still I didn't know how they got on to Mary. I'd only been seeing her for three years, so there would have been no record of her in my Service file.

I was about to carry Mary's drink into the bathroom, when she came out wrapped in a towel. She took the drink from me and sat in one of the armchairs. The towel settled around her, protecting her modesty like a shroud. I sat down opposite her.

"I don't want to see you anymore," she said.

It was a decision I had no right to argue with.

"O.K.," I said. I finished my drink.

"Do you mind?" she said.

"Ofcourse I mind," I said.

"You can find someone else to go to bed with," she said.

It was more a question than a statement.

"Yes," I said. I stood up.

"I was really frightened," she said.

"I know," I said. I started to say something else, then I thought what the hell. I headed for the door.

"You *are* a bastard," she said.

I looked back at her. She looked smaller wrapped in that towel.

"I don't want you to be frightened," I said. "You're right, I can get laid somewhere else."

"You're rotten in bed," she said. "You won't find anyone else who'll put up with it."

"It'll be fun looking," I said.

"No, it won't," she said. "You've got a thing about it. The harder you try the worse you are. At least with me you've stopped trying."

"I don't want you to be frightened," I said.

"If I'd known what they were after, it wouldn't have been so bad."

"They won't trouble you again," I said, wishing I could believe it.

"Would you come and see me if I didn't go to bed with you?" she said.

"Yes."

She sighed.

"I know you would. That's why I can't kick you out. You're fat and you're too old for me. You're selfish, your beard scrapes me raw 'cos you only shave once a day, and you're going bald. What the hell I put up with you for, I'll never know."

I tried out a smile from the door.

"You want to mother me," I said.

She stood up and the towel fell around her feet.

"Come and be mothered then," she said.

She smelled of lavender and fresh air after her bath. I nibbled her shoulder, then whispered in her ear.

"A going away present?" I said.

"I talk too much," she said.

We went to bed and I was so good that afterwards she pulled back and looked at me.

"You've been taking lessons," she said.

I was as surprised as she was, and in case we'd both made a mistake, we confirmed our findings an hour later.

⚜ ⚜ ⚜

I left her just after midnight. I thought that I was as near being in love with her as I had ever been. It was hell leaving the warm-smelling bed, but life's like that at times.

I drove to Victoria and left the car in Ebury Street. From there I walked. There were a few people about who seem to live out their lives close to main-line stations. If there was anyone following me, he must have been very good, far too good for me to be able to lose him, so I didn't bother taking any detours.

I walked past Dunning's house. It was closed up tight. At the end of the street I turned right and then right again down the parallel street. If I'd done that last night I wouldn't be here now, I thought. There was a small alley leading between two of the houses, and this in turn was intersected by another alley that ran along the backs of the houses in both streets. The older one gets the more one learns. I now knew that a dustbin in the front didn't mean there was no backway in, it just meant there were lazy dustmen.

There was a door let into the wall, and just so I didn't make a mistake, the house number was painted on the door in figures six inches high. The door was secured with a Yale type lock. I took something from the packet I had collected before I went to see Mary, and let myself in.

Inside was a minute garden bounded on three sides by high walls and on the fourth by the house itself. On the walls were painted views of a stately English garden. On my right, a path led half a mile down towards a tree-sheltered lake. On the left, two hundred yards away stood an oriental pavilion. The painting had been done by an expert in perspective, and in the vague light that leaked from the street, the lake looked real enough to swim in.

The back door was more difficult than the one to the garden. It was bolted on the inside. So I left it alone and went in through the kitchen window. Inside I put my foot in the sink, which still held last night's dirty dishes. The clatter was awful, and a dog started barking next door. By the time I had sorted myself out, the dog's master had succeeded in shouting it into silence again, the shouting effectively masking the rest of the noise I made getting in.

I crunched my way across broken crockery to the living-room. My pencil flashlight showed me that the place had been tidied up since last night. Some attempt had been made to scrub the blood off the walls, but complete redecoration was the only thing that would remove the last traces of the outgoing tenant.

The place had been searched of course. The books had been replaced on their shelves far too neatly, and there was still soot in the fireplace where somebody had probed up the chimney. The stairs were narrow and the bedroom opened directly from the top of the staircase. The bathroom lay beyond the bedroom.

I pulled open a drawer in the long dresser. It was full of Danielle's underwear, neatly and methodically placed in little piles, brassieres on the left, pants on the right, stockings in the middle. That meant they'd searched up here too. Danielle had always treated her personal possessions with a casual disregard for order that had made me grind my teeth at times, and five years isn't long enough to change the habits of a lifetime.

I thought for a moment of the patient, methodical men who must have spent the day taking the house apart. They would have slit all the upholstery neatly along its seams, and then sewn it up again afterwards; they would have tapped the walls and removed the skirting boards; they would have dismantled the electrical fitments, and reassembled them; they would have unscrewed the wall mirrors; they would have taken off the panels from the bath, drained the lavatory cistern, emptied the storage tank, and then still not finding what they were looking for, they would have put everything right again. Large, patient men, experts who knew what they were looking for.

Me, I didn't even know, but I had the edge on them nevertheless. I knew where to look.

On the dressing table among the scent bottles and cream jars there was a small Victorian jewel box, a present from me to Danielle when I had still thought a time would come when I would be able to buy her jewels. I ran my hand down the studs at the rear of the box and a small flat drawer at the bottom snapped open. It was empty. Danielle was saving it for the important piece of jewelry which I had never bought her, and which Dunning certainly wasn't going to be able to. Lots of these old Victorian pieces have secret drawers, a fact that the methodical searchers would be well aware of. But, again, I had the edge, because the thing that had really endeared me to this particular piece of cabinetmakers' art, was that the secret drawer had a secret drawer. It was necessary to remove the first drawer completely and use a pencil or pen to probe in the cavity for a small stud which released a catch so that the back of the cabinet fell outwards, revealing a narrow cavity just wide enough to hold a few banknotes or papers or, in this case, a flat, black, plastic-covered notebook.

CHAPTER THREE

I WENT to an all-night cafe in the Bayswater Road. Armed with a cup of tea and a Wimpey, I tucked myself into a corner table. I mopped the dregs of tea and coffee from the table top with a paper napkin, and opened the notebook for the first time.

Whatever it was saying, it started right out on page one without any form of heading. I read the first line:

24XB379yrc47aab986YYbBV

The rest of the page was like that. So was the second and the twenty-second. I flipped through to the end. The last fifteen pages were blank. I turned back to page one and looked at it until I was bug-eyed. In the old days I had known something about code, not much, but sufficient to know that without a key of some sort it's next to impossible to break down even the simplest cypher. This one wasn't simple.

I paid for my tea and Wimpey and took a taxi to Piccadilly Circus. I went into the all-night chemist and at the stationery counter I bought two notebooks as near similar to the one I had found as possible. From there, I walked to the all-night post office, where I bought two registered envelopes. I spent half an hour scribbling a mass of letters and figures into the two books I had just bought, then I put the real notebook and one of the phonies into the registered envelopes. I addressed them and posted them. The other phony notebook I tucked into my inside jacket pocket. The receipts for the postal registration I tore up and dropped in the wastepaper basket on my way out. I took a taxi back to Ebury Street, where I picked up the car and drove home.

I let myself into the flat, cold and tired. In the last twenty-four hours I'd had about three hours' sleep, and that in a police cell. I'd lost my raincoat, and while it wasn't much as coats go, it was all I had. All I wanted now was a hot bath, a large drink, and fourteen hours' sleep. What I got was a kick in the balls as I closed the door behind me. It wasn't too hard a kick, just hard enough to make me want to die quickly, and not hard enough to enable me to do so. I was so busy nursing myself for the next five minutes, that I didn't even look at the man who had kicked me. When I did, it wasn't too much of a surprise. It was Alworthy. He was sitting in my best armchair, holding on his lap a very large gun. At least it seemed large from where I was looking, the hole of the barrel gaping at me like the entrance to Blackwall tunnel. There was no silencer on the gun, a fact which didn't make me feel any better. The true professional doesn't use a silencer. It's bulky, it decreases accuracy, and it is generally more trouble than it is worth. Few people know what a gun sounds like. You can fire one in Oxford Street at high noon, and take money that no one will recognise the sound for what it is. Alworthy knew this, and so he didn't bother with a silencer. Funny, he didn't look queer any more, he just looked mean.

He watched me put myself together with an interested detachment, as though he were a spectator and not the cause. He allowed me to drag myself to my feet and lurch over to the side-board where I kept the booze. Fortunately, the bottle was on top of the sideboard. If I had been forced to reach inside, he would probably have shot me. I unscrewed the cap from the vodka bottle and took a belt that went straight down to my crotch. It didn't help much, but enough for me to unbend myself a little. I took another belt, slower this time. Then I put the bottle down carefully, screwed the top back on, and prepared to meet my doom.

"Sit down," he said. I sat.

"Fold your arms." I folded.

"Where is it?" he said.

I didn't even have time to look innocent. He leaned forward and tapped me on the kneecap with the barrel of the gun. It wasn't quite as painful as the kick, but it was on the way. My eyes began to water. "Where is it?" he said.

I unfolded my arms very slowly, and with two fingers I dipped into my breast pocket and extracted the notebook. He watched me like a predatory hawk, the gun as solid as the rock of Gibraltar.

"On the floor," he said. I held the notebook out to drop it on the floor.

"You," he said. "Face down."

I got off the chair and lay face down on the floor. He stood up, and bending over me he placed the barrel of the gun behind my ear. With the other hand he took the notebook. I heard him flip through the pages and then the barrel of the gun was withdrawn. I tried to remember whether a bullet in the back of the head killed outright, or whether you lingered for a few seconds. My nose started to tickle with dust from the carpet and I wanted to sneeze. Instead, I spoke, my voice muffled by the carpet.

"It's the wrong book," I said.

There was a moment's silence, then I felt the gun barrel placed behind my ear again, a little harder this time.

"You're lying," he said.

"So I'm lying," I said, trying to sound as though this sort of thing happened to me every day of the week.

There was a long pause while he digested this bit of information.

Then he gave me a jab with the gun barrel that nearly took my ear off.

"Up," he said.

He moved back six feet and watched me climb to my feet. Then he poked the gun towards a chair. I sat and folded my arms again before he could tell me.

"You're not as stupid as you look," he said.

I was, but I wasn't going to let him know.

"Where is it?" he said.

"I mailed it," I said. "Registered."

"To whom?"

"To myself."

"Where?"

"Here," I said.

"When did you mail it?"

"An hour ago." It felt like a week.

He managed to glance at his watch without seeming to take his eyes off me.

"What time is your first delivery?" he said.

"Seven thirty. But it won't arrive by first delivery. Registered mail always comes second."

"What time?"

"About eleven thirty," I said.

He thought about this for a moment, then he made up his mind.

"We'll wait," he said.

The thought of spending the night gazing down the barrel of that gun didn't appeal to me much, but as an alternative to having my head blown off, it didn't seem so bad.

At six thirty, I even managed to doze off for a few minutes. Not him though. I don't think he blinked his eyes once. Looking at him sitting there I wondered how I had ever thought he was a queer. He was as hard as nails and twice as sharp. It had been the clothes he was wearing, I suppose, and the general way he had camped around. It had been a good act, and that combined with the fact that I had been conditioned to expect a queer, had been sufficient.

But Dunning must have known him as a queer, and he would have required more positive proof. I tried to visualise the man sitting opposite me in bed with Dunning. I couldn't. All I could see was Dunning with his throat cut, and Alworthy as he was now, a hard case, about as queer as James Bond.

At half past seven, he allowed me to make some coffee. While I pottered back and forth, he stood in the kitchen door watching me, looking every inch the professional. But professional what? Killer certainly, agent probably, blackmailer possibly. He treated the gun with casual respect, and his behaviour towards me had been of the highest order right from the opening kick. Disable your opponent before you attempt to deal with him. Having me lay face down on the floor was good too. He'd learned his trade, whatever that was, in a good school. It would be interesting to see what he would do when the postman arrived.

After the coffee, he suddenly became talkative.

"You used to be quite a big wheel," he said.

I had never been more than one of the hired help, but to some I suppose it might have seemed important. But it was his knowing about it that intrigued me.

"Not for a long time now," I said.

"I heard you hadn't the stomach for it," he said.

"Something like that," I said. There was something seriously wrong with security somewhere. I didn't like it.

"You fellows who work for Max are all the same," he said, compounding my concern. "Big wheels until the going gets a little rough, then you quit."

"We all make mistakes," I said.

"Not me," he said. I could believe him too.

"It all depends who you work for," I said.

He looked at me for a moment then he grinned.

"For all the good it will do you, I could tell you," he said. "But I won't. Die ignorant, die happy."

I digested this with my coffee, and went to pour myself another cup.

He followed me into the kitchen again.

"What happens when the postman comes?" he said.

"He'll ring the outside bell. I'll ask who it is on the security phone. When he tells me, I'll go downstairs and sign for the letter."

"Does the postman know you?" he said.

"Yes," I lied.

"So you'll have to sign for it yourself?"

"He might let you have it," I said. "But I doubt it."

He followed me back into the living-room, thoughtful.

After five minutes, he told me what I was going to do.

"When you speak to the postman on the security phone, tell him you're sending a friend down to sign for the letter. Tell him you've got a bad leg or something."

"He may offer to bring it up," I said.

"Even better, you can sign for it yourself."

"What happens next?" I said.

He looked at me for a moment, then he laughed.

"You certainly have been away for a long time," he said.

I should have known. It's the sort of question a professional doesn't have to ask.

We spent the next three hours looking at each other. He had decided to stop talking, and after a couple of attempts to draw something out of him, I gave up, and started to try and work out what he would do when he opened the envelope and found another phony notebook.

Long before the postman arrived, I had worked out that I was going to have to get him to come up to the flat. If I suggested that my friend go down for the letter, my friend was going to kill me before he did so. With the postman up here, there was a chance that Alworthy would open the envelope and look at the notebook before he pulled the trigger. What he would do after that was anybody's guess. The only thing I could be sure of was that it would be painful.

At eleven twenty, he looked at his watch. He wasn't nervous or even concerned. He hadn't fidgeted and this was only the second time he had checked his watch. As though on cue, the doorbell rang. He looked up at me coolly.

"He's early," he said.

"It happens," I said.

He gestured towards the security phone with the gun.

I stood up and went to the phone.

"Yes?" I said.

"Registered letter for Mr. Smith," came the disembodied voice.

"Can you bring it up," I said. "I can't get downstairs."

"On me way, guv," came the voice.

I pressed the button that opened the front door and turned to see how Alworthy was taking it. He was grinning at me.

"You're grasping at straws," he said.

"I'm drowning," I said.

He stood up and moved so that he would be behind the door when I opened it. We heard the postman labouring up the stairs, and then the pause while he identified the apartment. Then the doorbell rang, at the same time as Alworthy jabbed me hard in the side with the gun, just in case I had forgotten.

I opened the door and there was Max. Behind him stood two members of the Heavy Squad, with hands tucked deep in raincoat pockets. Before I could say or do anything, he spoke.

"Sign 'ere, Mr. Smith," he said, handing me a gun.

"Thank you," I said.

Then I closed the door gently in his face and let Alworthy see the gun I was holding.

"Snap," I said.

For one moment, it looked as though he was going to chance it, and my finger tightened fractionally on the trigger. This is a dangerous thing to do if you don't know the tension of the gun you're holding. The gun jerked in my hand, there was a noise like the crack of doom, and Alworthy slammed back against the wall as though he had been hit by a truck. I watched him as he slid down the wall leaving a smear of red on my blue distemper.

After that, there didn't seem anything left to do but let Max in.

"You might have given me a gun that didn't fire as soon as I looked at it," I said.

"Sorry, old man," he said. He looked at Alworthy whose eyes were open and whose mouth gaped like a fish.

"Is he dead?" he said.

I hefted the gun in my hand. It was a .45, sufficient to stop a small elephant in full flight.

"As if you didn't know," I said.

"Pity," he said, lying like a cheap carpet.

"I've probably killed the family next door too," I said. There was a hole in the wall where the bullet had passed through after demolishing Alworthy. I handed the gun back to Max carefully.

"The landlord's not going to like that," I said.

"We'll fix it up," he said brightly, moving across to the phone. He dialed a number.

"Petersfield," he said. The Service were still getting their daily code words from the AA handbook. He waited a moment, then he spoke again. "This is Max. One disposal squad to flat 4, 27 Earls Court Garden Square."

He hung up and turned to me.

"You *have* been busy," he said.

I went to pour myself a drink. I didn't offer him one.

"This is Alworthy I presume," he said.

"You know bloody well it is," I said.

"He won't be much help to you as far as the Dunning killing is concerned, will he."

He was right. Without Alworthy, Max had me by the short hairs.

He shook his head.

"You shouldn't have killed him," he said.

"I'm sorry," I said. "It won't happen again."

"We all make mistakes," he said. He pulled from his raincoat the notebook that Alworthy had been waiting for.

"I bumped into the postman downstairs," he said. "I thought I'd save him a climb."

"Very considerate," I said.

"You've got a lot to thank me for," he said. "Alworthy would have been very disappointed."

"I don't have to thank you for anything," I said. "If you knew he was here, why didn't you come sooner?"

"But I didn't," said Max with injured dignity. "I just assumed you'd have a registered package this morning, so I waylaid the postman. Your excuse that you couldn't get downstairs didn't sound like you at all. So I came up."

"You're a lying sod," I said. After all, I didn't work for him anymore. He shrugged.

"Have it your way," he said. He held up the notebook.

"I assume by this that you *do* have the notebook somewhere."

"I have it," I said.

"Can we go and fetch it now old man," he said.

"No old man, we can't," I said.

I was delighted to see him start to look angry. It wasn't much, a slight tightening of the mouth, but it did wonders for my morale.

"I presume you have some valid reason for refusing," he said.

"You can presume whatever you like," I said. "You'll get the notebook when I'm good and ready to give it to you."

"Don't push your luck," said Max. "Diaman would just love to get his hands on you."

"But he won't as long as I've got the notebook," I said.

"You're not thinking of going into business on your own, I hope," said Max.

"I might."

"Don't," he said.

"If I don't, it won't be because you say so," I said.

He looked at me steadily for a moment, then he relaxed. He sat down and pulled his eyedrop bottle from his pocket. He unscrewed the stopper and squeezed two drops into each eye. Then he blew his nose loudly.

"Have you any idea what you're mixed up in?" he said finally.

"Something pretty murky, if you've got anything to do with it," I said.

"I suppose it is murky," he said. "But you were in the Service, so it shouldn't surprise you."

"Was," I said.

"Once an agent always an agent," he said.

"Balls!" I said.

"Would it help you to make up your mind about the notebook if I told you all about it?" he said.

"It might."

"Dunning was going to give it to the Chinese," he said. "Alworthy had a better idea. He was going to sell it to them."

"What's in the notebook?"

"Don't you know?"

"It's in code."

He nodded. "Dunning was a cypher man in the war. We got on to him three days ago. Before we could do anything, he'd met Alworthy and got his throat cut."

"He'd met Alworthy before that," I said.

"So I understand. But we weren't watching him, so we couldn't know."

"What about Alworthy?" I said.

"Freelance," said Max. "We've got a file on him, but we didn't even know he was in the country until you turned him up."

"Everyone else seemed to know," I said.

Max shrugged.

"As Kenning, Kentish, Schmidt or Josset, we would have known him. Alworthy was a brand new identity."

I glanced at Alworthy who had stopped bleeding and was beginning to stiffen. Fat lot of good it had done him. I turned back to Max.

"You still haven't told me what was in the notebook," I said.

"It's better you don't know," said Max. "You don't want to get yourself involved."

I tried to work out how much more involved I could get. But Max was saying nothing, so I let it go.

There was a lot more I wanted to ask, but the disposal squad arrived at that point. There were four very efficient young men who nodded politely at Max, gave me an incurious glance, and set about their business. The late Peter Alworthy, Kenning, Kentish, Schmidt, Josset was laid out on a rubber sheet and undressed quickly. The clothes and the contents of his pockets were put into a bag with a drawstring top. He had suffered a cadaveric spasm at the moment of death, and it was necessary to break his hand to remove the gun. This was done with an iron bar, the sound of the bones splintering like breaking wood. Then the edges of the rubber sheet were brought together across the body and stapled together. The bundle was then put into a small laundry basket, and three of the young men carried it downstairs. The fourth fetched a bowl of warm water from the kitchen. He added some chemical which he carried in a small plastic wallet, and washed down my wall and cleaned the carpet. Then he nodded politely and departed after his fellows. He had been quiet, efficient and quick. He also had a harelip.

I made some coffee while this was going on, and unbent sufficiently to offer a cup to Max.

Finally, we were alone again.

"I'll send a plasterer along to fix that hole in the wall," he said. "We might have to redecorate."

"Be my guest," I said.

Then there was a long pause while each of us waited to see which way the other would jump.

"What are you worried about?" he said.

"You know damn well what I'm worried about," I said.

"You think once I get my hands on the notebook, I'll throw you to the wolves. Is that it?"

"In words of one syllable," I said. "Yes."

"You know me better than that," he said.

I grinned at him. Even he must have seen the funny side of that remark.

"I could throw you to the wolves anyway," he said. "My wolves."

I knew about his wolves. I had thrown people to them myself.

"But you wouldn't do that," I said.

"Don't bet on it," he said.

There was a pause before I spoke again. I made it sound casual.

"How much was Alworthy going to sell it for?" I asked.

Max shrugged.

"It's a fluctuating market," he said. "Something worth fifty thousand today is worth nothing tomorrow."

"Today's price," I said.

"To the Chinese, fifty thousand," he said reluctantly.

"That's a lot of money," I said.

"You're a long time dead," said Max. "Anyway, a commodity only acquires value if you know where the market is."

"I know," I said.

I had the satisfaction of seeing him look surprised.

"They've made contact with you?"

"No," I said. "You have."

He got the point.

"You're offering to sell it to me."

"Half price," I said. "With that much money I could take a trip where I wouldn't have to worry whether you did the dirt on me with Diaman."

"I wouldn't do that John. I gave you my word," he said.

I didn't labour the point. I let him sit there and sweat it out while the computer he carries around in his head worked out the permutations.

"What exactly do you want?" he said finally.

"Twenty-five thousand pounds, a passport, and your solemn promise that the Diaman business stays as it is, with me off the hook."

He pretended to consider it. Finally, he nodded.

"I agree," he said. He stood up.

"You'll make the arrangements?" he said.

"I'll make the arrangements."

I allowed him to shake my hand. He did so vigorously.

"Good old John," he said. "You always did manage to land on your feet."

He walked to the door.

"You won't let me down, will you?" he said.

"Don't you trust me, Max?" I said.

He smiled.

"Ofcourse I do," he said. "I'll wait to hear from you."

"You do that," I said, and showed him out.

I changed my suit and went to the office. There I tried to locate Danielle. I telephoned a couple of friends she used to have when we were married. They were surprised to hear from me, but no, they didn't know where Danielle was. Wherever she went after she left my office, she wasn't advertising it.

I took from my pocket one of the notebooks I had made up in the post office last night. I flipped through the pages quickly. Assuming the code that Dunning had used was a good one, it would take some time before anyone realised that what I had written was so much gibberish. I stuck the

note-book in an envelope and addressed it to Max. Then I
wrote a little note.

Dear Max,
  Have the passport and the money sent Poste Restante
to Bloomsbury Street Post Office in the name of Harper.
I shall pick it up tomorrow morning. I'd like to say that it
was nice to see you again, but it wasn't.

I signed it, and put it in the envelope with the notebook.
Then I called Miss Roberts in. I told her to walk to Leicester
Square Post Office and be sure to post it in the outside letter box
marked London. numbered postal districts only. She put on her
fur coat, which didn't smell today, and left the office. The post
box was emptied every hour on the hour. At that time, any mail
addressed to United Rubber Estates Ltd., P.O.B. 17168, London.
E.C., was separated from the ordinary mail and taken by special
messenger to the Service building. I calculated that Miss Roberts
would post the letter in time for the two o'clock collection. Allow
another fifteen minutes for it to reach the Service and another
five for it to find its way up to Max. Give him ten minutes to
make up his mind that I was a complete idiot, and then either
make a phone call or not make one. By three o'clock, I should
know one way or the other. I looked at my watch. It was five minutes to two, so I had plenty of time.

As I left the office, there was a busty young hopeful waiting
to see Stubbs. She switched on a smile when she saw me, hoping
to impress. But when she realized, I wasn't the man she had come
to see, she switched it off again. I felt like telling her about Stubbs,
but instead I left her to her illusions. That's all she had.

I cashed a cheque for seventy pounds and left the bank
quickly before the manager could catch my eye. Two minutes
later, I was in Cecil Gee's, and the cashmere overcoat was mine.
I walked back to the office feeling ten feet tall. Miss Roberts had

returned and I allowed her to take my coat from me. Her eyes widened when she felt the material. "Ooh, Mr. Smith," she said.

I smiled at her grandly and patted her bottom as I walked through to my own office. She blushed furiously, loving it, and rushed to pour me some tea. It was now ten minutes to three. I sat back in my chair and put my feet on the desk.

At three o'clock on the nose, Diaman loomed large in the door of my office. He looked like a man who had lost a penny and found a thousand pounds. There was a plain-clothes sergeant with him, but it was Diaman's moment, and he intended to enjoy it.

"John Smith, I have a warrant for your arrest that you did on the night of September twelfth feloniously…" He went on and on, a truly happy man, while poor Miss Roberts stood petrified in the outer office, her eyes growing wider and wider.

Good old Max, I thought. How could I ever have doubted his double-crossing, twisted little mind. He had made his phone call, and at last I knew exactly where I stood.

CHAPTER FOUR

I
F the strings Max had pulled before had been slender and frag-
ile, the ones he had to manipulate now were like steel hawsers,
all snags and rough edges. I had been charged and the whole
business had now become documented and official.

I was in the same cell as before when Max came to see me.
He was livid.

"You've pushed your luck too far this time," he said. "I can't
help you."

"You'll manage," I said.

"Some of the big wheels want you to swing," he said. "I don't
blame them."

"You don't go along with them though."

"What a bloody fool thing to do," he said. "Have you any idea
how difficult it is going to be to get you out?"

"That's your problem," I said. "You got me in."

"Christ!" he said. "I could cut your throat."

He was in trouble, and he knew that I knew it.

"I'm liable to get chopped for this," he said.

"That's the best news I've heard this week," I said. He was on
his own hook. I wasn't going to help him off it.

He swore and he blustered for another ten minutes, stewing
in his own juices. He had to get down to business sooner or later,
and I wasn't going anywhere so I could afford to wait.

Finally, he cooled down a little. He squirted his eyes savagely,
blew his nose and got down to the purpose of his visit.

"We'll arrange a transfer in Switzerland," he said.

"France," I said. He agreed.

"The notebook from you, twenty-five thousand pounds in dollar notes and a passport from us."

"Fifty thousand," I said.

He went red, then white, then red again.

"You agreed twenty-five," he said.

"You agreed not to sick Diaman on to me," I said. "We both made a mistake."

"I'll have to get it authorised. It'll take time."

"I'm not going anywhere," I said.

We blocked out the basics in ten minutes. He agreed to everything I said. He had to. Just before he left, he had one further thing to say.

"It'll take about a week to get you out," he said.

I grinned at him.

"Take as long as you like," I said. "But you won't find it."

He snarled at me and banged on the door to be let out.

"And, Max," I said. "Leave my girlfriend alone. If I find you've been round there again, it's all off." He started to look innocent, then decided that it wasn't worth it.

"I don't know where you intend going afterwards," he said. "But make sure that it's a long way."

"It will be," I said. "See you in court."

And that was the next place I did see him. I had been charged, so a court appearance was necessary. Somehow, they managed to get the preliminary hearing in camera. I stood in the dock and watched Diaman being slaughtered by the solicitor that Max had arranged. I had an alibi as strong as a twenty-foot wall and equally insurmountable. Not only was I not at the scene of the crime, but I had been seen by twenty people, including a bishop and a chief constable, two hundred miles away. I didn't get the full gist of it, but I think I was addressing a political meeting on behalf of the Liberal party. Diaman knew what was happening, and he bled to death quietly in the witness box. I felt sorry for him. He was in way over his head and the way out wasn't easy for him to take. He was a good policeman, and the foundation stone of his beliefs was taking a severe belting.

I saw him just before I left the court without a stain on my character. He had been severely criticised by the presiding magistrate for misusing his authority, and he looked like a fifteen-stone schoolboy leaving the headmaster's study after a beating.

"If it's any consolation to you," I said, "I didn't kill Dunning."

He looked at me sadly. He couldn't even find it in him to be angry at me any longer.

"Son," he said, "you can go out right now and cut the throat of anyone you want to. If I see you, I'll look the other way."

He lumbered off unhappily.

I saw Max, too, after the hearing. But we made no attempt to communicate with each other. Everything we needed to say to each other had been said. The transfer had been worked out, and as far as I was concerned, I didn't have to come in direct contact with him ever again.

When I got home my ticket to Nice was waiting in my letter box.

Vindictive to the end, Max had booked me on a night tourist flight for the following evening. I telephoned a travel agent I'd had dealings with and booked a first-class ticket out on the morning Air France flight. Then I phoned Phil Bannister.

"Want to go to Nice, Phil?" I said.

"When?"

"Tomorrow night."

"How much?"

"Fifty quid plus expenses and you can stay as long as you like."

"You're on," he said.

I gave him a few minor instructions, then put the ticket Max had sent me in an envelope and addressed it to his home. He'd probably stay there a week, drooling over the birds in their bikinis. But I owed him a favour. He had done odd jobs for me before. He was a good friend, close mouthed and reliable.

I packed a suitcase and at eight o'clock I called Mary.

"Alone?" I said.

"Hello, darling," she said.

"Food?"

"Lovely."

"Nine o'clock," I said, and hung up.

I posted the ticket to Phil on my way to pick up Mary, and we went on to have a ball.

Halfway through the most expensive meal I'd ever bought her, she started asking questions.

"You've won the pools?" she said.

"Nope," I said.

"Your maiden aunt has died?"

"Nope," I said, spooning another dollop of caviare into her avocado.

"I give in," she said.

I leered at her.

"When we get home," I said. "That's when you give in."

"I've got the curse," she said.

I must have looked shattered. She burst out laughing.

"I'm joking."

"It's nothing to laugh about," I said.

"It is from where I'm sitting. You looked like a little boy who'd had his lollipop taken away."

"I felt like one," I said.

Ten minutes later she approached the subject again.

"You've robbed a bank?" she said.

I shook my head.

"I know," she said. "You've done a Doctor Faustus. You've sold your soul to the devil."

This was the nearest she'd got so far. It was near enough to make me feel uncomfortable. She noticed my expression.

"I'm getting warm, aren't I?" she said. She put her hand on mine. "You haven't done anything stupid have you?"

I told her to forget about it and finish her meal. But the gloss had gone off the evening, and later at her apartment, the whole thing was a dead loss. I blamed it on the booze, and she was good hearted enough not to give me an argument.

I left her at two a.m. and drove down to see Gunther. During the night, it's easy to see if you're being followed, and if you are it's simple to switch off your lights and lay by long enough to lose your tail. I wasn't being followed. Max had obviously accepted the deal and was prepared to wait for the pay-off we had arranged.

I found the front door key over the lintel, and let myself in. I made no noise going up to Gunther's room as I didn't want to wake his daughter. I opened the door of his room quietly and found myself looking down the barrel of a Luger, held steady as a rock. For a man like Gunther old habits die hard.

He grinned when he recognised me and the gun disappeared.

"I nearly shot you," he said.

"You bloody old pirate," I said. "You're disappointed it wasn't someone you could shoot."

"At my age I would probably have missed," he said. "Have some coffee?"

I still didn't want to wake his daughter so I said no. But he had a thermos jug beside his bed and he poured a cup for each of us.

"So tell me," he said.

I told him exactly as it had been since I had last seen him. When I finished he was very quiet.

"What have I done wrong?" I said finally.

He shrugged his massive shoulders.

"Nothing," he said. "Everything you have done is fine. It is what you are going to do."

"The money." I said. It was a statement, not a question. He nodded.

"It is not good that you sell your country's secrets."

"I'm selling them *to* my country," I said.

"It is still not good." He shook his head. "I cannot understand this thing, John."

He rarely used my name. It was a sure sign that he was angry or upset. Then he noticed something in my expression and he started to grin.

"What are you grinning at?" I said.

"You called me a pirate," he said. "Next to you I am an amateur."

"I don't understand you," I said.

"How much is Max going to have to pay?" he said.

"I'm a very expensive investigator," I said. "Twenty-five pounds a day, all expenses, and a thousand-pound bonus because I nearly got killed.

"How much will all that come to?" he said.

"Including the time, I spent in prison, and the fortnight I shall spend in the South of France, about twenty-five days. First-class round transportation, and a suite at the Hotel du Golf at Valescure. Say two and a half thousand pounds."

He rumbled into laughter.

"What will you do with the other forty-seven and a half thousand," he said.

"Give it back to the Service," I said.

"Not to Max," he said.

"I shall pay it directly to Accounts," I said. "Max will have to explain why he requested a fifty-thousand pound payment for a two and a half thousand pound job."

"That is good," said Gunther, still chuckling. "That is very good."

"I knew you'd appreciate it," I said.

"And the poor policeman, he cannot touch you any more for Dunning?"

"No. The case was dismissed at a preliminary hearing. Max threw away all his trumps."

He grew serious suddenly.

"That is not like Max," he said.

"He had no alternative," I said. "He had to get me out."

But I had worried him.

"Even so, Max is not a man to release a hold once he has one. He got you out of prison before without it being necessary."

"I hadn't been charged," I said.

But he still didn't like it, and I began to feel uneasy too. Gunther could spot a rotten apple in any size of barrel.

"Let's go through it all once more," he said.

So we went through it. We went through it from the beginning, then we started at the end and worked our way backwards. We tried picking it up in the middle and working our way backwards and forward at the same time. We checked, we cross checked, and then we checked again. After an hour, one point stuck out like a sore thumb. Where was Danielle? She had started the whole thing off, then she had disappeared. Had it been coincidence that she had set me on to her husband on the very day he got himself killed, or was there something we hadn't seen? But if there was, we couldn't dig it out.

At half past seven, Gunther's daughter brought him his breakfast. If she was surprised to see me, she didn't show it. She went downstairs again and a few minutes later she returned with some breakfast for me. I left Gunther's at eight fifteen and drove straight to the airport. I parked my car and checked in. In the departure lounge, I joined the people who were fortunate enough to be able to take their holidays this late in the year. They were mostly eager young couples, and exhausted parents who had finally got their children back to school after having them home for ten weeks. They were now going away to recuperate.

Max was expecting me to leave by the night tourist flight, so there was no reason for him to have anyone at the airport this early. This evening, if he had decided to have me followed, the tail would pick up Phil Bannister and spend the next week following him around the low-life joints of the Côte d'Azur.

The flight was called and we trooped our way to the bus where we were jolted back and forth as the driver took us across tarmacs and under tunnels, to the waiting Caravelle. I took my seat on the port side of the plane, next to the window. After five minutes, we started to trundle to the take-off point. I accepted a barley sugar and a *Daily Telegraph* from the stewardess, and settled back to enjoy the trip.

The uneasiness that Gunther had instilled in me had evaporated somewhat during the drive to the airport. It still lurked sneakily at the back of my mind, but I had no intention of letting it spoil the holiday that Max was going to pay for. I hadn't flown for a couple of years and before that only twice since I had left the Service. The money I earned in my business didn't run to holidays abroad any more than it ran to cashmere overcoats. Now I had both, and I intended to get the maximum enjoyment from them.

I had four glasses of champagne on the journey. Champagne always tastes better on an aeroplane, probably because it's free. I read the paper briefly and then did the crossword. I'd finished the crossword by the time we swung east over Toulon to fly along the coast to Nice. The pilot announced St. Maxime and then St. Raphael on our left, and by the time he pointed out the town of Cannes we were well strapped in and sucking barley sugar again. As always at Nice airport, one got the impression one was going to land in the sea. Then the edge of the runway flashed past underneath and we touched down gently.

We were instructed to remain seated until the aircraft had completely stopped and we were informed that the outside temperature was fifteen degrees. I tried to work out quickly whether that was overcoat weather. But I can never remember whether one has to multiply by nine and divide by five, or the other way round, and whether one adds thirty-two after or before. I finally settled for looking out the window to see what the people outside were wearing. On the restaurant balcony it was shorts and open necked shirts, and I surmised that it wasn't overcoat weather.

We straggled our way across the tarmac and queued to have our passports looked at. Then we waited fifteen minutes for our baggage. I collected my one suitcase, cleared the perfunctory customs barrier, and went to hire a car.

Ten minutes later, I was seated at the wheel of a Renault and bowling along the coast road with the impeccable blue Mediterranean on my left. Before reaching the Autoroute d'Estorel, I stopped for some lunch. The first meal eaten in France is invariably the best. The fish was superb and the wine was cold and complimentary. I capped the meal with a large brandy, and returned to the car with all doubts and uncertainties long gone and forgotten.

The Golf Hotel at Valescure, as the name implies is well known to golfers and very few others. It sits alone in a pine forest five kilometres behind St. Raphael.

My suite was on the fifth floor, and from my balcony I could look out across the tops of the trees to St. Raphael and the coast. The trees themselves looked like a sea of rich green waves piling one on top of the other, broken here and there by outcrops of white rock, which were the villas built in the forest. It was quiet, peaceful, and ten thousand miles away from London and Max.

I spent the balance of the afternoon flat on my back by the side of the swimming pool, soaking up the sun whose August savagery had mellowed to September benevolence.

Later, I returned to my room, bathed and changed then wandered down to the bar. I drank four *pastis* while I relearned elementary French from the bartender. Then I strolled out to the terrace for an early dinner.

I ate fresh grilled sardines, and drank a bottle of St. Roseline, while I watched the mosquitoes fry themselves to death on the electrical traps dotted about the terrace. They would fly up, attracted by the blue neon tube, then hit the exposed wires and explode with a crack. I was feeling so good it didn't even spoil my dinner. I lingered over coffee, and at half past ten I drove back into Nice. I parked the car at the airport and went into the terminal building.

I was upstairs in the bar when the night tourist flight from London was announced. I finished my drink and walked along the first-floor balcony until I could see where the passengers came out after clearing customs. Phil was the fourth person to come through, lugging a suitcase and dressed for a Soho bottle party rather than the South of France. He turned right and came across to the news-stand right beneath where I was standing. They were just about to put up the shutters, but he managed to buy a packet of cigarettes, and he stood there while he opened the packet and lit one. But I wasn't watching him, I was watching the other passengers who followed him out. They were the ones who travelled by night flights, and who for the sake of saving a fiver or thereabouts are happy to start their holiday with a sleepless night and indigestion from eating airline sandwiches at one o'clock in the morning.

None of them followed Phil, and I was beginning to think Max was getting soft in his old age, when Phil decided he had accomplished what he had been told to do. He picked up his suit-case and started out of the building with that lecherous preda-tory look that all Englishmen adopt when they arrive in France. As he did so, a small bald-headed man who had been dozing on one of the couches, woke up suddenly and trotted after him.

I could almost see Max's expression back in London. The report would have come through that the man travelling on John Smith's ticket, wasn't John Smith. So, what the hell was John Smith up to? Follow the man anyway. A phone call would have been made to Nice and Phil's description passed. Now Phil had a tail until he decided that the fleshpots of Soho were better than the fleshpots of Nice, and went home. And until I made the contact I had arranged, Max would sit in a cold sweat in case I pulled the whole thing down around his ears. So, let him sweat, I was only returning a favour he'd done me on a hundred different occasions.

I motored back along the autoroute at a steady fifty, while the Mercs and the Thunderbirds streaked past me at more than a hundred. The guests of the Golf Hotel are early-to-bedders; they're due on the first tee at seven thirty in the morning. So the hotel was shut up tight when I got back and it took me fifteen minutes to raise the right porter. He came grumbling to the door to let me in. I bought a bottle of Evian water from him, and tipped him sufficiently for him to forgive me for waking him up. I went up to my room and there I slept for ten solid hours, to be awakened at midday by ecstatic shrieks from the direction of the swimming pool.

But today was a workday, the day I earned my pay. I shaved and dressed while I drank my coffee, then reluctantly leaving my new overcoat behind, I went downstairs. I handed in my key, and after stopping for some petrol, I drove through St. Raphael to Fréjus Plage.

A couple of hundred yards back from the coast road is a large apartment development. There are four unsightly blocks of flats spaced round a dreary patch of scrub which is supposed to be a garden. I parked the car outside the West block and went up to the fourth floor. There was no elevator and I was puffing like a grampus by the time I rang the doorbell. I decided to cut down on the booze and get more exercise. The door was opened by a pretty young girl of nineteen or thereabouts dressed in a white bikini, with a small apron tied round her waist. The overall effect was highly erotic. She smiled at me and asked me what I wanted. Before I had time to bring a blush to her cheeks, she was pushed

out of the way by Gar Davies, who smothered me with enthusiasm. He was short, stocky, fifty-five years old, with the energy
and appetites of a man of thirty. He had been born in Egypt of
British parents and lived there until he had been slung out by
Nasser. He had tried to settle in England but decided the climate
would kill him, so he had moved to the South of France. Using
the compensation money the British Government had given him
by way of an apology for allowing him to be slung out of Egypt,
he had started a real estate business here in St. Raphael. He had
prospered in spite of the heavy anti-British and anti-Semitic sen-
timents of his competitors.

The girl continued to float around in the background until
he patted her backside and told her to go and sit in the kitchen.
He spent ten minutes telling me what had happened to him since
I had last seen him in England; then I gently pulled him back on
the rails. "The notebook," I said.

Every Frenchman—and Gar was a Frenchman by inclination
if not by nationality—keeps a safe in his home. The safe may only
be a hole in the floorboards or a cashbox stuffed at the bottom
of a dirty linen cupboard, but in it he keeps a few papers and a
vast amount of ready cash for doing business. Seventy per cent of
the business done in France is done in cash, which explains why
France is one of the poorest countries occupied by the richest
people in Europe.

Gar fetched his safe out. It was an old cashbox that could
have been opened by a disinterested boy scout. From it he pulled
something like twelve thousand pounds in five hundred-franc
notes, and the notebook I had sent him.

Inside the cover of the notebook he had slipped a few sheets
of paper, which were covered with his neat, spidery writing.

He spread the sheets of paper in front of me.

"This was a very difficult code at first," he said. "It was difficult
because it was so simple. There was no key word. It took me four
days to realise that. Afterwards it was still difficult. Every letter

is represented by a group of symbols, and there is no means of judging how long each group is. I had to resort to trial and error."

"But you managed," I said.

He smiled and nodded.

"I will show you," he said.

He pointed out the first line in the notebook.

24XB379yrc47aab986YYbBV

"The first group is 24XB37," he said. "That represents the letter 'H'."

"How do you know?"

"I worked it out," he said, as though I was asking a stupid question. "The next group is 9yrc4," he said. "That is the letter 'O'. The next group is longer for no other reason than the man who made this up wanted it that way. It is 7aab986Y. That is the letter 'M'. The next group includes the last four symbols on the line, YbBV, and also the next two on the next line, but reading from right to left. The letter is 'I'. And so it goes on, group by group, line by line, reading first left to right, then right to left." He slammed his hand down on the notebook. "I had a lot of fun with this," he said. "It was like the old days."

During the war he had been the top cypher man in Middle East Intelligence, and bloody good at his job. If he told me he had broken down the contents of the notebook, it was good enough for me. He continued.

"The first word appeared to be homing, and I thought I was well on the way. But then it didn't make sense with what followed. I thought perhaps it was a code within a code, and that now I would have to break a second cypher." He looked up at me suddenly. "You would have saved me a lot of trouble if you had told me there was Chinese involvement," he said.

"I didn't know when I sent you the notebook," I said.

"When I realised it was so," he said. "It was easy. homing wasn't one word, it was two. Ho Ming, you see, a name. It is followed by an address and by a small piece of information about the man."

"What sort of information?" I asked.

"He is a senior clerk in the foreign bureau in Peking."

I thought about this for a while.

"The whole book is the same?"

Gar nodded.

"There are fifteen names and addresses, and similar pieces of information about each person."

"Nothing else?"

"Nothing."

He watched me for a moment.

"Is it what you expected?" he said.

I hadn't known what to expect. For fifty thousand pounds the merchandise had to be pretty substantial. I think I assumed it would be the plans of the latest cobalt bomb, or whatever it is they're making now. But these fifteen names were far more important. The life of a spy or an agent or whatever you want to call him, is a pretty lonely one. Even his friends are his enemies when it suits them. His only ally is his anonymity. Here we had the names of fifteen men, or women for all I knew, who were working and living in the Peoples' Republic of China, and whose anonymity was only a shade from being destroyed. It was no wonder that the Chinese would pay high for the list, and that Max would pay equally high to make sure they didn't get it. The Far East had not been one of my territories when I was in the Service, but I knew enough about it to know that reliable agents there didn't grow on trees. Apart from any other consideration, they had to be Chinese. An Englishman, if he was expert at languages, could pass as native in most European countries, but try to slip him into China and see how far he'd get. I thought for a moment about those fifteen Chinese, living day by day under the shadow of the executioner's sword, or whatever they use in China, and I decided that the sooner I got the notebook back to Max, the better.

I thanked Gar and together we burned the papers he had worked on in solving the cypher. I declined the invitation to lunch, and left after promising to come and see him again soon. The girl in the kitchen saw me leaving and bounced to her feet in anticipation. Gar still didn't introduce me, so I contented myself with a leer, and left as she started to remove her apron.

Outside I lifted the engine cowling on the car and removed the battery. I put the notebook on the battery stand, and replaced the battery on top of it, screwing it firmly back into place. I put the phony notebook Max had thrown at me the last time I saw him into the glove compartment. Even now, I didn't trust him. I wanted my hands on that fifty thousand pounds before I turned over the goods. I know I was going to turn most of it back to the Service, but what with cashmere overcoats and jaunts to the South of France, my expenses were way over the top, and I had no intention of winding up out of pocket.

As I pulled away from the apartments, Gar waved to me from the balcony. There was a flash of white and brown behind him, and he disappeared inside. He had the sexual appetite of a pasha, and I had kept him busy for quite long enough. I still had two hours before making the rendezvous but I wanted to spy out the land first. Once before, when Max had thought he had got the notebook, he had shown that I was expendable, and I wouldn't have put it past him to send a couple of the Heavy Squad to take delivery, with instructions to see that I met with a fatal accident at the same time.

I knew what it was like getting money out of the Service treasurer, and the thought of paying out fifty thousand pounds must have been like a kick in the crotch to Max. He'd be no end of the fair-headed boy if he could do the job and not have to pay out.

There would be no sure way of knowing whether the men I met were Heavy Squad men. It had been five years since I'd been in the Service, and in that time most of the personnel would have changed. The mortality rate was the highest of any squad in the

Service. It was for this reason that I had chosen this particular rendezvous. I would be able to see a false move for two miles in either direction, and would be able to act accordingly.

The autoroute that connects Fréjus to Nice has been carved through the hills behind the coast on the premise that the shortest distance between two points is a straight line. It dips and curves in places, but in general it is like a great wide ribbon, loosely meandering between those two points without a single curve that can't be taken at a speed of a hundred miles an hour.

In places it is paralleled by sections of the old road, and in other places a bridge carries a less exalted road across the top of it. If you leave the autoroute at La Napoule, just before Cannes, and then double back for twelve miles, you find one of these bridges. This I did, parking my car off the bridge, out of sight. Then I walked out on to the bridge and looked down at the autoroute beneath me. I could see two miles towards Fréjus, and two and a half miles towards Cannes. Nobody was going to sneak up on me from either direction.

The road which the bridge carried was a different proposition. It wound down through the hills, crossed the autoroute, then climbed again the other side. But here I was banking on ignorance to keep me out of trouble. My instructions to Max had been simple and explicit. The rendezvous was to be on the autoroute exactly thirty-two kilometres from the Fréjus toll both. The man making the contact was to move on to the hard shoulder of the road when his milometer told him he had covered that distance. He was to wait for me there. I had made no mention of bridges, and I trusted Max's enthusiasm would override his natural caution, and that he would not have such a thing checked. If things worked out, I would make the transfer and then return to my own car and drive off. The man or men on the autoroute would be trapped there, unable to find an exit for the next fifteen kilometres, by which time I would be long gone.

It was a good, simple plan, one which enabled me to investigate who I was meeting before I actually met them, and which gave me an unbeatable start should they feel inclined to follow me. The fact that the whole thing turned into such a shambles had nothing to do with me; it was still a good scheme. There was an hour to go before my contact could be expected, so I returned to the car, removed my shirt and started to soak up some sun. But there is a difference between the sun that bathes you by the side of a swimming pool, and the sun that broils you when you're surrounded by acres of rock and scrub. Yesterday by the pool had been fine, here after twenty minutes I was sweating like a pig, and there was no way to cool off. I put my shirt on again and immediately it was soaking. So I sat in the car and roasted out the next half an hour while the sweat on my shirt grew cool and clammy. Ten minutes before time, I took the phony notebook from the glove compartment, slipped it into my hip pocket, and walked back towards the bridge. It was a little before four, an hour when the French are usually finishing their lunch, so there was very little traffic about. What there was zoomed past beneath me at speeds of seventy-five and above.

I spotted my man when he was still a mile away. He was in a small, three-year-old Simca, pottering towards me at a steady thirty miles an hour. I moved down off the bridge to a point where I could see and not be seen. As the car approached the point of contact, the engine started to cough, and a moment later the car moved over to the hard shoulder, and the engine conked out altogether. I didn't know what the men were going to be like, but the car was a bloody good actor.

There were two men, and they both got out. I didn't recognise either of them, but that wasn't surprising. One was about forty-five, and looked as though he had seen it all and didn't much like any of it. I could feel for him. The other was younger, about twenty-five or six. The older man stood close to the car, while the young one opened up the engine cowling and looked inside. He wasn't as good an actor as the car had been. They looked genuine enough; the older was too old to be a Heavy Squad man, and as the Squad always travelled in pairs, it was safe to assume the young one wasn't either.

I climbed out of the ditch and walked on to the hard shoulder about fifty yards away from them. As he saw me the younger man jumped as though he had been scalded. Max was scraping the barrel with that one. The older man didn't even blink. He reached into the car and when he straightened up again he was holding a black leather wallet about eight inches long and three inches thick. That one wasn't going to part with what he was holding until he had the notebook, he was too old a hand. As I reached him, he spoke to the younger man without turning his head.

"In the car," he said.

The younger man looked as though he'd have liked to give him an argument, but he didn't. He slammed the hood shut and got into the passenger seat.

The older man allowed his eyes to flicker past me, taking in the bridge and what it implied.

"Clever," he said. Then he looked back at me. "Do you want to count it?" he said.

"Just see it," I said.

He lifted the flap of the wallet and I saw the bundles of used dollar and sterling bills. I held out my hand for it, but he shook his head.

"After," he said.

"I'll get it," I said. I turned away.

"It's in your pocket," he said. He could see it sticking out of my hip pocket.

I took it out and flipped it to him. He caught it with one hand, opened it and looked at the first line that was written there. Then he looked up at me and nearly smiled.

"I'll wait," he said.

I walked back to the point where I had come on to the road. I was about to slither down the embankment when something I heard suddenly struck a jarring note. I looked back towards the car, the man standing beside it, and the autoroute beyond. In the minute we had been standing there, a couple of cars had passed us, and we hadn't even noticed them. There was another car coming towards us now, a large white Mercedes, and I realised what had made me turn. A quarter of a mile away the driver had changed down. There was no reason to change down, unless it was to stop, and there was no reason to stop.

The older man had noticed it too, he was looking back over his shoulder towards the approaching car. He said something I couldn't hear to the younger man, who started to get out of the Simca. He didn't make it. The Mercedes swept on to the hard shoulder still doing forty although the brakes were now hard on. It slammed into the back of the Simca, knocking it fifty yards up the road almost to where I was standing. I could see the younger man inside, as he was slammed backwards over the front seat, and then, as the Simca hit the side support of the bridge, stopping dead, he was pitched back to the front of the car again, his head and shoulders smashing through the windscreen.

The older man was still going for his gun when they shot him. Two men leapt from the back of the Mercedes, which had now stopped and ran back to where the older man was lying like a bundle of old rags. They picked up the wallet and the notebook from beside the body, then they jumped back into the Mercedes which had reversed to pick them up. There was a clash of gears and the Mercedes swung off the hard shoulder and was doing sixty before I could catch my breath. The whole thing had taken less than thirty seconds. From where I was standing, I could see a pool of blood seeping out from beneath the bundle of rags that was the older man. The younger man's head was still sticking through the windscreen, but I decided I wasn't going to do anyone any good by hanging around any longer.

I slithered down the bank and ran across to my car. I couldn't find the bloody key for a moment, then I remembered I had left it in my jacket pocket which I had taken off and thrown into the back. I found it and started the car, turning it so that I would be able to go back the way I had come. I'd started to sweat again, only this time it wasn't the heat. I hadn't got a very good look at the two men from the Mercedes, but good enough to see that one of them was Chinese.

CHAPTER FIVE

IT's surprising the number of Asians who live and work among us. They're so much part of the pattern that we don't notice them, that is until we're looking. Now it seemed that every third person I saw hailed from the East. They probably came from Japan, Thailand, Cambodia or Malaysia. But to me they all looked Chinese, and they all looked dangerous.

I was in a blue funk. After the autoroute incident, I drove up into the hills behind the old coast road and found a small restaurant that looked as though it hadn't had a client for the past twenty years. I parked the car well out of sight from the road, went in, and ordered a large vodka. They didn't have any vodka, but it was the end I was after, not the means, so I had a large brandy instead.

I was way up the creek without a paddle, and I didn't know what the hell I was going to do next. One thing was certain, I had to get the notebook back to Max as soon as possible. What is more, I had to advertise the fact that I no longer had it in my possession. It would take the Chinese no time at all to see that they had hijacked the wrong notebook. After all, they must already know the code. When they realised it, they would be after me like a modern day bunch of Genghis Khans.

The Chinese may be behind the West in matter of science and technology, but they have nothing to learn when it comes to spying and other miscellaneous thuggery. They had agents at work when the British were still painting themselves blue, and the only real American was the Red Indian. And that popular supposition about Asians being the most patient people on earth is so much eyewash. They can be as impatient as the next man when they want something really badly. And their means of obtaining it don't bear contemplation; they were the inventors of painful persuasion.

As far as I was concerned, the airport was out. So too, were the main-line stations. I could try driving across the border to Italy and catching a plane from Genoa, but they'd probably be watching the border as well. That left me one way out. Drive north, making for Paris, and pick up a plane there. They would be watching the main roads, the *Routes Nationales* 7 and 85, so I would have to do it by easy stages, sticking to the back roads. I didn't doubt for a moment that they knew what I looked like. If their organisation was efficient enough to have discovered my rendezvous with the Service, it was efficient enough for any-thing. For that reason, I couldn't go back to my hotel. I could see my new cashmere overcoat hanging in the wardrobe where I had left it but, as a measure of how scared I was, it didn't seem important any more. My hide would keep me warm enough, and if I went back to the hotel, I stood a good chance of losing that, too.

I finished my drink, had another, and then decided that I couldn't delay the decision any longer. I borrowed a touring map from the proprietor, and worked out a torturous route taking in Draguignan, Comps, Digne, then branching on to the RN 75 at Sisteron. I decided I would make my first stop at Rives, after by-passing Grenoble. I would plan the second stage of the journey from there.

It was dark by the time I left the restaurant. Going from the warmth and light of the small bar, into the anonymous dark-ness outside, took quite an effort, and I nearly succumbed to the proprietor's insistence that I stay for dinner. But I didn't. I settled instead for a couple of sandwiches and a bottle of wine which I took with me.

I passed over the bridge that I had left in such a hurry a couple of hours earlier. The wreckage of the Simca had been pulled well to the side, and I wondered if either of the two Service men were now resting in hospital, or in the morgue.

I cut across country to Draguignan and headed north through the wide beautiful country towards Comps. Not that I could see the country; it was dark. If it could have stayed that way for the next week, I would have been happy.

I made bad time at first, due to the number of times I stopped to make sure I wasn't being followed. Each time I picked up headlamps in my rearview mirror, I'd kill my own lights and coast into a layby. There I would wait in fear and trembling until the car behind me had passed. After Draguignan, I stopped doing this for each car that crept up behind me, and although it gave me a few uneasy moments, I made much better time. By midnight, I was past Sisteron and halfway towards Grenoble. I arrived at Rives at four in the morning, and the small town was closed up as tight as a drum. I parked off the road near a bar which looked as though it might open early, and tried to snatch a couple of hours sleep in the back of the car.

At six a.m., I saw someone moving about inside the bar, so I knocked on the door and was let in reluctantly. While the coffee was being made, I phoned Gar and asked him to wait a couple of days then collect my things from the Golf Hotel and send them to me in London. I just hoped I'd be there to receive them. Gar's nose for such things scented some excitement, and I almost told him to come and join me. But selfish as I sometimes am, I'm not that selfish. I finished by telling him I was in trouble with some girl and that I had to slip away unobtrusively. This he understood, and he promised to do what I asked.

By seven, I was on the road again. I reached the outskirts of Paris just as it was getting dark. I was nearly at the airport when I had a better idea. I swung west around Paris and picked up the RN 1 towards Calais. I would spend the night in a hotel I knew at Montreuil, and then drive into Le Touquet first thing in the morning. I could leave the car at Le Touquet and pick up the first plane to Lydd. The fact that I had virtually stolen the car, and that the hire firm would have no trouble in tracing me, didn't enter my calculations. Indeed, the thought of being safely locked away in jail, even a French jail, was quite intriguing. The other side of St. Germain, I stopped long enough to phone ahead and book my room. I had a couple of stiff drinks and then settled down to the last stage of my drive.

I arrived at Montreuil just after nine and drove straight to the Hotel Château de Montreuil. When the receptionist realised that I had no luggage, he had a quiet word with the manager. Full of *bonhomie,* the manager told me to leave my car keys with him and he would see that the car was washed for me. I didn't want anyone fiddling with the car, but as he had no intention of having it washed, I left them with him.

The dining-room was nearly empty as I had my dinner, and I went to my room immediately afterwards. I had a terrible night, dozing on and off. Each time I dropped off, my dreams were full of Fu Manchu-type characters chuckling among themselves because I thought I had escaped their oriental clutches.

I went downstairs at six thirty and borrowed a razor from the night porter. Half an hour later, I left and drove the twenty minutes to Le Touquet airport. There was a plane due out at eight o'clock so I bought a one-way passenger ticket, and then parked the car at the far side of the car park where it would probably stay for days before anyone noticed it.

I went back into the airport building and tried to get some breakfast to stay down. The airport was quiet at that hour in the morning. Trim young ladies in uniform were opening up the various enquiry and ticket desks, chattering among themselves in French and English. A captain who looked as though he should be in charge of a VC 10 and not just a Bristol Freighter, passed the time of day with a nubile looking wench who was supposed to be opening the perfume counter. It was all very ordinary and very peaceful, and for the first time since the autoroute business yesterday, I began to feel easier. I ordered another coffee and a brandy to help it down. The first plane over from England had arrived half an hour earlier and the English newspapers were on the news-stand. It wasn't until I went to buy one that I realised it was Sunday. I bought the *Sunday Times,* and moved over to the lounge to wait for my flight to be called. I could see two cars being readied for the plane, while their accompanying passengers were spending the last of their francs at the gift shop. I was halfway through the Colour Supplement, trying to locate the editorial content from the advertising, when I heard my name called on the public address system. "Mr. John Smith to the British United enquiry desk please." I started towards the desk, and I saw the girl who had sold me my ticket earlier point me out to a uniformed young man. He thanked her and headed across towards me.

"Mr. Smith?" he said as he reached me.

I nodded.

"If you want your car loaded, sir, you'd better hurry," he said politely.

That meant that somebody had seen me arrive by car.

"I'm not taking it," I said.

"In that case may I suggest that you lock it, sir? You've left it unlocked and the keys are still in the ignition." I thanked him, and feeling that I could cheerfully cut his throat, I started towards the exit doors. But he was full of good intentions, and was determined to follow it right through. He fell into step beside me. He talked as we walked.

"Lucky for you, sir, I noticed it," he said. "We try to take care of the cars that are left here, but we do like the owners to meet us halfway by taking normal precautions. It would be comparatively simple for someone to get in your car and just drive it off. Ofcourse, he wouldn't have the papers, but ..."

"Yes, he would," I said. "I left them in the glove compartment."

He was so bloody pompous and self righteous that I wanted to deflate him. He wasn't deflated, just superior. He talked to me as though I were a complete bloody fool.

"That's a very careless thing to do, sir."

"Yes, isn't it," I said, striding out across the car park to where I had parked the car in the mistaken impression it wouldn't be noticed.

They must have been waiting on the other side of the car park. As I reached in to take out the keys, I saw through the windscreen, an old black Citroen suddenly stop broadside on in front of my car. The only occupant was a cloth capped driver.

I pulled back out of my car so fast I hit my head a crack on the top of the door frame. My hand went involuntarily to my head to nurse the bump, and I turned to the pompous young man for protection. Even *they* wouldn't do anything foolish with a witness present. But the pompous young man had gone. At least he was still there, but he wasn't the same man. He didn't even look the same. It was the gun that did it. It was held steadily, pointing at my middle. Now he gestured towards the Citroen with it, and still nursing my head I did what was expected of me. I walked the six feet to the Citroen as the driver leaned back and opened the rear door. I got in, and the uniformed young man got in beside me. As he settled back, he removed his peaked cap and I realised that he wasn't wearing a uniform at all, but a well-cut navy blue suit. Put an ordinary chauffeur's cap on top of that and you've got a uniform, especially in an airport when every second person seems to wear one.

But that was the least of my problems. As the car pulled round in a wide circle and swept out of the airport gates, I made myself as small as possible in the corner of the seat and prepared to meet my doom.

Like a lot of people, I have a low tolerance to pain. Even a visit to the dentist is something of a traumatic shock, and my dentist isn't particularly painful. Let someone threaten to extract my fingernails one by one, or shove a red hot poker up my backside, then that someone can have from me, everything that his heart desires. In other words, I'm a coward. I have been told by people who are supposed to know me, that I have the faculty for covering up this fact, burying it beneath a stiff upper lip and an air of bravado. But I have never been aware of this fact and, if it is so, it is due no doubt to my belief that the person threatening me wouldn't actually carry out his threat. It takes courage of a different sort to physically torture another person, and the people I had dealt with in the Service were mostly as frightened as I was. But old-fashioned torture is not used much nowadays. There are so many medical ways to extract information that it has become obsolete like the bow and arrow and the atom bomb. A quick clean jab with a hypodermic is far less trouble than a pair of hot pincers. Under a truth drug, a man can be made to tell everything he knows, and there is the added attraction that what he tells is the absolute truth and not some fabrication screwed out of him by pain.

This was the general trend of my thinking as I sat in the back of the car. They were certainly going to sweat it out of me, and I hoped desperately that they were civilised enough to do it in a civilised manner. As an added bonus to not suffering any pain, one had the consolation that even the strongest man couldn't have resisted. This provided a salve to the conscience afterwards. If there was to be an afterwards. I looked sideways at the young man sitting next to me. He was staring at me, his gun loosely held on his lap. But it wasn't a stare of curiosity, it was the stare of a professional who knows that the only way to watch a man is to do just that. In fact, there was a complete disinterest in his gaze. If I suddenly sprouted another head, he wouldn't bat an eyelid. His only concern was that this particular bundle he had picked up didn't do anything stupid like trying to get away.

How they had found me I didn't even begin to consider. I learned later that they had checked at my hotel, and when I hadn't returned, they had simply put a man on every airport in the country. Don't ever let anyone tell you that the Chinese aren't well organised. Not that either of my two companions were Chinese, they were as French as the Eiffel Tower. They were hoods, plain and simple. Sixty-two per cent of the world's illegal drug supplies comes from Communist China, and if you are the principal suppliers to the French underworld of such a commodity and you ask for a little favour to be done, your wish is treated as a command. The two in the car were merely messengers. They were delivering a package without any knowledge of the contents. We went out of Le Touquet over the bridge at Etaples and swung left on to the coast road towards Boulogne. Ten miles after Etaples, we passed through a small village. The man sitting with me grunted something to the driver, who nodded. We stopped on the far side of the village.

As the man sitting with me got out of the car, the driver turned in the front seat so he could watch me. He, too, had a gun which he levelled at me across the top of the seat.

In the rearview mirror, I could see the first man walk back up the road into the village. He turned into a shop which announced by a sign that it contained a public telephone. Three minutes later he came out again, walked back to the car, and we were on our way once more.

At one time during the drive, I considered whether or not to appeal to these men's patriotism. After all, France was in this Western Alliance thing as much as Britain, however much de Gaulle argued to the contrary. It was Napoleon himself who said "Let China sleep, for when she awakens, the whole world will tremble." But hoods have no nationality, and without nationality there can be no patriotism.

We were two hours in the car, and during that time not one word was spoken. So I had plenty of time for thought, and I thought plenty. The principal thing that occupied my mind was that the notebook, which I was obviously supposed to provide, was still resting secure beneath the battery in the Renault at Le Touquet airport.

We turned off before Boulogne, and my visions of a slow cattle boat to China receded somewhat. Then forty miles beyond God knows where, we turned into the gates of an old château. At the back of my mind, habits of a lifetime had assimilated the directions we had taken, and I knew I could find the château again blindfolded. That, in itself, was ominous. It pre-supposed that they didn't care what I knew about them, because the knowing wasn't going to do them any harm. The only reason they could assume that was by assuming that I would be dead.

We pulled up in front of the crumbling façade of the château, which looked like something out of Charles Addams. If any money had been spent on the place during the last twenty-five years, it must have been on the cellars. It certainly didn't show above the ground. There were cracks an inch-wide meandering down the walls. Some of the shutters hung drunkenly, others had given it up entirely and fallen to the ground. These had left great holes in the walls where the stonework had rotted and crumbled around the rusty bolts that were supposed to hold them in position.

The grass, on what I assumed was once a lawn, stood knee high, and somewhere in that jungle there must have been a pool of some sort because the whole place smelled of long-stagnant water. Even the sun, which had been doing its best all morning, realised that it had met its match here. It had disappeared behind a large black cloud, and obviously had no intention of appearing again.

The driver got out and opened the rear door for me. In the moment when the man with the gun was off guard, getting out of the car behind me, the driver took his place. They were obviously under the illusion that, given the slightest chance, I would run. I had already run seven hundred miles and it had got me nowhere. There didn't seem much point in running again, especially as there was nowhere to run to. I walked up the wide front steps, nearly breaking a leg on a cracked piece of paving stone. The driver pushed open the door and we all went in.

The interior of the château fitted the exterior well. It was like an old, old man who had long ago realised that he was about to die, and in consequence had decided that nothing mattered anymore; no need to wash, or clean his teeth, no need to dress, or even get up. Just lie still while the barnacles grew and death crept down. It had been elegant once, the wide sweep of the staircase and the double height of the hall showed that. At the far end of the hall were huge windows, the glass miraculously intact, which looked out on to a sloping vista of land which still bore traces of the formal garden it had once been. Beyond lay twenty miles of hazy countryside.

I was steered to the left of the hall, through a pair of double doors into what had once been the drawing-room. There was an ornate Louis Quinze fireplace complete with chipped marble cherubs, and the remains of a huge gilt framed mirror above it. Like the hall, there was no furniture.

I started across the room towards a door at the far side, assuming it was expected of me. Then halfway across the drawing-room I was prodded gently in the back with the gun and told to stop. I didn't turn for a moment, wondering if I was going to get it now, and not wanting to see it coming. Finally, when I did turn, my two companions were already walking out of the door to the hall again. They left without so much as an "au revoir".

I was still standing there with egg on my face when I heard a car start up outside. I moved over to one of the front windows in time to see the back of the Citroen as it disappeared down the drive. Then the sound of footsteps from the hall pulled me round. I debated whether to make a dash for the far door, but I was far too intrigued by now. Instead, I crossed the room and went out into the hall to meet whoever it was I could hear.

There was a tall, thin man coming down the stairs. He was brushing some dust off the sleeve of his jacket. He smiled at me like an old friend.

"Mr. Smith isn't it?" he said.

I nodded.

"Fascinating place," he said. "It must have been quite beautiful once upon a time."

His accent was barely noticeable, and certainly insufficient from which to judge his antecedents. His suit was a charcoal grey shantung, his shirt and tie silk. He looked like one of those "men of distinction" advertisements, and as out of place as Dracula in a creche.

He reached the bottom of the stairs and stood looking at me for a moment, still smiling.

"I must apologise for meeting you here," he said. "It doesn't belong to me; it was loaned to me by a friend."

"The same friend who loaned you those two men who just left?" I asked.

"Exactly," he said. "You're very observant. But then observance has always been a strong point of yours hasn't it?"

"Has it?" I said.

"Don't be modest, Mr. Smith. Rio, seven years ago."

I *had* been in Rio seven years ago. Something to do with an ex-Nazi who had offered us something in exchange for saving him from the Jews. What he was offering hadn't been of much value, but I had accepted it anyway, and then told the Jews where to find him. It had been a bit of a balls-up from start to finish, but somehow I had come out of it well, and even Max had congratulated me.

"I don't remember you," I said.

"I wasn't there," he said. "But I read the reports on the case. Very impressive."

"Whose reports?"

"Mine," he said.

"You don't look Chinese," I said, fishing desperately.

"Albanian," he said. "Although I do spend a great deal of time in China of course."

"Of course," I said.

"But how rude of me," he said suddenly. "I haven't introduced myself."

He stuck out his hand.

"My name is Igor," he said.

I was obviously supposed to shake his hand, so I did. His handclasp was dry and surprisingly strong for so lean a man.

"Just Igor?" I said.

"Just Igor."

I was playing for time now, sorting through the card index in my mind, looking for an Igor. But it was five years out of date, and any filing system falls flat after that length of time.

"I hope you'll excuse the manner in which I had you brought here," he said. "But I had to see you before you returned to England. If I hadn't known better, I'd have thought you were trying to avoid me."

"Why should I want to do that?"

"That's exactly what I said to myself," he said. "Come."

He started towards the glass doors at the end of the hall. I followed him.

The catch on the doors was rusted beyond recall, and after fiddling with it for a moment, he stood back and kicked at it with the bottom of his shoe. The doors flew open, letting in a gust of fresh air, which made me realise how dank and musty the château was.

"We'll walk in the garden," he said.

If that was what he wanted, who was I to stop him? I followed him out on to the terrace, and at that moment the sun decided to come out again.

It was very pleasant in the garden. We walked, and we talked. We sat for a while on an old stone bench and we talked some more, the château looming in the background. It was all very civilised and I wondered when the crunch was going to come.

"I followed your exploits with interest," he said. "You were a highly successful operator. We couldn't understand it when you dropped out of sight—six years ago, wasn't it?"

"Five," I said.

"We thought you had gone underground," he said. "You had us worried for a time. But then we found you again and we realised what had happened."

"What?"

"Disillusionment," he said. "The occupational hazard of our profession. We look beneath the flag-waving and the patriotic slogans, and what do we find? We find that we are in the dirtiest business of all, doing nasty little jobs for very little money."

He was no fool. He knew what he was talking about.

"After a couple of years, we marked your file closed and that seemed to be that."

He looked at me suddenly. His eyes were grey and vaguely glassy. I decided that he wore contact lenses.

"Why did you decide to come back?" he asked.

"You know why," I said, hoping desperately that he would come up with an answer that I could tag on to.

He continued to stare at me for a moment, then he nodded.

"Yes, of course," he said. " 'Tis a consummation devoutly to be wished.' "

So he quoted Shakespeare. I wasn't impressed.

"What is?" I asked.

"Financial independence. Opting out of the rat race. I'd have done the same thing in your place."

He was beginning to lose me, but I didn't want it to show.

"It's not unusual," I said.

"No, it's not, and I commend you for it," he said. "The question is, where do we go from here?"

I waited for him to tell me.

"You are a seller in a seller's market," he said finally. "That's always a strong position."

"The strongest," I said.

"I am one of the buyers for what you wish to sell. The other is your man what's-his-name."

He knew bloody well what his name was.

"Max," I said.

"That's him, Max," he said. "Max was willing to pay you fifty thousand pounds-worth of dollars for it. I can be more generous, I'll give you seventy-five."

"That's not being more generous," I said. "You've already got fifty thousand of it from Max."

"But I *do* have it," he said. "And I am prepared to add twenty-five thousand more. I couldn't be fairer than that, could I?"

"What about the passport?"

"That, too," he said. "But I give you fair warning. You cheated Max. You sold him a counterfeit. I will not be so treated. Before I pay you the money, I shall want to be absolutely sure that I am buying the genuine thing."

"If I allow you to open the merchandise and check its authenticity, there'll be no need for you to pay me the money," I said.

"Then we must devise a scheme where both our interests are guaranteed," he said.

"What do you suggest?" I asked.

"I suggest we arrange a rendezvous. I come alone with the money, you come alone with the notebook. It will take me five minutes to authenticate the contents. If I am satisfied, we can both leave together and go our separate ways."

Stated like that it sounded very simple, but there were holes in it large enough to drive a horse and cart through.

"Who chooses the rendezvous?" I said.

He shrugged.

"It doesn't matter," he said. "As long as we both agree."

That seemed fair enough, and I said so.

"Paris?" he suggested.

"London," I said.

"Why London? I should have thought you wanted to stay well away from Max's clutches."

"The best way to stay out of Max's clutches is to get so close to him he can't see you," I said. "Besides, that's where the merchandise is."

He thought about this for a moment, then he nodded.

"Very well," he said. "London."

We started to walk back towards the château.

"Your Max would have been very angry if we hadn't interrupted your transaction yesterday," he said.

"I shouldn't think he's over-delighted about it even now," I said.

"A hijacking he can understand," he said. "It's an occupational hazard. But to have carried through with the transaction and paid out the money in good faith only to find that you had cheated him—that would have been far worse."

There wasn't much I could say to this, so I said nothing.

"I presume you intended contacting us eventually," he said.

"Of course," I said.

"And selling us false information too?"

"Probably," I said.

"Extremely clever," he said. "You would have been in possession of a permanent pension. Every time you needed more money you could have played us off against each other."

I decided that we'd gone far enough into the realms of fantasy, and I started looking for a few answers.

"How did you get on to Dunning in the first place?" I asked. He didn't seem to mind.

"Dunning approached us through diplomatic channels," he said. "We, of course, were extremely interested."

"So was Alworthy," I said.

"Naturally," said Igor. "I wonder what happened to him."

"I killed him," I said, trying not to sound like Humphrey Bogart.

"I imagined you had," said Igor. "For a man who had so much at stake, he behaved extraordinarily foolishly."

"Yes, didn't he," I said, wondering what the hell he was talking about. Then he allowed me to slip off the hook.

"Tell me, how did *you* get on to Dunning?"

"Connections," I said.

"Through your ex-wife I suppose."

"Exactly," I said. I was groping around in the pitch dark and any moment I was going to say the wrong thing. But once more he steered the conversation away from the edge.

"You are a patient man," he said. "I admire you for it, To wait as long as five years before moving in for the big kill requires self-control of the highest order."

"There was no point in moving in for a kill that wasn't big," I said.

"Tell me," he said. "When your nose for such things detected what was afoot, did you realise that the pay-off would be so high?"

"Of course," I said grandly. "It needs all of fifty thousand to assume a new identity in comfort."

"And now you have seventy-five thousand."

"That's the difference between comfort and luxury."

"Where will you go?"

"South America," I said.

"Very sensible," he said.

We reached the terrace and I was about to go in through the french windows when he redirected me.

"My car is round the side," he said. "I'll drive you back to the airport."

We walked along the terrace and round to the side of the château. Parked close to the wall was a large grey Rolls with Italian number plates. Sitting behind the wheel was a Chinese chauffeur.

He got out of the car as we approached and opened the rear door for us. I got in first, and Igor behind me. As I settled back in the comfortable smell of real leather, the chauffeur got back behind the wheel and started the engine. Or rather, I assumed he started the engine. I couldn't hear anything.

Igor lowered the partition window and told him to drive to Le Touquet airport. Then as the car purred off towards the château gates, he raised the partition again and sat back with a little sigh that denoted that as far as he was concerned, all was right with the world.

"Things must be looking up in Albania," I said, looking round the interior of the car. Igor pulled a face.

"It's a terrible country," he said.

"You must make a splash when you drive up to party headquarters in this," I said.

"I don't take the car to Albania," he said. "When I am there, I use a bicycle. Fortunately, I am not there very often."

I tried to visualise him cycling along the road with all the other good little Communists. I couldn't get the picture at all.

"The Party are very lenient in the matter of expenses." he said. "As long as the results are satisfactory, their tolerance is unbounded."

"You should try working for Max," I told him.

"He's an interesting person, your Max," he said. "He possesses an unusually devious mind for an Englishman."

I suppose you could have called Max devious, I preferred to call him pig-headed and mean.

"This whole business worried me a little at first," he said. "There were an extraordinary number of loose ends which I didn't like. Not least was the fact that the admirable organisation Max runs hadn't started to suspect Dunning far earlier."

This had worried me too, but I let it go.

"Then I heard that Alworthy had moved in and I worried even more," he went on. "He had the homosexual's nose for intrigue, which was why he made such a formidable opponent."

"He was an idiot," I said.

"Yes, wasn't he. Still, it is through such idiots that people like you and I can work. When he failed to get hold of the notebook, I thought Max had located it and I was prepared to see the whole thing go out of the window. Then came your arrest and that extraordinary farce Max was forced to arrange in the English courts. I knew then that you must have something he wanted very badly."

He was very well informed, and I told him so. He shrugged it away as something of no particular importance, and took no credit for it. I almost began to like him at this point.

A couple of miles further on, he got down to business.

"How long do you need to set up the rendezvous?" he said.

"Two days."

"Where will it be?"

"I'll contact you," I said. He gave me a London number through which he could be passed a message.

"I shall be in Paris," he said. "When I hear from my contact, I will come over to London. Allow me eight hours from the time you make the call."

I memorised the London number and then lapsed into silence. I now had to work out how I was going to get the notebook out of the Renault without his being aware of it. There was a possibility he would remain at the airport until my plane had left and I didn't want to have the complication of coming back for it. Neither could I afford to let him know of its existence on this side of the channel. If he did, he'd have it off me so quickly I wouldn't be able to duck the bullet he would give me in exchange. Likeable as he was, he was still a professional and would cut me down like a piece of grass if it suited his purpose.

This problem occupied me for most of the journey, and I was still no nearer a solution when we reached the airport.

It was just past mid-day, and the airport was busy. The car park was full of cars waiting to take their places on the outgoing flights and becoming tangled up with those which were arriving on the incoming ones. Their passengers milled about in family groups with the lost look that most people have at airports.

We drove straight to the main entrance and the chauffeur got out to open the door for me.

"I'll wait to hear from you," said Igor.

"I'll be in touch," I told him.

At least he wasn't going to hang around until I boarded the plane. It was a help, but not much.

As we had driven into the airport, one thing had struck me immediately and with considerable force. In spite of the general confusion, with cars going every which way, it stuck out like a sore thumb. The Renault had disappeared.

CHAPTER SIX

WATCHED the Rolls sweep imperiously from the airport on its way to Paris. No doubt Igor would stop at the first telephone and arrange for someone to pick me up at Lydd airport. He had got his hooks into me and he wasn't likely to let go. I didn't doubt that he was prepared to pay the promised seventy-five thousand pounds, but only as a last resort. For the next few days, until I fixed the rendezvous, I would have to be prepared for a tail that would stick like glue. But that was the least of my problems. The vanishing Renault had first priority. Without the car, there was no notebook, and without the notebook, I was as low on the totem pole as it is possible to be.

I started with the RAC. No, they knew nothing about it. Why not try the police? Next I tried the AA. No, why not try the police? I tried the airport manager's office. No, better try the gendarmerie. All roads seemed to lead to Rome so, much as I hated the idea, I went to the police. They had an office at the airport and I was shown into a room where I was kept waiting for twenty minutes while they looked for Monsieur l'Inspecteur.

They found him in the middle of his lunch. As he came into the office he was buckling on his belt and looking livid.

"How can all this bloody nonsense about a missing motor car be important enough to interrupt my lunch?" That isn't exactly what he said, but that's what he meant. I explained to him how I had left the car and how when I had returned it had gone.

"How long were you away?"

"Four hours or thereabouts," I said.

He called in a sergeant and ordered that a call be put out to watch for the car.

"The number?" he said, turning to me.

"I don't know," I said.

"It is on the papers," he said.

"I don't have the papers," I said.

"Where are they?"

"In the car."

I was forced to go on to tell him that just so it didn't inconvenience the thief too much, I'd left the keys in the ignition as well.

His red face became even redder, and realising that he could say 'au revoir' to his lunch, he got down to business.

"The car is yours?"

"No, it belongs to a hire firm in Nice."

"In Nice?" he said. "Do they know their automobile is a thousand kilometres from home?"

No, they didn't, I said. He booked a call to Nice, explaining that I would have to pay for it. Then, while we were waiting for the call to come through, he started on another tack.

"You say you purchased a ticket on the eight o'clock plane. Why didn't you take it?"

"Something came up," I said.

"You only purchased a passenger ticket. What were you going to do about the car?"

"Leave it here," I said.

"You told the owners in Nice of course?"

"No, I didn't," I said.

And so it went on, with me putting my foot in my mouth every time I opened it. I believe he almost began to welcome being called away from his lunch. As far as he was concerned, the case had started to develop interesting sidelines that lifted it above the level of a mundane car theft. The call to Nice came through and, as I was paying, the inspector took his time. He asked about the weather on the coast, and remarked how he envied those who lived there all the year. He reported on the weather here in Le Touquet, and finally, after five minutes, he condescended to get down to business. Yes, Mr. John Smith had hired a car from them. No, they didn't know Mr. Smith was going to drive to Le Touquet and abandon it, and if it had been stolen, they would inform the insurance company, knowing meanwhile that Monsieur l'Inspecteur would use all the forces at his command to retrieve it for them. *Au revoir* and *bonne santé.*

There was a further hour of questions before the inspector grew tired of the whole thing. He apologised that there was nothing he could charge me with and suggested I wait around the airport until he had some news. Then he left abruptly, presumably for his tea.

I didn't feel much like hanging around the airport, so I left a number with the sergeant and took a taxi into the town. I walked into the Hotel Westminster and as I was telling the receptionist that I might be getting a call from the police, the call came through.

They had found my car abandoned in the forest, about two miles from the airport. It had been driven off the road into the trees. Would I please go and identify it. They said they didn't have any transport to spare so would I take a taxi. They gave me the directions and I had a taxi drive me out. Funds were running pretty low by this time, and if somebody at British United wasn't going to be broad-minded enough to take this morning's plane ticket in exchange for a new one, I could see myself spending the rest of my days in Le Touquet. The taxi driver had some trouble in finding the spot and, when he did, there was one bored constable waiting for me.

All the seats had been taken out of the car and the floor covering stripped off. Apart from that, it was the worst bit of searching I'd ever come across. I can only assume that the men Igor used were more used to looking for five-pound boxes of heroin than they were for slim thirty-five page notebooks. Which only goes to show that a man should stick to the trade he knows and only employ experts in the same trade to do his odd jobs for him. If they'd even bothered to lift the engine cowling, it didn't show. I identified the car for the constable and offered to drive him back to the airport. He accepted with alacrity, and after putting the seats back we drove to the airport, where I dropped him off. I then drove to the far side of the car park and under the guise of fiddling with the engine. I removed the notebook from beneath the battery. I collected the car papers, locked the car carefully and went back to the police office in the airport building. Fortunately, the inspector wasn't there. I phoned the hire firm at Nice and arranged for them to pick up the car. Then I left the keys and the papers with the sergeant and went to see British United. They were extremely helpful and changed my early morning ticket for one out on the next flight. At two-thirty I was on my way.

The journey takes twenty minutes, and I was at Lydd and through customs and immigration by three o'clock. The customs officer looked at me a little strangely when he realised that not only did I have nothing to declare, but I actually had nothing at all. Still, they can't pinch a man for travelling without luggage and, after waving his bit of chalk around, wondering what he could mark, he passed me through.

As I had expected, there was a tail waiting for me. He was a youngish man with a sickly white pallor which looked as though it had never seen the light of day. He was quite good, inasmuch as he didn't jump a mile when he saw me, but he was so out of place at the airport that I spotted him long before he saw me. Knowing he was going to be with me for the next couple of days I christened him for ease of reference. I called him Horace.

On the plane, I had started a conversation with a return-ing holiday family named Cummings. There was forty-year-old father, thirty-year-old mother, and three children whose ages were indeterminate. Father was so glad to find someone to talk to after having the family around his neck for the past fortnight, that he offered me a lift into London. This had been my point in starting the conversation, and I had accepted gratefully. In the car park, mother and the children were shoved into the back of the car with the luggage, and I was given the seat of honour next to the driver. As we drove out of the airport, I saw Horace get into a Vauxhall to start earning his pay.

Cummings turned out to be one of those drivers who feel the public highway is their own private road, and that nobody else has any right to be on it at all. Within ten minutes of leaving the airport, I was regretting the whole thing. The family must have been used to it. They chattered away happily in the back, while I quietly died in the front. Horace, I'm sure, had thought he was on to an easy pitch following a family saloon, and the fact that he managed to keep up with us at all sent him up in my estimation. We reached the outskirts of London at five thirty and twenty minutes later, I said good bye to the Cummings family. My right leg was as stiff as a board from applying a non-existent brake for the past sixty miles. How I had avoided shoving my whole leg through the floor of the car was a miracle.

About now, Horace became a little confused. Following a car had been all right, but now I was on foot and he was still in his car. Added to this, Cummings had dropped me near Victoria, and Horace wasn't going to be able to find anywhere to park. I watched him drive past where I was standing, frantically looking for a hole where he could tuck his car. I allowed him to drive past me, then I crossed the road and caught a bus going in the opposite direction. Half a mile down the road, I got out of the bus and went into a tube station where I bought a ticket to Piccadilly Circus.

At Piccadilly, I fought my way out against the down-pouring commuters. In the concourse, I rented a left luggage locker, and I locked the notebook in it. Getting rid of it was like discarding a ball and chain. The thin book had weighed a ton in my pocket. I went to the public toilet and paid the appropriate fee for the privilege of taking a crap, and I dropped the key of the locker into the water cistern. Then I went home.

Horace was parked fifty yards down the road in his Vauxhall. He must have been very relieved to see me. I resisted the impulse to wave at him, and I let myself in. The flat, which is pretty crummy at the best of times, felt and smelled as if it hadn't been occupied for a decade. But however it felt and smelled, it had nothing on me. I'd been in the same clothes since leaving the hotel in Valescure two days before. Since then, I'd sweated on the autoroute, driven seven hundred and fifty miles, spent a terrible night in Montreuil, sweated some more when I was picked up by Igor's men and sweated some more under the influence of Cummings' driving. My shirt was so stiff I practically broke it taking it off and I smelled like an old gymnasium. I poured myself a massive drink and took it to the bath with me.

I lay in the bath for two hours, freshening it periodically by turning on the tap with my right foot while removing the plug with my left. During that two hours I did some very hard thinking. By the time I got out of the bath, I was as red as a pillar box, and my skin had crumpled so that it looked as though it didn't fit me any more. But my thinking bout had served its purpose. I now had the whole thing neatly set in order and analysed. I'd judged every move since the whole mess had started. The conclusion was final and absolute. I was still in it up to my armpits, with even less chance of coming out of it than I had had before.

I know I had the notebook. And all I had to do was to take it to Max. But then Igor would be after me and I'd seen enough of him to know that once he got his teeth into something he'd not let go until he'd shaken the life out of it. It would be useless to ask Max for protection. Once he got the notebook back, Max would do the necessary to me—but quick. On the other hand, I couldn't let Igor have the notebook either. I'm pretty stupid most of the time, and this was one of those times. Even for seventy-five thousand pounds I couldn't allow those fifteen Chinese names in the book to go for the long chop. But if I didn't contact Igor by the day after tomorrow, he was going to contact me. And this time it wasn't going to be a polite discussion in an elegant old château, it was going to be a noisy killing in a dark and dirty alley.

After I clambered out of the bath, stupefied with the booze and the heat of the water, I came into the bedroom and started across to the wardrobe with the intention of getting my dressing-gown. I sat on the bed for a moment to scratch my stomach, and one thing led to another. The pillows looked very comfortable, and I liked the feel of the mattress beneath me. I lifted my legs on to the bed and stretched out experimentally. The moment my head hit the pillow, I died.

I must have been in the same position when the Heavy Squad arrived three hours later. I was conscious first of a very bright light obtruding into my sleep. Then, before I could identify or even be fully aware of it, somebody clouted me on the side of the head, and I rolled off the bed. Still stark naked I was jerked to my feet, with a hand under each arm. A man is at his most vulnerable when he's wearing no clothes, added to which I was still half asleep and didn't know what the hell was happening. I stood, supported on each side, my mouth hanging open, trying to organise some sense out of the chaos. I was helped in this direction as I received another clout round the head, and was dropped into the bedroom chair. I started to get out of the chair and was pulled back by four large hands from behind. Then, from the shadows, a towel was thrown at me.

"Cover yourself up, you look revolting," said Max.

I draped the towel primly across my lap as Max stepped into the light. When Max is feeling benevolent, he's a formidable character. When he's feeling mean, one is hard put to find any comparative depth of meanness. At the moment he was obviously feeling just as mean as he could.

He had a thin, tight, smile pinned on, which fooled no one, least of all me.

"Been having yourself quite a little jaunt," he said. I said nothing. When the Heavy Squad hit you, you knew you had been hit, and the bells hadn't yet stopped clanging.

"How much did you take them for?" said Max.

Rather stupidly, I told Max to go fornicate with himself and immediately received another clout which practically took my ear off. Max just stood there, his hands stuffed deep in his coat pockets, looking mean.

"How much?" he said.

"Nothing," I said. I braced myself to lose the other ear but nothing happened.

Max fetched an upright chair and carried it over towards me. He sat on it back to front, his face fourteen inches from mine. I could see that his conjunctivitis was giving him hell and I could have spat straight in his eye if I'd had any spit. But my mouth felt as though it were stuffed with dusty carpet.

"Marchesson was a good operator," said Max.

Marchesson must have been the one who was shot on the autoroute. If I hadn't known Max, I would have thought his anger was due to the shooting of Marchesson. But I did know him, and I knew that Marchesson could have been hung, drawn and quartered in Max's living-room, and he wouldn't have batted an eyelid. It was the money that was sticking in his gullet, and the fact that he'd lost the notebook. He would look on happily while twenty Marchessons were killed if he could rectify either.

"Try looking to your own bloody security," I said. "Our meeting place was blown."

"You're a liar," he said.

"So I'm a liar," I said.

I saw Max shake his head quickly, and I realised I had narrowly avoided being thumped again.

"If the rendezvous was blown," said Max. "You blew it."

"I suppose I killed Marchesson, too," I said.

"I wouldn't put it past you," said Max.

I said a rude word, and when the expected blow didn't come, I started to regain some of my confidence. Not much of it, but sufficient to ask if I could put something on. It was cold and I was beginning to shiver. Max nodded his agreement.

As I put my dressing-gown on, I saw the two Heavy Squad men for the first time. They were large and anonymous. I didn't know either of them. They stood behind the chair I had just left with a hawk-eyed indifference. One wrong move and they would have knocked my head off. When I'd done up my dressing-gown I sat on the bed. If I was going to be hit again it would have to be from the front.

"If they got what they wanted, why were you picked up at Le Touquet?" said Max.

"If you knew I was picked up at Le Touquet, why didn't you stop them?" I said.

Max brushed this away indifferently.

"They had the notebook. What did they want with you?"

"Perhaps they didn't like the notebook they had," I said.

Max's eyes flickered briefly like one of those panels on a computer as it digests a problem and hasn't yet pumped out the solution.

"They haven't got it?" he asked.

"Right," I said.

He expelled his breath slowly. Then he looked up at the two Heavy Squad men.

"You can go," he said.

They left quietly and unobtrusively, without a backward glance.

"What happened?" said Max.

I told him about the abortive meeting on the autoroute, and the opposition's departure with the wrong notebook and the fifty thousand pounds.

"What about Le Touquet?" he said.

I told him. At the mention of Igor's name, he sat up a little.

"Igor Berat?" he asked.

"Just Igor as far as I'm concerned," I said.

"It must be Berat," he said, half to himself.

"Should I know him?"

He looked up at me as though he had forgotten about me. Then he shook his head.

"No. He's only been around for four years. And very long years they've been."

"Big wheel?"

"You could say that. What was his proposition?"

"Your fifty thousand and twenty-five more."

"You agreed, of course."

"I agreed," I said.

"So why didn't you let him have it while you were still in France. What made you come back to London?"

"I found out what was in the notebook," I said.

This didn't impress Max.

"So?" he said. As far as he was concerned it might have been a grocery list in the notebook. People don't rate very high in Max's scheme of things.

"So if fifteen people are going to get the chop, I'm not going to wield the axe," I said.

"Not even for seventy-five thousand pounds?" He couldn't believe that anyone could be so stupid. Then he had an idea. "You think I'm going to offer you more?"

I let him get on with it for a while. It's fascinating sometimes to watch a snake screw himself up.

"What kind of a bastard are you?" he said. I could see he regretted having dismissed the Heavy Squad. "You'd sell out your own mother if the price was right. We made a deal—fifty thousand pounds for the notebook. I've come up with the fifty thousand pounds and by Christ I'm going to get the book in exchange."

"I've been offered seventy-five," I reminded him.

"I don't care if they offered you the Great Wall of China. By Christ, I'm going to turn you over to the Heavy Squad with a black ticket." He was already halfway to the telephone when I stopped him. He was practically rigid with anger and his eyes had started to stream. He must have gone over the top to have even thought of turning me over with a black ticket. The colour codes for the Heavy Squad were white, which meant a little roughing up with not too many bones broken: grey was designed to be used on people who were reluctant to divulge information needed by the Service and was always very painful. The only people who were issued with black tickets were those who were going to die alone in some far away place where their dying inconvenienced no one, least of all Max.

"It's not for sale anymore," I said as he reached for the phone. He'd worked himself into such a pitch that I wondered if I'd got through to him. He had the phone halfway to his ear when he started to relax. He put the phone down again, and fumbling in his pocket he produced his eye drops. He squirted them into his already streaming eyes, and then mopped up the deluge with his handkerchief.

Then he came and sat on the bed beside me. I got up and moved to the chair.

"What do you want?" he asked.

"All I want from you is enough to cover my expenses," I said.

"And?" said Max. He knew me.

"And twenty-four hour protection until Berat decides to stop chasing me."

"He's not chasing you."

"He will be as soon as he realises I'm not going through with it."

"Where do you keep the booze," said Max suddenly.

He followed me into the living-room where I poured two drinks. I handed him his and watched while he walked over to the window and looked out into the street.

"You're being followed," he said.

"I know."

"Shall I have him removed?"

I shrugged. It didn't make much difference. I wasn't trying to hide. Not yet, anyway. Then he turned from the window, his mind made up.

"We'll kill two birds with one stone," he said. "You get Berat over here. You get the money from him and turn back to me my fifty thousand. You can keep half the balance."

"There won't be any money unless I give him the notebook."

"Give it to him," said Max. "We'll pick him up immediately afterwards. I've got a lot to talk over with Mr. Berat. It should be very interesting."

"It's risky," I said. "What if you don't pick him up? He's got the notebook."

"We'll be sitting on his head two minutes after you hand it over," he said. "The meeting place is your choice. We'll find a place we can button up so tight that no one will get away."

"Not even me?" I asked.

"That's a nasty thing to say," said Max.

"I've got a nasty mind," I said.

He didn't give me any arguments.

"You'll have to trust me as much as I'm going to have to trust you," he said.

This was a pretty poor arrangement, but there wasn't much I could do about it. I told him so.

"Good," he said. "I'll contact you when I've sorted out a suitable meeting place."

He headed for the door, then he turned back.

"How much is 'enough to cover your expenses'?" he asked.

"It doesn't matter anymore," I said. "I'm going to get half of twenty-five thousand."

He looked at me steadily for a moment. His eyes were dry now.

"Nevertheless, what do you consider your services over the past few days have been worth?"

"Why?"

"I'm curious," he said.

"Two and a half thousand," I said, naming the sum I always intended to keep.

"As much as that," he said. "I'm obviously in the wrong business."

"We're both in the wrong business," I said.

"You should be happy. You're going to get a very large fee and do a bit of good at the same time."

"Good for whom?"

"Your country," he said. I laughed in his face. He looked as though he wanted to say something but bit it off short, and he left.

He was right, ofcourse. I should have been happy. I would get paid. I'd get shot of the notebook and Max would take Igor off my neck. So why wasn't I happy? There was a little crawling creature lurking around inside my head. I couldn't pin him down and the harder I tried, the deeper he crawled. There was something wrong somewhere. And I didn't have any idea what it was.

After Max had left, I considered going down to Box Hill to see Gunther. But I'm a big boy now, I thought, and I must learn to stand on my own two feet. Apart from that, Horace was still outside, and while I didn't doubt my ability to lose him again, I could have been wrong, and there didn't seem any point in taking the chance of dragging the Old Man into it.

It was still only just after midnight, and I was wide awake now, I thought about calling Mary, but decided I wouldn't do her the unkindness of wishing myself on her in my present state of mind. Instead, I cooked myself some bacon and eggs. The bacon had been in the fridge for over a week and was a little tired round the edges. But it tasted all right. I made myself a pot of coffee and started to think about things. Somewhere along the line I fell asleep.

On my way out at nine thirty the following morning, I saw that Horace's place had been taken by another man. He was using the same car, sitting low in the driver's seat, with a newspaper held up in front of him. He gave me fifty yards start, then he got out of the car and started following me. He was cut from the same mold as Horace. He could have been his brother. I called him Wallace.

Miss Roberts was ecstatic when I walked into the office. It had been two weeks since she had seen me, and what with the appearance of the police just before my disappearance, she had begun to doubt that she would ever lay eyes on me again. She fussed around like a mother hen, bringing me three cups of tea in the first five minutes. She gave me a quick rundown on what Stubbs had been up to, which turned out to be exactly nothing. Then she brought me my mail. There were three circulars, seven assorted bills, and a postcard from Phil Bannister in the South of France. In it he said he was having a ball, and he knew I wouldn't mind if he stayed over for a further week. I'd forgotten about Phil. That was another item for my expense sheet. There was also a printed form from Her Majesty's Customs and Excise saying they were holding a suitcase at London Airport, addressed to me. Would I please go and collect it? So I hadn't lost my overcoat after all.

Miss Roberts also gave me a list of telephone messages, none of which meant anything, except the last name on the list. Mrs. Robert Helix had called. Barbara Helix had been one of Danielle's friends I had telephoned when I was looking for her. I was still looking for her, so I called Barbara and identified myself.

"Would you like to take me out to lunch?" she said.

I said that I wouldn't, and what did she want.

"I'm not sure I'll tell you if you don't take me out to lunch."

"I can take you to the Corner House," I told her.

"I was thinking of the Caprice," she said.

"You can think again," I said. "I can't afford it."

"Well, I'm not going to the Corner House," said Barbara. "Not that I don't think it's very good," she added. Her husband had once been a Labour M.P. and, as much as it went against the grain, Barbara tried to help him with his image.

"Does that mean you won't tell me?" I enquired.

She told me, as I had known she would. It seemed that a couple of days after I had phoned enquiring for news about Danielle, Marjorie Adams, another mutual friend, had returned from Madrid where, she reported, she had seen Danielle.

"So there you are," said Barbara. "She's in Madrid—or at least she was."

I thanked her and was about to hang up when she continued:

"Don't you want to know who she was with?" she said.

I didn't, but I asked nevertheless.

"Michael Lumsden," she said, like he was the Aga Khan.

I said, "Oh really!" or something equally fatuous, but she wasn't going to let go.

"He's that terrible man who was married to Katherine Lumsden. All four of them used to go around together when they were married."

"When who was married?" I said.

"All of them. Nathaniel and Danielle, Michael and Katherine."

I knew Dunning's death had been kept out of the papers, so I dug a little.

"You mean Michael and Katherine are divorced now?" I said.

"Of course," she said. "They all got divorced about the same time."

"All of them," I said.

"Nat and Danielle, Michael and Katherine. You knew, surely."

I said I didn't.

"No reason why you should really," admitted Barbara. "It was all very quiet and discreet."

"How long ago did all this happen?" I asked.

"Two years. No, two and a half. I remember because Danielle asked if she could use the cottage while she was waiting for her decree thing, and she couldn't because I was there getting over an abortion."

I thanked her politely, and hung up.

I thought of Danielle's clothes I had found in Dunning's bedroom, of her make-up and perfumery laid out on the dressing-table. And I thought of the place where I had found the notebook, in Danielle's secret hiding place. There was a mistake somewhere, and Barbara must have made it.

I sent Miss Roberts down to Somerset House. Because it was urgent, I told her to take a taxi there and back. She was back inside the hour. And there it was, in black and white. My ex-wife had asked me to obtain evidence so that she could divorce a husband she hadn't been married to for over two years. Whichever way you sliced it, Danielle had set me up and led me to the chopping block.

I was still trying to work out the whys and wherefores when Miss Roberts buzzed me on the phone.

"There's a gentleman to speak to you," she said. "He won't give his name."

A lot of my clients are like that, and I didn't want to be bothered with clients right now. I told Miss Roberts so, and she buzzed me back thirty seconds later.

"He says his name is Oxford," she said.

Oxford had been a name I'd occasionally used when I had been working for Max. I asked for him to be put through, at the same time telling Miss Roberts to bring me another cup of tea. She would listen happily at the switchboard for hours if I didn't do something about it.

It was Max.

"Can you come and see me?" he said.

"Don't forget I'm tailed," I said.

"I'll take care of it," he said. "Leave your office at exactly twelve forty-five. I'll expect you at one."

As I left the office at twelve forty-five, a young lady was hitting Wallace about the head with her handbag, and screaming that he'd made indecent advances towards her. Two policemen were ambling over the horizon, and as they moved in on either side of Wallace, engulfing him, I hailed a taxi. Then, in case Wallace had seen the number of the taxi, I paid it off around the corner, and walked the rest of the way.

Max must have been feeling very pleased with himself. He got to his feet as I was shown into the office, and even came round the desk to pull up a chair for me.

"Sit down, John," he said. I sat.

"Cigarette?" he offered. I took one.

"It's all laid on," he said.

"What is?" I said.

"The meeting place for you and Berat. We've got to play it very cool. Berat is expecting you to come alone, so we'll stay well out of sight until after the transaction. Then we'll pick him up."

"What happens if he decides he's not going to part with the money and tries to pay me in kind?"

Max looked at me fondly.

"There'll only be the two of you," he said.

I remembered the surprising strength of Igor's handshake, but I nodded.

"What happens after you pick him up?"

"You give me the money, after the deductions, and go on your merry way."

"No repercussions?"

"None."

I thought about it for a moment. There didn't seem to be any way I could get out of it, so I agreed.

"Where's it to be?" I asked.

"Psychologically, the place has to be dead right. It has to be a place that Berat would expect you to choose if you were meeting him alone. A place where neither you nor he can call up the cavalry at the last moment."

"Where is this place?" I said.

"If it's not dead right, he'll smell a rat and won't turn up at all."

"Where is it?"

"It took a little thought, but ..."

"Stop flannelling me, Max," I said. "Just tell me where the bloody place is."

He looked mean for a moment, then he shrugged it off. He reached into his centre drawer and pulled out a map. He turned it so that it faced me and stuck his finger on a point about twenty-five miles east of London. I leaned forward and removed his finger so that I could see what he was pointing at.

"You're kidding!" I said.

"It's an ideal place," he said.

I got to my feet.

"What's the matter with it?" he said.

"It stinks, and you know it."

His mouth tightened up and his eyes started to water.

"Any better ideas?"

"Dozens. And so have you. What are you up to, Max?"

He started to bluster with his number two indignant expression. I'd seen it before and I wasn't impressed.

"I don't like your choice of rendezvous," I said. "What's more I don't like anything about the whole bit."

He stopped blustering and grinned at me.

"So, what are you going to do about it?" he said.

There was nothing I could do about it and he knew it. I sat down again and he got down to business, showing me exactly where and how I should meet Berat, and where and how the Service were going to pull him in afterwards. He had all the details worked out meticulously. Every move was plotted and counter-plotted. But I still wasn't impressed. To my way of thinking, the whole thing had assumed melodramatic proportions quite out of keeping with the essential simplicity of the operation. And the operation *was* simple. If one forgot for the moment the ramifications built into the notebook, the whole operation boiled down to a simple exchange—notebook for money. It was the sort of thing that could be done in an Oxford Street cafe in two minutes flat. Yet Max detailed to me a plan which was complicated enough to have been used for the Great Train Robbery.

I left the office an hour later with one thought uppermost. Max was up to something sneaky. And when Max got sneaky, someone usually got hurt. It didn't take three guesses to know who that someone was liable to be. I went straight back to my own office. There was no sign of Wallace. He was probably languishing in Saville Row police station by now, waiting for the magistrate to sit next morning. I spent ten minutes trying to locate Marjorie Adams's number, and finally got her on the line.

"Yes," she said. "I saw Danielle in Madrid."

"Any idea which hotel she was staying at?"

"Why?"

"I want to contact her."

"I know that, but why?" she said.

I spun her a yarn about a second cousin in from the colonies who wanted to see her. I thought for a moment that she wasn't going to bite. She relented finally.

"The Hilton," she said. I thanked her and hung up. I should have guessed. If there was a Hilton hotel, Danielle would be in it. She had an affinity for the streamlined, super-efficient, completely impersonal atmosphere Mr. Hilton has scattered across the globe. In a Hilton hotel she knew she could drink the tap water, and she knew that the cooking wouldn't be foreign if she didn't want it that way and the beds would be without bugs. She was a little like a Hilton hotel herself, streamlined, efficient and impersonal.

I asked Miss Roberts to place a personal call to Mrs. Dunning at the Castellana Hilton in Madrid. Then I remembered that she wasn't Mrs. Dunning any longer. It was no good trying to work out what name she was now living under, so I took a chance and asked for the call to be made to Mrs. Lumsden. If she was staying with the man in Madrid, there was a fair chance that she would be using his name, if only to keep the hotel management happy.

The call came through an hour later.

"Danielle?" I said.

"Who is it?"

"John."

"John who?" she said. After three years of being married to me, she had to ask that.

"John Smith," I said.

There was a moment's pause.

"Hello darling," she said. "How are you?"

"I want to talk to you," I said.

Considering I had bothered to phone her clear across a continent, it was a pretty fatuous remark. But it didn't make any difference, as it was the last thing I had a chance to say.

"Darling, this is a terrible line, I can't hear a thing," she said. I could hear her as clearly as though she were in the next room. I started to say so, but she didn't let me finish.

"It's no good, darling, can't hear you. I'll be back next week. I'll call you then." And she hung up.

The English operator asked me if I had finished because my party had cleared. I said I hadn't and asked to be reconnected. Then something went wrong with the lines between here and Madrid and it was half an hour before I got through to the hotel again. I was told that Mr. and Mrs. Lumsden had checked out ten minutes ago and left no forwarding address.

CHAPTER SEVEN

THE street was the same, with the house still looking like an ageing queen. But now there was an air of decay added to the overall impression. It was the window-boxes that did it. The flowers hadn't been attended and they had withered and died. They drooped over the edges of the boxes like the dried brown fingers of a long dead mummy. The coaching lamps hadn't been cleaned either, and the brass was dull and lifeless.

I walked past the house and knocked on the front door of its immediate neighbour. I worked my way up the street, then I started down the opposite side. Halfway down, I re-crossed the road and worked my way back up, finishing at the next door house on the opposite side. Out of the twenty houses I tried, I found seventeen people at home, and from fifteen of the seventeen, I learned nothing. The other two, while not exactly turning up trumps, at least meant that I hadn't wasted my time.

I called in at the pub at the end of the road, the one I had visited on the night it had all started. I greeted the barman like a long-lost friend, and he pretended to recognise me. Because he didn't, and felt that he should, he became more voluble than he would have been normally. His information, combined with what I had just learned, made the whole trip worthwhile.

Mrs. Jacoby lived in a building that was put up to celebrate the Crimean war, and should have been pulled down to celebrate the Boer War. She had a two-roomed apartment on the fourth floor, and she shared tap privileges with three other apartments

on the same floor, the tap being located on the communal landing, next door to the toilet, which was also shared.

She answered the door to my knock, and over her head
I could see into the apartment. There was a truculent looking
youth in leather sitting at a bare wood table forking his dinner
into his mouth. He didn't even look up as Mrs. Jacoby came out
on to the landing quickly, and closed the door behind her. She
started straight in on why she had fallen behind on the TV pay-
ments and it took me ten minutes to get across to her that I didn't
come from the finance company, from the landlord, or from the
police. But once she had got that fact firmly fixed in her head, she
showed signs of becoming loquacious.

Yes, she had charred for poor Mr. Dunning, what took
sick and died, two hours a day five days a week. Not Saturday
or Sunday 'cos her Bob was at home and had to be fed. Having
ascertained that fact, I told her to fetch her hat and coat and took
her down to a handy pub and we really talked.

Horace was back on duty when I arrived home. No doubt he
was wondering what had happened to Wallace. Between the two
of them, they had made a complete balls of keeping me under
surveillance. It wasn't really their fault, but I didn't imagine that
Berat would be too pleased. He had struck me as a man who
didn't make mistakes himself, and wouldn't tolerate them in others. Still, that was their problem. I had others of my own.

I poured myself a large drink, and read the evening paper. I
washed up some dirty dishes and rinsed out a couple of pairs of
socks. I washed a nylon shirt and hung it up to dry. I had another
drink which I took with me to the bath. I trimmed my toenails,
had a crap, read the evening paper again, and then had a shave.
After that there seemed nothing left to do but to phone Berat's
contact and tell him about the rendezvous.

I called the number he had given me and identified myself.
Then I gave the time and the place. The message was repeated
back to me by the person on the other end of the line, who then

hung up. It was now seven thirty. I had twenty-six hours to wait. I broke all the rules and called Mary before eight o'clock. Fortunately, it was all clear, and after snarling at me gently for breaking the rules, she said she'd have dinner with me.

I got dressed and went out. I still hadn't picked up my stuff from the airport, which meant that I didn't have a topcoat. The evening was chilly, but I warmed myself up during the next twenty minutes while I was losing Horace. It is next to impossible for one man to tail another, if the one under surveillance knows that he is being followed. There are a thousand different ways to shake a tail, and I lost Horace round about number three. Having left him stranded on the down escalator at Sloane Square station, I called a taxi and gave the driver an address in Cheapside.

I am not a man who is normally disposed towards violence. I will walk ten miles to avoid trouble, and if trouble comes, I will try to talk my way out of it. As a last resort I will turn and run. But there comes a time when running is no good any more, for no other reason than that there is no longer any place to run to. Then all one can do is to turn and fight. The question then arises as to how one fights—clean or dirty. I'd learned very early in life that the man who fights clean winds up with his head in a sling, while the dirty fighter leaves the field of battle with nothing more painful than a troublesome conscience. That's always assuming he knows what a conscience is, which isn't usually the case.

The address I had given the taxi driver was Solly Weisman's. Solly runs a clock and watch repair shop just off Cheapside. At least, that's what he runs in the front of his place. What goes on in the back is anybody's guess. As far as I was concerned, what went on was a bit of judicious blackmail, so that I left the shop twenty minutes later with a gun.

Solly and I have known each other for years, and since leaving the Service. I have used him as my private armourer. My ability to do this is based on the fact that Solly deserted from the British army early in 1942, and, by a pure stroke of luck, I found out about it. The British army has a long memory, and even now, twenty-five years later, Solly could still be put away for a few years if they got their hands on him. So, while he hated me, if I asked for something hard enough, I got it.

What I asked for in this case was a Smith and Wesson .38 Police Special, and twenty-five rounds of ammunition. I don't like guns; I never have, but as a functional piece of equipment, they have their points. If I was going to be left alone with Berat for any length of time at all, I wanted to level the odds as much as possible. The gun, I felt, would help.

Solly tried to get me to take a holster as well, a soft chamois shoulder holster. This, in itself, was a sure sign that he hated me. A holster is strictly for the birds, or for those people who have no intention of using their gun. If a gun is going to be used, it should be tucked in the waistband of the trousers where it is easily accessible, and clearly visible. The sight of it by the opposition is often sufficient to obviate the necessity of using it. A gun in a holster is difficult to reach, and having reached it, difficult to get out. A man is liable to be dead three times over before he can clear a gun from a shoulder holster. Solly knew this, so he practically begged me to take one. I told him "no thank you" and promised to let him have the gun back in a couple of days. His soft brown eyes told me that he would be happy never to see the gun again, if it meant that I disappeared with it. I was his one link with the past, and while he was practically sure that I would never turn him in, the fact that I was in a position to do so offended his peace of mind.

Because of this, I checked every round of ammunition as soon as I got home, examining each round individually. Then I selected three cartridges at random and prised the lead from the cartridge case. I tipped out the powder in each case, and struck a lighted match to it. Each time it flared convincingly.

Then I wrapped the gun and the remaining ammunition in an old pair of pyjamas, and buried the bundle at the bottom of my dirty linen basket. Anyone adventurous enough to delve through *that* deserved to find something.

Then I brushed my teeth, took two Amplex, and went out to exercise my urges.

I took Mary to a small fish restaurant behind Eaton Square. There I stroked her thigh gently throughout dinner. She wanted to know where I had been and what I had been up to. But it was a polite curiosity rather than a genuine desire to know. Our relationship was so adjusted that any interest we had in each other was confined to those times we were together. Apart, we led completely individual lives with no strings and no comebacks. I watched her tucking into her food like there was no tomorrow and I wondered, as I often did, what the hell I was going to do when this girl got married. The thought crossed my mind, as it had the habit of doing, why didn't I marry her myself? I'd never asked her, and the reason was buried deep in my subconscious. Not deep enough however, that it didn't poke its murky little head up sometimes long enough for me to recognise it. I didn't ask her because I was frightened that she would say no. I am realistic enough to know that I am no catch yet, like a number of realists, I can fool myself quite adequately when I want to. As long as she didn't turn me down, I could bask in the fact that she might have said yes. So, I didn't ask her. I consoled myself with the fact that she *wasn't* married and at least while we were together this lovely, gentle, humorous creature was all mine. Dinner over, we went back to her flat and to bed.

I emerged into the early morning at three a.m. and drove home. I could see Horace a little way down the road, asleep in his car. I thought for a moment that I should go and waken him. At least he would know that I had come home. Then I thought the hell with him. I let myself in, made a cup of hot chocolate, and went to bed.

According to the label on the tin, deep undisturbed sleep should have followed. It didn't. I wrestled with my pillows for an hour; then I got up and made myself a strong, black coffee. I took it back to bed with me, and wide awake now, I did some top-grade thinking, mostly about Mrs. Jacoby.

She had warmed towards me after the second port and lemon, and although her speech had started to slur slightly, she had been very positive about what she had told me. She had arrived at Dunning's house the morning after the murder, unaware that anything had happened. She found the place full of large young men in lounge suits, the police long ago having been chased out by Max's staff. They had told her that Mr. Dunning had suffered a heart attack the previous evening. Then they had asked her to look around the house to see if she could spot whether or not anything was missing. She had done so, and reported that as far as she was concerned everything was where it should be. They had thanked her politely and driven her home. Unfortunately, or fortunately, depending on whose point of view one took, she had forgotten her handbag. So later that evening, after she had fed her Neanderthal son, she had gone back to the house to fetch it. The Service men had gone and she had let herself in with her own key, which for some extraordinary reason she wore on a piece of string around her neck. She knew where she had left her handbag and she went straight to it in the upstairs bathroom.

Then, as she put it, she "'ad the shock of 'er life". The bedroom was full of women's clothes. There were dresses hanging in the wardrobe, and the drawers were full of sweaters, blouses and underwear. The dressing table held perfumery and other such female accoutrements, the like of which she had never seen in Dunning's house before.

"I thought for a moment as 'ow I'd come into the wrong 'ouse," she said. "But I knew I 'adn't, so I thought as 'ow the 'ouse had been sold to someone else already, and poor Mr. Dunning not even in his grave yet. So I just grabbed me 'andbag and left quick afore anyone 'cused me of trespassin'."

She had a spot of bother with the word "trespassing" but I was well satisfied by now. I bought her two more port and lemons and left her in the Snuggery with a group of her cronies who had been eyeing us for the last hour dying to know what it was all about. They weren't the only ones. I was pretty desperate to know what it was all about myself.

I made myself another coffee, took it back to bed, and went all over it again. But, whichever way I tried to work it out, it always led back to Danielle. And Danielle wasn't going to give away one little thing, not to me anyway.

Then, about five thirty, I started to get a nasty idea. It was buried deep in the back of my skull and it took me more than an hour to ferret it out. When I finally made it, and spread it out in the cold dawn light, it didn't look as feasible as I had first thought. It still looked nasty, but much too nasty to take really seriously. But Max was the prime mover, so I took it seriously.

Finally, at seven a.m. I dropped off to sleep. My alarm was set for eight, so waking up was like returning from the dead. I staggered around the flat like a man suffering from shell shock, dragging myself awake in easy stages between coffee, bathroom and three cigarettes which tasted like dirty blotting paper and set me coughing like an advanced tubercular case. By nine thirty, I judged myself fit to communicate with my fellow creatures. I telephoned Miss Roberts and told her I wouldn't be in. Then I unwrapped the gun from its hiding place, and nearly ruptured myself trying to tuck it in the waistband of my trousers. I began to wish I had listened to Solly and accepted the offer of a holster. I put all the ammunition loose in my jacket pocket and left the apartment.

I got into my car and after giving Horace plenty of time to manoeuvre his car out, and start to follow me, I drove to London Airport. I parked the car and went into Number Two Building. I walked up the stairs, where I joined a stream of passengers going through to Customs and Immigration, bound eventually for

Majorca. I caught a glimpse of Horace's face as he watched me leave. His mouth was hanging open. Then, as he dashed for the nearest telephone, I walked over to a customs officer and showed him the note I had received reporting the arrival of my luggage from France. He told me that I could pick it up in the bonded warehouse that dealt with freight. I thanked him and remarked on the weather and how fortunate people were to be going away to the sun this time of the year. He agreed with me, and said how some people have all the luck, and how he couldn't afford to go abroad even if he did have the time, which he didn't. With embellishments, this took up ten minutes, so by the time I walked out again, Horace was long gone. I hoped that Berat wouldn't take the report that I had left the country too seriously.

I picked up my suitcase and my overcoat, signed a couple of forms and returned to my car. Just to be on the safe side, I peered under the bonnet before I got in. I wouldn't have put it past Horace to have exceeded his duties somewhat, and prepared a surprise for me. But there was nothing under there that wasn't supposed to be, and wrapped in cashmere, I piloted my way out of the airport and pointed the car towards Box Hill. My early morning flights of fancy were far too wild to accept without a second opinion, and Gunther's was the only opinion, apart from my own, that I could trust.

He pretended indifference when I arrived, and I let him sweat at it for a while. Finally, he could wait no longer.

"So tell me!" he said.

I told him, right from the time I had last seen him just before I left for France. I didn't realise how much there was to tell until I laid it all out on the line like that, and it took me more than an hour. He didn't interrupt me once and, when his daughter appeared with lunch, he merely snarled at her to serve it quickly and get out.

"That's about it," I said finally, sitting back. He didn't say anything for a couple of minutes and I let the silence rest between us.

Then he asked a couple of questions. They were questions of fact, not theory, and I answered them as accurately as I could. There was another silence, which lengthened to six minutes before he spoke again.

"You have drawn conclusions?" he asked.

"Plenty," I said.

"So let's have them," he said impatiently.

"The first one is a little far out," I said. "But it could fit, if you've got a strong stomach."

I gave him the nasty idea I had conceived at five thirty that morning. Here, with the birds racketing and the sun shining, it seemed even further out than I had at first visualised. Halfway through I started to say so, but he dragged me back on the rails and made me finish.

"It fits," he said at last.

"Like a tailor-made coffin," I said. "But even Max wouldn't dream up a scheme like that."

Gunther didn't say anything. He just looked at me, and finally I nodded my head.

"Yes, he would," I agreed.

"But that is only one story, one set of conclusions. Let us examine some others," he suggested.

But each one we examined had holes in it large enough to drive a bus through and we found ourselves coming back to the first idea time and time again. It was the only theory that fitted all the circumstances.

"It's sick," I said.

"It's a sick world," said Gunther.

I agreed. It was a sick world, and nowhere was it sicker than in the grey half-world which was ruled by Max and men like him. I had opted out of it once before, and now here I was again, in so deep that I needed a sludge dredger to get me out. This time there was no pretty young girl with blood where her face should have been, but there was a trail of dead and dying bodies stretching back to the beginning. There was Dunning and Alworthy and there were the two Service men on the autoroute. There was also the fifteen names in the notebook who were as good as dead, and there was yours truly who was still walking around on two legs, but who might as well be in a coffin six feet down as far as the overall plan was concerned.

I thanked Gunther for his time, and for once I wasn't embarrassed when he kissed me goodbye. He, better than anyone else, knew that if we were correct in our diagnosis, I stood about as much chance of getting clear of the set-up as Max getting religion. Something of Gunther's grimness must have transmitted itself to his daughter because she gave me the first kind look I had ever received from her. She even unbent sufficiently to wish me luck as she showed me out.

I drove back to London and parked in a no waiting area while I went down to pick up the notebook. The toilet where I had hidden the key was occupied and I hung around for a few minutes while the attendant eyed me mournfully. He was just working up enough enthusiasm to start getting awkward, when the toilet was vacated, and I slipped in and slammed the door behind me.

For one moment I thought they must have had the plumbers in and the key was gone. I fished around desperately, elbow deep in the cistern, and then I found it lodged in the most inaccessible corner.

Up in the concourse, I opened the left luggage locker and extracted the notebook. Then, feeling that everyone in the place had eyes only for me, I walked up to street level and went back to my car. There was no policeman hovering around the car and no parking ticket taped to the windscreen, the first bit of luck I'd had since the whole mess started.

Just before I drove out of London, I thought about calling Mary. But there didn't seem much point. There was nothing I could say to her except good-bye, and I hate good-byes.

I stopped for a few minutes in a lay-by about twenty minutes out of London. There I loaded the gun, and did one other little job. Then I restarted the car and pointed it towards the rendez-vous Max had chosen with such loving care.

Twenty-five miles east and slightly south of London, you are slap in the middle of Kent. It's beer growing and farming country, dotted with oast houses and tidy, prosperous farms. The Garden of England it's called, and in some circumstances, I suppose I could have enjoyed a leisurely drive along country roads lined with neat hedges that marked out fields full of cows and sheep and other agricultural impedimenta. But this wasn't the circumstance. To me the cows looked bovine and stupid, and the sheep reminded me too much of my own predicament for comfort—that of an innocent being fattened for the not-too-distant slaughter. But there was an edge I had over my wool-bearing compatriots—I *knew* I was being led to the chopping block and I had enough meanness in me to work on some form of protest.

In the centre of a triangle formed by Wrotham, West Malling and Aylesford, there is an airfield. Or rather there *was* an airfield. It formed part of the Greater London defence system during the war. After the war, when the Americans had left and the shouting had died down, an enterprising local tycoon had started a flying club there and promptly gone broke. Since then, the huts that had once provided billets and administration buildings for upwards of twelve hundred men had been used successively by squatters and itinerant hop pickers down from London. More recently, they had been used as cow sheds, but as there was no one willing to spend any money on their upkeep, they had become so dilapidated that even the cows wouldn't use them any longer and they had started to collapse gently, one by one. In the centre of the airfield was the only building that could lay any claim to having withstood the ravages of time. This had been the control tower and, although the operational section of it had long ago been stripped of all its trappings, there were still four concrete walls and a roof.

This, then, was the infallible rendezvous picked by Max as a place where his men of the Heavy Squad would be able to pick up Berat the moment the transfer had been made. There were twenty-five different ways of approaching the place and, naturally enough, twenty-five different ways of leaving it. To be sure of picking up Berat, Max would have needed to call out the entire Brigade of Guards. The reluctant conclusion I had been forced to was that Max didn't want to pick up Berat at all. But this was reasoning that, while fitting all the known facts, still remained within the area of speculation. And because I could no longer afford to speculate, I arrived at the airfield a full two and a half hours before the appointed rendezvous time.

I drove round the perimeter once, then turned off on to a side lane and parked my car half a mile away, well off the road. Then I walked back the way I had come. I reached the edge of the airfield at five p.m., still two hours before time and, feeling rather foolish, I selected a tree and climbed it.

I suffered a scraped knee, a bruised elbow and a severe attack of vertigo before I was satisfied that I had clambered high enough. Resting uncomfortably in a junction of trunk and branches, I looked around. I could see the whole of the airfield, right round the perimeter to the cluster of collapsed walls that had been the administration centre. The control tower stood alone and phallic in the middle of the airfield about seven hundred yards from where I was. It was a fine, clear evening and, with the binoculars I had brought along, I could pick out detail with absolute clarity. After ten minutes, I had satisfied myself that I was the only person anywhere near the airfield. It was so bloody quiet and peaceful that it wouldn't have taken much effort to convince myself that I was the only person for five hundred miles, but the idea was so tantalising that I banished it severely.

After half an hour, I realised that if I didn't come down from the tree soon, I was going to do irreparable damage to my spine, which was jammed against the main trunk, and my crotch, which was wrapped around a particularly knotty branch. Moving about just made it worse, so I started to tuck the binoculars back in their case, when suddenly my aches and pains were forgotten. There was a car moving slowly around the perimeter road. Using the binoculars again, I could see that there were at least four occupants. One of them could have been Max, but it was impossible to tell for certain.

I followed the car as it made a complete circuit of the airfield, passing almost beneath me. Then, as it reached the far huts once more, I lost it for a moment behind the walls. When it reappeared, it was minus two of its passengers. It figured—two detachments from the Heavy Squad, two men in each. One detachment had been dropped off at the far side of the airfield, and it was reasonable to assume that the other pair would station themselves somewhere near where I was perched. But the Heavy Squad didn't interest me at this moment. It was Max I wanted to see.

I didn't doubt that he would be lurking around somewhere nearby. He enjoyed field work, as long as it wasn't too dangerous, and providing it was somewhere in the British Isles. He used to say he liked to get out to see how "his boys" operated. But he would no more have left the country than he would have taken up knitting. Somewhere deep in his shifty mind there was the fear that, should he leave the protection of these shores, he would be spirited away to some Red dungeon, there to suffer torture, brainwashing and worse. He was probably right. The number of people who would have liked to get their hands on Max was formidable.

The car stopped three hundred yards away from my perch, but the two occupants didn't get out. They were still ninety minutes early for the rendezvous and they weren't going to get off their arses until it was absolutely necessary. But they had chosen their parking spot well. Although I could see both them and the control tower, it would be impossible for anyone in the control tower to see the car, due to half a dozen strategically placed trees. If Berat followed his instructions carefully, he would turn off the road on to the airfield perimeter just to the left of the huts and drive straight to the tower. He'd never see the waiting car, and it was safe to assume that the two men who had been dropped off near the huts would remain well under cover.

So far everything seemed above board, as long as you were willing to discount the actual site. Max had said he would have Heavy Squad ready to pick up or pick off Berat after our little transaction, and here they were. If I'd had a less suspicious mind, I'd have accepted the whole thing at face value and proceeded as planned. But I had no intention of proceeding anywhere until I had located Max.

And locate him I did. Ten minutes after the first car stopped, away on my left, I picked up another car as it meandered round the perimeter. There was only one occupant, the driver, and halfway round the airfield I identified him through the binoculars. As though to confirm my identification, I saw him take a hand off the wheel and mop his eyes with a handkerchief. If he thought his eyes were giving him trouble now, just wait until I was through with him. I started to clamber down to the ground.

I ripped my jacket halfway down, and I silently thanked the powers that I had left my new overcoat in the car. By the time I dropped to the ground, Max's car must have passed the one with the waiting Heavy Squad, and I cut through the bushes and out on to the perimeter just in time for Max to see me and stick on the brakes.

He didn't get out of the car, but at least he had the courtesy to wind down the window.

"You're early," he said.

I leaned on the side of the car looking down at him.

"So are you," I said.

"Checking the disposition of the troops."

"How many men?" I asked.

"A dozen," he said. I let it go.

"Any changes in the plan?"

He shook his head.

"After the transaction, you get him to leave first. Give him five minutes. We will have picked him up by then. You can come out safely after that and I'll meet you here."

"How do we know he'll come alone?"

"He probably won't," said Max. "But while you're doing your bit of business, we'll wrap up whoever he's brought along. Simple."

I decided the only simple thing about the whole bit was me for letting it go so far—and Max for thinking I'd let it go any further.

"I spoke to Danielle today," I said.

He covered up very well.

"Danielle?" he repeated. His eyes had started to water again.

"You remember Danielle," I said. "I used to be married to her."

"That's right," he said. "I remember now."

He pinned a very convincing look on his face which was meant to convey polite curiosity at my mentioning something that couldn't possibly have any bearing on the issue at hand.

"She was married to Dunning too," I said.

"Yes?" He had decided to humour me.

"Until two years ago," I said.

He decided he had had enough.

"That's all very fascinating," he said. "But this is hardly the time or the place to discuss your domestic failures."

"How did you get to her?" I persisted.

"To whom?"

I didn't even bother to answer. There was a long pause while he thought about this latest development and the repercussions it could have. Then he decided to ignore the whole thing. He started the engine.

"I'll meet you afterwards," he said.

I had to hand it to him. Even at this stage he was prepared to bluff it out. He stopped bluffing when I poked the gun across the edge of the door. I let him get a good long look at it, and the little lead snouts poking at him from the chambers.

"Switch it off," I said. He switched off and started to play it cool.

"You haven't got a licence for that."

"Sue me," I said.

"Put it away, John," he said affably. "Let's talk."

"So talk." I didn't move the gun.

"You know this area is swarming with Heavy Squad."

"Four men don't swarm," I said. "Especially when two of them are nearly a mile away."

He looked from my face to the gun and back to me again.

"You're getting yourself into trouble," he said. He had started to look mean.

"I'm already in trouble," I said. "This is getting cut."

"With a gun?"

"If it helps."

"What trouble are you in?" he said. It was an old habit of his. You started off by asking the questions and two minutes later he was asking them and you were so busy defending yourself you didn't have time to remember what it was you started out to discover.

"You tell me," I said.

He started to look innocent until I jabbed the gun into his throat, just below his right ear.

"Tell me about Danielle," I said.

He thought it over for a moment. Then he decided that I was a *schmook* and he might as well tell me anyway.

"Would you have come in if I'd asked you?" he said.

"No."

"That's what I thought. I wanted you in. She seemed as good a way as any."

"You paid her?"

He shrugged.

"A couple of hundred pounds." Danielle would have sold her own mother for fifty; Max had got no bargain.

"And Dunning?" I asked him.

"He had the names. We had to get them from him before the Chinese did."

"Why didn't you just move in and take them?"

This one worried him for a moment, but only a moment.

"We didn't know where the notebook was," he said. "Dunning could have hidden it anywhere. It was important enough for him to keep quiet about it, whatever form of persuasion we used."

From what I could remember of Dunning, he had seemed the sort that would have wanted an anaesthetic to have his toenails cut.

"You're lying Max," I said.

He started to look indignant, then he changed his mind.

"So, I'm lying," he said.

"Why did you think I could find the notebook if you couldn't?"

"You found it."

"Because I was supposed to. Danielle told you about the hiding place."

"You're talking nonsense," he said.

"I haven't started yet." I gave him a little jab with the gun, just below the ear. "Now you listen to me, Max. When I go wrong you can tell me. Until then keep your big fat mouth shut, or I'll take your ear off." He started to reach in his inside pocket and I jabbed him again.

"My eye drops," he said.

I nodded and watched him extract his eyedrops and perform the necessary.

"Ready?" I said finally. He nodded.

"This is the way I read it," I said. "I was *meant* to find the notebook and the whole business about my involvement with the Dunning killing and Inspector Diaman was designed to look good to the other side, to Berat. I had something which you wanted badly enough to get me off a murder charge and pay me fifty thousand pounds for. Therefore, says Berat, it must be pretty bloody important. You rig a convincing handover in France, put up the money for the notebook, then you blow the rendezvous. It didn't matter a toss to you that you were sending two of your own men to the chop. All you wanted was Berat to get the notebook there and then. But that's where your scheme fell flat on its arse. There were only two dead men instead of three, me being the third. You must have been choked. Two men dead, fifty thousand quid out of pocket, and nothing to show for it. It couldn't have looked very good upstairs. So you devise a salvage operation— and if you tell me you're going to pick up Berat after he gets the notebook, then I shall tell you that you're a bloody liar. He *gets* the notebook, he has always been going to get it. Your only problem was to make sure that it didn't look like the plant that it is. Which raises the question, what's in the notebook?"

"Names," said Max.

"I know that. Whose names?"

"Agents," he said.

"Whose?"

"Russian," said Max. And the whole thing fell into place. Berat would get the names believing they were those of Western agents, and the Chinese would act accordingly. Doors would be broken down in the middle of the night, and fifteen people would be driven away in fast motor cars, or rickshaws, or whatever they use in the People's Republic. There would be no trials, just fifteen empty places where once there had been people. The Russians would be unable to scream because the agents shouldn't have been there in the first place. But the cold front between the two countries would widen considerably, and that could do the West nothing but good. But it had to have been made to look genuine. If Berat or his employers suspected that the names were Russian and not Western agents, then the two big enemies would come closer together, united against the common foe.

It was a fine scheme until one started to count the dead bodies that Max had strewn along the wayside. I think about here he expected me to congratulate him. He had started to look a little smug.

"Who got the names in the first place?" I asked him.

"Dunning. He was on a mission to Moscow. One of our people over there contacted him."

"Why did he wind up with a cut throat?"

"Alworthy was a Russian agent. They found out about the leak and tried to plug it."

"By killing him?" I said.

"Alworthy knew we were on to him. He got impatient."

"Dunning was above board," I said.

"Completely," said Max. "He brought us the names as soon as he came back from Moscow. That's when I took over."

The little bastard was proud of himself. I felt like shooting him there and then, and hang the consequences. But I resisted the temptation.

"What's supposed to happen now?"

"Berat gets the notebook, you get paid, and I get my fifty thousand pounds back," said Max.

"And the names in the book?"

He shrugged.

"Occupational hazard," he said. He didn't feel any justification was needed, but in case I wanted one, he threw it to me casually. "Anyway, they're Russian agents."

I suppose I'd been too long out of the Service, because it didn't help much. When I spoke again it was slowly. I wanted him to get the full benefit of what I was saying.

"Max," I said. "You can go and stuff yourself." I didn't use that particular verb, but the meaning was the same.

He looked at me blankly. He honestly didn't understand what I was getting at.

"It all ends here," I said. "I don't meet Berat, and I take the notebook away and burn it."

This got to him where it hurt. He could see the whole torturous business going out of the window. What really upset him was the thought of the eventual post mortem, where he would have to account for two dead agents and a petty cash voucher for fifty thousand pounds. That was on the debit side and he would have nothing with which to balance the book.

"You can't do that," he said.

"Don't take any bets on it," I told him. But I wasn't feeling as confident as I sounded. He was taking the news badly, but not nearly as badly as he should have been.

"You've got no choice," he said.

"Prove it to me."

"If you don't turn up, Berat will go after you, and in case he has any difficulty, I shall give him a hand. It's a small world, John, not nearly big enough for you to hide in, especially as you're broke."

All too true I decided. Then he helped me on my way.

"On the other hand," he said. "You do everything as planned and you wind up with half of twenty-five thousand pounds and nobody chasing you."

"What about Berat when he finds out I've sold him a plant?" I asked.

"He's a professional," said Max.

He had a point there. If a deal went sour, that was that. The professional would write it off and get on with the next. Revenge was for the birds.

Max could see he was getting to me, so he pursued his advantage in the area where it would do the most good.

"You must be way out of pocket by now," he said. "I checked—and you were on your uppers before you started. So to add to your problems, if you don't go through with it, you'll probably wind up inside for debt."

I was weakening fast and he knew it.

"So be a good fellow," he said. "Take that gun out of my ear and I'll forget I ever saw it."

I took the gun out of his ear. There didn't seem to be anything else I could do. He leaned forward and restarted the engine.

"Don't forget," he said. "Give him five minutes before you come out."

"So's you can wrap him up," I said.

He grinned at me, a nasty little grin.

"So's he can get well clear," he said. "I'll wait for you here."

I tucked the gun back into my trousers.

"All right, Max," I said.

He continued to grin at me as he drove away. If anything, the grin was nastier than it had started out, and suddenly I felt cold.

I walked back to the car and fetched my overcoat. Still cold, I walked back to the airfield and, avoiding the car with the Heavy Squad, I carried on to the control tower.

It was nearly dark when I reached it. Before going in, I looked around the silent airfield, feeling the three sets of eyes that were no doubt watching me. I felt like giving them a stiff two fingers, but as a gesture of defiance it would have fallen as flat as I felt, so I just turned and went into the control tower instead.

There was nothing much left of it except the four walls and the roof. There was a dilapidated concrete staircase leading up through a hole in the roof. This had once provided access to the first floor, but as the first floor had been constructed entirely of wood and glass, it had long since gone. All the staircase now provided was somewhere for me to sit while I waited for Berat.

Before settling down, however, I removed the notebook from my hip pocket and hid it beneath a pile of rubble in the corner. I placed the gun on the sixth stair from the bottom, and covered it with a piece of sacking that had been used for God knows what. Then I sat down and waited.

While waiting I did some retrospective thinking. If my greed for one hundred and fifty pounds hadn't blinded me into taking the job Danielle had dangled in front of me; if I hadn't barged into Dunning's house like a drunken Irishman on St. Patrick's night; if I hadn't allowed myself to be conned by everyone and his mother; if I hadn't...I gave up. The trouble was, I *had,* and that's why I was here.

I tried occupying my time with dreams of what I could do with my share of the loot, but as I didn't really expect to lay my hands on it, it proved an abortive process.

I was still trying to think of other ways to occupy my time when Berat arrived. He appeared suddenly in the doorway and frightened me to death. I had been expecting him to arrive by car, and his sudden, silent appearance, put ten years on to my life. He looked the same as he had at the château, immaculate and just as incongruously out of place. His eyes flicked once round the inside of the control tower, then back to me and he smiled.

"You're punctual," he said.

"I didn't have so far to come as you did," I told him.

"The journey was well worth it," he said. Then when I didn't move, he added a codicil. "Wasn't it?"

It wasn't that I was feeling rebellious again; it was just that suddenly I felt a hundred years old and he could have shoved a stick of dynamite up my backside and I wouldn't have been able to find the energy to pull it out. He stepped further into the building.

"Are you all right?" he asked.

There was concern in his voice and I wondered how soft his shoulder would be for crying on. But then I pulled myself together. His concern was for the notebook, not for my peace of mind.

"I'm sorry," I said. "I'm getting old."

"Old and rich," he said.

He stepped out of the door and reappeared a moment later with a briefcase. I wondered whether he had picked it up or had it handed to him. Then I decided that I didn't much care. I nodded towards the stairs.

"I'd like to see it," I said.

"Of course," he said.

He moved over to the stairs, and opening up the briefcase, he up-ended it. It was a grandiloquent gesture, but a little impractical, as everything tumbled out every which-way. Two hundred and ten thousand dollars in negotiable currency is a lot of paper. It spilled from the third stair, on to the second and the first, covering all three stairs with impressive ease. It was lucky there wasn't a wind blowing or we'd have lost the lot. As it was, a gentle evening breeze caressed the edges of some of the notes, causing them to rustle with hynoptic effect.

I stepped towards the loot, but he held up his hand suddenly.

"Please," he protested.

He was right of course. I fetched the notebook from where I had hidden it and pitched it to him. He caught it neatly and backed away from the money. I watched him as he flipped it open on page one. He checked the contents of page one quickly, and satisfied, he riffled through half a dozen pages and checked another entry. If he looked at the last page, I was dead. I measured the distance between me and the place where I had hidden my gun, and tried to coax some energy into my tired old legs. But it wasn't necessary. He looked up at me and smiled.

"That all seems to be in order," he said. He nodded towards the money.

"You're satisfied?"

I walked over to the money, and picking out a couple of notes I ran a quick check on them.

"Satisfied," I said.

He turned to go. Then, at the door, he turned back again.

"You worried me at first," he said. "I didn't like the way you kept losing the tail I provided."

"It wasn't hard," I said. He smiled.

"Perhaps not, but I couldn't see why you considered it necessary."

I shrugged.

"Old habits die hard," I said. He waved his arm, embracing the surroundings.

"Then this," he said. "When I heard about it, I thought the whole thing was beginning to become too melodramatic to be genuine. I nearly didn't come."

"But you did," I said.

"Yes, I did." He held the notebook up. "One way or another, I had to get hold of this. I expected a trap, but I came anyway."

"Expecting a trap, you must have come prepared," I said. He produced a gun suddenly. Or, rather, a gun suddenly appeared in his hand. I had a vague glimpse of a holster, low beneath his arm, before his jacket flapped back. So much for my theory on holsters. He held the gun loosely but efficiently. There was no threat implied.

"I'm impressed," I said. I was, too.

"It wasn't meant to impress," he said.

"I know. That makes it even more impressive. Personally, I don't like guns."

"Then I suggest you leave yours buried under that rubble when you leave," he said with a grin.

"*Touché*," I said. "But I still don't like them."

"Nor do I," he said. "But they do have their uses."

He looked at me steadily for a moment. Then he reholstered his gun. It disappeared almost as quickly as it had appeared. For a man who didn't like guns, he handled one remarkably well.

"It's a pity you're going out of business," he said. "We could have done some work together in the future."

"Would you continue in business with this?" I indicated the money.

"Yes, I would," he said. "I enjoy it."

I started to go off him round about here. Anyone who enjoyed doing the work that he did must have had something seriously wrong with him somewhere.

"Perhaps we'll meet again," he said.

"I doubt it."

He smiled again and then went out of the door. I checked my watch and started to gather up the money, stuffing it back into the briefcase. Berat might have had a dozen men out there with him, but I couldn't even be bothered to find out. As far as I was concerned, our dealings were over and if I never saw him again, it would be too soon.

I repacked the briefcase in three minutes. I collected my gun and blew the cement dust out of the barrel. I tucked it back in my trousers and checked my watch once again. The five minutes were up and I started out to meet Max.

Just as I reached the door, I heard a shout from away on my left.

"Smith!"

I turned towards the voice and caught my foot on a chunk of cement and stumbled. Because of this the bullet missed me, chopping a chunk of concrete from the outside wall just where my head had been a second before. Instead of regaining my balance after tripping, I followed through and went flat on my face. The second bullet would have castrated me if I hadn't hit the deck. And there I lay, my nose buried in mud, petrified with fear, and so angry I could have eaten nails.

That elegant, double-crossing Albanian bastard, with his beautiful suits and his silk shirts! Next time he flashed his pearly choppers at me, I'd knock them through the back of his head. Then I realised that, unless I got my arse off the ground pretty soon, there wouldn't be a next time. It was pretty dark, so they must have been using some form of infrared sight. I wondered for a moment whether Max would call up the Heavy Squad to get me out of trouble. But the idea was so ludicrous, it only served to remind me how scared I really was.

I fumbled beneath me trying to pull my gun out, but due to my fall, it had slipped below my waistband and was now flopping around inside my trousers. I couldn't remember whether I'd put the safety catch on, and I spent a frantic minute groping inside my trousers wondering whether I'd accidently snag the trigger and blow my own balls off.

I extracted it finally, still face down in the mud and tried to work out what I was going to do with it. As long as I lay where I was, I was obviously all right. If they had still been able to draw a bead on me, I would be dead by now. The trouble was I couldn't work out from where they were shooting, so I didn't know whether to wriggle backwards, forwards or sideways. I settled for backwards. At least the walls of the control tower would offer some form of protection.

I ripped my overcoat to shreds in the next few minutes, and if I'd been angry before, now I was livid. Once through the door, I wriggled sideways and then clambered to my feet. There was a hole in the far wall which had once been a window, so I kept well clear of it. I had no idea how many men Berat had with him and, knowing him as I did, he was probably covering all exits.

My immediate panic began to abate somewhat. I was still frightened, but no longer petrified. This was probably due to the fact that I was now perpendicular instead of horizontal. I knew I wasn't as frightened as before because now I started to try to analyse a way out of the mess. First, I couldn't go out of the door. Whoever he was, he wouldn't miss next time. Second, I couldn't go out of the window, because that was obviously covered as well. Third, I couldn't stay where I was; there was no future in it.

So I went on to the roof. I was clambering through the hole at the top of the staircase before I realised that I was still clutching the briefcase. In fact I'd never let go of it, even when I had fallen flat on my face, and afterwards when I was groping one-handed for my gun. I'd been half an inch off dying and I had clung to the money like it really mattered. I decided that I was an avaricious bastard and left it at that.

Climbing on to the roof meant that I had to stick my head through the hole first. This I did in easy stages, bobbing up for a split second the first time, slightly longer the second, longer still for the third. Finally, I managed to hold it up there for a full five seconds before my nervous reflexes jerked it down again. But behaving like an irrational jack-in-the-box wasn't going to achieve anything, so stamping firmly on my screaming nerves, I stuck my head up once more, and kept it there. The top of my skull remained where it was and a minute later I wriggled out on to the exposed flatness of the roof, dragging the briefcase behind me. There was a foot high parapet around the edge of the roof which effectively screened me from anyone at ground level, and I just prayed that Berat's men hadn't taken to tree climbing like I had done. But nobody shot at me again, so I made myself as comfortable as possible, and began to wait.

The hunted has an advantage over the hunter inasmuch as he can go to ground and then wait for the hunter to come for him. Whereas the hunter, with orders to kill, must continue to advance until he is satisfied that his task has been successfully completed.

They waited an hour before they moved in. When they did, it was quietly and efficiently. Wherever Berat had got these men, it wasn't from the same stable as Horace and Wallace. I was reluctantly forced to the conclusion that Berat himself would be long gone by now. The notebook was too valuable to risk in deeds of idle assassination.

There was a small scuff of sound from the front of the tower, and a similar sound from the back. They had approached from two directions simultaneously. I edged myself forward so that my head was inches away from the stairwell. A moment later I heard another sound as a man climbed in through the window. There was a pause, then he spoke to his companion who had obviously reached the door.

"He's gone," said a voice.

There was another pause, then a flashlight clicked on. The light leaked up through the stairwell, inches from my nose.

"Look on the roof," said another voice. He was the bright one.

A sudden shaft of light streamed up through the stairwell. I backed away quickly to the edge of the roof, and for the first time I let go of the briefcase. I left it on the roof, while I lowered myself over the edge and dropped to the ground. To me it sounded like a bag of coals dropped forty feet onto corrugated iron, but then I'm sensitive. The two men in the control tower didn't hear a thing, probably because the one on his way up to the roof was concentrating on not getting his head blown off, while the other one was blundering around in the dark.

I edged my way along the outside wall until I was level with the window. I drew my gun carefully and checked that the safety catch was off with my finger. Then I offered a silent prayer that Solly hadn't filed away the firing pin, because I was going to have to use the bloody thing in about ten seconds.

"He was up here," said the voice from the roof. "He's left the briefcase."

The one inside uttered an exclamation I assumed to be of satisfaction. I heard the footsteps on the roof as they crossed to the briefcase, then returned to the stairhead. Then as the footsteps started to descend, I risked a quick peek through the window. As it turned out there was no risk. One man was standing at the bottom of the stairs, looking up towards the other who was coming down. Just to make it easier for me, the one descending was shining his flashlight on to his companion.

I shot the one at the bottom first, and as the flashlight swung instinctively towards me, I shot at the light. He must have been holding it at waist level, because the bullet hit him in the stomach. The flashlight fell from his hand, bounced down the stairs, and finished on the ground, still switched on. The light that it gave was sufficient for me to see that the first man I had shot was as dead as he would ever be. The second was taking his time. He clutched his stomach, and stumbled down two more steps. Then he let go of the briefcase, and covered the last five stairs on his face.

An unholy silence suddenly clamped down, and I realised I was sweating like a pig, and my hand was shaking like I had the palsy. There was the stink of gunfire in the still night air and a lot of dust and smoke just beginning to settle.

At first, I was physically incapable of stepping back through the window, but after a moment the briefcase reasserted its old hypnotic effect and I scrambled through. I held the gun ready just in case, but my first diagnosis had been correct and both men were dead. I picked up the briefcase and then the flashlight. Out of curiosity, I flashed it on the faces of the two men. The first one didn't have much of a face left, my bullet having caught him just below his left eye. I didn't hold the flashlight on him longer than it took my stomach to heave. The second man was still clutching his stomach. His face wasn't pleasant by any means, but at least it was unmarked. It was an ordinary face as faces go, an anonymous everyday face, but the shock it gave me was twice that of the bloodied mask of his companion. The last time I had seen him had been through binoculars. He had been sitting with his partner in a car on the edge of the airfield, warming his bottom and waiting for the action to start.

No wonder Max hadn't felt it necessary to call out more than four of the Heavy Squad. He had assumed that four men were quite capable of taking care of little old me.

CHAPTER EIGHT

RELOADED my gun, more to gain thinking time than for any other reason, then I sat down for a moment to try to work it all out. There had been four of the Heavy Squad, one pair on either side of the airfield. These two men had approached the control tower from opposite sides, so it was safe to assume that they comprised one from each pair. That meant there were still two men out there, one some place near the old huts and one near the parked car. As my own car lay in that direction, I decided to deal with the man near the car. Just how I was going to deal with him, I hadn't worked out, but by this time I was too angry to care. Berat pulling a double-cross had irked me enough, but Max doing it, that really choked me.

I gathered up the briefcase, picked up the flashlight and started out. It wasn't as dark as I had at first thought. There was a moon somewhere up there behind the clouds, and sufficient light leaked through to enable me not to have to use the flashlight all the time. But when I judged I was about two hundred yards from the car, I switched it on anyway. A man behind a torch is next to impossible to identify. I walked confidently, whistling a vague tuneless dirge between my teeth, for all the world like a man returning from a job well done. At least this was the impression I was trying to create, and it was successful. I'd nearly reached the car when a figure materialised behind it.

"O.K.?" he said.

I grunted an affirmative and walked closer. He came round to the front of the car, and the first he knew that all was not as it should be was when I showed him my gun.

To his credit, he didn't try anything stupid. His hands, which had been stuffed in his raincoat pockets, came out empty and he put them behind his head without having to be told.

"Into the car," I said.

He climbed into the car and I slammed the door behind him. I rested the gun across the top of the door, and still he didn't say a word.

"Take a message to Max for me," I said.

His eyes looked at mine. They were flat and expressionless. He was just a fellow doing a job and if the job had gone sour, it wasn't his fault.

"Tell him he can whistle for his money," I said. "And tell him not to hold his breath waiting for his grand scheme to pay off."

I withdrew the gun. The man was good, he knew the interview was at an end. He started the car and drove off without a word.

I waited until I judged he could no longer see me through the rearview mirror, then I bolted. By the time I reached my own car, I was practically useless. I threw the briefcase into the back and flopped into the driver's seat. I was puffing so hard I misted up the windscreen before I'd even started the engine. I followed the lane I was in for half a mile, then turned off on to a wider road. A mile further on I turned on to a minor road once more, all the time heading more or less south.

By three a.m. I was outside Lydd. I drove the car off the road into a small wood. Fifty yards into the trees I left it and walked back to the road. Then I waited two hours before I was able to hitch a ride to the airport.

There was a Geneva plane due out at seven thirty. I bought my ticket, and when the restaurant opened, I just had time for a substantial breakfast before catching the plane.

Two hours later I was in Geneva. I checked into the best hotel in the city, throwing Max's money around like a drunken sailor on Saturday night. From my suite, I called Gustave Holbecker. He agreed to meet me at the bank at one thirty.

During my days in the Service when I travelled Europe extensively, I had made Geneva my jumping off point both outwards and inwards. Returning to London after a job, I would invariably re-arrange my flight schedules so that I could stop over in Geneva, sometimes for a couple of days, sometimes only for a matter of hours. It became a habit and Max hated it. He couldn't understand why I did it and I never enlightened him.

If there is one thing that the Swiss treat with the respect that it deserves, it is money. To the Swiss, money is not something to be spent, but a commodity in its own right. It's the only place where money is not just a means to an end, but both the means and the end. And it is because of this that they make the arrangements that they do.

A safe deposit box in most countries is a place to store valuables so that the light-fingered fraternity can't get their hands on them. But should anything happen to the owner of the safe deposit, it is comparatively simple to obtain a court order whereby a responsible official can gain access to the deposit. I had £75,000-worth of Max's money, and there wasn't a single place in England where I could hide it. I owned safe deposit boxes in five different places at home, but knowing this, Max had only to exterminate me and set in motion the processes of law, and he would have had every one opened inside twenty-four hours.

But the Swiss don't go along with this at all. There you can rent safe deposits that can only be opened by the owner. And if the owner drops dead somewhere along the line, that safe deposit will remain closed until the crack of doom.

Needless to say, I owned one of these. In it, over my years in the service, I had deposited various documents and photographs that I considered necessary to insure my peaceful old age. After each job, I'd leave a small memento in Geneva, a little something that could effectively screw Max if he had come up with any bright ideas as to how important I was.

I hadn't been in Geneva for five years, but I knew that my box would still be there, untouched and inviolate. I also knew that only I, in person, could open it, and only then with the help of Gustave Holbecker. Because the Swiss are very careful. To obviate the possibility of anyone trying to impersonate a safe deposit owner, you can make it a rule at the bank that there must be two signatories for access to the deposit. One of them is the actual owner, the other is a local man of some standing, a lawyer, a doctor, or even a town councillor. Gustave was my man, a self-important little lawyer who had lived and worked in Geneva all his life. Unless he accompanied me to the bank, and identified me as being the man I said I was, I couldn't get into my deposit box even if the man in charge had been my own brother. For this small service I paid him a fee of £10 every time he came to the bank with me. He had about two hundred and fifty other clients for whom he performed the same service and, all in all, he probably made more money out of it than he did with his lawyering.

I waited for him outside the bank, clutching my briefcase like a mother with her firstborn. He bustled up to me through the lunchtime promenaders and looked at me shrewdly for a moment through rimless spectacles, while he sorted through his card index mind and identified me.

"Mr. Smith. It has been a long time," he said when he was satisfied that I was me.

"How are you, Gustave?" I said.

He spread his fat little hands.

"Business is not improving," he said. "But then neither is it deteriorating. And you?"

"So, so," I said, lying like a veteran.

"You wish access to your safe deposit?" he said.

I replied that I did and we went into the bank.

First we signed forms, then we waited while records were checked. They all knew Gustave as well as they knew their own families, but the whole rigmarole of identification was carried out as though he hadn't been near the place for ten years.

Finally, after much bowing and hand rubbing, we were escorted to the elevator. As an extra security measure, the elevators are constructed so that only one person at a time can get into them. I squeezed myself and my briefcase into this vertical coffin, and creaked downwards into the bowels of the earth. The door was opened at the bottom and I was greeted by another bank official who examined my pass and made me confirm that Gustave was in my party. Then the elevator was sent back up for Gustave, while we both stood there waiting. A minute later, Gustave joined us and the examination process was repeated.

Gustave and I were shown into a small room with a table and a couple of chairs. Two minutes later the bank official placed my safe deposit box in front of me. He bowed and walked out, and I heard the lock on the door click into place behind him. Gustave and I were now locked in the room and a "No Entry" sign was flashing outside the door. Until I rang the bell to be let out, Jesus Christ himself couldn't have come in.

There was a six number combination lock on the box and for one frightening moment I thought I had forgotten it. I spun the first four numbers, hesitated for a couple of seconds groping around in the past, and then it came to me. The lock clicked back and I opened the box. I would have liked to have spent a little time looking through the papers just to remind myself how much I hated Max, but it was a luxury I didn't really need to indulge in, so I let it ride. I opened the briefcase, and while Gustave stared fixedly at the opposite wall, his fat little face completely expressionless, I transferred the contents into the box. It was a tight squeeze, even after I'd taken out three thousand dollars for petty cash. But I managed, and I slammed the lid shut and spun the combination to relock it.

Then I pressed the bell and a bank official took the box away. As I watched it disappear from my sight, I felt like a mother must feel as she loses her only child.

We went up in the elevator one at a time, and upstairs I paid Gustave his fee. He shook me by the hand and puffed off to his next assignment. I settled the outstanding account for the safe deposit rental and paid up for the next ten years. I gave the brief-case to the doorman at the bank entrance and said I would pick it up later. Then I went shopping.

I'd arrived in Switzerland with the clothes that I stood up in, which included a badly torn cashmere overcoat. I went into Au Carneval de Venise in the Rue Montblanc, stripped down to the buff and bought half a dozen of everything from the skin outwards. I topped this sartorial binge with a new overcoat and, because I felt good, I made it vicuna this time. Then, feeling like Aristotle Onassis, I strolled back to my hotel. I hung a "Do not disturb" notice on the door and went to bed. I slept for eighteen hours straight.

It took Max three days to find me, which wasn't bad going, all things considered. Things had to come to the crunch eventually, and I didn't want to make it too difficult for the Service to locate me, so I spent most of those three days seated prominently outside a terrace restaurant on the main street.

In fact, I spotted them at the same time as they spotted me. I was enjoying my first bottle of Dom Perignon on the third morning, when I saw a small anonymous car pull up on the opposite side of the street. There was a hurried conversation between driver and passenger, then the passenger erupted from the car and dashed off to find the nearest telephone. The driver unfolded a newspaper and disappeared behind it.

I finished my champagne and paid the bill. I over-tipped outrageously and strolled back to the hotel slowly, so as not to make it too difficult for them. The Geneva office had never been too bright and I didn't imagine much would have changed in five years.

I settled my hotel bill before going upstairs to my room. There I packed and five minutes later when they exploded into my room, bristling with muscle, I was waiting for them. I believe they were sorry that I was so amenable. It had been a long, quiet year in Switzerland and they hadn't leaned on anyone for quite a time.

I was driven to the airport sandwiched between two men of the Swiss office. There I was handed over to two of the London men. They were a little nervous in case I started to scream that I was being kidnapped, so they stuck very close and didn't really relax until we were airborne. On the plane there didn't seem much point in trying to start a conversation, so I sat quietly for the hour and a bit to London.

Max pulled strings with immigration and customs and I was escorted into a car, straight off the plane. My suitcase came with me. Max wasn't going to have any customs officer rummaging through *that*.

We drove straight to the Farm. It's a place thirty miles out of London which the Service has owned for more years than I can remember. I believe things do get grown there, and there are certainly cows and suchlike wandering around. But the real business goes on in the farmhouse itself and, whatever it is, it's not agricultural. The Farm exists as a place to hide people, as a place to keep people, and sometimes as a place to kill people.

I was shown straight into the interrogation room, a tiled room with a drain let into the centre of the floor, containing a table and two chairs. Max was sitting behind the table, while beside him stood an anonymous looking member of the Heavy Squad. I didn't see the one behind the door, but I knew he was there. The point was emphasised a moment later when I felt a cold ring of steel pressed into the base of my skull. But I was giving nobody any arguments. I stood perfectly still and allowed the ball to stay in their court.

"Sit down," said Max.

The man standing beside Max moved round the table and dragged the chair into position for me. The one with the gun eased me into it.

"I'm going to kill you," said Max.

"Again?" I queried.

He ignored this.

"Before I do, though, I want some answers."

"I'll bet you do," I said.

"What was the meaning of the message you sent me?"

"About whistling for your money?"

"You said the plan wouldn't pay off. Why?"

"Because it won't."

"You told Berat?"

"No."

"Then why?"

So, I told him. I told him how I had started to smell out his plan and how I didn't like the stink. I described how I had stopped on my way down to the airfield and added a note of my own in the end of the notebook. It had been a simple note, one which I could have torn out before handing the book to Berat had I felt my suspicions were groundless. But they hadn't been, my interview with Max just prior to the rendezvous had proved that. Berat would have seen the note when he examined the book more carefully. It was a short note, four words only. I quoted them to Max verbatim.

"This is a plant," I said.

There was a long silence after this. Max sat there bidding a fond farewell to his grand design. Then he shrugged manfully and got to his feet.

"There's not much point in killing you then," he said.

I agreed.

"Give me the money and we'll call it quits," he said.

"No money," I said.

The room grew cold suddenly.

"The money," he said.

I shook my head again.

"My expenses have gone up," I said. "When I'm shot at by my own side and have to shoot people in return, then I come very high."

"How high?" said Max, knowing the answer.

"About seventy-five thousand pounds high," I said.

He looked at me steadily for a moment, his eyes as dry as dust. Then he nodded to the man standing behind me. For one blinding moment I thought I had overplayed my hand. Then I felt a quick, sharp jab low down on the side of my neck and, before I was able to climb to my feet, my mind slipped sideways and skidded off into the unknown.

When I came round it was purely a temporary arrangement. There was a large man in a white coat who I later learned was called Bruno. He asked me questions which I answered truthfully. With the stuff he pumped into me, I couldn't have done otherwise. I told him all about the safe deposit, and about the Swiss laws of access and about Gustave and about every other damn thing there was.

After these bouts of question and answer I was helped off to sleep again. Max's face appeared occasionally during these short periods of semi-consciousness, but that may only have been a hallucination.

My main hope now is that I can get out of this place before they yank my teeth. The ones I've got aren't anything to write home about, but at least they belong to me, and I prefer them to the National Health choppers which would be all I'd be able to afford on the outside.

Because whichever way you slice it, Max is going to have to get his money back. It's my only way out of this snake pit. The delicate piece of the operation comes in judging just how long

I can keep him sweating before I throw in the towel. I'm rather proud of myself that I've hung on as long as I have, what with the food they give you here and Bruno's happy needle.

But other urges are starting to obtrude. I want to see Mary again before she forgets I exist. I want to drink a bottle of good wine, and I want to feel the sun on my back. Unimportant things in themselves perhaps, especially when balanced against the trouble Max must be having from upstairs, but they are beginning to weigh heavier in the scales. By the end of the week they'll probably be sufficient to swing the balance the other way. Then I shall have to tell Bruno to contact Max.

Max and I will have a little talk, and I will try to convince him to let me hang on to a couple of thousand quid to cover my expenses. He'll scream a little, but he'll have to wear it. Then will come a short, swift trip to Geneva, and that will be an end of it.

The trouble is, that after I have seen him and our financial transactions have been sorted out, he'll have his hooks deep enough into my hide to give him a pretty strong edge should he decide he wants me for anything in the future. If he starts waving my medical file around, I'm dead and buried. And with an edge like this, it doesn't take three guesses to know who Max will come to the next time he's got a particularly nasty job to be done. And knowing Max as I do, if he's got an edge, he'll use it like a hopped up axe fiend.

So perhaps I'll hang on longer than the end of the week. After all, I don't actually need my teeth to eat the muck they hand out here and the board and lodging is free. But if Bruno comes at me with that needle again, I'll shove it into him so far he'll need major surgery to get it out.

It's late now, and there's a fellow along the passage screaming like the maniac that he undoubtedly is. But the bed isn't uncomfortable and Bruno removed my strait-jacket half an hour ago. I think sleep is in order, and we'll review the whole situation again tomorrow.

FOREIGN EXCHANGE

PUBLISHER'S NOTE

This book was originally published in the United Kingdom in 1968 and reflects the cultural and sexual attitudes, language, and politics of the period. ... as well as the punctuation and spelling.

CHAPTER ONE

Sometime back I read an article which said that London was the most swinging city in the world. I don't think the man who wrote the article had ever been to London or, if he had, he hadn't been to my part of it. My part doesn't swing, it just hangs there. I also read that London was timeless. If, by timeless, the writer meant that everything stays the same uniform shade of grey, then I can go along with him. Grey people in grey buildings, living grey little lives. And the greyest life of them all is mine.

It had been a long, hard winter. Expenses had been running at their customary level of stupidity, with income limping along in the rear falling further and further behind. And now it was Monday. It's a rotten stinking day, Monday. And just lately I've started to believe that every day is Monday, even Friday. Everyone who could had spent the weekend away from London, leaving it to the grey people. Being a founder member, I had stayed with them.

Mary, the only light in the murk of my existence, had recently taken up horse riding. She would disappear each weekend into the country, there to exercise her urges on the back of a horse. She had started by asking me to come along with her. If she could learn to ride, then so could I, was her attitude. But after making a number of fatuous excuses I was finally forced to admit that while horses for betting on are fair enough, horses for riding on scare the living daylights out of me. Their superior bloody attitude intimidates me, and the distance from the ground one is required to perch is, to my way of thinking, suicidal. So our long weekends doing nothing except each other had come to an abrupt end. Booted and spurred, she would drive away on a Saturday morning and return, sore and satisfied, late on Sunday night. I was too pigheaded to want to hear about her equine prowess, or how the nineteen-year-old riding instructor had developed a serious crush on her. So I left her alone on Sunday evenings, and gradually my weekends deteriorated into a slough of boredom. This one had been no exception.

Saturday had been shopping in the morning and 'Grandstand' on the box in the afternoon. About six I had thought for a moment about taking myself out to dinner. Then I had decided that I couldn't be bothered. I had ended up with bacon and eggs and more television.

Sunday had been Sunday papers and a lunchtime drink in a Chelsea pub. At this pub, the thing to do was to drink cider and sit on the pavement. I drank brown ale, sitting on a bar stool with my elbows in a pool of stale beer. A hundred years ago I had sat on the pavement to drink my cider, but now cider gave me a headache and the pavement aggravated my piles.

Sunday afternoon had been television again, and Sunday evening another pub. This pub was supposed to be chic, but there weren't any chic people in London, and to me it was just another pub where beer was two-pence a pint dearer to help pay for the regency striped curtains.

That had been my weekend in the swingingest city in the world and now, rejuvenated by all that excitement, I joined the commuters on the way to the office.

My office lies between a coffee bar and a strip joint just off Old Crompton Street. This is in Soho, the 'wicked' section of the

Swinging City. To a fourteen-year-old it may be wicked. To me it's just plain nasty.

Sometime over the weekend some joker had peed through the letter box all over the entrance hall. But this was a common occurrence and I didn't even notice the smell any more. Occasionally I'd indulge in flights of fancy that ran to setting some sort of jaw toothed trap inside the letter box. But, with my luck, if I'd hooked anything I would have been arrested for causing grievous bodily harm.

I avoided the fourth stair, which could break the leg of the unwary, and opened the outer door of my office. Miss Roberts was already there, rattling the teacups. She smiled at me as I came in.

'Good morning, Mr. Smith,' she said. 'Did you have a nice weekend?'

I told her that I had spent a quiet weekend.

'We went to the coast,' she said brightly.

Miss Roberts had been working for me for three years, and I had never asked her who 'we' included. It couldn't have been a boyfriend. If it wasn't for the fact that she wore a skirt and used the 'Ladies' on the third floor, I would have taken money that she was a fellow. She had a trim little moustache and her voice could best be described as a full-toned baritone. But under this formidable exterior lurked an excited young girl of motherly inclinations. She was kind to the point of embarrassment, and she looked after Stubbs and me like a protective hen. Stubbs shared the offices with me. We each used the outer office and the services of Miss Roberts, and we each had our own room leading off it. While I ran a sometime private investigation business, Stubbs ran a sometime theatrical agency. Occasionally this would cause the outer office to be graced with expectant young female hopefuls who had somehow been recommended to Stubbs as a man who could further their artistic careers. If he did further their careers, it must have been straight into the arms of another agent, as I never saw the same girl twice.

As for Stubbs himself, I saw little of him. Three or four weeks could go by without us bumping into each other. On the odd occasions when we did meet, the encounters were overlaid with a subtle form of embarrassment, due to us both knowing everything about each other, courtesy of Miss Roberts. If I knew that he hadn't paid his share of Miss Roberts' salary for two weeks, I also knew that he knew that I'd been served with a writ for nonpayment of my car instalments. We were both dead losses at our chosen professions, and we both knew that the other was aware of it. The sensible thing to have done would have been to slap him on the back and ask him out for a beer. That way we could have cried in it together and to hell with the embarrassment. But I never did, and neither did he. So we went our separate ways, tied together by Miss Roberts and our common failure to scratch a decent living.

All this made it quite a surprise when Miss Roberts followed me into my office, clutching the first of an endless supply of cups of tea.

'Mr. Stubbs would like to see you,' she said.

My first thought was that he wanted to borrow money. Then I remembered that he knew me as well as I knew him, and he would have been aware of the futility of such an idea.

'Is he here now?' I asked.

'Yes, and he'd like to see you just as soon as you can spare him a moment.'

'Wheel him in then,' I said. He was the one requesting the interview, so let him come to me. While Miss Roberts went to fetch him, I took off my coat and hung it up. There was no mail, so I took a couple of old reports from my drawer and spread them around on top of my desk. If he was going to ask for my time, as opposed to money, I wanted to create the impression that it was valuable.

There was a tap on the door and he came. He's a small, birdlike man, with neat precise movements. But this morning it was different; his movements were sluggish and his feathers bedraggled.

'Good of you to spare me a moment. John,' he said.

So he did want something from me. He'd never called me anything but Mr. Smith before.

'Sit down, Harvey,' I said. I, too, could use Christian names. He sat and plucked nervously at his trouser crease for a moment. He was on a hook and, being ignorant, I couldn't help him off. I waited.

'How's business?' he asked finally.

'Just fine, Harvey,' I said. 'You?'

'Good,' he said. 'Very good.'

Having lied our way through the overture, he opened the first movement.

'There's a girl,' he said. And there he stopped.

There was nothing I could say, so I just sat and tried to look interested and intelligent at the same time. The former wasn't difficult, I *was* interested. I'd long had Stubbs tagged as a homosexual. As for looking intelligent, I've been told that if I frown a little and can manage a slight squint, the effect is passable.

He coughed twice, cleared his throat, and twitched in his chair.

'There's a girl,' he said again. I gave him all the help I could.

'Yes, Harvey?'

'There's a girl,' he said for the third time. But from there on in he needed no help. Once he stepped over the edge, there was no stopping him.

'She came to see me four months ago. Perhaps you saw her in the office? Pretty little thing with blonde hair, blue eyes and big knockers.' They all had blonde hair, blue eyes and big knockers, but I kept my mouth shut.

'Not much talent, but quite a nice singing voice and beautifully built. I took her on to my books. I liked the kid as a matter of fact. I told her she weren't no Marilyn Monroe, likewise she weren't no Barbra Streisand. But I said that, handled properly, she could no doubt earn herself a fair to middling share of scratch on the number two type circuits. She didn't seem to mind. Seems she knew about the Monroe-Streisand bit, and all she wanted was a small forty pound a week job, and to hell with her name in neon.'

Right then I could have done with a small forty pound a week job myself, but Stubbs was in full flow now and I didn't interrupt.

'So I booked her for a one-nighter down a pub in the City. Sort of dummy run. She went down fine and I fixed her three or four more dates on the same circuit. She weren't earning no forty a week, but then she weren't on Assistance either. I took to visiting the places she played. The neighbourhood's a bit crumbum, and so I'd take her back to her pad after she'd done her show.'

There was a pause. I jumped in.

'And?' I said.

'And nothing,' he said. 'Never set foot inside the front door.'

'But she's pregnant and she wants you to pay for the operation,' I suggested.

Stubbs looked at me wide-eyed. If I'd just promulgated the theory of relativity, I couldn't have impressed him more.

'How did you know?' he asked.

'I guessed,' I said. 'You don't think she's pregnant?'

'She could have fifteen buns in the oven for all I know,' he said. 'But one thing's for sure—I'm not the baker.'

'What does she say when you tell her that?'

'Nothing,' he said. 'She says nothing at all. She just smiles at me in a special way.'

'Special how?'

'Like one of those adverts for insurance where the bird's looking at her husband who's just taken out a bloody great policy. Like "Drop dead, but don't make too much noise about it".'

I know the look well.

'What do you want me to do, Harvey?' I said.

'Go and see her. Tell her it's Harvey Stubbs she's got her hooks into, not Lew and Leslie Grade. Ten per cent of what my clients earn doesn't add up to two hundred guinea abortions.'

'Is that what she's asking?'

'She tells me she's got the quack all picked out,' he said.

'For two hundred guineas, he's no quack.'

'He is if he manages to get *my* baby out of that cheap hooker.'

'Have you tried telling her to go jump in the lake?'

'Sure I told her,' said Stubbs. 'She just smiles that smile some more and says she'll sick the law on to me.'

'There's no law against poking,' I said.

'There is when you poke a fifteen-year-old,' he said.

He continued fast, before I could comment. 'So help me, she looks twenty-two,' he said. 'And I didn't anyway.'

'She's got quite a case,' I said.

'Then why doesn't she lay it before the guy who packed it?'

'Perhaps she has,' I said.

He thought about this for a moment. Then his eyes widened. 'Clip us both,' he said.

'Why just the two of you? If she'd like to spread her net a bit, there's no limit to the number of suckers she can con.'

'There is as far as I'm concerned,' he said. 'I don't have no two hundred guineas, and if I did, I wouldn't hand it over to her.'

'What would you hand over?' I said.

'You mean to make a deal?'

I nodded.

'With that cheap whore,' he said. 'Why should I let her screw me?'

'She already has. We've got to make sure the screw isn't too tight.'

He thought about this for a moment; then he came up with an alternative.

'You wouldn't like to lean on her a little, would you?'

My leaning days were long gone. Not since I quit the Service had I leaned on anybody. At least, not physically. I told him so.

'How big a deal?' he said finally.

'How much can you afford?'

'Nothing,' he said. 'But I could scrape up twenty-five at a pinch.'

Even I could have managed twenty-five. Business must have been worse than I thought.

'I'll put it to her,' I said.

'How will you put it?'

'I'll tell her if she lets you off the hook, she can have twenty-five guineas.'

'Pounds,' he said.

I ignored the interruption. 'If she doesn't want to accept it, you'll fight.'

'You bet,' he said. 'I'll have her teeth knocked down her throat.'

'I didn't mean fight fight. I meant legal fight.'

'Oh,' he said. I thought he looked disappointed. He had a nasty streak in him, I decided. Funny I hadn't noticed it before.

'Let's have her name and address and I'll go see her,' I said.

He hesitated for a moment. 'About your fee?'

I decided to be magnanimous, mainly because, whatever fee I named, I wouldn't be getting it.

'No fee,' I said. 'Perhaps you can do me a favour one day.'

I was going to be pretty hard pressed on the day I needed a favour from Harvey Stubbs, but it never hurt to make a person beholden to you, especially if that person shared the same office.

Maybe one week I wouldn't be able to find my half of the rent. Then I could remind him of how big I'd been. Apart from that, I was quite interested in taking a look at the girl who had managed to con a sharp operator like Stubbs with one of the oldest tricks in the book.

'Her name is Anne,' he said. 'Anne Ballard. Flat 625, Chelsea Park Towers.'

It figured. I knew the block of flats well. It was known in the trade as The Rabbit Warren. There were ten floors with fifty one-room apartments on each floor. You can't really *live* in a one room apartment, but you can do just about everything else. And that pretty well covered it as far as The Rabbit Warren was concerned.

I brushed aside Stubbs' effusive thanks, telling him to save them until I was able to do some good. He parted with a twenty-five guinea cheque like a man parting with his eye teeth, but I promised to let him have it back if I wasn't successful. He seemed to forget the fact that if I wasn't able to make her take it, he was liable to be lumbered with one for eight times the amount. But I knew how he felt as he watched me fold the cheque and put it in my notecase.

He thanked me again, and again I reminded him not to be premature. As he left the office, his movements were neat and precise, and he was birdlike once more. As far as he was concerned, the ball had been passed out of his court, even if only temporarily. I hoped for his sake he hadn't misplaced his trust. At least I had discovered he'd got balls, which was something I hadn't known before. And having made the discovery, I found myself almost liking him.

I didn't believe for one second that he hadn't poked the girl. People just aren't like that. If a girl sleeps around, people oblige her, especially people like Harvey Stubbs. Anyway, even the sloppiest con artist isn't going to try to palm the offspring on to a fellow who hasn't even been there.

✤   ✤   ✤

I hadn't visited The Rabbit Warren since a small affair I'd had going for me about five years ago. It hadn't changed. The porters still studiously ignored everyone who came in or out, minding nobody's business but their own. The tenants preferred it that way. I rode one of the elevators up to the sixth, and then walked down what seemed like half a mile of dark corridor until I located 625. I rang the front door bell and, for good measure, I knocked as well.

A girl answered the door and right about there I started to think there was something seriously wrong with Harvey Stubbs. She didn't look twenty-two, she didn't even look fifteen. She was about ten.

'Yes?' she said primly.

'Miss Ballard, please,' I said.

'She's gone to the shops. Would you like to wait?'

She stood back, holding the door open for me and, although I should have known better, I walked in. The apartment was neat and clean. There were two divans, both made up as settees, and the sort of anonymous furniture one finds in multi-apartment blocks.

'Would you like to sit down?' she said.

I sat down and the child stood four feet away from me and regarded me solemnly for what seemed like six long months.

'Anne usually asks gentlemen callers if they'd like a drink. Would you like a drink?'

'Very much,' I said. She smiled and trotted off through the door which I knew from memory led to the tiny kitchen. Some people have the happy knack of being able to communicate with children. I even have trouble communicating with my own age group, and anyone below the age of twenty might as well be from a different species, so vast is our lack of communication.

A couple of minutes later the little charmer reappeared carrying a glass full of what I took to be gin or vodka, but in fact turned out to be water.

I sipped it and made appreciative noises. Then I decided that, as I was supposed to be working, I might as well work.

'Does your mother have many gentlemen callers?' I said, feeling like a bastard.

'I don't know,' she said. 'She lives in Barnsley.'

'Miss Ballard is your ... ?' I let the question hang.

'Anne's my sister,' she said. 'I've lived with her ever since Mum ran off with the telly man and Dad went inside for doing him over.'

As a potted family biography, it seemed to cover all the salient facts. I sipped my water again and tried to think of something amusing to say.

'It's been a nice day,' I managed finally.

'Very nice,' she said.

'It was terrible yesterday,' I sparkled.

'Awful,' she agreed.

And there the conversation ground to a halt, where it remained for five minutes until Anne Ballard arrived.

She came in behind a parcel of groceries which hid her face from me. So I looked at the rest of her, as she headed straight for the kitchen without being aware she had a gentleman caller. It was no hardship at all, and I started to hope that her face wouldn't let the rest of her down. She swore fluently in the kitchen as she dropped something on her foot, and her little sister didn't bat an eyelid. Then she came out of the kitchen and saw me sitting there clutching my glass of water.

'Hi!' she said.

'Miss Ballard?'

'That's why you're here, isn't it?'

She had wide blue eyes, a small nose and a mouth that looked good enough to make you want to be eaten.

'I gave him a drink,' said the little girl.

'So I see,' she said, looking at my glass. 'Tell me what you want and I may offer you another.'

'My name is Smith. John Smith,' I started.

She grinned, showing perfect teeth.

'I'd hate to be with you when you're signing a hotel register,' she said. 'And you can have that drink, whatever you want.'

She took my glass and disappeared into the kitchen again. My main thought about now was that if Stubbs hadn't slept with her, he must be queer after all; and if he had, he was a dirty rotten bastard. If this girl was the sleeping around kind, there must have been a queue from here to Piccadilly Circus every night. And I knew who was going to be first in line next time. But even while leching in my mind, other wheels were clicking. She couldn't be just fifteen, that was for sure. And I'd just about decided that Stubbs had got the whole thing screwed up, or we were dealing with two different people, when she came back with my drink. This one looked like water, too, but it was vodka. And it was on the rocks, the way I like it. If it had been possible, she would have gone up a couple more notches in my estimation, but there wasn't room. She may have been no Barbra Streisand or Marilyn Monroe, but she didn't need to be from where I was sitting.

'I suppose Harvey sent you,' she said, dragging me back to earth with a jerk.

'He didn't send me,' I said. 'I came of my own free will.'

'Harvey Stubbs nevertheless?' she said.

'Nevertheless.'

'I saw your name on the door the day I went to see Harvey,' she said by way of explanation. 'Darling, slip downstairs and get me some cigarettes from the machine.'

She handed her sister some money and the little girl left dutifully. Then she sat down in the armchair opposite me and crossed her legs neatly and elegantly. They were good legs, very good.

'It's your move,' she said.

I lifted my eyes and cleared my throat.

'Harvey thinks you may have got a mistaken impression as to his earning capacity,' I said. 'He is quite incapable of finding the sum you mentioned.'

She didn't bat an eyelid. 'Tell him if he leaves me alone, he's off the hook.'

I didn't say anything. There didn't seem to be anything to say.

'Surprise, surprise,' she said finally. 'The whore has got a heart of gold.'

Now that I'd done what I came for, I couldn't think of any excuse for staying around, so I made movements preparatory to getting to my feet.

'Aren't you intrigued?' she said.

I nodded. 'Very.'

'Shall I tell you something?'

If it meant I could stay a little longer she could have told me anything. And I *was* intrigued. I subsided again, regretting that I'd downed the last of my drink. She must have been a thought-reader. 'I'll get you another drink,' she said, and took my glass and disappeared into the kitchen again. I looked around the flat from where I was sitting. It was neat and tidy, and somehow the anonymity of the furniture was dispelled by the small personal possessions that lay around. There were a couple of large teddy bears, one on each bed, and a few snapshots of the two of them on holiday. One snap was tucked in the corner of a picture frame holding the photograph of a weak chinned man about forty-five. If this was Dad, I couldn't see him doing over a disinterested boy scout, let alone an amourously inclined telly man.

She returned with my fresh drink and sat down again.

'Are you married?' she said.

I shook my head. 'I was. But not any longer.'

'What do you do for sex?'

'The same as everyone else,' I said.

'I don't mean that. I mean, do you chase nineteen year old girls?'

'I'm too old,' I lied.

'That makes you about the only man in London who is. This flat is a bloody citadel, where I defend my honour nightly. A man walks me to the front door—and let battle commence. I've talked to them, argued with them, wrestled with them. I've even banged one on the head with a bottle. Because I sing in a couple of clubs and live alone, I'm supposed to be easy meat. I'm not knocking sex, I like it. But it's got to be on my terms and when *I* want it. I'm sick of everything in trousers between the ages of seventeen and seventy behaving like a stag in rut just because I'm polite and don't bang them in the mouth when they start to leer.'

'You're not pregnant?' I asked.

'I'm not that stupid,' she said. 'Neither am I fifteen years old.'

I grinned, trying to make it look avuncular and not like a leer.

'I didn't think you were.'

'But it works,' she said. 'Tell a man you're only fifteen and you need a two hundred guinea abortion and it's amazing how quickly his blood pressure goes down.'

'Harvey Stubbs was persistent?'

'Harvey Stubbs was a bastard,' she said. 'He was the one I had to use the bottle on.'

'Bully for Harvey,' I said.

There was a pause.

'Satisfied?' she said finally.

I took that as a signal that I'd outstayed my time. I swallowed my drink and clambered to my feet.

'I'll tell Harvey if he lays off, he's got nothing to worry about.'

She stood up. 'But I don't want to see him around here again,' she said.

'You won't,' I said. Then I suddenly remembered the cheque. I fished it out of my pocket and showed it to her.

'Want it?'

She shook her head. 'He probably needs it more than I do.'

She followed me to the door. Just before she opened it, she looked at me steadily for a beat.

'What *do* you do for sex?' she asked.

'I get by.'

'You're not every girl's dream of home,' she said. 'But I imagined you did. Come and hear me sing one night.'

'Where?'

'Ask Harvey. He's still my agent, even if he is a bastard.'

She opened the door and I nearly collided with kid sister, who was just coming in. The little girl smiled brightly at me as she slipped past me into the flat.

'Apart from anything else,' said Anne. 'This is a one-roomed flat.'

'Yes,' I said.

She closed the door quietly behind me and I retraced my way along the corridors back to earth.

'I met some competition today,' I said. Mary looked up from her scrambled eggs.

'Competition for whom?'

'You.'

'You're frightening me to death,' she said, as she resumed eating.

Mary is the lovely, leggy blonde with whom I have my arrangement. It's not much of an arrangement; I'm in love with her, I think. She feels sorry for me, I believe. She has the casual elegance of the model, combined with a devastating charm that has been known to stun the most hardened buyers. But underneath her professional shell she is as soft as marshmallow, the gentlest, warmest thing I've ever snuggled up to.

'You're not the only fish in the sea,' I said.

'I am in yours,' she said, not even looking up. 'No other fish would put up with you.'

'I was led to believe that if I cared to make an advance, it would not be unkindly received,' I said.

'You were conned.'

She shoveled up her last mouthful of scrambled egg and, getting to her feet, she headed for the kitchen. She limped heavily due to an altercation she had had with her horse that weekend.

'Your leg's going to be black tomorrow,' I said.

'So's your eye if you don't stop throwing up your girlfriends in my face.'

This was the first time she had ever intimated that there might be a shade of jealousy in her and I felt unreasonably pleased. Like the idiot I often am, I pursued the idea.

'I'll bet she doesn't waste her weekends climbing all over horses and nearly breaking her leg.'

Mary rattled a couple of dishes in the sink. 'I bet she doesn't waste her evenings feeding a *schnorrer* like you.' Being in the rag trade her speech could at times lapse into the Jewish vernacular, especially when she was feeling angry. And I still didn't leave it alone.

'At least now I might have someone with whom to spend those long, wet weekends.'

Mary suddenly appeared in the arch that led to the kitchen. 'You spend one long wet minute with her and you can go somewhere else to get laid.'

'I don't come here to get laid.'

'So you keep telling me, but you give a pretty good imitation of it three nights a week.'

I realised I had overstepped the mark, so I tried some back pedaling. 'I'm joking,' I said, trying to look contrite.

'You're not,' she said. 'You're trying to needle me. And you're making a bloody good job of it.'

'Are you needled?'

'Yes, I am,' she said, and flounced back into the kitchen.

I gathered up a couple of plates and followed her in. 'I'm sorry,' I said, trying to nuzzle the back of her neck. She brought her head back sharply, catching me on the bridge of the nose.

'Ouch!' I yelled.

'Serve you right,' she said. 'You're a sadist.'

'You don't bash a sadist,' I said. 'You allow him to bash you.'

My eyes were watering, but I made more of it than was necessary, and her face started to soften into the gentle expression I loved.

'Did I hurt you?' she asked.

'Yes, you did.'

She put her arms around my neck and kissed me on the nose. 'There,' she said. 'All better.'

Then she pulled back a little and looked at me with her wide, grey eyes. '*Did* you meet a girl today?'

'As a matter of fact, I did. Professionally, of course.'

'Yours or hers?'

'Mine. I thought she was a con artist. Turned out she wasn't.'

'What was she?'

'Just a girl alone in the city trying to protect her virtue.'

'I can feel for her,' said Mary. 'It's not easy.' She walked back into the living-room and started to unzip her dress.

'I'm not complaining,' I said. 'But isn't it a little early for bed.' It was seven thirty.

'I've got a date,' she said, stepping out of her dress.

I watched her walk over to one of the wall cupboards and fish around for another dress.

'Have we got time to...?'

She didn't even let me finish. 'No. He'll be here in half an hour.'

I felt like reminding her that the day I could last half an hour, someone should give me a medal. But she was way ahead of me.

'It'll take me twenty minutes to put a face on, and you know how terrible I look after we've made love.'

I thought she looked marvelous after we'd made love. She looked warm and soft and defenceless. But obviously tonight's date didn't require her to look warm or soft, so I started looking round for my shoes which I'd taken off as soon as I had arrived.

I didn't ask her who her date was with. I never did. As long as I wasn't prepared to offer her any more in our relationship than I did already, I was in no position to pry into what she did when she wasn't with me. It was a pretty unsatisfactory arrangement, but it was the best I could manage. Besides, while our affair was kept on the casual side, I wasn't forcing her into making any decision about me which could have backfired and blown up in my face. Because whichever way you sliced it, I was no gift. I was pushing forty (not too hard) and I was constantly on my uppers. I was losing my hair and fighting a constant battle against overweight. My sexual prowess ranged wildly between the indifferent and the downright bad. So why put this lovely creature in a position where she was going to have to decide that I was all, or nothing at all? I wanted to, but I was scared of the way she would decide.

I found my shoes and jammed my feet into them. I could see her reflection in the mirror on the wall as she rummaged through the wardrobe. Brown flesh and white lace, and I felt myself weakening fast. So, I got out of the place before discretion really took a belting and I asked her to marry me.

She called me back when I was half way down the stairs. She was standing at the door to her apartment, having slipped on a housecoat.

'I'll be home by eleven,' she said.

'Not a very heavy date?'

'You're my only heavy date,' she said. 'Idiot that I am.'

She kissed me and shut the door in my face.

❖ ❖ ❖

On my way home I bought an evening paper. There was the usual crisis on the front page along with a picture of the Prime Minister gazing blandly from a two-column photograph. He'd just made a speech in which he had said that we must all put our shoulders to the wheel, increase our productivity and cut down on our spending. If I cut down any on my spending I'd starve to death. Beneath the photograph, which was as inspiring as a plate of cold custard, was another story about how fifteen hundred car workers were out on strike because one of their number had said 'fuck' to the foreman and been given the sack.

The Antonov story was on page four. Gregori Antonov had been sentenced to fifteen years. About bloody time too, I thought. I'd been out of the Service for five years, and I'd been working on the case a year before that. Gregori Antonov, sometime Ukranian, sometime Albanian, sometime any other nationality that took his fancy; a forty-five year old agent-cum-con-artist *par excellence.* He had arrived in this country ten years ago and armed with unlimited funds and a black-mailing turn of mind, had proceeded to screw or buy classified information from any or everybody who could lay the remotest claim to know anything of value. It took the Service four years to realise he was at work, and then, it seems, another six to do anything about it.

I read the story casually at first. Then I read it again. Nobody knew better than I did that the Service was capable of making a balls-up. Indeed, when I had been working for them five years ago, I'd been personally involved in, and sometimes responsible for, some monumental cock-ups. It was one of these hideous miscalculations that had caused me to pack it all in. Even today, with five years of comparative poverty behind me, I'd still break out in a cold sweat at some of the things I'd done in the cause of patriotism and sixteen hundred pounds a year. So I had no illusions about the Service. But six years to pin down one man seemed to be going it a bit, even for Max.

Dear Max! I'd managed not to think about him for nearly six months now, and was becoming pleasantly accustomed to the happy state. I hadn't clapped eyes on him since he had conned me into a triple cross involving a book of names, a Chinese Albanian by the name of Berat and a particularly murky shooting match in the wilds of Kent. After that I had been forced to hand him back a considerable sum of money in exchange for my release from a mental institution into which he'd had me thrown complete with certificate of insanity.

Perhaps he was no longer at the helm. Perhaps he'd met with a fatal accident. I rolled these thoughts around in my mind luxuriously for a moment. Then I thought: 'What the hell?' Somebody had to do the incredibly dirty work that went on just below the surface and, if you're going to work with mud, it's as well that you've got a muddy mind. Max was right for the job, his mind was like the bottom of a bog.

I put the Antonov story out of my mind. I donned my best blue worsted and a pint of after-shave, and drove down through the City to the pub where Anne Ballard was singing that night.

The place was really jumping. It took me three minutes to locate the bar through the smoke haze, and another five to elbow my way through to it. The noise was catastrophic; a mixture of laughter, shouting, chatter and yelling. I don't go much on the East End. It depresses me more than it should, but you have to hand it to them; when it comes to enjoying themselves they have no equal. I contrasted this place with some of my local pubs, usually decorated by pasty faced boys or girls—one couldn't be sure—who only raised their nasal voices above a whisper to insult the barman. Here, the men looked like men, and the women looked the way a woman was supposed to look—feminine. Most of the customers in the place would have put a boot in your face as soon as look at you, but they were off duty now and having a ball. If they knocked their birds about when they got home, that was their business; here in public they mostly treated them with a courtesy that unfortunately went out with Edward VII.

I screamed my order to the barmaid and, when she shoved my drink at me and gobbled up my money, I managed to get it across to her that I wanted to know what time Anne Ballard came on. She glanced at the clock behind her.

'Five minutes,' she yelled. 'After the group.'

It was only then that I realised there was a group playing. Jammed on to an undersized stage against the far wall, four young tearaways were slamming away at electric guitars and singing lustily. I assumed they were singing, because their mouths kept opening and closing. I certainly couldn't hear them. I doubt if they could even hear themselves. If Anne Ballard had to make her living singing to this lot, my heart bled for her. I started to regret that I hadn't forced her to take Stubbs' twenty-five guinea cheque. But if I couldn't hear her, at least I could see her, so I started to shove my way over towards the stage so as to be ready when she appeared.

I reached the edge of the stage just as the group bellowed their last chord. Standing with my nose practically inside the bass guitar I could hear that they *had* been singing, and I felt a little sorry for them. But they didn't seem to mind. They took four quick bows to an audience who hadn't even been aware that they had started, let alone finished. Then they scrambled down off the stage and elbowed their way towards the bar in a wedge formation.

A man got up from a chair to go to the toilet and I managed to beat an old lady to it, dragging it up close to the stage. And then, quite suddenly, all noise in the bar ceased. If a Black Maria had driven in through the doors, the effect couldn't have been bettered. I looked around to see what the excitement was all about, and there was Anne Ballard. Unfortunately, she wasn't using the stage. There were some stairs leading up to a half landing on the far side of the pub, and that's where she was standing, a good fifty feet and five hundred people away from me. But even from there she looked good. She was wearing a simple little black dress and a black ribbon in her blonde hair. And that was all. No sequins, no jewelry, no trimmings. She looked about sixteen and as defenceless as a babe at a Mafia convention.

Somebody started to play the piano somewhere, and she picked up a hand mike and started to sing. I've got a tin ear myself; to me, Sinatra sounds like someone reading the weather report. But even I could tell that Anne Ballard certainly wasn't no Barbra Streisand. Neither was she a Shirley Bassey, nor a Peggy Lee. In short, she wasn't a singer. Her voice was quite full and, wisely, she spoke the words rather than tried to sing them. When she did actually go for a note, her aim was terrible. But it didn't matter a toss. She was virginal and sexy at the same time, and there's nothing more exciting than a sexy virgin. I can't even remember the numbers she sang. I think she murdered a couple of Cole Porters and badly mauled Jerome Kern. But the audience loved her. At least, the male half of them did. When occasionally somebody, usually a woman, made her voice heard above the singing, she was intimidated into silence by three hundred freezing looks or, in one case, by having a pint of beer emptied on to her lap.

I had started to push my way towards Anne as she started to sing, but I gave it up after a couple of yards. A very large man had glared at me and then stepped on my foot. He kept his foot where it was threatening to crush my instep if I moved a muscle, so I stayed where I was. Just before the end of her last number, Anne saw me. At least, I assumed it was me she smiled at and half raised her hand towards. My assumption was confirmed a second later as the large man removed his foot and glared at me again.

'Jammy bastard,' he hissed.

I grinned at him to show there were no hard feelings, but he was already staring at Anne again, anxious not to miss a moment of her act. I tried to analyse what it was that riveted the attention of every male in the room. Sure she was sexy, but so was the barmaid if it came to that. Certainly the barmaid had bigger knockers, and there was an open invitation in her shrewd eyes and in the wide open front of her silk blouse. Anne looked like everybody's sister, and you've got to be real kinky to fancy your sister. But fancy her they all did, in spite of the fact that in most cases the women they were with gave infinitely more promise of a successful and satisfactory roll. I decided that analysis was for the birds. Everybody fancied her and she fancied me. At least, she had hinted that way.

As I pushed my way through the crowd after she had finished, I felt a twinge of guilt about Mary. But she was out swinging somewhere and, being the bastard that I am, I never let my conscience get in the way of anything I want to do. And right now, I wanted to do Anne Ballard.

Another large man stood at the bottom of the stairs where she had disappeared after taking six bows to tumultuous applause. I started to mount the stairs, but he moved in front of me.

'Miss Ballard, please,' I said.

'Get lost!' he said.

'I think she's expecting me.'

He looked down at me from his six feet five inches. 'You've got to be kidding.'

'Business,' I said, playing it cool. He looked at me a moment longer, making up his mind.

'Get lost!' he repeated. To add a little weight to his argument he put a hand like a bunch of bananas flat on my chest.

I'm a mild mannered fellow by nature, and I dislike violence of any kind. Especially I dislike violence that is directed towards me. Putting it another way, I'm a coward. My standard opening gambit if someone threatens anything physical is to beat a hasty retreat. I had just about decided that is what I would do when Anne appeared at the top of the stairs. There's something of the little boy in every man, evincing itself in a desire to show off in front of the opposite sex. Here was this bruiser about to shove me heartily in the chest and, while normally I'd have allowed him to do just that, the fact that Anne was to be witness to the scene upset my metabolic balance to the extent that discretion and good sense took a jump out of the window.

When I was in the Service a number of hefty ex-army instructors had endeavoured to teach me judo and karate. They'd failed miserably. To me, a black belt was something for keeping up a dark pair of trousers. But two things I *had* learned. One was the way to kill a man with a stiff fingered jab in the side of the throat. But this seemed a little too drastic a ploy just to impress a bird. So, I used my other gem of knowledge in the noble art of self defence. Stated simply, this is never to give the other fellow an even break. Ninety-nine point nine per cent of the men who are going to use some muscle announce the fact beforehand. They threaten, they bully, and finally they take two seconds to weigh up the consequences of what they are about to start. Only then do they haul back and let fly. If you've got a nasty turn of mind like I have, this winding up period can be used to settle the argument before it starts.

The other fellow had also seen Anne and, like me, he was gripped with the urge to impress. I was five inches shorter than he and his hand on my chest hadn't felt any real resistance. He weighed up the pros and cons carefully and, conscious of his physical superiority, he decided to thump me. But, like I said, this took time. Long before he had reached his conclusions, I had stepped back a pace and kicked him hard where it would do the most good. As far as he was concerned all further thought or action became superfluous.

I turned apologetically to Anne as he reeled back clutching himself and being sick down the front of his suit. She was looking sorry for him.

'He was going to thump me,' I said.

'You should have told him you were a friend.'

'I did. I think that's why he was going to thump me.'

I was aware suddenly that there were three more large men, each of whom could have taken Cassius Clay with one hand tied behind his back. My childish satisfaction at having downed the bully in front of my girlfriend evaporated miraculously. One of the trio had now slipped on brass knuckles. I assumed he was the gaffer. I turned to him.

'He was going to thump me.'

'So are we,' he said companionably.

'He's a friend of mine,' said Anne quickly. 'Pete thought he was a trouble maker.'

The gaffer got a soppy look on his face as he turned to Anne. 'Is that right, Miss Ballard?' She nodded. He looked at me. Now he really wanted to work me over, but he managed a smile that nearly fractured his jaw.

'Sorry,' he said.

I decided to be magnanimous. 'A natural mistake,' I said. 'I'm glad to see that Miss Ballard is so well looked after.'

He managed to hold the smile in place, although his eyes were black with hate. 'We'd cripple anyone who upset Miss Ballard,' he said. I believed him implicitly.

Anne took my arm and devastated the three of them with a show of teeth. 'Thank you all so much,' she said. 'I hope Pete's ... I hope Pete is all right. Good night.'

'How did you like my act?' she said in the car.

'Very much.'

'Why?'

'It's a good act.'

'But I can't sing.'

'Joan Sutherland can,' I said. 'But she'd die in there.'

'I know it,' she said. 'So, what's so good about my act?'

'*You* are.'

'Sex?' she said.

I just managed to stop myself from saying 'Yes please', as I realised that she was still talking about her act.

'Virginal sex,' I said. 'It's a short supply commodity in these parts.'

She giggled, a sound which usually grates on my nerve ends, but which in this case only served to make me feel a little hornier than I did already.

'Where would you like to go?' I asked.

'Are you going to feed me?'

I had four pounds ten shillings in my pocket, but I took a chance. 'Of course.'

'You choose,' she said, settling back.

I chose Carlo's Place at the far end of the Fulham Road, where the food is good, the price right and the service friendly without being overwhelming. Halfway through the second course I began to deploy my troops.

'Who looks after your sister when you're working?' I asked, calling up the left flank.

'Nobody, she's quite happy on her own.'

'She lives with you all the time, does she?' I enquired, gently alerting the right flank.

'Friday to Tuesday she stays with our aunt in Camden Town.'

For one blinding moment I couldn't remember whether it was Monday or Tuesday. Then it came to me, and I called up the whole bloody army and advanced with banners unfurled.

'She's away tonight then?' I said. I tried to throw the line away casually, but my aim was way off. It landed between us with a thump that rattled the crockery.

She glanced up at me through eyelashes that just had to be false, but I knew they weren't. 'That's right,' she said.

I had to do something to change the conversation fast. I turned round and casually waved my arm at the waiter. The waiter didn't see me, but I knocked my wine glass over and the contents emptied into my lap.

By the time we'd mopped it all up and spread a serviette over the stain on the tablecloth, we were on to the coffee and I was temporarily off the boil. I sat simmering through the coffee and was ready to cut the waiter's throat when he suggested liqueurs. Anne, bless her, declined and there was a banging of the table and a scraping of chairs as I galloped her out of the place, cursing the time it took to pay the bill.

I covered the Fulham Road in four minutes flat and parked in the forecourt of The Rabbit Warren. We both got out and I held her arm across the lobby, trying not to smirk at the two night porters, who watched us casually.

There are those among us who say that a girl who allows a man to tumble her the first time they go out is a tramp. I don't go along with this. You might as well say that a girl who doesn't allow a man to tumble her after they've been out a dozen times is automatically *not* a tramp. It's an argument that just doesn't hold water. If the basic attraction is there, it doesn't take a month to work out whether to hop into the sack or not. This is being dishonest with yourself and with your intended sackmate. Bed is only an extension of a natural physical attraction and, if the attraction is there, it's hypocritical to deny its fulfilment. That's how I looked at it, anyway. So I felt like a right idiot when Anne flatly refused to let me past the front door.

'Thank you for dinner,' she said, blocking the way as efficiently as a Harvard fullback. My face must have fallen six inches. She patted me on the cheek like someone consoling a desolate child.

'Cheer up,' she said. 'I'm not your type.'

It was such a basically stupid remark that I couldn't think of anything to say for a moment. I had been sitting on my hands all evening, and I'd had great difficulty in not misting up the cutlery with my heavy breathing. And now, here she was, as good as saying I didn't fancy her.

'Yes, you are,' I managed to croak.

She looked at me steadily for a beat and I felt like a predatory rapist. I looked away and by the time I looked back at her, she'd gone, closing the door in my face.

It was the porters' turn to smirk as I slunk out of the building. I started the car, revving the engine savagely. I drove out of the forecourt, narrowly missing a taxi which was coming in. I shouted an obscenity at the driver and was answered in kind. Right then I felt for Harvey Stubbs and all of the other men she must have left outside her front door. It was downright dishonest for a girl as sexy as she was not to come across. I recalled the thumping in the pub that I had nearly received on her behalf and felt even angrier.

❖ ❖ ❖

I slotted the car into a space outside Mary's place and clumped my way upstairs. I tapped on the door of her apartment and tried to organise my face into a semblance of normality before she opened it. She finally opened the door, dressed for bed bed, as opposed to sex bed. Bed bed consisted of curlers in the hair, cold cream on the face, and the most sexless pair of shorty pajamas imaginable; black I think, with white polka dots, or the other way round.

'Well?' she said.

I started to step into the flat and she jammed the door on to my foot. I must have looked surprised.

'I had dinner at the 'Durrel Arms',' she said.

The significance escaped me for a moment. So, her date had fed her at a pub, I thought; she thinks *she's* got problems. Then the significance didn't escape me any longer. The 'Durrel Arms' was right opposite Carlo's Place. She'd seen me with Anne.

'It was business,' I said.

'So's this,' she said. She opened the door a little wider, then slammed it hard against my foot. By the time I'd finished hopping around, she'd shut it once more, this time for good. I limped downstairs, got into my car and drove home. For a Monday, the day had been about par for the course.

CHAPTER TWO

It was raining on Tuesday, too. I fetched the newspaper and carried it into the kitchen to read while I was having my coffee. The Antonov story had made the front page this morning, due to the fact that a keen leader writer had started to ask how a man like Antonov could successfully operate in this country for ten years without being caught. It was a good question, especially as I knew that he had been under investigation for at least six of those years. Fortunately, the newspaper man didn't know that or heads would have started to roll.

It seemed that during his ten years on the loose, Antonov had successfully corrupted countless atomic physicists, Foreign Office employees, Admiralty clerks, and two minor generals. Not a bad score, considering that the people who were supposed to prevent such things knew all about him.

It didn't really take much intelligence to work out that there was something fishy going on and I'd just about deduced what it was when the post arrived. There was a final demand from the London Electricity Board and an exhortation to do myself a favour and order *The Great Book of Art and Artists* at fifty per cent below list price, for selected customers only, this offer limited to three months. Fifty per cent below list price would have paid my electricity bill for the next six months. I dropped the letter in the wastepaper basket along with the final demand for the electricity. I didn't have the money to pay it and there was no point in having it lying around the flat where it could only depress me. The third letter was in a plain typed envelope. This one I opened last for no other reason than that it was at the bottom of the pile. In it was a newspaper cutting reporting the Antonov trial. Written in a broad hand in the margin were the words: *See me at your convenience.*

There was no signature, but I knew who it was from nevertheless. The handwriting was Max's and, that being the case, 'at your convenience' meant pretty damn quick, unless I wanted the Heavy Squad knocking down the front door.

I thought about me and Max while I was dressing. When I had worked for him, he had been omnipresent, a first-water *eminence grise*. It was he who had patted me on the back and sent me out on jobs that, even to think of them these days, curled my hair. I'd done those jobs for more years than I could remember, until even my pretty revolting standards could take no more. Then I had quit. He hadn't wanted to let me go. He didn't like anyone leaving the Service, unless it was feet first. But as my insurance against old age, I had started to build my '*dossier* on Max' in which I had outlined in detail some of the more savoury episodes he'd instigated. He had let me go in the end. He'd no alternative. I'd looked both ways before crossing the road for a while and hadn't wandered up any high places. But he really had let me go and, much to my surprise, there had been no repercussions. Apart from that painful incident six or seven months ago, he'd left me strictly alone, which was the way I liked it.

Unfortunately, during this last episode, he had managed to get a severe edge on me which to some extent nullified the efficacy of my '*dossier* on Max'. He'd got me certified as criminally and incurably insane. If I knew my Max, my medical file was reposing right now in his filing cabinet and, unless I jumped when he said jump, I was going to be back in a padded cell before I could turn around.

So, if he said 'see me', I wasn't going to give him an argument. I got dressed and went to see him. He greeted me like the prodigal son. He's a small man physically, with thinning hair and a sharply defined face, all planes and angles. He has a thin, humourless mouth and very good teeth. His eyes are prominent and he's a permanent martyr to conjunctivitis. He uses eyedrops as frequently as another man uses a pocket handkerchief, pulling out a small bottle and squeezing the drops into the corners of his eyes. He did this as I sat across from him in his upper echelon civil service office. He blew his nose hard and put the bottle away. Then he looked at me, his eyes swimming.

'Good of you to come so promptly,' he said.

I kept my mouth shut. The best way to talk with Max is to say as little as possible. He has a remarkable knack of fashioning your own words into a noose which he uses to hang you.

'You read about Antonov?'

I nodded.

'Made you wonder a bit, I imagine?'

I hadn't really been all that interested, but I was forced to admit that I had wondered a bit.

'Thought we'd dropped a clanger?'

I admitted it had crossed my mind.

'Well, we haven't.'

I knew he hadn't or he would not have had me up here to tell me about it.

'So knowing we haven't dropped a clanger,' he went on, 'what's your opinion of what has happened?'

I thought about it for a moment. Not about what had happened, because I was pretty sure I'd worked it all out over my coffee that morning, but about whether I should expound my theory. I'd long ago learned it was safer to volunteer nothing to Max. But time dulls the sharpest reactions, and whereas five years ago I'd not have opened my mouth, now I did, stepping in with both feet.

'I think you got on to Antonov five years ago and instead of eliminating him, you conned him into becoming a double agent. You've used him for the past five years to feed back duff information.'

'And?'

'And now his usefulness is at an end. He's probably been blown, and he's an embarrassment. So you put him away.'

Max smiled, showing perfect teeth. 'Half right,' he said.

'Which half?'

'The first. We turned him four years ago. He's been feeding them back the biggest load of codswallop you could imagine.'

'Now they've got wise,' I said.

'Now they've got stupid,' said Max. 'They're impressed with friend Gregori. They think he's no end of a bright-eyed boy. He's held up as a number one example to all the new embryonic spies.'

He'd lost me, I'm afraid, and I told him so. 'So why lock him up where he's no good to anyone?'

'Because we've decided he can be more use to us working someplace else.'

'Like at home?' I asked.

'Like at home,' said Max. 'If they had him now, he'd be given a section at least. Imagine that, John, a whole bloody section, and the leader is our man.'

It was a pretty fanciful idea and one that Max would have given someone's eyeteeth to achieve. And about here I started to get the trend. If I'd been sensible, I'd have trotted out of the office there and then and gone home and put my head in the gas oven. It would have been quicker and less painful. But I didn't. Like the idiot I sometimes am, I stayed and listened to Max confirm what I had already worked out.

'If we'd have left him free, they'd have been content to leave him here. He was doing good work, they thought, and there was no need to upset the *status quo*. First we had to convince them that his usefulness here was at an end. So we pinch him. Now they're faced with one of their best men being out of action, while they'd like him working. The only way he can work is for them to get him back. The only way they can get him back is through an exchange.'

I was right on the button and now was the time to leave. I started to get to my feet.

'I've an authorisation to pay ten thousand pounds,' said Max.

I sat down again. Money does that to me at times; it paralyses the back of my legs. Max allowed me to sweat for a while before he continued. 'We can't be expected to swap him for any old rubbish,' he said. 'So we've got to find a man who ranks in their eyes equal with Antonov.'

'Yes?' I said.

'You did some pretty good work before you got cold feet,' said Max. 'They must have a substantial file on you somewhere in the archives.'

'I've done nothing for five years,' I said.

'Files are longer than that,' said Max. He was right of course. Somewhere in the Kremlin, or wherever it is they keep these things, there must have been a dossier six inches thick on John Smith. It would have gathered a fair amount of dust by now, but dust could always be blown off. I sat there chewing my lower lip for a while.

'Ten thousand pounds,' said Max.

'How long?' I asked.

'One month to set it up, three months to negotiate once they get you inside. Four months altogether.'

Twenty-five hundred pounds a month, more than six hundred pounds a week. It was pretty fair scratch, as long as you ignored the side issues. I decided to ignore them for a few minutes to see what happened. Max took my silence for partial acquiescence. 'I knew I could rely on you, John,' he said.

As I've said before, Max can be as wrong as the next man. I wouldn't have cut a hang nail for Max or the whole Service put together. But for ten thousand pounds, I'd cut my own throat which, as it turned out, I damned near did.

⚜ ⚜ ⚜

It seemed there was a trade mission going over to Moscow the following week. This was to provide my entry permit. Once there I would be contacted by various shifty individuals in Max's employ. They would spin a web around me and, when I was well and truly entangled, they would blow the whole thing to the KGB. There'd be a showy trial and I'd get fifteen years. The moment sentence was announced, negotiations would commence and, all being well, Max said, I'd be back in London four months and ten thousand pounds from now.

The actual details of what I was going to be arrested for, we didn't go into at this stage. Max in his infinite duplicity had decided the less I knew about what was going on behind the scene, the more convincing I would appear. The prime requisite of a scheme like this was that I should appear absolutely genuine. John Smith, agent of long standing, quiet perhaps for the last five years, but still with an impressive record of espionage and counterespionage. Truly a worthy swap for Gregori Antonov.

'You'll have to go down to the Farm for a few days,' said Max eventually.

'Why?' I knew the Farm of old. It was a place in the country kept by the Service for hiding, or doing away with people when the occasion arose.

'Briefing,' he said.

'Brief me here.'

'Can't, old son.'

'Why not?'

'Too many distractions,' he said.

'Distractions like what?'

'Birds. Things like that.'

I started to get suspicious. 'What's wrong with birds all of a sudden?'

'Nothing,' he said. 'So long as they're used just for sex.'

'So?'

'You're involved two ways in London and it's on a deeper level.'

Mary he knew about, so he had to be talking about Anne.

'How long have you had me lined up for this?' I asked.

'Couple of weeks.'

'You've been tailing me.'

'You're getting old, John,' he said. 'Time was when a tail couldn't hold you for two minutes without being spotted.'

'You've got a bloody nerve.'

'I know ... The Ballard girl worries me.'

'She worries me, too.'

'I know what you're like when you're not getting your oats,' he said. 'And from her you're not getting them.'

'Christ, I only met the girl yesterday.'

'Exactly,' he said. 'Can't allow you to get involved in any deep level courtship just before going out on a job like this. Might have a change of heart.'

He was right, of course, but he'd got well and truly up my nose by now. 'You can go and jump in the lake,' I told him. 'I'm not going down to the Farm.'

'At least down there you'll get your ration,' he said.

The Service kept a list of phone numbers which were used occasionally, as required. The girls who lived at the ends of these numbers were quite extraordinary. Not true whores, or so they told themselves. They slept around for money only if they could be convinced that they were doing their patriotic duty at the same time. Their true identities and backgrounds were kept well shrouded, but when I had been in the Service I had known two of them. One had been the wife of a senior civil servant and the other had been the girlfriend of a junior minister. They were paid a small retainer by the Service, which arrived in their letter box in the guise of some obscure pension. And they were given bonuses whenever they were required to give their all for Queen and Country. If their domestic arrangements intruded on their duties more than three times in succession, they were quietly paid off. I never knew who the selection board consisted of, but whoever they were, they did their job well. The girls were lovely, intelligent, and marvelous in bed. When they eventually left the Service, whatever the reason, they did so discreetly with never a murmur of a come-back. I say they were marvelous in bed, because that is what I had been told. I'd never been important enough to warrant their professional services. Now, it seemed, I was. There had been one girl in particular I had met.

'Is Margaret still on the payroll?' I asked. They were all known solely by Christian names.

'Margaret has three children and weighs thirteen stone,' said Max. Five years was a long time.

I digested the Farm bit for a couple of minutes and I was finally forced to the conclusion that what Max was suggesting was the only sensible solution. With a major briefing on my back, I couldn't afford to get myself into a state about Anne Ballard. And if I did manage to storm the ramparts before I left for Moscow, then I was going to be in two minds about going at all. Mary, I wasn't worried about. Our affair had been going on long enough for me to leave her for six months at a stretch and then pick up again as though nothing had happened. I knew with Mary that if she met the right man, she'd marry out of my life and, while I dreaded the day, I knew that if it was going to come it would do so whether I was around or not.

So, having sorted out my immediate domestic life, and with the prospect of a gargantuan payday looming on the horizon, I threw caution to the wind and agreed to what Max outlined.

I had decided to leave Anne Ballard strictly alone, at least for a couple of days, so I called around at Mary's that evening, armed with a bunch of flowers and a new model vintage car for her collection. She opened the door and, seeing who it was, she turned and walked away. But at least she left the door open, so I went in and closed it behind me.

'Peace offering,' I said, holding out the flowers.

She took them from me without a word and went into the kitchen. I followed her in.

'Am I forgiven?' I asked.

She shook her head vigorously without turning round.

'Shall I work on it?' I said in my little boy lost voice. I thought for one moment she was going to shake her head again. But she didn't. She nodded almost imperceptibly. It was enough for me. I walked back into the living room, feeling ten feet tall, and started to unwrap her present.

Much later, when I was leaving, I told her I was going away for a while.

'How long a while?' she asked.

'Three or four months at least,' I said.

'Do I see you before you go?'

I shook my head. 'I don't think so.'

She looked at me steadily for a beat, then brought up her hand and laid it flat on my cheek.

'Take care,' she said.

And that was it. I left quickly before I burst into tears.

Max had given me a day to clear up before I went down to the Farm. I went to the office on Wednesday and reported to Harvey Stubbs that all was well.

He bounced to his feet. 'She took the twenty-five?'

'She took it.'

The cheque was still in my pocket and, although it was made out to cash, I had no intention of keeping it. Neither did I intend him to have it back. He would be more inclined to keep away from Anne if he thought she *was* fifteen and *was* pregnant. He came round the desk and proceeded to pound me on the back.

'Good old John. I knew you wouldn't let me down. Good old John.'

'I went to see her sing,' I said.

He pulled a face. 'Terrible.'

'They loved her.'

He spread his hands. 'I know it. That's why I ain't going to tell her to sling her hook. Working clients I need. But as far as I'm concerned, socially, she might as well be clapped up to the eyeballs.' Which suited me fine.

I returned to my own office and put the cheque in an envelope. I addressed the envelope to one of my favourite charities, the one devoted to the welfare of unmarried mothers.

Then I called in Miss Roberts. 'I'm going away,' I said. 'I'll be gone about four months.'

Her face started to fall. I caught it before it hit bottom as I handed her a cheque and she read the amount I had written on it.

'This will cover your salary, your holiday money, the office rent and anything else that comes up.'

She fingered the cheque as though it were going to vanish in a puff of smoke. 'Are you sure it's all right?' she asked. She had good cause. Yesterday if I'd written a cheque for that amount it would have bounced from here to Shannon. Max had promised to deposit twenty-five per cent of my fee in the bank that morning and he was far too dependent on me at this stage to let me down. The cheque would be good and I told Miss Roberts so. About then she started to get worried.

'Mr. Smith, I hope … I mean … well … you're all right, aren't you?'

I nearly kissed her. She was worried that I'd been up to something illegal. I assured her that my new-found affluence was legitimate and she burst into tears. 'I'll miss you, Mr. Smith,' she said, sniffing hard through her moustache.

'You've still got Mr. Stubbs,' I said.

She brightened up a little, but not much. 'I'll keep everything exactly the way you like it. When you come back you won't even realise you've been away.'

I doubted that, but I let it ride.

I spent the rest of the morning tidying up, and telling Miss Roberts how to handle anything that might come up. Any new enquiries I told her to refer to Phil Bannister, an old mate of mine who could do with the work as much as I could have done yesterday. Finally, I couldn't think of another thing to keep me busy. I stared hard at the telephone for ten minutes wishing it would disappear, thus obviating the necessity of welshing on myself. But it didn't, and I did. I called Anne Ballard.

'How did you know my number?' she asked.

'I was in your flat, remember?'

'What do you want?' she said, not unkindly.

'Take you out to dinner?' I said. There was a moment's pause.

'You're a glutton for punishment.'

'I'm a masochist,' I said.

'Pick me up at the pub?'

'No, thank you,' I said. 'I'll meet you at Carlo's Place.'

It was unlikely that Mary would see me twice in three nights. Anne agreed, and I hung up, feeling a bastard about Mary once more. But Anne had got her hook deep enough into me for me to want to settle it one way or the other. Either she'd have to start hauling in the line, or I'd remove the hook and cauterise the wound. I wasn't even sure which way I wanted it, but whichever it was going to be, it had to be settled and settled fast.

I said good-bye to Miss Roberts, who burst into tears again. I went home and packed a suitcase. I fished around in the wastepaper basket until I located the electricity demand. I wrote out a cheque, stuck it in an envelope and put the envelope in my pocket. The London Electricity Board had struck lucky. I even considered doing myself a favour and subscribing to *The Great Book of Art and Artists,* but reason prevailed and I let it stay in the basket.

Then, there being nothing else to do for the next few hours, I put my head down. I emerged a few hours later, bathed, dressed, locked up the flat and took the suitcase down to the car. There was someone lurking in the front seat of a car a few yards up the road, and I must have been an idiot not to have noticed him before, considering he'd been there for two weeks. But if I bothered to lose him now, Max would get suspicious. And anyway, Max had as good as told me to leave Anne alone.

So, because I don't like being told what to do, and because I get pig-headed when I am, I wanted him to hear that I'd taken no notice of his wishes in the matter. As I started the car and drove away, I gave the man behind me plenty of time to maneuver his own car out and slot into a space about two vehicles behind me. There he stuck all the way to Carlo's place. As I parked and went into the restaurant, I saw him reach into the glove compartment of his car and start in on some tired looking sandwiches. Life can be hell.

Anne arrived at eleven-thirty, by which time I was well stoned. Not so stoned though that I didn't get a lurch in my breastbone as she came in the door and across the restaurant towards me. Every man in the place watched her surreptitiously and, when I didn't even get to my feet as she sat down at the table, most of them would happily have cut my throat.

'Hi!' she said.

'Hi, yourself!' I countered. 'How's Pete?'

'He's worried,' she said. 'You really kicked him very hard.'

'I wasn't even trying,' I said. Here I was, on to the little boy act again, trying to impress. And tonight was my night for playing it cool, I had decided. I pulled myself together, and I played it so cool the soup nearly froze over. Half way through the meat and veg., she began to figure me out.

'You're sulking,' she said.

'Nothing of the sort.'

'I liked it better when you were on the make.'

'You could have fooled me.'

'I didn't say I would have liked it better if you'd succeeded, I just said you were better company.'

'You don't have to worry any more,' I said. 'I made my pass and you saw fit to turn it down. It won't happen again.' It was the booze talking, of course.

'So why did you ask me to dinner?'

'To say good bye. I'm going away.'

I'd like to say that her face fell, but it didn't. She shoveled a mouthful of kebab into her mouth and, like the brave little girl she was, she didn't flinch.

'I'll probably be away about four months,' I said, continuing to flog a dead horse.

'Have fun,' she said.

Then I really did start to sulk. The whole evening gathered rapid momentum on its downhill run. By the time we reached the coffee, five minutes had gone by without a word being spoken. She weakened before me, as I was sure she would.

'Pass the sugar,' she said.

On the way back to her place I tried to rally the troops a little. I had been a first water shit all evening; so much so that even I felt a little guilty.

'You were right,' I said. 'I was sulking. I'm sorry.'

She patted my knee in a sisterly fashion. 'Apologies accepted,' she said. 'And I *am* sorry you're going away.'

'I could postpone it,' I said, grasping at straws.

'Not on my account,' she said.

And that seemed to be that. She rewarded me with a kiss on the cheek and a door closed gently in my face. Perhaps she needed a bit of brute force, I thought. Should I kick down the door of the apartment and rape her on the carpet. Then I remembered it was Wednesday and little sister was at home. This gave me the excuse I needed not to make a bigger fool of myself than I already had and, slinking out of The Rabbit Warren for the second time that week, I climbed into the car and drove down to the Farm.

Agricultural things may go on at the Farm. If it is to provide a truly effective cover for what goes on inside the main building, I suppose they must plant and dig and slaughter sheep and milk cows, or somesuch. But it had never interested me and I had never bothered to find out. The only part of the place that had ever concerned me was the main farmhouse. It was a large, rambling building, with distorted corridors on three different levels, bedroom doors that didn't fit properly and low ceilings for bumping heads on. In the cellars were a couple of interrogation rooms of dazzling clinical whiteness, but from the ground floor up it was furnished in stockbroker rustic and was warm and comfortable.

If anyone was surprised at my arriving at three in the morning, they didn't show it. The door was opened by an anonymous young man who showed me to my room and then took my keys so as to put my car away. He told me I could breakfast at any time I wanted and, if there was anything I needed, would I be so kind as to ring the bell behind the bed. He called me 'sir', which was a fair indication of my general importance in the overall scheme of things. Later, I overheard him on the phone downstairs, reporting my arrival.

Just before I dropped off to sleep, I wondered just what the hell I had let myself in for, apart from ten thousand quid. But I was tired, the bed was comfortable and my thought processes ground to a halt as I slipped over the edge of sleep and died for eight straight hours.

It was midday when I resurfaced, too late for breakfast. I rang my bell and a minute later the young man tapped on the door gently and came in. I suppose he did sleep sometimes, but I never caught him at it. I asked if I could have some coffee and he brought it to me while I was shaving. Lunch would be served in half an hour, he said, and there would be one other person apart from myself.

'Max?' I asked.

'No, sir,' he said, and left as unobtrusively as he had arrived.

I finished shaving and dressing and went downstairs. The main living room, which served as the dining room as well, was large and pleasant. The sun was streaming through the leaded windows, splashing pools of light on the highly polished, dark oak floor. The booze was located on the sideboard against the far wall. I crossed towards it and poured myself a healthy snort.

'Hello, Smith,' someone said.

I turned towards the door. There was no-one there. Then he stood up from where he had been sitting in a high backed wing chair. It was Leo Tamir. He looked as large as life, which was pretty bloody disturbing considering that I had personally shot him to death seven years before.

CHAPTER THREE

Seven years earlier I had been a fully-fledged, paid up, card carrying, prize winning operative for the Service. Admittedly the rot had already started to gnaw away at some of my nerve ends, but not sufficiently as yet for me to lift my fat ass out of the way of Max and his little schemes. That came a couple of years later. I was a one-man team. I liked it that way. I didn't even trust myself overmuch, so I was quite incapable of trusting anyone else.

I had been in West Berlin on a job and was about to fly back to London when Max contacted me. It seemed there was a fellow who wanted to come over the Wall and our people wanted him very badly. I was to cross into the Eastern sector, make contact, and bring him safely back into the fold of democracy. It wasn't a difficult job technically, just highly dangerous.

I had a couple of men on the other side whom I used from time to time. It was reciprocal; they used me when they needed me. There is a certain level of the spy game where agents of opposing sides do each other small favours. It's quite a low level and the top brass, while being aware of it, are completely powerless to do anything about it. But Joe Red is doing the same job as John Blue; they're both overworked and underpaid; they both heartily despise the anonymous, desk-bound individuals who send them out on impossible tasks. So there is a certain affinity towards each other in spite of the fact that they work for opposite sides. In the past. I'd used my men in the East to help smuggle over some unimportant people and they'd used me to ship back some undesirables we didn't want anyway. It was all very shifty and, as I said, only worked on low levels. The fellow Max now wanted me to bring over was not low level; he was extremely high. So my opposite numbers on the other side couldn't be expected to help. At least, not consciously. They needed to be conned into it. And a right royal conning it turned out to be.

I told them I wanted to get my hands on an East German railway worker who was passing forged ten dollar bills. They said fine, but could they please have Otto Heidler, who had come over the Wall a month before, leaving a wife, a mother-in-law and eleven children to be cared for by the State. The deal was arranged and, at the last minute, the man I wanted quietly dropped out of his usual domestic and social pattern and became the railway worker. He came across the Wall gift-wrapped and I bunged Otto Heidler across to them. Fat Otto was delighted to be going back, mother-in-law and eleven children notwithstanding. He had missed the whole bunch of them and had himself been trying to work out a way to get back to them. But such was the nature of my job at that time, I would have delivered him back anyway, even if he had screamed blue murder all the way. I was like that in those days.

The plan was then to shift my man out of West Berlin on the first available aeroplane; to get him well clear before the balloon went up across the Wall. But about here the whole thing started to backfire. My man dug his Germanic heels in and said he wouldn't leave Berlin unless his wife and two children were smuggled over the Wall to join him. He was immovable in this decision and, bar hitting him over the head and sending him air freight, there was nothing I could do about it. So I did the only thing left to me. At great personal risk to life and limb, I smuggled over his wife and two kids. This I had to perform all by myself. I couldn't get on to my regular contacts because that would have blown the identity of the man I'd just conned them into sending over.

Unfortunately, they were already two jumps ahead of me, having found out that they had been duped. They didn't care about the wife and the children; they were only interested in the head of the family. So they allowed me to sweat a few days while I worked out a way to re-unite the family; then they allowed me to sweat some more while I carried out my plan. There were even some shots thrown at us to make the whole thing look real. They must have been laughing like a row of buckets, especially as they had sent Leo Tamir along behind us.

He spoiled the family reunion I had arranged by arriving five minutes after I had left and shooting the lot of them, kids and all. There was no one we could scream at for this bit of skullduggery; it was an occupational hazard. The only thing that lifted it out of the realm of the everyday was my part in it. For three days I had been living with the wife and the children and, bonded somehow by our common fear of discovery, we had grown closer together than we had any right to allow. She was a gentle, pretty girl of twenty-eight or thereabouts. The children, a boy and a girl, were seven and nine years old respectively. We had crouched in dirty cellars, slept under a common blanket, crossed a muddy frontier, and at one moment I had even started to entertain wild ideas about not delivering her back to her husband at all. But what with the children, and the fact that she was a very sensible girl to boot, I *had* delivered her to her husband and five minutes later all four of them were drowning in their own blood. And **I** developed a king-sized needle.

I phoned Max and told him I wanted a month's leave. I didn't have any due to me, but he guessed what I wanted to do and, as it fitted in with his scheme of things, he happily granted my request.

It took me three weeks to locate and catch up with Leo Tamir. I did so finally in a disused garage five miles inside East Berlin. As an executioner he was ideal type casting; tall, colourless and very thin. His body seemed to be completely devoid of any flesh; just a thin layer of skin stretched tightly over an animated skeleton. He sidled into the garage, looking for the contact I had conned him into believing he was to make. I let him get one good look at me so that he would know why he was dying. In those days I considered myself a pretty dab hand with a firearm and I put two bullets an inch each side of his navel. He was rolling around on the floor, dying painfully, when I stepped over him and walked out. That was the last I saw of him. Three or four months later we learned circuitously that he was no longer with us, having been given a State funeral, third class.

And now here he was, seven years later, as large as life and twice as ugly. He still looked like an animated skeleton, only now the skin wasn't so tightly stretched. There was a wrinkle here and there, as though it had been badly dry cleaned somewhere along the line. I looked at him for a long moment, the bottle still poised over my glass.

'It must have been one of my off nights,' I said.

'Fortunately, that wasn't the case with the surgeon they took me to,' he said. His English was almost perfect, with just a trace of an American accent buried somewhere not too deep. I held up the bottle.

'Drink?'

He shook his head and patted his stomach lightly. 'Thank you, no,' he said. 'I have trouble with my stomach if I am not careful.'

I remembered the two bullets I had placed there. 'Yes, you would,' I said. I finished pouring my drink and carried it across to a window seat where I sat and studiously studied the trees and fields through the window. The sun had gone in suddenly. Behind me Leo cleared his throat. It sounded like someone scraping their fingernails across sandpaper.

'We have things to discuss, Mr. Smith,' he said.

I didn't turn round. Even after seven years the very thought of Leo Tamir made me want to throw up. Before I had ended his career, he had been hatchet man extraordinary for the East Germans. The little interlude which directly concerned me had been just another four notches in a gun butt that had already been sliced to ribbons. We knew of sixteen murders that could be laid at his door and there must have been God knows how many others. He had been the true professional in his day, working on the principle that loose ends can be woven into a noose, so cut the loose ends. The wives, girlfriends or children of his victims were all loose ends as far as he was concerned, so they all went to his own private wall; butcher *par excellence* was Leo.

'We have things to discuss,' he said once more.

The view out of the window wasn't as impressive as I had first thought, so I turned towards him. 'What do you want?' I asked. 'Apologies?'

He looked at me blankly for a moment, then he grinned without humour.

'You are joking,' he said.

'You tell me.'

'Next week you are going to Moscow,' he said. 'There are things you must know about.'

'For instance?'

'It is my task to acquaint you with certain names, addresses and pieces of information which will be of use to you while you are there. They are designed to make your eventual arrest appear authentic.' His English wasn't so good after all; he talked like a page from the manual on How Not to be a Spy in Five Easy Lessons.

'Why you?' I asked.

'Because it is my job,' he said. 'I have been sent here specifically for this purpose.'

'Sent by whom?'

'My employers.'

'KGB?'

'CIA.'

So that was where he'd been for the last few years.

'What's the CIA got to do with this?' I asked, not keen to know the answer. I didn't like the CIA, they were too big. When an organisation has upwards of seventeen thousand agents in the field, it's natural that there should be slight deficiencies when it comes to servicing them. I'd known CIA men in the old days who'd stayed out in the field three times as long as anyone else because their Control had too many men to deal with and some-one had mislaid their file. Max hadn't mentioned the CIA when he was giving me the deal.

'It's a joint operation,' said Tamir. 'Your department and the CIA.'

This made it worse; it conjured up visions of interdepartmen-tal rivalries, petty jealousies and, above all, not letting one hand know what the other was doing. If I'd have had any sense I'd have quit there and then. Unfortunately the time for quitting had passed the moment that I saw and recognised Tamir.

'So discuss,' I said. And we discussed.

We talked over lunch and we talked all afternoon and into the evening. Or rather, he talked, and I only opened my mouth to shovel in food and drink and to ask an occasional question. One of these I asked fairly early on. How was it that Leo Tamir, who was supposed to be dead, was working for the CIA?

'I was very ill for a long time after our meeting,' he said, with-out particular rancour. 'My employers thought it advisable to announce my death. That way, when I returned to work, I would have the benefit of additional cover. After a year in hospital, I returned to the field.'

'Same job?'

'No. I'm afraid my taste for the old job had soured a little. My English was good, and I spoke three other languages, so I became an interrogator.'

That was like saying he had become fed up with killing people quickly, so he started killing them slowly. I started to dislike him even more than I had done originally, which wasn't easy.

'I worked at that for two years,' he said. 'And then I received this offer from the Americans.'

Just like that. He received an offer of employment from a rival firm, so he accepted. What price patriotism? I thought. But this thought only served to remind me of just how long I had been out of the game. In the old days, patriotism had been a dirty word.

'Your original employers couldn't have been overjoyed,'
I said.

'They were extremely unhappy,' he said. 'They have tried to kill me on more than one occasion.'

It was a pity they hadn't succeeded, then I wouldn't have had to sit here looking at his animated death's head.

The instructions he gave me covered the broad outlines of what I was to do when I got to Moscow. Names and addresses were committed to memory, identification phrases were gone over, and along towards the end of the day I started to get very suspicious. But my suspicions needed airing in front of Max, not Leo Tamir, so I allowed him to plough on while I sat there soaking it all up and disliking him more each minute.

Finally, it was bedtime, and Tamir disappeared upstairs with a glass of warm milk. The young man came into the sitting room to see me.

'Is there anything you'd like, sir?' he asked politely.

I thought for a moment about Max's extravagant promises to lay on a Service whore, should I feel so inclined. Then I decided that I didn't feel so inclined, so I bid the young man good night and went up to bed myself.

Leo Tamir was with me all the following day, retracing the ground he had already covered. I purposely made a couple of stupid mistakes so that I could watch him get the needle. He didn't. He corrected me with infinite patience and re-explained the point I had so obviously missed. Then he moved on to the next one. My suspicions were confirmed some time during the day and that evening I told the young man I wanted to make an outside telephone call.

He smiled apologetically. 'That's not permitted I'm afraid,' he said.

'I want to talk to Max,' I said.

'He left no instructions.'

'Take your pick,' I said. 'Either I call him from here, or I go down to the village and do it from there.'

His eyes flicked over me briefly, working out how much muscle he might have to use. It wouldn't have been much. He was a trained man, and a swift kick in the cobblers wouldn't have worked here like it did in Anne's pub. But then he decided that he'd better not damage the goods he was supposed to be looking after, so he excused himself politely and returned three minutes later.

'Max is on the line,' he said.

The phone was in the hall, a direct line to Max.

'What do you want?' he said.

'I want to see you.'

'What for?'

'I'll tell you when you get down here.'

There was a pause at the other end.

'Is it important?'

'Anything that could make me want to see you would have to be important,' I said. He muttered something unintelligible at the other end of the line.

'What did you say?' I asked.

'I'll come down tomorrow.'

'Before six,' I said. 'Or I won't be here.' And I hung up.

Tamir disappeared upstairs early again with his glass of milk. I'd not seen him eat or drink anything except warm milk for two days, and I began to think my aim seven years ago hadn't been as bad as I had thought. Seven years is a long time to nurse a sore tummy.

When I came down to breakfast the following morning, Tamir wasn't there. But there was a nervous young man sitting at the table alone. He jumped to his feet as I came in as though I were important. 'My name is Harcourt,' he said.

'Smith,' I said, helping myself to orange juice.

He started to smile, then looked embarrassed. 'Good morning, Mr-er-Smith,' he said.

'Just Smith,' I said, sitting down.

'Yes, sir,' he said. 'When do you want to start?'

I hadn't the faintest idea what he was talking about.

'Why not now?' I suggested. He seemed relieved. He got to his feet once more and fetched a bulging briefcase from the sideboard. He sat down again and, rummaging in the briefcase, handed me a pile of multi-coloured pamphlets.

'This is our latest model,' he said. 'It's a diesel, of course, and we can deliver with clutch or brake band and drum steering. It has removable cylinder sleeves, variable governor throttle control, adjustable radiator shutter. It will deliver 85 per cent of its horsepower at the drawbar, or it will perform beltwork at one half pound per horsepower hour at rated load.'

'What is it?' I asked.

He looked at me with a slightly pained expression. 'It's the diesel multi-purpose Mark Ten,' he said. I must have looked extremely stupid. 'It's a tractor,' he said, nearly bursting into tears.

I glanced at the pamphlets. It *was* a tractor. 'I think you're talking to the wrong person,' I said. 'The farm's out there, I'm just a house guest.'

'You're Mr. John Smith?'

I agreed that I was.

'You're going to Moscow next week?'

Again I agreed.

'Well surely,' he said, 'if you're going to demonstrate the Mark Ten, you've got to know *something* about it.'

So I was to be a tractor salesman. Max couldn't put me on the booze stand, or in ladies' underwear. He'd given me tractors. That was something else I was going to have to talk to him about. But having crossed the initial hurdle, young Mr. Harcourt really stretched out. He bombarded me with pamphlets, drawings, specifications, and enough technical data to fill a small encyclopaedia. It all went in one ear and a good part of it spilled out of the other. But enough of it stuck and by half past five, when Harcourt left, I was pretty conversant with the multi-purpose Mark Ten. I couldn't have pulled it apart and put it together again blindfolded, as I'm sure Harcourt could, but at least I knew how to start the bloody thing.

Max arrived on the dot of six, his eyes streaming. He was a city man, grass and trees doing terrible things to his particular brand of conjunctivitis. What with that and the fact that he hadn't wanted to come at all, he arrived in a foul mood. This suited me, because when he lost his temper he was inclined to become unsubtle.

He poured himself a small whisky, drowned it with soda and stood in front of the fireplace, his legs spread wide.

'Well?' he said.

'What about Tamir?' I said.

'What about him?'

'You didn't tell me he was here.'

'I didn't know,' he lied. 'The CIA said they were sending a man. They didn't say who.'

I let it ride, it wasn't all that important. 'What's going on?' I said.

'You know what's going on?' he answered a little warily.

'I bought your original scheme,' I said. 'I needed the money sufficiently for me to ignore some of the rough edges. The pay was good.'

'Bloody good,' he interjected. 'So what's the complaint?'

'Side issues.'

'Ah,' he said. He rocked back and forth for a few seconds trying to work out how much he could get away with not telling me.

'Big operation, John,' he said. 'Large appropriation. Got to show as many results as we can.'

'Sort of bonus,' I said.

He smiled with his mouth only. 'Exactly.'

I went to fetch myself a drink. 'I don't like it,' I said.

'You're not required to,' he said. 'It doesn't affect your part of the job.'

'Yes, it does,' I said. 'You're asking me to make contact with a VIP.'

'Right.'

'A Russian VIP.'

'Right again.'

'And what happens to this VIP after he's been contacted by a British agent?'

'I don't think they'll shoot him,' said Max.

'Then they must be getting soft since I turned it in.'

'Yes,' said Max. 'They have eased up a bit. He'll probably get the salt mines or somesuch.'

'What exactly have you got against this poor slob?'

'Nothing,' said Max, surprised that I should ask. 'He works in a department of the KGB. He's not a Controller yet, but he's a bright lad and soon will be. Nothing like chopping down the tree while it's still an acorn.'

'It stinks,' I said.

'I know,' said Max. 'But as long as we had to fake something for you to get up to, I thought this was as good as anything and better than most.'

'*You* thought?' I asked.

'CIA actually,' said Max. 'Your man's an expert on American affairs.'

'So you do their dirty work now, as well as your own.'

'We co-operate,' he said.

'What have they got to do with Antonov?' I asked.

'Nothing.'

'Then how did they know what we were about?'

Max thought quickly. 'They had some information on Antonov. When they heard we'd pulled him in, they offered to let us have it.'

That was a bloody lie for a start; the CIA never volunteered anything.

'They didn't know Antonov was a double?'

'No,' said Max. He was lying every time he opened his mouth now. 'But we had to tell them of course.'

'Of course,' I said.

❧ ❧ ❧

Then we moved on to this and that and, after twenty minutes, during which time he sweated a little more than normal, he plucked up enough courage to glance at his watch and say that he had to get back to town. I walked to the door with him and he shook me by the hand, saying it was unlikely that he'd see me again before I left. I watched him walk back to his car and saw the driver get out to open the door for him. It was a lady driver, a mousy looking thing from the motor pool, who obviously disapproved strongly of evening drives into the country. Just before Max stepped into the car, I shouted at him from the front door.

'I thought you said I could get laid down here,' I said.

He stopped, halfway into the car, and I saw him glance sideways at Miss Mouse. He stepped out of the car and walked back towards me. I suppose I should have met him halfway, but I didn't. When he was a good ten feet away from me, I spoke again, just as loudly. 'There's no one here except Leo, and I don't fancy him.'

He reached me, his mouth a thin, straight line. I smiled at him broadly.

'Do you really want a woman?' he asked.

'I don't know till I see her, do I?' I said.

He sighed. 'All right,' he said. 'Tomorrow.'

He walked back to his car and Miss Mouse. Just before he got in, I called to him again. 'A big redhead,' I shouted. He didn't acknowledge it. He got into the car quickly and the driver slammed the door after him. She marched round the front of the car, and as she was about to get in to the driver's seat, I delivered my parting shot. 'With tits,' I yelled.

The engine started up with a snarl of disapproval, and I watched the car until it disappeared between the chicken house and the barn, on the way out. Then feeling childishly pleased with myself, I went back in.

At dinner, Tamir appeared for the first time that day. He sat there sipping warm milk while I tucked into soup, meat and veg., the lot. With it I sunk a whole bottle of very good wine, capped the whole thing with three large brandies, and then went to bed. I slept like a log until half past five.

The dawn is a cold, lonely thing. It is not a time for constructive thinking. On the rare occasions when I wake up with the sun, I get up straight away rather than lie in bed and reflect my problems. This morning I reflected and it was a pretty murky exercise. I decided that my feeling of well-being of the previous evening had been built on a liquid foundation, and now the whole thing was on the point of running down the plughole, taking me with it. But I was deeply committed by now and, if I had tried to wriggle out, Max would have become very nasty. And a nasty Max has to be seen to be believed. I decided I was better off taking my chance with the Russians.

I got up about seven and went for a walk. There was nobody downstairs when I went out and, by the time I came back at half past eight, the young man in charge had done everything bar call out the Marines. He'd phoned Max, he'd made discreet enquiries at the local police station, and he'd ordered half a dozen men in London to start looking for me. His relief at seeing me walk in the door only just outweighed his desire to cut my throat for causing him to get into such a state.

'Morning,' I said. 'What's the excitement?'

He pinched back his first remark and tried to smile at me. 'You're not supposed to leave the farmhouse,' he said.

'You should have told me.' I helped myself to some bacon and eggs and sat down at the table. 'What's on the agenda today?' I said. 'Tractors or Leo?'

'Political history,' he said primly.

'You're kidding,' I said. But he wasn't. At half past nine a man named Greeley arrived and I spent the day learning about the people I would have known about already if I hadn't quit the Service five years before. So-and-so now ran the Middle East office, having succeeded whatsisname who had been put in charge of the American Bureau; a man at the Italian Embassy was always a good bet if you wanted something leaked to the Russians; Carey, a second secretary at the US Embassy was the local head of the CIA; and so on and so forth. This went on through lunch and up until tea time, when Greeley packed his case and left.

I was pouring myself a large drink when Leo Tamir appeared. He probably didn't know, but I thought I'd ask him anyway.

'I've been given a lot of information today,' I said.

'More tractors?'

'People. An A to Z on who does what on the Moscow spy scene.'

'Necessary information,' he said.

'Too necessary,' I replied. 'I'm not in this for glory. If anyone asks me anything, I shall tell them. Nobody's going to have to pull any of *my* fingernails.'

'Then you must assume that the information that has been given you is designed with that in mind.'

'I'm being underpaid,' I said. 'Not only am I doing the job I was told I would be, but I'm spreading fringe benefits round like there was no tomorrow.'

'Please?' said Leo.

'First there's the man you've been briefing me on. The poor slob who's to be contacted by a British agent. And now there's half a dozen other pieces of choice information which I'm supposed to divulge.'

He pulled his mouth back, exposing his teeth. I think he thought he was grinning. 'If you have enough information to give away, they may grow tired before they can get you to give away the true purpose of your visit.'

It figured in a roundabout sort of way. The stuff I now knew would keep my interrogators busy for a couple of weeks. If I provided them with sufficient pseudo-genuine information, they might accept my cover without peeling off the last layer.

Over dinner Leo grew quite loquacious. He told me how he had gone to America and spent a year there engaged in what amounted to total recall of his ten years in the service of the East Germans. The number of people he must have sent to the wall during this opening up of his mind would have been impressive by most standards. But for his career it was an anti-climax. He had merely taken his own finger off the trigger and aimed the gun for someone else.

'Do you sleep nights?' I asked.

'My stomach gives me trouble,' he said.

'Not your head?'

He looked at me for a moment, not understanding. Then he got it. 'You mean conscience,' he said. I nodded. 'No,' he said. 'It was a job like any other. I did it as best I knew how.'

'But you enjoyed it,' I said.

He shrugged indifferently. 'I never considered whether it was to be enjoyed or not. It was just a job.'

That was even worse. If he had been a sadist and had got a kick out of murder, it would have been understandable, if not commendable. But indifference put it on a completely different level. I called him a very rude name and left the table.

I was crossing the hall on the way upstairs to bed at the same time as our young man was opening the front door. He stood aside politely and a girl came into the hall. She was tall, very fair, and thin. She had muscular legs that looked as though they could squeeze the life out of you if she ever got a good hold. She was everything I didn't like in a girl, and this was confirmed a moment later when she spoke to the young man. 'Max asked me to come down,' she said.

She had a flat, nasal intonation in her voice which set my teeth on edge. Max knew my taste in women and he must have gone to great pains to find this girl. It was his way of paying me back for last night. As she came across the hall to say hello, I mumbled something fatuous and fled upstairs. It was just one more indication of how long I'd been away; Max *always* had the last snigger.

I spent four more days on the Farm. I talked with Leo Tamir some more and had two more visitors from London. One of them tried to show me how to work a small transmitter-receiver. I told him to stuff it; I was taking no radio sets to Moscow. There was a hurried phone conversation with Max, and the man left in high dudgeon, taking his radio with him.

The other visitor brought my documents. There was a passport, well used, a National Insurance Card, a driver's licence, a Diners' Club Card and a membership card to the Playboy Club. All these were made out in the name of Harrison King. Then there were a couple of photographs of an anonymous looking woman with two kids, and two personal letters that a man like King might have been expected to keep. To cap this do-it-yourself spy kit, there was a wallet containing dirty photographs and a packet of french letters. I decided I didn't much like Harrison King. But I was obviously going to have to live with him for the next few months, so I took the large file on my new found background up to my room, where I read it carefully, getting to know myself as well as I could.

On Monday morning, bright and early, a car called for me and, with a suitcase full of clothes that I normally wouldn't have been seen dead in, I was driven to Gatwick Airport.

At the airport I met some of the other delegates to the Trade Conference. They were about equally divided between dedicated men, who were determined to return with order books crammed, and the others, whose dedication lay solely in having a ball during the next two weeks while they were away from hearth and home. I gravitated towards this bunch who already, at ten thirty in the morning, were well on the way to getting smashed on airline champagne.

The aircraft was chartered, and my half of it swung vigorously all the way across Europe. After half an hour the hostesses refused to come up to our end of the aeroplane at all and we were forced to collect our own booze from the galley. This we did with inexhaustible enthusiasm.

Before we knew it, the captain, who had wisely remained in the driver's seat for the whole journey, announced that we were approaching Moscow.

The liquor I had consumed over the past few hours evaporated suddenly. The fun was over, let battle commence.

CHAPTER FOUR

L ooking back on the whole Moscow bit, it's a bloody miracle that I managed to stay alive for more than forty-eight hours. The fact I *did* stay alive was not due to any particular ability of mine. Rather it was a long series of errors of judgment and execution by everyone concerned. I was merely a pawn, to be shoved this way and that, in the hope that I could be made to cause as much damage as-possible before someone from the other side moved his queen and swatted me from the board.

It was dark when we touched down at the International Airport at Sheremetevo, about eighteen miles from Moscow proper. There was an official welcoming party of minor state officials, and we were hurried through the airport formalities with a haste that was almost indecent. Our entire party was bundled into a fleet of Ziv limousines, with one Intourist guide to each car. The drunken bunch I was with drew an attractive, serious faced young girl, who spoke better English than I did. Ideas of extra-curricular activities entertained by any of our party in her direction were quickly squashed when Harbottle, an aggressive North Country idiot, laid a sweaty hand on her knee. She blasted him with a stream of Russian delivered in a tone cold enough to take his arm off above the elbow. As he snatched his frostbitten hand away, she switched back to English, without batting an eyelid, continuing at the point at which she had been interrupted.

She pointed out with pride the vast building programme which was gobbling up the outskirts of the city. Huge, multi-storied blocks of apartments, hung with scaffolding and topped by cranes, stuck up against the night skyline. Nearer the centre of Moscow, the scaffolding had disappeared and the same buildings were occupied and blazing with light. Then we were in Moscow proper, with its wide, straight streets. Here, the buildings were not so uniform in design as the workers' apartments on the outskirts; here there were still relics of pre-revolutionary architecture. This was the first time in Moscow for me, and I managed to find enough respite from my problems to show a reasonable interest in my surroundings.

The hotel was a genuine piece of Victoriana. The room I was eventually shown to on the fourth floor was large enough to hold a diplomatic reception. The ceiling was so high as to be almost out of sight, and the furnishings were comfortably ugly. There were heavy plush curtains, over-stuffed armchairs with dainty antimacassars, and a huge iron bed with a feather mattress deep enough to drown in. There was a connecting bathroom, with a hot water geyser that looked efficient enough to launch the entire hotel into orbit. There was a telephone and a pile of official notices in five languages. There was also a small printed notice in English welcoming me, as a member of the Trade Delegation, to the USSR. In small letters at the bottom it informed me that anything I wanted while I was in Moscow, I was to refer to my Intourist representative. I wondered what the serious young lady would say if I told her that I wanted to get arrested for spying. She would probably have found it as unbelievable as I did.

There was some sort of a wingding laid on for us that evening, and after a suitable time had been given to us for washing and changing, we reassembled in the lobby of the hotel.

We were bundled into the fleet of limousines once more and, accompanied by our young Intourist guide, were driven across Moscow to the monolithic pile that housed the Overseas Trade Centre. The booze consumed on the aeroplane that day had, by now, started to take its toll and my group was looking a very sorry bunch of high-powered sales executives. Even the amorously inclined Harbottle was subdued, and the sight of our guide in a neat little black dress with discreet decolletage, did nothing to revive his spirits.

The party, if it could be so called, was held in a vast room into which they seemed to have crammed the entire population of Moscow along with diplomatic representatives from five different embassies. I think the Big Man himself was there, but I couldn't be sure; since the exit of Khrushchev I've never been quite sure who it is and, anyway, all Russian politicians look the same to me. There was a sprinkling of large Russian wives, and some slimmer women who obviously came from the embassies; there was a mess of interpreters, smooth eager young men in ill-fitting lounge suits; there were photographers and reporters from the accredited news agencies; and there was half a ton of caviar and a seemingly inexhaustible supply of champagne and vodka. I spent three-quarters of an hour talking to four large Russians about the multipurpose Mark Ten. Fortunately, I had to do this through an interpreter, so the more glaring holes in my discourse could be laid at his feet as examples of bad translation. Even so, I thought they looked at me a little strangely when I was explaining the slip differential. But, on the whole, the discussion passed off reasonably well.

They excused themselves after a while, when they went to discuss the merits of a new type of combine harvester, and I found myself alone for the first time since I had arrived at the party. Not wanting to get involved in another technical talk, I side-stepped two more men who were dragging an interpreter towards me, and pushed my way through to the bar. I ordered three vodkas and, pouring them all into one glass, I started to make my way to a distant corner of the room where I imagined I might be able to sit out the remainder of the evening undisturbed. I didn't make it. Halfway across the room, I felt my elbow grabbed from behind. Turning, I saw a short, dapper man, with sandy coloured hair and rimless spectacles.

'Comrade King?' he enquired politely. I confirmed that I was indeed Comrade King, and he stuck out his hand.

'Alexei Alexandrovitch,' he said. I shook his hand. It was dry, yet still managed to give the impression that it was clammy. I decided I didn't like him.

'You are the representative of the tractor people?' he asked.

'Multi-purpose Mark Ten,' I said. 'We can deliver with clutch or brake band and drum steering. It has removable cylinder sleeves too.'

'Interesting,' he agreed.

'It will deliver eighty-five per cent of its horse-power at the drawbar.'

'Very interesting,' he said. 'What else will it deliver?'

'When performing beltwork, it will deliver one half pound per horse-power hour at rated load.'

He nodded a couple of times as though he knew what I was talking about.

'Will it deliver Vladimir Karkov?' he said finally.

I nearly asked him what the hell was a Vladimir Karkov. There was nothing about one in my pamphlets. Then through the booze came a flash of light. Vladimir Karkov was the man I was supposed to put the big finger on, the bright young man of KGB who was an expert on American affairs and would one day grow up to be a Controller. Except that he wasn't going to be allowed to grow up at all if Max and the CIA had their way. Three hours I'd been here and already they were sharpening the chopper.

'No doubt we could adapt the basic model to deliver anything you'd care to ask for,' I said.

'Later this evening,' he said.

I looked around the room and the number of people in it. Then I looked back at him. 'It is a little crowded,' I said.

He sidled closer to me. He had halitosis. 'When this is over, come to forty-four Kotelnicheskaya Street, apartment seventeen.'

'Which street?'

'Kotelnicheskaya,' he said.

I couldn't even pronounce it, let alone find my way there.

'Write it down,' I said.

'Too dangerous,' he hissed. He pronounced it again, syllable by syllable like a teacher taking a four-year-old through a primary reader. I must have got it eventually, because suddenly he wasn't there anymore. He slapped my back, causing me to slop my drink, and with a hearty 'Good night, Comrade,' he was gone.

His place was taken by an earnest young man whose only interest in tractors was as a means of introducing himself. Once that had been established, we got on famously. He wanted to know about Western authors. Did I know the work of Ernest Hemingway? I told him that old Ernie and I had practically been born in the same bed. Had I read *The Sun Also Rises?*

'*Read* it? The hero was based on me,' I said.

He looked sympathetic. 'It must be terrible to be impotent,' he said.

I agreed that it had its disadvantages and resolved to read *The Sun Also Rises* as soon as I got home. We had covered Galsworthy and Chesterton and touched on Maugham, all bosom friends of mine, before I was dragged away by an interpreter to extol the virtues of the multi-purpose Mark Ten to a group of yokels up from the Urals. A couple of hours later the party broke up. We were picked up again by our Intourist guides, who shepherded us into neat little bundles and drove us back to the hotel. There we were bidden a polite good night, indicative of the fact that we were supposed to retire to our rooms and remain there until we were fetched the following day.

❖   ❖   ❖

On every floor of every hotel in Russia there is a big woman who sits at a desk in the corridor. The desk is strategically placed so that she can see the doors to all the rooms and the stairs as well. I don't suppose it really is the same woman, but it might just as well be. From her eyrie she is supposed to command the efficient running of the floor. Maids, messengers, waiters are all summoned by her, and report back to her after they have performed their duties; towels, linen, keys are all organised by her. She also serves very well the purpose of keeping an eye on the comings and goings of the guests. She certainly phones down any unscheduled movements to the reception desk and it's an even money bet she's got her own hot line direct to the KGB. So subterfuge was in order if I was to keep my appointment.

I asked for, and received, a bottle of vodka and, nursing it tenderly, I enquired from her the room number of my good old pal Harbottle. We argued back and forth for a couple of minutes until she got the gist of what I was asking. Rigid with disapproval at this obvious example of drunken Western decadence, she phoned down to Reception and ascertained that Harbottle was on the third floor, the one below mine. She wrote the room number down because, being a stupid idiot who didn't speak a word of Russian, I couldn't be expected to understand what she was saying.

Thanking her profusely, I tottered off towards the stairs, giving a creditable imitation of a man who was three parts stoned and was about to complete the course. This part wasn't too difficult, because I *was* three parts stoned. The rest was simple. I just continued to walk down the stairs until I reached the ground floor, where I strolled across the lobby, like a man who had every right to, and out of the front door. The two women behind the desk didn't even look at me.

Once I got outside, my troubles really started. There were no taxis and, even if there had been, I wouldn't have taken one. Neither did I have any idea in which direction I was supposed to go. A hundred yards from the hotel I stopped a man and tried to pronounce the name of the street I was looking for. It took me five minutes to get it over to him that I wanted Kotelnicheskaya Street, by which time we'd gathered quite a crowd. Fortunately, among the interested spectators was a student whose command of English, while not being by any means fluent, was at least comprehensible. He started to explain how I should get there, and then he got into an argument with the man I had stopped as to the relative merits of taking first left and second right, as opposed to second left and first right. Luckily they sorted it out before the police arrived to break up an illegal gathering. I gave them the bottle of vodka I was still clutching to share between them and, as I left, they were just starting another argument as to who deserved the lion's share.

Forty-four Kotelnicheskaya Street was an old, brown-stone apartment building, sandwiched between an office block and a depressing looking clothing store. I mounted the steps to the lobby and was striking matches, looking for the bell push of apartment seventeen, when Alexei Alexandrovitch grabbed my elbow for the second time that evening, pulling me back into the darkness of the hall. Coming out of the dark like he did, he scared the life out of me and it was only by hanging on to my tattered nerve ends that I refrained from bolting back to the security of the hotel. As it was, it took me half a minute to pull myself together and listen to what he was telling me.

It seemed that Vladimir Karkov had a mistress. There was nothing illegal or even indiscreet in this. He was an unmarried man with normal appetites and the KGB were only concerned with his private life insofar as it reflected on his work for the department. The girl in question was apparently well cleared for security and the arrangement was satisfactory to all parties. Up until now. Alexei had made a phone call to Vladimir, purporting to be delivering a message from his girlfriend to the effect that she was in serious trouble, and would he please meet her right away at apartment seventeen, forty-four Kotelnicheskaya Street. He was due here in five minutes. The ruse was simple to the point of stupidity; it had the stamp of a second-rate melodrama. And about here I began to question the validity of the statement that Vladimir was a bright young man who would go far. If he was *that* bright he would have smelled a trick of some sort.

'What if he phones his girlfriend to check you out?' I asked Andrei.

'She is out of town.'

'You're sure?'

'She was phoned three hours ago and asked to meet Vladimir in their dacha thirty miles from Moscow. There is no telephone there.'

I hastily tried to think of another objection that would warrant my calling the whole thing off, but I couldn't. 'What am I supposed to do with him when he arrives?' I asked.

'Nothing,' said Alexei.

'What do you mean, nothing?'

'Just that. He will do all that is necessary.'

I had a quick vision of Vladimir pulling out a gun and shooting holes in me. But Alexei was way ahead of me.

'He never carries firearms,' he said.

'How do you know what he does when he's rescuing damsels in distress?'

But Alexei was insistent. 'He never carries firearms.'

He gave me the key of apartment seventeen and pointed me towards the stairs.

'Good luck,' he said. Suddenly I was alone and scared gutless.

Apartment seventeen was on the second floor. The building was silent except for the muffled sound of a radio from one of the floors above me. I located number seventeen and let myself in. It was a spacious three bedroomed apartment of the old style which reflected the Russian passion for high ceilings and lots of elbow room. It was completely empty of any furniture, provided you discounted a battered, upturned packing case in the centre of the main room. I toured the apartment quickly. In the old days, the first thing to do in a situation like this had been to make sure of your line of retreat. Always locate and check the way out, whether you thought you would need it or not. It took me thirty seconds to locate and check the fact that, in this instance, there wasn't a back way out. There was only the one door into the apartment, the one I had come in by. If Vladimir and I both decided that we had had enough, then we were going to trample each other to death on the way out.

After that, there seemed nothing left to do but sit and wait. Not the least unnerving thing about the whole bit was not knowing what I was waiting for. I knew that Vladimir Karkov would come hot footing it to rescue his girlfriend, but rescue her from what? If Alexei had told him she was being raped, then in spite of his apparent dislike of them, he'd likely arrive bristling with firearms. With my non-existent command of the Russian language, I was going to be bleeding all over the floor before I could set him straight. On the other hand, if Alexei had concocted some milder type of story, where was I going to be left when he arrived and started to ask me questions? It was all very well for Alexei to say do nothing, leave it all to Vladimir, but Alexei wasn't going to be here, and I was. I decided that speculation was for the birds and sweated out the remainder of the time with my teeth chattering. I'd like to have blamed it on the cold, which it undoubtedly was. But not that cold.

Alexei's timing was dead on. Five minutes to the second Vladimir Karkov arrived. If he had come by car, I didn't hear it. The first sound I heard was that of hurried footsteps coming up the stairs. There was a moment's pause while he located the door of the apartment, and then the door bell rang. I remained where

I was, sitting on the packing case facing the door, and wishing I was twelve thousand miles away. After a pause, the bell rang again, and a few seconds later the door started to open slowly. There was sufficient leaklight from the street lamp outside for me to see him pretty clearly. He was wrapped up against the cold in a fur collared overcoat and a fur hat; but I could still see enough of him to recognise him again if I had to. He was about forty years old, a fact of which I was already aware. He had a fine-boned face and dark, bushy eyebrows. There was a healthy growth of whisker on his upper lip which didn't quite hide a mouth that looked hard enough to break rocks. It was difficult to see his eyes in this light, but I found out later they were grey and flat like a Russian winter.

He saw me when the door was half open and he stopped, staring straight at me. Then he said something fast in Russian. It was obviously some sort of question and, not understanding a word, I kept my mouth shut. Then he stepped across the threshold and repeated the question. This time there was an edge of anger in his voice. I thought I'd better contribute something and, being unable to think of anything particularly witty, I fell back on the Englishman's standby. 'It's chilly tonight,' I said.

I might as well have said I'd just flown in from Pluto, so great was the effect. He stiffened visibly, right down to his toes. His eyes swept the apartment quickly, looking for my flying saucer perhaps. Then they settled on me for a full ten seconds. It seemed like ten days. Then he turned abruptly and ran down the stairs. I heard the outside door slam hard behind him, and I was alone once more with only the upstairs radio to keep me company.

And that seemed to be that. I was obviously doing nobody any good hanging around getting colder by the minute. I stood up and waved my arms about for a few seconds to restore my flagging circulation. Then I followed Vladimir out of the apartment. I left the door open and the key in the lock. What happened to it was none of my business. There was no one in the street outside and, turning up the collar of my inadequate overcoat, I trudged back to the hotel.

The large woman on my landing glanced up at me as I emerged from the elevator. If she knew that I had been anywhere other than to visit my old pal Harbottle, she didn't show it. I could feel her eyes boring holes in my back as I walked to my room and let myself in. I tried a tentative 'good night' in her direction, but it was met with stony indifference, her rimless spectacles making it look as though she had two large holes drilled in the front of her skull. I slammed my bedroom door hard, hoping it would annoy her and started to get ready for bed. Fifteen minutes later I was sound asleep, engulfed in my feather mattress.

It took six hours for them to draw together all the strings and weave them into what amounted to my noose. That made it half past five in the morning when they came for me. There were four of them, two in the room and two more hovering about outside. They were very polite and didn't throw their weight about. Not that I gave them cause. As soon as the light snapped on, I was wide awake and already halfway out of bed.

'Mr. King?' asked the elder of the two men in the room. I concurred. 'Please, you will come with us.'

I made the requisite noises of bewilderment trailing into protest and back into bewilderment. All this while I was getting dressed, watched with evident disinterest by the older man, while the younger stood just inside the door, hands deep in pockets, ready to blow my head off.

As I was ushered out by these two, the other pair, who had been waiting outside, came into the room and proceeded to dismember my belongings. My large Russian lady was still sitting behind her desk, her expression no more disapproving than it had been before. No doubt, in her mind, sneaking out in the night clutching a bottle of vodka was just as bad a crime as that which caused the KGB to collect me at crack of dawn. Perhaps she even thought that was the reason they *were* collecting me. I felt like goosing her or sticking out my tongue, anything to get beneath that monolithic shell. But by the time I had made up my mind not to, it was too late anyway. I was shuffled across the deserted lobby and out into the Moscow dawn.

If I had thought it was cold before, now it was really something to write home about. My overcoat, designed for a London winter, was no match for its Moscow equivalent. The wind carved straight through to the bone so quickly that by the time I had been escorted across ten feet of pavement and bundled into the back of an anonymous looking black car, my teeth were chattering like castanets. Privately, I was delighted, because they would have been chattering anyway. This way I could afford to let them without losing face.

The ride to God-knows-where took twenty-five minutes and was conducted for the most part in silence. I made one half-hearted protest, babbling something about the British Embassy, but I only did this because I imagined it was expected of me, and not because I thought it would do any good. Here, I was right; it did no good whatsoever, and I spent the remainder of the journey preparing myself for the nastiness that was to follow.

The building outside which we disembarked was as anonymous as the men and the car. There were no guards on the door, and no official signs or notices proclaiming its function. It was just another building, like all the others in a nondescript street. This fact gave me no encouragement at all. There are buildings like this all over the world where the really nefarious things take place, things far too messy to be conducted in official places. I was hustled up the steps and through a door that opened in front of us when we were still four feet away from it. I had a momentary glimpse of a mournful looking man standing behind the door as I was marched across a grey, stone floored hall, and through a door on the far side. This gave on to a corridor with half a dozen doors leading from it.

My escort knew exactly where they were going. They ignored the first three doors, then jerked me to an abrupt halt outside the fourth. The younger man opened it, and the elder indicated with a nod of his head that I was to go through. I did so and the door was closed quietly behind me. I didn't hear a key turn, but when I tried the handle a moment later, the door was locked solid. The room was furnished lower echelon civil service, and I could have been in the office of any ministry in practically any damn country in the world. There were two standard filing cabinets, a two-drawer wooden desk with one chair behind it and one in front. Against the wall was a small table which in London would have held the tea making paraphernalia, but here in Moscow they obviously took their tea drinking seriously; on the table were two dirty glasses and an empty vodka bottle. The walls were grey, like the floor and ceiling, and were covered with a slight film of condensation. Although the room was a good twenty degrees warmer than it was outside, it was still bloody cold.

I wasn't sure what was expected of me, so I sat on one of the chairs to wait it out. But in case anyone was watching me, and not wanting to look as scared as I was, I reversed the chair and straddled it, trying to behave nonchalantly, as if this sort of thing happened to me every day; and even if it didn't, I was wrapped up and protected by my obvious innocence. I don't know whether anyone *was* watching, but two minutes later the door opened quietly and Vladimir Karkov walked in.

This was a turn up for the book and no mistake. My rendez-vous with him was designed solely to plot his downfall and now here he was, as large as life, and obviously acting in an official capacity, about to start asking me questions.

I remained seated while he closed the door behind him. He looked at me, a little sadly I thought, for a long moment. Then he sighed gently through his moustache. He pulled the other chair out from behind the desk and sat down so that he was facing me, his face a few inches away from mine. He continued to regard me stolidly for another thirty seconds, during which time I tried not to blink, and failed three times.

'What's it all about?' he said suddenly. It was a surprise; he looked so bloody Russian that I had expected at least the trace of an accent. There was none, unless you could classify minor Oxford as an accent. It was no good my pursuing the outraged British Citizen with Karkov, so I didn't bother. I tried the innocent tack.

'What's all what about?'

'Why was it arranged that you and I should meet in Kotelnicheskaya Street?' he said. Then, before I had time to open my mouth, he answered his own question. 'No,' he said. 'Not why. I know the reasons. What I now must know is what follows.'

Not knowing, I said nothing. After a pause he continued. 'In situations such as this your people will, one, have had me watched; two, will have planted evidence to incriminate me. I must know who was watching, to whom he will report, and the nature and the whereabouts of the evidence. You understand?'

I understood only too well, and I felt sorry for him. He was bright enough to have spotted the whole set up from the moment he walked into the room at Kotelnicheskaya Street and heard my English voice. He had known he was going to be framed and he had acted quickly. By having me picked up immediately he might have been able to neutralise the whole bit before the trap snapped shut on him. To do this, he had only to learn phase two in my operation and he would be able to clear himself before he was even under suspicion. Unfortunately for him, that's where he hit the snag. I couldn't tell him about phase two, because I didn't know what it was myself. The funny part about it was that he believed me. And, having accepted this fact, he grew mournfully conversational.

'We are tools, you and I,' he said. 'We are like the stone, the scissors and the paper in that stupid game. Stone blunts scissors, scissors cut paper, paper wraps stone. The unfortunate thing for us is that we don't know which we are. In this case, you are the scissors and I am the paper. It could have been the other way round.'

I was following him admirably and, in some places, I was way ahead of him. What he didn't know was that while I was scissors to his paper, there was a bloody great rook to my scissors waiting in the background ready to blunt me to hell and gone. But knowing it wasn't going to help him any, so I kept quiet.

The conversation moved on. He had already accepted that he was dead and buried as far as his professional life was concerned and he grew comparatively loquacious. This meant that he assumed that I was dead and buried alongside of him. Although he was going to get the sharp edge of the chopper from his employers, he was still sufficiently professional not to give away any secrets unless he was dead sure the giving away would harm no one.

He told me a great many things that I didn't know. And it wasn't because I had been out of the Service for six years; these were things that I was sure Max himself was unaware of. Normally I would have been both interested and fascinated by some of his disclosures, but all I could see now was that each new revelation was just another nail in my coffin.

After half an hour he had a bottle of vodka sent in and we killed it together, drinking solemn toasts to one another. I wasn't aware of the fact at the time, but I suppose I should have been grateful that he didn't stick bamboo splinters under my finger-nails or red hot pokers up my ass. In similar circumstances, had our positions been reversed, I am not at all sure that I would not have descended to such vulgarities, especially had my entire life been hanging in the balance, as his was. For the next ninety minutes we grew steadily more drunk and our conversation veered from the professional to the sentimental.

He told me all about his girlfriend, the one whose name had been used to involve him. I told him all about Anne Ballard, assuming that the telling could do no harm whatsoever; which only goes to prove how wrong you can be when there is half a bottle of vodka slopping around inside your stomach.

But the crunch had to come eventually. After two hours Vladimir suddenly pricked up his ears at some sounds in the corridor outside. To me they were just sounds, like all the others we had been hearing since we had been closeted together. But Vladimir knew different. He rose to his feet dramatically. He raised his glass and toasted me once more, this time in Russian. Then, like something straight out of Tolstoy, he flung the glass over his shoulder where it shattered on the wall behind him. Feeling that something was required of me, I, too, rose to my feet and lifted my glass, which was unfortunately empty, and intoned *my* farewell toast.

'Mud in your eye,' I said.

I upended the empty glass and, with an equally grandiloquent gesture, I flung it backwards over my shoulder. Unfortunately, I was standing with my back to the door, which was opened from the outside as my glass flew over my shoulder and shattered, inches away from the head of a thin, hawk-faced individual who was just entering. Not surprisingly, one of the uniformed men who had accompanied him, and who were standing outside the door, scrabbled for his revolver, assuming no doubt I was making a desperate attempt to escape. Vladimir shouted something in Russian and Hawkface repeated it. The uniformed man subsided, looking disappointed.

There followed a staccato exchange in Russian between Vladimir and Hawkface. Vladimir was obviously getting the worst of this interchange, but he went down with all flags flying. After half a dozen rapid sentences, he drew himself up to attention, bowed stiffly towards Hawkface, turned, bowed towards me and walked out of the room with his head held high. I would have liked to have told him that everything would be all right, but I didn't believe for one moment that it would. So I kept quiet and, when Hawkface indicated that I should precede him out of the room, I also drew myself up to attention, executed a stiff little bow, and did as he asked, crunching my way across a pile of shattered glass.

I had thought Vladimir and his men were efficient, but Hawkface and his crowd soon put them to shame. I was out of the building and in the back of a car before I could catch my breath. At our destination I was whisked out of the car and into a building so quickly that it was impossible for me to take in any of my surroundings. It wasn't until much later that I discovered that I was actually inside the walls of the Kremlin.

I was rushed down two or three anonymous corridors so fast that my feet barely touched the ground and was finally deposited in a cell. It wasn't bad as cells go; there was a reasonable looking bed, a table, a chair and a flush toilet lurking behind an inadequate screen in one corner. But it was a cell nevertheless, and I am of the opinion that even if one got David Hicks to design the interior, a cell will always be a cell. There are bars on the windows and a lock on the door; these have a psychological effect that no amount of flim-flam or chintz can disguise.

It was only after the door had been slammed shut behind me that I realised that nobody had spoken a single word to me since Vladimir had made his dignified departure. This could have been merely anti-social but was more likely due to the fact that from here on in my every utterance was to be recorded for posterity. They, with a capital T, didn't want my words wasted on the hired help. Hawkface I now relegated to this category. It was going to be interesting to see how high up the KGB ladder They considered they should climb before they reached an interrogator worthy of my importance.

❧   ❧   ❧

Somewhere in the Manual, it says that a suspect should be left alone for at least five hours before interrogation commences. This is designed to put the fear of God into the suspect, undermining his confidence and giving him serious doubts as to what his eventual fate will be. Either the Russians did not use the same manual or they considered my confidence was already undermined to a degree where further waiting would be superfluous. In this, they were right. The last vestiges of my confidence, courage, or what-have-you had leaked out of me back there in Kotelnicheskaya Street.

I hardly had time to use the toilet and ascertain that the plumbing was not as efficient as it looked, when the door was opened again. Two uniformed men stood outside and one of them barked something at me in Russian. I suppose I must have looked uncooperative, standing there doing up my flies, because a moment later the two of them came into the cell, grabbed an arm each, and hustled me out through the door.

I was taken to a large, well lit, efficient looking room, where I was fingerprinted and photographed before being escorted to a smaller room which was furnished even worse than my cell. There were a table and two upright wooden chairs, and I had been in the trade long enough to know that this was where we got down to business. There were no windows and the walls were tiled to a height of six feet. The floor, too, was tiled and very slightly funnelled to a soakaway drain set in the centre of the room. There was a water tap bolted to one of the walls, with a short length of hose fixed to it. They had obviously removed the thumb screws and the rack for the time being, but their message was there for all who had eyes to see. I was shoved hard into one of the chairs and a moment later the two uniformed men snapped to attention as Comrade-Colonel Nicolas Borensko came into the room.

I have a reasonably good memory for faces; but, more important, it is a selective memory. This means that I can recall the
important faces that crop up now and again, without having
the filing system cluttered up with the unimportant ones. This
one was a very important face. I had never seen it in the flesh
before, but in the old days Max had kept a file in which there were
photographs and details of the dozen or so men he would most
have liked to get his hands on. Even after six years I recognised
Borensko from the top of Max's file. This wasn't as difficult as it
sounds, because Borensko had just about the ugliest scar I have
ever seen. It started somewhere near his left temple, pulling back
the skin of his eye socket to such an extent that it was a wonder he was ever able to close his eye; it meandered down across
his cheek bone, clipped the corner of his mouth and trailed off
under his chin down into the collar of his tunic. It was a revolting
looking scar and he could easily have had it corrected by plastic
surgery. But in his job he had discovered that the mere sight of it
gave him such a psychological advantage that he even refused to
grow a beard to cover it up.

He was supposed to have come by his disfigurement during
the revolution when a White Russian officer had sliced open his
face with a sabre. But, if appearances were anything to go by, he
didn't look old enough to have been involved in the Revolution
and it was generally agreed by people whose job it was to know
such things that his face had been opened up with a broken bottle
wielded by an irate whore when he had been stationed in Macao
early in his career.

He came around the table and sat down in the other chair.
He examined the top of the table for a minute and then, seemingly satisfied with it, he shifted his gaze to me. This was
extremely off-putting, as no doubt it was intended to be. The
whore's bottle or the Czarist sabre had done its work extremely
well. In addition to disfiguring him, it had somehow severed
some of the muscles that controlled the movement of the eyeball

so that his left eye swung free within its socket. I have seen plenty of wandering eyes in my time, but Borensko's really travelled. It flopped about in its socket, darting hither and thither as though it were trying to escape. But, frightening as it was, it was soon forgotten when you looked into his good eye. That one was like a piece of chiselled quartz, muddy grey in colour, and far more intimidating than its wildly erratic companion, the scar, the interrogation room, the KGB or the entire bloody Kremlin.

'Mr. King,' he said. I tried to look intelligent. 'You are Mr. King?'

I nodded.

'Mr. Harrison King?'

I nodded again. Then I did the standard indignant bit which I felt was expected of me. 'I don't know what this is all about,' I said. 'But I want to see the British Consul.'

'No doubt,' said Borensko. 'But I feel the British Consul would not want to see you. No doubt you would be a considerable embarrassment to him.'

I blustered my way through a couple more indignant phrases and then subsided into silence.

'Have you quite finished,' he said. I nodded. 'Good. Then we can get down to business,' he said. 'First, your reason please for being in Moscow at this time?'

'I'm with a trade mission,' I said. 'I sell tractors.'

'I'm not interested in your cover,' he said. 'Only in the purpose of your visit.'

'Tractors,' I said.

He smoothed the surface of the table with his stubby, well kept hands. 'Mr. King,' he said. 'I must assume that you are not a fool or you would not be here. Would you please do me the courtesy of assuming the same as far as I am concerned. Now please, your business with Vladimir Karkov?'

'Who?'

He gave me one more chance. 'Your business with Vladimir Karkov?'

'I don't know anyone by that…' Anything further I had to say was superfluous. One of the men standing behind me fetched me a clout on the side of the head which lifted me clear out of the chair and deposited me against the wall seven feet away. There was a high-pitched singing in my ear as I was dragged to my feet and dropped back into the chair.

'Your business with Vladimir Karkov?'

I decided about here that enough was as good as a feast and, if I wanted to end the day with my head still on my shoulders, now was the time to start talking.

'I was told to contact him,' I said.

'Told by whom?'

'A man I met in London,' I said. 'I'd never met him before. He gave me five hundred pounds and said I was to contact this man at an address he gave me, and take from him whatever he had to offer, and fetch it back to London.'

'All this for five hundred pounds?' said Borensko.

'I'd cut my own throat for five hundred pounds,' I said.

His good eye regarded me bleakly for a moment. 'I think you have,' he said. He allowed me a few seconds to digest this remark before he continued. 'However, if you are telling the truth, and if you continue to co-operate, perhaps we can salvage something from the wreckage.'

By 'wreckage', I assumed he was referring to me personally.

'I'll be only too happy to co-operate,' I said.

'Please,' he said. 'The name of the man in London?'

'What man?' I said, courting another thump on the head. But I needed time right now. Borensko was not supposed to enquire too deeply into my association with Karkov. The whole Vladimir bit had been designed as a side issue, having no real bearing on the purpose of my visit. And until such time as they were able to compare my fingerprints and photograph with the file on John

Smith that must have been somewhere in their archives, I was forced to continue playing the role of the innocent victim of circumstance. I sincerely hoped that their records department was as efficient as their strong arm boys. You can flannel some people for a fair amount of time; a man like Borensko, with luck, you could flannel for ten seconds dead. But somehow over the years, it seems I had lost my knack. I didn't even get ten seconds.

While I was still making up my mind how long I could stretch the current trend of the conversation, he spotted me for the phoney that I was. When interrogation is your business, and you are a master at the job, you can read signs in your subject, without the subject even being aware that he has made any. To this day, I don't know what the sign was that gave me away to Borensko, but whatever it was I was grateful for it. There was bound to be a certain amount of table thumping, and even a modicum of John Smith thumping, but at least I would now be getting on to ground that had been partially prepared for me back at the Farm.

He announced the fact that I had not fooled him by suddenly slamming his hand flat down on the table.

'We are wasting time,' he said. 'You are not Harrison King, tractor salesman.'

'Oh,' I said. 'Who am I?'

'I don't know who you are,' he said. 'Just who you are not. And you are not who you would have me believe. Perhaps our records will turn up something.'

As far as I was concerned the pressure was now off, even if only temporarily, and the record department could take as long as they wanted. I wasn't going anywhere. But in the meantime Borensko decided to try to short circuit his filing system and gather his own information. 'If you are not a tractor salesman, then you can only be one other thing; a professional agent. And, if you are a professional agent, then there is more to the Vladimir Karkov affair than you or your employers would have us believe.'

In fact, there was considerably less to the Vladimir Karkov affair, but it turned out that this was what he meant anyway.

'A professional agent,' he continued, 'would never contact a man like Karkov in the manner that you did unless he had a special reason. In your case, I believe that the reason was discovery. It was intended that we here should know about your meeting with Karkov. He should be grateful to you. While knowing that he was a good man, we were not aware that he had attained such importance in the eyes of the West. The dispatch of an agent to Moscow, purely for the purpose of discrediting him, makes him a very important man indeed.'

He was right; Vladimir had considerable cause for gratitude. Five minutes ago, he had been as good as bound for the salt mines. Now it looked as though he was in line for rapid promotion. But we were still on unsafe ground. Borensko had accepted the fact that I was not King, tractor salesman, and that I *was* a professional agent, but he still believed that my sole purpose in visiting Moscow was to discredit Vladimir.

But records didn't let me down. There was a discreet tap on the door, which was answered by one of the uniformed men who had been standing behind me, and a file was handed over and then placed on the table in front of Borensko.

In happier circumstances, I would have been extremely flattered. The file was more than two inches thick. Considering I had not worked for the Service for six years, it was a pretty impressive indication as to how effective I had been during my earlier career. As the file was placed in front of him, Borensko looked at me bleakly for a second before examining it. I think he, too, was impressed with the size of the file, but it was impossible to read anything in the flat grey of his single eye. It was remarkable how quickly one forgot its roving companion. It was still wandering around like a lost soul within its strict orbit, but I hardly noticed it at all.

He bent over the file and there was silence for the next ten minutes. The only sound to break the monotony was the occasional rustle of paper as he passed from one document to another. Once he flashed a look at me and I would have liked to have known what he had just read that caused this deviation. Perhaps it had been that fiasco in Algiers, the one that had led me to quit the Service; then again, it might have been a report on my part in the crippling of Gustav Heidecker, who we all understood had been no end of the bright-eyed boy under the Stalin regime. But whatever it was, he didn't let on. He continued to shuffle through the file until he gently closed it up. Then, resting his hands palms down on the blank cover, he stared at them for a full minute and a half.

Finally, he looked up at me once more. 'Mr. Smith,' he said, 'there seems to have been a slight inefficiency in our records department. The last entry on your activities is dated two years ago and before that another four years. Tell me, please, where have you been during all this time?'

'Retired,' I said.

'But you are still working,' he said. 'You are here now.'

'I'm staging a comeback.'

He was pleased with himself; there was no doubt of it. His eye wasn't actually twinkling, but at least it had begun to look as though it had some sort of life in it. I could understand his satisfaction and a moment later he confirmed it for me.

'We thought we had caught a little fish. It seems we have caught a very large one.'

'Not that large,' I said.

'Come, come!' he said. 'You have an impressive record. Do you realise that at one time you were number three on our list of most wanted enemy agents?'

I hadn't realised it, but I wasn't going to let him know. 'That was a long time ago,' I said.

He flicked through the file once more, then stopped halfway. 'You shot Leo Tamir,' he said.

There didn't seem much point in denying it. I nodded.

'It's a pity you weren't on your true form that night,' he said.

That made two of us who felt the same way about Leo. I shrugged. 'We all have our off days,' I said.

'Much trouble would have been averted,' he said, as he leafed further through the file. 'There is a flattering report on you by Berat, the Albanian,' he went on, picking on another sheet of paper.

'I didn't know you were still chummy with the Chinese.'

'We're not. This is two years ago.'

'We got on quite well, all things considered,' I said. We had, too, considering we were on opposite sides of the wall.

'And since then you say you have been in retirement?' I nodded. 'You don't expect me to believe you?' he said.

'You might as well. It's true.'

'And the purpose of your present visit?' he said, coming to the crunch.

'Karkov?' I asked.

He shook his head. 'No. Karkov was a side issue, I think. A sort of bonus.' And having hit that nail right on the head he proceeded to bash away some more, his aim becoming even more accurate. 'Let us assume your main purpose in coming here was not to discredit Karkov,' he said. 'It follows that you must have had another reason. And yet you still kept this foolish rendezvous knowing that it was bound to lead to your eventual capture.' His good eye regarded me steadily as though he had asked me a question and was expecting a reply. But he hadn't and he wasn't. 'It's an interesting situation,' he went on. Looking at it from his side of the desk, I suppose it was. 'Of course, there is only one set of conclusions we can draw. Right?' This time he *was* asking a question.

'You tell me,' I said.

'You wished to be captured. It's the object of your visit here. The whole object.'

I said nothing. He was doing very well, thank you, all on his own, and Max's plan was running downhill fast. For if Borensko even began to guess that I had been planted for an exchange, then there wouldn't be one. If Max had been the only consideration, I would have chucked the towel in there and then, and a pox on his grandiose scheme. But there was a far more important aspect which had started to hammer around in my head. With no exchange, I had bought a one-way ticket to the salt mines. So right here, I started to get busy.

'Ofcourse I didn't intend to be caught,' I said. 'What do you take me for? Some kind of a nut? You've got my file there. That's the file of a man who knows what he's doing because he's done it all before. It's the file of a professional, not a half-assed amateur.'

'So?' he said.

'So you want to know why I'm here, I'll tell you. But you'd better get a stenographer in here, because I'm only saying it once.'

My goodness, I was brave! Nobody talked to Nicolas Borensko that way. But self-preservation is about the only strong basic emotion I can lay claim to and, when it comes to the fore, discretion takes a back seat. And anyway my file showed that I was a tough experienced customer, so I decided that I'd better start acting like one. Because if he truly started to believe that I was a hard-up ex-agent, long retired, then I was dead and buried already.

He jabbered something to one of the soldiers behind me and, while the soldier trotted off to find a stenographer, we sat and looked at one another. It didn't seem the time for small talk so, while attempting to look casual and completely at ease, I desperately tried to marshal my thoughts into a semblance of what I hoped he would take for credibility.

The stenographer arrived, a prematurely bald man with thick glasses. He brought his own chair with him and we all watched him while he made himself comfortable.

'First you will tell me in your own words,' said Borensko. 'Then later I will ask you questions.'

I looked toward the stenographer, who nodded, and I was away.

I trotted out all my recently learned information, adding a little here, missing out a little there. I embroidered parts of it and other parts I just sketched in. The important thing at this stage was to leave enough room for enlargement at some later date. The names I trotted out from time to time were just names as far as I was concerned. They may have had people attached to them; I just didn't know. Nor did I much care. They were the names that had been given to me to use, so I used them like. If these names, or the material I was spewing forth, meant anything to Borensko, he didn't show it. He just sat there, the only movement coming from his duff eye. If it hadn't been for that, rolling around in its fixed orbit, he could have been dead and embalmed.

I talked for two solid hours, while the stenographer wore out six pencils and filled two notebooks. The soldiers behind me grew bored some way through the proceedings and started to shuffle their feet occasionally. I was being so bloody co-operative that I was surprised Borensko didn't send them off to supper or some such. But he didn't, and for two hours there were just the five of us with me making all the noise. Then, when I started to get tired, I stopped. There was a long silence during which the stenographer kept his pencil poised. When he realised I had finished he lowered his pencil and closed his notebook quietly. The silence stretched and finally Borensko called an end to the proceedings. He said something to the man behind me and I felt a tap on my shoulder. I got to my feet.

'Thank you, Mr. Smith,' he said. 'We will talk later.'

'Any time,' I said, generously.

Two minutes later I was in my cell once more and, three minutes after that, I was sound asleep. There were dreams, of course, a huge conglomeration of all that had happened to me in the past twenty-four hours, mixed up so that they made no sense whatsoever. But even awake it didn't make much sense either, especially when viewed from the standpoint that I had walked into the situation with my eyes wide open. However, I slept, and while I slept Borensko put the wheels in motion.

The names I had trotted out so casually were checked and run to ground. The facts were examined, re-examined, and noted upon. A line was opened up to London where a check was made on my movements prior to leaving for Russia. Max had already made provision for this and I passed with flying colours. Everything possible was checked against my statement, then rechecked and verified. My personal effects at the hotel were dissected and disembowelled. No doubt all sorts of goodies came to light there, especially as Max's people had done my packing.

And while all this was going on, I slept for twelve hours, until Borensko called for me again.

'You are in grave trouble, Mr. Smith.'

'I know it.'

We were alone this time. The same room, but without the guards. My typed statement lay on the table in front of him and I could see where he had scribbled notes in the margins.

'Very grave trouble,' he said, as though the point needed emphasis. 'But there are aspects here which I do not understand. We will now examine some of them.'

That was the first session. It continued for three hours. Then there was a break of a couple of hours, and we started again.

About here I started to realise that Max hadn't chosen me for this assignment because he liked the colour of my eyes, or even because he thought I could do with the money. He had chosen me because for five years I had been out of the business. Consequently, anything about the internal workings of the Service that I inadvertently gave away was so out of date as to be harmless. And yet I was still steeped in sufficient genuine background material to keep Borensko interested. If it hadn't been for me, I don't think Max would have even contemplated the scheme, I was so damned right for it. At the back of my mind I started cursing the fact that I hadn't asked for more money. But I wasn't in any position to go back and ask for a raise now. So session after session followed with Borensko probing deeper and deeper, until I started to get seriously worried.

Then, just as I was about to run out of answers, it was all over. On the fourth day, as I was getting ready for my morning session in the interrogation room, the door of my cell opened and in came a man I hadn't seen before.

He was neatly and, for a Russian, almost elegantly dressed. His hair was cut short and he wore a pair of rimless spectacles. When he spoke, it was slowly, as though he was carefully examining each word in this foreign tongue before allowing it into circulation.

'My name is Chenkov,' he said. 'Boris Chenkov.'

He held out his hand and, because it seemed expected of me, I shook it. His handclasp was dry and not very firm. It was as though he would have had a good solid handshake had his heart been in it. In fact, his whole attitude was that of a man whose natural inclination was to be friendly, but whose inbuilt caution slowed him up a little. This turned out to be the situation exactly, as he explained in his next sentence.

'I have been appointed by the State as your defence council,' he said.

I felt like offering him my sympathy. Instead, I smiled and asked him to sit down. He did so, taking the only chair. I sat on the bed, facing him. 'What happens now?' I asked.

'Your trial is set for a week today,' he said. 'We do not have much time to prepare a defence.'

We could have had ten years and it wouldn't have made any difference. I hinted this to him delicately, not wanting to discourage him this early in the proceedings. 'I've signed a statement,' I said.

He looked away from me quickly, then back again. He was actually embarrassed. 'My task will be to persuade the court to reduce your sentence as far as it is possible. As you point out, guilt or innocence are not in dispute.'

'Reduce it from what to what?'

'The death penalty will be demanded,' he said. 'I shall endeavour to get it reduced to life imprisonment.'

'Bully for you!' I said irreverently. I was feeling choked. I didn't know what it was Max had set me up for, but it must have been a beaut for them to have been talking about the death penalty. What price Max's exchange if I was in a box, I thought, and I turned back to friend Chenkov, who was looking a little upset. 'I'm sorry, Mr. Chenkov,' I said. 'I know you'll do your best.'

He smiled very slightly. 'If I succeed,' he said, 'then things may not be as black as they now seem. Perhaps sometime in the future an exchange will be made.'

Hello, I thought, the plot thickens. I tried to see if there was anything lurking behind the smile, but there didn't seem to be. On reflection, it was a perfectly natural assumption of his; exchanges were the lifeblood of the trade. That's why I was here. I returned his smile.

'What can I do to help you?' I enquired.

It seemed there wasn't much. I should express remorse and shame in equal proportions; I should throw myself on the mercy of the court; I should confess to my errors and to my conversion to the Russian point of view, delivering a hefty thump to the capitalist warmongers in the process. It all added up to my saying that I had been a bad, bad boy and, if you don't spank me too hard, I promise not to do it again.

None of this would, of course, be believed by anyone, East or West, but the whole bit had become formalised in procedure like a badly staged farce. He then asked me if there was anything I wanted and I told him I could do with some decent toilet paper. He promised to speak to a friend at the American Embassy.

'A new toothbrush and some soap,' I added. He made a note in a small black notebook which he took from his jacket pocket.

'And some cigarettes,' I said, beginning to warm up. 'And matches, of course; some paper and pen and ink; a couple of books—murder stories; an English newspaper or two; a copy of *Time* magazine would be handy, and I could do with a new mattress. The one I've got…' He stopped me by snapping shut his notebook. It was a decisive moment, one which signaled that I had overstepped the mark somewhat. He still looked apologetic as he stood up, but there was no sign of it in his voice.

'Please bear in mind, Mr. Smith, that you are in prison charged with a capital offence. This is not a holiday resort on the Black Sea.'

'Sorry,' I said.

He smiled once more. 'I shall come and see you again tomorrow and we shall start to prepare the statement you will read out in court.'

He shook my hand again, a little harder this time, and off he went.

Me, I went to bed. There wasn't anything else to do in the cell and exercise appeared to be a dirty word as far as my gaolers were concerned. So I climbed into the sack, pulled the blanket over my head and curled up as tight as I could, wishing I could return to some sympathetic womb.

CHAPTER FIVE

The trial was a full, showcase affair; foreign press, diplomats, the lot. There hadn't been such a show of righteous indignation since the U2 business. It continued for three days of rock bottom boredom as far as I was concerned. They had provided me with earphones through which the flat voice of the interpreter droned on and on. But, as I knew practically verbatim the course the trial was going to take, it only served to enhance the boredom and after the first couple of hours, I realised that if I had to listen to this voice for the next three days, I would be a basket case. So when no one was looking, I managed to rip out the wires built into the phones. Wearing them after that effectively blotted out what was actually being spoken in the courtroom, so I was spared both the Russian and the English versions.

Occasionally I would see in the courtroom a face I knew, but not often. Neither Vladimir Karkov nor Borensko appeared. As undercover men it was necessary for them to remain undercover. There was an attractive-looking bird who, I later learned, was from the British Embassy, and I spent most of the trial staring at her and indulging in lewd flights of fancy. She must have been able to read the outer edges of my mind because, after the first couple of hours, she started to blush and pull her skirt down round her knees. After that she wouldn't catch my eye again.

I was driven to the courtroom each morning, escorted by three men, and driven back to my cell each evening. My clothes were taken from me when I went to bed and returned, laundered and pressed, before setting out the next day. I was shaved each morning by a vast sergeant who didn't speak a word and who wielded a cut-throat razor like he was decapitating an entire Cossack division. The food improved somewhat and I was even given half a bottle of Russian wine with my dinner.

The case against me, as presented by the Russians, was extremely lucid and beautifully documented. I had come to Moscow disguised as a tractor salesman and had then proceeded to contact various subversives who somehow still managed to exist in Russia. I had offered them money in an attempt to set up some sort of network which was to be used to feed back classified information. The whole thing was straight out of James Bond and far too infantile to fool any but the most gullible. But the Russians were fooled, or so it seemed, which only goes to prove something.

The evidence against me mounted slowly and methodically until even I began to wonder if I hadn't overplayed my hand somewhere along the line. If everything they were saying about me was true, I was too valuable to swap for a brace of Pontecorvos with a Fuchs and a Blake thrown in for good measure. But there was nothing I could do about it except sit and wait.

Comrade-Lawyer Chenkov did his best, but his heart wasn't in it. He pleaded a reasonable case based first on the premise that I wasn't the man everyone thought I was and, when that obviously died the death, he subtly switched tactics and presented me as an ignorant tool of the capitalist system. Here, he fared a little better, and on the fourth day of the trial, with me standing in the dock and looking suitably penitent, I heard the verdict: *Guilty on all counts. Sentenced to fifteen years' hard labour.*

That evening in my cell there was no wine and the dinner was diabolical. I felt as low as it was possible to be which, considering how low I had felt for the past couple of weeks, was pretty abysmal. The attitude of my guards had changed too. While not exactly thumping me, they gave every indication that they would like nothing better, and they gave me the impression they were just begging for an opportunity. So I was good—so good it hurt. I did everything I was told, when I was told. I didn't answer back and I kept myself strictly to myself. Mysteriously, my flush toilet went on the blink and, when I mentioned it apologetically, I was handed a bucket.

After the morning exercise period I lay on my bed and tried to analyse the reason I felt at rock bottom. Discounting the petty inconveniences, none of which really amounted to much, I should have been laughing. The whole plan was working exactly the way Max had predicted it would. All that remained now was for the wheels of international commerce, espionage division, to start grinding and, before you could say Kim Philby, I'd be a free man. A *rich* free man at that—and my mind started to slip sideways to visions of Anne Ballard, Mary and the girl from the British Embassy I had seen in court, and the first girl I had ever laid and the twenty-first. Just as the whole thing was beginning to become embarrassing and I was wondering what to do with my hands, the cell door opened and I was gestured at by a guard. I picked up my bucket, but another gesture from the guard told me it wasn't mucking out time. It seemed that it was visiting time instead.

It was Chenkov. He came into the cell and so good were his manners that he didn't even wrinkle his nose. He sat down on my only chair and smoothed the creases in his trousers.

'I did the best I could, Mr. Smith,' he said.

'You did very well,' I lied.

'After all,' he said. 'Fifteen years isn't a lifetime. With time off for good behaviour, you could be back home in ten years.'

'That's a great comfort,' I said. He had performed a thankless chore to the best of his ability and a pat on the back wasn't going to cost me anything.

'I have arranged that you will be transferred to Malensk. It will not be so bad there.'

'What's at Malensk?' I asked.

'It is what you call an open prison. The inmates work on the neighbouring farms. It is healthy work. You will eat well and the time will pass quicker.'

'That's very civil of you,' I said. 'Where is it?'

'It is near Vilyuisk, two hundred miles South of the Arctic Circle.'

'Siberia?'

He nodded. 'But it is not as bleak as people make out. During the summer the snow melts for as long as two months.'

'That must be hard on the farmers,' I said, not really interested. He then launched into a discourse on farming near the snowline which, if I had read about it in the *National Geographic,* I would have found quite interesting. But knowing that I was to be personally involved somehow robbed it of its fascination. Sure, I'd be home in three months, but even three weeks of what Chenkov was describing sounded sufficient to kill me stone dead.

He talked on for half an hour, then he rose to his feet. 'It is unlikely that we shall meet again, Mr. Smith,' he said. 'If you like, and if it is permitted, I shall write to you occasionally. I shall of course lodge appeals on your behalf every three years for the reduction of your sentence, but I am of the opinion that they will not be granted.'

'By all means write to me,' I said. 'Perhaps they will permit me to write back.'

'I understand that you will be allowed to send and receive one letter every two weeks. Is there anyone at home you wish me to contact?'

I thought briefly of Mary and Anne Ballard. Both would have read of my exploits in the newspapers, so there didn't seem much point. I would like to have assured Miss Roberts that everything was not as black as it obviously looked. But even she would survive for three months, by which time I would be home again, as large as life and twenty times richer.

'There's no one,' I said.

He bowed slightly. I believe he was a bit embarrassed. Between him and Vladimir Karkov, the Russians I had met hadn't been at all bad. I'm not by nature a gregarious person, but I could have made friends with either of them had the situation been different. I shook hands with him and he knocked on the cell door to be let out. Then I had an idea. 'Do the Embassy know where I'm going?' I asked.

'They do. But there is nothing they can do for you.'

'Still,' I said with a smile. 'It's a comfort.'

He returned my smile, a little vaguely. The guard opened the door, and that was the last of Comrade-Lawyer Chenkov.

Half an hour later my cell door was opened once more and a young officer I hadn't seen before appeared. He spoke atrocious English, but sufficient for me to ascertain that I had three minutes to gather my personal effects together. My personal effects consisted of a toothbrush, half a roll of toilet paper and a bent comb. He told me I wouldn't be needing the toilet paper, which sounded ominous, and with my toothbrush and comb clutched in my hand, I was marched out of my cell for the last time.

It was cold in the yard. I stood with half a dozen bedraggled looking prisoners, while our names were checked and rechecked on innumerable lists. Then we were signed for by an enormous officer with a great bushy moustache. He barked at his sergeant and we were all bundled into the back of a closed van. During our short ride I kept myself to myself, staring steadfastly at a spot on the wall opposite me. This lot were real criminals, not the sort of company I was used to at all. I may have killed a dozen or so assorted villains in the course of my ex-career, but the men sitting with me in the van were thieves, black marketeers and deviationists; it was downright humiliating to be included with them. And it was an even money bet that none of them spoke English anyway. There were two guards sitting in the rear of the van with us, nursing automatic weapons on their laps. But they were expecting no trouble and were plainly bored with the whole operation. As far as I was concerned, trouble from me was one thing they weren't going to get. Didn't I have my passport out of here? All that was needed was the stamp of official approval and I'd be on my way.

The van was driven to one of the main line stations and straight on to the platform. We were herded out and into two reserved compartments. The passengers standing around the platform regarded us with a disinterested curiosity. Once in the compartment, the blinds were drawn. I was with three other prisoners and one of the guards, so there was plenty of room. By judicious use of an elbow I managed to corner a window seat on the assumption that once the train started they'd raise the blinds. If we were going to do a 'Doctor Zhivago', and travel clean across Russia, I might as well have something other than my companions to stare at for the next four or five days.

The train remained motionless for the next twenty minutes and then, to the accompaniment of shouting and whistling from outside, it jerked and rumbled its way into motion.

For two whole days I sat on that train. Sure enough, they *did* pull up the blinds soon after we left Moscow but, as far as I was concerned, after an hour they might as well have lowered them again. There was nothing to see except mile after mile of flat farmland, stretching from here to God knows where. One hears of food shortages in Russia, when they rush off to buy wheat and cereals from Canada; all I can say is that they must be terrible farmers. There seemed to be enough farmland out there to feed all of Russia and half of China thrown in for good measure. Occasionally the train would roar past a small village, most of them no more than a collection of half a dozen wooden buildings; and once we slowed down to pass through some sort of industrial complex. But just as it was getting interesting, the officer with the whiskers appeared and barked at the guard to pull down the window blinds. This he did, letting them up an hour later, when we were back to the wide-open spaces.

I suppose the journey *did* take five days; I never found out. On the evening of the second day there was an unscheduled stop. Through the window I could see a tiny platform, backed by a couple of corrugated iron huts. I was trying to work out where we were when Whiskers put in one of his infrequent appearances and I was beckoned out into the corridor. There Whiskers informed me, through an interpreter, that I was to be taken off the train and returned to Moscow immediately.

I was driven from the station to a small airfield where I was escorted into an army plane. It was a big one, with four jets, and my spirits began to lift somewhat. If someone had considered it worth sending a plane this big, they must have wanted me back to Moscow very badly indeed. I seriously doubted for one moment that the pilot would be able to get it off the ground in the limited space that the airfield offered and, well strapped in, I watched through the window as we gathered speed towards a point where the airstrip ended and the ploughed fields took over. But a couple of seconds before we would have been among the cabbages, there was a great thump, I was slammed back in my seat, and the aircraft seemed to rise vertically, the engine noises drowned out by the roar of the rocket assisted takeoff. Very impressive, I thought, as I was quietly sick into a paper bag.

The journey to Moscow, which had taken two days on the train, took three hours in the plane. We touched down just after midnight and there was a car waiting at the end of the runway. I was bundled into the back with my escort and we were driven to a forbidding looking building somewhere in the centre of the city. There I was handed over with my documents, signed for, and escorted down a mile and a half of corridor. I was steered into a cell, the door was clanged shut behind me, and that seemed to be that.

At eleven o'clock the following morning, after I'd had a reasonable breakfast, Comrade-Lawyer Chenkov stepped into my life once more. He was all smiles and greeted me as though we hadn't seen each other for God knows how long.

'Mr. Smith. How are you? You look fine,' he said, wringing my hand. I mumbled something appropriate and waited for him to get to the meat. I knew what was coming and I prepared to look suitably surprised and grateful.

'You have been brought back to Moscow on the instructions of Comrade-Colonel Borensko,' he said.

'Why?' I asked, slipping easily into my part.

He smiled again, unable to contain himself. 'It is not official of course, but I understand there is the distinct possibility of an exchange being made.'

I widened my eyes in surprise. 'Really?' I said. 'What sort of an exchange?'

He was dying to tell me everything he knew, but discretion took the upper hand. 'I can tell you no more,' he said. 'But no doubt Comrade Borensko will want to see you personally.'

I doubted that. Borensko wouldn't become personally involved in an exchange, any more than Max would. They would both push their respective buttons and the machinery would do the rest. All of which goes to show that I didn't know what I was talking about because, at ten the following morning, I was taken to see Borensko.

Obviously, this was 'let's-be-friends' day, because he was wearing an eye patch. It didn't hide his scar, but it blotted out his erratic eye and made him considerably easier to look at. He even got to his feet when I came into the room he was using and, in case there were still lingering doubts that we were pals, he dismissed the guards immediately.

'Sit down, Mr. Smith,' he said. I sat. 'Cigarette?' He handed me a long brown Russian cigarette and then lit it for me with a lighter that could have been silver, but which I knew was platinum. 'What did Chenkov tell you?' he said when he was sure I was comfortable.

'Nothing,' I said. Then I qualified it. 'Nothing that I fully understood.'

'Then I shall start at the beginning,' he said. He then went on to explain that immediately after my conviction, the lines of communication to London had been opened up and, after careful probing, a meeting had been arranged in East Berlin between one of his men and one of Max's. It seemed that we in England were holding a man whom the Russians wanted back here in the fold, one Gregori Antonov. It also seemed that the English wanted me back where I belonged. So, being civilised human beings, what could be more natural than to arrange an exchange. I did the full Olivier bit, while he was explaining all this, registering surprise, delight and relief, all in equal proportions. When he reached the end of his little dissertation Borensko spread his hands, for all the world like a Russian peasant explaining why he couldn't pay his taxes. 'So you see, Mr. Smith, in two or three weeks' time you will be back at home where you belong, and so will Comrade

Antonov. Of course, you will give me your personal undertaking that you will never again resume the job that you do so well.' Here he patted my file which was on the table beside him.

'Of course not,' I said.

'No, of course not,' he agreed, convinced I was lying, and convinced that I knew that he knew I was lying. The funny thing was that I was telling the truth. I'd been hooked into this by the short hairs of my own avarice and I had no intention of going anywhere near Max or his kind ever again.

'We on our part,' he said, 'have given your people a similar undertaking with regard to Antonov.'

'Naturally,' I said. The whole thing was a pantomime and we both knew it. But there are formalities that have to be observed, and we observed them meticulously.

'I apologise that you were brought here last night,' he went on. 'Things moved too quickly for me to make proper arrangements for your comfort.'

They hadn't moved so quickly that he wasn't able to organise a bloody great rocket-assisted jet to pick me off a train in the middle of Russia, but I let the matter ride.

'As soon as we have finished here, you will be taken to a place I am sure you will find more agreeable.'

'I could do with a change of clothes,' I said.

'That has all been arranged,' he said, getting to his feet. 'And now I shall say good-bye. It is unlikely that we will meet again.' And here he showed me the gold in his teeth. I think he was smiling. 'I do not think I shall be visiting your country,' he said. 'And I sincerely hope that you will not be visiting mine again.'

I made polite noises, shook his hand, and was escorted out of the room by the same guards who had brought me there. I didn't even return to my cell. I was whipped out through a back door and into a car, which headed out of the city at a rate of knots.

Two hours later we pulled on to a side road and the country started to get wooded. Three miles into the trees, we stopped outside an impressive looking pair of gates. They were set into a wall, fifteen feet high, topped with insulated barbed wire. The wall disappeared into the trees without break for about three hundred yards in either direction. There was a guard-room just inside the gates and our papers were carefully checked. Then one of the guards climbed into the front of the car and started directing the driver.

We were in what looked like a large private park. The main drive headed slightly uphill, but after half a mile we turned off this on to a smaller track. A moment later I caught a glimpse through the trees of what lay at the end of the main drive. It was an old house, slightly smaller than Buckingham Palace, but not much. As a relic of Czarist Russia, the Communists could have charged visitors five roubles a head on bank holidays. But ever practical, they had put it to better use. I learned later that the whole place, the house and the grounds, was nothing more than a detention centre. A four star, de luxe, Category A type detention centre to be sure, but a prison nevertheless. Here came the V.I.P.'s; the deposed leaders, while the Party was making up its mind what to do with them; and the foreigners, who had earned detention, but not so conclusively that the Russians weren't sure what sort of fuss the detainee's Government might kick up.

Apart from the main house, there were a number of chalets dotted about among the trees. It was to one of these that I was taken. There I was handed over politely to the man whose job it was going to be to look after me. He was six feet seven inches tall and built like a brick outhouse. He spoke no English and, when he smiled, which he did often, he exposed a set of extremely ill-fitting false teeth. His name, of course, was Ivan and after the first ten minutes, when I was sure he could speak no English, I started to call him Terrible. He pointed out to me in Russian that it was his job to buttle for me and, while he gave every outward indication that his only purpose was to serve, he left no doubts that if I put so much as a foot wrong, he'd cut it off at the knee.

The chalet consisted of a living room, kitchen, bathroom, and two bedrooms. The bedrooms were arranged in such a way that to get to mine, it was necessary to pass through Terrible's. My room was pleasant enough, with a wardrobe, dressing table, double bed and full-length curtains; but the curtains were for effect, because there was no window. I also had to go through Terrible's room to get to the bathroom. This didn't disturb me unduly, but the combination of the cold and my unreliable bladder was going to rob Terrible of a lot of sleep.

My suitcase, which I had last seen when I had been dragged out of my hotel, was waiting for me. Terrible helped me unpack and hang up the awful clothes that Max's men had chosen to fit the image of Harrison King, tractor salesman.

After that, I sat in front of a roaring fire in the living room, while Terrible sat across from me, examining his fingernails and occasionally grinning broadly in my direction. About four o'clock, I heard noises in the kitchen and I glanced towards Terrible for enlightenment. He called out something and a moment later a pleasantly plain girl came in from the kitchen. She was wearing an apron and looked like domesticity personified. It seemed that she was our non-resident housekeeper. She cooked the meals and did the general chores while Terrible sat on my back, making like a butler-cum-companion, and failing in his attempts not to look like a gaoler.

The girl smiled shyly at me and bobbed a strictly non-Party-line curtsy in my direction. I leered back at her and she returned to the kitchen. A moment later Terrible got to his feet and dragged me over to a cupboard which he opened proudly, showing me that it contained a fair assortment of booze. He made extravagant gestures signifying that I should ask for what I wanted. I pointed to the vodka bottle and, beaming, he poured me three fingers. Three of *his* fingers practically filled a tumbler, but I wasn't driving, so I took it and began to anticipate the delights of getting stoned out of my mind. I pantomimed for him to have one too, but he shook his head emphatically. From the size of him he could have drunk me under seventeen different tables, but he was obviously going to take no chances. But while he wasn't going to drink with me, he was prepared to keep me amused. He dragged out a chessboard and, when I nodded, he happily set out the pieces. I decided that I would show this bumped up yokel that the Russians weren't the only chess players in the world and I started right out to massacre him. Fifteen minutes later he had me tied up so tight that I counted his pieces to make sure he hadn't sneaked a couple of spare queens on to the board when I wasn't looking. He hadn't, and I magnanimously conceded the game to him. He offered to play me again, this time without his queen, but I declined.

I was getting smashed by now; I wasn't talking funny or staggering around the place, but I had begun to entertain lecherous thoughts towards the domestic help. And while one section of my mind indulged in lewd flights of fancy, another kept reminding me that she really was a very plain girl, with a figure like a badly packed laundry sack. Terrible meandered off towards the kitchen—perhaps he wasn't as particular as I was—and with the fire going and a gentle background of voices mumbling in the background, the booze finally gained the upper hand. The next thing I knew was Terrible shaking me awake and pointing me in the direction of the dinner table. It was a good dinner, but I didn't do it justice. All of a sudden the past few weeks seemed to catch up with me. The arrest, the interrogations, the trial, the train journey, the return by plane, the bad food, the cells, the cold and the damp. I must have fallen face forward in my *borscht*, because I was vaguely conscious of being lifted to my feet and propelled towards the bedroom. There Terrible had me out of my clothes and into bed before I knew what was happening. The last thing I remember was his amiable face bending over me as he tucked me in. Then the lights went out and I died for thirty-two straight hours.

A week passed pleasantly enough. Terrible and I would go for walks in the parkland, and occasionally I'd see other members of our little community through the trees, each with his own version of Terrible. But we were never allowed to meet and, on the odd occasions when it looked as though head-on collisions would be unavoidable, my Terrible, or the other man's, always managed a diversion of some sort.

But by the end of the first week, the novelty of living like a human being again was beginning to wear a bit thin. There had been no word from Borensko or from anyone else. I was sick of being beaten at chess by Terrible and he didn't know how to play anything else. The half dozen books in the chalet were all in Russian and my requests for something in English fell on stony ground. So, on the morning of the seventh day, I woke up deciding to be ugly. I sulked at breakfast and, when Terrible suggested a walk, I snarled at him with fluent obscenity. But if I hoped to get him annoyed or to hurt his feelings, I was unlucky. He nodded politely as though he understood and went to sit across the room on his own. When I got up to go to the toilet, he followed me as always, and took up his usual position outside the door. I was so bloody bored I even contemplated breaking the mirror and slashing my wrists. Terrible would see that I didn't come to any real harm, and it might have relieved the monotony somewhat. But reason prevailed and all I did was to stay there long enough to worry Terrible sufficiently for him to come in and get me out.

I refused to eat my lunch and was rewarded by a hurt look in the eyes of our cook. But it was during the afternoon that I really came into my own. I started drinking in lieu of lunch, and by four o'clock I was well and truly zonked. Terrible was sitting off in a corner working out a chess problem and, full of booze and pent up irritation, I walked over to him and swept all the pieces off the board.

'What are you going to do about *that?*' I said, looking at the two of him sitting there.

He gazed at me placidly for a moment from all four of his eyes, then he reached down and started to pick up the chessmen, putting them back on the board.

While he was bending forward, I emptied my glass down the back of his neck. He jumped to his feet quickly and, in doing so, quite accidentally, he bumped into me. That was it as far as I was concerned. I aimed a swipe at him designed to take his head off, at the same time lining up another blow which I was going to use when he ducked out of the way of the first. But he didn't duck. He just stood there and my first blow, the decapitating one, landed dead on target, just in front of and slightly below his left ear. He made no effort to ride the punch, and it was just like hitting a lump of concrete. I swear he didn't even blink, but I couldn't be too sure of this as I was too busy nursing a hand in which I was willing to bet that every single bone was shattered. Perhaps he thought I hadn't finished, because the next thing he did was to raise a hand, with one finger extended, and poke it into my diaphragm. All coordination and control left me suddenly, and he caught me deftly as I collapsed to the floor like a tent that has had all the guy ropes and poles removed at the same time. He carried me into the bedroom and laid me out tidily, where I stayed for the next three hours trying to rebuild myself from scratch.

For the next three days I behaved myself. I wasn't affability, but at least I pretended to be civilised. If Terrible bore any grudge, he didn't show it. He was the same, amiable bear of a man he had been before. Only once did he show that my afternoon's stupidity had made any impression on him. That was two days later when I stopped in the woods to have a pee, and for two seconds he didn't realise that I wasn't still with him. When he *did* realise it, he moved incredibly quickly and in a moment he spotted me standing behind a tree poisoning the roots. He relapsed immediately into his ambling self, but he permitted himself a little shake of the head to signify that I shouldn't frighten him like that again; and to add weight to his argument, he held up the finger he had used to demolish me, and waggled it at me like a nanny admonishing a naughty little boy. I waggled back at him, then put myself away and did up my zip.

The fourth day dawned like any other. I was lying on the edge of sleep, wondering what the hell I had to get up for, when Terrible came in and gestured that I was to get dressed. When I showed signs of turning over and going back to sleep, he picked up my bedside clock and with a bit of absurd pantomime he indicated that a car was coming for me in half an hour. This was it, I thought—the moment of truth, pay day. I was shaved, dressed and packed in twenty minutes, waiting outside when the car arrived. Terrible and his female helper stood on the doorstep to say their good byes. I shook them both by the hand feeling for all the world like a country squire saying good bye to two faithful old retainers.

Then into the car and back to Moscow. I sat comfortably in the back with visions of being home and dry by the end of the week. I expected to be driven straight to one of the better hotels, where I would stay while the final formalities were gone through. I wasn't. I was driven straight back to the gaol I had left ten days earlier.

There didn't seem much point in yelling and screaming at the guards; and, anyway, I was far too frightened. Something had gone seriously wrong somewhere. I sat in my cell chewing my fingernails to shreds and feeling sick, until half an hour later I was hauled out and escorted to an interview room.

Waiting for me was a tall, thin man in a black jacket and pinstripe trousers. There was a bowler hat and an umbrella on the table, beside them a leather briefcase with the legend EII R stamped on it. I was dose to panic by now.

'It's about bloody time,' I said, before Pinstripes could open his mouth. 'I've been in and out of gaol for the past five weeks, and you're the first indication I've had that we've even *got* an Embassy in Russia.'

'My name is Beamish,' he said. 'Philip Beamish.'

'I don't give a fuck what your name is,' I said, in full flow now. 'Just tell me why I've been brought back here, then do something about getting me out.'

His left eyelid had started to twitch; whether from anger or embarrassment at what he was about to say, I didn't know. Nor did I care. 'Calm yourself, Mr. Smith,' he said, trying to keep his voice on an even keel. 'Histrionics will get us nowhere.' He glanced at the guard who was minding his own business in the corner of the room. It was important to Beamish to preserve the British image of stiff upper lip and all that nonsense. But my upper lip had lost its starch way back, and I wasn't about to re-stiffen it just so Beamish could keep the Union Jack flying.

'I'll behave any damn way I please,' I stormed. 'Now tell me what's going on before I lose control.'

If he could have cut my throat there and then, he would have done so with pleasure. Instead he sat down and indicated for me to do the same. I did so reluctantly.

'As you know,' he said. 'An exchange was in the process of being arranged. Yourself for Gregori Antonov.' I nodded, not trusting myself to open my mouth. 'There's been a slight snag,' he went on.

'How slight?'

He cleared his throat. 'Not slight at all as a matter of fact.'

'So tell me,' I said, bracing myself for disaster.

'The snag lies with Antonov himself,' Beamish continued.

I jumped in on him. 'The bastard doesn't want to be exchanged,' I said. 'So tell him to get stuffed and deliver him here anyway.'

'It's not as simple as that,' said Beamish primly.

'It is for me,' I said. 'I want out of here, and friend Antonov is my ticket. Now get moving on it and don't come to me with any more balls about snags. You tell Max he won't know what the word 'snag' means until I get started. And if he doesn't get me out of here in one week flat, I'll open my mouth so wide you'll be able to lose the entire British Embassy in it.'

Beamish had looked horrified when I mentioned Max's name and glanced over his shoulder toward the disinterested guard. Now he turned back to me, tight lipped, livid with anger, and relishing what he was about to say next.

'It will be impossible to arrange an exchange between you and Antonov,' he said. 'Because two days ago Gregori Antonov suffered a heart attack.'

Then, in case the full import of what he was saying had failed to impress me sufficiently, he hammered in the last nail.

'He's dead.'

CHAPTER SIX

Having entered my life with such dramatic effect, the British Embassy couldn't wait to get out of it again. Apart from that one traumatic interview with Beamish, I never saw hide nor hair of them again. As far as they were concerned, I was the *persona* most *non grata* in existence. Russian diplomats would drop my name casually when they were arguing delicate points of diplomacy with their British counterparts; while the British tried to pretend I never existed. For while both sides were fully aware that spies and other such villains existed, there was a tacit understanding that the fact was never referred to. But I had upset the *status quo* and committed the unpardonable sin of being caught, with all its attendant publicity. So for a short time the Russians made hay of the fact, and the British wished I would disappear into a large hole.

As for me, it took me twenty-four hours to recover from the shock. Then I started to yell. I yelled so loudly and so consistently that someone *had* to take notice. I wanted to see Borensko and I wanted to see him before they put me back on that bloody train. This time there would be no aeroplane to pluck me from the middle of the Steppes and, if I was going to have to spend the next fifteen years digging up Russian potatoes, I wanted to leave a lot of bleeding corpses behind me. And I wanted Max to be the bloodiest of them all. He'd got me into this impossible situation and I was determined that he was going to suffer for every furrow I had to hoe.

So I yelled. I yelled at the guard who escorted me with my bucket and I yelled at the guard who brought me my food; I yelled at the officers who inspected the cells twice a day, and I yelled at anyone in uniform who I saw in the exercise yard. I tried to get hold of Chenkov to yell at him too, but he never appeared, so after a while I forgot about him and concentrated on trying to get through to Borensko. And somewhere along the line I must have succeeded, because just after lights out on the third day, the guards came to my cell and gave me two minutes to get dressed. I thought for a moment the train had arrived and I started to protest, until one of the guards who had been forced to listen to me for the past three days, jabbed me with the barrel of his submachine gun. It wasn't as painful as Terrible's finger, but well on the way. So I got dressed and was escorted along corridors, upstairs, and along more corridors until I suddenly found myself in a room with Borensko. My immediate relief evaporated somewhat when I realised that it was an interrogation room and he wasn't wearing his eye patch. He was sitting behind the table, looking one part bored and three parts angry.

'You have been making a great deal of fuss, Mr. Smith,' he said.

'I wanted to see you.'

'If it wasn't for the fact that I don't like my name shouted around the place, I would have left you to rot.'

'That's why I shouted it.'

'I could also have had you silenced.'

'You couldn't do that,' I said. 'I'm a much publicised, well-documented prisoner.'

'So what have you to say to me?'

'I want to go home,' I said, trying to keep my lower lip from trembling.

'No doubt,' he said. 'And with time off for good behaviour, you will probably be released in ten years.'

'I want to go home now. And I want you to send me home.'

His good eye stared at me unblinking. The less said about the other, the better. He digested my remark well, before answering. 'What reason would I have for sending you home?'

'You'll think of something,' I said.

This time the silence was longer.

'You are offering me some sort of a bargain?' he asked finally.

'I made a bargain with Max that backfired,' I said. 'Perhaps I can make one with you that won't.'

'What bargain did you make with Max?'

So I told him the lot. Before I was halfway through, he was on the phone. Having found out that their prize man in the U.K. was working for the home team, there were a lot of readjustments to be made, and quickly. Between calls he prompted me to continue. Finally it was all over, and he relaxed slightly. 'Gregori Antonov did us a great favour by dying,' he said.

'He didn't do me much good though.'

'True.'

'So?' I said, wondering whether I'd lost him forever.

'So now you want to work for us?'

'Not in any permanent capacity,' I said. 'Just one job that will buy me my ticket home.'

'For example?'

I shrugged. In for a penny, I thought.

'You want someone killed perhaps?' I said, not too hopefully.

He shook his head. 'No, Mr. Smith. I have executioners for that sort of work.'

'Men like Leo Tamir,' I said, merely stating a fact, but as it turned out unconsciously turning the key in the door marked Exit.

'Yes,' he said. 'Men like Leo Tamir.' And as he said it, his one good eye suddenly got itself a withdrawn expression. What the other eye was doing was anybody's guess. Me, I was busy looking at his good eye and wondering whether I'd hit a jackpot without knowing it. 'If I remember rightly, you tried to kill Leo Tamir once.'

'A long time ago,' I said, starting to feel my way.

'He was no good to us after that. We should have let him die.'

'You should indeed,' I said, starting to feel solid ground under my feet.

'We've lost track of him,' said Borensko.

'He's working for the CIA,' I said.

Borensko dismissed the fact with a wave of his hand. 'We know that,' he said. 'What we *don't* know is where, and at what.'

'He was in England five weeks ago,' I said. 'He briefed me on part of this job.'

'Is he still there?'

'Could be,' I said. 'If he isn't, he could be got.'

'How?'

'Something could be arranged,' I said.

'Could it really, Mr. Smith?' He was asking me a direct question now, and on the answer hung fifteen years of my life.

'Definitely,' I said, without hesitation.

He was nibbling at the bait. I tried to think of something that would make him bite hard. 'I might say I could almost guarantee it,' I said after a moment. He still said nothing and I could practically hear the wheels in his head clicking over, sorting out the various permutations and complications of what I was offering. It would be a big feather in his cap. Not only would he be bringing back a defector for retribution but he'd be getting a window into the workings of the CIA. After all, Leo Tamir had been working for them for a long time now and he must have packed away a pretty useful store of information in that time. I didn't doubt for a moment that Borensko would be perfectly capable of extracting every ounce of it before Leo finally succumbed. He had closed his good eye while digesting all this. The other one continued to revolve erratically. I waited for the good one to appear again; therein lay the key. He reopened it finally.

'I will think about it,' he said. I'd have liked something a little more concrete, but there was no point in pushing my luck any further than I already had. I got to my feet. 'Take your time, Colonel. I'm not going anywhere.'

He smiled. At least, I think it was a smile. 'No, you're not,' he said.

And that was the end of the interview.

The following day a draft left the prison bound for the long train ride to the wide-open spaces. And I wasn't included, which made my day. I'd thought that Borensko would have had the good manners to change my accommodation, seeing that we were now on the same side, and I even began to look forward to seeing Terrible again. But nothing happened in that direction and when I was sent for, seven days later, I was still languishing in the same cell.

They came for me at eight o'clock in the evening and I was taken to a dressing room where I was told to change and to bring my overcoat with me. Then I was escorted out into the prison yard to a large black car. Borensko was waiting for me in the back of the car. He was out of uniform and wearing an eye patch, which was encouraging. He said 'Good evening' to me politely enough, and that was all.

We had been driving for ten minutes before I got curious enough to open my mouth.

'Where are we going?'

'To the theatre,' he said flatly.

Ask a silly question, I thought. But to the theatre we went. We pulled up outside a small theatre fifteen minutes from the centre of the city. Once inside the foyer we were hurried upstairs by a man I assumed was the manager, and through a door into a box. The show was already in progress and the theatre was full; the Russians will go and see anything, and what they were seeing at the moment was an acrobatic act composed of two men and a girl. It was pretty diabolical, as acts go, but the audience seemed to like it. I was too busy wondering what I was doing here to pay much attention, until one of the men in the act, stepping forward to take his bow, distinctly said: 'Thank you, ladies and gentlemen.' And he said it in English. I glanced sideways at Borensko, but he was watching the stage and didn't or wouldn't catch my eye. But I knew what was going to happen and I started to feel sick.

Sure enough, the acrobats finished, the lights dimmed and when they came up again a piano had been wheeled on to the stage. Two seconds later, there was Anne Ballard, looking like a million roubles, and twice as beddable as when I last saw her.

She still spoke her songs rather than sang them, and the effect was still the same, sexy virginity. The audience may not have been able to understand the lyrics but they loved her anyway. Me, I just started to curse fluently under my breath and, if I'd had a knife handy, I would happily have cut my throat. Because it was me who was to blame, me and my big drunken mouth. A bottle of vodka with Vladimir Karkov, and I had presented them with Anne on a platter.

I found out later that Borensko had moved very fast after our last conversation. A member of the Russian Embassy had called on Harvey Stubbs and asked him to book an entire variety bill for a week in Moscow, followed by a tour of some of the Russian cities. Once Harvey had gotten over the shock, he borrowed two acts from another agent, parceled them with three of his own clients including ofcourse Anne, who was an integral part of the deal, and four days later, here they were.

Borensko allowed me to sit through all of Anne's act. As she left the stage to loud applause, he stood up. 'Charming,' he said. 'Shall we go?' We went.

'It is perfectly straightforward,' he said to me later that evening. 'Miss Ballard and her companions will be in Russia for five weeks. That means you have five weeks to deliver Leo Tamir to us.'

'How?' I asked.

'That is your problem. It was your idea, remember?'

'And if I don't?' It was a silly question.

'Miss Ballard will remain in Russia.'

'There'll be a fuss.'

'Come, Mr. Smith.' He was right. There'd be an accident, and exit Anne, clean and simple. I tried to tell myself 'so what?', but I'm a selfish bastard from way back and I knew that it was more than just Anne's future in the balance; my own was there right beside hers. If I didn't produce Leo, not only would Anne go to the wall, but I'd be discovered in some dark alley with my head beaten in with a hammer and my heart cut out with a sickle. When I didn't say anything, he continued: 'You wanted a bargain. Now you have one. A simple case of exchange. Anne Ballard for Leo Tamir.'

'It was a simple case of exchange before,' I said.

He shrugged. 'You must make sure this one doesn't go wrong, mustn't you.'

'Yes, sir,' I said. And that seemed to be that.

East Berlin was as depressing as it had always been. And the way over the Wall was just as simple, provided one knew the right people. Borensko had seen to it that I knew the right people, and two hours after landing in East Berlin, I was checking into the Hilton in the Western sector.

My passport said I was a Mr. Barnet Wimpole, salesman. I wasn't sure what I was supposed to be selling, but it didn't really matter. The passport was designed to get me out of West Berlin. After that I could use it or not, as the fancy took me. I certainly wasn't going to fly into London Airport. Max always had the odd man hanging around watching arrivals and departures, and I hadn't decided yet when I wanted Max to know that the prodigal had returned. One thing was for sure, when he *did* find out, it was going to be on my terms and not because some eagle-eyed flat foot spotted me coming through customs.

I showered and shaved, mutilated half a bottle of vodka, and went out to exercise my urges. You can find anything you want in West Berlin, providing you know where to look. I used to know where to look, but five years had washed an awful lot of people under the bridge. There had been a time when I'd been quite a big wheel in the seamier side of the Berlin social scene. But everyone seemed to have moved, married, or died. Three frustrated hours later, I was back in my hotel room alone. I had been propositioned by a woman who reminded me of my grandmother, and by a beautiful young girl who, on closer examination, proved to be a beautiful young boy.

I asked the hotel switchboard to give me an eight o'clock call and by ten I was on an aeroplane to Paris.

At Orly airport I hired a self-drive car and drove the three hours to Le Touquet. I left the car there, flew British United to Lydd, where I hired another car. Ten minutes later I was on the main road to London, wondering where the hell I was bound for. My own flat was out; that would have been too obvious. Mary seemed a natural choice, but I didn't want to mix her up in the nastiness that was to come. But thoughts of Mary led me to thoughts of Anne, and thoughts of Anne led naturally to The Rabbit Warren. With Anne away, her kid sister would be staying with her aunt, and The Rabbit Warren was about as anonymous a place as I could wish for.

I parked my car at the back of the block and used one of the rear doors. On the sixth floor, I walked along to 625 and rang the bell. Nobody answered the door and, after ringing once again just to be sure, I let myself in with a visiting card. The apartment was exactly as I had last seen it, complete to the teddy bears on the two beds. The whole place was spick and span and clean as a new pin. Considering the short time she must have had to prepare for a trip to Russia, she'd done well.

I poked around for a while until I found a spare front door key; then I moved a few things out of one of the drawers and unpacked. I stripped off and had myself a bath, liberally laced with some of the bath salts scattered all over the place. Then, wrapped in one of Anne's bath towels, I turned back one of the beds, lay down, and composed myself for a bit of heavy thinking.

Item one; how was I to get hold of Leo Tamir? He sure as hell wasn't going to answer any invitation, even if I knew where to deliver it. Item two; having sorted out item one, how was I going to manage the physical side of shipping him to Russia? Borensko had laid on all sorts of schemes for my approval, but a prime requisite for all of them was Leo himself. Item three; Having taken care of one and two, how was I going to make sure that Anne was returned safely? Item four; I fell asleep.

It was dark when I woke up and my watch had stopped. There wasn't much traffic outside, so it was fairly late. I wasn't interested enough to dial TIM and, finding an unopened bottle of vodka in the kitchen, I became even less interested. I started a list, heading it 'one bottle of vodka', which I left in the kitchen to be added to each time I swiped something else. Back in bed I started to marshal some of the random thought processes that had flitted back and forth on the edge of sleep. It was getting light outside and I'd killed half the bottle before I could honestly say that I had a rough idea of what I was going to do. 'Rough' was the operative word, and if ever there was a situation that was going to have to be played by ear, this was it. But at least I'd worked out stage one. Stage two could branch off in seventeen different directions, fifteen of which could turn out fatal for me. But fifteen to two were the best odds I could muster for the time being. I set the alarm for mid-day, pushed the bottle under the bed and started in on a little serious sleeping.

A bell jerked me awake. I was groping around for the alarm clock when I realised that it was the front door bell. This was a turn up for the book. I lay still, hoping whoever it was would go away eventually. But the bell continued to ring as though someone was leaning against it and had no intention of doing otherwise until the door was opened. So I clambered out of bed and, clutching the bath towel around me, I opened the front door. I'd quickly composed a story that I was Anne's uncle, down from the North for a week in the Smoke. But my story wasn't necessary. The two men outside the door had Max written all over them. As I opened the door, they stepped in without a word. The fact that they had to elbow me out of the way to do so, didn't worry them a bit. Not that I took much elbowing. With one hand clutching my modesty about me, I couldn't have resisted even if I'd wanted to. And, anyway, one didn't resist Max's Heavy Squad unless one wanted a broken arm at best, and a broken head at the other end of the scale. They were both large, hard-eyed men, neatly dressed and quietly spoken. I didn't know either of them. This wasn't surprising, because even in the old days when I'd worked for Max, I'd rarely had anything to do with the Heavy Squad. Most of their work was conducted in sound proof rooms or anonymous alleyways.

One of them stood in the minute hall, keeping me company, while the other examined the apartment quickly. Then having ascertained that I was alone, I was prodded into the main room.

'Get dressed,' said Number One.

'Why?' I asked.

'Max wants to see you.'

'He'll have to wait,' I said.

'He wants to see you now.'

'So? He knows where I am.'

Number Two sighed gently, but Number One shook his head quickly. Obviously, I wasn't to be thumped. Not yet anyway. 'He'd appreciate it if you could pay him a visit,' said Number One, obviously wishing he could belt me.

'I'll pop in and see him tomorrow,' I said.

Number One started to flounder a little. He'd been told to bring me in without bending me too much, and here I was being difficult. Number Two just looked nasty. 'He hoped you'd be able to see him right away.'

'Then he's going to be unlucky,' I said. 'Tell him I was coming to see him anyway. He owes me seven and a half thousand quid.'

The two men flashed a look at one another. This was news to them, as no doubt it would be to Max.

Number One made the final effort. 'We could fix an appointment for this afternoon,' he said hopefully.

'Ten-thirty tomorrow morning,' I said, heading for the front door. They shambled after me reluctantly. I opened the door and stood aside. 'Incidentally,' I said, as they moved past me. 'How did you know where I was?'

They looked at one another for a moment, then Number One shrugged as though it didn't matter. 'You were spotted out of Berlin,' he said.

I closed the door quietly behind them. I might just as well have caught a plane straight to London. But at least there was some satisfaction in knowing that Max must have tied up a dozen men to keep tabs on me from Paris, through to Le Touquet, across the Channel and into London. If nothing else I had given the tax payers a belting.

And having said I wouldn't go to see Max until next morning, I now had nothing to do. I'd intended calling on him that afternoon, but the fact that he had sent the Heavy Squad to fetch me had got up my nose. So let the bastard wait!

Now that he knew I was in circulation again, there didn't seem much point in staying at The Rabbit Warren. I dressed and packed, then I phoned the off-licence to send up a bottle of vodka to replace the one I had used. Because I was an evil bastard with lecherous intent, I kept the spare key that I had found. I phoned the hire company and told them where they could pick up the car. Then I went home.

The flat smelled like a disused graveyard and looked just about as inviting. There was an even coating of dust over everything and a stale smell like a bad embalming job. A bottle of beer had iced up in the fridge and exploded. This had put the fridge out of commission so that a packet of frozen fish fingers had gone way off. It took me five minutes to locate the source of the smell and, when I finally opened the fridge door, I was practically knocked off my feet.

I slipped down to the local grocers, where along with bacon, eggs, bread and milk, I purchased one of those Fresh-Aire squirters. Back in the flat I sprayed it liberally over everything. It helped, but not much. Then I pulled out my battered old typewriter and started work. Many years before, I had decided that, as long as I was doing a dangerous job, I might as well take out some form of insurance. My insurance consisted of carefully documented reports about what I was doing, and what conclusions I drew. These reports I deposited in a safe deposit box in Switzerland. My long suffering London bank manager had the number of my deposit box and my instructions to open it should anything untoward happen to me. In the deposit box were detailed instructions as to what to do with the contents. If my head had rolled at any time, it would only have been the first of many, and Max's would have been close behind. It wasn't much as insurance policies go, but it had kept me alive through six years of working for Max, and six subsequent years, so it must have had something going for it.

I finished typing, sealed the stuff in an envelope, and addressed it to my Swiss bank. When I went out to buy stamps, there was a man sitting in a car twenty yards down from my front door. He could have been asleep, but I knew he wasn't. He followed me to the post office at a respectful distance, then back to my apartment. As I went in, he climbed back into his car to continue his vigil.

As my presence was now public knowledge, there seemed no point in keeping out of Mary's way any longer. I left it until eight, then showered and shaved and went to pay my respects. 'I'd like to have said that her expression when she opened the door to me was a compound of amazement and delight; but if it was, she concealed it admirably beneath a cloak of what can only be described as indifference.

'Hi!' she said. At least she stood aside to let me in. She allowed me to kiss her chastely, then she stood back and looked at me closely. 'You look terrible.'

'I've got the curse,' I said, trying to make light of something that was annoying me no end.

'You've been having yourself quite a time,' she said. 'You made page one.'

'I'm surprised you noticed,' I said, miffed as hell.

'Fifteen years wasn't it?'

'Time flies,' I sparkled.

'Indeed it does. I expected you yesterday.'

I really was surprised at this, and said so.

'Two unpleasant gentlemen called on me and said if you contacted me, I was to let them know,' she said. That was Max again. Not content with tailing me clear across Europe, he had been making sure that if I slipped his tail, there'd be no place for me to go. Which only goes to show how little he knew Mary.

'Do you want to know what happened?' I asked.

'No,' she said firmly. Then she softened sufficiently to qualify the remark. 'What I don't know can't hurt me. And I don't want to get hurt anymore because of you.'

I wasn't aware that I'd managed to hurt her already, and I said so.

'Because you're a fat, balding, insensitive bastard,' she said. Fat and balding I may have been, but I was sensitive enough to know that I wasn't insensitive.

She turned on me about then. 'You pop in and out of my life like a bloody yo-yo. And I'm supposed to be happy and grateful to see you every time you condescend to put in an appearance.' I started to say something, but she stopped me, in full flow now. 'And it's no good saying you don't make demands on me. Just being there is the biggest demand of the lot. You put on your whipped spaniel look and I start thinking I'm a first water bitch. Well I'm not, and I don't like being made to feel guilty for something that isn't any of my doing.'

The evening wasn't going at all the way I had planned, and I began to panic a little. 'I love you, you know that,' I said, casting caution to the wind.

'No, you don't,' she said. 'If you did, you'd ask me to marry you.'

'So marry me,' I said, completely demented by now.

'I wouldn't marry you if you were the last man on earth,' she said. In a lifetime of dealing with illogicals, I'd never learned to fathom the illogicality of women, because suddenly she smiled and it was like the sun coming out.

'But at least you asked me,' she said.

I admitted that I'd asked her, failing to get the point.

'You're a bastard most of the time,' she said. 'But you're rather sweet.' She patted my cheek affectionately, rather like she would have done one of her horses.

'Dinner or bed?' she said.

'Bed,' I said, getting back to firmer ground.

'No,' she countered. 'Dinner.' And she started to strip off. I made a tentative grab at her as she padded across to the bathroom, but she evaded me easily. 'After dinner will be better,' she said. 'Booze improves your performance.'

'I can booze now,' I said, beginning to work up a fornicator's sweat. But she disappeared into the bathroom, and in case I hadn't got the message, she locked the door loudly behind her.

So we dined leisurely in one of our regular restaurants, while the manager frantically searched for a bill I had run up that he hadn't expected to collect on for fifteen years. When he presented it to me, all he said was that it was nice to see me back. It was that sort of restaurant, all candelabra and discretion. We played footsy under the table while Mary tucked away a meal that would have done justice to an Irish navy, and during the sweet and the coffee I began to champ at the bit. I paid the bill and galloped Mary back to her apartment and into bed. It was like coming home again. Familiarity may breed contempt in some areas, but as far as I was concerned, the familiarity of Mary's warm, gentle body bred only affection and extreme gratitude. Afterwards I lay smoking while she idly picked fluff out of my navel.

'Was it terrible?' she said.

'It was sensational.'

'Not me, idiot! Russia.'

'It wasn't too bad,' I said.

'Why did they let you go?'

This I couldn't tell her. No doubt there'd be something about it in the newspapers tomorrow, put there by Max. But until I knew what story he was going to concoct, I could do nothing but keep quiet.

Mary didn't seem to mind when I didn't tell her and, after an hour, she pushed me out of bed.

'Why can't I stay?' I asked.

'Because the bed's too small, and you snore. Tonight I've got to sleep, I've got a heavy day tomorrow.'

She was right about the bed being too small. I'd been on at her for longer than I could remember to get a double bed. But she said that, as a single girl, a double bed would give the impression that she was promiscuous. I think the true reason she didn't have a double bed was her fear that I might move in with her permanently, but we kept up the pretence. The odd nights I *had* stayed had invariably been sleepless ones for both of us.

I got dressed reluctantly and kissed her good-bye. She was asleep before I was out of the flat. I was using my own car now and, before going home, I drove to Fleet Street and picked up a copy of tomorrow's paper. Max had excelled himself. There was a terrible picture of me on page one with a story that said that due to the vast improvement in East-West relationships the Russians, not wanting to throw a spanner in the works, had decided to be magnanimous and suspend my sentence, provided I never returned to any of the Iron Curtain countries. That would hand Borensko a laugh. But as far as he was concerned, they could say what they bloody well liked; none of the people who mattered would believe a word of it anyway. My watcher, or his double, was still parked outside my apartment, and I saw him acknowledge receipt of me to the man who had followed me for the entire evening. Max was taking no chances of my failing to keep my appointment.

I turned up promptly at ten-thirty and was shown straight into Max's office. He was sniffing away at an inhaler when I came in. He smiled apologetically at me as he put it away and mopped his streaming eyes. 'Doctor said it might be better than eye drops,' he said.

I hoped fervently that the doctor didn't know what he was talking about; one of the few pleasures left in life was watching Max suffer. While he was mopping up the deluge, he pushed a newspaper across the desk towards me.

'I've seen it,' I said.

'Good?'

'Adequate.'

'So what happened?'

'They let me go,' I said.

'Why?'

'With Antonov dead, there was no point in keeping me.'

'They didn't arrest you because of Antonov.'

'But that was the whole idea, wasn't it?'

'You and I know it,' said Max. 'They didn't.'

'They do now,' I said. 'I told them.'

Max leaned back in his chair, his hands flat on the desk in front of him. The clock on the wall ticked away a noisy minute.

'Mmm,' said Max.

'I'm sorry,' I said. 'But I didn't feel up to doing fifteen years.'

'You told them that the whole job was a frame?'

'I did.'

'And they let you go?'

'They did.'

'You're a liar.'

'So I'm a liar, and please can I have the rest of my money?'

Max grinned, a thoroughly unpleasant baring of his immaculate teeth. 'You're joking of course.'

'What do you think?'

'You're not joking?'

'Right,' I said. 'Cash please, no cheques.'

'Did they knock you about?'

'Some,' I admitted.

Max nodded thoughtfully. 'I thought so,' he said. 'You've had a bash on the head, it's affected your thought processes.'

'You'll have to do better than that.'

'So try this,' said Max. 'I slap a lien on your bank account and get back the twenty-five per cent I've already paid you.'

'But you won't do that.'

'Why won't I.' He was still smiling.

'Seller's market,' I said.

He put his teeth away. 'What's the commodity?' he asked.

I shook my head. 'It's not for you.'

'For who?'

'Your friends in the CIA.'

Now he started to look nasty. 'What have you got that they might buy?' he asked.

'Not might,' I said. 'Will.'

'What?'

'I'll tell the customer. In the meantime, give me my seven and half thousand quid and I promise not to spill too much mud over your name.'

'It's been muddied before,' he said.

'Not with the brand of mud I'll use.'

'You're bluffing, John,' he said.

I got to my feet. 'Suit yourself,' I said. 'But I'll get it in the end. If not from you, from the CIA.'

I started for the door, then I remembered something. I turned back. 'Incidentally, what did Antonov die from?'

'A coronary,' said Max. I thought I saw a momentary flash of something in his eyes, but it could have been the water that was still streaming out. 'Don't try to treat the CIA like you treat me,' he added, just before I went through the door. 'They're hard cases when they need to be.'

'You're frightening me to death,' I said. And I left.

I hadn't for a moment expected to get any money from Max but at least I'd got him wondering, which was the purpose of my visit. I'd also rattled him a little by way of a bonus. Now all I had to do was to wait for the CIA to contact me. I knew that they would. Max would see to that, even if it was only to satisfy his own curiosity as to what I was up to.

They didn't take long either. I'd been home for an hour when there was a polite tap on the door and I opened it to two of my American cousins. CIA men come in all shapes and sizes. There are the part timers, who do other, normal-type work; then there are the scholarly individuals who work with computers and such like in the offices that the CIA runs all over the world; there are CIA men disguised as soldiers, Peace Corps workers, students, minor diplomats, and plain common or garden tourists. But somewhere behind this bunch there is the hard core of professionals, who do the dirty and the dangerous work. And, with my luck, it was a natural that I should draw two of these.

As they removed their topcoats they introduced themselves. Harvey Dacron was six feet two inches, slim and sporting a crew cut; Martin Rich was shorter by a good few inches, more heavily built, and nearly bald. Both wore neat, navy blue, lightweight suits, and button-down shirts with plain knitted ties. They could have been anything from Madison Avenue to Wall Street. They were polite, almost deferential, and they would have cut my throat as soon as look at me. Martin Rich had obviously been elected spokesman and, while he chatted me up, Harvey meandered around the apartment, apparently aimlessly, but in fact making sure I didn't have the place wired for sound. There's something almost pathological in the way Americans expect everything to be bugged; to me, a bug is something you find in a dirty bed and I didn't know one end of a tape recorder from the other. But while Martin talked inconsequentials, Harvey ran an unobtrusive, but thorough, check over my establishment. Obviously satisfied, he gave Martin an invisible sign, and business started.

'Max said you wanted to see us, John,' said Martin with the customary American irreverence for anything but Christian names.

'I didn't say that.'

'He said you'd got something to sell us,' prodded Martin.

'I hadn't anticipated making contact as soon as this,' I lied. There was no point in letting them take over the entire proceedings. But I hadn't allowed for that old American 'get up and go'.

Martin persisted gently. 'There's no time like the present. That's what we always say, eh Harvey?' Harvey nodded. He wasn't really listening; he was watching me through a pair of the clearest blue eyes I'd ever seen. He looked as though he were measuring me for a box. 'So suppose you tell us what it is you're selling, and we'll tell you if we're interested in buying.'

'You'll buy all right,' I said. 'But I can't sell to you personally.'

There was a moment's pause.

'To whom then?' said Martin finally.

'Leo Tamir,' I said, holding my breath. I needn't have bothered. They accepted it without batting an eyelid.

'When do you want to see him?'

About here I should have started to get suspicious, but I was so relieved at having crossed what I had anticipated as a nasty hurdle that my natural mistrust of Americans in general and the CIA in particular took a back seat.

'Just have him call me,' I said. 'I'll arrange the meeting with him direct.'

'Why not give us the details?' said Martin. 'It'll save time.'

'Time I've plenty of,' I said. 'Just have him call me.'

There was another pause while Martin digested this. Then Harvey decided to take an interest in the proceedings.

'What's so special about Tamir?' he asked.

'Nothing special about him,' I said. 'Just that what I've got to sell I'm only going to sell to him.'

'He won't have the money with him,' said Martin.

'Don't you trust him yet?' I enquired lightly.

Martin smiled gently. 'You know better than that, John. Like you, we don't trust anybody.' It was the first really sensible thing he'd said since he arrived.

'If Tamir isn't allowed to carry money, how do I get paid?' I asked, not unreasonably I thought.

'You give him sufficient information for head office to judge whether it's worth the price you're asking. If it is, another meeting will be arranged. You 'can give him the balance of the information and he'll give you the money.'

'So you *do* trust him to carry money,' I said.

'Ofcourse we do,' said Martin.

'It's you we have doubts about,' said Harvey. 'If Tamir is carrying twenty-five thousand dollars with him first time round, what's to stop you banging him on the head and making off with it?'

There were all sorts of loose ends to this argument, but I let them all go while I seized on the point that really interested me.

'Who said anything about twenty-five thousand dollars,' I asked.

'It was just a figure of speech,' said Martin.

'Then try figuring your speech up near the hundred thousand mark.'

Martin looked sad. 'That's a lot of money, John,' he said.

'I've a lot to sell.'

'Perhaps. Perhaps not. We shall see. After we know what it is, then will be the time for haggling about the price.'

'Sounds fair,' I lied. 'I'll wait to hear from him then.'

I started towards the door to show them out. Harvey was standing in my way and he didn't move. 'You wouldn't be putting us on, would you, John?' he said.

'Why on earth should I do that, Harvey?' I asked, with righteous indignation.

'I don't know,' said Harvey. 'But I don't like the smell.'

'Some fish fingers went off,' I said, realising that he wasn't quite as simple as the button-down shirt and crew cut implied.

Martin came up behind me. 'Harvey is merely intimating that should all not be as it seems, there could be trouble. Serious trouble.'

'Trouble's my middle name,' I said.

'Not our sort of trouble, John, believe you me,' said Martin politely, and the two of them let themselves out of the door as quietly as they had entered. 'Bay of Pigs to you,' I muttered as I closed the door behind them.

That seemed to be that. Wheels had been set in motion and all I could do now was to wait. But while waiting I decided to investigate the gleam I had spotted in Max's eye when I had mentioned the death of Antonov. It fitted in with an idea I had formulated somewhere along the line, but which I had rejected as being too far out, even for Max. On consideration, I remembered that there was nothing too far out for Max. So I went and bought some back-copy newspapers. Being a bit of a masochist, I bought editions that covered my arrest and trial, as well as those I needed. The whole trial bit was a fascinating exercise in journalistic double talk. It was obviously a big story at the time, but D notices had been issued to cover various portions of it, and so the facts were liberally laced with fiction. There were a couple of indignant editorials and a number of interviews with political pundits and foreign correspondents, whose opinions of the fiasco ranged from indignant disapproval of the British for employing such a stupid person as John Smith right through to outrage that the Russians should arrest an innocent British tractor salesman, even if he were a spy. The colour of the reporting was governed solely by the political shade of the particular newspaper, and none of them from *The Times* to the *Morning Star* had the remotest idea what they were talking about.

But reading all this provided a pleasant enough interlude prior to getting down to work. The work in question involved learning as much as I could about the death of Antonov. As a man recently arrested for spying, his obituaries were decidedly sparse. Briefly it boiled down to the fact that while he was in prison awaiting trial on umpteen counts under the Official Secrets Act, he had suffered a heart attack. He'd been transferred to the prison hospital, where he had lingered for a couple of days before giving up the ghost. It all sounded very simple and straightforward. But there was a nasty smell somewhere and it had nothing to do with fish fingers.

I searched out one particular report and then made a phone call. The call was to the author of the report, who had gently hinted that perhaps all was not as it should be. He'd obviously had his knuckles rapped later, because there was no follow up. Half an hour later I answered the door to Fred Terry, a sometime freelance newspaper man, and a not-very-often novelist. We'd known each other on and off for a long time. I'd saved his life once by marrying the girl he was going steady with. He must have recognised her for what she was long before I came on the scene because, instead of taking umbrage when I appeared with flowers and chocolates, he treated me like the best friend he'd ever had. We'd met on and off during the disastrous five years of my marriage and during the divorce we'd almost become bosom buddies. We'd spend hours talking about the failings of women in general, and our common link in particular. After that we went our separate ways again, meeting only now and then. I'd steered him into a couple of stories before anyone else knew of their development and he had pointed me in the direction of some minor jobs which helped pay the rent. Also, he had introduced me to Mary and, even if I'd hated his guts, I had to be grateful for that.

He's a long, gangling man, with arms and legs sticking out every which way. He holds his head slightly to one side as though he is listening for something all the time. All in all, he looks like a human assembly kit that has been badly put together, which one good shove would cause to fall apart. But behind his ragbag appearance there was a reasoning mind of sorts and, in my telephoning him, he sensed a story. Thirty minutes after I hung up on him, he was spread all around one of my armchairs clutching a drink.

'The traveler returns,' he said. 'What happened?'

'Don't you read your newspapers?'

'They only print the sort of balls I write. Are you going to give me a story?'

'You couldn't use it even if I did. They'd lock you up.'

'Not even a little story?'

'Perhaps, but later,' I said. 'Right now, I want a favour.'

He downed his drink rapidly and started to wind himself up preparatory to getting to his feet. 'Favours for you usually involve someone getting their head bent,' he said. 'I'll see you around.'

But I bullied him into hearing me out and, after he'd probed around for a while trying to dig the grain of an idea from what I was asking, he agreed to help me. There wasn't any need for him to make such a big deal about it as all I was asking for was a couple of introductions. He knew it, too, but he made drama out of it so that the next time he asked me for a favour the ledger would be well balanced in his column. I went along with him, slapping him on the back a couple of times and telling him what a good fellow he was. He made some phone calls and a meeting was set up. Just before he left, he remembered something. 'There's a fellow outside watching this place,' he said.

'Nothing to do with me,' I told him. 'They're running a brothel in the flat upstairs and the law can't decide whether to do anything about it.'

'He didn't look like a policeman,' said Fred, suspiciously.

'Vice squad never do,' I said, pushing him out of the door. I watched him gangle down the stairs, no wiser and a little drunker than he had been when he arrived.

The meeting Fred had arranged was for that evening, and this was one get-together that I didn't want Max to know about. So, two hours before the appointed time, I put on my coat and went out to lose my tail.

Unfortunately, I chose to go out just as the shifts were changing over, and the off-going worker decided to put in a bit of overtime helping his mate. This gave me two to contend with, which is infinitely more difficult than one. Anyone can lose one tail, but with two men on the job, one can follow you into the shop, while the other goes round and covers the back door; one can travel on the same bus with you, while the other follows in a taxi; one can make a call for reinforcements while the other keeps tabs. It's a difficult operation which requires a little thought and concentration; particularly in this case as they didn't mind one little bit that I knew they were tailing me. This allowed them practically to sit in my pocket. I played it cool for the first half hour, lulling them into a sense of false security. This put me in Oxford Street at rush hour, where a man with three heads could lose himself in the crowd if he had a mind to.

I joined the commuters battling their way into Oxford Circus tube station where I bought a ticket while Mutt and Jeff queued three places behind me, buying theirs. I managed to insinuate a few more people between me and them on the down escalator. Just before we reached the bottom, a train came in and a great mob of people poured towards the up escalator. I made it just ahead of them and, by the time Mutt and Jeff crossed over, there were thirty to forty people jammed between us. My way ahead was clear and I started to mount the moving staircase two at a time. I heard once that this is bad for the heart. It didn't do my heart any harm, but it must have played havoc with Mutt and Jeff's.

At the top of the escalator, I crossed back to the downside. We were only ten feet away from each other when we passed, going in opposite directions. But they were so busy looking upstairs to where I had disappeared and trying to shove their way through the crowd that they didn't even see me.

At the bottom, I caught a train and got out one station later at Regents Park. There I picked up a cab and gave him the address that Fred had given me.

It was an insalubrious looking pub and Fred was waiting for me in the saloon bar. With him was a sad little man with a large moustache and boils on the back of his neck. Fred introduced us, then discreetly withdrew to chew his fingernails, while I got down to business.

Two hours later I was back home. Jeff had gone, no doubt regretting his offer to put in some overtime, but Mutt was still there and he glared at me as I got out of my cab. He'd be getting a rocket up his ass from Max tomorrow and, if he could have jumped on my face right there, he would have done so happily. But what Max was going to do to him was nothing to what I was going to do to Max. My little man with the boils had turned over a large stone for me and what I had found underneath was just about as nasty as anything I'd come across for a long time

CHAPTER SEVEN

amir called me the following day.

'Mr. Smith, this is Leo Tamir,' he said when I answered the phone.

'Hello, Leo, how's the stomach?'

'Not good, Mr. Smith. You want to see me I understand?'

'That's the general idea,' I said. 'When can you make it?'

'I am at your service.'

I arranged to meet him at the White City Greyhound Racing Stadium. Being a Saturday, the place would be crowded enough to be anonymous and noisy enough to prevent anyone from over-hearing our conversation. I telephoned the restaurant to reserve a table; as long as we were going to talk, we might as well eat while we were doing it.

I then wrote a cheque for one thousand pounds and trot-ted round to my bank to cash it. The teller looked at me a little cross-eyed when I pushed it across the counter at him but, after a hurried consultation with the manager, he paid me out with one hundred ten pound notes. I left the bank feeling much better. If Max was going to block my bank account, he wasn't going to find much economical advantage.

Having nothing further to do until the evening, I went to my office. Harvey Stubbs was a five-day week man, so Miss Roberts wasn't there either. I let myself in and, after hanging up my coat, I searched through Miss Roberts' desk until I found the file where she had stored my mail. I carried it through to my own office, put my feet on the desk and proceeded to catch up on the last few weeks.

There were a few bills, for which I promptly wrote cheques; there was a note from Phil Bannister thanking me for pushing some business his way; and there was a small cheque from a client I thought had died. That and a dozen pamphlets was the sum total of my absence. I left a note for Miss Roberts saying I wouldn't be in for a couple of weeks as I needed a holiday after my shattering experience. Then I shut up shop and went to see Solly Weisman.

Solly runs a clock and watch repair shop, just off Cheapside. At least, clocks and watches are the front; in the back you can buy anything from a Bren gun down to a bow and arrow. He could probably have provided a Polaris missile if your references were good and you had the money to pay for it. He was the armourer for the local villains, reliable, tightlipped and very expensive. But only expensive to everyone else; I got what I wanted for free. Somewhere back in the dim distant past, I had stumbled on the fact that Solly had deserted from the British army during the war. I used this piece of information whenever I needed hardware to bolster up my courage. This wasn't often because, while I didn't have much courage most of the time, my antipathy towards guns usually outweighed my cowardice. I didn't like guns and I never have; as a functional piece of equipment I suppose they have their uses, but my recipe for a long and healthy life is to stay out of situations where guns are needed. Still, there came times when even I felt the need of outside support and this was one of those times.

While Solly watched me through his sad eyes, I took my pick of what was in the back room. I chose a Smith and Wesson .38 police special and twenty-five rounds of ammunition. I drew the ammunition from a box holding two hundred rounds. I didn't want Solly picking out the cartridges for me; he'd as soon have put talcum powder in them as gunpowder. I was the only link with his past, the only person who knew about his desertion, and it offended his peace of mind. It bothered him not one little bit that what he was doing every day could put him inside for ten years. As far as he was concerned, what he was now engaged in was honest villainy, whereas desertion had a sneaky connotation quite out of proportion to the gravity of the charge. Also, there was the knowledge that his customers were villains themselves and would cheerfully have cut their own throats before grassing. Whereas I wasn't a villain. A bastard maybe, but I would have sung like Nelly Melba if it would have got me out of trouble. And Solly knew it.

So, he watched me sadly as I took my pick of his stock, and tried to talk me into taking a holster as well. A holster is for people who carry guns without expecting ever to have to use them. They are nasty, dangerous things which are liable to snag in the gun at the critical moment leaving blood over everything. And, while I hoped fervently that I wasn't going to have to use the gun, at least if I did have to, I had no intention of cluttering myself up with a holster. I declined Solly's offer politely, tucked my acquisition deep in my raincoat pocket, and left Solly wishing he could shoot me in the back.

Tamir was right on time. We met outside the restaurant entrance to the White City, where I bought two tickets. We went straight upstairs and were shown to the table I had reserved. The first race was about to start and, while Leo looked around the place and wondered what on earth he'd choose from the menu that wouldn't upset his stomach, I trotted up to the tote window and laid out a little of my hard-earned money. By the time I got back to my table, the race was over and I'd struck lucky. This meant I had to go back and collect my winnings. While I was doing this, I bumped into someone I knew vaguely and we talked for five minutes, so by the time I got back to the table once more, it was time to bet for the next race. All in all, three quarters of an hour passed before Leo could pin me down to any sort of talking.

He did so finally, while I was noshing into an *escalope Holstein*, and he was toying with some boiled fish.

'Please, Mr. Smith. I am not enjoying myself and I would like to get down to business.'

'I'm having a ball,' I said. 'I've won a hundred pounds already.'

'I'm glad,' he said. 'Perhaps now you will tell me what it is you wish to see me about.'

'Don't you know?'

'Only that you have something to sell and that you will deal only with me. What I can't understand is …'

I cut in on him quickly. 'I didn't say I would deal only with you. I said I would sell only to you.'

'But why?'

'Because you're the person with the most interest in buying.'

His flat eyes became even flatter. He toyed a moment with his revolting looking meal, then pushed it aside. 'What you are trying to say is that the CIA would not be interested, but that I, as an individual, would.'

'I didn't say they wouldn't be interested. It's just that you would be more interested.'

'Please get to the point, Mr. Smith.'

'I spent some time with Borensko,' I said.

There was a moment's pause. 'So?' he said finally.

'He told me all about you,' I said.

'What did he tell you?'

I flashed a look over my shoulder, then leaned forward conspiratorially. 'You don't have to worry,' I said. 'I'm on your side.'

He'd not the slightest idea what I was talking about and he said so.

'Come on, Leo,' I said. 'I know you're working for Borensko.'

If I'd emptied my *Holstein* over his lap, he couldn't have looked more surprised. I reached across and patted his arm. 'You certainly had me fooled,' I said.

He pulled his arm away from my hand. 'You are talking non-sense,' he said. 'Dangerous nonsense.'

'It's not dangerous as long as only you and I know about it.'

'This was what you wanted to see me about?'

I sat back. 'What else?' I said.

He looked at me steadily for a while and it was only by con-juring up a vision of the umpteen people he had murdered that I was able to stop myself from feeling sorry for him.

'I believe you know this isn't true,' he said finally. 'The prob-lem that now confronts me is—why?'

'Yes,' I agreed. 'It's quite a problem.'

'I am realistic enough to know that if you told my present employers, it would cause me a great deal of trouble.'

'Indeed, it would.'

'Regardless of whether or not it is true.'

'Regardless,' I agreed.

'So, the problem resolves itself purely on the basis of how much money you will accept.'

'No,' I said.

Then I left him for a few minutes to make another bet. When I returned, he hadn't moved and he picked up the conversation as though it hadn't been interrupted.

'Why not?' he asked.

'It goes deeper than that,' I said. 'I may be working for Borensko myself, but there is the faintest chance that he is lying to me and you are telling the truth.'

I thought I saw a flash of hope in his eyes, but it was extin-guished immediately.

'So?' he asked.

'So, I'm going to give you a chance to get out.'

'Why?'

'Because you're going to pay me,' I said.

'And if I don't?'

'Then no doubt the CIA will hear about your defection. And as you say, true or not, it can only bring you trouble.'

'What's your price?'

'A hundred thousand dollars. Fifty for you and fifty for me.'

He almost smiled. 'And where am I going to get a hundred thousand dollars?' he asked.

'You're here to negotiate with me on behalf of the CIA so negotiate.'

'You'll have to have something worth selling first.'

'I can give you the names of three officers on the NATO staff, none below the rank of colonel, who all work for Borensko. I can give you the sailing orders of two of their nuclear submarines, both working off the Newfoundland coast. And, best of all, I can give them *you*, unless you can convince them that what I am selling is worth the money.'

A waiter grabbed his boiled fish and pushed an ice cream under his nose. He wasn't even aware of it. He was looking at me steadily, hate oozing from his eyes.

'Why are you doing all this?' he asked finally.

'I like money. I don't like you. And I don't like Borensko, even if I do work for him.'

He glanced down at the ice cream, then pushed it aside and stood up.

'You'll hear from me,' he said.

I smiled at him. 'I'm sure I will.'

I watched him as he threaded his way through the tables towards the elevators. There was one simple solution to his problem and I didn't believe for a moment that he hadn't thought about it. Killing used to come easy to him and there was no reason why an upset stomach should have spoiled his aim. Until I next heard from him, I was going to have to be very careful. Apart from murdering me, there was no way out for him other than what I had suggested. He knew he wasn't working for Borensko, and he'd a pretty good idea that I knew it too. But a word to the CIA would be all that was needed to have him put away permanently. Even if they weren't fully convinced, they couldn't afford to take that sort of chance. After all, he'd done an about-face once before. There would be a quiet little accident somewhere, which might make a page two story in a local paper, and that would be that. In effect, I was blackmailing him with material that didn't exist. It was a pretty fanciful idea and it couldn't have happened to a better person than Leo Tamir.

I stayed for the next couple of races, paid for dinner, and left. I had a medium sized alcoholic glow on me, I'd won fifty quid, and the necessary wheels had already been spun into motion. Life was good, and getting better. Wait until Anne Ballard learned what I was going through on her behalf; she'd be so bloody grateful it would be sickening.

In fact, I was feeling so good, I didn't even mind when Leo tried to kill me. He'd obviously allowed American culture to get the better of his original training, because what he tried was straight out of prohibition. I had picked up my car from the car park and was driving slowly back into town when this car ran into the back of me at the traffic lights. It wasn't a large bash, but sufficient for me to switch off the engine and get out to go and inspect the damage. My fender was badly bent as was the paneling at the rear. Preparing to swap insurance companies, I walked towards the car that had done the damage. I realised that there was no driver behind the wheel—and at the same time I saw Leo. He had obviously climbed out of the car on the passenger side and was now leaning in through the passenger window for all the world like an interested bystander looking to see what it was all about. I was supposed to lean in through the window on the driver's side and get a face full of bullet. Instead I moved round behind him and, before he knew what was happening, I had grasped his arms just below the elbows, keeping his hands shoved deep in his topcoat pockets. His arms were like matchsticks, which goes to show what a diet of boiled fish can do for a man. I made a disapproving, clucking sound.

'Silly man, Leo,' I said. 'You must know me better than that.'

Suddenly the stiffness went out of him. People were gathering now, and I could see a bucket shaped helmet bobbing towards us over the heads of the crowd. I released Leo's arms and he turned towards me, pulling his empty hands from his pockets. He looked almost embarrassed.

'You're right, Mr. Smith,' he said. 'It was stupid. But only because it didn't work.'

'Never mind,' I said, consolingly. The policeman was nearly with us by now. 'But in case you feel like trying it again, I've got it all written down.'

I don't know whether he believed me or not because the policeman finally got through to us. 'Have to move those cars, gentlemen,' he said. 'Blocking traffic.'

'Certainly, officer,' I said in my best public-spirited voice.

'And you, sir,' he said to Leo. Leo looked at him blankly.

'It's not my car, officer,' he said. Obviously, he'd knocked it off in the White City car park, just to follow me. While the policeman was looking round for the nonexistent driver, Leo gave me a small nod and started to push his way out through the crowd.

The policeman took my name and address and radioed his mates that he'd found an abandoned car. The patrol car arrived and more details were taken. Finally, an hour later, I was allowed to go about my business.

I drove home, parked the car, and let myself into my apartment. Max was sitting in my best armchair. There were two of his Heavy

Squad with him. One was going through the bureau where I kept my unpaid bills and the other appeared in the doorway of my bedroom as I let myself in. All three of them were looking at me steadily and I decided to play it very cool indeed.

'Come on in, John,' said Max generously. 'Sit down.'

I took off my coat and sat.

'What are you up to, John?' he said when he thought I was comfortable.

'I told you yesterday,' I said.

He waved my answer away with his hand. 'What are you really up to?'

'Making a living,' I said.

'By selling information to the CIA?' I nodded. 'Not good enough, John. Not good at all.'

'Then you tell me,' I said.

He leaned forward. 'Let's try this,' he said. 'You're working for Borensko.'

'Who's Borensko?'

He treated this with the contempt which it deserved, ignoring it completely. 'You made some sort of deal with him to let you go. I want to know what that deal is.'

'If you find out, be sure to tell me,' I said.

He sighed gently and pulled out his eyedrops. I was glad to see the inhaler hadn't done him any good. I waited while he squirted more liquid into his already streaming eyes. And while I was waiting, I hoped that his two associates wouldn't decide to poke around in my raincoat pocket. The gun was still there. But hopes like that usually turn out to be futile. Before Max had even put away his handkerchief, one of his men brought him my gun and the ammunition. He looked at it as the man held it out to him, butt first. But he didn't touch it. He looked at me again.

'A gun, John?'

I admitted it was a gun.

'Not like you. Not like you at all,' he said, like he was disappointed. 'What's it for?'

'To shoot people,' I said. He smiled, a thin exposure of his teeth.

'Like who?'

'Like you, if you don't take your two boys and get your ass out of here.'

He shook his head slowly. 'It wouldn't be for Leo Tamir would it?' he said.

'I've already shot him once.'

'To stop him from shooting you?'

'Now why would he want to do that?' I said, beginning to feel uncomfortable.

'I can think of a number of reasons,' said Max.

'You could think of reasons for a man to shoot his own mother,' I said, trying to head him away from the course the conversation was taking.

'Does Borensko want Leo killed?' asked Max. 'Is that the bargain you made with him?'

'Who's Borensko?' I said, flogging a dead horse.

He sat forward, putting his hands on his knees. An edge came into his voice, a cutting edge. 'Leo Tamir works for the CIA,' he said. 'While he is over here, he comes under my protection. I'm responsible for him. If anything happens to him, it would cause me considerable inconvenience.'

This was a bonus as far as I was concerned. To cause Max inconvenience was as good as a holiday. But I decided that the conversation had gone far enough. I didn't think Max had anything to go on, he was just fishing. So, I decided to call his bluff and get ugly.

'I don't give a fuck for Leo Tamir,' I said. 'And I don't give a fuck for you or your two boys here. If you want to pinch me for having a gun, go ahead. But I don't have to sit here and listen to any more balls from you and I don't intend to. So, if you've got anything bright and scintillating to say, say it quick before I throw you all out.'

I could feel a tightening of the atmosphere in the room, a backwash caused by the heavy boys flexing their muscles. I braced myself for a thump from behind, all the time watching Max in case I could recognise a signal which would give me time to take evasive action. But no signal came. Max sat where he was tor a moment longer; then he got to his feet slowly and headed for the door. His men beat him to it and opened it for him. Just before he went out, he turned back to me. 'Be careful, John,' he said. And he was gone.

I poured myself a drink, and it wasn't until I'd downed it that I saw they had left my gun on the table. I felt unreasonably pleased with myself. Max had dropped a clanger. His visit went towards confirming something I was already three parts sure of, and made what was to follow a whole lot easier.

I spent the next couple of days just hanging around waiting for Leo to contact me. My apartment was still being watched so, to relieve the boredom, I played games with the men whose job it was to shadow me everywhere, losing them time and time again. After the third time I was gratified to see that they had doubled the watch. This made the game even more interesting, and I spent a fortune on bus and taxi fares, getting a childish satisfaction each time I managed to slip out from under.

On the third day I was letting myself into the flat after leaving two men stranded on top of the Post Office tower, when the phone started to ring. I answered it.

'This is Leo Tamir.'

'Hello, Leo,' I said affably.

'My employers like the sound of your commodity and they agree to your price.'

'Good,' I said. Then because I knew that he was waiting for me to continue, I let him sweat a little and said nothing. The silence grew as I listened to his breathing on the other end of the phone.

'Are you still there, Mr. Smith?' he said finally.

'I'm still here, Leo,' I said.

'The arrangements, please?' he said. This required a bit of thought. It was better than fifty-fifty that my line was being tapped and Leo would know this. Therefore, the arrangements he wanted to hear were those designed for public consumption; namely an official exchange of money for information, all normal and above board. The arrangements I was supposed to have made for him personally, whereby he could abscond with fifty thousand dollars of the CIA's money, were for his ears alone; he would expect me to tell him about these later.

'You come here,' I said. 'The key's under the mat. Be here at six-thirty exactly.' Before he could say anything else, I hung up.

At five o'clock I went out. My two tails were waiting for me and they dutifully followed me to the nearest call box. There I made a call to a number that Borensko had given me. I came out of the call box, nodded politely to the two men, who were propping up the railings, and went into the pub.

There I sat, supping ale until exactly six-thirty. The two shadows were at the other side of the bar, trying to stretch one drink as far as they could and trying to look everywhere except at me. At six-thirty I borrowed sixpence from the barman and went to use the pub phone. I dialed my own number. It rang ten times before Leo answered it. He was out of breath, apparently having run upstairs. I didn't give him a chance to say anything once he had identified himself.

'O.K.?' I said.

'Yes, Mr. Smith. O.K.,' he replied, and hung up. I'd left a note under the mat with the key, telling him where to meet me. Now it was up to him. If there was a tail on him, he'd have to lose it. That was his problem. Mine was in the shape of the two men who had followed me into the pub. Clutching my own drink, I went to join them at the bar. At first, they tried to pretend I wasn't there; but eventually they realised they were looking rather stupid, so they accepted my invitation.

'Thank you, sir, I'll have a bitter,' said the larger of the two.

The smaller looked a little panicky for a moment, then he also nodded. 'Same for me, please.'

I bought and paid for their drinks, wished them good health and then got down to business.

'Which one of you is in charge?' I asked.

They looked at one another, then the large one turned to me. 'I am,' he said.

'What's your name?'

'I don't think that's ...'

'It doesn't really matter,' I said, cutting in. 'I'll call you Fred.'

'It's Jim,' he said. I looked at the little one.

'Bob,' he said, as though he were ashamed of it.

'All right, Jim,' I said. 'Here's what I want you to do. You go and phone Max while Bob here keeps his eye on me. You tell Max that unless I walk out of here in five minutes, leaving you two propping up the bar, I'm going to get on to our mutual friend on the other side and tell him what I know about Antonov.'

Jim looked at me empty-eyed for a moment. I could see the wheels beginning to turn in his head. 'I'm sorry, sir, I don't know what you're talking about,' he managed finally.

'Have you ever seen Max when he's got the needle?' I asked. It was obvious that he had. 'So be a good lad and do what I say. I'm walking out of here in five minutes—*alone*, O.K.?'

He looked at Bob for help, but got none. Then, weighing up the pros and cons, he made up his mind. He borrowed sixpence from Bob and lumbered off to telephone. Left alone with me, Bob was even more embarrassed than he had been at first.

'How did you like the view from the Post Office Tower?' I asked. He'd have liked to have glowered at me, but he was unsure of his ground, so he contented himself with grunting an unintelligible monosyllable into his beer.

Three minutes later Jim returned, looking red in the face. He ignored me completely. 'Come on Bob,' he said. 'We're off duty.' Bob started to down the remainder of his drink.

'Me first,' I said. 'And give me ten minutes.'

He nodded unhappily and I left them at the bar, two cogs in a wheel which obviously wasn't as well oiled and orderly as they had always imagined.

I took a taxi straight to a small garage I know where a car can be borrowed with a minimum of fuss and three sets of licence plates. I drove around for a couple of hours until I was certain I wasn't being followed. Then I pointed the car west, and put my foot down.

It took me forty-five minutes to reach where I was going and the whole time I wasn't conscious of the road once. My thought processes were far too involved, sorting and classifying the permutations of what had been going on for the past few months. For the sake of accuracy, I cleared out all the garbage in my mind to start with and then, with a clean slate, I started to slot back the facts as I saw them. Whichever way I put the material in, it came out the same way.

It had started when I had read the report of Antonov's death. He'd had a preliminary heart attack and been moved from his cell to the prison hospital. Now prison hospitals may be fine for removing home-made shivs or mending bashed skulls, but intensive care units they definitely ain't. A man of Antonov's notoriety and importance would have been hot footed to the nearest large hospital where there was equipment and personnel to take care of coronary failures. Therefore, it was logical to assume the heart attack had killed him right off. But, in that case, why the fiction of the two days lingering in the prison hospital? Unless he hadn't been in prison at all.

This was where my little man with the boils had come in. Fred Terry had dug me up a genuine, *bona fide* prison officer. Warmed by the fifty pounds I'd given him, he was adamant that not only had there not been a death in the prison hospital where he worked, heart attack or otherwise, but neither had there ever been a man named Antonov anywhere inside the walls. What he did recall very clearly was an occupied coffin arriving late one night with a minimum of fuss and a great deal of secrecy. The following morning the coffin had been collected and whipped off for burial to the accompaniment of sufficient publicity to spread the fact around.

'I must admit it 'ad me wonderin' at first,' he had said to me, scratching one of his boils with a dirty finger nail.

'Why only at first?' I'd asked.

He'd gone on to explain that once he'd read the official report in the newspapers, he'd stopped wondering because it was obviously being taken care of by Them.

'Who's Them?' I'd asked.

'Them,' he reiterated. 'You know—*Them. They.*'

It had taken me a couple of minutes to work out what the hell he was talking about. But then I'd got the drift. He'd gone on to say that who the hell ever knew what They were up to; They said all sorts of things whenever it suited Them; and it wasn't up to the likes of us to question what They were doing. As like as not They were doing it for our own good. I disagreed with him heartily on this point; not only did They do very little for anyone but Themselves; what They did do, They invariably cocked up. But They notwithstanding, Antonov had not died in prison, nor had he been anywhere near the place until he was long dead.

Once having digested this fact, it wasn't much of a problem to deduce that the announcement of his death had been delayed for a specific purpose. The timing was such that the purpose could only have had something to do with me. Antonov was dead before I went to Russia. Therefore, I had been sent for a completely different purpose. I'd worked out a pretty fanciful theory as to what that purpose was, and tonight would see me right or dead.

If I was going to be dead, I'd chosen a pretty crummy place for it. Just outside Beaconsfield, there's a disused gravel pit that covers about forty acres. There was still gravel in it, but they'd dug so deep over the past twenty years that it had become uneconomic to continue. Five years earlier, they had realised it was costing them more to dig the stuff out and transport it than they could get for it. The company had gone broke and the receivers had stepped in. Faced with a lot of clapped out gravel shifting equipment, they did the most economic thing they could think of; they left it there to rot.

I pulled off the main road and bumped my way over half a mile of rutted track, trying to avoid the more obvious hazards. Finally I stopped the car and switched off the engine. The car gave a grateful grunt as it eased its tortured springs and silence took over. I climbed out of the car and transferred my gun from raincoat pocket to the waist of my trousers. I made sure the safety catch was on—there was bumpy ground ahead and I didn't want to trip over and blow my own balls off. Leaving the car, I started to grope my way off to the left. There was a thin moon which spread sufficient diffused light to make the whole place lighter than a pitch-black cellar, but not much. After two or three minutes and a badly bruised shin, my eyes adapted themselves sufficiently for me to check that I was heading in the right direction. Confirming this, the path I was on started to go downwards. I plodded on, the only person, as far as I could tell, for a couple of hundred miles in any direction.

I reached the bottom of the slope and pressed on. There was a quarter of a mile of flat, muddy ground, and then the path started upwards again. This one was steeper and by the time I reached the top, I was fit for bugger all. I was blowing like there was no tomorrow and my leg muscles were shaking like autumn leaves. It took me five minutes to recover. Finally, I put myself back together again and got under way once more.

I'd chosen this particular place because when I had seen it in daylight it had seemed to provide everything I was looking for. If I had realised then the energy I was going to have to expend just to arrive at the meeting place, I would have settled for Hyde Park. What I couldn't see in the dark, but which I knew was there, was a huge, shallow basin, like a saucer, the side of which I had come down after leaving the car. On the far side of the saucer, there was a wedge-shaped, flat-topped hillock, and this was what I was now traversing.

At the far side of this projection was the dilapidated wreckage of what had once been the gravel working equipment. There was a tall gravel washing tower, which had originally been fed by tipper trucks which reached it on a small gauge railway. I was reminded painfully of this as I tripped over one of the rails and landed with my knees on its companion. I dropped the torch I was carrying, and hadn't used yet, and spent three minutes feeling around trying to locate it. I was on the point of giving up all attempt at concealment and lighting a match, when I heard, very clearly and unmistakably, a foot shifting on gravel. For a few seconds after that all I could hear was my own heart thumping like a steam hammer from somewhere right between my ears. Then I managed to swallow hard and replace my heart where it belonged before introducing myself.

'Leo?' I whispered. It came out like a dying croak. There was absolute silence for the space of five seconds. It seemed like five days. Then I heard the shifting of feet on gravel once more.

'Over here,' said Leo. He sounded damn near as frightened as I was. I climbed to my feet and, in doing so, I kicked the torch I had been groping for. I picked it up and, still not switching it on, I tried to locate where 'over here' was. I didn't need to; Leo suddenly loomed up beside me so silently that he nearly had me going again. But I controlled an urgent desire to scream out loud, and endeavoured to sound like the master of the situation.

'You're early,' I said.

'So are you.'

'You've got the money?'

He nodded. 'I've got it. But first, what happens?'

'What should happen. You give me my half of the money and we go our separate ways.'

'The information?'

'What information?'

'What you are selling.'

He must be barmy I thought. 'What good is it to you,' I said. 'You're not going back to the CIA.'

'It still has a financial value,' he said. So that was it. He was going to buy information with the CIA's money, then sell it to someone else. It was pretty sneaky and he went up a notch in my estimation. But it didn't really matter as from here on in he wasn't going to do a thing that I hadn't already arranged for him. I fished around through the slit in my raincoat pocket, ostensibly searching for what I was supposed to be selling, but in fact easing my gun from where it was tucked into the top of my trousers. I didn't bother to release the safety catch as I didn't expect I was going to have to use it. He, in turn, reached into his inside pocket and produced a flat, bulky envelope that could have held fifty thousand dollars. He handed me the envelope at the same time as I jabbed the gun into his stomach, just about in line with where I had shot him seven years ago. And he didn't bat an eyelid. In fact, as far as I could see in the poor light, he seemed to relax slightly as though I had settled a point that had been worrying him. Keeping my gun tucked well into his middle, I groped around for the gun I knew he would be carrying, but which he wasn't. Feeling a mite safer I relaxed a little, but kept my gun where it was.

'Brought your suitcase?' I said.

'What's that supposed to imply?'

'You're going on a trip. Didn't you know?'

'I've made my own plans,' he said.

'I'll bet you have,' I said. 'But you may as well forget them. My plans are better.'

'Better for you, perhaps.'

'You'll survive,' I said, not believing it for a moment.

He was almost enjoying himself. 'And where will my survival take place?' he asked.

'Where else?' I said. 'Back home in Mother Russia.'

Through our connecting thirty-eight calibre umbilical, I thought I felt a stiffening of the muscles. Then he relaxed again.

'No, Mr. Smith,' he said. 'It is not I who will be going anywhere; it is you.'

'Where?'

'Wherever Max decides to send you. To the grave I trust.'

'You don't want to take any notice of Max,' I said. 'He's a pathological liar. What did he tell you? That he'd send his cavalry in at the last moment? Is that what he said?'

I'd obviously hit it right on the button because he stiffened up again. And to confirm the fact even more positively he glanced quickly over his shoulder. Although what he expected to see in the pitch dark, I had no idea.

'You're a pigeon, Leo,' I said. 'You're going to Russia. Not because I made a deal with Borensko, but because the CIA and Max intend you to.'

I'd got through to him in spades now.

'I work for the CIA,' he said, as though it made a difference.

'Indeed, you do,' I said. 'What delicious little tidbits of information have you picked up during the past three years? You'd better start remembering because Borensko will want to know the lot.' He was silent for a moment, trying to take in what I was telling him. 'Think about it, Leo,' I said. 'Doesn't it strike you as odd that just because you decided three years ago that you wanted to change sides, the CIA fell over themselves to employ you. Why? You were mediocre at your job and they'd already got a full quota of mediocrities.'

'I gave them a great deal of useful information,' he finally managed.

'And no doubt they were grateful. As far as they were concerned it was a bonus. You were the man they wanted, not your information. For three years they've been filling you full of guff intending to deliver you back to Borensko at some later date for him to torture it out of you.'

'This can't be true.'

'I'm afraid it is. Did you know that Antonov was dead before I went to Russia?'

'No.'

'So why did they send me?' He didn't answer. So, I filled him in, laying it out for myself at the same time. 'There had to be another reason, and you were it. They took a calculated risk that Borensko and I would come up with the idea ourselves. If we hadn't, I would have done my fifteen years and they'd have thought of something else.'

'But Max said...' He didn't finish.

'You went to Max after we met and made our little deal. You told him all about it and I'll bet I can quote you verbatim what he said. Meet Smith, pass over the money, and we've got him for working for the Russians. I'll have men standing by to pick him up. Right?' He didn't answer, but I was right nevertheless. 'So, forget it, Leo, you've been conned, same as me. There's no cavalry waiting to gallop to the rescue.'

'But they're here. I saw...' Before he could finish we heard the helicopter. It must have come in very low because it was only seconds after we first heard its chopping roar that it swooped past overhead. Still keeping the gun on Leo, I fished out my torch and switching it on, I waved it about a bit. A moment later the helicopter swung round, half a mile away, and started back towards us. At the same time a giant floodlight was switched on beneath the fuselage, bathing everything in glaring white light.

Then we were both ducking from the downdraft of the helicopter as it put down delicately, twenty-five feet from where we were standing.

'Come on,' I said, giving him a prod with the gun.

'No,' he said.

I jabbed him again. 'Yes,' I said. And all fight seemed to leak out of him. He started towards the helicopter with me following half a pace behind. As we drew near, the door in the side of the fuselage was opened and I could see a crewman standing, waiting. We reached the helicopter and Leo, an old man suddenly, started to climb in.

But during that short walk something he had just said suddenly cracked me on the back of the skull.

'*They're here. I saw ...*'

He was right, of course. Leo *would* have seen them. He would have pointed out the meeting place and told them how he was going to play it. They may have been there just to keep Leo happy and play up the deception, but Max had always been a great one for killing two birds with one stone. I suddenly knew who the second bird was going to be. I jabbed Leo with the gun as the crewman reached down to help him in.

'Not this trip, Leo,' I said. He turned and looked at me, not understanding. 'I'm going instead,' I said.

I stepped past him and climbed into the helicopter. I nodded to the crewman as he closed the door and he signaled forward to the pilot. The helicopter shook beneath us and started to rise almost immediately. I turned to the window, looking down at the diminishing figure of Leo, who was staring up at us, oblivious to the enormous downdraft.

'Switch off the light,' I yelled to the crewman, hoping Borensko would have had the sense to send someone who could speak English. The man pressed a switch and for a moment Leo was lost in the blackness below. Then suddenly another light flashed on. It was a spotlight located somewhere on the other side of the gravel pit. It hovered, searching for a second, then it fixed on Leo. He turned towards it and I think he realised what was going to happen a split second before he died, because he put his hands up, waving them wildly, and started to run in the direction of the light. There were half a dozen stabs of flame from behind the spotlight. I thought I heard the sound of the shots over the noise of the helicopter, but it was probably imagination. The figure of Leo was arrested in mid-flight, as though he had run straight into an invisible wall. Then he was knocked backwards off his feet. The last I saw of him, as the helicopter swung round and made off fast, was a lifeless rag doll figure, sprawled out in the beam of the floodlight. Then that, too, was extinguished, leaving nothing but blackness.

I walked up front to the pilot's cabin and tapped him on the shoulder. The crewman was close behind me, not having any idea what was going on. He was nervous and he fingered the holstered gun at his belt as though there was a possibility he might have to use it. I shouted to the pilot.

'You've got about five minutes before Max realises he's had the wrong man killed.'

The pilot grinned up at me and, taking that as a sign that five minutes was all he needed, I moved back into the passenger cabin. I sat down and a moment later the crewman, who must have been watching my face, handed me a plastic bag. I didn't even have time to thank him before I was noisily sick.

❧   ❧   ❧

It was Leningrad this time. Men like Borensko didn't often travel outside Moscow, but it seemed there was a minor purge on in Leningrad and he was here to see that there wasn't any fair play.

When he recovered from his initial nastiness, he was affability itself. He'd been expecting a valuable Leo Tamir; what he got was an apparently worthless John Smith. But when he'd settled down a bit and put away the thumbscrews, I managed to explain how well off he was.

'The whole thing was designed to get Leo Tamir back here,' I said. 'For three years he's been working for the CIA and they've been feeding him false information. All he knew was what the CIA intended you to find out, and you can guess how useful *that* would have bean.'

Borensko poured me another drink, even getting to his feet to do so.

'Max knew I was going to push Leo into the helicopter. That was the whole idea. Then, to make sure I didn't get loud-mouthed afterwards, he had his Heavy Squad waiting to gun me down the moment Leo left. That's why I got on the 'copter and left Leo. They thought it was me. Bang, bang! Good-bye, Leo. And good-bye grand design.'

He refilled my glass.

'What do we do with you now, Mr. Smith?' he asked.

'You give me Anne Ballard, your blessing, and two first class aeroplane tickets to London.'

'We don't have first class on our aeroplanes. Ours is a classless society.'

I grinned at him to show that I didn't believe it either.

'What is to stop me from sending you back to prison?'

'You wouldn't do that,' I said. 'There'd be no point.'

He knew I was right. I'd been framed into the whole deal from the off, and it was going to do no one any good at all to lock me up for fifteen years. Also, in the back of his mind, there was no doubt lurking the nasty idea that perhaps, somewhere in the future, he'd be able to use me now that contact had been established. I didn't disillusion him.

'What are you going to do?' he asked.

'Pick up Anne Ballard and go back to London.'

'Is that safe? Max will be very angry.'

'He'll be even angrier when I ask for the seven and half thousand pounds he still owes me.'

'He won't pay.'

'He'll have to. Because if he doesn't, I'll tell the CIA that it was his men who killed Leo. The CIA have worked very hard for three years on this little scheme. They're going to be choked that it's gone up in smoke. Max will have spun them some yarn to cover up his cock-up. But you can bet your life it won't be the true one. Only I can do that. And that's why he'll pay me.'

The conversation drifted on after that. Borensko asked a few more questions and I answered them as best I could. Then he grew bored with the whole thing.

'You are fortunate, Mr. Smith,' he said getting to his feet. 'Miss Ballard's theatrical group are performing in Leningrad this week. I'll have you driven to the theatre.'

At the door he shook my hand warmly, and I almost liked him for a moment, revolving eye notwithstanding.

'You and Miss Ballard,' he said, just before he let me go. 'You have something between you?'

'I'm working on it,' I said. He looked curious for one moment.

'You've not ... I mean to say, have you yet ...?'

'No,' I said. 'But we've our whole lives in front of us.'

He laughed then, the first genuine laughter I had heard from him. He threw back his head and he roared. I thought his bad eye was going to revolve its way clean out of its socket. I stood there politely, with an inane grin on my face, wondering if he was going to enlighten me. But he didn't. Finally, he pulled himself together.

'Good-bye, John Smith,' he said. Then he handed me over to his driver.

The driver had been given his instructions and, while I sat in the back of the car sharpening up my hormones, he drove me to the theatre. There, he had a word with the stage door keeper, and I was passed through backstage.

I saw Anne almost immediately. She was standing in the wings, waiting to go on. She was with one of the acrobats I had seen perform in Moscow. They were holding hands and, as I watched, they turned to each other, smiled a secret sort of smile reserved for lovers, and they kissed. It was the sort of kiss that left no doubt as to their relationship.

I backed out of the theatre quietly and had the car take me straight to the airport.

Borensko had been wrong; there was a first-class section on the aeroplane. But it was full up, and I sat with the peasants.

I put Anglo-Soviet relations back ten years during that journey. I shouted at the stewardess; I complained to the captain who was ill-advised enough to ask me how I was enjoying the flight; I sent back the caviar; I insulted three other passengers; and if I'd had a razor I would probably have slashed the seats.

No wonder Borensko had laughed. No doubt in ten or twelve years I'd see the funny side of it myself. After all, I had been through a great deal for that bird and now here she was, in love with someone else. I don't think I'd have minded as much as I did if she'd chosen one of the other acrobats in the group. But out of the two fellows and the girl, Anne had chosen the girl.

THE END

ABOUT THE AUTH

Jimmy Sangster was an acclaimed screenwriter (*Curse (Frankenstein, Deadlier Than the Male, The Legacy*, etc), director (*Lust for a Vampire, Banacek*, etc), TV writer (*Wonder Woman, Cannon, BJ and The Bear, Kolchak*, etc) and novelist. His many books include *Touchfeather, Touchfeather Too, Blackball, Snowball, Hardball, The Spy Killer* and *Foreign Exchange*. He died in 2011.

A movie adaptation of *Foreign Exchange*, written and produced by Sangster and directed by Roy Ward Baker, was released in 1970 and starred Robert Horton as John Smith, Sebastian Cabot as Max, and Jill St. John as Mary Harper.

www.ingramcontent.com/pod-product-compliance
Lightning Source LLC
Chambersburg PA
CBHW031017030726
47497CB00004B/894